SHADOWS OF THE APT

BOOK TWO

Dragonfly Falling

ADRIAN
TCHAIKOVSKY

TOR

First published 2009 by Tor
an imprint of Pan Macmillan Ltd
Pan Macmillan, 20 New Wharf Road, London N1 9RR
Basingstoke and Oxford
Associated companies throughout the world
www.panmacmillan.com

ISBN 978-0-230-70415-2

1 3 5 7 9 8 6 4 2

A CIP catalogue record for this book is available from
the British Library.

Map artwork and illustration on p.iii by Hemesh Alles
Typeset by SetSystems Ltd, Saffron Walden, Essex
Printed and bound in Great Britain by
CPI Mackays, Chatham ME5 8TD

Visit www.panmacmillan.com to read more about all our books
and to buy them. You will also find features, author interviews and
news of any author events, and you can sign up for e-newsletters
so that you're always first to hear about our new releases.

For Alex

ACKNOWLEDGEMENTS

A very big thank you to everyone who's encouraged and helped me over the last year, including Simon; Peter and the folks at Macmillan; Al, Andy, Emmy-Lou and Paul; the Deadliners writing group; and all the folks at Maelstrom and Curious Pastimes.

A Map of the LOWLANDS and environs

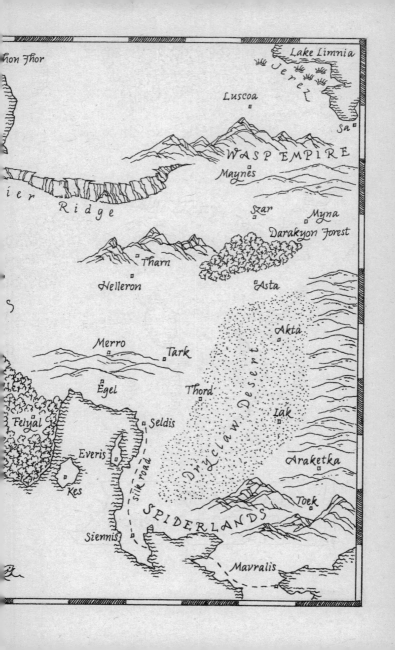

Glossary

Stenwold Maker Beetle-kinden spymaster and statesman
Cheerwell 'Che' Maker his niece
Tisamon Mantis-kinden Weaponsmaster
Tynisa his halfbreed daughter, formerly Stenwold's ward
Salma (Prince Salme Dien) Dragonfly nobleman,
    agent of Stenwold
Totho halfbreed artificer, agent of Stenwold
Achaeos Moth-kinden magician
Scuto Thorn Bug-kinden artificer, Stenwold's lieutenant
Sperra Fly-kinden, agent of Scuto
Balkus Ant-kinden, agent of Scuto, renegade from the
    city of Sarn

Thalric Wasp-kinden major in the Rekef
Ulther Wasp-kinden governor of Myna, killed by Thalric
Reiner Wasp-kinden general in the Rekef
Te Berro Fly-kinden lieutenant in the Rekef
Scyla Spider-kinden magician and spy

Lineo Thadspar Beetle-kinden Speaker for the Assembly
    of Collegium
Kymon of Kes Ant-kinden master of arms in Collegium
Hokiak Scorpion-kinden black-marketeer in Myna
Skrill halfbreed scout in Stenwold's service
Grief in Chains Butterfly-kinden dancer

Places of import

Asta Wasp-kinden staging post for the Lowlands campaign

Collegium Beetle-kinden city, home of the Great College

The Commonweal Dragonfly-kinden state north of the Lowlands, partly conquered by the Empire

The Darakyon forest, formerly a Mantis stronghold, now haunted and avoided by all

Helleron Beetle-kinden city, manufacturing heart of the Lowlands

Myna Soldier Beetle-kinden city conquered by the Wasp Empire

Sarn Ant-kinden city-state allied to Collegium

Spiderlands Spider-kinden cities south of the Lowlands, believed rich and endless

Tark Ant-kinden city-state in the eastern Lowlands

Tharn Moth-kinden hold near Helleron

Vek Ant-kinden city-state hostile to Collegium

Organizations

Arcanum the Moth-kinden secret service

Assembly the elected ruling body of Collegium, meeting in the Amphiophos

Fiefs competing criminal gangs in Helleron

Great College in Collegium, the cultural heart of the Lowlands

Prowess Forum duelling society in Collegium

Rekef the Wasp imperial secret service

For many years the Wasp Empire has been expanding, warring on its neighbours and enslaving them. Having concluded its Twelve-Year War against the Dragonfly Commonweal, the Wasps have now turned their eyes towards the divided Lowlands.

Stenwold Maker realized the truth of the Empire's power when it seized the distant city of Myna. Since then he has been sending out covert agents to track the progress of an enemy whose threat his fellow citizens will not recognize.

Among these agents are his niece Cheerwell, his ward Tynisa, the exotic Dragonfly prince Salma, a humble half-breed artificer Totho . . . and staunchest of his allies is the terrifying Mantis warrior Tisamon.

But can their efforts bring the Lowlands to their senses before it is all too late?

One

The morning was joyless for him, as mornings always were. He arose from silks and bee-fur and felt on his skin the insidious cold that these rooms only shook off for a scant month or two in the heart of summer.

He wondered whether he could be accommodated somewhere else – as he had wondered countless times before – and knew that it would not do. It would be, in some unspecified way, *disloyal*. He was a prisoner of his own public image. Besides, these rooms had some advantages. No windows, for one. The sun came in through shafts set into the ceiling, three dozen of them and each too small for even the most limber Fly-kinden assassin to sneak through. He had been told that the effect of this fragmented light was beautiful, although he saw beauty in few things, and none at all in architecture.

His people had been building these ziggurats as symbols of their leaders' power since for ever, but the style of building that had reached its apex here in the great palace at Capitas had overreached itself. The northern hill-tribes, left behind by the sword of progress, still had their stepped pyramids atop the mounds of their hill forts. The design had changed little, only the scale, so that he, who ought to expect all things as he wanted, was entombed in a grotesque, overgrown edifice which never truly warmed at its core.

He slung on a gown, trimmed with the fur of three

hundred moths. There were guards stationed outside his door, he knew, and they were for his own protection, but he felt sometimes that they were really his jailers, and that the servants now entering were merely here to torment him. He could have them killed at a word, of course, and he needed to give no reason for it, but he had tried to amuse himself in such capricious ways before and found no real joy in it. What was the point in having the wretches killed, when there were always yet more, an inexhaustible legion of them, world without end? What a depressing prospect: that a man could wade neck-deep in the blood of his servants, and there would still be men and women ready to enter his service more numerous than the motes of dust dancing in the shafts of sunlight from above.

His father had taken no joy in the rank and power that was his. His father had run through life, never taking time to stop, to look, to think. He had been born with a sword in his hand, if you believed the stories, and with destiny like an invisible crown about his brow. The man in the fur-lined gown knew what that felt like. It felt like a vice around the forehead forbidding him rest or peace.

His father had died eight years ago. No assassin's blade, no poison, no battle wound or lancing arrow. He had just fallen ill, all of a sudden, and a tenday later he just stopped, like a clock, and neither doctor nor artificer could wind him up again. His father had died, and in the tenday before, and the tenday after, all of his father's children bar two, all of this man's siblings bar one, had died also. They had died by public execution or covert murder, for good reason or for no reason other than that the succession, his succession, must be undisputed. He was the eldest son, but he knew that the right of primogeniture ran thin where lordly ambitions were concerned. He had spared one sister only, the youngest. She had been eight years old then, and something had failed in him when they presented him with the death warrant to sign. She was sixteen now, and she looked at him always with the carefully bland adoration of a subject, but he feared the thoughts that swam behind that gaze, feared them enough to wake, sweat-sodden, when even dreaming of them.

And the order lay before him still, to have her removed, the one other remaining member of his bloodline. As soon as he had a true-blood son of his own it would be done. He would take no pleasure in it, no more than he would take in the fathering. He understood his own father's life now, whose shadow he raced to outreach. Yet how envied he was! How his generals and courtiers and advisers cursed their luck, that he should sit where he did, and not they. Yet they could not know that, from the seat of a throne, the whole weighty ziggurat of state was turned on its point, and the entire hegemony's weight from the broad base of the numberless slaves, through the subject peoples and all the ranks of the army to the generals, was balanced solely upon him. He represented their hope and their inspiration, and their expectations were loaded upon him.

The servants who washed and dressed him were all of the true race. At the heart of a culture built on slavery there were few outlander slaves permitted in the palace, for who among them could be trusted? Besides, even the most menial tasks were counted an honour when performed for *him*. Of foreign slaves, there were only a handful of advisers, sages, artificers and others whose skills recommended them beyond the lowly stain of their blood, and though they were slaves they lived like princes while they were still of use to him.

His advisers, yes. He was to speak with his advisers later. Before that there were matters of state to attend to. Always the chains of office dragged him down.

Robed now as befitted his station, his brow bound with gold and ebony, His Imperial Majesty Alvdan the Second, lord of the Wasp Empire, prepared to reascend his throne.

★

The Emperor kept many advisers and every tenday he met with them all, a chance for them to speak on whatever subject they felt would best serve himself and his Empire. It was his father's custom too, a part of that clamorous, ever-running life of his that had taken him early to his grave as the Empire's greatest slave and not its master. This generation's Alvdan would gladly have done without it, but it was as much a part of the Emperor as were the throne and the crown and he could not cut it from him.

The individual advisers were another matter. Each tenday the faces might be different, some removed by his own orders, others by his loyal men of the Rekef. Some of his advisers were Rekef themselves, but he was pleased to note that this was no shield against either his displeasure or that of his subordinates.

Some of the advisers were slaves, another long tradition, for the Empire always made the best use of its resources. Scholarly men from conquered cities were often dragged to Capitas simply for the contents of their minds. Some prospered, as much as any slave could in this Empire, and better than many free men did. Others failed and fell. There were always more.

His council, thus gathered, would be the usual tedious mix. There would be one or two Woodlouse-kinden with their long and mournful grey faces, professing wisdom and counselling caution; there would be several Beetles, merchants or artificers; perhaps some oddity, like a Spider-kinden from the far south, a blank-eyed Moth or similar; and the locals, of course: Wasp-kinden from the Rekef, from the army, diplomats, Consortium factors, members of high-placed families and even maverick adventurers. And they would all have counsel to offer, and it would serve them more often than not if he followed it.

His progress into the room was measured in servants who opened the doors for him, swept the floor before his feet, removed his outer robe and the weight of the crown.

4

Others were serving him wine and sweetmeats even as he sat down, food and drink foretasted by yet more invisible underlings.

His advisers sat on either side of him in a shallow crescent of lower seats. The idea was that the Emperor should look straight ahead, and only hear the words of wisdom that tinkled in his ears, without being in any way swayed by the identity of the speaker. Ideologically brilliant, of course, though practically useless, since he had an ear keen enough to identify any of the speakers from a single uttered word. Instead, all they gained for themselves were stiff necks as everyone craned around to look at whoever spoke.

I could change this. He was, after all, the Emperor. He could have them sitting around a table like off-duty soldiers on a gambling spree, or kneeling before him like supplicants, or hanging on wires from the ceiling if he so wanted. Not a day went by without some petty detail of the imperial bureaucracy throwing thorns beneath his feet, yet he always found a reason not to thrust his hand into the works of the machine: it would be bad for morale; it had worked thus far; it was for a good reason, or why would they do it like that?

And in his worst dreams he heard the true reason for his own reticence, for at each change he implemented, each branch he hacked from the tradition-tree, they would all doubtless murmur, *He's not the man his father was.*

He had sired a legion of short-lived bastards and no true-blood sons, and perhaps that was why: the burden of the imperial inheritance that he did not want to pass to any child of his. Still, *that* problematic situation was looming closer each year. The imperial succession was a matter he had forbidden his advisers to speak on, but he felt the weight of it on him nonetheless.

The assembled advisers shuffled in their seats, waiting for his gesture to begin, and he gave it, listening without interest as the first few inconsequential-seeming matters were brought before him. A famine in the East-Empire, so perhaps some artificers should be sent to teach the ignorant savages something approaching modern agriculture. A lazy gesture signalled his assent. A proposal for games to celebrate the first victory over the Lowlands, whenever it happened. He ruled against that, judging it too soon. Another proposal, this from the sad-faced Woodlouse-kinden Gjegevey, who had a sufficient balance of wisdom and acumen to have served Alvdan's father for the last nine years of his reign and yet survived the purges that had accompanied the coronation.

'It might be possible to proceed more gently in our invasion plans,' the soft-voiced old man said. He was a freakish specimen, as all his people were: a whole head taller than any reasonable man, and with his grey skin marked by pale bands up over his brow and down his back. His eyes were lost in a nest of wrinkles. 'These Lowlanders have much knowledge of, mmn, mechanics, philosophy, mm, logistics . . . that we might benefit from. A, hrm, gentle hand . . .'

Alvdan sat back and let the debate run, hearing the military argue about the risk inherent in relying on a slow conquest, while the Rekef insisted that foreigners could not be trusted and the Consortium pressed for a swift assault that would see their Lowland trading rivals crushed. All self-interest, of course, but not necessarily bad for the Empire. He held up a hand and they fell silent.

'We have faith in our generals,' was all he said, and that was that.

Before speaking, the next speaker paused long enough that Alvdan had a chance to steel himself for the words to come.

'Your Imperial Majesty.' General Maxin, whose frown could set the entire Rekef trembling, began carefully. 'There remains the matter of your sister.'

'Does there?' Alvdan stared straight ahead with a tight-lipped smile that he knew must chill them all.

6

'There are those who would—'

'We know, General. Our dear sister has a faction, a party, but she has it whether she wishes it or not. They would put her on this seat of mine because they think she would love them for it. So she must be put to death like all the others. Are you going to counsel us now about the place of mercy in imperial doctrine, or lack of it?'

He heard nothing, but in the corner of his eye caught a motion that was Maxin shaking his head.

'Do you remember General Scarad?' the Emperor continued. 'I believe he was the last man to counsel us about mercy. An unwise trait in a ruler of men, he claimed.'

'Yes, Your Imperial Majesty.'

'Remind us of our response, General.'

'You agreed with him, praised him for his philosophy and then had him put to death, Your Majesty,' replied General Maxin levelly.

'We praise you for your memory, General, so pray continue.'

'An alternative disposition of your sister has been suggested to me, Your Imperial Majesty,' Maxin said, picking his way carefully. 'She cannot be married, obviously, and she is not fit for office, so perhaps she should find some peace of mind in some secular body. Some philosophical order, Majesty, with no political aspirations.'

Alvdan closed his eyes, trying to picture his sister in the robes of the Mercy's Daughters or some such pack of hags. 'Your suggestion is noted, General, and we will consider it,' was all he would say, but it appealed to his sense of humour. Yes, a nice peaceful life of contemplation. How better to drive his little sister out of her mind?

When he was done, and his advisers had no more advice to give, the servants repeated their rigmarole, but this time in reverse. Once he had stood up, his advisers began to sidle out of the room, leaving only General Maxin, who seemed to be taking an unaccountably long time to adjust his swordbelt.

'General, we sense by your subtlety that you wish to speak to us.'

'Some small diversion, Your Imperial Majesty, if you wish it.'

'The Rekef are becoming entertainers now, are they, General?'

'There is a man, Majesty, who has fallen into the hands of my agents. He is a most remarkable and unusual man and I thought that Your Majesty might welcome the chance to meet this individual. He is a slave, of course, and worse than just a slave, not fit to serve any useful purpose. In private he is full of strange words, though. Your Imperial Majesty's education might never have another chance such as this.'

Alvdan at last looked at Maxin directly, seeing a slight smile on the stocky old soldier's face. Maxin had not advised his father, the late Emperor, but he had been wielding a knife on the night after Alvdan's coronation, making sure that the next morning would be free from sibling dissent or disunity. He was not one for jokes.

'Well, General, we are intrigued. Take us to this man.'

The flight had been like something out of a fever dream, nightmarish, and unheard-of.

Thalric had come to Asta expecting to be punished. He had anticipated encountering the grim face of Colonel Latvoc or even the pinched features of General Reiner, his superiors within the Rekef, because he had failed the Empire. There had been a mission to seize the rail auto-motive that the city of Helleron had called the *Pride*, which was then to have provided the spearhead of an invasion to sack Collegium and have any dreams of Lowlands unity die stillborn. Instead, motley renegades under the command of Stenwold Maker had destroyed the *Pride* and even managed somehow to cast suspicion of that destruction on the Wasp-kinden who had so stalwartly tried to save it.

A small setback for the Empire, which must take by force, now, what might have been won by stealth. A great setback indeed for Captain Thalric of the Imperial Army, otherwise Major Thalric of the Rekef Outlander.

And yet there had been no court martial for him to face in the staging town of Asta. It seemed that the race for the Lowlands was now on, and even a flawed blade like Thalric could be put to good use. There had been sealed orders already awaiting him: *Board the* Cloudfarer. *Further instructions to follow.*

And the *Cloudfarer* itself: it was a piece of madness, and no Wasp artificer had made her. Some maverick Auxillian technologist had come up with that design and inflicted it upon him.

It had no hull, or at least very little of one. Instead there was a reinforced wooden base, and a scaffold of struts that composed a kind of empty cage. There was a clockwork engine aft, which two men wound by pedalling furiously, and somewhat stubby wings that bore twin propellers. Thalric had boarded along with a pilot-engineer and Lieutenant te Berro, Fly-kinden agent of the Rekef, who was to brief him. Then the *Cloudfarer* had lifted off, a fragile lattice of wood shuddering up and up through the air under the impelling force of her propellers. Up and up, rising in as tight a spiral as her pilot could drag her into, until they were sailing across the clouds indeed, and higher. Then the pilot let go the struts to either side, and the *Cloudfarer*'s vast grey wings fell open left and right, above and below, and caught the wind. The vessel that had seemed some apprentice's mistake was abruptly speeding over the world beneath it, soaring on swift winds westwards until they were casting across the Lowlands as high, it almost seemed, as the stars themselves sailed.

And it was so *cold*. Thalric was muffled in four cloaks

and layers of woollens beneath, yet the chill air cut through it all, an invisible blade that lanced through the open structure of the *Cloudfarer* and put a rime of white frost on him, and painted his breath into white plumes before the wind whipped it away.

They would reach Collegium faster than any messenger, eating up any lead that Stenwold had built, so that despite Thalric's detour to Asta it was anyone's guess who would arrive first. They were so high, up in the very icy roof of the sky, that no flying scout would spy them. Even telescopes might not pick out their silvery wings against the distant vault of the heavens.

And as he suffered through this ordeal, from the cold and the wind, he hunched forward to catch te Berro's fleeting words, for these were his instructions, his mission, and he would need to remember them.

'You're a lucky man,' the Fly said, shouting over the gale. 'Rekef can't spare an operative of your experience simply for a disciplinary trial. Lowlands work to be done all over the place. You get a second chance. Don't waste it.' They had worked together before, Thalric and te Berro, and a measure of respect had grown between them.

'We'll put you down near Collegium,' te Berro continued. 'Make your own way in. Meet with your agents there. There can be no unity allowed for the Lowlands. There are two plans. The first is swifter than the second, but you are to enact both of them if possible. Even if the first succeeds, the second will also help the war effort.'

And te Berro had explained to him then just what those plans were, and whilst the first was a commonplace enough piece of work, the second was a sharp one and the scale of it shook him a little.

'It shall be done,' he assured the Fly, as the *Cloudfarer* continued its swift, invisible passage over the Lowlands so far beneath them.

★

He walked into Collegium without mishap, entering at the slow time near noon when the city seemed to sleep a little. Collegium had white walls but the gates had stood open for twenty years, had only been closed even then because the Ants of Vek had harboured ambitions to annexe the Beetle city for themselves. There was a guard sitting by the gate, an old Beetle-kinden who was dozing a little himself. Collegium was not interested in keeping people out. If it had been, then he might not have needed to destroy it.

Thalric had been granted a short enough time in the city when he was here last. Two days only and then he had been bundled onto a fixed-wing flier to go and catch Stenwold Maker on the airship *Sky Without*. At that thought he tried to discern where the airfield lay from here and see whether the great dirigible was moored there today, but the walls were too high, the buildings looming above him, for much of Collegium was three-storey, and the poorer districts were four or five. He knew that the Empire had much to learn here. The poor of Collegium cursed their lot and complained and envied, but they had never witnessed how the poor of Helleron lived, or the imperial poor, or the slaves of countless other cities.

If we destroy Collegium, will we ever regain what is lost in the fires? Because it was not only a matter of writing down some secret taken from one of the countless books in the College library. This was a way of life, and it was a good thing to have and, like all good things, the Empire should have it. Imperial citizens should benefit from the knowledge of the men and women who had built this place.

But the second plan that te Berro had given him would kill all that, and he had his orders.

The kernel of discontent that had been within him for a while now gave him a familiar kick, but he mastered it. If the Empire wanted things in such a way, the Empire would have it. He was loyal to the Empire.

He stopped so suddenly in the street that a pair of men

manhandling a trunk barged into him and swore at him before they passed on.

What a heretical idea. Better keep that one hidden deep in one's own thoughts. To even think that loyalty to the Empire, to the better future of the Empire, was not the same as loyalty to the Emperor's edicts or to the Rekef's plans, well, that sort of thinking would get a man on the interrogation table in a hurry. He had avoided a well-deserved reprimand for failing at Helleron and he wasn't about to start playing host to that kind of thought now, that was just asking for trouble.

But in the deepest recesses of his mind the idea turned over, and waited for another off-guard moment.

There had been Rekef agents before him in Collegium, of course. Whilst the Inlander branch of the Empire's secret service purged the disloyal at home, the Outlander had been seeding the cities of the Lowlands with spies and informants. Thalric had made contact with them when he was here last but their networks were four years old. Thalric sent Fly messengers across the city with innocuous letters into which codewords had been dropped like poison into wine. Those men and women the Rekef had infiltrated into this city had been making everyday lives for themselves. Now that was to end. He was calling them up.

He met with them in a low sailors' taverna near enough to the docks for them to hear the creak of rigging through the windows. It was a place where people would forget who it was that met with who, or what business might have been done there – and that was just as well, too. They made an ill-assorted quartet.

The most senior was a lieutenant in the Rekef, and when Thalric had needed a pair of assassins to catch Stenwold Maker in his home he had gone to Lieutenant Graf, trueblood Wasp-kinden, who was working here as a procurer for the blades trade. That, in local parlance, meant that he made introductions between fighting men and prospective patrons, and it put Thalric's operation here on a sound footing straight off. Graf was a lean man, his face marred by a ragged sword-scar from brow to chin that Thalric knew for a duelling mark from the man's days in the Arms-Brethren. The eye traversed by that scar was a dark marble of glass.

The other three were all unranked on the Rekef books, mere agents. Hofi was a Fly-kinden who cut the hair of the rich and shaved the mighty, and Arianna was a Spider and a student of the College. The fourth man, Scadran the halfbreed, worked as a dockhand, catching all the rumours going in and out from both ways down the coast. Wasp blood adulterated with Beetle and Ant, his heavy features displayed the worst of all three to Thalric's eyes, but he was a big man, a brawler. That might be useful, in the end.

He had them at a corner table, drawn far enough from the others that low voices would not carry. They had come in plain garb and armed and they looked at him expectantly. If he sent them out into the city to kill that very night, they would be ready.

'Tell me about Stenwold Maker,' he said.

Lieutenant Graf glanced at the others and then spoke. 'He arrived the day before you, sir. Quite a tail of followers, too.'

'Was there a Mantis-kinden with them?' Thalric asked. His mind returned abruptly to the night battle at the engine works at Helleron that had seen the *Pride* destroyed. There had been a Mantis there, making bloody work of every man who came against him – until Thalric had burned him. Tisamon, Scyla's reports had named him, and his daughter had been Tynisa. *Tynisa*, who had very nearly done for Thalric when he came to finish the matter. In his heart he had hoped that the man had died from his wound, but Graf's next words surprised him not at all.

'Yes, sir, his name is Tisamon. I've learned he was a

student at the College many years ago, at the same time as Maker. Even from back then, he had a reputation.'

'And well deserved,' Thalric confirmed. 'What movements?'

'Maker's settling his men in. He's applied to speak before the Assembly, but that's likely to take a few days. He's not exactly popular. A maverick, they think, and he leaves his College duties too often. They'll stall him with bureaucracy for a while, maybe even a tenday, before they let him in. A slap on the wrist.'

'And the rest?'

'Many of the others are now at the College,' Arianna said. 'Some are in the infirmary, in fact. They brought some wounded with them from Helleron. There's a monstrous little wretch with them, though, some spiky kinden I've never seen before, and he's been going about the factories a lot, the engine yards and the rail depot.'

'That would be Scuto,' Thalric explained, 'Stenwold's deputy from Helleron. He's an artificer, I understand, so some of that might just be professional curiosity.' Thalric remembered his one meeting with Stenwold Maker, a few brave words over a shared drink: two men in the same work on opposite sides, but common ground nonetheless; they were two soldiers who had suffered the same privations under different flags.

And now I stalk him to his lair, and I must destroy him. Because I must believe he would do the same to me, I shall feel nothing.

'I have your orders,' he addressed the foursome. 'We'll need armed men, Lieutenant – and craft from the rest of you. Stenwold Maker is not long for this world.'

Two

To live in an Ant-kinden city was to understand silence, and he had spent time in a few. There was the silence of everyday tasks which meant that one heard only the slaves cluttering about, whispering to one another. There was the silence of the drilling field where there were marching feet and the clink of armour but never a raised voice or a shouted command: five hundred soldiers, perhaps, in perfect formation and perfect order. There was the silence after dark when families sat together with closed lips, while the slaves stayed huddled in their garrets or outbuildings.

Then there was *this* silence, this new silence. It was the silence of a city full of people who knew that the enemy, in its thousands, was camped before their gate.

Nero hurried through this silence bundled in his cloak. All around him the city of Tark was pacing along at its usual speed. At the sparse little stalls local merchants handed over goods wordlessly, receiving exactly the correct money in return. Children ran in the street or played martial games and only the youngest, eight years old or less, ever laughed or called out. Men and women stood in small groups on street corners and said nothing. There was an edge to them all and, in that unimaginable field extending between their minds, there was a single topic of unheard conversation.

It was once different, of course, in the foreigners' quarter where he was lodging. A tenday ago it had been a riotous bloom of colour, penned in by the Ant militia but shaped by countless hands into a hundred little homes away from home. Now there was a hush over that quarter as well because all but the most stubbornly entrenched residents had fled.

And I should have gone with them.

He had been in Tark a year, not long enough to put down roots, but at the same time perhaps the longest he had spent anywhere since Collegium.

What keeps me here?

Guilt, he decided. Guilt because he knew this day would come, when the gold and black horde would pour into the Lowlands, and he had done nothing. He had walked away, once the knives were out, and not looked back.

He attracted little notice from the locals, for he was well known in this part of the city, which meant in any part, given that the local opinion of him could be passed mind to mind as easily as passing a bottle in a taverna. They looked down on him because he was a foreigner, and a Fly-kinden, and an itinerant artist. On the other hand he had friends here and he stayed out of trouble, and therefore he was tolerated. Not that staying out of trouble was an infallible recipe: three tendays before, a house had been robbed beyond the foreigners' quarter. The militia, unable to track down the culprit, had simply hanged three foreigners at random. Visitors, they were saying, were there only on sufferance and were expected to police themselves.

He was an ugly little man, quite bald and with a knuckly face: a heavy brow and broken nose combined with a pugnacious chin to make a profile as lumpy as a clenched fist. Fly-kinden were seldom the most pleasant race to look at, and his appearance was distinctly nasty. If he had been of any other kin he would have hulked and intimidated his way through life, but no amount of belligerent features could salvage him from being only four feet from his sandals to the top of his hairless head.

His name was Nero and he had made a living for the last twenty years as an artist of such calibre that his name and his work could open select doors all across the Lowlands. In his own mind that was just a sideline. In a land where most people never saw much beyond their own city's walls, unless for commercial purposes, he was a seasoned traveller. He rolled from city to city by whatever road his feet preferred, imposed on the hospitality of whoever would take him in, and did whatever he wanted.

Which brought him back to the present, because he now wanted, if his continuing presence was anything to go by, to be involved in a siege and bloody war. He himself was unclear on this point, but so far he had not felt inclined to leave, and shortly he suspected that he would not be able to do so without being shot out of the sky by the Wasp light airborne.

Ahead of him the city wall of Tark was a grand pale jigsaw puzzle of great stones, adorned with its murder holes, its crenellations, passages and engines of destruction. In its shadow the Ant-kinden were calm. This wall had withstood sieges before when their own kin of other cities had come to fight against them, just as Tarkesh armies had been repulsed by the walls of those kinfolk in Kes or Sarn.

Nero knew that the army now outside was not composed of Ant-kinden, and would not fight like them. Whenever he had that thought, he had a terrible itching to be gone, and yet here he still was.

Parops was of unusual character for an Ant, especially an officer. His friendship with Nero had begun on rocky ground when the universal grapevine had informed him that the woman picked out as his mate was sitting nude before the Fly's easel, and he was a joke across the city before he had stormed across to remonstrate. Ant pairings were a strange business, though, made for the convenience of the city and the furtherance of children, and they lacked the personal investment, the jealousies and passions, of other kinden. In truth, after their coupling was achieved, the two of them had grown bored of one another. Nero had been one of a line of diversions she had taken up.

And of course Parops had been expected to kill the Fly on the spot, both by his mate and the city at large. Not from rage, for Ants were rarely given to it, but for the affront to his racial, civic and personal dignity. Instead, he had passed most of the night up on the roof by Nero's side, looking out over the city and talking about other places.

Parops was a wild eccentric by Ant standards, which meant that he entertained unusual thoughts occasionally. His natural intelligence had brought him just so far up the ladder of rank and he knew that he would never receive further promotion. In the opinion of his superiors he was not wholly sound. So here he was, a tower commander on the walls of Tark, a position considered more bureaucratic than military until now. Now he stood at the arrowslit window of his study and looked down over the chequerboard of the Wasp army. The late sunlight played on his bleached skin.

'How are the negotiations going?' Nero enquired, for a Wasp embassy had been admitted to the city earlier that day. While Parops was not privy to their debate, news of its progress loomed large in the collective mind of the city, silently passed from neighbour to neighbour in rippling waves of information.

'Still keeping them waiting,' the Ant explained.

'It's their prerogative,' Nero allowed. 'So what are they doing meanwhile?'

'There are some Spider-kinden slavers left in the city,' Parops said, 'and some of them have Scorpion-kinden on their staff. It seems that the Scorpions and the Wasps go way back, mostly in the same trade, so we have people paying the Scorpions for their recollections. The Royal Court is busy putting the picture together.'

'How seriously are they taking it?'

'There are thirty thousand soldiers at our gates,' Parops pointed out.

'Yes, but you know how politics goes. Everyone's city is the greatest, and everyone's soldiers are invincible, at least until they get vinced.'

Parops nodded. 'They're taking it seriously, plentifully seriously. They've gone to the tunnels and spoken to the nest-queen herself, woken up the flying brood. They're putting in readiness every machine that can take to the air. Everyone who can pilot a flier or handle artillery is getting marching orders, and it's crossbows for everyone else. It's a flying enemy we face, and that much we understand. It's something new.'

And Ants did not like new things, Nero reflected, but at least the complacency had gone. The ant nest beneath the city, which produced domesticated insects that laboured for their human namesakes, was a valuable resource. To utilize the winged males and females as mounts of war would kill off an entire generation of them, a tragedy of economics which meant they were only brought out in the worst of emergencies. The Royal Court of Tark had finally conceded that this was nothing less.

'You've had some dealings with these Wasps,' Parops noted.

'As few as I could but, yes, a long time ago.'

'Tell me about the other kinden they have in their army. Have they formed an alliance against us?'

'The Wasp Empire doesn't do alliances,' Nero said with a harsh laugh. 'Those are slaves.'

'They arm their slaves?' The Ants of Tark, as with Ant-kinden almost everywhere, kept slaves for the menial work and would not dream of putting so much as a large knife in their hands. It was not so much for fear of rebellion as pride in their own martial skills.

'It's more complicated than that. They deal in very large armies, and they swell their ranks with the conquered – Auxillians, they call them. They enslave whole cities, you see. Then they ship out fighters to some part of their Empire remote from their homes, and set them to it. It's as though here you got sent out to . . . Collegium or Vek, or somewhere. I imagine sometimes it doesn't work, but mostly the men sent out there will have family back home and they'll know that if they run, or turn on their masters, then their kin will suffer. And so they fight. They'll either be skilled help, artificers and the like, or just bow-fodder, first into the breach. It can't be much of a prospect.'

Parops nodded again, and Nero felt a shiver as he realized that his words would be at large in the city now, darting from mind to mind, perhaps even reaching the Royal Court itself.

'There are still some foreigners leaving by the west gate,' the Ant said carefully. 'In fact there are still foreigners coming *in* by the west gate – mostly slavers hunting a late sale. It's probably time you made your move.'

'I'll stay a little while,' Nero said casually.

'I get the impression that when these fellows draw sword they're not going to care what kinden you are, if you're found inside the walls.'

'More than likely true,' Nero admitted.

Parops at last turned from the window and his obsessive scrutiny of the near future.

'Why are you here, Nero?' he asked. 'Your race is hardly renowned for its staying power in the fray. You run further to live longer, isn't that it? So why haven't you done what any sensible human being would do, and run while you can?'

Nero shrugged. Partly it was due to his friendship with Parops, of course, but there was another reason, and it was such a personal, trivial thing that he was ashamed to admit it. 'I've never witnessed a war,' he said. 'I've put a few skirmishes under my belt, over the years, but never a war. Not really. I did a study once, the Battle of the Gears at the Collegium gates, you know, and shall we say critical reception was lukewarm. That's because it was beyond my experience, and I couldn't capture it. And so that's my reason, as good as any other – and it's a poor one, I know.'

'You are quite mad,' Parops told him.

'Probably. However, my own kinden are very good at squeaking out at the last minute, and there are still a few grains of sands in the glass. You never know, perhaps I'll reclaim my heritage after all.'

'Don't leave it too long,' Parops warned, and then some fresh word came to him, invisible through the crowded air of the city. 'They have taken the ambassadors in, at last,' he announced.

When Skrill came running back she was ducking low amidst the sprays of man-high sword-grass. Her progress involved a series of sudden dashes across less covered ground, moving with her long legs at a speed Salma knew he himself could not have matched. Then she would freeze into immobility, hunched under cover, an arrow already fitted to her bowstring. He and Totho were dug in together beneath one of the great knots of grass that arched over them with its narrow, sharp-edged fronds. They watched Skrill's punctuated progress impatiently.

Then she had flung herself to a halt beside them, bowling into them in a flurry of loose earth. She was a strange creature, halfbreed of Mynan Soldier Beetle and something else, and with no manners or education to recommend her, but she had led them flawlessly to within sight of the Wasp army as if she knew every inch of the terrain.

'What did you see?' Totho asked her.

'Did you see her – or the Daughters?' Salma interrupted.

She gave him a wide-eyed, mocking look. 'Did you perchance not notice those many thousand soldiers out there, Your Lordship? Wherever your glittery lady is, she ain't paradin' herself about their camp, now, is she? So no, I din't happen to meet her and invite her over here for a pint and a chat.' She shook her head, one hand coming up to tug at her pointed ears as though trying to make them longer. 'I didn't even get close to the camp because they got a thousand men on sentry duty, or that's like it looked to me. A whole ring of them, and earthworks, palisade, even little lookie-outie towers. And the sky! Don't even get me started. If you was thinkin' about just swanning in with those wings of yours you best put that candle right out. They got men circlin' and circlin' like flies on a tenday-dead corpse. They plainly reckon the Ants'll give 'em grief – and why not? I would, if I was runnin' things at Tark Hall.'

'Ants are too straight for that, aren't they?' Totho asked. 'I thought they'd just line up and fight.'

'Don't believe it, Beetle-boy,' she told him. 'Ants'll play the dirty tricks same as anyone. They do *war*, Beetlie, and war means day and night work. Nobody ever won a war just by fighting fair.'

'Don't call me that,' Totho said, for the nicknames she used were starting to gall him. 'I'm no more a Beetle than you are a . . . a whatever it is you are, or aren't.'

'Am I a Beetle? No. Is His Lordship a Beetle? No. Then you get to be Beetle-boy unless we can get a better Beetle than you,' she told him without sympathy.

'Will the pair of you be—' Salma had started to hiss, and then the Wasps were in sight, skimming at just a man's height and touching the tops of the sword-grass as they came. In that same moment they had clearly spotted the three spies.

There were half a dozen of them, light airborne out

merely on a scouting mission, but Wasps were a pugnacious lot and never ones to shirk a fight. Their leader shouted an order and two of them broke off, arrowing back towards their camp. The others sped towards Salma with swords drawn and palms outstretched to unleash their energy stings.

Skrill shot one straight off, leaping up with her sudden speed and loosing an arrow that split the second oncomer's eye. The Wasp flier recoiled in the air and then dropped from sight amidst the tall grass.

Salma had no time to string his own bow. As the three remaining soldiers launched the golden lightning of their stings he let his wings take him straight upwards, his shortsword – stolen Wasp-make itself – clearing its scabbard.

Skrill had already dashed to one side but Totho had no option but to cast himself to the ground and hope. He felt one sting lash across his pack as though he had been punched there by a strong man. Then he was up with a magazine slotted into his crossbow.

One of the men had skimmed upwards in pursuit of Salma and it struck Totho how they seemed nimbler in the air than most Wasps, obviously hand-picked as scouts. He raised his bow and loosed.

The man coming for him jinked aside and the bolt sped past him. Totho saw the man's face split into a grin in the knowledge that there would be no reloading of such a cumbersome weapon as a crossbow in time. By then Totho was racking back the lever and shooting again and again, seeing surprise and dismay splash across those same features. The man dodged the second shot but not the third, nor the fourth or fifth, and he ploughed dead into the earth six feet away. They were a race of builders and artificers, the Wasps, but for all their numbers and ingenuity they were behind the Lowlands yet in craft.

He heard a shout nearby and saw Skrill fighting furiously

with another enemy, sword to sword. She was swift, her blade lunging and darting like a living thing, but her opponent was a professional, and the metal plates of his armour kept turning aside her blows. Totho knew he couldn't risk a shot in their direction and drew his own blade, breaking cover to run to her aid.

Above them Salma dived and spun in a deadly aerial ballet with his opponent. For them, distance was all: too close and they would foul each other, too far and the Wasp would have more chance to use his sting. Amidst their aerobatics their swords flashed rarely, each seeking a second's opening to strike against side or back.

Salma was Dragonfly-kinden, born to the air, and his race prided themselves on their grace and control while on the wing. The Wasp, for his part, was as fleet and nimble as his kind ever were, but there was a distance even so. Salma had abruptly cut away, seeming to falter in the air, allowing the Wasp to draw up to shoot at him. In that same moment Salma reversed his motion, wings powering him forwards. The man tried to angle down to face him head-on, sword sweeping in a broad parry, but Salma was through his guard on the instant, driving the blade between the Wasp's ribs where his armour left off, and then using the pull of the man's heavy descent to drag the steel from his corpse.

He touched down, looking around for more enemies just in time to see Totho and Skrill finish off the last Wasp scout together.

'Get your kit together!' Skrill urged him. 'There'll be more!'

Salma scooped up his satchel, seeing Totho shoulder the big canvas bag that held his tools and belongings. *I travel very light these days*, the Dragonfly thought wryly, but of course, being captured and stripped of your possessions would do that to a man. He had only what the Mynan resistance had been able to find for him.

Skrill's kitbag was already strapped on her back, a position it never left save when she was using it as a lumpy pillow. She pelted past him even as he and Totho were collecting their gear, and they ran after her, knowing it was vain to try to catch up.

The Wasp armies had yet to invest the city of Tark in siege. *But for us the war has already started.*

He remembered his talk with Aagen, the Wasp artificer whose information had originally sent him south to Tark – the same who had been given the Butterfly dancer named Grief in Chains and then released her with the name Aagen's Joy. Salma had now killed another Wasp, his first since then. There had been no hesitation at the time. After all, the man had been trying to kill him.

And yes, the Wasp had been another human being with all a man's hopes and aspirations, and now snuffed out by eighteen inches of steel. But also, there had been enough Dragonfly dead during the Twelve-Year War to make the numbers now massed outside Tark pale into insignificance. Amongst them, his own father and three cousins, including his favourite, Felipe Daless. Not just kinden but *kin*: blood that called out for a levelling of the scales; three principalities of the Dragonfly Commonweal that groaned under the boot of the Empire.

He hardened his heart. There would be more blood spilled before the end of this, and some of it could easily be his own.

Skrill had stopped ahead, waiting for them. Totho blundered up to her.

'And how did they find us?' he demanded.

'Scouts, Beetle-boy. What do you think they were doing?'

'They followed *you*.'

'You take them words back, or we're lookin' to have a disagreement right here,' she said hotly. 'Nobody asked you to link with us.'

Totho swallowed whatever words he had been going to utter and, after a moment's thought, said, 'Well it's just as well I did, or you'd have been spitted right back there. What do you think of that?'

'Will the pair of you be quiet?' Salma grumbled without much hope.

'I was playing with him,' Skrill said. 'I was—' Suddenly she fell silent, turning away from Totho with her hand plucking an arrow from her quiver.

'Put the bow *down!* Put the swords *down!* Put the crossbow *down!*' barked a voice from somewhere within the grass. There was an uncertain pause, and then a bolt spat out of a nearby thicket, ploughing the earth at Totho's feet. Even as they watched men began emerging in a crescent formation in front of them, swathed in cloaks of woven grass and reeds, but all with crossbows levelled. For a moment Salma thought it was the Wasps that had them, but they were Ants – Tarkesh Ants – with their pale faces smeared with dirt and green dye. Beneath the cloaks they wore armour of boiled leather and darkened metal.

'Weapons *down!*' shouted their leader. 'Or I shoot the lad with the crossbow. This is your last chance.'

Totho dropped the bow quickly enough, and his sword as well. Salma did the same, trying to gauge his chances of taking to the air. He counted ten Ants in all, and they would be in each other's minds. The least wrong move and they *all* would see it. Salma did not rate his chances of dodging so many bolts.

Skrill gave a hiss of annoyance and placed her bow on the ground, replacing the arrow in her quiver.

'What in blazes have we here?' the Ant officer asked, aloud for their benefit. 'A bag of halfbreeds, it would seem.'

Salma could only guess at the silent thoughts going meanwhile between him and his men.

'We're not with that army out there,' he said hastily. 'In fact, we're from Collegium.'

'I can't see a crew like yours fitting in anywhere outside a freakshow,' the Ant officer replied levelly. 'But what you are right now, lad, is prisoners. You come along with me, and anyone who does any tricks gets a bolt up the arse, and no mistake. There're folk in the city just waiting to speak to folk like you.'

'We're not your enemies,' Salma tried again. He tried a smile, but the officer was having none of it.

'You might be all sorts, lad, but I think you're spies looking to get inside the city. Looks like you got your wish too, doesn't it, although not in the way you might prefer.'

Three

The Prowess Forum had never seen the like. This was no formal event, no meeting of teams from the duelling league, and yet the backsides of the onlookers were packed all the way up the stone steps that rose in tiers at every wall. The aficionados of the duel were crammed in shoulder to shoulder, from College masters through the ranks of students and professional bladesmen to the children who followed their favourites with the fanatical loyalty of Ants to their city.

The fighters stood ready in the circle, which had been scuffed by a hundred hundred feet in the past. Neither participant was new to it. They had faced each other before, and there was nothing the crowd liked better than a rematch of champions. The Master of Ceremonies, the old Ant-kinden Kymon of Kes, had tried to start the duel three times, but the crowd was refusing to quieten down for him.

To one side stood the acknowledged champion of the Prowess Forum. He was Mantis-kinden, as the very best of the best always were. They were born with blade-skill in their blood: it was the Ancestor Art of their nation. They came to the College sporadically, one or two in every year. When they fought they inevitably claimed the prize, and then mostly they left. Piraeus of Nethyon had stayed on, however, preferring the life of a champion of Collegium to anything his homeland might offer. He made his living in private duel and by hiring out his skills to any duelling house so desperate for victory as to show the bad form of buying in a champion. Nor had he been short of offers this last year, for winning had ousted taking part as the fashionable thing. Now many magnates of Collegium kept duelling teams to further their prestige.

But the crowd were here to see more than a haughty Mantis-kinden win yet another bout. Enough of them had gathered there to see his opponent. The less charitable said that they wanted to see her before some stroke dealt by Piraeus ruined her, for he was a misogynist at the best of times, and this match . . . The Mantis-kinden saved their utmost barbs of loathing for one target. Why they hated the Spider-kinden quite so much was lost in time, but they did, and they never forgot a grievance.

Like most Spider-kinden, she was beautiful. She was also unusual in that she was a daughter of Collegium, not some arrogant foreigner. The name on the lips of the crowd as she entered was 'Tynisa'. Properly she was Tynisa Maker, but she was so obviously none of the old man's blood that just the one name sufficed.

Piraeus was tall and lean, his face chiselled with distaste. The bruises he had given Tynisa when they had last met had healed, and it was obvious he was ready to gift her with another set. She was shorter than he and slighter, an eye-catching young woman with her fair hair bound into a looped braid and her green eyes dancing.

There was something in the way she stood that told the best of them this was going to be a new kind of contest. She did not stand like a Prowess duellist or like a Spider-kinden. In her time away from the city she had learned something new.

She had learned who she was and what blood ran in her veins, but only Tynisa and two spectators there knew it.

Kymon called for silence once more, striking the two

practice swords together in a dull clatter of bronze-covered wood.

'I shall not ask again!' he bellowed. 'Silence now, or this match shall not take place!'

At long last the crowd quieted, under threat of its entertainment being removed. Kymon nodded heavily and passed the swords out. They were, in the hands of these fighters, graceless things. Those two were meant for swords more slender and crafted of true steel.

'Salute the book!' Kymon directed, and they turned to the great icon carved at one wall of the forum and raised their blades.

'Clock!' barked the Master of Ceremonies and stepped back hurriedly. Neither of them moved even as the ponderous hands of the mechanical timepiece ground into motion. For a long moment, to the hushed anticipation of the crowd, they merely faced each other. Tynisa studied Piraeus's face and knew that, while she was seeing just what she had seen before, he could tell how she had changed.

But he was proud, and he was a blur of motion as he now came for her, his ersatz blade swinging in tight arcs to trap her.

She gave before him, barely parrying, making the fighting-circle her world, backing around it so the darts and sweeps of his sword clove empty air. She thought he might get angry, since she had seen him provoked before, but he retained his icy calm and his moves became tighter and tighter, and she was going to have to do something soon . . .

In a sudden flurry she had taken his sword aside and in that instant she was on the offensive. She did not keep it long, but after that it was anybody's. She and Piraeus circled, stopped, circled back. The air between them rattled with the clash of their blades. The audience were on the edge of their seats but the two combatants had forgotten them. Their world had contracted to that duelling ring. The

Prowess Forum with its clock and book had ceased altogether to exist for them.

He never gave up pressing his attack, for he knew the natural order of things was for him to advance, his foe to give way before him. He tried and he tried to turn the fight back to that familiar territory. He had done it before when, not so very long ago, he had beaten her two strikes to none. Now she was holding him off, constantly turning his attacks into her own. Her guard was iron. He could not breach it, no more than she could break his.

And the thought came to Tynisa, *If these were live blades, I'd have killed him by now.* Her own Mantis blood was rising in her and she saw Piraeus then as his own kind would. *Look at this coward playing with children.* He was all skill and poise, but the pride of his heritage had died within him.

So let's call it real. And she gave her blood full rein. The orderly, calculated exchange of the Prowess Forum fell in pieces around them. She cut straight through, his blade passing inches from her face, and the point of hers rammed into his stomach.

He doubled over, hit the ground shoulder-first, and it took all of her will's work to hold back a second strike that would have broken his neck in lieu of opening his throat. She stepped back carefully with the slight, sad thought that she could not return to this place. Her skills, once made here, had been reforged in blood, in the outside world. The reflexes and instincts honed between life and death were not tame beasts for her to teach tricks to.

Piraeus was slowly getting up, trying to catch his breath. She waited for him, motionless, and amongst the crowd not a word, not a fidget.

He lunged at her, as swift a move as they had yet seen, and it would have caught her if she had been a mere duellist. She had moved before her eyes had registered his strike, the point of his sword missing by inches. She struck

31

him a numbing rap to the elbow that sent the blade tumbling from his hand.

After she had left, with the crowd baying her name, standing on the seats and cheering, few had eyes to watch Piraeus stand up again. His face was thunderous as he rubbed his injured arm. He made to leave by another door but a voice stopped him. The doors to the Prowess Forum were left open always, and there was another Mantis-kinden lounging there, a man older than he in an arming jacket of green.

'An interesting fight.'

Piraeus narrowed his eyes. 'The fight isn't over.'

'Yes it is.' The older man pushed himself off the wall, and Piraeus noticed that he had a claw over his right hand, a glove of metal and leather with a blade that jutted a foot and a half from the fingers. It was the weapon of choice for Mantids from the old days, and Piraeus recognized the stranger's sword-and-circle brooch a moment later.

'Weaponsmaster,' he stated, and it was obvious he had never met one before.

'We live yet,' the man acknowledged. 'You're not going after her, Piraeus.'

'She's a Spider.' Piraeus's face twisted. 'I'll have her in the next pass, don't you worry, and I'll have her with steel.'

'No, you won't.'

The young duellist shook his head, missing something, he knew. 'Are you *protecting* her? She's Spider-blood. She's our enemy.'

'She's *my* blood, boy,' the old man said, and let that sink in.

Piraeus's look of bafflement slowly decayed into horror. 'But she—'

'What, boy? You've a problem with me? Want to call me out, I'll wager?'

'I don't even know who you are.'

'I am Tisamon, and I earned this badge and this claw, and she is of my blood. You should keep that in mind before you say anything else.'

The name bit into the youth's memory, Tisamon saw. Piraeus had heard of him, even it was just through Collegium's duelling circles. There had been a time when Tisamon, too, had played with his skills just like this young man.

'So it would be unwise of you to take this further with Tynisa,' he said. 'Lick your wounds and learn from them, but if you come after her with a real blade in your hands—'

'You'll be there,' spat Piraeus, disgusted.

Tisamon smiled slightly. 'I won't need to be. She will.'

'Why all the hurry?' Che complained. Almost as soon as she had left the Prowess Forum, hastening to congratulate Tynisa, she had run into one of her uncle's agents. The big Ant called Balkus, who in Helleron had seemed just a part of that city's gritty tapestry, looked woefully out of place amidst the understated order of Collegium.

'If you move quick, they can't follow you so easily,' was all he said, so Che was forced to jog after him.

It was strange to be back after seeing what she had seen. Collegium, with its peace, its petty one-upmanship, its learning, all seemed like a mummer's show where the backcloth could be torn down at any moment to reveal the chaos behind. She knew that Stenwold wanted to speak before the Assembly, who were currently snubbing him, but he had not let his plans wait on them. He had not told her what they were, either, or what role she might play in them. Instead he had closeted himself away with Scuto, or else he had gone on rambling and random hikes about the city with Balkus or Tisamon watching over him. It was probably all to confuse their watchers but it served to confuse Che just as well.

Was she herself under surveillance? With the thought she began scanning the faces, but Collegium was a diverse city and the native Beetle-kinden played host to people from all over the Lowlands and beyond. Even here, making her rapid progress down the Haldrian Way that led to the metal market, she could pick out every kinden that called the Lowlands home, together with a mix of halfbreeds, and a few others that might be other kinden entirely, from distant lands. Any one of them could be an imperial agent, and she knew it was more likely to be some innocuous-looking Beetle wood-seller than that Wasp-kinden man on the street corner perusing a bookseller's discounted stock.

It was a strange feeling, exciting and uneasy, to think that she could be important enough to be watched.

Balkus abruptly turned into the shop beside the book-seller and, when she moved to follow him, he signalled for her to continue on down the Haldrian. With no idea of where she was going, she kept wandering, with less and less enthusiasm, through the bustle until he caught up with her again.

'Wanted to see if we were being followed,' he explained, his thoughts obviously on the same tracks as hers.

'And were we?'

'No bloody idea,' he admitted. 'I'm not so good at all the sneak stuff. A fighter, me.'

And he was. She had seen enough evidence of that. The voice of his nailbow, spitting its powder-charged bolts with a sound like thunder, remained with her from the battle around the great railway engine called the *Pride*.

'Here,' he said at last and ducked into a little taverna that seemed mostly deserted. The owner, a greying Beetle-kinden, nodded cheerily to him, and did not object when he hurried Che into a back room. She had a brief glimpse of a Fly-kinden in a broad-brimmed hat, sitting apparently asleep at one table, who was one of her uncle's men here.

He had one eye still slightly open, enough to watch the door.

'So what is going on?' she demanded, and fortuitously it was Stenwold himself beyond the door to answer her questions.

She was reminded of the Taverna Merraia, where she and her friends had been briefed by Stenwold the first time, then sent off at short notice to Helleron and the first step in a course of events that had brought her betrayal, slavery, love, and the stain of a dead man's blood on her hands.

Balkus sat down by the door and unslung his nailbow, taking up a filthy rag in a vain effort to clean it out. Stenwold sat at a table with a mess of papers strewn across it. Beside him was thorny Scuto and Sperra, a young Fly-kinden woman who was still recovering from the injuries she received during the *Pride* battle. Across the table sat Achaeos, and Che went over to him instantly. She was aware, as she was still always aware, of their eyes on her as she hugged him. They certainly made an odd pair. Partly it was that she was broader than he was, and not so much shorter, for the Moths were a slight kinden, but mostly it was because Moths generally resented Beetles, despised them and loathed them for their invasive technologies and their crass profiteering. In truth, Achaeos was no different, for he had fought her race over the mines at Helleron. He would make an exception for her, though, having already done many things and travelled a great many miles specifically for her sake.

'We move within the next hour,' Stenwold announced. 'They've been watching me close enough but we're in the clear here, and when we leave it'll be underground. By the time they pick me up again, we'll be in business.'

'You've a plan,' Achaeos observed.

'We've always got a plan,' Scuto agreed. 'And just like before, last minute's best.'

'When we leave here, Scuto is taking the rail to Sarn,' Stenwold explained. 'I will see the Collegium Assembly soon enough, and if I have to tattoo the threat of the Wasp Empire on every Assembler's forehead to get my point across, I'll do it. But Collegium cannot stand alone. Sarn has been our ally now for just a little while, but the Ants of Sarn have proved themselves faithful before. They came to relieve the siege when Vek had us invested. We need them to rally to our flag now too. Scuto, you've still got your contacts in Sarn, yes?'

'Oh they've been quiet enough.' Scuto's grotesque, thorn-pocked face wrinkled. 'A decent shout in the earhole'll get 'em moving, don't you worry.'

'Then you're to go shout at them. I need you talking to the Royal Court at Sarn, or at least to someone within it. Tell them about Tark. Tell them about Myna and Maynes. Tell them about the Empire, most of all.'

'They ain't going to want to see me,' Scuto said. 'Ain't nobody wants to see me. I'll get a mouthpiece, though. I'll get your message through.'

'Good man. Take Balkus and Sperra to help you.'

Balkus cleared his throat. 'Excuse me, Master Maker, but you might just notice my skin-shade here.'

Stenwold looked at him blankly, seeing only a Sarnesh Ant, larger than most, and wearing a glum expression at that moment. Then he recalled another such: Marius, who had died at Myna. They had both been considered rene-gades, and if an Ant turned from his city there was no easy way of going back.

'I suppose you won't be going back to Sarn any time soon,' Stenwold admitted. Marius had left Sarn because all those years ago his superiors would not listen when he warned them about the Wasps. Yet he had left to better serve his city, while Balkus, Stenwold was sure, had left for less noble motives. The outcome was the same.

'I'll be good just with Sperra,' Scuto said. 'I ain't no greenhouse flower, chief. You up for a trip, Sperra?'

The little Fly-kinden nodded wearily.

'You up to go speak to a Queen for me?' Scuto pressed.

'Not on your life,' she said.

'Sure, you'll come round to it,' Balkus told her. 'Now for me, I'll stay right here and look after the chief. That sound like a good plan? I'm a handy fellow to have around.'

'Might not be a bad idea,' Scuto agreed. Stenwold looked from him to Balkus and back again.

'I'm going to have Tisamon and Tynisa right here should I need them, but . . . fair enough. Another pair of hands and eyes won't go amiss.' He looked over at his niece and her lover. 'Che and Achaeos, you're going to Sarn as well, but for different reasons.'

Che put on a stern expression. 'You wouldn't be trying to keep me safe again, would you? Because that didn't work so well the last time you tried it.'

Stenwold's smile was bleak. 'The Wasps are invading the Lowlands, niece, so there isn't anywhere that's safe any more. Scuto and I operated out of Sarn for a while, way back, and we had some unlikely misadventures that owed nothing to the Empire. Specifically, we had a fairly heated run-in with a band of fellows called the Arcanum.'

Achaeos hissed at the word. 'What kind of run-in?' he demanded.

'They fought with us at Helleron, didn't they?' asked Che. 'They're the Moth army or something?'

'A secret society of sorts,' Stenwold explained. 'But mostly they're spies and agents for Achaeos's people. All a misunderstanding, the trouble we had then, but it's left us knowing a little about them that should be useful. Between what Scuto can furnish you with and the fact of having Achaeos on our side, I think we can hope to make contact.'

'You want *us* to convince the Arcanum to fight on our

side?' Achaeos asked, in a tone of voice that suggested it could not be done.

'I want you to do whatever you can. Your people in Dorax have been left alone more than those in your own city, and that makes them, I think, less leery of outsiders,' Stenwold said. 'We still get a steady trickle of them at the College, at least, and they send the odd ambassador to Sarn. I'm hoping that they will at least consider lending us some aid. I know we can't expect armies from them, but even a little information would be useful. Will you do it?'

Achaeos looked to Che. 'And you?'

'I'll do whatever I have to,' she said. 'I've met with your people before. These Arcanum can't be worse than the Skryres at Tharn.'

His face wrinkled at that reference, but he turned back to Stenwold. 'I cannot promise anything, but what can be done will be done.'

Stenwold had chosen that same taverna because it had possessed an underground exit leading to the river, from way back when the temperance drive was running riot in the Assembly and the wine-duty had been sky-high. He now watched Scuto and Che, Achaeos and Sperra disappearing down it, to make their way to the rail station as swiftly as possible. At the same time another man of his, dressed in a spiky wooden harness and swathed in a cloak, would be poking about the automotive works located along the Foundry West Way. Stenwold and Scuto had discovered a long time ago that difference could provide a disguise in itself if, like Scuto, you were so different that the difference was all people saw.

Tisamon and Tynisa would be back at the College by now, unaware that the wheels of the plan were turning already. He had lied to Che in the taverna's back room. Sarn was by no means safe, but he had a feeling it would be safer than Collegium over these next few days. He would get to see the Assembly sooner or later, and put his case to them, though the Wasps no doubt had men bribed there to speak against him. At this late hour nobody could predict whether the old men and women of Collegium might recover the wisdom of their predecessors. For this reason, he knew, the Wasps would be looking to stop him making his speech.

With Balkus lumbering behind him he set off back for the College. The big Ant was something of a mystery to him, being Scuto's man, not Stenwold's own. He knew him for a mercenary and yet the man had asked for no payment. That was either a happy turn of events or a suspicious one.

'Tell me, Balkus, what's in it for you?' he asked boldly.

'Don't trust me, is it?'

Without even glancing around, still presenting his broad back to the theoretical knife, Stenwold shrugged. 'It's not a trusting business.'

'That it's not,' the man agreed. 'Look, I'm no hero, right? I plied my trade from Helleron down to Everis, and I must have signed on with everyone from crooks to Aristoi at one time or another. It's a fine stretch of land thataways, so between Helleron and the Spiders there's always work for a man like me. Wasps will change all that. A man like me under their shadow is either a slave waiting for the chains or he gets slapped with rank and papers and made to do their dirty work for them. If I'd wanted that I'd have stayed in Sarn.'

'There are always frontiers,' Stenwold pointed out. The white spires of the College were visible ahead now. 'You could have just moved on.'

'You're trying to get rid of me?'

'I'm curious, Balkus. If I'm going to rely on you, I need to know you. I know Scuto trusts you. So that's a good start.'

'Yeah, well.' Stenwold heard an awkwardness in the Ant's voice. 'Scutes and me go way back. We used to take turns bailing each other out. This is . . . what, almost before *you* knew him. And some of the lads and lasses with him, they were fellows of mine, and a lot of them are just ash and dirt now. And you get to wondering how it's going to be, you know.'

'I do,' Stenwold agreed. 'Well don't think you're not appreciated. I saw you fight before the *Pride*. You did good work there.'

'So did you, and your niece and a whole lot of them,' Balkus agreed. 'And some that didn't leave that field alive either.'

They passed by the twin statues of Logic and Reason that adorned the east gate of the College. Stenwold paused a moment to rest a hand on Logic, carved as a female Beetle of mature years wielding a metal rod marked with the gradations of an artificer's rule. The Great College was where learning was to be had here for the youth of all kinden and, while the rich paid their way, there were scholarships for the poor as well. The Moths might keep their secrets in the dark of their mountain fastnesses, but here learning was light to be spread to all corners of the world. There was nowhere else like it, and there never had been. And now the Wasps wanted to destroy it.

At the gates he turned to the Ant-kinden. 'I have work for you. An opportunity.'

'Name it,' Balkus told him, and Stenwold did. From the man's expression the duties outlined did not suit him, and it was a test, in a way, to see whether he would accept it. In the end he nodded, perhaps just because Ant-kinden were bred to take orders. With a final grimace and a shake of his head Balkus set off, heading away from the College.

Stenwold saw knots of students point him out as he entered. He was aware that, all unsought, he had a reputation within these grounds. He was considered a free-thinker, apparently: he dared to teach that which the orthodox Masters of the College would not touch. He had been warning of the Wasp Empire for a decade now, and this very year they had finally come to the Lowlands. First they had competed at the Great Games, taking a pointedly diplomatic second place in any contest they chanced their hand at. Now the news was seeping in of armies on the move, the drums of war sounding from the east. Stenwold the panic-monger had become Stenwold the prophet.

There was a far greater murmur now as he crossed the College grounds, and all of a sudden he realized what it must mean. Concrete report must have come to Collegium that Tark had been attacked, that the invasion had actually started. He turned to look at all those young faces, and he saw hope and fear, doubt and admiration, all mixed in. Seeing him stop, many of them approached him, calling out questions.

'Master Maker, where will the Empire go when Tark throws them back?'

'Master Maker, how do they fight? Do they use automotives?'

'What happens if they smash down the walls of Tark?'

This last question silenced them. It was something most of them had never considered, for a dozen Ant-kinden expeditions had been turned back by that city's defences. The political balance of the Lowlands had been stagnant for generations. Change, on such a scale, was unthinkable.

'If they take the city of Tark,' Stenwold said, speaking quietly enough, but the silence hanging over the students was eerie, 'they will come west.' He knew that his words would be taken as truth by them, simply because he spoke them, but he knew that they were indeed true and so did not care. The girl who had asked the question pushed forward from her fellows.

'But they can't, surely? What do they want?'

He tried to place her. She had attended some of his

history classes earlier that year. 'Power. Control. Their Empire is like a spinning top that must keep moving lest it falls.'

'But can't we do anything?' she asked. She was a young Spider-kinden, pretty without the cutting beauty that some of them possessed.

Achaeos's words recurred to him. 'What can be done, will be done,' he said, and in that moment he placed her – placed her name, Arianna. A promising student, one with a lot of potential.

Four

The main difference between Wasp hospitality and Ant hospitality, Salma decided, was that Wasps could fly. When he had been locked up by the Wasps in Myna they had wrenched his arms behind his back and tied his elbows together with Fly-manacles so that he could not have manifested his Art-wings even if he had somewhere to go.

By contrast the Ants had now bound his hands before him and then slung him into a windowless, pitch-dark cell, and left him for what seemed like a day and a half.

The cell itself was too small to lie down straight in, also too low to stand up. He ended up hunched in one corner, trying to listen for any movement from without, but the cell was dug into the earth, with stone walls and a solid wooden door. Not an echo got through to enlighten him.

They gave him some water, stale-tasting, in a bowl he nearly upset trying to find it with his fingers. No food, though, which did not bode well. It suggested they were going to keep him around for a little while, but not for long.

He had protested, of course. The three prisoners had done their best to explain that they were not spies and that the Wasps were their enemies. The soldiers who had captured them had simply not been interested. They had a specific role and it did not include talking to prisoners. Nothing Salma or the others could say would make a dent in that.

He hoped that Totho and Skrill were doing better than he was, although it seemed unlikely.

Then he heard the hatch slide in the door, and he froze, wondering if there might be some opportunity here, but even if they opened the cell for him and he could somehow, with hands tied, overpower his jailers, then he would still be underground somewhere, and likely to be killed on sight after that.

Light beyond, dim lantern-light that seemed as bright as the sun to him, spilled across the cramped little space to climb the far wall.

There was the clank of a key in the lock and the heavy door was hauled open. Even as Salma got to his feet the world exploded, searing into his brain. He found that he had fallen onto his side, his hands up to shield his eyes. They had suddenly turned on some kind of lamp, some artificer's thing, just as he had been looking straight at it. After so long in complete darkness his eyes burned and he felt tears course down his cheeks as two men lifted him to his feet and hauled him out of the cell.

By the time they found another place for him he could see again through watering eyes. He was in a starkly bare room, with a single slit window high up, illuminated by hissing white lamps burning on two walls. He turned to question one of the soldiers and the man punched him solidly below the ribs, doubling him over. As Salma struggled to recover his breath, his wrists were hauled up and their bonds hitched over a dangling hook. He heard the rattle of chains and his arms were jerked abruptly over his head, yanking him onto his toes.

The two soldiers then stood back, clearly satisfied with their work. They could have been brothers to each other, and, equally, to the men who had captured him: short, solidly built types with flat, pallid faces and dark hair, dressed in hauberks of dark chainmail.

There was a single door to this room, and Salma eyed it

as he waited for the interrogator to arrive, as he must. This position was intended to be painful, he guessed, but he could have stood on his toes for hours. His race owned a poise and balance that the Ants had never known. Salma allowed himself to relax into it, recovering from the knocks and scrapes of the last few minutes.

Lovely fellows, these Tarkesh. Remind me why we're on their side again?

Of course that was the point. Nobody ever claimed the Lowlands were populated by paragons of virtue, only that the Lowlands free were of more service to the world than the Lowlands under imperial rule. This was doubly the case from Salma's perspective, for if the Lowlands fell it would open to attack the entire southern border of his own nation, the Dragonfly Commonweal.

The door opened, at last, and a woman came in, a sister to the soldiers' fraternity. She might have been some higher official than they but she wore chainmail just as they did, and carried no badge of rank. He supposed that they sorted all that kind of thing out in their heads, communicating it between their minds. Creeping in behind her was a Fly-kinden girl, no more than fourteen, who sat down by the door with scroll and poised pen. A scribe slave, Salma guessed.

'Name,' the interrogator said. Her tone gave the word no hint of questioning, just a flat statement.

Salma decided to be fancy. 'Prince Minor Salme Dien of the Dragonfly Commonweal.' The pen of the scribe scratched the words down without hesitation.

The Ant woman, however, looked unamused. 'Do not play games with me. You must know that you are under order of execution.'

'Because you think I'm a spy.'

'You are a spy,' she told him. 'There can be no other reason for your skulking about to the north of our city where you were found. Tell us about your masters, then, their weapons and their military capacity, their tactics and weaknesses, and you might be allowed to serve Tark as a slave.'

'I'm not with the Wasps,' he insisted.

She pursed her lips and slipped something from her belt. It was a glove, he saw, with metal rivets studded across the knuckles, and she drew it on without ceremony.

'I am indeed a spy, however,' he said hurriedly and she raised an eyebrow, 'but not for the Wasp Empire. But I do know something about them, and I'm more than willing to reveal to you all I know. They're my enemies, too, and my people have fought them – I've fought them myself, been their prisoner, even.'

She seemed not to have registered most of what he said. 'If not for the army currently beyond our gates, then which other city are you spying for? Kes would seem most logical.'

Salma had to think a moment before he recalled that Kes was yet another Ant city-state and the one closest to Tark.

'I'm not spying for any of the Ant-kinden,' he told her.

'I fail to see any other option. Who else would profit from this situation?'

He looked into her bland, uninterested gaze. 'I was sent here by Stenwold Maker: a Beetle-kinden, a Master of the Great College. He has been working against the Wasps for years, and he sent me and my companions just to observe and report back to him. His only interest – our only interest, is in stopping the Empire.'

'*We* will stop this Empire,' she replied, with a curl of contempt. 'Why should some Beetle academic care?'

Salma knew that his next words might not help him, would in fact hurt him, so he tried to find another way of putting it, but he could not paint Stenwold as a Tarkesh sympathizer any believable way.

'Stenwold Maker firmly believes that the Wasps will not be halted at the walls of Tark,' he said quietly, and waited.

One of the soldiers actually strode forward to strike him for his insolence, but some unheard command of the interrogator turned him back.

'Explain yourself,' she said, still expressionless.

Salma took a deep breath. 'The Empire has been expanding rapidly for two generations,' he said. 'They have met Ant-kinden before, and triumphed over them. You have proof of this, if you've even looked over your walls at the enemy. We ourselves saw Ant-kinden amongst them before your scouts took us. Not as mercenaries or allies, mind, but as slave-soldiers.'

She remained quiet for a moment, and he wondered what was now passing between her and her kin. 'They have fought Ants, yes,' she agreed at last. 'They have not fought Tark.'

Salma tried to shrug, but couldn't. 'Whatever. Perhaps. Maybe you'll just kick the dung out of them and they'll go limping back east dragging their dead with them. If that happens, no one will be happier than I. But Stenwold fears otherwise. What else can I say?'

He knew that there was now a mental debate going on. The soldiers were in on it too, for he could see the interrogator's eyes flicking between them. Perhaps in time the whole city would be arguing the merits.

Then the interrogator turned and left him without warning, her slave scribe hurriedly following. The soldiers hoisted him off the hook, and it was downwards all the way from there, back to the pitch-darkness of his cell.

Some time later, the extent of which he found impossible to judge, he heard them coming for him once more. On seeing there was light, Salma hid his eyes quickly behind his bound hands, in case they tried the same trick again.

'Come out here!' one of his guards barked roughly.

'Not if you're going to blind me again.'

He heard them coming into the cell and backed off,

finally dropping his hands. The time had almost come for an escape attempt, he was thinking, however doomed to failure.

'Now calm there! No need to turn this into a diplomatic incident!' It was not an Ant voice, not even a Tarkesh accent. The leading soldier stepped to one side to reveal the ugliest Fly-kinden Salma had ever seen. Bald and broken-nosed, the little man looked him up and down critically.

'I see our hosts here have been their usual warm-hearted selves,' he said.

'Are you a prisoner, too?'

'I'm your ticket out of here, son.'

Salma's eyes narrowed. 'You're a slave-buyer?'

The Fly laughed loudly at that. 'If I had that kind of money I wouldn't be where I am now. No, I'm your secret guardian, boy, and I'm getting you free. Or at least as free as anyone around here is right now.' Something glinted in his hands, and with a single twitch he had cut the bonds about Salma's wrists. 'Come on, let's get you out of here.'

He turned and left and, keeping a suspicious eye on the guard, Salma followed. The Fly might be small but he walked fast, so Salma had to jog to keep up with him.

'Who are you?' he demanded.

'I've never liked repeating myself, so just let me get us safely into this room up here and I'll spill all.'

Without warning the Fly took a sharp left and pattered up a flight of stairs. Salma, following, found himself in an antechamber with two of the familiar high-up windows and, more importantly, with Totho and Skrill.

He almost knocked the Fly over in his haste to get over to them. Skrill looked decidedly weary, while Totho had a fistful of bruises about his face and a split lip.

'What's going on?' Salma hissed.

Totho shook his head. 'I think this fellow here is about to explain.'

Then Salma saw there was another Ant in the room, a man of middle years who was regarding the three of them dubiously.

The Fly jabbed a finger towards him. 'First,' he said, 'this is Commander Parops, into whose custody you're now being put.'

'I thought you said we were free,' said Salma.

'You are but, just so you know, this is the man who gets it in the neck if you turn out to be something other than what you claim you are.' As the Fly was explaining, the Ant officer gave him a wry look.

'So who's you then, little feller?' Skrill interrupted.

The Fly gave her a crooked smile. 'My folks called me Nero on that most auspicious day whereon I was born – and that's all the name I've ever needed.'

'I know that name . . .' Totho said, and paused, trying to bring it to mind. Then: 'Are you an . . . do you draw pictures?'

'No, I do not draw pictures, I am in fact a particularly talented artist,' Nero said, somewhat sharply. 'More than that, I'm an old drinking pal of Stenwold Maker, and when Parops told me that was a name being passed along the grapevine, I decided I had better spring you, if only to see what kind of kiddies ol' Sten's using these days.'

'Well, Master Maker sent us here to witness what happened when the Wasps attacked Tark,' Totho explained. 'We need to get out of the city and find a decent vantage point.'

Nero and Parops exchanged glances. 'Son,' the Fly said, 'you've got yourself the best vantage you're ever likely to get. You're inside the city, the siege's already started and nobody's getting in or out.'

'Your man,' the Dragonfly woman declared, 'is late.'

The old Scorpion-kinden scratched his sunken chest with a thumb-claw. 'First off, lady, he ain't my man. He's just this fellow what fitted your call. Second off, he ain't late – not in this business anyway. We ain't all got clocks and motors.'

She stalked up to him, her cloak swirling. The four of his heavies that he had stationed about the room went tense. He held up his hand, the one with the broken claw, to calm them.

'Do you know what happens if you betray me, Hokiak?' she asked.

Hokiak put on an easy smile that was a nightmare of jutting gums. 'Don't bandy threats, lady. I ain't got this old by being scared of 'em.' With measured unconcern he took up his walking stick and hobbled away from her, pointedly showing her his back if she wanted to take the opportunity. Inwardly, he waited for the blow and sighed raggedly when it did not come.

This one's trouble, he decided. Hokiak had taken on a lifetime of trouble, from his half-forgotten youth as a Dry-claw raider to his current station as a black-marketeer in the occupied city of Myna. He had made a living out of trouble, more money than he could ever spend now. If this trouble-woman did kill him, it was not as though she would be cutting many years off his life.

But she was a mad one, no doubt about it. He could smile casually at her but he avoided her eyes. They burned, and there were fires there that would be raging when the world went cold.

Dragonfly-kinden. He didn't know many of them. They had to go off the path of virtue early to become wicked enough to end up in his business. Otherwise they were all peace and light as far as he knew. *So where'd this waste-blasted woman come from?*

She was tall, almost as tall as he had been when he could still stand straight and without need for a cane. She kept herself cloaked but there was armour beneath it, and a blade that seemed always in one hidden hand. But she had money and, when she had talked to him, the money seemed to outweigh that drawn and hungry sword.

Now he wasn't too sure. He was going to be in real trouble if his contact didn't show, and equally so if the Empire had got wind of this deal and sent along more than he could handle. Either way he guessed that her first move would be to stick him for it, his fault or no.

Risk, risk, risk. He used to say he was getting too old for pranks like this, but then he *had* got too old for it, and still not given up the habit.

He hobbled back across his backroom's width, cane bending under his weight at each step. Propping it against a table he took his clay pipe out and filled it, trusting that his age would excuse any shaking of his hands. He had dealt with murderers, fugitives, revolutionaries, professional traitors and imperial Rekef, but *this* woman, now, she gave him the shudders.

She called herself Felise Mienn and, apart from the name of her mark, that was all he knew.

At last a Fly-kinden boy dashed in, making everyone start.

'He's here, Master Hokiak,' the boy blurted out.

'How many's he got, boy?'

'Got three. Three and hisself.'

'Then get out of here,' Hokiak advised him. As the boy dashed off again he looked about him at his other lads. They were regulars of his and three were Soldier Beetle locals: blue-grey-skinned and tough, wearing breastplates that had the old pre-conquest red and black painted out. The fourth was an innocent-looking Fly-kinden who could puncture a man's eyeball with a thrown blade at twenty paces. They all looked ready, relaxed. In contrast, Felise Mienn seemed to be shaking very slightly and very fast. Hokiak decided that discretion was a good trait in an old man, and poled himself behind the vacant bar counter.

The men who stepped in were also locals, less well

armoured but with swords at their belts and one with a crossbow, its string drawn, hanging loose in his hand. They inspected the room suspiciously, and then stepped aside for their patron.

After all the tension he was an anticlimax: a plump Beetle-kinden with a harrowed expression who looked as soft as they made them. He wore a cloak but the clothes beneath it were of imperial cut and colour.

'Draywain,' Hokiak greeted him from behind the bar. In a moment's inspiration he added, 'Fancy a drink?'

'Never mind the wretched drinks. Where's the money?' Draywain demanded. He was some manner of Imperial Consortium clerk, Hokiak gathered. He had been quite the big man under the previous governor but, since that man's mysterious death, the former favourites, those who had survived him, had been having a hard time of it. Sometimes a fatal time.

'She's the money,' Hokiak said, and Felise Mienn stepped forwards.

Draywain flinched from the sight of her. 'A Commonwealer? You must be mad! Where could I spend *her* gold?'

'She's got good imperial gold. I seen it myself,' Hokiak assured him, privately reckoning she had taken it off good imperials.

'Do you have what *I* want?' Felise asked impatiently.

Draywain narrowed his eyes. 'Let me see the money.'

'Do you have what I want?' She asked it more slowly, emphasizing each word separately. 'If you don't know where Thalric has gone, nothing for you.'

'Thalric of the Rekef? That bastard!' Draywain barked. 'Oh, I know where he went, don't you worry. Now let me see the money.'

Without taking her eyes from him she unshipped a pouch, emptied it onto the table. A flurry of gold and silver spilled out, and Draywain and his men pulled closer to inspect it.

'One hundred Imperials – our agreed price,' she said. It was a decent sum of money, Hokiak decided, for just a piece of information. Not a fortune, certainly, but an awful lot.

Draywain looked up from the money, and he had obviously come to a slightly different conclusion. 'It's not enough,' he said. 'Not enough for imperial secrets that nobody else'll sell you. My life's hit the rocks recently, Dragonfly-lady. I need to relocate myself somewhere an honest man can do business, and that isn't cheap.'

'That is not the arrangement,' Felise snapped.

'Well then the deal's changed places when you weren't looking,' Draywain replied. 'Now you double what you've got there and I'll start talking.'

'That is not the arrangement.' Again the words were slower, more pointed, as though she was clarifying some simple matter for a simple man.

'I have what you want, Wealer,' Draywain told her. 'Cough up the goods or I'm taking it right back out with me.'

'Draywain—' Hokiak began, but the Beetle cut him off sharply.

'Stay out of this, old man!' he snapped. 'I'm doing business here.'

That's all I need to hear. Hokiak rubbed the two claws of his good hand together, seeing his men pick up the signal.

'So let's see the rest, Wealer,' Draywain insisted.

'You knew the terms I offered,' she said. 'I need that information.'

'I'm a merchant and this is a seller's market,' he responded without sympathy.

And she smiled and Draywain took that for a good sign.

Then the sword came out from under her cloak, the whole gleaming length of it that had been held close down the line of her body. The cloth was flung back as she lunged into action, revealing armour beneath that was iridescent blue and green and mother-of-pearl.

She had the blade through the first bodyguard's gut before he could react, drawing it smoothly out to smash the next man's crossbow and the half-fired bolt on the back-swing. The crossbowman fell backwards, reaching for his blade, and the remaining bodyguard went for her.

He was not bad, that man. Clearly he had seen a few fights before. It was a waste, Hokiak decided, but that was the nature of this business.

Felise Mienn's sword was four feet long, but half of that was the hatched and bound metal hilt. The blade itself was straight and double-edged, tapering only towards the very point. She swung it with both hands and in either hand, dancing it round and past and over his guard as the luckless man tried to defend his patron. In a single fluid move she had sidestepped his strike and put the blade across his neck with far more force than her slender arms looked able to muster, half taking his head from his body.

Draywain bolted then, and she flung the sword at him as if without thinking. It slammed into the wall right alongside his head, cutting a line across his cheek. He screamed and stopped there, tugging at the hilt. The point of it had pinned his ear to the wall. His *ear*? Hokiak had never seen such a throw, and it had been solid enough that the Beetle could not yank the sword free using both hands.

The crossbowman had his blade now and he went for the unarmed woman. She stepped back and back as he came, cloak swirling about her, and then blades flicked out from her thumbs. It was the first Hokiak knew of the weapons that their Ancestor Art gave to Commonwealers. They were two-inch curved razors and she now stood poised with them ready, fingers clenched inwards but thumbs ready to strike.

The last bodyguard paused, weighing up the odds.

'Kill her!' Draywain screamed weakly. 'For blazes' sake, just kill her.'

He was a professional man now torn between his reputation and safeguarding his health. In that moment Felise went for him, claws slashing across him three times before he could even get his sword between them. He stumbled back, blood trailing from his face. Lunging forwards, Felise caught his head with both hands, as though she was a lover about to kiss him. Then she gashed both claws across his throat and he fell at her feet.

She looked at Hokiak then, and if her eyes had been burning mad before there were whole fiery suns of demented rage there now.

He forced himself to lean peaceably on his cane and indicate, with a twitch of his chin, that not one of his men had moved to intervene. He was not sure that she would understand him, but then she was stalking across the bloody floor towards Draywain.

'Keep away!' he shrieked. 'Someone help me!' but Hokiak knew that his backroom had thick walls and people around this part of the city always minded their own business.

She put one hand up, stilling the quivering hilt of her sword.

'Thalric,' she said simply, conversationally.

'Thalric, of course!' he gasped. 'They sent him away. They sent him west, to the new-found lands. The city Helleron, where the foundries are. He's Rekef Outlander. You know what that means?'

'Oh, I know exactly what that means,' she said. Only Draywain could see her expression just then, and his voice dried up to a whimper.

'Do you know where this Helleron is, Hokiak?' she asked, without turning.

'Sure I do,' the old Scorpion said. *Seems like every month I'm shipping people west.*

'Good,' she said and pulled her sword out of the wall effortlessly. As Draywain gasped in relief she rammed the point of it double-handed through his chest and then whipped it out, all in one movement. He was dead instantaneously, without even realizing what was happening. Perhaps, Hokiak thought, that was her way of mercy. Or her thanks. *Charming thought.*

'You will find me means to get to Helleron,' she told him. 'And supplies. A map that I can read.' That last was because she was not Apt, of course, not one for machines or crossbows or technical drawing.

'I got an old Grasshopper chart,' Hokiak said. 'Ain't what you'd call recent but I don't guess they moved the cities that much. Look, this all is going to cost. I earned my one-in-ten for bringing him here, no matter what he did.'

She turned then, smiling, and she was a lovely-looking woman, when she smiled – and more likely to kill a man than any Spider-kinden seductress.

'But Master Draywain has just chosen not to collect his fee. What's one-in-ten of nothing, Master Hokiak?'

The Scorpion gave out a sigh, and his men around the room tensed, ready. 'Now that ain't how we do business around here. You got what you came for.'

'Do you think I care about gold?' she asked him. 'Do you think that I can't find more? Do you think for me this is about *money*?' She snarled at that last. 'I would empty the coffers of the Empire and the treasuries of the Commonweal to find this man Thalric. You want money? Take it *all*.' She gestured at the pile, the not-quite-a-fortune, that she had left on the table. 'Just get me what I want.'

Five

'I was right here in my front office,' Parops told them. 'I had a crossbow and a telescope, but after I while I just used the telescope. It was quite something to see.' He indicated the view from his slit window.

'Nothing's happening now,' Totho pointed out. There was a tray of bread and spiced biscuit on Parops's desk, and he was aware that Skrill seemed to be working her way through it all methodically.

'That's war: boredom and boredom and then everything's far too interesting all of a sudden,' Nero confirmed. He was sitting on the desk looking at Skrill and obviously trying to decide what she was.

'So what happened?' Salma asked.

Parops put his back against the wall beside the arrowslit. 'Take a look at the disposition,' he invited. Salma did so, seeing only a large extent of land between the city walls and the Wasp camp, which was dotted with a few tangled heaps of wood and metal.

'First off, they moved their engines in,' Parops explained. 'They started shooting straight off and they must have some good artillerists, because in only a few shots they were sweeping the wall-tops with scrap from their catapults, forcing everyone's head down. They were loosing some at the walls, too, lead shot rather than stone, I think. We were shooting back from embedded positions like the one atop my tower. You can see evidence of some of our successes out there, but with our lot flinching back all the time it took a while to make the range to them. And of course nobody was getting a peaceful time of it. They had their men flying over the wall amidst the rocks.'

'Sounds risky for the men,' Salma said, studying the tents, making out what he could with his keen eyes.

'A good few of the incomers got squashed, no doubt, but nobody seemed to care on either side,' Parops confirmed. 'They were frothing mad, attacking everything along the length of the wall itself, or just charging off into the city in bands of eight or ten. Shields and a chitin cuirass was all they had, most of them, and javelins, and that fiery thing they do with their hands. They didn't seem like proper soldiers, to be honest – more like a rabble.'

'A rabble is what they were,' Salma confirmed. 'The Wasps call them Hornets, but they're just Wasps really. We saw a lot of them in the Twelve-Year War when they invaded my own people's lands. They're from the north-Empire, nothing but hill-savages. Your average Wasp is a touchy fellow at the best of times, but the Hornets are downright excitable.'

'And clearly expendable,' Nero added.

'Right,' confirmed Salma. 'So what happened?'

'Well, we had crossbowmen on the walls, and line soldiers defending the artillery,' Parops explained. 'Their first charge, coming with all that rock and lead, took its toll, but we knew they were a flying kinden, so we had ranks of crossbowmen stationed beyond the walls as well. Any that lingered on the battlements or tried to press into the city were picked off. We think the toll was about four hundred of them, in all, and just thirty-seven of ours. Most of those fell to their artillery and first charge, too. After that we were well dug in.'

'And are you calling it a victory?' Salma asked him.

'Opinion is divided,' Parops admitted. 'Some who

fought on the walls say it was, but I, who was just watching from inside here, say not. They had their tacticians out, carefully seeing how it went, so I'm suggesting to my superiors that they'll do better next time.'

'Wise man, good advice,' the Dragonfly told him.

'So what are *we* supposed to do in the meantime?' Totho asked. 'We can't just sit here. We have to get word to Stenwold.'

'The city is sealed,' Parops said sadly. 'That's the one thing we and the Wasps seem to agree on, as we're not letting anyone out, and neither are they. If you left without permission from the Royal Court you'd be shot by our crossbows, and even if you weren't, they have flying patrols on the lookout all the time.'

'They'll try to recover the broken engines after dark,' Totho said suddenly. 'They'll send slaves to do it, probably.' He had taken Salma's place at the slit window. 'Your artillerists should keep the ranges, and keep watch.'

'Night artillery's always a challenge,' Parops said. 'I've said it, though. Let us hope they take it up.'

Totho frowned at that 'I've said it,' and then realized what the man meant, remembering the mindlink that the Ancestor Art gave to all Ants. It united them within their own walls and equally divided them from their brothers in other cities.

Skrill finished another mouthful of bread, and took a swig of beer from the nearby jug. 'I ain't fighting no siege,' she said.

'They wouldn't have you anyway,' Nero told her.

'Now I ain't good enough for your siege?'

'We fight together, as one,' Parops explained. 'Foreigners on the walls would only get in the way. No offence, but that's how it is.'

Skrill shrugged.

'On the other hand,' Nero said, 'if the walls do come down, then we're *all* invited.'

'Did their engines break through anywhere, when they turned them on the walls?' Totho asked. He closely examined the arrowslit, seeing how its flared socket was set into a wall three feet thick at least.

'A few stone-scars but nothing structural,' Parops said. 'They're going to need a bigger stick to get through these walls. Nero tells me my kinden aren't renowned for having new thoughts, but one reason for that is that the old ones have always served us pretty well. We know how to build a wall that won't come down.'

'And of course, this is another thing their . . . tacticians out there will have noted. That they will need more . . .' Totho mused. 'What are their artificers like, Salma?'

'I'm no judge,' the Dragonfly admitted. 'They're like people who put big metal things together. That's about my limit.'

'It's an odd thing,' said Nero, 'but the best imperial artificers, in my experience, are Auxillians: slave-soldiers or experts from the subject-races. True Wasps always prefer to be proper warriors, which is more about the fighting and less the tinkering around. I've had a good look out there and a lot of the big toys are in hands other than the Wasps'.'

'Can they be turned?' Totho asked immediately. 'They're slaves, after all. If they turn on their masters, with our help, they could escape into the Lowlands—'

Salma was shaking his head and Nero chuckled. 'You'd assume, with all their experience as slave-owners, that the Wasps would have spotted that one, boy. Which is exactly why they have. Any funny business from those poor bastards down there, and their families will get to know about it in the worst way. And, besides, if some platoon of Bee-kinden, hundreds of miles from home, does decide to go it alone, you think they'll be welcomed any, in Tark? Or anywhere else? And home for them is now within the

Empire's borders, so any man jumping ship will never get to see it again.'

Salma nodded. 'I should tell you something, I think, at this point.'

Nero and Parops exchanged glances. 'Go on, boy, don't hold it in,' the Fly-kinden prompted.

Salma's smile turned wry. 'I didn't come here just for Stenwold's war, or even my own people's war. Not just to fight the Wasps, anyway.'

Totho nodded, remembering. Salma had barely mentioned the lure that had drawn him on this errand, which had originally been Skrill's errand alone. Totho had almost forgotten that himself, amidst the catalogue of his own woes.

'Don't keep us in suspense,' Nero said.

'A woman, I'm afraid.' Salma smiled brightly. 'I came here after a woman.'

'A Wasp woman?' Parops asked.

'No, but I'm told she's with the camp. With some order of theirs, the . . . Grace's Daughters, is it? No, Mercy's Daughters.'

'Never heard of them.' Nero said. 'So what about it?'

'I will be leaving Tark at some point,' Salma said, 'whether your monarch approves or not. Because she's out there somewhere and I have to find her.'

Nero's glance met that of Parops. 'Must be wonderful, to be young,' the Fly grumbled. 'I almost remember it, a decade of making a fool of myself and getting slapped by women. Marvellous, it was. Your mind seems set, boy.'

'I mean what I say.'

'Then at least choose your moment,' Parops said. 'Work with the city and let us get to trust you. Because there will be a sortie sooner or later. We're not just going to sit here and watch them ruin our walls, you realize.'

'Forgive me, but so far your city doesn't seem interested in working with any of us,' Totho pointed out.

'That was then,' Parops told him, taking the jug from Skrill and taking a swig from it. 'Now you are, nominally, on our side, and people want you to talk to them.'

Salma's grin broadened. 'Now that's unfair. There was a delightful Ant-kinden lady earlier who wanted nothing more than for me to talk to her.'

And at that there was a rap on the door and, when Nero opened it, she was standing right there, the Ant interrogator, staring straight at Salma.

Alder made a point of not wearing armour. Not only should there be some privileges for a general, but he hated being fussed over by slaves and servants, for with one arm he was unable to secure the buckles.

The largest tent in the Wasp encampment was not his living quarters but his map room. If assassins chose to head for it at night in search of generals to kill then that was entirely agreeable with him. He had sent a call out to his officers to join him, and if he had known that an Ant tower commander had dubbed them 'tacticians' he would have found it highly amusing. The term might just fit himself but, as far as planning this siege went, his was a perilously lonely position.

He was a man made for and unmade by war: lean and grey, though athletic still. He remembered a time when the title 'General' was reserved for men commanding armies. Now back at the imperial court there were generals of this and that who had never even taken the field. In his mind he preserved the purity of the position.

He was of good family, in fact. That had taken him to a captaincy. After that each rung of the ladder had been hard-won, climbed under enemy shot, and slick with blood. His face had a rosette of shiny burn-scar across nose and right cheek. His right arm had been amputated by a field surgeon who had not expected him to live.

That surgeon still received, at each year's end, twenty-five gold Imperials from the amputee's personal coffers. General Alder remembered the competent and the skilled.

So why, he asked himself, *am I left with these misfits as my command staff?* He lowered himself into one of the four folding chairs, watching his staff file in. The Officer of the Camp was Colonel Carvoc, an excellent administrator though an almost untried soldier, now seating himself to the general's left. His armour was polished and unblemished. To Alder's right came the Officer of the Field, Colonel Edric. Edric was a man of strange appetites and humours. An officer of matchless family, he spent his time amongst the hill-tribe savages that passed for shock troops in this army. He always went into battle, by his own tradition, in their third wave. He even wore their armour, and a chieftain's helm with a four-inch wasp sting as a crest. With coarse gold armbands and a mantle of ragged hide, he looked every inch a tribal headman and not at all an imperial colonel.

The fourth chair remained empty, but Alder's third and most problematical colonel was usually late and kept his own timetable. The general's hand itched to strike the man every time he saw him, but some talents were precious enough for him to suffer a little insolence. *For now at least.*

The others were assembling in a semicircle before those seats: field brigade majors, the head of the Engineering Corps, the local Rekef observer posing as military intelligence. Behind them were the Auxillian captains from Maynes and Szar, their heads bowed, hoping not to be singled out.

Still Alder waited, whilst Colonel Edric fidgeted and played with the chinstrap of his helm.

His missing colonel remained absent, but *she* came at last. He had not ordered her to attend. Supposedly he could not, although he could have had her marched into his tent or out of the camp any time he wished. Instead, he kept a civil accord with her because an officer who was seen to drive away any of the Mercy's Daughters was an officer soon disliked by the men.

'Norsa,' he said, although he had greeted none of the others.

'General.' Norsa was an elderly Wasp-kinden woman in pale lemon robes, walking with the aid of a plain staff. Alder's respect for her was based in part on that staff and the limp it aided, which had been gained in battle, retrieving the wounded.

'Colonel Edric. The morale amongst your . . . adherents?' Alder asked.

'Ready to make a second pass on your word, General,' Edric confirmed.

'I suppose we should be grateful that they're all so stupid,' Alder said, noticing the sudden crease in Edric's forehead. *The fool believes it. He's gone native.* In that case it was an illness that time would soon cure.

'Major Grigan. We lost three engines, I counted.'

The Engineering Corps major nodded, not meeting Alder's eyes. 'We can retrieve parts, and we have enough spares in the train to construct six new from the pieces.'

'Your estimation of their defences?'

Grigan looked unhappy. 'Maybe we could go against them again tomorrow. Don't think we made too much impression. Can't be sure, sir.'

'I want your opinion, Major,' Alder said sternly.

'But he doesn't have one, General,' snipped out a new voice, sharp and sardonic. Here was the errant colonel at last and, despite the man's usefulness, Alder always preferred a meeting where he did not appear.

'Drephos,' Alder acknowledged him.

'He prefers to defer to my opinions, since my judgment is sounder.' The newcomer swept past Grigan with a staggering disrespect for a man of his heritage. He wore an officer's breastplate over dark and decidedly non-uniform robes. A cowl hid his face. 'General, the normal engines just won't dent those walls.'

'Well, Colonel-Auxillian Drephos, just what do you suggest?'

'I have some toys I'm longing to set on the place,' Drephos's voice rose from within the cowl, rippling with amusement, 'but I'll need the cover of a full assault to do so. Specifically, throw enough men at those emplacements atop the towers, as their crews are too skilled for my liking.'

'Well we wouldn't want to see any of your toys broken,' Alder said.

'Not when they're going to win your war for you.' With his halting tread Drephos took up the final seat, on the other side of Colonel Carvoc. 'We all know the plan, General,' he continued. 'And the first part of the plan is to knock a few holes in those walls of theirs. Give me the cover of a full assault and I'll work my masterpiece. Stand back and watch me.'

'A full assault will cost thousands of lives,' Carvoc noted, 'and it will be difficult to sustain it for long.'

'Don't think I'll need all that long. Mine are exquisitely clever toys,' Drephos said, delighted with his own genius as usual. 'I'd suggest that you start by putting your usual tedious engines up front, give them something to aim at. While you're at it, give the archers on the inside something to think about. We all know Ant-kinden: if it works, they won't change it. Which always means they only try to mend something *after* it breaks. And if something breaks messily and finally enough, well, we artificers know that sometimes things just can't be fixed.'

Salma awoke as she slipped from his bed. There was wan light spilling sullenly from the two slit windows up near the ceiling, and it caught the paleness of her skin. He had never known skin so pale, like alabaster with ashen shadows. In that grim, colourless light she seemed to glow, picked out from all the surrounding room.

Her name, he recalled, was Basila. Her second interrogation had been gentler than the first, and the third, after the hours of night, gentler still. He had not believed, quite, that these Ant-kinden even possessed a concept for the soft arts, as his people called the intimate act. They seemed all edges and planes and cold practicality. There had been heat aplenty, though, until he wondered just how many women across the city he was making love to simultaneously. She was stronger than he was, and fierce, constantly wresting control from him, an officer commandeering a civilian. For a man used to casually seducing women, it had been quite an experience.

He watched, eyes half open, as she pulled on her tunic and breeches. She was lacing her sandals before she noticed his watching attention.

'You might as well sleep,' she said.

'I'm awake now. It's dawn already?'

'It is. I have duties.'

He watched as she shrugged on her chainmail, twisting for the side-buckles from long practice. He knew, or at least suspected, that they would not lie together again, that it had been merely curiosity that had drawn her to him. For his part it had been, at least, a way of showing the world and this city that his destiny had not escaped entirely from his own grasp.

Back in Collegium his liaisons had been the titillation and scandal of the Great College, scandal most particularly among those he had passed over or those who would have indulged in the same liaisons if they had dared. The strait-laced of Collegium would not have believed it, but Salma's own kinden had a strict morality of coupling. It divided the world of the preferred gender into two parts, not based on race or social standing or anything other than the subjective feelings of the individual concerned: sleep where you wish, amongst those who mean little to you, and amongst those to whom you mean little. Amuse yourself as you will, but with those close to you, those who love you or those you love, bestow your affections only where they are sincerely meant.

He had never elaborated on this creed for Collegium, for there it would not have been understood. He had never lain with Tynisa who had, he knew, wanted it. Particularly he had never lain with Cheerwell, who would have agreed, for all the wrong reasons, if he had asked.

Basila buckled on her sword and, seeing Salma smiling at her, ventured a small one of her own.

'Off to a hard day's beating people?' he asked, and her smile slipped. He assumed it was annoyance at him, but then she said, 'It is dawn. The enemy is advancing on the walls.'

He dressed as fast as he could, his belongings having been returned to him. He took up the stolen Wasp sword without even buckling on a scabbard. Basila was now gone to join her unit or await prisoners or whatever she had to do. She had left him to cower here behind doors like the slaves of Tark and await his fate, and that cut deep.

He found Totho emerging from the next-door room just as he left. For a second he had time to wonder whether the halfbreed artificer had heard anything of the previous night's activities, before recalling that Basila, of course, had been silent throughout.

So Totho heard nothing but the whole city knows we did it. He had to grin privately at that.

'What's going on?' Totho asked sleepily.

'The Wasps are attacking. Get your sword and bow.'

'But the Ants won't let us fight—'

'Totho, if enough of the Wasps get over the wall, then our hosts' preferences won't come into it.'

Salma bolted up the stairs as Totho turned back for his gear.

They had been billeted in the rooms beneath Parops's tower. Salma chose the first outside door, the ground-level door, and stopped with it half open, frozen.

The space before the gate was filled with ranks of Ant-kinden soldiers with crossbows and plenty of quarrels. Above them the walls, their crenellations slightly scarred from the previous day, were lined with more of them, and some of those had greater weapons. There were nailbow-men there with their blocky, firepowder-charged devices, and two-man teams with great winch-operated repeating crossbows resting on the walls.

They were shooting. All the men on the walls were shooting, either straight ahead or slightly upwards. Salma heard the grinding thunder of mechanisms, and the arm of the trebuchet atop Parops's tower flung itself forward, slinging its load of man-sized stones in a high arc. All along the slice of wall that Salma could see, other engines were busy doing the same.

Then the Wasps were at the wall itself, and what he had only been told about became real.

The first wave was a great ragged sweep of spear-wielding savages who hurtled into a field of crossbow bolts. There were already deep holes punched in their scattered mass. Salma watched almost three in four get ripped from the sky in that first instant, as soon as their silhouettes appeared in the sky above the walls. Some were killed outright. Others screamed and plummeted from the air to be finished on the ground with pragmatic brutality. The surviving attackers paid them no heed. Some alighted on the walls. Others ploughed into the waiting men below or scattered across the city. They were in a blood-rage, foaming at the mouth, hurling their spears and blasting with their stings, drawing great slashing swords from their belts to lay about them. One came down close to the tower's entrance, flinging his lance with such force that it punched right through an Ant's chainmail, knocking the man off his feet. Salma leapt out instantly, taking to the air and dropping on the attacker with sword extended. Another Ant was there already, and the Wasp savage took both sword-blows simultaneously. He howled in something that was more rage than pain, swinging his own blade at Salma and then at the Ant soldier, cutting a long dent in the latter's shield before falling.

There was a second wave of them at the walls already, coming too swiftly for many of the soldiers to have reloaded, although the repeating bows had taken a savage toll of the incursors. There was now hand-to-hand fighting all along the wall, and attackers kept dropping, or sometimes falling, down into the courtyard before the gates.

Salma had never seen Ants in combat before. There was no confusion here, no hesitation. The invaders were set upon efficiently, without haste. All found that any Ant they attacked was ready for them as those they tried to surprise turned to see them. The Ants had a hundred pairs of eyes watching each one's back. The Wasps took a toll with their stings and their frenzied hacking, but how small that toll was! Most of their second wave had been turned into corpses, all for the loss of no more than two dozen defenders.

'Get back inside, you!' one of the Ants shouted over at him. 'No place here for a civilian.'

'I'm not a civilian!' Salma called back. 'Look, I have a sword!'

The man was about to answer him when something pulled his attention upwards. They were all looking up, and across all those raised faces one expression was asking: 'What . . . ?'

And then they were moving. Without a word, without panic or cries of alarm, they scattered as best they could. Those at the edge of the square were backing quickly into the side streets, others were pushing up against the wall itself. Some found the shelter of doors or doorways. All this in the space of seconds. Salma would have remained standing still if an Ant had not cannoned into him, pushing him back into the tower door, where he collided with Totho so that all three of them fell in a heap.

The first explosion came across the other side, just left of the main gate. A crack of sound, a burst of fire and stone and dust, flinging half a dozen soldiers up and away, shearing through the next nearest squad with jagged metal and shards of stone. Up above, the trebuchet was winching itself ponderously round, while other enemy missiles were landing now, some right before the gates and others impacting on nearby buildings in a sporadic and random rain of fire. Wherever they struck, they split and burst, cracking stone and flinging pieces of their shells in scything arcs. Soldiers everywhere were holding their shields up, falling back to what cover they could find. Each second yet another fireball burst close about the gates, and there had been so many soldiers gathered there a moment ago that each missile claimed at least one victim. Salma, clinging to the doorframe, saw shields punched inwards by the invisible fists of these explosions, a nearby door smashed to kindling, men and women given a second's notice before being blown apart.

Yet there were no screams, and it seemed horribly unreal with that essential element missing. The Wasps that had come in first had screamed and shouted in fury and terror, but the Ants even died in silence, save for whatever last words they conveyed through that essential communion between them. In their last moments, he wondered, was that link a blessing for the fallen, or a torture for those still standing?

The artillery atop the wall was still pounding away, and Salma could see the Ant-kinden weapons, the ballistae, catapults and all the other murderous toys of the Apt, pivoting and tilting to get the range of the enemy siege engines. Totho went struggling past him, repeating crossbow cradled in his hands, even as another wave of Wasps passed overhead. These were the ones that Salma was familiar with, more disciplined and better armoured: the imperial light airborne. There were crossbows enough to deal with them but they had seized their moment and swiftly struck before the defenders had regrouped. Some circled overhead, spitting down with their stings, while others bedevilled the wall or passed into the city. There were strangers amongst them, Salma spotted: men of another kinden wearing breastplates and leathers in the imperial colours. One of these passed low over the crouching soldiers, and cast something behind him that erupted in a plume of fire and shattered paving flags.

Salma felt his wings flare into being before he had even decided what to do next, and an instant later he was springing for the wall-top. He caught a descending Wasp as he did so, the force of his flight driving his blade between the man's armour plates and doubling him up in agony. Salma let the sword go, pushing upwards the height of the wall to leap up next to another Wasp soldier while the man was grappling with one of the defenders. Salma twisted the blade from his hand and stabbed him with it before even alighting on the stone walkway.

It was not chaos, but it was not far off. Beyond the wall the plain was crawling with war machines. Many of them were still flinging their explosive burdens inside the city despite the presence there of their own men. The walkway of the wall had become a mass of small skirmishes. The Ants were stronger and more unified, but the Wasps could fly and they took full advantage of it, dragging men and women off the walls or stinging their victims from on high and swooping down on them from all angles.

But the defenders below were rallying. The crossbow-shot began to pick up, Wasp attackers plucked from the air by the increasingly thick and accurate barrage. There would be no chance for Salma to take wing now without the risk of being taken for an invader. He looked about for a chance to intervene and then a Wasp leapt at him from over the battlements, almost knocking him off the walkway altogether. He grappled fiercely with the man, each keeping the other's sword away. The Ants were fighting all around him but each would be waiting for a mental cry from him for help and Salma could not give it.

The Wasp was the stronger and he began forcing Salma back so that he was pushed half out off the wall, hanging over the battlefield beneath. The rough stone ground into Salma's ribs, but then he got a knee up into the man's groin and twisted around, using the soldier's own force to pitch him headfirst into space.

The man's wings rescued him, but he took a crossbow bolt even as they did, and fell. Salma dropped to one knee behind the shelter of the crenellations and tried to take stock of what was going on. Most of the flying attackers had been dealt with but their artillery was still moving. Salma risked a quick look over the wall.

Some of the enemy engines had been destroyed, but others were still active and an explosive missile struck Parops's tower even as he watched. The Ant artillery seemed to be concentrating on the engines that were still advancing. He could see two of those in particular that seemed mostly armoured metal plates, like great woodlice, grinding forwards with their own mechanical power. One rocked under the impact of a scattering of great stones that put huge dents in its armour.

There were more fliers streaking overhead. One of the firepots landed on the walkway close by, throwing him from his feet and casting three Ant-kinden off the wall entirely, down onto their brethren below. As the next flier streaked close over the wall-top, he jumped up and rammed his sword home. The impetus of the man's flight nearly dragged Salma from the wall, but he succeeded in wrestling his opponent onto the walkway.

Something beyond the walls exploded thunderously, with enough force to shake every stone beneath his feet. He dropped onto the man he had just stabbed, his head ringing with the din, and then dragged himself upright to look.

The armoured engine was gone. Instead there was a crater ten yards across, and splintered metal thrown ten times that distance.

Its brother engine was unfound by the artillery so far, and now it began to attack. A fat nozzle in its front opened and spat a great stream of black liquid out onto the wall, coating and clinging to the stones. The Ants were shooting down on it but it was inside the arc of their artillery fire and crossbow bolts simply shivered to pieces or bounced from its plating. Salma watched in horror as the black stain spread across the face of the wall, before the flood slowed to a trickle and stopped.

The engine began to retrace its steps towards the Wasp camp, crawling backwards without even turning round, and the artillery did not assail it. Instead, the Ants were waiting to see what happened.

Nothing happened. The black liquid simply hugged the wall. Whatever terrible effect the Wasps had anticipated did not materialize.

Salma dropped back down and rested his back to the stone crenellations. He saw beside him the body of the last man he had killed. It was one of the others, not a Wasp but a stocky, dark-skinned man in partial armour, with flat, closed features. He still lived, just, his eyes moving to seek out Salma's own. Then he died.

What city? What kinden? Where had the Wasps taken this luckless man from, to force him to fight enemies not his own, to have him die in panic and pain far from his home?

On the face of the wall, the black liquid had evaporated,

leaving only a great blotchy stain to disfigure the walls of Tark.

The plated engine's retreat was the signal, and the Wasp assault slowed, the commands moving around as fast as they could be shouted. One more wave of soldiers, too enthusiastic for their own lives, flew out unsupported into the Tarkesh crossbow-shot, while the wall artillery made the imperial engines' return a hazard, sending rocks and ballista bolts hurtling at them to the very far extent of their range. The imperial soldiers who regained their camp were the whole ones, or those with only light wounds. All others had been left to the sharp-edged mercies of the Ant-kinden. If they could not fly, they died.

General Alder watched the survivors, so few of them now, struggle back into camp. The two waves of Hornets had been wiped out to a man, and only a third of the light airborne had made it back, with half of the Bee-kinden engineers he had risked. By traditional military standards the assault had been a disaster. Generals had been executed for such performances, he thought bleakly. *This had better not be the battle they remember me for.* Morale would be low in the camp tonight, and would only get lower. His soldiers would still fight, but they would lack fire, for the discipline of the Ants would destroy them. The Wasps would inevitably batter themselves to death against the defenders' steel resolve. *Of all things I hate fighting Ant-kinden. Every step forward's nothing but bloody butchery.*

He cursed wearily. Those wounded fortunate enough to have returned would be under the care of the field surgeons now, or else the healing skills of the Daughters. Later he would walk amongst them, as was his tradition, and it was more than just show put on for the men. The general felt the responsibilities of his position keenly.

For now, though, there was one meeting that he was anxious to get over with, and the spark of anticipation he now felt was that it might just give him an excuse to have the maverick artificer killed.

'Get me the Colonel-Auxillian,' he snapped at his attendant staff, and one of them flew off to locate the man.

Colonel Edric was at that moment coming over to make his report, in all his barbaric splendour. Alder found himself vaguely surprised that the man was still alive, but then recalled: *Third wave is his tradition. Lucky for him we pulled out when we did.*

'Colonel, speak your piece.'

'Sir.' Edric had not forgotten himself so far as to miss his salute. 'We made progress, sir, we really did. I'm told that the combination of engines, troops and the grenades broke up the defenders so that we were able to send a whole wave of the airborne over the wall without resistance.'

'Really, Colonel? And amongst the hill-tribes, this is considered progress?'

'Sir?'

'And will you take the city with just one wave of the light airborne?' Alder shook his head. 'Go see to your men, Colonel. Those few that are left.'

There was a bitter taste in his mouth, and he had nobody to share it with. *That is what it means to be in command.* But of his subordinate colonels, Edric was too savage and Carvoc too dull. Only Norsa, of the Daughters, could possibly understand his feelings. He promised himself that he would visit her tonight, share a bowl of wine and talk of this in tones that would not be overhead. *An imperial general shows no weakness to his men.* His bleak thoughts could not hide from his own scrutiny, however, nor would he disown them. *We have done poorly today, and that bastard Drephos is to blame.*

He saw the man in question now, swathed in his robe as always, with not a crease or scratch on him. As he watched the Colonel-Auxillian make his way over, his gait slightly offset from some old injury, his face was just a blur under the cowl, but Alder was sure that he could glimpse a smile there.

'Drephos,' he growled, 'explanations, please?'

The cowled man made an amused noise. 'It's war, General. Surely you know your own business.'

Alder's one remaining hand caught him by the collar, twisting the cowl half across his face. 'For what cause have you spilt the blood of so many of my men?' he demanded.

'For *your* cause, General,' said Drephos, his voice showing no sign that Alder held him by the throat.

'I don't see any of the walls down, Drephos,' Alder snapped. He knew that Wasp lives were less than nothing to this man. Spending life in the Empire's name was one thing, while spending it to fuel the Colonel-Auxillian's private games was quite another.

'Let us have this conversation again in two days' time,' Drephos suggested. 'Then you might see something quite different.'

Six

Tisamon and Tynisa were duelling, passing rapidly around the circle of one of the practice halls of the College. There were a dozen or so spectators, students garbed or half-garbed as Prowess contestants, sitting on one of the tiers of steps. There was none of the cheering and shouting of a public performance; instead, the watchers murmured to one another on technique as they compared notes.

Nor was it the formalized shortsword technique of Collegium's duelling circle being practised here. The pair carried rapiers, live steel blades, and the air between them flickered and sang with the lightning clashes of the weapons. It struck Stenwold, as he entered, that he had never seen Tisamon with a rapier in his hand before: the folding blade of his clawed gauntlet had always been his first choice. Rapiers were a Mantis-kinden weapon nonetheless and he was showing his proficiency here. They dodged and lunged so abruptly, father and daughter, that Stenwold felt that they must have rehearsed this between them. Each move was matched by the other and he thought, at first, that the entire bout, starting however long before his entrance, must have continued entirely without contact.

Then he heard Tisamon's voice coming in at irregular moments. 'Strike,' he would declare, and then after another furious pass with the weapons, 'Strike.' He was marking his touches, Stenwold realized. Unlike any sane or civilized duel the fight did not pause on a hit. There was no moment permitted for Tynisa to regain her composure or her balance. Sweat gleamed on her forehead, soaking her arming jacket, but Tisamon's brow was pearled as well. Stenwold could not tell if it was the injury from Helleron or the pace of the current duel that strained him.

'Strike,' Tisamon noted again, and they fought on. Neither was cut: the blows had been delivered with the flat of the narrow blades only. Their faces had so much the same expression of intense concentration that in that moment Tynisa truly resembled her father. The features of her dead mother were momentarily banished.

Stenwold sat down a little way from the rapt students. Tisamon had promised to train his daughter – the one gift he could give – and he took that vow as seriously as the Mantis-kinden always did.

'Strike,' he said again. Stenwold expected Tynisa to become frustrated now, stirred to anger that would be fatal for a duellist. Instead she seemed calmer after each call, focusing more and more within herself.

Stenwold glanced around at the students. They had stopped murmuring now, were watching the action with almost as much concentration as the protagonists themselves. They were all young, in their first year, local Beetle-kinden mixed with a few visitors. No Tarkesh Ants, of course. They had been recalled, all of them, when the news broke of the threat to their city.

'Strike,' came Tisamon's voice, and then, 'Strike!'

The sound of swords stopped, and Stenwold struggled to disentangle what had happened. Only when he saw the line of her blade pressed against her opponent's side did he realize that the last call had been Tynisa's.

They were all watching Tisamon now for his reaction. It was a nod, just a small, sharp nod, but Stenwold read volumes of approval in it. The Mantis ran a sleeve over his forehead, fair hair flat and damp with sweat there, and then came over to sit by Stenwold. Close to, the strain was clearly visible, more lines about his eyes and an added pallor to his face.

'You should perhaps take things easier for a while,' Stenwold suggested, knowing the suggestion was futile.

'I'm getting old.' Tisamon smiled a little. 'I used to heal faster than this.'

'You've healed faster than anyone has a right to,' Stenwold told him. 'You took quite a scorching there.'

'It has been a while since someone put such a mark on me,' the Mantis agreed.

Tynisa had meanwhile been accepting the congratulations of the students, who seemed to appreciate that fighting Tisamon was like fighting a force of nature, and that even one strike was equivalent to a victory.

'Of course, you killed her a dozen times there,' Stenwold remarked.

Tisamon shook his head. 'Practice is always different to blood, even using a real sword.'

'I notice she wasn't using the sword you gave her.'

Tisamon seemed to find that amusing. 'It is crafted for killing, Stenwold. It wouldn't understand.'

'What will you do, when she's good enough?'

'She is already good enough, or nearly.' There was hard pride in the Mantis's voice. 'She was on the edge of good enough before I even met her. Blood will out, and all she needed was real blood on her hands to call to her heritage.'

Stenwold shifted uncomfortably. 'So what will you do now?'

'When this is done and when we can, I shall take her to Parosyal.'

'I can't even begin to imagine what that means for you, but surely your people . . . ?'

'They will hate her, and despise her,' Tisamon said flatly. 'Not one of them will look at her, or even at me. We will be pariahs in my people's holy place. But they will not

79

deny her, because she has the skill. If she can pass the trials they set, then in the end . . . in the end she will be one of us and then their hate must drain away, and they must accept her.'

'"Must" . . . ?' Stenwold prodded.

Tisamon was silent.

'Well, if Cheerwell can be accepted by the Moth-kinden, then anything is possible,' Stenwold allowed, and rose to greet Tynisa as she approached.

It was late when they finally returned to Stenwold's townhouse. Tisamon had cautioned him to reside elsewhere after the last attack on it, but Stenwold had a stubborn streak when it came to giving up what was his. He would not be harried out of his own home, his own city. Besides, with Tynisa and Tisamon under the same roof with him, he reckoned it would be a brave assassin that tried it.

After watching the duel he had gathered reports from some of his people within the city. They were not his agents as such, but he had slipped them a little coin to keep their eyes and ears open. He knew that the Assembly still kept its doors closed to him, out of pique more than anything else. Until that attitude changed, the Wasps had time and, while they had time, they would move carefully.

But there would come a moment, as there had in Helleron, where the metal met, as the saying went, and caution went out of the window. A night of knives, it would be. He was glad to have Tisamon and Tynisa with him, glad also to have sent his niece Cheerwell to the relative security of Sarn.

In the quiet of his own room he shrugged out of his robes, letting them pool on the floor. The night air was cool on his skin through the knee-length tunic, and the water he splashed on his face made him shiver. They were forecasting a cold winter for Collegium – for the Lowlands as a whole. Cold, of course, meaning a few cloudless and icy nights. Salma, hailing from north of the Barrier Ridge, had claimed that nobody in the Lowlands knew what winter really meant.

It was still warm enough to sleep in his bare skin, so he stripped off the tunic and cast it on the floor, then turned the flame of the lamp out. Finding his way in the moonlight to his bed he threw himself down on it. His mind was alive with stratagems, shreds of information, clues and counter-intelligence. The threat of the Wasps was bad for his sleep patterns.

And then he became aware that he was not alone in the room. Somewhere in the darkness someone moved.

All at once he went colder than the night could make him. At first he was going to call out for Tynisa or Tisamon, but if he did so then it would only mean a swift blade – a blade that might come at any time, but would surely come now, right now, if he called.

Why couldn't I have listened to Tisamon?

He reached out. There was always a sword within reach of his bed, a judicious precaution that had borne fruit more than once. His fingers brushed the pommel, so he stretched a little further to grasp the hilt.

'There is no need for that, Master Maker,' said a woman's voice, one he knew, he realized, although he could not immediately place it.

'Who's there?' he asked, excruciatingly aware that who-ever it was could obviously see better than he could in the dark.

'Wouldn't you be more comfortable if you lit the lamp again?'

Yes. Yes I would. He crawled backwards off the bed, sword in one hand, still sheathed, and in the other a sheet clutched demurely to his chest. He thought he heard a snicker from the unseen woman which helped not at all. Then he realized that he would need both hands free to light the lamp.

Both hands. His sword-hand included. Or perhaps not. He let the sheet go, modesty playing second fiddle to mortality, and opened the lamp hatch single-handed. Thick fingers fumbled across the cabinet top until they located his steel lighter. He flicked at its catch until it caught, and then brought the fragile flame to the oil. It lit with a gentle, golden glow and, with his sword firmly presented, he turned to face the intruder.

She had a hand over her mouth, in hilarity or horror, and it was a moment before he recognized her. When he did, he swept the sheet back up so fast that he almost lost his sword in it.

'Arianna?' he gasped. 'What are you . . . what are you doing – in my *house*?'

She was desperately trying to hide a smile. It was hilarity then, which was the worse of the two reactions. 'You do not bar your windows, Master Maker.'

'That's not an answer.' But she was right of course. He still thought like a Beetle, having just one entrance to his home, on the ground floor.

'I . . . I wanted to speak with you, privately.'

'Well this is about as private as I get.' He clutched the sheet close to him, tried to drape it about him like a robe, and found it would not stretch. In front of the young Spider-kinden's unabashed gaze, he felt acutely aware of all the physical parts of him that had never been slim to begin with, and that time had only expanded.

'I would have said something when you came in, only . . .' Her shoulders shook a little. 'Only you started getting undressed so fast and . . . I didn't know what to say.'

How old I feel, at this moment. 'Would you mind . . . turning your back while I at least put a tunic on?' he asked.

Then the door burst open and Tisamon was there.

The Mantis had his claw on ready and he saw the intruder at once, bounding across the room towards her.

She shrieked, falling down beside the bed and tugging desperately at a dagger that was snagged in her belt.

'Tisamon, wait!' Stenwold yelled, and the Mantis froze, claw still poised to stab down. Arianna was now completely hidden behind the bed, but Stenwold could hear her ragged breathing.

'What is this?' the Mantis demanded.

'She's just a . . . student,' Stenwold said, feeling the weight of providing some explanation descend on him. 'You can . . . let her get up now.'

Tisamon backed off from her cautiously. 'She's Spider-kinden,' he remarked.

'I don't think that's an objection you can make any more,' Stenwold pointed out, reasonably.

Arianna stood up slowly, one hand nursing the back of her head. The dagger was still caught in the folds of her robe.

'She's armed,' Tisamon said, sounding less certain now.

'She has a knife. I wouldn't advise anyone over the age of ten to go about the city without a knife these days.' Stenwold realized that Tisamon's attention was focused on him now, rather than on Arianna.

'I was . . .' Stenwold looked down at the rounded bulk of his own body, so inadequately hidden by the sheet. 'I was just retiring . . .' he began lamely, acutely aware that the harsh lines of Tisamon's customarily severe expression were trembling a little.

'Retiring with . . . ?'

'No!' More harshly than Stenwold had meant. 'Or at least not knowingly.'

'So,' Tisamon's mouth twisted. 'What does she want?'

'Good question.' Stenwold looked at the girl.

'I want to help,' she stated.

'Help how?' He had his tunic on again, which felt like armour beyond steel plates under the gaze of this young woman. Here in his study, the desk between them, he could feel a little more like the College Master and less the clown. She sat demurely where he had placed her but there was merriment still dancing in her eyes.

'Everyone knows how you've been to the east. Everyone knows there are enemies waiting there. I mean, the Empire, that you taught us about in history. Nobody else has ever dared point the finger. None of the other masters would even answer my questions. And yet it was always there, and those soldiers – the Wasp-kinden – had come from there for the games. And that's when a few of us started to realize that you'd been telling the truth all this time. That those men weren't here just for the sake of peace and trade.'

'Some people believed me, anyway,' Stenwold said heavily, 'understood that they are the threat I made them out to be. But the Assembly? Perhaps not.'

'I believe you,' she said, without hesitation. She was staring at him so earnestly that he became acutely aware of how young she was, how old he was. She was an odd specimen for a Spider. Her coppery hair was cut short in a local style, and she had freckles that made her look even more desperately earnest. He found himself looking at her in a different light: how very slender she was, how pale the skin of her bare arms where the short sleeves of her robe ended.

He gave himself a mental shake. 'Why?' he asked, refocusing.

'Because for one, my people are good at reading truth and falsehood, and I believe that when you're up before us students telling us all this, you are sincere, that you know what you're talking about. Since you left for wherever you went, we've all had a chance to see the Wasp-kinden at large in Collegium. Oh, they're on their best behaviour and they've always got gold ready to pay for breakages, but they're . . . ugly, do you know what I mean? Not physically, but something inside them. And the way they brawl. A little drink and a harsh word, and they'll fight to kill. I know one student of the College who was killed in a taverna, only the Wasp officers paid out gold to keep it quiet. And they're all trained soldiers, which is just what you said, too. Every one of them, even the artificers, even the diplomats who speak to the Assembly.'

'Arianna . . . you Spider-kinden have never cared much what wars have racked the Lowlands,' Stenwold said. 'So why—?'

'You think I'm here on behalf of my people?' she asked him incredulously. 'You think I'm some agent of the Aristoi? That . . . that would be grand, Master Maker.' Bitterness was rife in her tone now. 'But I'm not Aristoi. I'm of no great family to help me get anywhere in the world. I'm the last daughter of a dead house, and all we had left went to pay my way into the College. This is my home, Master Maker. The College is all I have. And you, to me you are the College.'

In the face of all that solemn youth, he could only swallow and stare.

'Most of the Masters just get lost in their own disciplines, Master Maker . . . Stenwold. May I . . . ?'

He found that he had nodded.

'They don't care, you see, what happens elsewhere. And some others are worse, lots of the ones in the Assembly, they look only to their pockets and their social station, and little else . . . I've seen enough of that snobbery in Everis where I grew up. But everyone knows it's *you* who has gone out there and seen the world. And you've come back with a warning, and nobody is listening to you. But a lot of us students do. Master . . . Stenwold. I want to help you.'

'How?' he asked. Suddenly the words were difficult to reach for. 'What do you . . . how can you help me?'

She moistened her lips with her tongue, abruptly nervous. 'I . . . I hear things, see things. I learned to stay out of the way, back home, so I'm good at not being seen. You . . . that was one reason I came through your window like that. So that you'd see . . . so you'd know.'

'I understand,' he said, thinking, *One reason? And what are the others?* He did not want to involve this young girl in what was about to happen and yet she was so desperate to help, and if he now said no? Why, she would surely go off and do something rash on her own, just to prove herself to him. Just as Cheerwell would have done, doubtless.

And he *could* use her, certainly.

She reached out and put a hand on his, a touch that dried his throat suddenly.

'Please,' she said, and he found that he could not refuse.

'It's wonderful, isn't it!' Cheerwell exclaimed. 'I don't often get the chance to travel by rails.' She had taken the bench end closest to the open window, watching the dusty countryside pass by, feeling the wind blast at her face. The rumble of the automotive's steam engine tremored through every fibre of her being. Out there, craning forward to peer along the carriage's length, she could see the duns and sand-colours of the land turning into the green marshes that surrounded Lake Sideriti, whose eastern edge the rail line would skirt, posted up on pillars to keep it clear of the boggy ground.

Achaeos huddled beside her, wrapped in his cloak and looking ill. It was the smell of the automotive, or the motion, or all of it. This was not a way that Moths travelled comfortably, and he could not even fly alongside. The carriage had no ceiling, just an awning to cover the seats in case of rain, but the steam automotive made such pace that if Achaeos went aloft he would get swept away, left behind.

Beneath her feet, through the slatted floor, Che could see the ever-turning steel wheels strike occasional sparks along the rails, and the ground in between hurrying past in a constant blur. This truly was the travel of the future, she decided, and even though Achaeos disliked it so much, they would reach Sarn in two days. Even Fly messengers took the rail these days to retain their boasted speed of delivery.

On the bench in front of them Sperra slept fitfully, leaning against the carriage wall. Che had carefully shuttered that part of the window closest to her, in case the little Fly-kinden should stir in her sleep and just pitch straight out of it. She was still not entirely recovered from her injuries at Helleron, poor woman, but it had been her decision to join Scuto in his journey to Collegium. The Thorn Bug himself was off inspecting the engine, Che gathered. He might be an agent in Stenwold's spy army but he remained an artificer first and foremost.

Of course that made her think of Totho, and she suddenly found no pleasure either in the journey or the machine that transported them.

Poor Totho, who had left them for the war at Tark for one reason only. She herself had never fully told Stenwold the truth, although he had probably guessed most of it. Only Achaeos and she knew with utter certainty. Totho had left them because he could not bear to be with her without having her affection. For that reason he had come all the way from Collegium to Helleron with her. He had come to rescue her from the Wasps, travelled into the Empire itself, for no other cause, and she had never seen it because she had never looked. There had been Salma to worry about. There had been Achaeos, too, who had become bound to her by forces she could not explain, and who she loved.

Poor Totho had fallen between the slats of her life and only in his misplaced farewell letter had he been recalled to her guilty attention.

She had told him casually, *You are like a brother*, and she, who had experienced her share of rejections and even derision, knew just what that felt like. Yet how easily the words had slipped out from her.

There had been no word yet from Tark. That the siege

had started seemed clear, but Totho and Salma should have kept a safe distance away, watching the moves of Ant and Wasp like a chess match. Yet they should have been able to send word somehow. Which meant that something had gone wrong, and poor clumsy Totho, who had never been able to look after himself, not really, was there in the middle of it.

She put her arm round Achaeos, and hugged him to her. His blank eyes peered at her from beneath his hood.

'You're thinking about him again,' he noted.

'I am, yes.'

'No doubt we will find word from him when we return,' he said weakly. Sickened by their method of travel, he was not in much of a position to offer comfort.

The first margin of Lake Sideriti was passing them by now. The water was stained a bright turquoise by the sun and the plants that lived in it, as though beneath the surface was a great blue jewel that caught and reflected the light. Even Achaeos perked up somewhat at that sight.

'They don't make 'em any more like this old girl!' came Scuto's voice as he rejoined them, pushing his way down the carriage's length to the amazement and disgust of the other passengers. He had his cloak flung mostly back, so the full spiky grotesquerie of his face and hunched body was there for anyone jaded enough to want to peruse it. Even his garments only emphasized the lumpy form beneath them, torn in a hundred places by his hooked spines. 'I ain't never had a chance before to see one of these up close and working.'

'Scuto,' she said, but he had seen the radiance of the lake, dotted with reed islands, that stretched virtually from their window to the horizon.

'Well if that don't beat the lot of 'em,' he murmured, sitting down beside Sperra. She shifted sleepily, jabbed herself on his spines and woke with a start.

'Wretched spickly bastard,' she muttered, stretching and thus pricking herself again with a curse. 'Are we there yet?'

'Look,' Che gestured, and the Fly glanced over the lake without much interest.

'Lovely. Can I go back to sleep now?'

'You got no heart,' Scuto told her.

'You can tell that, can you?' She rubbed her arm where he had pricked her. 'You're a wretched nail-studded menace, that's what you are.'

Cheerwell knew very little about her, other than she had worked for Scuto for years now. She was no artificer, but she was Apt and a good hand with a crossbow. She had some doctoring skills as well and a bag of salves and bandages, and so she must have trained a little. Fly-kinden got everywhere in the Lowlands and did all manner of work, legal or not, but Che realized that she had never really got to know one well. They tended to keep to their own kind and stay out of the way of larger folk. Sperra was about typical of her race: standing a few inches under four feet in her sandals, with a lean, spare frame. She kept her hair quite long but tied behind her, and she wore dark, unassuming clothes without any finery or ornament. Everyone claimed that Flies liked valuables, preferably those belonging to others. Whether they wore them openly in their own communities of Egel or Merro to the east, she did not know, but she could never recall seeing a Fly-kinden flaunting any such treasures.

To the east . . . Of course, if Tark fell, then Egel and Merro, those two Fly-kinden warrens in the Merraian hills, would lie in the path of the encroaching army. Would they merely hide in their homes? Would they take up what they could carry and flee? They were no fighters, certainly not before an army of such magnitude. She wondered whether this thought was at the back of Sperra's mind too.

We are all at risk here: Achaeos's people, Sperra's and mine.

Even Tisamon's precious Mantis-kinden cannot stay apart from this.

The sun was lowering in the sky and the gleam of Lake Sideriti grew duller, the beautiful allure of its waters dimming and dimming as the night loomed in the eastern sky.

Seven

They called Capitas the City of Gold, but it was only at dawn that the name struck true. The tawny stone it was built from, which had gnawed up quarry after quarry in the hillsides to the north, took that moment's morning light and glowed with it. After that it was just stone.

This artificial flower of the Empire was young enough that old men could remember when the river wound untroubled past the hills and the homes of herdsmen. Alvdan's father had planned the city and seen most of it built before his death. Alvdan himself had let the architects and craftsmen follow the same plans, another binding promise he had inherited from his father's reign. Even now, if he chose to look for it, he would see scaffolding where the Ninth Army barracks were still being constructed.

But he liked the place at dawn. Now here he was, breakfasting on his balcony and looking down the stepped levels of the great palace and over the elite of his subjects. Capitas was a place that could never have grown naturally. The land was insufficient to support it. It was the heart of Empire, though, and the taxes and war plunder of the Wasp-kinden flowed relentlessly to it. If they did not then the Rekef would soon ask why.

The Emperor was breaking his fast in company today. Often he dined with concubines, sometimes generals or advisers that he wished to favour. Once in a tenday, though, he made a point of sending for his sister. She was installed in a palace of her own across the city that was as much a padded prison as anything else. He knew that to arrive here on time for a dawn breakfast she would be roused from her bed not long after midnight. After all, the daughter of the Empire must be correctly dressed and perfumed and painted.

As Emperor he took his victories where he wanted, so here she was.

They sat at a table, almost within reach of one another, and servants scuttled to serve them with seedcakes and new-baked bread and warm honeydew. The city beyond was waking up, a hundred dashes of glitter showing his subjects taking to the air. None of the airborne would approach the palace, of course. There were guards enough on the tier above them who would shoot any intruder without question.

And one more guard, of course, to stand uncomfortably close behind his sister, to remind her of her situation.

'Your name came up in council again,' he remarked, sipping his honeydew. He seemed all ease here, slouching in his chair, smiling at the servants. She, on the other hand, sat with a spear-straight back, eating little and delicately. Eight years his junior, barely a woman, she had been living in fear now for half her life.

'General Maxin wishes, I think, to be remembered to you.'

He was adept at reading her. Now, seeing her lips tighten, he broadened his own smile. *There* was a name she was unlikely to forget. Three brothers and a sister that had separated the two of them in age had all fallen, if not to Maxin's knife then to his orders.

'I am sure,' she said, 'that I am grateful to the general for his concern.'

He laughed politely. 'Dear sister Seda, they are all so anxious that you find some direction in your life.'

'I am touched.' Seda took a minute bite of seedcake, her eyes never leaving his hands, watching for any signal to the guard hovering behind her. 'Although I can guess at the *direction* they have in mind.'

'They don't understand how it is between us,' Alvdan continued. A servant brought him more bread and buttered it for him.

'I am not sure that I do, Alvdan.' She sensed the guard shift behind her and added, 'Your Imperial Majesty.'

'They think I am so soft-hearted. They agonize over it, that the Emperor of the Wasps should have such a flaw in his character,' he told her.

'Then you are right that they clearly do not understand you.'

'Insolence, sister Seda, does not become one of our line,' he warned her.

She lowered her head but her eyes stayed with his hands.

'You and I understand each other, do we not?' he pressed.

'We do . . . Your Majesty.'

'Tell me,' he said. She glanced up at him, and he repeated, 'Tell me. I love to hear the words from you.'

For a second she looked rebellious, but it passed like the weather. 'You hate and despise me, Majesty. Your joy is in my misery.'

'And an Emperor deserves all joys in life, does he not,' he agreed happily. 'My advisers and their plans! They do not understand your potential. Last year they were plotting to marry you off, to make an honest wife of you. They do not realize that you are not like other women of our race. You are no mere adornment for some *man*. You are a weapon, and if your hilt were in a man's hand he would turn your edge on me. I think General Maxin would marry you himself, if I was mad enough to let him.'

She said something quietly, and he rapped his knife-hilt on the table impatiently.

'I said I would rather die, Your Majesty,' she answered him.

He smiled broadly at that. 'Well then perhaps I should hold the option open. I can always have Maxin slain on his nuptial night. That would be a fit wedding present, no?'

'Your Majesty forgets who he most wishes to hurt,' she said tiredly.

'Perhaps. But now they are trying to parcel you off to some order, so as to make an ascetic of you. As though you could not be recalled from there, once my back was turned. And that is the crux. Alive, you will always threaten me. Yet dead . . . My throne will always require defending and, with your blood staining my hands, who can say from where the next threat might come? So, alive and close you must stay, little sister.'

'You will keep me only until the succession is secured, Majesty, and then you will have me killed. Perhaps you will even wield the knife yourself, or break me in the interrogation rooms.'

'Do you tire of life, Seda?' he asked her.

She reached out for him, then, but the cold steel of the guard's sword touched her cheek before she could touch even his fingers. With a long sigh she drew back.

'I have had no life since our father died. What I have had since then is nothing more than a long descent, and every tenday the ground is moved one tenday further off, so that I drop and drop. But one day the ground will stay where it is, and I shall be dashed to pieces.'

'Beautifully said,' he told her. 'Your education has not been wasted after all. Seeing the good use you have made of it, I decide that I shall broaden it.'

This was a change from the usual routine. 'Your Imperial Majesty?' she enquired cautiously.

'A little trip to the dungeons, dear Seda,' he said and, when she sighed, he added, 'Not yet, dear sister. It is not your turn yet. Instead there is a most interesting prisoner

94

that General Maxin has brought for me. I think you should see him. Furthermore, I think he is desirous of seeing you.'

The Wasp Empire was all about imposing order. Alvdan the Second's grandfather Alvric had forced it on his own people, who were a turbulent and savage lot by nature. The original Alvdan, first of that name, had then turned his need for order on the wider world and his namesake son had followed his lead. The imposition of order became all. The multiplicity of ranks and stations within the army, the precise status of the more powerful families, the honours and titles that were the gift of the throne, even the station and privileges of individual slaves – everyone had a place, and those above, and those below.

The maxim applied even to prisoners. There had developed a whole imperial art to the treatment of prisoners – how often they were fed; whether they had a cell a man could stand in, or even lie straight in; whether they were kept damp, kept cold; whether they were dragged out to lie on the artificer-interrogator's mechanical tables for no other reason than it was their turn, their lowly contribution to the Empire's sense of order.

Such prisoners as had something to offer the Empire, they could do well for themselves. They could even make the leap, eventually, from prisoner to slave – just as the threat of becoming a prisoner kept the lowest slaves in line.

Judging by such exacting standards, this man her brother had found must have a great deal of potential, for his cell lay on the airiest level of Capitas's most accommodating prison. He had two rooms to himself, and an antechamber, and the guards even rattled the barred door in advance to announce that he had visitors. In the antechamber there sat three young pages, two boys and a girl, presumably to run errands for the prisoner's needs. As she considered that, Princess Seda noticed how pale and drawn they all were, and that one was visibly trembling.

She was not really a princess, of course. That was a Commonwealer title that one young officer, desperately gallant and politically naïve, had once given her. What fate had befallen him since she did not know, but he had been a brief ray of sun through the clouds that perpetually clogged her life.

The prisoner's reception chamber was lit by great windows, latticed with metal bars, that extended across almost an entire wall, and opened up part of the ceiling as well. There were no curtains, she saw. The sun flooded unopposed across the floor until it met the doorway into the sleeping chamber. That room was quite dark, muffled in drapes, and impenetrable to her gaze.

'Your Emperor is here,' one of the guards announced. 'Present yourself!'

For a moment it seemed that nothing would happen, and then Seda heard a shuffling from within the darkness, and at last a hooded figure in tattered robes came forward tentatively to the brink of the dazzling light. One hand, pale as death and thin as bone, was raised against the sun.

'Come forward, we command it,' Alvdan instructed, and Seda saw how he was enjoying himself, watching the wretch quail before the sunlight.

The guard began uncoiling a whip from his belt and, with a shudder, the slender creature crept forwards, head turned away from the windows. She could see nothing of him yet but those two delicate hands, long-fingered and sharp-nailed.

'We have brought our sister to you, since we thought that you might be of interest to each other,' Alvdan sounded pleased with himself no end. The cowl shifted and sought her out, and she imagined watery eyes within were trying to focus on her.

'Introduce yourself, creature,' Alvdan said. 'Have your kinden no manners?'

The robed thing gave a long, tired hiss and crept closer,

until it was almost within arm's reach. There were blue veins prominent against the translucence of its arms, and something about the creature sent a deep shiver through Seda.

'This is Seda, youngest of our father's line, as we are oldest,' Alvdan announced. 'Name yourself.'

The voice was hoarse and low. 'Uctebri the Sarcad, Your Imperial Majesty and honoured lady.' It was a man's voice, as accentless as though he had been born here in Capitas city.

'And is it good-mannered to conceal yourself behind a cowl?' Alvdan demanded. 'Surely my sister deserves better than that? Come, unmask yourself, creature.'

The figure that called itself Uctebri shuddered again, one hand gesturing vaguely towards the windows. The voice murmured something that might have been a plea.

The crack of the guard's whip made Seda start. Uctebri flinched back from it, though it had not touched him. She feared that, had the lash struck his wrist, it might have snapped his hand off.

Trembling, those hands now rose to draw back the cowl.

The sight was not so bad, at first. An old man, or an ill one. A pale veiny head with a little lank hair still clinging behind it. A thin, arched neck bagged with wrinkles. The lips were withered, his nose pointed, and there was a florid bruise on his forehead.

Shading them with both hands, he painfully opened his eyes to stare at her. They were protuberant, with irises of pure red, and they stared and stared at her face despite the glaring daylight. Seeing those, she saw also that the mark on his brow was not a bruise after all, but blood, a clot of blood constantly shifting beneath his waxy skin. .

'I don't understand,' she said to her brother. 'Who is this old man?'

'Do you hear her, Uctebri?' Alvdan smirked, as though he and the withered thing were sharing some joke at her expense. 'Well even we were unsure when first we looked upon you. Even with General Maxin's urgings, we were slow to believe – and yet here you are.'

Uctebri's head turned to squint at him, and then his crimson attention focused back to her. He would have been just some old man except for those eyes. They seemed to look through her. She could feel the force of that crimson stare as a queasiness in her stomach, an itch between her shoulder blades.

'Touch her,' Alvdan commanded. Seda drew back at once, but the guard, the man who had spent all morning at her shoulder, was now gripping her arms. Uctebri shuffled forwards, those unnatural eyes craning up at her, and she saw his tongue pierce between his lips, a sharp dart of red.

Something terrible was about to happen. She could not account for the premonition but she began to struggle as hard as she could, twisting and writhing in the soldier's grip as the old man approached her.

And then he was before her and she saw his mouth open slightly, the teeth inside sharp and pointed like yellow needles. One of those slender hands reached out to pincer her wrist.

He was not strong, but stronger than his frailty suggested nonetheless. She wrenched her hand from that cool touch, and Uctebri said, 'I must feel the blood, your great Majesty,' in that same calm, low voice.

She heard the whisper of Alvdan unsheathing his dagger, and then the cold steel at her throat. The old man raised his hands urgently.

'A point, the prick of a pin only, Lord Majesty. Just for the savour of it. No more, not yet. All in good time.'

They had surely all gone mad. If there was any fraternal feeling in Alvdan's heart she would have pleaded with him. Instead she closed her eyes and turned her head away as he seized her hand and cut across a finger.

Uctebri grasped eagerly for the weapon, but Alvdan only presented the blade of it.

'Have no ideas above your station, creature,' the Emperor said. 'You know what you are. Now act as you should.'

The crabbed old man craned forwards, hands cupping beneath the stained blade to catch any drips, and then licked the steel, his sharp tongue cleaning her blood from it in scant moments. Even that small taste of her seemed to bring a new strength to him. His next glance at her was nothing other than hungry.

'Will she serve?' Alvdan demanded of him. 'Or must we mount a hunt for more distant relations?'

Uctebri smiled slyly. 'She shall more than serve, your worshipful Majesty. She is . . . perfect. A most delicate savour.'

'Brother—' Seda's voice shook but she did not care. 'What is this?'

'Some small diversion,' he told her. 'Merely an entertainment. Fear not, dear sister. You have your part to play, but need learn no lines or dance-steps. Come, bring her.'

She was bundled after him back into the antechamber, where the pale servants waited.

'What is he?' she stammered.

'Can you not guess, sweet sister?' Alvdan's smile was now broad indeed. 'Think back as far back as childhood, when we sat by the fire together and listened to stories.'

And it was worse that she knew what he meant, that he did not need to explain. 'He cannot be . . .'

'Quite a discovery by General Maxin's Rekef, is it not?'

They come at night for the blood of the living, the ancient sorcerers, the terrible night-dwellers, who steal bad children from their beds, never to be seen again . . .

'But there are no Mosquito-kinden. There never were. They were just tales . . . surely?'

But confronting that gleeful smile of his, she knew otherwise.

Eight

Collegium was a city of laws. The underhanded could not easily purchase respectability, nor were they of great service or use to the Assembly. Such businesses as Lieutenant Graf had been practising were therefore done by word of mouth and behind closed doors.

Graf's office sat behind a small-package exporter run by a copper-skinned Kessen Ant who had long been renegade from his native city. The exporter's own work was on the shady side of the legal line and he asked no questions nor answered them. Behind his store was the back room where Graf bought and sold the talents of swordsmen to whoever required them. He was well known. He had a good reputation amongst buyers and sellers of blades.

Regular business was now closed for the evening, though, and he set out five bowls, poured wine into only one. His true line of work was a more uncertain business. There was no telling which of the chairs would sit out the night empty.

Thalric came first, unpinning his cloak and casting it off. 'Concerns, Lieutenant?' he asked, straight away.

'All going like clockwork, Major,' Graf confirmed. Thalric took the bowl of wine he was offered and swallowed deeply.

'Local?' he asked, and when Graf nodded, remarked, 'They have good vineyards hereabouts.'

Graf shrugged. 'Never was much of a man for it myself.' The lieutenant's speech and accent told Thalric that here was someone who had risen through his own efforts, without any help from family or friends. A doubly useful man, then. Mind you, merit got you further in the Rekef than it did in the regular army.

Scadran and Hofi, large and small, arrived together. At a gesture from Graf, the Fly-kinden barber hopped up onto a stool to pour two more bowls of wine.

'We'll start,' Thalric decided. 'Your report first, Scadran.'

'Arianna's not here, sir?' the big man asked.

'I've had word from her. She's in place and the plan is working well enough, but she decided it was best not to arouse any suspicion by breaking cover. The hook is set and the fish looks to be gaping for it, so to speak.' Thalric shook his head. He had only met Stenwold the once, and he had rather liked the man – as much as he could like any enemy of the Empire. Stenwold was a man who took his duties seriously, even when they might endanger those closest to him. Admirable, perhaps, but he was a tired old man, whereas Arianna was Spider-kinden, born to be devious, sly and cunning from her first breath.

Poor old man, but who would not be flattered to have an innocent young girl like that hanging on his every word? Who would not be swayed?

But it was for the good of the Empire, and that was the first rule of Thalric's life. Stenwold was altogether too much of an obstacle to ignore.

'So, Scadran, report,' he said, slightly irked that he needed to ask twice.

'Lot of news about Tark,' the dockworker began. 'Spider ships are coming in saying the north road from Seldis is cut, impassable. They're saying that they can sell to the . . . well, to us as well as they could to the Tarkesh. The slave trade and the silk trade haven't been dented. That's what they're most bothered about.'

'Anything more?'

'Nothing but the usual trouble,' Scadran continued, and then, as Thalric gestured for him to explain, 'Mantis long-boats from Felyal are on the rise. Spider shipping is being attacked. That happens every few years, then the Spiders get some mercenary navy in and everything quiets down.'

'Could be to our advantage, Major,' Graf remarked, and Thalric nodded.

'The more little wars being fought in the Lowlands right now the better,' he agreed. 'Hofi, the news with you?'

'All good as gold.' The Fly-kinden barber grinned happily. 'I snip a few grandees from the Assembly, in my place, and they love to boast about their doings. With a few words dropped, I can have them talking about anything I like. In this case, I got them – two or three of them waiting for the curl – talking on the subject of our dear friend Master Stenwold Maker.'

'In your own time, Hofi,' Thalric said, finding the little man long-winded.

'Of course, Major, of course. He's not a well-liked man, because they don't appreciate troublemakers. They don't think he takes the College seriously enough. There's even a motion tabled to strip him of his Masterhood. That's not the first time, but it could be passed.'

'Are they going to give him a hearing?' Thalric asked pointedly.

'Oh, of course they'll see him, in the fullness of time. For now, though, they're still debating just when. That debate alone could last thirty days.'

'Or?'

Hofi blinked. 'Or what sir?'

'Or it could be decided tomorrow?' Thalric suggested. 'And then they'd see him in a day after that?'

'Not likely, sir.'

'It's just as well I don't deal in likelihoods, then, when I can avoid it. I'll let Arianna know that the trap needs to be ready to spring at any time. Let's hope she has had the chance to worm her way fully into Stenwold's graces.'

'Rely on her,' Graf told him. 'She's a good agent.'

'I'm sure.' Thalric nodded again. 'What about *your* duties, Lieutenant?'

'I have men for you,' Graf confirmed. 'This city's never brimming with fighting men, but I have a dozen confirmed reliables so far.'

'Let's hope they're better than those last two you sent at him,' Thalric said.

'They're as good as I can get without compromising our position here, Major. And I have one special treat – one with a particular grudge against Stenwold's girl.'

'Against Cheerwell?' Thalric frowned. He could hardly imagine it.

'Not her, sir. The Spider girl. I've hired us a Mantis duellist.'

Thalric felt his heart skip despite himself. *No of course he hasn't hired* that *Mantis-kinden*. But the reaction was automatic. He had taken that man down, he had burned him and yet, after the Mantis's wretched daughter put her sword through Thalric's leg, he had seen the same man get up and fight like a monster.

He forced himself to stay calm. They would meet again, he assured himself, and the Empire would triumph over the backwoods belligerence of the Mantids.

But secretly he hoped they never met again.

'Our man's name is Piraeus. Apparently the daughter, or whatever she is, gave him a public whipping at one of their little fencing games, and for once we've found a Mantis who doesn't care just how he gets even. He's more than happy to stick her from the shadows. Or her old man, come to that. He's not particular.'

'Thalric,' she said, 'a Wasp-kinden. That is who I'm looking for.'

The paunchy Beetle-kinden looked down on her from his throne. It was meant to be a throne, anyway. A built-up chair atop some steps with gold and stones hammered into it. Perhaps he had been aiming for barbaric splendour.

'Name rings a bell,' he allowed. This seated dignitary was known as Last-Chance Fraywell. Felise understood this name came from his final words to those who crossed him. 'I'm going to give you one last chance,' he would say to them, and then proceed to kill them in whatever way appealed to him. So she was led to understand, anyway.

Fraywell leant down from his throne, peering at her suspiciously. She was standing a fair way back and she had come without her sword but, even so, there were a dozen of Fraywell's bullies carefully watching her. She looked from face to face: Beetle-kinden, Ants, halfbreeds . . . there he was, the man she was told to watch out for: a tall Spider-kinden, the only one here of his kind. His was the face she knew.

She moved in worlds far from home these days, always amongst the faces of strangers. It was better that way, for she could not have guaranteed recognizing faces from the Commonweal any more.

'Why do you want him?' Fraywell asked her. 'I've got no brief for Wasp-kinden, but this doesn't ring true.'

'Why I want him is my own business,' she replied flatly.

'Well then maybe where he's gone is mine.' Fraywell sat back, looking pleased with himself. He was one of the smaller gangsters in Helleron, and his fief, as they called a criminal's holdings, was pitiful, but it had been expanding recently. The word was that he had done well out of the recent visit by imperial troops, peddling all kinds of muck to them: drink, drugs, women. Certainly he had the clout to jostle for elbow room now.

'I must know,' she said. 'I *will* know. I have followed Thalric a long way and I will not give up now.'

'Well maybe your business can stay your business if only

you've got the wherewithal,' said Fraywell, sounding bored all of a sudden. 'Come on, let's wrap this up. You're taking up my valuable time, woman. Show me the stamp of your coin.'

She found that she was smiling, and it was disconcerting Fraywell and his men. 'I am not here to buy,' she explained. It was such a simple concept and yet the Beetle had still not grasped it. 'I am here to make payment.'

Fraywell glanced at his men, baffled, and she now was advancing on his seat smoothly, so smoothly that two of his people barely got in her way in time. Her hands flashed out, the razor edges of her thumb-claws folding forwards, and she cut them down with swift economy.

Fraywell screamed and kicked away from her so hard that he toppled his would-be throne backwards, leaving only his boots showing. She turned, looking over the room of stunned thugs and held a hand high.

The Spider-kinden that she knew stepped back and took her sword from within his cloak, pitching it to her above the heads of his fellows in a smooth arc. She hardly had to move her hand at all to catch it.

With her blade restored to her, she let them all draw their own weapons. That seemed only fair. Ten of them, and they tried to rush her, but she was already leaping forwards from the steps, descending on them with blade first.

They were not skilled but they were many. She made their numbers her ally, as they crashed into one another, fouling each other's blows. Her blade moved among them like lightning, like sunlight. She sent them reeling back in bloody arcs, and moved – quicksilver past lead – to evade their clumsy thrusts and grasping hands. Behind them the Spider-kinden traitor had a long dagger out and was picking and choosing his targets, putting the point in with the care of a surgeon.

And suddenly there were none left. It was so sudden she

could not quite work out where they had gone until she saw the bodies. She was used to that now: the jarring of cause and effect, the sudden returning to herself to discover blood on her blade and the fallen around her. There was some part of her, some innocent part, that had come loose inside her head, leaving only cold skill to hold the reins and whip her on.

She stalked over to the throne where Last-Chance Fraywell was now clambering to his feet, his broad face a-sheen with sweat.

'Whatever they're paying you, I'll double it,' he gasped, but they were paying her with the next chapter of Thalric's story, and how could he double that?

'I will not take up any more of your valuable time,' she said, and ran him through. Only afterwards did she notice that he had been holding a sword. It had not done him much good, she supposed.

Then she turned, like a performer to her audience.

The Spider-kinden man clapped politely. 'So much for the Last-Chancers. My employer will be over the moon. Serves them right for getting above themselves, say I.' He was a man past middle years, hair long and greying very slightly, wearing clothes whose flamboyance had been cut down, she guessed, to suit his purse. His voice was cultured, though, and she could only wonder where he had fallen on hard times from.

'Thalric?' she said questioningly, the sword still very much ready in her hands.

'Do you want it from my employer's mouth, or mine?' The Spider's name was Destrachis, she recalled, although she could not exactly remember now who his employer was.

'Tell me,' she directed.

He nodded, taking a seat on a bench there. 'Well our man Fraywell was here with a whole load of Wasp-kinden not so long back, and they got involved in something bad. Some people say they destroyed some big Beetle machine called the *Pride*, although that doesn't make much sense to me. They were kicked out in a hurry, though, and your man along with them. They went to Asta, which is a Wasp-kinden—'

'I know Asta,' she said. 'So he is there? Or at least that is where I travel next.'

Destrachis raised a hand. 'We pay in good coin in this fief, lady. He's not at Asta, we're sure of that. There's a fellow known to us, trades secrets all over, and to the Wasps as well. He's heard of your man. Thalric's a name that's being talked about after the wheel he knocked loose here. You're not the only one who's keeping him fingered.'

She stared, waiting for more, and he smiled, suddenly.

'Your man's been posted way out west of here. Do you know a city called Collegium?'

She shook her head. 'I shall find it, though.'

'I don't doubt it. You've got quite the way of asking questions.'

She merely nodded, and cleaned her blade on Fraywell's tunic before returning it to its scabbard. 'West. Collegium. Well I must go then,' she announced, and was at the door of Fraywell's hideout before his voice called her back.

'You know . . . you're a remarkable person,' he said. She turned, frowning. One hand was close to her sword. She sensed a trap here. At her expression he put his own hand up to forestall her.

'I've been all over the Lowlands,' he explained. 'I can do business in Collegium. If you wanted a guide, I could go with you.'

Her hostile expression remained. 'Why?'

'Because when I look at you, I recognize something. I see someone who's lost everything, and yet lost nothing.' He was not telling her why, she could see. It was just words.

She found her hand now on her sword's hilt, her heart speeding all of a sudden, and something clamoured away at the back of her mind.

'I used to be someone of consequence, down south,' Destrachis continued, watching her face intently. 'Not Aristoi, but not far off, but now look at me: some Beetle gangster's errand boy and quacksalver, betraying one brute for another at the drop of a kerchief. I lost it all, you see. You, at least, have retained a purpose.'

She stared at him. She could not discern his meaning.

'I can get you to Collegium the fastest way, and that way, you might actually catch this fellow of yours, instead of just walking his trail.' His eyes flicked over hers, reading her carefully – or at least what was left of her that was legible.

'What do you want from me?' she asked him outright.

'I don't know,' he told her, 'but probably I'll think of something. Perhaps there's someone I want dead. Perhaps it's just money.'

'I will not give myself to you,' she told him.

His eyebrows twitched. 'Never entered my mind.' He said it so smoothly that she knew it was a lie.

He claimed he could speed her progress, he could take her to Thalric. Then she could finish this hunt. The thought sent a shiver through her, oddly discomfiting, but the offer seemed too good to ignore.

And she could always kill him if she had to.

She nodded curtly, and the deal was done.

Doors had been opening recently to Stenwold that he had not guessed at. In all his years of lecturing at the College, of hand-picking some few students each year who might be able to serve his cause, he had never believed that he was being *listened to*.

Now he was a cause in his own right. His name had

been passed from student to student, year to year. The more the Assembly and the other Masters looked down on him, the more he had become something like a folk hero.

These last few days he had found that he need not simply wait on the indulgence of the Assembly. If they would still not hear him he need not let his voice go rusty.

Arianna, of course, was the architect of it all. He had not imagined it possible, otherwise, that so many of those bored faces he recalled from his years of teaching could have actually paid so much attention.

In these last few days he had twice gone with Arianna to some low dive – a taverna's back room once, and then an old warehouse near the docks – where he had met them. A dozen the first time, and then in the warehouse three score of them. They believed him because they had heard of the siege of Tark that was even then under way. They had heard disturbing news from Helleron. They had heard other rumours, news even to him. Some were Spider-kinden and had watched the imperial shadow encroach south-west towards their borders. Some even had some snippets of the Twelve-Year War the Wasps had waged against the Commonweal.

They watched with shining eyes as he told them the truth, the scale of the imperial threat: unity or slavery.

That became the slogan and they left with it on their lips. Yes, they were mere students, young men and women whose idealism had not yet been calloused by the everyday world. They were merchants' sons and daughters, youngsters from the Ant city-states, Flies of good family from Merro, paupers on scholarships from Collegium's orphanages and poorhouses. But they were not powerless: they could watch for him and spread word for him.

And they would fight for him, if worst came to worst. He knew he did not want them to do so, but many of them had held a blade before, the Ant-kinden certainly. Some were duellists of the Prowess Forum, some were artificers and all of them had volunteered to put what they had at his disposal.

Tisamon's words of not so long ago came back to him. Stenwold had become what he hated, the Mantis had said. He had become a spymaster sending the young to die for him. Times had changed even since those words were spoken. The first blood had been shed by an imperial army in the Lowlands. *Unity or slavery*. These young men and women might be the first stones to precipitate an avalanche.

In his dreams, he saw flames erupting in the Collegium streets he knew so well, young men and women with blades and crossbows. Stenwold awoke with the sound of clashing steel fading in his mind.

The Wasps knew that Collegium *must* fall, for it was the key to the soul of the Lowlands. They had tried once. They would try again. Stenwold stared at the dark ceiling of his room, seeing through the slats in the shutters that dawn was still distant.

They would try again soon. Sands in the hourglass had become a constant hissing and hissing of lost time. It was an hourglass in a dark room, though, so he could not see how much sand was left.

He moved to turn over and realized that she was beside him. The last hours of the previous night fell back on him and he opened his eyes wide.

There had been cheering for him, at the warehouse: all those bright-eyed faces. Unity or slavery! He had left for his own rooms feeling ten years younger, buoyed up in spite of himself. He was not alone now, and neither was Collegium.

Back at his house there had been wine. Tisamon and Tynisa had not stayed long. They had been on their way elsewhere, some Mantis training session. He had found himself alone with Arianna, drinking wine and talking about old times. An old man's failing, yes, although he still did not actually think of himself as *old* – though perhaps no longer young. An old man's failing nonetheless, and yet she had listened. He had talked about his own College days, his travels; about Nero the artist, of whom she had heard; then, darkly, of the fall of Myna; the Wasp plans he had seen; his own personal experience of their ambitions.

How she had listened, and it had seemed to him that her eyes had shone more brightly than any of the other students', and at the last he had convinced himself that there was more than simple zeal behind their gleam.

It had been a while since he had last slept with anyone – not that it was an excuse to say so. When he was a student himself there had been the usual ill-conceived liaisons, and after that a few tentative, short-lived ventures. Later there had been the occasional affection purchased on a commercial basis from a professional. His raising of Tynisa and Cheerwell and his crusade against the Empire had taken up all his time and his energy, until the latter endeavour had somehow led him to this place.

Well, there goes my place at the College. Or perhaps not, because he would not be the first by any means. He had always reserved his greatest contempt for Masters who preyed on their students in such a way, and now a clear pane of glass through which he could shine his judgement had become a mirror for himself.

But it wasn't like that. But of course it was like that. He was a College Master and she a student. He had plied her with wine, until her judgement had been sufficiently afloat that a night with him had seemed irresistible, or at least grimly inevitable. True, that was not what his blurry memories of the previous evening were saying, but it must have been what happened, by any objective standard.

She shifted slightly, the curve of her back pressing against him, moving her feet, surprisingly cold, to curl about his ankle. Despite all he had just thought, he felt himself stirring. Oh, it was the dream, though, wasn't it?

The dream all young Beetle lads had, when coming to the College. For they were the sons of tradesmen and merchants and artificers, and they would go home to wed a respectable Beetle wife, most likely. It was ever the dream, to sleep with a Spider-kinden woman before you die.

And I could die any day now, he told himself. Some part of Stenwold that was still the custodian of his schoolboy ego was crowing, distantly, for all the immorality of it.

She moved again and then turned restlessly, as though she knew what he was thinking, throwing an arm across his broad chest, and hooking a smooth leg across his. He closed his eyes but the responses of his body were beyond his ability to master. He gently freed his arm and fed it around her shoulders, and she nestled closer to him. He was able to put off thinking about what her reaction might be when she fully woke.

Waking past midnight, with the bulk of Stenwold sleeping beside her, her thoughts had been bittersweet. She had now done what the job required of her. He had moved and groaned on top of her, and she had considered him analytically, like a whore not yet wholly jaded.

Beetle men! she had thought and, though he was strange for a Beetle, seeing further, thinking more, in this way he was just like the rest of them.

Arianna, with the stillness of the night about her, considered her options, for her brief from Thalric had not taken her this far. His instructions had been limited to the student meetings she had lured Stenwold to. She knew her trade, though: she was Spider-kinden, after all. For Thalric to instruct her would have been as pointless as her giving an Ant counsel on going to war.

And Thalric had not said to kill the man, but here was her chance, and there would never be a better one. Thalric might be planning Stenwold's capture perhaps, his interrogation, but she knew with cold certainty that if she came to him with Stenwold's blood on her hands Thalric would not turn her away.

She slipped from beneath the sheets without disturbing him. He had drunk a lot, last night, but Beetle constitutions were sturdy. It had certainly not hindered his later performance.

It would be the work of a moment to take up her dagger and put it through his ear. Forty years of life and learning brought to a certain point and then cut off.

Would he boast, she wondered, if he survived to see the morning? Would he tell his College peers of his prowess? Or that evil-eyed Mantis friend of his? She thought not, because even in so few days she had come to know Stenwold Maker.

With her bare feet she searched her discarded robe for the blade, feeling along the braided cord of her belt. The work of a moment to kill him, the work of another to slip from the window and vanish into the night. Thalric would be surprised but pleased.

But the dagger was not there. She narrowed her eyes so as to pick out her pale robe in the darkness. She knelt by it, feeling. She had shrugged the garment off for him, not in haste, measuring his reaction as she unfurled her bare skin piece by piece. She did not recall the weapon dropping away, so it must still be here.

She stopped, clutching the robe to her. She was suddenly afraid, but it was a moment before she could pin down the cause.

The door was ajar, just a sliver. The doors in this house were all kept ajar, she recalled. Of course they were. They were Beetle doors with complicated catches. She could never have opened them if they were fully shut. The locking mechanism, simple though it might be, would have baffled her.

As it would also baffle the Mantis, since they were similarly of the old Inapt strain who had been left behind by the revolution. Spider-kinden might bar their doors, or fasten them with hooks, but never some twisting turning thing like this device. And so the doors were all ajar, because of Stenwold's household, and of her.

Knowing that, feeling across the floor for a blade that was not there, she abruptly *knew*. Standing, with the cool of the night on her skin, she looked across the room, seeing just a little in the faintest of moonlight from between the shutters. She and Stenwold were alone.

But *he* had been here and he had taken her knife. As tactfully and gracefully as that, because he was a Mantis and he did not trust her. She did not fear that he had broken her cover. It was all merely part of the loathing his kinden had for hers.

She saw now, in her mind, that gaunt shadow appearing in this room as she slept peacefully; his closed face, looking from Stenwold to her. He might have had his metal claw on his wrist. He could have killed her. She would not have known and she had not even woken. Instead, he had withdrawn. Stenwold's misplaced respect had kept him from ending her, but he did not trust her. He had removed her blade.

Arianna felt a strange feeling of relief. This was not over Tisamon's forbearance, she realized, but because she would not now stand over Stenwold's sleeping form with that blade in her hand, having to make that choice. The emotion took her by surprise. Surely she would not hesitate, but . . . how the man spoke! He had been to so many places, seen so many things. Now he had come to what he considered was home but he was wrong. She could hear the words he left unsaid almost more clearly than those he actually spoke. He was an outsider in his own city. He had made himself someone apart. He was struggling to save something that had already shunned and snubbed him. Yet Collegium had such a broad palette of colours to it that he had never quite noticed how he was not a native any longer.

Not so different, after all, she thought. She had told the truth when she had said that the Spiderlands offered no home for her any more. She had fallen in the dance, as her whole family had, and with nobody to help them back up.

She examined her hands and then clenched them into fists, watching the needles of bone slide from her knuckles. The knife was better, but Mantids were not the only kinden that the Ancestor Art could arm.

Stenwold would die just as easily.

She stood over him and watched the rise and fall of his stomach, the total relaxation of expression. It struck her that she had never seen him before without a look of vague worry. Except last night, when he had drunk so much and she had taken her robe off her shoulder and let it fall in careful stages to the floor.

If she had the dagger, things might be different. With her hands, with her Art-drawn claws . . . She felt abruptly crippled by something, some hindering and atavistic feeling. If she had the dagger, or the orders, but just now she had neither.

Perhaps Thalric would prefer him captured and talking. The rationalization – and she knew it for one – calmed her. Thalric had a plan and she was sure this moment of reticence on her part would make no difference, in the end.

She carefully tucked herself under the sheet again, her back to him, feeling him shift slightly. After the cool of the air she let her back and feet rest against him, stealing his warmth. When he moved again she turned automatically, her hand moving across his chest. There were scars there. She had seen them. It was a strange life, that had made this man scholar and warrior both.

When he put his arm around her she felt, for one instant, trapped, and in the next, safe, before she recalled herself to her role. Whether it was her role or herself that reached out for him she could not have said.

Nine

General Alder woke as soon as the tent-flap was pushed aside. By long practice his one hand found the hilt of his sword.

'General,' came the hushed voice of one of his junior officers. 'General?'

It was ridiculous. 'Either you want me awake, soldier, in which case speak louder, or you don't, in which case what in the Emperor's name are you *doing* here?'

'I'm sorry, General, it's the Colonel-Auxillian.'

Drephos. There was only one Colonel-Auxillian in the army. 'What does that motherless bastard want?' Alder growled. It was pitch-dark within the tent, too dark for him to even see the man a few paces away. 'What's the hour?'

'Two hours before midnight, General.'

'And he wants to speak to me *now?* Can't he sleep?'

'I don't know, General—'

'Get out!' Alder told the man. He sat up on his bed, a folding, metal-sprung thing they had made especially for him in the foundries of Corta. Drephos was a menace, he decided. The twisted little monster was taking his privileges too far.

Still, the man had a reputation, and it was a reputation for being right. Alder spat, and then dragged a tunic one-handed over his head and slung a cloak over his shoulders. Barefoot, he stepped out of his tent.

The camp had enough lights for him to see the cowled and robed form of Drephos standing some yards away. The agonized junior officer was hesitating nearby and, when Alder raised a hand to dismiss the man, Drephos's voice floated towards him.

'Don't send him away just yet, General. I think you will have orders to issue before long.'

Alder stalked over to him. 'What is it now?' he demanded. 'Your precious plan failed a day and a night ago.'

'Did I admit its failure?' Drephos enquired.

'You didn't have to.'

'I did not, General, nor do I. Have your men gather for an attack. The moment is at hand.'

Alder stared at him, at the featureless shadow within the cowl. 'Then—'

'Tark's walls are thicker to be sure, and of a stronger construction than I had thought, but the reagent has permeated the stone.'

'And you know this?'

'By the simplest expedient, General. I went and looked.'

Alder shook his head. 'I don't believe it.'

'Darkness is a cloak to me, General, but a blindfold to my enemies. I simply walked up to the enemy's walls and knew what I was looking for. In three hours, perhaps less, you will have your breach. I would therefore have your response standing by.'

'A night assault?' Which would be messy, Alder thought.

'They're bound to notice their walls coming down, General. Wait till morning and they'll have barricades up. We must force the issue now. And while they're busy fighting it out over the breach, in the darkness which will whittle away at their crossbows' effectiveness, we can try to put a few more holes in them. I've not been idle these last few days, and one of the leadshotters is now converted into a ram.'

'Major Grigan mentioned as much. He was not pleased.'

A derisive noise emerged from within the cowl. 'Major Grigan, of your precious engineers, is a dull-minded fool.'

'Major Grigan is an imperial officer—' Alder felt his temper rise.

'He is a *fool*,' Drephos repeated. 'He should be over on their side of the walls, hampering them. I am ten times the artificer he would ever be even if he opened his eyes to the world mechanical. A fool, General, and you would best give me what I ask for if you wish this war won.'

At this late hour it was too much. Alder's one hand clutched Drephos by the collar again, drawing the man up onto his toes. 'You forget your place, Auxillian.'

The general felt Drephos's left hand, gauntleted in steel, take his wrist and, with an appalling strength, remove it from its owner's person. Still maintaining that grip, which was gentleness backed with the threat of crushing force, Drephos's unseen face looked straight into his.

'Judge me on this, General,' he said. 'Prepare for your assault. If the walls still stand, then do what you wish.'

Not half an hour had passed before Alder had his command staff woken and rushed to his tent: Colonel Carvoc for the camp; Colonel Edric for the assault; the majors, including the sullen Grigan; the Auxillian chiefs and other unit leaders.

'We are going to attack,' he informed them, seeing blank incomprehension on all sides. 'Drephos assures me that the wall will be down shortly and I want to be ready for it.'

He saw Grigan's lip curl at the name, but when he fixed the man with his gaze, the major dropped his eyes.

'Colonel Edric.'

'Yes, General.'

'Get me all of your Hornets that are still able to fly. Back them with two wings of the light airborne and a wing of the Medium Elites. Go and organize them now.'

Edric saluted and ran from the tent.

'Carvoc.'

'Yes, General?'

'I want three wings each of Lancers and Heavy Shield-men, and our Sentinels. Go now.'

When Carvoc had gone, a worried frown already appearing on his face, Alder turned to the Auxillian officers. Discounting the maverick Drephos there were two of any worthwhile rank. Anadus of Maynes was a ruddy-skinned Ant who was either the army's swiftest dresser or slept in most of his armour: a solid, bitter man who detested the Empire and all it stood for. Alder knew all that, just as he knew that so long as the man's city-state of Maynes, his family, his people, were all held hostage to his behaviour, that hatred would be turned on the Ants of Tark. Besides, Ants fought Ants. All the subject races had flaws, and that feuding was theirs.

Beside him was Czerig, a grey-haired Bee-kinden artificer from Szar. There was never any trouble from that direction, fortunately. The Bee-kinden were loyal to their own royal house and, since the Emperor had taken their queen from them and made her his concubine, they had served the Empire as patiently as if they were its born slaves.

'Captain-Auxillian Anadus,' Alder said, enjoying the dislike evident in the man's eyes, 'assuming Drephos is correct, your brigade gets to take the breach.'

Anadus's eyes remained bleak. The worst danger, the greatest glory, a chance to kill Ants of a city not his own? Alder could only guess at the thoughts going on behind them. 'Go and prepare your men, Captain. If there's a breach I want it packed end to end with your Maynesh shields before the Tarkesh can fill it.'

'It shall be so, General,' said Anadus, his tone suggesting that he considered death in this other man's war the only way out with honour for him and his men.

Which concept I have no concern with.

'Captain-Auxillian Czerig.'

The old man looked up tiredly. Like all his kinden he was short, strong-shouldered, dark of skin.

'Get the new ram Drephos has tinkered with ready for the gates. You know the one?'

Czerig nodded. He said nothing that was unnecessary, and when he spoke it was mostly about his trade.

'Good. And I also want the Moles.'

Czerig pursed his lips.

'What is it, Captain?'

'They . . . are not happy.' Czerig twisted, clearly less than delighted himself. 'They say . . . they are not warriors, General.'

'So what makes a warrior?' Alder enquired. 'If they have the ill luck not to be born Wasp-kinden, then they have this: they have armour, they have weapons and they are going to war. Tell them they're all the warrior they need to be. I want them against some patch of the walls within a hundred yards of the breach – if it ever happens. So I can support the main assault. Is that clear?'

Czerig nodded glumly and saluted.

Awake. Totho's eyes were abruptly wide in the darkness. It was not the sound, although there were sounds, but a shudder that had awakened him. He clung to his pallet because the floor was shaking.

People were running about in the hall outside. He was in Tark – that was it. Not in Collegium. Not Myna, which for some reason had come to him as a second guess. The Ants of Tark. The siege . . .

He stumbled up from the floor, feeling it twang again like a rope pulled taut. Part of him was desperate to believe he was still dreaming. He tripped over his discarded clothes on his way to the door and pulled it open. There were lamps outside, and he stared at them blearily: simple globes over gaslight, but one of the covers had fallen and smashed, leaving the naked flame guttering.

A squad of soldiers charged past him, heading for the outside. They were armed and armoured, but there was an uncharacteristically slipshod look to them: warriors who had harnessed in haste. He called after them, but not one of them looked back.

'Totho, lad.' The small figure of Nero almost tripped down the stairs, his wings flaring as he caught himself. He was wearing only a nightshirt. 'What's happening?'

Totho could only shake his head, and a moment later Nero was displaced by Parops, his chainmail hauberk hanging open at the back. Totho expected him to say this was no place for civilians, that they should go back to bed and let the army deal with it. Instead Parops hissed, 'You've arms and armour? Put them on!'

'Parops, what in blazes is going on?' Nero demanded.

The Ant commander's face was haunted. 'The wall's down.'

'The *what?*'

'The wall's down,' and the floor shook as he repeated himself. 'It's coming down right now, and the Wasps aren't far behind.'

And then Parops was charging back upstairs, his loose armour flapping. Even as Totho watched, Salma bolted from his room, heading for the outside, his sword in his hand.

Nero shook his head. 'I have a bow upstairs in my room,' he remarked philosophically. 'I think I shall go and string it.' He left Totho gaping.

But gaping would solve nothing. Totho stumbled back into his room and wrestled on his leather work-coat: that would serve as armour better than his bare skin would. He had the repeating crossbow that Scuto had given him and he slung on his sword-baldric that had a bag of quarrel magazines hanging from it.

I am no soldier, he inwardly protested. But the Wasps would not care.

Totho blundered out into the hall again.

'Hey, Beetle-boy? You fighting now?'

It was Skrill. She wore her metal scale vest and her bow and, to his surprise, she looked more frightened than he felt.

'I suppose,' he said uncertainly.

She clapped him on the shoulder. 'I'll stick right with you then, Beetle-Boy. Whole world's coming apart at the seams.'

And it was. Another shudder racked Parops's tower, and Totho pushed his way to the door and flung it open.

Behind him, Skrill uttered something, some awed exclamation, but his ears were so crammed with the sound from outside that he heard not one word.

The wall was down. The wall beside the tower had fallen and was still falling. Totho saw the stones of the lower reaches bulge and stretch like soft cheese, shrugging off the colossal weight of their higher-up brethren, so that to the left and right of the breach whole stretches of wall were bulging inwards or outwards as though pressed either way by a giant's hand.

There were Ant soldiers running for the gaping breach, each man and woman falling into formation even as they ran, shields before them, locked rim over rim. The stones fell on them as they massed forwards.

There were other soldiers charging the breach from the outside. For a moment Totho could not work it out at all. The shields of the defenders were meeting the same locked rectangles of the attackers, and in the poor light of the moon he could see no difference between them. Ant against Ant, shortswords stabbing over shield-tops, second-rank crossbows shooting, almost close enough to touch, into the faces of the enemy, and all happening in silence: metal noises aplenty but not a cry, not an order yelled on either side. The battle line twisted and swayed over the breach, which widened and widened, dropping further stones that slammed gaps into the ranks of both sides.

The skies were full. He found himself dropping to one knee, a hand up to shield him. The skies were crowded tonight with a host of madmen out for blood. There were Wasp soldiers darting and passing there above, and the spear-wielding savages in their howling hosts. From the roof-tops of nearby houses, from the ground and the still-standing wall, Ant crossbows were constantly spitting. As Totho's wild gaze took in the archers, he saw that most were merely in tunics, others were near naked. They were citizens, off-duty soldiers, the elderly or children no more than thirteen straining to recock their bows by using both hands.

The skies were busy with more than just flying men. Even as Totho watched, a great dark shape cut through a formation of the Wasp light airborne, its powering wings sounding a metal clatter over all the rest. Totho saw the flash of nailbows from within and knew it must be a Tarkesh orthopter. More of the machines flapped, some loosing their weapons against the airborne while others were dropping explosives on attackers beyond the wall.

Beyond the wall: there were more, then. Totho craned up and saw the trebuchet on Parops's tower pivoting, lean-ing at an angle, launching a missile past the section of wall that still held the gate. Then something thundered over it, and there was the flash of incendiaries that briefly silhouetted the siege weapon in sharp detail. Moments later it was on fire, and Totho saw one of its crew drop blazing down onto the soldiers fighting below. He hoped Parops was well clear.

The juddering machine flew on, a great ugly heliopter clinging to the air with its three labouring rotors. It would have been a simple matter to dispatch it with artillery or with the orthopters but the Wasps had given Tark all manner of distractions tonight.

Totho raised his crossbow, but the sky was such a

jumble that he could find no sense in it. He fell back against the tower wall, feeling the stones shift against one another. He had never been intended to see this: it was a world the sedate College had no words for.

Cheerwell, he cried in his mind, but no doubt she had already forgotten him in his self-imposed exile.

Skrill crouched beside him, tracking a passing Wasp with her bow and sending the arrow off, a hiss of annoyance already on her lips as she saw her shot fall short. Totho himself could not even manage to shoot, though. The assault on his senses was overwhelming.

He had put his sword into Captain Halrad, all those tendays before, put it right into his back as they had escaped the *Sky Without.* The first blood he had ever shed and it had been spilled for Che Maker. He had been there, as one of Stenwold's men, but only for Che.

He had fought in Helleron and then tracked her into the very Empire, stealing into the Governor's Palace in Myna. He had used this same crossbow to kill Wasps there, and it had been to rescue Che, to bring her safely home.

But in gaining her he found he had lost her. Her heart had been stolen from him. Stolen, because she had barely met the other man, Achaeos, the Moth-kinden deceiver. And in the end, for her sake, he had left to go along with Salma, to go to war.

He knew a great tide of despair that almost eclipsed him, and when it receded he found himself standing, shooting into the soldiers passing overhead, dragging the lever back over and over until the wooden magazine was empty, and then reaching for another from his bag.

Outside the city wall the advancing infantry of the Empire was almost untroubled, as the defenders sent their missiles at the flying corps or at Anadus's Ant-kinden. Captain Anadus's men had not been able to press into the breach, for the Tarkesh were holding them at bay, although the carnage on both sides was unspeakable. The very bodies of the dead were now starting to clog the gap. This was the ancient war that the Ant-kinden had always waged upon themselves. Shield rammed against shield, neither side would give an inch.

Drephos's new engine was almost at the gates, shielded from above by a great curved iron coping. It was a lead-shotter in essence, a siege engine that should launch great powder-charged balls of stone or metal. Drephos, however, had given it a new purpose.

Captain Czerig himself had taken on this duty, along with two of his artificers. The three of them now sheltered under the eaves of the machine's metal roof, and guided it forwards until it was mere feet away from the gate. Behind them came a mass of Wasp armoured infantry, bristling with spears and desperate to join the fight.

The sound of missiles above them was more persistent now. If the Tarkesh got a siege engine to bear on them it would be over. The Tarkesh had other things to think about, he knew.

The Wasp army had ramming engines, of course, but they traditionally relied on their engines' power to push through the barriers. Drephos had a better plan, though. Czerig gave the signal and his artificer had the great machine ratchet back, cogs and gears moving the foot-thick arm into place. There was a firepowder charge in the chamber that could have hurled a stone from the Wasp camp all the way over Tark's walls, but its force would now be concentrated into the three-knuckled metal fist. Czerig did not like Drephos: the man made him shiver to his very core. Nevertheless, there was no denying his skill as an artificer.

'Stand clear,' he said, and his men scurried back, raising round shields against the engine itself in case it failed.

He took a deep breath and released the catch. The powder exploded, swathing them instantly in thick, foul smoke, and the trapped power of the charge went into the ram that punched against the gates of Tark. Czerig heard them bend inwards, heard the crunch of ruined wood, the snap of metal fixings.

His artificers were already moving to draw the ram back and put a second charge in place. Something heavy struck the coping above and bounded off, either engine-shot or a stone hurled from the walls. Czerig remained phlegmatic: the ram would succeed or fail, he himself would live or die. He was a slave of the Wasps without hope of freedom and he found he cared little enough.

Across the field his fellow slaves of war were marching into battle, dwarfing the Wasp soldiers all around them. The giants were striding forth and Captain Czerig felt a stab of sorrow. They were so wretched, he knew: they hated the fighting even more than he did, had less hope even than he.

In his heart he wished them luck – or a swift death.

There were a dozen of them only, half of their kinden's unwilling contingent currently serving with the Wasp Fourth Army. As tall as two men, as broad as three, sporting massive slabs of metal armour and thick sheets of studded leather that would crush a normal warrior, they bore great spade-headed spears and seven-foot shields of metal and wood. They now moved with five-foot strides towards the walls of Tark. Mole Cricket-kinden they were and, like the other Auxillians, they were slaves whose families were held hostage to their loyal service. Few and reclusive, to them it seemed that they had always been slaves to someone or other. They had laboured and built for the Moth-kinden and Spiders when the world was younger and the revolution still a dream, but at least their masters had known where their true skills lay. Now the Wasp-kinden had garrisoned their towns and their mines, and turned them into warriors.

There was some shot coming from the city walls now and they put their shields up, feeling the metal shudder as crossbow bolts bounced from them. Their kind were onyx-skinned and pale-haired, huge and strong, but, though they were armoured like automotives, a keen shot with a crossbow could finish them, just like any mortal man.

But their present enemies were creatures of the surface and the sun, while the Mole Crickets saw better at night than in daylight. They were closing on the walls.

Their leader glanced left, seeing old Czerig with the ram and that the gates were almost broken through. No doubt it was important to the Wasps that all these holes be made in one go. He had no wish to learn strategy himself.

A fistful of grenades suddenly landed all around them, dropped from an orthopter already burning, even as it passed overhead. An instant volley of explosions erupted about them, killing three and wounding another, denting and splitting shields. The remainder picked up their pace. Their orders were to go through the wall, they knew, and then through the men beyond.

None of them would survive. So much seemed certain. The Mole Cricket leader braced himself as the great stones loomed before him.

Pardon this violence, he said silently, dropping his spear and shield. His great chisel-nailed hands found the gaps between the stones, and he called upon his ancestors, called upon the Art they had given him. The stones within his grasp – and those his brothers grasped – began to soften and to shift.

Totho found himself crouching against some of the fallen wall, frantically slotting another magazine in place and knowing he was almost out of ammunition. Skrill was behind him, her back to his, sending sporadic arrows up at the enemy. More and more Ants were coming to help hold the breach, and even Totho could see how the attacking force was being made to give ground, every inch of it bought in blood. Above them the cavalry had arrived, Ant-kinden soldiers riding great winged insects, cumbersome in flight as they buzzed ponderously through the darting Wasp airborne. Each flying beast had a big repeating crossbow mounted above its thorax and soon the newcomers were taking a savage toll of the enemy.

Knowing that Salma was up there somewhere, Totho just hoped he would be safe, but he could spare him no further thought.

Yet more Ant-kinden were coming to join the defence. Some had brought packs of giant ants under leash, drawn from the nest of tunnels beneath the city. The creatures were the guards and soldiers of the nest below, and another resource the city could barely spare, but they had stings and jagged mandibles. As soon as they were within sight of the enemy their leashes were loosed, and they scuttled towards the foe with jaws gaping in idiot threat.

Totho tried to track another Wasp soldier while the man darted overhead, hands spitting golden fire. Then one of the Wasp heliopters rumbled past, and Totho noticed it was failing, one of its rotors torn and still. The ponderous, blocky machine limped through the air, tilting and tilting further. One of the great flying insects was clinging to its side, riderless, peeling at the metal casing with its jaws. Then it went out of sight over the rooftops, but Totho felt it come down, felt the ground shake and heard the sudden blast as its engine ruptured and its fuel exploded. Looking over the rooftops he saw the night was punctuated by a dozen red gleams where Tark was burning.

There was a sudden sense of movement around him, Ants pushing into him, wordless but eyes wide as some unheard alarm went through their heads.

A bright light, a sound – he was lifted up by a great hand. He heard Skrill scream and then . . . and then . . . Nothing.

*

Totho's head was ringing, and he did not know why. He was aware of lying on some uneven surface and there seemed to be a great deal of noise and confusion going on. He sat up, clutching his head, and then saw what he was lying on.

Bodies.

He was lying on corpses, dead Ant-kinden from Tark, dead Wasp-kinden from the Empire. He stumbled to his feet, fell over almost immediately. His artificer's coat was bloody and ragged, and he picked a metal shard from it curiously. All around him a lot of people were rushing back and forth, but he felt it was his duty as an artificer to identify the piece of metal he had found.

It looked like the sort of fragment that would be left behind by an exploding grenade, he thought. A crude ball-type grenade, not one of the hatched-metal ones the Beetles made in Helleron.

Awareness ran through him like a swordblade: Tark; the siege; the night attack. *It was still going on.* He must have been knocked flat by an explosion.

'Skrill?' he shouted, remembering how she had been there with him. 'Skrill?' but there was absolutely no chance of being heard. Even his own voice sounded muted and far away. Another thirty or forty Ant soldiers went charging past, trampling their own dead. Some stopped to shoot upwards, and he fell to his knees once again, looking into that asylum sky full of fighting men, beasts and machines.

Hands found him and helped him to his feet. He leant back into them, feeling shaken and sick, the impact of the grenade still thundering in his head.

'Che!' he got out. 'You found me.'

'You better get your head on straight!' And Che turned into Skrill, her voice high with fear. 'Where's your piece?'

He looked around, but Scuto's marvellous crossbow was now nowhere to be seen. He plucked another – a Tarkesh soldier's – from its dead owner's hand, dragging a quiver off a second body.

They had moved further from the breach, he saw, but the gate itself was now open. Or rather there were splintered pieces of it left barely clinging to the hinges. There was the great engine there that had powered through the gateway before it had finally been stopped and disabled. Ants and Wasps were fighting there. Totho stumbled towards the machine.

'Where're you going?' Skrill shouted after him. She had lost her bow, he noticed. She should find herself a crossbow as he had, but of course she surely derived from some primitive old race that didn't know about crossbows and how clever they were.

The ramming engine was partly blocking the gateway. Wasp spearmen were trying to push through, but the Ants were holding them back. The engine itself looked really interesting, though, and that seemed the most important thing to Totho's addled mind. As the Ants swarmed around it, he struggled to make his way to its battered head. It had not been intended for this use, he now saw. Some brilliant hand had cunningly reshaped it.

There was a litter of bodies about it, mostly Wasp-kinden. Some were still moving, and he eyed them dully. The engine was slewed a little on its side, and he saw corpses in Wasp colours scattered there, but not actually Wasps. *Artificers?* Of course they were the machine's artificers. The Wasps themselves had no respect for such skills.

He reached out and, as the Ants continued fighting all around him, he put his back to the skewed machine and forced it up, working to free one of his brother artificers from under its weight.

Skrill was yelling again, and he glanced around in time to see the city wall by the gate begin to shift. He suddenly felt so very calm about it, because he was right in the wall's shadow, and there was nothing he could do about it in time.

Stones began to bulge out of it, only one at first, and then in whole fistfuls. A man emerged: Totho could see his shape by the light of the fires, but it seemed impossible, for it was a man ten feet tall, armoured in great metal plates and wielding an eight-foot mattock. There were others behind him, and they lumbered out of the gap as still more Ants rushed in to engage them. Just before they clashed Totho was struck by the expression of hopeless misery on those giants' faces.

The huge creature in the lead swept his spade-headed spear around him like a club, flinging three or four of the Ants aside with ruined shields, but then the soldiers were on him, and their attack-insects as well. Totho watched with numb amazement, seeing how easily the giants fell. There were Wasps following behind them though, armoured Sentinels pressing forward, their plate-mail easily turning the swords of the defenders. Some dozen of them plunged into the Ant line and shattered it, even as the last giant fell, and then there were savages bursting out along with them, shrieking and casting their spears. Behind them, in turn, came the armoured Wasp infantry, already lancing out with its stings.

Totho felt the fallen man he held stir in his arms and he forced the ruined engine an inch further off him. The man clutched at him as Totho pulled him free, now seeing the wreckage the fallen engine had made of his legs.

With conflict still all about him he dragged the dying man away, aware only that this was an artificer, and therefore a brother in craft.

'My queen!' the man cried. 'I am done at last.'

Totho lowered him to the ground. He felt cold and getting colder, but his eyes found Totho's. 'You, Lowlander . . . I am sorry—'

Totho nodded, not knowing what to say. The man's hands tugged at his coat, and perhaps there was some returning recognition there, on feeling the pockets lined with tools. 'You must know . . . the air . . . airships! It is the end. I have . . . died for them, never to be home again. But the airships . . . you must guard . . . !'

There was nothing more said, just one more death amidst so many.

Salma dived through the sky like a mad thing, slashing at every Wasp that came near him, though missing most of them. The aerial forces of Tark were token only. They had their orthopters and their flying insects, but coming against them the entire sky was dense with Wasps.

He pulled out of his dive on coming level with a handful of the winged ants. Ahead of them a mass of the Wasp savages was gathering like a cloud, spiralling upwards. Salma looked over to the lead Ant rider, and for a moment there was a touch of mindlink with him, two soldiers in perfect accord, as if he saw the man's thoughts and passed back his own.

You lead, we follow, was the man's message, because Salma was vastly more at home in the air than they were.

Sword extended, Salma kicked out towards the circling Hornets, sword extended, and he got close, very close, before they even saw him. Then crossbow bolts from the insect-mounted weapons started punching into the flight of Wasps and they scattered wildly. Salma veered to the left, seeing spears and bolts of light dash past him. Briefly something caught his eye about their formation, then he was lancing through them, bloodying his sword on at least three before turning to dance back towards them. The insects were on them by now, thrumming heavily through the air, jaws clacking at their nimbler opponents. The crossbows were never silent, funnel-fed bolts from their hoppers cracking out every second into the mass of the enemy. Then two of the insects were down and in a moment Salma saw why.

The Ants were not the only airborne cavalry deployed above the field. Diving directly past his view came a giant wasp the size of a horse, with a soldier clinging gamely to its back. There was no crossbow, in fact no weapon at all, but the man's hands yanked and tugged to get the monster to cooperate. It dodged and spun in the air and then fell on one of the ant-riders, lancing the insect he rode on with its sting, and crushing the rider's shoulder with wedge-shaped jaws.

Another buzzed past, spinning Salma in its wake. Its rider tried to let loose his energy sting, but the beast began bucking the moment he took a hand from its harness. And then he was gone, and Salma was slicing through the air towards the scattered savages.

He saw what had snagged his attention before. There was a leader amongst them, a man in a spike-fronted helm bawling out orders that sent them hurtling across the city. Salma adjusted his angle, so as to come in from above and put his sword through their commander.

Colonel Edric continued sending his Hornet soldiers out to loot and burn, to create as much confusion as possible, when one of the men pointed over his shoulder and began shouting a warning. Edric turned in the air, wings dancing, to see a man – a Commonwealer! – almost upon him. He threw himself aside, losing his hold in the air and dropping ten feet before his Art caught him, and the Dragonfly flashed past him, slicing open the soldier who had warned him. Edric was after the Commonwealer in a moment, knowing that a score of Hornets would follow faithfully, and then had to hurl himself backwards as a great dark shadow roared down from above. It was one of the Empire's own heliopters, and for a second Edric's entire sky was obscured by its metal-plated hull. He heard a bitter shearing sound as several of his men met the rotors, and then the machine was trying sluggishly for height, spilling out grenades in a non-stop cascade.

He tried to locate the Dragonfly, saw the man again spearing towards him. Edric shot a blast of his sting, but his adversary flitted out of the way. The bulk of the heliopter was still clawing for height, and he dropped beneath it to give himself space to think and manoeuvre.

But the Dragonfly was veering off suddenly, and Edric looked about to see what he was avoiding.

It was a Tarkesh orthopter with red flames blazing from its cockpit. The heliopter shuddered in the air as it tried to correct its course, but the orthopter, even as its wing cables were snapping, shifted its aim lazily and struck against the bigger machine's side, staving it in. A second later and one or the other had exploded, and then they both had, and Edric was hurled head over heels through the air and across the city.

Feeling a wave of hot air roll over him, Salma caught himself in the air, still seeking out his target. There he was, blown almost up against the wall by the force of the two dying machines. He was right at the gatehouse, amongst the wrecked artillery. Even as the colonel got to his feet on the stones of the wall, Salma was stooping down on him.

Barely in time, Edric saw him coming and dragged his sword from its scabbard. It was a Hornet piece, big and heavy-edged, and he slashed furiously at Salma as the Dragonfly fell on him, but Salma was a natural in the air, pitching aside to let the great blade pass him. His own lunge scored across the colonel's side and then he had knocked the man down, and the two of them went tumbling end over end towards the broken edge of the wall. Edric was now on top and with one hand to his side he straightened up, raising his sword to split Salma's skull. At the same time, Salma stabbed upwards, his blade punching through his opponent's light armour and up to the hilt beneath the man's ribs. The Wasp colonel's sword fell from his hand, spinning through the air until it struck the ground far below. A moment later, Salma sent the man's body heading in the same direction.

Ten

'What it is,' Destrachis shouted above the wind, 'is that the money goes to Collegium. That's the way it works.'

Felise clung on grimly, trying to catch his words as the rushing air swept them past her.

'If you do well for yourself in Helleron . . .' he continued, quite happy, apparently, to carry on this conversation at the top of his lungs, 'if you own a string of factories, make a mint, then you retire to Collegium. That's where the respectables live, and having money like that buys you a lot of respectable, you see?'

She nodded, still trying to understand. Their automotive jolted at that point, some join or flaw in the rails, and she nearly lost her grip. If she fell now, though her wings would catch her safely, she would never catch up with this machine again. Nobody could fly as fast as the engine was propelling them.

'And so,' Destrachis went on, 'there's a market for luxuries. The Collegium rich like to flaunt it, same as everywhere. Spiderland goods come in up the coast, but for anything from the north, there's a real battle to be the first with it. And that's' – he waved an arm perilously around, having hooked onto the automotive's side with the other – 'where this comes in.'

The machine they were riding was mostly open cage-work. The middle section was for the cargo, five or six heavily padded crates lashed together on a low-sided hold. At the front was the engine, which had originally sounded like thunder rolling across the hills to the west of Helleron, but the sound of it was now mostly merged with the wind. Parts of it glowed red-hot, while other parts were constantly being tightened by the three-man crew of artificers. It ran on firepowder and seemed, even to Felise who knew nothing about such matters, like a dangerous beast waiting for its moment to attack.

At the back of the machine was the meagre space the thing set aside for its crew. Two men were forward now, keeping the engine in tune. One was watching some dials and gauges that were wholly occult to her. Behind him, Destrachis and Felise clung on tight.

They were close-mouthed, tough-looking men, those three. Black Guild artificers, contraband runners, Beetle-kinden, all of them, and loosely allied to the fiefdom that Felise had served so well by eliminating the Last-Chancers. They were, above all, supreme opportunists, as this venture showed.

'You see, this was going to be the big business,' Destrachis further explained. 'The Iron Road from Helleron to Collegium by a direct and unbroken rail, instead of having to go the square way round Sarn. Only they got the rail finished and then some fool blew up the engine. Thing called the *Pride*, most expensive automotive ever made, and they blew it up. You'd think someone else would step in, but no, the fellow who owned the *Pride* has the contract, and he's blasted if he's going to let anyone else get the first ride, so he's having a new engine built, and meanwhile all these miles of shiny rails are just sitting here, doing nobody any good! So you see, these lads decided to jump at the chance. They tell me it's easy enough to make an automotive run on rails, and once it's running on the rails it goes a lot faster than if it wasn't.' He was grinning wildly, his hair streaming and, in the face of that, she had to smile back. 'So these lads cornered the market!' he finished, and she nodded to show she understood.

'I love machines!' he told her. 'They fascinate me!'

'But you can't, really,' she called back, and she knew that, downwind as she was, her words would not reach him. He read the remark in her face, though, and his grin merely widened.

'I don't *understand* them, but I love them. All the little parts and pieces!'

Despite the lack of available space, the artificers had taken them aboard willingly. They were engaged in a high-risk venture, for there could be brigands or even militia in their way, but Felise Mienn was the woman who had killed a dozen Last-Chancers single-handed. When she had asked Destrachis why they were taking him too, he had told her it was for the same reason.

'You're a fighter?' She had sounded sceptical. He was a man for the underhand knife, perhaps, but no warrior.

'I'm a doctor,' he had said, with some dignity. 'Or at least that was my training. I've been a lot of things since. Anyway, it's a risky trip we're on now. Injuries are likely from the journey or the machine itself. They'll be glad to have me patching them up.'

The nameless little automotive scorched across the miles, the fastest thing in the Lowlands, according to its crew. Even the *Pride* itself would not be able to do this journey so swiftly, they boasted, since the power of its ingenious engine would be hindered by the weight of its carriages.

Felise was amazed that she could even catch her breath, amazed that the constantly churning engine did not fly apart or the crewmen get caught in its works or burned at any minute. The rush of the engine, the sweep of the countryside as it was hustled past them, the occasional brief image of some small village or herder's croft, it all seemed to sing in her heart.

Would this be such a bad life? Perhaps she could find these men again, when she was done, after—

After what? For surely there would be no after. The one task that had sustained her this far would take the world with it once it was done. As though peering from a brightly lit room into the clouded night skies, she could see no after.

But this thought, with so much else, was soon blown past her by the incessant wind, and Destrachis was still grinning at her, so she smiled back at him and allowed herself to enjoy.

Destrachis woke with the tip of a blade at his throat. For a second he twitched uncontrollably, instincts yelling at him to do something, anything. He suppressed them, lying calmly for a moment to gather himself. Then he opened his eyes. There was a little moonlight slanting across them, and his eyes – and hers, he knew – would pick out enough from it to see their way.

'I'm awake,' he said quietly. They were in a Wayhouse located not far from Collegium. She had paid the surprised Way Brothers for a private room, and let Destrachis take a place on the floor, but now she had apparently had second thoughts.

Felise Mienn studied him down the length of her sword, and he thought she was trembling slightly in the faded moonlight.

'How do I know I can trust you?' she demanded.

He allowed himself a slight smile. He knew from experience that, on his slightly lined face, it seemed an expression of infinite reassurance. 'Felise—'

'You are too convenient,' she said. 'I think . . . I think you may be working for him. For Thalric – or for his masters. You are here only to stop me. Or else to warn him.'

She *was* trembling, he saw, but for all that the sword was

still. Its tip was close enough to dimple the skin of his neck, but it drew no blood.

'Felise, please listen to me.' It was long practice that allowed him to lie there, as calm as a cloudless sky, and speak in such reasoned and measured tones.

'Why would you leave your work in Helleron?' she asked.

'I am a mercenary at best, I have no roots—'

'And why come along with me, just like that?'

'You have money, do you not?'

'And why—?'

'But most of all,' he said, risking much to cut across her increasingly urgent questioning, 'we have had this conversation before.'

Dead silence from her. He stared into that face, beautiful as it was, and, in that instant, he saw nothing whatsoever alive behind her eyes. He granted her a long moment, and then continued.

'Three days ago, camping beside the automotive, we had this exact conversation. Remember, it scared the squits out of those smugglers we were with? You accused me of being a Wasp agent. You had me pinned like this, almost exactly the same. It was the middle of the night, just like now. And then we talked, and I explained to you that, no, I wasn't a Wasp agent, and that if you wanted me to leave you, then I'd do it, but I'd rather not. I'm simply a travelling companion who is, for the moment, heading in the same direction as yourself. And I'm not overly fond of the Empire, either. And I have watched you fight, and I find you admirable.'

'Admirable,' she echoed. He was not entirely sure she had understood his words.

'Capable of being admired,' he explained lazily. 'I have lived in a great many places, both inside and outside the Lowlands, Felise, and I have never met anyone quite like you.'

She was trembling again, and he knew that this was the point where the loose string in her head that was keeping her in check might snap, or not. He fought down his own anxiety and made himself wait.

'I . . .' There was the look of a lost child on her face, and the 'I' she spoke of was someone else, someone surfacing from long ago to take brief possession of a body long vacated. 'Where am I? What is this place?'

'Just a Wayhouse on the road. We'll go to Collegium tomorrow.'

'What's . . . Collegium?' She seemed dazed.

He wondered what would happen if he led her deliberately astray now, invented some other purpose for her. How long would the deception last, and could it be that simple? But, no, here came her familiar expression once more, ice spreading across her face and making her cold and hard again.

Abruptly her sword was back in its scabbard. '*He* is there,' she reminded herself.

'Or has been there,' he corrected, allowing himself to sit up, gingerly touching his throat but finding not a mark on it.

'*He* is there,' she repeated. 'And I will fall on him, and all his allies, and leave not one alive.'

The worrying thing, for Destrachis, was how this thought seemed not to fire her up but to calm her down.

Lieutenant Graf perused the dispatch, keeping his expression carefully blank. Amidst the scars, his one eye flicked back and forth over the few words it contained, looking for a way out.

'Major?' he began at last, and Thalric saw that, like so many in his position, he was a man who had forgotten, until this moment, what really frightened him.

'Never underestimate the cowardice of a subject race,' Thalric said, and Graf studied him cautiously.

'I had not thought . . .' Graf twisted in his chair. It was something Thalric had observed before, when underlings had sudden sight of the spectre of authority at his shoulder. Graf was a man who could, perhaps, have bested him, certainly a man who had no reason to believe he could not. Thalric was his superior, though. Most of all, Thalric was higher within the ranks of the Rekef. And, although it was Thalric's plan as much as Graf's, it was, here and now, the subordinate's role to bear the blame.

'We neither of us predicted it, because we are Wasps. This development is merely a result of the weakness of our enemies,' said Thalric, growing tired, letting the other man off the hook. 'Perhaps we should have foreseen, but the plan seemed sound enough to me when you first outlined it.'

Graf visibly relaxed into his seat as Thalric took the paper from him. It was advance word from a man he kept fee'd in the Amphiophos, where the Assembly met. This man was just a servant, but he saw everything that went on there.

'Well, the endgame can be salvaged, even though we might look like fools for all the rest.' It had seemed reasonable, for Stenwold was already no friend of the Assembly. He had dangerous ideas and he left his post too often to undertake private ventures. He associated with dangerous and unsavoury types, yet now he wanted to speak to the Assembly, and they wanted to make him wait, to consider the error of his ways. Graf and Thalric had wanted to drive a wedge between Stenwold and his peers, so that the wait might become an eternity, so that his voice might never be heard.

'So what happens?' Thalric asked disgustedly. 'He is constantly seen, agitating, rousing up the students of the College, going to dubious places to speak the very words that have so riled their precious Assembly in the past. And would you not think that this disgraceful behaviour would sour matters further, that they would cast him from their ranks and have done with it? If this were a place with any decent rule of law the man would have been crucified as a troublemaker before now.' He crumpled the piece of paper and threw it across the room.

'Yet now they want to speak to him,' he spat. 'All his rabble-rousing has them quaking in their sandals. They're desperate, now, to have him where they can see him, and if that means they must allow him his hearing then so be it. They're too feeble or too frightened to take the beetle by the horns and have the wretch arrested.'

'But at least they won't be well disposed to him, when they meet,' Graf suggested.

Thalric turned a hard gaze on him, 'They won't meet, Lieutenant. We're going to see to that. Our final move is to happen *now*. Get word to Arianna straight away. Tonight would be best, and let's hope that word of the Assembly's decision won't even have reached him. Then gather your men. I assume they've been briefed on who lives and who dies?'

'Death for the Mantis and his daughter,' confirmed Graf, 'but Stenwold lives, if possible.'

'And dies if not,' Thalric completed. 'And when he disappears or dies we'll put the word around that the Assembly had him dealt with after all, and then see how badly his precious students take it.'

Arianna left Stenwold dozing on his back again, lulled asleep by her latest embrace. The house was quiet, and she washed and dressed swiftly, and left even as dawn was creeping up the skirts of the eastern sky.

The stalls of the markets were in place already, the earliest business of the day commencing. Arianna wandered through them casually until she was sure she was not being watched or followed.

Her feet then found the path into the richer district of

the mercantile quarter, close to the white walls of the College itself. The shopfronts here were just being unshuttered, for the rich could afford to rise later and with more leisure. Most of those out on the street already would be servants, waiting for one place or the other to open its doors for business. She passed on.

On the next street she paused at the barber's shop. The Fly-kinden who was giving the floor inside a final opening sweep was Hofi, of course, but he did not look at her, nor she at him. Her attention instead wandered over the placards he kept in his window. Anyone who wished could pay him a few coins to tell the world whatever they wanted announced. There were some goods reported for sale, goods similarly required. Rather more were personal valedictions, anonymous accolades for lovers, sly insults, even challenges. Her eyes skipped over them until she found her latest brief: a poem penned in a blocky hand, idolizing some woman named Marlia, but she recognized the key words in the first line and followed the stanzas down until she knew her new instructions.

So soon! Her heart lurched. She had been keeping the pot boiling so deftly. She could not think what had happened for Thalric to hasten the pace so violently. *And tonight?*

It just could not be done.

But of course it could be done. It would be easy enough. It would, in fact, pose no problems. Her instant reaction, though, was to kick away from it.

She had now been staring too long, and Hofi inside would note it. She turned and walked on, but stopped two shops down, peering through an iron grille at the jewellery behind it, yet seeing none of the gold or glitter. When she had been standing over Stenwold, her claws had been out ready to kill him, or at least she had told herself she was ready. Now her readiness would be put to the test, for now she had direct orders.

Direct orders and no luxury of choice. Of course she must do what she was told. She was Spider-kinden, so betrayal and double-dealing were in her blood. Stenwold Maker would not be the first to find her loyalty buckle beneath him just as he trusted his weight to it, nor the last either, no doubt. It was a game she once had played badly in Everis, but everyone was an expert out that way. In Collegium, amongst the plain and simple Beetle-kinden, she was superb at what she did.

She got back to Stenwold's townhouse in good time. The smell of new bread was in the air, his servant making breakfast. Despite all that was on her mind, she felt hungry at once, passing straight through the hall and into the kitchen.

She stopped abruptly, for Tisamon was seated at the table, and before him lay her scabbarded dagger.

As his eyes met hers, a chill went through her. In Everis nobody had worried much about the Mantis-kinden. They were few, and across the water, and they were savages. Oh, dangerous enough out there in the wilds, but stout walls and civilized company, good wine and good conversation, could keep the threat of them at bay.

And here she was, and here he was, and although they were within Collegium's walls it was as if he had brought the wilds inside with him.

Her eyes flicked down to her weapon, back up to his face. She, who was so skilled a reader of minds and faces, could see nothing past the shield of his dislike.

'Good morning, Master Tisamon,' she tried, her voice shaking a little.

He blinked, said nothing.

What did he know? And did it matter, for surely he would as easily kill her without a reason, or for such a reason as bedding his friend, as for the real one: the real reason that she was in the pay of the Empire, rather than the general cause that she was an ancient enemy of his blood.

The servant put down a plate of warm bread and a pot of the nut and honey mixture that Beetles seemed to favour. The man looked from her to the Mantis, and made a quick exit.

'I hope Tynisa is well,' she began conversationally, spreading some honey over a chunk of bread, while determinedly trying to keep her hands from trembling. Only when she had finished that did she reach out and reclaim the dagger, pushing it into the belt of her robe. 'I had wondered where I left it,' she said. 'D-did you find it somewhere?' Desperate attempts at normality in the face of that blank disdain.

At last he spoke. 'You should be more careful.' Was he warning her away from Stenwold? Was he acknowledging that her association had not harmed his friend? It was impossible to tell.

'Thank you,' she said, and looked away from him as she began to eat, aware all the time that his eyes were fixed on her.

Up above she heard the sound of Stenwold himself stirring. He would be down soon enough, adding one more layer of awkwardness to their little gathering. Then she would tell him how there were more students waiting to hear him speak, that they would be gathering tonight, and that he was eagerly expected.

She would announce it to him flawlessly. She would play her role without any catch in her voice or a single moment of doubt, even under the loathing stare of the Mantis. Whatever she might feel on the inside was quite irrelevant.

When Stenwold appeared, her story came out evenly, convincingly, over breakfast. He nodded at her animatedly, smiling widely at the prospect. *He thinks he's getting somewhere*, she thought. But it was at her that he smiled most. It cut her more deeply than she would have thought, how much encouragement he took from the mere fact of her. *Oh Stenwold, for all your learning, you are a fool.*

'Tonight then,' he said. 'And perhaps the Assembly will finally get the message. The longer they leave it, the more a meeting with them will become irrelevant. I'll have the whole city up in arms soon enough, if they hold off.' He grinned at Tisamon, who gave him a brief nod that contained all anyone could ever want of ready violence.

And you are right, Stenwold, Arianna thought, *which is why we must do this to you. I'm sorry.*

It was almost time to leave, with dusk stealing about the Collegium streets. Stenwold had his academic robes swathed about him, but wore his sword as well. The students liked to see him bearing it. It showed he was serious – not just some typical all-talk-no-action Assembler. He paused to examine himself in his mirror, a full-length Spider glass that had cost a fortune, and had once adorned Tynisa's room.

Every inch the hero? he thought, *Or are there simply too many inches to me?* There was a barely contained excitement in him, for he had been wrestling with the city's inertia for a tenday and now he was winning. The word had come, during the day, that the Assembly would deign to see him after all. That meant his loyal students would truly have something to celebrate.

He then reminded himself of the grim realities. This was no game he was playing, and all those who listened to his words might be signing their own death warrants once the Wasps came. Still, Stenwold felt light-hearted, too much so to brood on things. *A new lease of life, is what I have.*

He came downstairs to find Tisamon waiting at his hall table, less than a metre from the spot where his daughter Tynisa had killed her first man – an assassin sent by the Wasp officer called Thalric.

'Where's Tynisa?' Stenwold asked him.

'She said she would meet us there,' the Mantis confirmed. He was eyeing Stenwold slightly oddly, so the

Beetle paused a moment to make sure his robe was hanging straight, the sword not caught in it. A growing feeling that he ought to explain something overtook him and eventually, after some moments of awkward silence, he did.

'Ah . . . Tisamon . . . last night . . . it's only that . . .' He was caught by that Mantis stare, not knowing what the man had seen, what he knew of the lines he had crossed with Arianna.

'I was wondering whether you would mention it,' said Tisamon. 'I know, Sten.'

'You do? Ah, well . . .' Stenwold could not decide whether to smile or not. 'And do you . . . what do you think . . . ?'

'Whatever I think, it is not as it was with Atryssa and myself,' the Mantis said, conjuring up his long-ago liaison with Tynisa's Spider-kinden mother.

Meaning that this is not true love, just some old man's foolishness. Stenwold's heart sank at the implied judgement. *But of course, he's right.* He opened his mouth for the admission, but a hand rose to stop him.

'Whatever wrong you have done is nothing,' said Tisamon flatly. 'In clasping to Atryssa, in siring a halfbreed between our two peoples, I broke with my kinden and betrayed them.'

'Tisamon, you did nothing wrong—'

'It is between myself and my conscience.' A wan smile. 'It is a Mantis thing, Sten. You wouldn't understand. But we were talking about you.'

'You think I've been a fool?'

'Of course I do, but we're at war.'

Stenwold frowned, sitting down heavily opposite him. 'I don't understand.'

'You could easily die tonight,' Tisamon told him. 'Or in a tenday. In a month, we all could be dead – you, Tynisa, your niece and her lover . . . myself. My end could come, though I am better equipped to avoid it. War, Sten, and

148

war such as the Lowlands has not seen since the Days of Lore.'

'I still don't see . . .'

'So live,' Tisamon shrugged, 'while you can, while your heart still beats. This is no handfast, no building of the future together. So bed the girl and who should care?'

'I . . . didn't expect you to see things like that,' Stenwold admitted.

Tisamon nodded. 'My people, they would not understand. We also live as though we might all die the next day, but in our case it is so they may say, in our memory: he was skilled and honourable. Nobody says that this skilled and honourable dead man might have had a hundred other things he wished to do. I have been too long away from my own, Sten, and seen altogether too much of the world. Why do you think we keep to ourselves so much, we Mantids, save that there is so much outside that would tempt us? I envy you, Stenwold.'

It was an uncharacteristic speech, coming from regions in himself that Tisamon usually kept shut and barred. 'You've been thinking about her,' Stenwold guessed.

'I have, yes. Last night, after I knew what you had done . . . I think I cannot be blamed for seeing Atryssa in my mind. And Tynisa is . . . so much her image. A mercy, I think, as I would not wish her to carry these features of mine. I envied you, last night, for having someone . . . anyone.'

'You could—'

'Never another, Sten. It's the Mantis way. When we clasp hands, it is for life. We do nothing lightly, and least of all taking a mate.'

Stenwold had never quite thought of such things. Even now, it was hard to contemplate. 'But . . . seventeen years . . .'

Tisamon shook his head. 'For life,' he repeated. 'And who could there ever be to stand in her place? But you saved us in the end, Sten. You preserved our daughter. And once I would have killed you for it. I'm sorry for that.'

It was embarrassing to see the man so maudlin. 'She was beautiful,' Stenwold recalled. 'I remember, at the time, how the envy was all mine. Mine and everyone else's. We were all in love with her, a little. Even Marius, whose true love was his city. But it was you she saved her love for.'

For a long while Tisamon stared at the tabletop, while Stenwold looked blankly at his own hands, and they both remembered friends gone and times past, all the moments that time's river carries away, never valued until their absence is discovered.

'We are,' murmured Tisamon at last, 'a pair of old men. Ten years older, surely, than our true ages. Just listen to us, gumming over the past.' He stood up abruptly. 'And tonight you have young minds to corrupt.'

Stenwold levered himself up, making the table groan a little. 'I have indeed. And an Empire to foil. Shall we go?'

'We shall.'

Arianna joined them at the door and Tisamon dropped back tactfully, at least nominally out of earshot. As they traversed Collegium streets towards the quay quarter and the docks, there was little enough said between them. She named those students she hoped would be appearing, and she spoke of slogans scrawled on the College walls that were strongly in his support – all the rigmarole of falsehood that was expected of her, until she became aware that he was saying nothing.

And at last, after many covert glances, Stenwold said to her, 'About last night, Arianna . . .'

She cocked an eyebrow and walked on in silence, waiting.

'I should not have done what . . . I mean, I had no right—'

But she was smiling now. There was an edge to that smile, of course, because, knowing what she did, the incongruity of the situation made it impossible to restrain. A smile, nonetheless, and she said, 'Stenwold, what I did last night was by my will, no more and no less.' At that she saw relief on his face and, yes, pleasure. A candle lit just for him that was about to be so brutally snuffed.

'After all,' she could not help adding, knowing that it would not be taken for the warning that it was, 'I am Spider-kinden.'

And here was the warehouse she was taking him to. A secluded enough place on the edge of the docks quarter. Somewhat run-down and just the place for a clandestine meeting of the disaffected. Or an ambush.

She glanced behind, where the Mantis had now been joined by Tynisa. There was a puzzle there that Arianna had not been able to work out, because the girl was clearly as Spider as herself, and yet she had passed from being Stenwold's ward to Tisamon's. There would be no time now to work it through, and shortly it should not matter, not if the plan went right. Arianna bore Tynisa no malice, though she would shed no tears over the Mantis's corpse. The plan demanded that both of them be laid in the earth and that was what must happen tonight.

She tugged at the door, and Stenwold stepped forward to help her open it. There was a young Ant-kinden waiting inside, who recognized them and nodded. He looked plausible for a student, one of the older ones at least, and there were hundreds of young scholars that Stenwold had never taught or even met. No clue therefore that he was no student at all but a mercenary on Graf's books.

'You'll keep watch out here like last time?' Stenwold murmured to Tisamon, and the Mantis nodded.

So Stenwold went in alone, just like the other times, leaving the Mantis with Tynisa under the evening sky, all of it happening as smooth as a blade drawn from its sheath.

Although he was *not* alone, of course, because Arianna was with him.

In the gloom of the warehouse three lamps were lit, and Stenwold stopped short, for the people ahead were not the youthful faces he had expected. A handful of men and one woman, but all with no need of any College lessons in their chosen trade. Scadran loomed at their centre, a large man even amongst large men. Arianna found the distance between her and Stenwold was growing as though a tide was pulling her from his side.

And it was Thalric himself who flared into view as he lit a fourth lamp. Two men lunged for Stenwold from the shadows even as he heard Tynisa crying out in pain outside. The first grabbed his left arm but he was already hauling himself away and the other man missed his catch. And then Stenwold had his blade out, lashing it across the arm of the Beetle-kinden mercenary who held him, making the man let go and fall back.

'Master Maker!' Thalric snapped out, one hand extended, fingers splayed. The sounds of steel on steel carrying from outside were increasing.

'I can't offer you a drink this time, Master Maker,' Thalric said. 'But I'll have your sword.'

Eleven

There was smoke on the air but, at this distance from the walls, Alder knew that it was not the fires of the city in his nose, but the pyres of the dead. Many of the wounded had not survived the retreat, although the surgeons had this time at least been given a chance to work on them. It had not been the same scrambling rout as last time, having to abandon their fallen so shamefully.

There would be a lot of bloody faces to see, if and when he chose to. The dawn was lighting up an ugly scene in the camp, but that was the countenance of war. Alder had lived with it for decades now and it held few horrors for him any more. He was willing to bet that the scene within Tark was worse. At night, with surprise and three holes punched in the walls, the Ant-kinden losses had for once been greater than those of the attackers.

Which means that Drephos has done well, curse the man. Alder was a good soldier, though. He would happily postpone the pleasure of having the Colonel-Auxillian hoisted up on crossed spears, in return for the taking of this city. He would even add to the man's long list of commendations, all equally grudgingly given.

Colonel Carvoc found him just then, thrusting a hurriedly tallied scroll into his hand. The assault was over and the Ants still held the walls, but taking them had never been the objective. The idea had been to inflict as much damage as possible whilst keeping the bulk of the imperial army intact. Alder surveyed the first lists of Wasp casualties and the estimates of Tarkesh losses, and found himself nodding. *I can live with this. My record can live with this. We have done well, this past night.*

'Have we achieved enough, General?'

'It wasn't cheap, Carvoc,' Alder admitted. He recalled that Captain Anadus had brought back less than a quarter of his men, bitterness etched deeper into his face at the fact of his own survival. The Moles he had sent out were all dead, and Captain Czerig was assumed dead as well, or at least he had not been seen amongst the living.

Colonel Edric was dead, for sure, though Alder found himself only mildly surprised that it had not happened before. When a man chose to live with savages he was likely to die like one, and they had died in their hundreds. The dregs of them that were left were barely worth using.

'Send word to all captains involved in the attack,' he told Carvoc. 'I want the men congratulated for their discipline and order. Night attacks are normally a chaos, but they did well, all of them.'

'Of course, sir.'

Alder's eyes passed on across the list. 'Half a dozen of the heliopters are down,' he murmured, knowing that left eight still able to take to the air.

'But they did their job, General,' came Drephos's voice in his ear, and Alder glanced back to see the hooded man reading over his shoulder. His instinct to strike the man or flinch away was ruthlessly surpressed. Instead he met the shadowed gaze calmly.

'You witnessed it all, I suppose.'

'I saw as much as I needed. What will they be flying, when tomorrow comes? You have destroyed most of the artillery on their eastern walls, and the walls themselves have seen better days. Endgame, General. Their air cavalry, their flying machines – what remains of them?'

Alder nodded soberly. It had indeed been a bloody night. The Mercy's Daughters were filling every bed, giving help to the less wounded and last comfort to the dying, but Drephos was right: the endgame was at hand. He was glad of it. He had seen the Maynesh rebellion a few years back and he hated fighting Ant-kinden. Still, he felt a glowing coal of pride that it was him they had chosen to crush this first Lowlander city. *Even if I have had to rely on this wretched monster to do it.*

'What do you want from me, Drephos?' he growled. 'You'll get yourself a fair report, don't worry. They'll know what you've accomplished.'

A little cackle of a laugh came from within the cowl. 'Oh, General, not so soon. Write nothing yet, I implore you. I've only started. Write your eulogies when the city has surrendered.'

For he has his scheme, Alder knew. *I'd ask if it will work, but when has he been wrong yet? The entire military establishment despises this man, and yet it seems we cannot do without him.*

'I was at Maynes,' Alder said. 'I remember Ant-kinden.'

'Maynes was a lesson to be learned, General,' Drephos told him. 'A lesson I have learned from. Tark shall be yours in a fraction of the time.'

'For a fraction of the loss?'

Drephos paused as though considering. 'Imperial losses? Almost certainly. Tarkesh losses? Alas no, but in war one must always anticipate a little destruction, mustn't one?'

He then went on his limping way, and Alder knew the man was fully aware of the stares of hatred he attracted, the narrowed eyes and curses from the other men. Aware, and enjoying it.

Later, Alder permitted himself a visit to the Daughters. They had lashed three long tents together end to end and the wounded were crammed into them shoulder to shoulder. There were Wasps here, and Ants from Anadus's contingent, a few of the Bee-kinden engineers and a couple of Fly messengers who had been just plain unlucky. He caught the eye of Norsa, the most senior Daughter here, looking tired and drawn. She and her coven had been labouring all night, bandaging the lucky and holding the hands of the rest. It would do no good, he knew, to insist she took the Wasp wounded in first. The Daughters made no distinction between kinden, just as they accepted into their ranks any penitent who showed herself willing to serve. Norsa had all kinds here to help her, from across the Empire and beyond.

They exchanged a look, he and Norsa, that was familiar to both of them, and then he turned to that part of his duty that he felt signified a true officer: to walk amongst the wounded, to acknowledge their whimpers and cries and not to shy away from them. To take ultimate responsibility for the inevitabilities of war.

In dawn's unforgiving light, Totho found himself wandering along the line of the ruined wall, trying to find some way in which to account for what he was seeing. The smoke gusting past him was a fickle mercy: for every scene it concealed there were a dozen more clearly visible wherever the eyes turned – the tangible testament to the events of the night.

The sheer numbers of the dead! The dead were everywhere, all across the city, but mostly here by this stretch of wall and non-wall. To his right were three houses staved in like eggshells by the twisted hulk of a crashed heliopter. The metal of the machine and the stone of the buildings was smoothed off into one tangled whole by the soot, with a single rotor blade jutting proud like a standard above the jagged roof-edges. The ground that he picked his way across was a litter of windfall dead, some savage encounter between the light airborne of the enemy and the defenders' crossbows. Fallen to the earth like so much rotten fruit,

Wasp soldiers and the savage Hornet bolt-fodder lay twisted all over the place, so that he had no clear footing, but stumbled on over broken limbs and the spines of quarrels, spears snapped like matchwood, swordblades sheared from their hilts, and everywhere the vacant, empty faces of once-angry men. Wasp-kinden, certainly, but here in death that stigma was gone from them. They were brothers now with the fallen of the city: all members of that great and inclusive society of the dead.

Totho paused beside the corpse of a great ant, its wings shattered to shards, its legs curled in on themselves. The crossbow had been shorn from the saddle-mountings, the rider also. Not so far from it lay most of the wing of a Tarkesh orthopter, and for a moment Totho stopped, unable to conceive of any string of events that could leave just the wing, with the bulk of the craft falling elsewhere. He crouched by the great twisted vane, examining where its cables and struts had sheared. Just one more casualty, but it came to him that this wing could serve again, could even be reunited with its original body to fly again, unlike the broken wings of the insect. Thus the artificer became a magician beyond the dreams of the Moth-kinden.

But in the end it had been those Moth dreams she had preferred.

And here was where the giants had broken through the wall, the gap they had excavated with their Art and their hands. Their bodies lay, overlapping, where the quick swords of the Ants had found the gaps in their armour. In death, sadness still ruled their faces, not the anger or hatred of the other combatants. The breach they had carved still supported itself, a rough but perfect arch within the wall. Around them the bodies of the defenders and of the Wasp soldiers who had followed after them seemed paltry, like children.

Now the footing became trickier because here was where the gate had been and gone. The charred corpse of the great ramming engine was still here and Totho looked for, but did not find, the body of the man he had dragged clear – the artificer. It had seemed strange to him, then, that artificers should go to war. Now it was all beginning to make sense.

Despite their engine, the Wasps had not made it through the gate, though the gap between the strained hinges was choked with their corpses and their enemies'. Besieger and besieged lay over and beside one another in a frozen jumble of black and silver, black and gold, pale skin and the dark stains of dried blood.

And beyond there, the wall gave out entirely of course. Here was where it had started, and at the broken edge of stone closest to him he could see some of the lower stones squeezed out of shape where the reagent of the Wasps had softened and distorted them. Here was where the defenders' main force had met the Ants of Maynes, and the slain were piled so high that Totho could not see past them to the field beyond. There was no sense to be made of it, this tangle of arms and legs, shields and swords. It was like one of those clever pictures where a series of shapes interlocks so perfectly that there is no gap between them that does not form another shape, another Ant body. He found himself backing away from the sight but, even as he did, he was thinking, *Meat, just meat.* The Ant-kinden had been killing each other like this since history cared to record. If the Wasps wanted to join in that pointless bloody round, why should they be dissuaded? The Tarkesh were fighting for their homes now, but how many years would he have to track back before he found them assaulting another city's gates? Certainly, had Totho been caught outside their walls at any other time, halfbreed and foreigner that he was, he would have been chained as a slave here without hesitation. There could be no special plea for Tark's virtue.

Something was moving amongst the dead: he saw children, searching over the bodies of both their own kin and the enemy. He watched them, saw them gathering crossbow quarrels that had not been broken, saw them pulling swords from cold hands, meticulously undoing the buckles of armour. They called out to each other to announce their finds. It shocked him at first, to hear those thin, high voices in this silent place. They were too young, he realized, to have learned the Ancestor Art of the Ants, so they must have been taught these words by their parents, mouth to ear, before they would be able to speak them back mind to mind.

They were gathering only what was valuable. Not the mere flesh that was spent, not even the purses or effects of the dead. Only the harder metals, that could be used again or smelted and reforged. It seemed to him so fitting, what they did, for they were cogs, and war was the machine. Here on the battlefield was where the machine's wheels ground hardest, where the metal met and the end process was written in bodies and blood. Had he not seen, in Helleron, where the raw materials of war were cast, all the swords and bolts and engines? Here was where the process came full circle, where the discarded pieces of a war were made as new, ready to go back into the mix. Only the meat, transient and replaceable, would not be saved. There was always more of that. Meanwhile, here came Ant-kinden soldiers to carry the stripped corpses to the pyres, and who knew whether the next ones to fall in this very place would be the same men who now hauled the bodies away? Interchangeable, the living and the dead. All meat.

He had not intended, when he left the others, to see this. His world had been complete without this. He had been happy in his ignorance, for ignorant Totho had been. But he was an artificer and this war was an artificer's thing, a mechanical process cranked over and over by the constant refinement of the weaponsmith and the armourer, the automotive engineer and the volatiles chemist. Seen in that light, in that harsh but clear light, the whole business became somehow admirable. If he looked past the meat, contrived not to see it, then it was just another process that sharpened and honed itself each time it was set in motion.

'Hey, Beetle-boy!'

He looked up without curiosity to see Skrill picking her way over to him, with Salma following a little way behind. Her arm was bandaged tightly, bound up in a sling. 'I ain't pulling any bow no time soon,' she informed him. 'Got me good, they did. Thought they'd got you too, when you took off.'

Totho merely shook his head. It seemed so long since he had spoken that the words had dried up inside him, making him envy the Ant-kinden and their voices of the mind.

'Well, if this ain't a right mess,' Skrill decided, dismissing the butchery with that. The air was thickening with flies, an intrusion Totho had not noticed before, from the littlest ones to fist-sized blood-drinkers. *Where do they come from?* Was there some machine churning them out? Surely all these insects had not been just waiting around in Tark for a massacre.

'The Ants think they won, last night,' Salma said, 'though I'm not so sure. The Wasps eventually pulled back, but to their own tune, not ours.' He used to smile a lot, Totho remembered, but his face was tired now, without even the ghost of that grin left.

'They're all over the gaps in the wall, our lot, putting up stuff to fill 'em,' Skrill added. 'Ain't going to make much difference is my thinking.'

'Parops reckons they can hold against one more attack before the Wasps take the wall, anyway,' Salma continued. 'Their soldiers got the measure of the Wasp infantry last night, and the Tarkesh think they're superior. If the Wasps want the wall they'll have to pay for it, or that's what they're saying.'

Totho surprised himself by laughing. Salma stared at him.

'What? Is something funny?'

'You,' said Totho, feeling his voice rasp in his throat. 'You, fighting an Ant war. Where's Parops?'

Wordlessly, Salma pointed to where a squad of Ants was labouring at one edge of the breach, fixing stone and wood into place to make some kind of a barricade.

'Let's talk to Parops,' said Totho, but Salma gripped him by the shoulder.

'Are you hurt, Toth?'

The halfbreed artificer looked him right in the eye, but without quite focusing. 'I've just . . . seen . . . Salma, I made a mistake. You know why I came?'

'I think I do.'

'How could . . . ? Surely this isn't what I meant, by coming here.'

Salma let out a long breath. 'I don't think anybody meant this. I never saw it, but I heard reports during the Twelve-Year War. There were single days of fighting that you could have fitted these corpses into five times. And if Tark falls, then where next? Helleron? Collegium? This is why we have to fight them.'

Totho shook his head, feeling it throb in response. 'If we wanted to stop this, then we should just not fight them at all. We should just give in. But we don't, and so we don't want to stop it. We fight them to create war, and this' – a vague gesture across the strewn ground – 'is just a by-product. War is what it's about, and we all work hard at it.'

'Listen to you, Beetle-boy,' Skrill said nervously. 'You got knocked on the head or something?'

'There may have been a grenade,' Totho said vaguely. 'Close, perhaps. We should speak to Parops.' Without a further look at them he wandered away.

Parops glanced up as they came over. Helping build barricades, he still had his armour on and it was still unfastened at the back. In all the night's chaos there had been nobody yet to secure it for him. Nero was sitting nearby, watching the busy activity but pointedly taking no part in it.

'You're wasting your time, Commander,' Totho announced for all to hear. Parops raised an eyebrow.

'And why's that?' he asked. Salma came up quickly and took Totho's arm.

'He's taken a beating,' he explained. 'You shouldn't mind him.'

'They won't come in by this door. They wanted to draw you out. I've understood it,' Totho explained.

'Since when were you a tactician, lad?' Nero asked him.

'I don't have to be. There was a man . . . a slave of the Wasps. He told me. He warned me, I think. "Airships," he said. I would use airships, if I could.'

Staring at Totho, Parops had gone very still. 'Airships,' he echoed.

Totho shrugged, still finding it difficult to concentrate. None of it seemed that important. 'That was what he said. I think it was what he said.'

'Totho!' Salma took him by the shoulders and pulled at him. 'Come back to us,' he said. 'I don't understand what you're saying, but if it's important . . .'

The world shifted and slid sideways in Totho's head, and he blinked. 'He said airships,' he told Salma softly. 'I pulled him out from under the engine. He was an artificer, Salma, like me.'

'You'd better come with me,' said Parops, and set off for his guard tower at a jog.

He took them up to his arrowslit, noticeably slanted now. Parops's entire tower seemed to be at a slight tilt. His commandership there might be living on borrowed time, Salma reckoned.

Out beyond the wall they could see the broad swathe of the imperial camp, and there was little new there, save that their numbers seemed barely touched by the atrocities of the previous night.

At the camp's far end, though, lay the enemy's makeshift airfield, where a few of the heliopters could be made out. There, beyond those blocky, graceless things, something was now rising up.

Several things, in fact. Half a dozen bloated shapes were slowly, imperceptibly swelling. Already they were bigger than the heliopters ranged before them, and Salma had the impression they still had a way to expand yet.

Parops had passed round his telescope, which Salma had no idea what to do with. It showed him nothing but blurs but Totho took it and peered into it keenly, seeming more focused than he had been since Skrill had first found him.

'They would do the job,' the artificer observed. 'I can see that. Now there are no air defences left.'

'Little enough,' Parops agreed. 'Most of the nest crop is gone, and we only have a couple of orthopters that could even be repaired on time. They threw a lot at us last night.'

'Of course, and for that very reason,' Totho murmured, still scrutinizing the distant gasbags. 'An artificer's war.' He looked back at the others, seeming more himself, more the avid student Salma had known. The animation with which he spoke of his trade was macabre. 'Airships are very vulnerable to any flying attack. That's why they've not been used much in warfare.' Right now he might have been a College master delivering his lecture.

'So what *are* those things out there?' Skrill demanded. Totho gave her a frustrated look.

'They're *airships*, of course, because there will be no airborne opposition to them now. They just have to float them over the city. It makes perfect sense. It's just that the Tarkesh don't think like Wasps. Parops, your people fight ground wars, and so your air power is secondary, kept just for spotting and the occasional surprise attack, but the Wasps think like you should think, Salma. They think in the air and now they've opened the city on the ground, and stripped its wings away, they'll proceed to attack it from above. Those heliopters are too heavy, and they fly too low. You could shoot them down with your wall artillery, maybe even with sufficient crossbows. The airships, though . . . they can go so high, only the best fliers could reach them. So what will you do?'

'But what can *they* do?' Nero asked. 'They can spy us out, but we can shoot their troops if they drop down—'

'They can do whatever they want,' Totho said, leaning back against the wall, his mind still full of airships. 'The whole of Tark will be spread below them. Explosives, incendiaries – it would be like dropping boiling oil onto a map, you see. Drop – drop – drop, and three buildings gone. And all we will be able to do is shake our fists at them.'

Twelve

Che had never before seen an Ant-kinden who was actually fat. If it were not for Plius's distinctive Ant features she would have thought him some kind of halfbreed. That was not the only surprise about him. He was not a Sarnesh Ant, which was even more remarkable given the Ants' propensity to make war on others of their own kind. His skin was icy blue-white while the irises of his eyes were dead black, which had the effect of making them seem huge. She had seldom seen such colouring before, and had no idea what city-state he might have come from.

'Scuto,' he called out from the table he had to himself in the taverna, leaning back in a capacious chair. He wore an open robe over an expensive-looking tunic that strained over his belly, but there was a shortsword slung over the chair-back, to show he had not entirely left his belligerent roots behind.

Scuto glanced about, but none of the other patrons, few enough of them, seemed interested. It was still before midday and most of the inhabitants of Sarn's foreign quarter were out taking care of business.

'It's been a while,' Plius remarked, as the Thorn Bug approached. He kicked another chair out for him, and then glanced quickly from Che's face to Sperra's. 'Pimping now, are you?' he asked. Despite his louche appearance, he spoke in an Ant's voice, with its characteristic clipped precision.

'This lady here is Cheerwell Maker. You remember Sten Maker? Well this is his niece. The other's called Sperra.'

Plius waved the introductions away. 'So I heard you were looking for me, Scuto. It's been a while,' he repeated.

'It has that,' Scuto admitted. 'Didn't know how much of the old cadre would still be here for me.'

Plius shrugged. 'There's Dola over at the Chop Ketcher Importing place but, if you've not heard from her, she's probably keeping her head down. As I said, Scuto, it's been a while since then, and we've all had the chance to make some money here in Sarn.'

Scuto's pause for breath, his moment of hesitation, opened a book for Che on his relations with Plius: revealing that they had never really trusted one another, and that Scuto had no guarantee that the other man would be of any use to them.

'So where are we now?' Scuto asked.

Plius shrugged. 'We're in a city where I have a good business going, Scuto, but if you want something, then ask and, if it's not too much out of my way, maybe it will happen.'

'What *is* your business, if I can ask?' Che put in. This man seemed so corrupt, but she knew the Ants were ruthless with crime, even here in Sarn.

'Ah, well.' Plius coughed and grinned. 'It happens I'm the most successful milliner in Sarn.'

'The most successful *what?*' Che asked.

'I used to be the only one, but now there are two more, which shows you how profitable the trade's become.'

'A milliner? You mean hats?'

Plius's grin widened. 'The way it was, you see, there weren't any here, because Ants would wear helms or go bare-headed, but of course Sarn has a foreign quarter that covers almost a third of the city these days, and Sarn is half again as big as most Ant states. So there was a call for them, and business was good. And you know what? Now the Ants have started buying as well. Now they can see the foreigners having a good time, they themselves start to change how they dress and the like. They still all look like they're ready for a funeral, but at least they're not all dressed exactly the same.' He turned his attention back to Scuto. 'So what is it, then? What brings you back here for me?'

'You know what,' Scuto told him. 'It's happening, Plius. It's time.'

'Yes, well, I've heard the news.' Plius spread his hands. 'The Empire, which was your man Sten's bedbug back in the old days, is away battering Tark even as we speak. Things may have changed in this city, but not that much. Nobody in Sarn's going to lose sleep about the Tarkesh taking a few punches.'

'We ain't here to ask for Tark's sake,' Scuto said flatly. 'It's too late, anyway, by my reckoning. This lot'd never get there in time. Now I ain't a diplomat or a pretty speaker, so I'll put it plain as I can. Sure, you've heard about Tark. Well, soon enough you'll hear about Helleron, too.'

'What about Helleron?'

'Soon enough,' Scuto said again. 'And probably Egel and Merro, once they're done with Tark. Who knows where next? They'll be marching up the coast towards Collegium, and from Helleron it's not such a jump to take Etheryon. Or even Sarn.'

Che expected Plius to laugh this off, but something in Scuto's tone, maybe his very lack of emphasis, had drawn the Ant's face longer and longer. 'You mean it, don't you?' Plius said. 'You're serious?'

'Ain't never been more,' Scuto confirmed, sounding tired. 'Look, Plius, I saw the start of it at Helleron, when they tried to get a thousand men by rail into Collegium to shake the place up. They're not really after Tark. It's the Lowlands they want. The whole of it, from Helleron all the way to Vek and the west coast. They've got more fighting men than five Ant cities put together, and a dozen slave-towns to pull more soldiers from. You know the Commonweal?'

'Yes, I know the Commonweal,' Plius said testily.

'Well then you know they've spent the last dozen years carving out a great lump of that, and now they're ready for us,' said Scuto. Plius's easygoing manner had evaporated entirely now, and he was looking a little stunned.

'So what do you want?' he asked, and Scuto replied, 'We need to speak to the top, Plius. To the Royal Court.'

Plius let out a long breath. 'If you'd asked that straight off I would have said you were mad. Now, though . . . I have some contacts. Not high-up contacts, but they're there. I can try for an audience, but it'll use up just about all my credit with them.'

'What,' Scuto said pointedly, 'were you saving it for?'

On their arrival, Che's first view of Sarn had been of a city split by the line of the rail track. As the automotive pulled in to the depot it had seemed to her that somehow – by Achaeos's magic perhaps – there were two cities, as close as a shadow to each other, but each blind to its neighbour.

To the right was Sarn, the Ant city-state comprised of low, spartan buildings, pale stone and flat roofs without decoration. The people there moved briskly but without haste, and they did not stop to speak to one another or gather to converse. Everyone knew precisely where they were going. Soldiers were on hand to watch the automotive and make sure, she suspected, that only native Sarnesh alighted through the right-hand doors. Everything looked clean and orderly and the streets of the city ran at precise angles to one another, all in the shadow of the city wall.

To the left lay the foreigners' quarter, which presented a totally different world. To start with, its limits had begun outside the walls, with stalls, wagons and tents extending a hundred yards down the road that ran alongside the rail track. Inside the walls, it fairly bustled. Even the depot's goods yard had suffered a hundred encroachments, with market stalls pitched ready to ambush the unwary visitor, peddlers and hawkers and dozens of kinds of traders converging or waiting or looking out for each other. There were a lot of Beetle-kinden amongst them, mostly Collegium-grown and many even College-educated: merchants and artificers and scholars all mingling, clasping hands, making animated conversation with frequent gestures, as though to compensate for the quiet world just across the track. There were others, too, especially Fly-kinden – dozens of them, from ostentatiously well-dressed merchants to grubby peddlers of trinkets, their eyes keen for a loose purse or dropped coin. There were also some from breeds not commonly found within the Lowlands: a Commonweal Dragonfly mercenary in piecemeal armour of glittering hues and a long-faced Grasshopper in College-styled robes discoursing with two Beetle scholars. Spiders, she saw, though not so many as Collegium regularly knew, and small wonder, for she had never seen so many Mantis-kinden in one place in her life. Some were in bands, lounging about and watched carefully by the guard. Many went singly, at the shoulder of some wealthy foreigner or other as a tactful and tacit warning to thieves and rivals. With their strongholds of Nethyon and Etheryon just north of Sarn, a lot of Mantis-kinden young bloods came down here looking for excitement, hiring themselves out as mercenaries or bodyguards.

The Sarnesh were to be found in the foreigners' quarter as well, of course. She had expected their armoured men and women patrolling through the throng and keeping a careful eye on exposed weapons and their owners. She was struck, though, by the many brown-skinned Ant-kinden, robed or dressed in simple tunics, doing patient business with their visitors, or simply walking through the crowd, taking a vicarious interest in all the bustle that was going on within their walls.

Scuto had found them a taverna going under the sign of the Sworded Book, which suggested that its owner, past or present, had been a duellist at the Prowess Forum. Certainly it was decked out in Collegium style, with a great clock perched over the bar in imitation of the Forum itself. Now Che sat at a window and watched the foreign-quarter marketplace, a bizarre halfbreed venue that seemed wrenchingly close to home and yet completely distant. Meanwhile, only three streets away, the Sarnesh proper continued to hold their normal silent communion with one another.

'I've never really visited an Ant city before,' she admitted. 'It's not at all what I expected.'

Sperra, virtually sitting in her shadow, snorted. 'This isn't just any Ant city. Sarn's different. I've been in Tark and Kes before and it wasn't fun.'

'But they have their foreign quarters too,' Che recalled from her studies.

'They do, only there're guards watching every wretched thing you do, waiting for you to take a step out of line, and nobody talks any more than they have to, so's to be like the locals. And if you're Fly-kinden like me, you're on double guard, because if something goes wrong and they don't know who did it, they just hang the first person they don't like, and they always assume it's us. And, ah! The slaves. There are slaves everywhere, and what their masters overlook, the slaves'll spot. And you just know they'll tell their owners, because the Ants don't have any use for slack slaves.'

Che grimaced. However bad Ant-kinden masters might be, a severity surely bred of frugality and efficiency, she had herself become a slave to the Empire, and she was willing to wager that was worse. 'Your kinden don't keep slaves – do you?' she enquired. The Fly-kinden fielded no armies, nor had any great repute as artificers, scholars or social reformers. They tended to slip off the edge of the College curriculum.

'Oh they'd tell you that in Egel or Merro,' Sperra said disdainfully. 'But don't you believe them. It's all about the money – families owing other families. And if your family can't settle what's due, they'll sell you. Indenture, it's called, only basically it's slavery.'

'Was that what happened to you?'

'Would have done,' the Fly replied, 'only I was smart enough to skip out. Everyone thinks it's so homey to be one of my kinden: all family and sticking together and everyone mucking in, all rosy cheeks and cheeky banter. If it's so wonderful, why do you think so many of us are living anywhere but home?'

The two of them silently watched the ebb and flow of Sarnesh business for a little while, until Sperra added, 'But here, I could like it here. No slaves here in Sarn, and outlanders seem to get a fair deal.'

'If you'd come here three generations back, it would have been just like Tark and Kes,' Che observed, and instantly saw that Sperra did not know what she meant. 'It's all down to a man called Jons Pathawl. A reformer.'

'Never heard of him,' Sperra said. 'What did he do?'

'He came to Sarn from the College and started preaching about freedom and equality and all that.'

The Fly stared at her. 'You're telling me that one man just talking did all this? And they didn't lock him up or anything?'

'Actually they did lock him up, and he was going to be hanged as a warning to other outspoken scholars. He had a band of followers, though, and they made a bid to free him. In the process they got in the way of Vekken assassins come to wipe out the whole Royal Court prior to one of their wars. So, as a mark of thanks, the Queen and her court agreed to listen to what Pathawl had to say. *That* was what changed everything. He must have been a very persuasive speaker. Still, look at Sarn now. There's more money here than in any of the other city-states, and instead of a force of slaves who are a liability as soon as things get hot, you've got a resident population of experts and advisers who will fight to defend what they view now as their home. Plus, Sarn gets all the best of the Collegium scholars after Helleron's had its pick.'

Achaeos slipped into the taverna at that point, sitting down at their table with a quick glance towards the door.

'I have made contact,' he began.

'With the – the Arcanum?'

He nodded, his expression suggesting that it was a name best not spoken openly. 'We can speak to them. I have a name now. A place to go.'

'You want me to come?'

'I have thought about it. To them I will be only an intermediary. A Moth bringing the word of Collegium will seem wrong, to them. It is best that *you* speak for Stenwold.'

The 'place to go' turned out to be a tall-roofed house almost beside the wall of the city, just where the foreign quarter met the river. Sarn had no inferior districts as such, and Che understood the appeal to foreigners of doing business where the Ant militia was always tough on robbery and double-dealing. Even so, the place that Achaeos had found stood in the murkiest district that the city had to offer.

There was no sign, no indication of the building's use, but they went along at dusk when the street was nearly deserted, a pair of Ant soldiers on patrol just turning off at the far end.

'Is there going to be trouble here?' Che asked him cautiously.

'It's possible,' he admitted. 'I have not been told so outright, but I believe that the Sarnesh are inclined to turn a blinder eye here than they do elsewhere in the city. I suspect their rulers benefit somehow – perhaps their own spies can deal here for information, or goods not sold openly. This place is a gambling house, also a brothel, where the rougher kind of foreigner comes to deal and talk. I'd guess every so often the Sarnesh raid it, and no doubt the owners arrange in advance who gets caught and who is given warning to flee. A dangerous line to walk.'

She nodded. 'I hate to remind you, but we're not exactly the rougher kind of foreigner.'

He gave her a smile that was almost rakish. 'Try me,' he suggested.

Inside the place was dark. There were two half-shuttered lanterns hanging low on the walls but, if she had not had the Art to see through the gloom, she would have tripped over every projecting foot and every chair. As it was, although Achaeos slipped between the tables deftly, she had to push her way through the narrow gaps. The occasional patron gave her a baleful look, but she realized that it was those who minded their own business and did not look up who were likely to be the more dangerous.

The clientele were a ragged pack. She saw plenty of Fly-kinden, who always seemed to throng these kinds of places. There were a couple of Spiders, too, and several Mantis-kinden who looked perennially ready for a fight. There was even a Mantis warrior in attendance on a sly-eyed Spider lady, a partnership which stretched Che's imagination, and two robed Moth-kinden, who watched them pass with blank white eyes while sharing a sweet-smelling pipe between them.

There was no bar as such; instead a Beetle-kinden sat at a small table by the rear door and sent a young Fly girl back for beer when it was requested. Achaeos went up to him and exchanged a few words before palming a gold Central to him, whereupon the man nodded to one of the occupied tables.

It was a gaming table, five-handed, with cards being snatched, turned and discarded almost faster than Che could follow. There was something nearly Ant-kinden about it, for none of the players spoke, each just following the course of the game by mutual consensus. There was no room to stand back a step, so she ended up right at the shoulder of one of the gamblers. He was holding his cards at such an acute angle that she wondered how even he could read them.

One of the players was a Mantis, who also seemed to be the dealer. Her hard face, with its pointed chin and ears, should have been attractive, except it was frozen with the cold disdain of her race, which made her seem only hostile and bleak. As her hands made automatic motions with the cards she glanced up at Achaeos and nodded briefly.

'Last hand, last hand,' she said, 'then break for drinks and begin again.'

They ante'd up, and Che noticed the stock lying in the middle of the table was partly coins and partly rings, brooches and other small items of jewellery that had probably recently changed ownership. There was a flurry of cards, back and forth with increasing urgency, and the hand fell to a copper-skinned little man seated to the Mantis's left, someone resembling a Fly-kinden but not quite. When he had scooped up his winnings, three of the gamblers rose and took their leave, with curious glances at Che, leaving only the Mantis and the diminutive man with the winning streak.

'Sit,' the woman instructed. 'Master Moth, you've been spotted, and you've been asking some questions. I'll have your name.'

'Achaeos, Seer of Tharn,' he replied easily, taking the seat across from her.

'Who's your doxie,' the small man asked. 'Are you selling or renting her?'

'My *patroness*,' Achaeos said pointedly, 'is Cheerwell Maker of the Great College.'

The little man snorted, but the Mantis nodded thought-fully. 'An interesting pairing, Master Achaeos. My own name is Scelae. This creature is Gaff. You understand that those whom we serve have greater emissaries than we. We are merely convenient to greet new arrivals.'

Achaeos nodded, as Gaff produced a pipe from within his leather jerkin and lit it – Che blinked in surprise – by a flicker of flame issuing from his thumb. Some Ancestor Art of his kinden, she realized, whichever kinden that was.

'She's your patroness, let her talk,' said Scelae, leaning back in her chair.

Che looked to Achaeos for support but he remained without expression, waiting for her to speak. She swallowed uncomfortably. 'You . . . You and your masters have heard of the Wasp-kinden, of course,' she began.

Eyes hooded, Scelae nodded. The little man stopped puffing on his pipe for a moment and then started again.

'Your business is information, I'm sure,' Che continued, hearing her voice tremble with nerves, 'so you've heard the news from Tark.'

'And from further,' Gaff agreed. He glanced from Scelae to Che. 'If Tark's your high card, lady, then I'll raise you.'

'Quiet,' Scelae told him. 'Assume we are aware of the Wasp-kinden, their armies and their Empire, and assume, as you say, that information is our business. What would you say to our masters?'

Che screwed up her courage, trying to present the words as Stenwold would have done. 'That old divisions must be put aside,' she said. 'We need your help, and you need ours.'

'Who is "we"?'

She was about to say her uncle's name, which would surely mean less than nothing, and then Collegium, but what should that matter to the Moths of Dorax living so many miles away?

'The Lowlands,' Che said at last.

Scelae looked at Gaff, and the little man shrugged.

'Nobody tells me anything,' he said, 'but I hear on the wind that the big men in Tharn have done a whole lot of considering of their position recently. But then I hear all sorts, and most of it's rubbish,' he added conversationally to Achaeos.

'Where are you staying?' Scelae asked Che.

'I—' Che stopped, torn. The Mantis smiled sharply.

'You are asking us to trust you. In return, you will have to trust *us*. We reserve the right, Cheerwell Maker, to take what action we will. If that means that we are told to aid you, then you will receive our aid. If instead that means that a Beetle-child who should not even be aware of our name disappears from Sarn then that also shall happen, and in which case do you really think we could not find you?'

'I'm at the sign of the Sworded Book,' Che said. 'But I tell you that not because of threats, but because you're right: somebody has to make the first move, with trust. I trust Achaeos to have brought me to the . . .' Just in time she swallowed the name 'Arcanum', 'to the right people. And I trust the right people to consider seriously that the Lowlands is no longer in the same position as this time last year. And whether you're in a College by the coast or in a city up a mountain, that's just as true.'

The other gamblers were returning now, and Gaff began shuffling the cards.

'We will speak with our masters,' Scelae told her. 'No more than that.'

Thirteen

She was very nearly too quick for it, Tynisa turning as she heard the faint scuffle, but the arrow sliced across her shoulder nonetheless, making her yell with pain and shock. By the same token she was very nearly too slow. So thin was the difference between a clean escape and a fatal strike.

The archer was up on a rooftop and Tynisa was already moving towards the building's shadow to put her out of sight. There were men bursting out on them, though, eight or so of a varied and well-armed crew. The leader, a rangy halfbreed, had an axe already raised behind his head and hurled it even as Tynisa spotted him, the weapon spinning end over end towards Tisamon. The Mantis did not sway aside from it but caught it in his left hand, the force of its impact spinning him on his heel. Then the axe had left his hand, flying at an angle to embed itself in the chest of the archer.

Tynisa's rapier was now in her hand and she fell into line behind it. The ancient weapon, Mantis-crafted from before the revolution, took her straight at a barrel-chested Beetle-kinden in chainmail. He swung his great mace at her, flicking it through the air faster than she expected and then dragging it across her approach on the backswing, forcing her to keep her distance. He had a buckler shield in his off-hand and, when she drove towards him, he tried to take her point with it. She turned her wrist and snaked the rapier past the shield's edge, gashing his arm and then dropping back as the mace swept over once more.

There were two other men shifting to either side of the mace-wielder. One was a Spider-kinden spearman, his face painted with darts of white, and the other was the tall halfbreed axe-thrower who held a second axe now, a two-handed piece. She gave ground before them, watching their approach. She decided they were all skilled, but not used to working with each other. She could exploit that.

Tisamon passed behind them, keeping ever on the move whilst a full half-dozen men tried to pin him down. He closed for a second, his claw cutting and dancing, making them scatter, and one of them went down, blood spurting from over his steel gorget.

Abruptly Tynisa went sideways, slipping under the thrust of the spear to lay open a line of blood across the Spider's ribs. The axeman tried for her but held his stroke as the mace-wielder stepped in its path. Grimacing with pain, the spearman was lunging for her, anticipating she would continue her move further out.

She stayed close to him, still within the reach of his weapon, coming up almost within his extended arms to put an elbow across his nose. He reeled back and, while the mace-wielder tried to avoid hitting him, she drove her sword past the man's shield.

He twisted aside and the point struck his chainmail, but it clove through the metal rings with only a little more force and went deep into him, so that the mace fell from his hand. He tried to clutch the blade but it sheared across his fingers. Then she was darting away, the greataxe sweeping past where she had just been. She rounded on the two of them, seeing the spear coming in towards her. Instead of staying back she moved in and caught the spearhead with the guard of her rapier, driving it towards the ground, using her sword-hand as a pivot for her whole body, dancing over the spearhead and bringing a knee down on the shaft.

It was too good a piece to snap, but it bent and then sprang back, and she leapt past the spearman's startled, painted face and, when she had passed, her sword followed and slashed his throat.

Tisamon was still fighting, one against four now, so she turned to the axeman, who was staring at her and backing away. She fell into her duelling stance, began advancing step by step. To her surprise and gratification he turned and ran away.

She looked round for Tisamon, saw him trading blows still with three men. They were obviously the pick of the lot. There was another Spider whose rapier moved like light and shadow, the second a rogue Ant-kinden complete with shortsword and tall shield, and the final man was some kinden she did not recognize, white-haired and whirling some kind of bladed chain about his head.

As she moved to join Tisamon something cut across her back, just a brief slash of the blade. She whirled, ducking into a crouch, silently cursing herself that she had not heard the newcomer.

He stood there sneering, a rapier in his hand, a tall, angular figure that she recognized.

Piraeus the Mantis-kinden, and he had a lean and hungry smile on him.

'Enough play, Spider-girl,' he said. 'Let's try it for blood now. Then we'll see who's best.'

'Aren't you going to ring a bell?' Stenwold said softly, holding them at his sword's point, trying to keep his eyes on both the men who were trying to reach for him.

'A bell?' Thalric asked, wrong-footed for a moment.

'Oh you know, sudden betrayal, with Tisamon about to kick the doors down to save my sorry hide. It just reminded me of poor Elias in Helleron. Never mind. If you want my sword you'll have to take it, and I'll make that point-first if I can.'

Thalric glanced at Scadran, who began to move forward on Stenwold, his two companions going left and right so that the Beetle was now in a circle of five. He kept turning and turning, sword first this way and then that, waiting for the moment when everything turned to chaos.

'Master Maker,' Thalric said, 'I would rather take you alive, but that's just personal sentiment.' Arianna had joined him there, alongside Lieutenant Graf, and he saw the way Stenwold's eyes followed her for a moment. 'You've been in the trade too long,' he said harshly, 'to lament over *that*. Sentiment is folly, Master Maker.'

'Perhaps I just have higher expectations of people,' Stenwold spat. He lunged at Scadran abruptly, making the big man stumble away, then he dropped back into the centre of the circle.

With a pained look Thalric extended his hand towards Stenwold, fingers open. 'Scadran, take him now. If you can't, I'll shoot the man myself. Go!'

On the word 'Go' one of the grimy, high-up windows to his left exploded in shards of dirty glass and the man directly across from Scadran was punched from his feet, dead even before he hit the ground with a hole torn in his chest. In the echoes ensuing, like small thunder in the space of the warehouse, Scadran fell back quickly. Only one of his band tried to rush Stenwold. The luckless man had got a hand on the Beetle's collar before he realized he was alone in his courage, and Stenwold rammed his sword up to the hilt in his stomach. Even as the dying man dropped away his sword was wrenched from its scabbard as Stenwold took it and ducked low. Thalric's sting scorched across his shoulder, charring his robes black, and then Stenwold was running for whatever shelter he could find. A stack of crates suggested itself, but the top one exploded into splinters even as he neared it. He glanced back wildly, and just then there was another hollow boom from above, and then two more. Another man of Scadran's pack was dashed to the ground, and the one next to him pierced through the leg by a finger-long missile that then buried itself entirely in the floor beyond.

Stenwold kept running. Thalric's shots smashed a jagged hole in the planks of the floor nearest the entrance and he veered away, knowing he was being drawn full circle. He put on more speed, as much as he could manage, and raised his sword high. If this was to be it, if there was no more than this, then he would make an account of himself that even Tisamon would respect.

Another sting blazed past his cheek and he suddenly changed his mind, diving to one side, bouncing awkwardly on the floor where he had intended merely to roll, but ending up crouching behind a solid-looking box. In a second he felt the shudder as Thalric's sting seared into it.

Piraeus dropped into his own favoured stance and saw Tynisa do the same. He had been waiting for this moment. She should realize his kind never forgot. She had blackened his reputation, slurred his previously untarnished name. When she now disappeared, no finger could accuse him, but everyone would *know*.

And blood-fighting, that was his kinden's game. Let the Spiders dance and prance and win their false battles, he decided. He was a champion duellist in the Prowess Forum, but he was also Mantis-kinden. Revenge and murder were imbued in his very sinews.

He lunged forward, a simple move to start with, noting her style, her steps, as she backed away from him. Perhaps he should have killed her when he stood unnoticed behind her, but that would have given him scant satisfaction. He wanted her to *know*. To know who and to know why.

He had never challenged her with a rapier, only the clumsy practice blade of the Prowess, but it was a weapon that both their kinden knew well. She was some Spider dilettante, though, while he had been fighting since his tenderest years. He was a warrior from the Days of Lore, when his kind were acknowledged as the iron fist of the old ways.

He pressed his advantage, driving her back, enjoying the frown of concentration on her face. *Go on, try your tricks on me*, he sent his thought to her. He quickened his pace, his sword constantly testing hers, batting it from side to side, making his opening.

He blinked suddenly, staring at her. She was abruptly much closer than she had been a moment ago and his sword . . . she was inside the reach of his sword, which must mean that he was inside the reach of hers.

He glanced down, but he saw no more of her sword than the hilt. His own, in the meantime, was no longer in his hand.

He frowned at her, at that expression of concentration that had seemed so ludicrous before.

'What?' he said and began to fall backwards.

She had been fighting for blood, he realized at last, and he had still been playing.

Tynisa drew her blade from Piraeus's body, already looking around. Tisamon was still making heavy work of the last two, the Spider and the man with the chain. The Ant-kinden lay nearby, having been gashed across the throat over the rim of his shield.

Tisamon glanced at her, and shouted, 'Go get Stenwold out of there!'

She turned instantly and kicked her way through the doors to the warehouse. There was a scene of utter confusion, several bodies on the floor already. She located Stenwold, though, or at least his back. He was crouching behind a great box, but he had his sword in his hand and looked ready to make an unwise move any moment. There was a scattering of men across the warehouse from him, busy taking what cover they could, but it was not the threat of

Stenwold Maker that had sent them there, for a great roar erupted from a broken window high on one side, and she saw wood splinters spray from the floor three, no, four times, punching a line of shot towards them.

'Come on, Stenwold! We're going!'

Stenwold heard her, then threw himself to one side, his sword clattering away from him, as the box he hid behind cracked in half. The unseen bowman high above loosed another shuddering round of bolts at the Wasps, making them duck away, and Stenwold reversed his course yet again, running for her and the door.

Tisamon was done when they emerged, standing over the two last bodies, and waiting for them.

'They could have more men nearby,' he said, his breath ragged. 'We have to go.'

'Not quite yet,' Stenwold wheezed back, looking as though he could no more run than fly just then. A few moments later, Balkus came running for all he was worth round the corner of the warehouse, his nailbow in his hands.

'Now . . . now we go,' said Stenwold, as the Ant joined them. 'I hope it was worth waiting for,' he added, to Balkus's sudden grin.

Back in Graf's office they remained quiet for some time, watching their leader. Thalric stared into the fire, his hands clasped behind him, and it seemed that he was fighting to repress a great deal of anger that might spill out at any moment.

Lieutenant Graf stood to attention, his eye staring fixedly across the room. It was his hired men that had let them down, and it was obvious he expected the worst of the lash. The other three sat cowed and quiet. Scadran was attempting to staunch and then bandage the gash across his leg that a nailbow shot had made, grimacing as he struggled to tie the knots but not letting anyone else help him. Hofi and Arianna exchanged silent glances. Hofi, for his part, was strictly not a fighter and had not even been there, while Arianna felt she could claim that her task, at least, had been completed to specification.

Or had it? Stenwold's glance at her had suggested genuine betrayal, but they had been ready for the trap nonetheless, with one of their men waiting on high to ambush the ambushers. What had tipped them off?

Or had Stenwold just been more cautious than she expected? After all, he was an old campaigner in the intelligence trade. Perhaps that nailbowman had been hanging out of a window every time that Stenwold went to meet the students. In Stenwold's business it was not whether things would go wrong, but when.

And she knew, as Hofi knew, that this was all immaterial. If Thalric now decided to take it out on them, because of some dislike of them as individuals or lesser kinden, or simply to safeguard his own career, then reason need not enter into it. Graf would be only too glad to offload the blame onto them.

At last Thalric spoke. 'Playing your enemy in his own city is always a risk,' he declared. 'I had hoped that we could at least strip a few of his bodyguards away from him, but the Mantis and his girl seem to have survived this as well. So where are we now?'

He turned to them. Arianna noticed a muscle in Graf's jaw twitch.

'There are plans and plans,' Thalric said. He no longer seemed angry, had clearly conquered that. 'I was sent here with two, but one has come to nothing. Stenwold will be speaking his piece at the Assembly soon enough. Now, we have our own people on hand in the Assembly, who have taken our gold, but the Empire has seen how those old men and women of Collegium cannot leave well alone. Look what they did to Sarn. They think they have all the answers, and yet the philosophy they peddle is an enemy to the Empire in its own right.'

He sat down at last, and only then did Graf allow himself to relax.

'I had hoped to take Stenwold tonight,' Thalric said. 'This next part would be so much the easier if we could pick over his brains. I still hope the Assembly will refuse him. All that is now effectively irrelevant. We have a greater matter at hand.'

Arianna and Hofi glanced at one another again, because this meant something Thalric had not mentioned, and the comment surprised even Graf.

'I sent a messenger to Vek two days ago,' Thalric told them. There was a thoughtful pause at that, and he knew that he stood on a very narrow line, and must cross it soon enough. There was little expression on Graf's scarred face, compared with the wary looks of the other three, but it was Graf who spoke.

'The Ants of Vek, sir?' They all knew how difficult Ant city-states were to infiltrate in the spy trade, for it was nigh impossible to place agents within a city's power structure where everyone knew the inside of his neighbour's head. They had to kick about the edges like any other foreigner.

'Do we have agents in Vek, Major?' Hofi asked.

'Not spies as such,' Thalric said. 'An embassage, however. Official, formal, very respectable. They got there about a tenday before I arrived in Collegium. Nothing underhand, merely trade deals, talks of a possible compromise between their city and the Empire. After all, Vek is a long way from our borders and, like all the Ants, they are vain about their strength. Our envoys have been taking things leisurely but now I've sent them word, they're going to change pace. They're going to arrange for me to see that city's Royal Court, and I'm going to put a proposal to them that they won't turn down.'

'Dealing with the Vekken?' rumbled Scadran. 'They are

not at all trusted, here.' He glanced sidelong to see Hofi nodding agreement.

'Nor should they be. They're an ambitious and grasping lot, always looking for a chance to extend their borders,' Thalric declared. He smiled at that, but kept the next thought unspoken. *Just like the Empire in miniature, I suppose.* Still, with empires size was everything and, in the fullness of time, Vek was small enough to fit easily within the Empire's jaws.

'We're going to offer to split the Lowlands with them,' he explained, and let that drop into the room and silence them.

'Sir . . . ?' Graf began slowly, after a long moment.

'We can't trust them,' Arianna interrupted. 'And they won't trust us either, I'm sure.'

'You're right. It's all nonsense of course, and they'll know it for that, but they won't believe that they can't beat us if they need to. Someone here please tell me Collegium and Vek's recent history.'

'Vek was at Collegium's gates in living memory, sir. Thirty years back, or so,' said Graf.

'Nobody here's forgotten,' Hofi added.

'So what happened?' Thalric prompted.

'They wanted inside the walls quick,' Hofi said. 'But they got held off so long at the gates that a Sarnesh army came to attack them, and they had to retreat.'

'Right,' Thalric agreed, 'because Sarn and Collegium are close allies, these days. So our offer to Vek will be simply this: an army will be on the move towards Sarn, through Helleron, soon enough. With that keeping the Sarnesh on their toes, Vek can take Collegium at last, which they have been wanting to do for a very long time.'

'They'll sack the entire city,' said Arianna. 'Everyone here knows they haven't forgotten their defeat. When they were forced to withdraw from the walls they burned the crops in the fields and razed a dozen of the tributary villages. They're a vindictive lot in that city.'

Thalric nodded. 'Nobody much likes them, that's plain.' Privately he was not overjoyed with the plan, but his own wishes were entirely secondary. 'The Empire's path into the Lowlands is fraught with difficulty as it is,' he reminded them. 'The Ants and the Mantis-kinden will fight, and there will be a great many miles that will have to be bought with blood. However, the real danger is here. If these scholars and pedagogues all end up pointing in the same direction, they could conceivably forge the enemies of the Empire into a single blade. If that happens, not only will the conquest of the Lowlands become much more difficult, but if it fails the Empire will have that blade at its own throat, because they will not stop at simply defending their own lands. So, Collegium must fall and, if Vek is our agent in that, then what outrage the Lowlands can muster will fall on them, and away from us. That is why I sail for Vek tomorrow.'

'What about us, Major?' Scadran asked.

'Right now, go and prepare your fall-back positions. Find places to lie low when the fighting starts. I will have specific tasks to assign all of you, and we will meet again tomorrow before I leave for Vek. After the Vekken arrive here, you will all be on hand to disrupt the city's defence in any way that seems profitable. For tonight, though, you are dismissed.'

The Amphiophos had not seen such a rabble thronging its antechambers in living memory, Tynisa thought. The Assembly's guards were having fits about the situation. With things as they were, though, it could be no other way. There could be a hidden knife here stalking the halls of power as easily as on the streets of the city.

So it was that Stenwold, Master Gownsman of the

College, artificer, Assembler, was waiting for his audience in the company of a Mantis-kinden Weaponsmaster, his halfbreed duellist daughter, and a hulking Ant renegade with a loaded nailbow. Tynisa could only guess how the sight of them evoked horror and dismay amongst Stenwold's opponents within the Assembly. They must think he had come here in a bid to take over the city.

'Now we are here, I am leaving Stenwold in your care,' Tisamon said to her, appearing abruptly at his daughter's shoulder. 'You and the Ant must watch over him as best you can.'

'Where are you going?' Tynisa asked.

'Hunting,' the Mantis said. 'I have played Stenwold's game long enough, all this polite spying of his. Now the Wasps have made their move, and I will play my own game. They are still in this city and I will hunt them down.' Here in the antechamber of the Amphiophos he looked wholly out of place, a savage shadow of the past.

They both turned as Stenwold approached, wearing his best Master's robes. He had obviously caught Tisamon's last words, for his broad face carried an unhappy expression.

'Tisamon . . . ?'

'Yes?' The Mantis gave him a challenging look. 'You disagree, Sten?'

'No, but . . .' Stenwold's face twisted. 'If possible, could you take a prisoner, at least. It would help, it really would help, to discover what they were up to.'

'A prisoner?' Tisamon considered. 'If it is possible, I shall do.' And as Stenwold seemed to relax he added, 'But as for *her*, she dies.'

'Tisamon—'

'No, Sten. She betrayed you.'

'Yes, but—'

'And in betraying you she betrayed us all, including me. And she knew it, Sten. As soon as she saw me, she knew the risk she ran – and she ran it willingly. They had their chance, and they failed, and now there is a price that must be paid. All kinden understand this, Sten. Except for yours.'

Stenwold grimaced, and Tisamon continued, 'If you have one real reason to prove me wrong, let me hear it.'

He waited, giving the Beetle plenty of time to reply, and then shook his head. 'I'm sorry, Sten, but some things just have to be.'

He then looked to Tynisa, who nodded, taking on the duty he had offered her. Then Tisamon turned on his heel and left the antechamber of the Amphiophos.

'I'm sorry too, Uncle Sten,' Tynisa said.

Stenwold tried to smile, felt it slipping on his face. 'I'm a foolish old man, Tynisa. I'm too old for this game, really I am.'

'It's not exactly the time for that thought, Master Maker,' said Balkus. He had his nailbow plainly displayed over one shoulder, so that the three Beetle-kinden guards in there with them were giving him nervous looks.

'You need to think now about what you have to do,' Tynisa agreed. 'And, for what it's worth, I think Tisamon is right. Maybe it's just my blood talking, but if he wasn't setting off now I think I would go do it myself.'

'Who am I to judge?' said Stenwold sadly. 'The world, I think, has more need of those like Tisamon and yourself than it does of me.'

'Master Maker?'

They turned to see a middle-aged Beetle-kinden, robed as Stenwold was, step out into the antechamber.

'The Magnates and Masters of Collegium are assembled and waiting,' the man announced. 'You have your day, Master Maker. You had best make the most of it.'

Stenwold nodded. 'You and Balkus must wait here,' he explained. 'They will not let you in there, armed as you are, and I would rather have you armed out here and watching, than unarmed in there and blind to what goes on outside.'

Tynisa nodded, and Stenwold clasped hands with both of them, and then followed the usher in.

He stopped just within the doorway, so that the usher had to return to lead him over to the podium. Lineo Thadspar was already there, one of the oldest Assemblers and the Assembly's current Speaker. He was a white-haired and dignified old man who had always treated Stenwold with at least a distant courtesy. Now he nodded as the other man approached him.

'Master Maker, in the past, I think, you have believed that we did not take you seriously,' he said, with dry humour. 'Let this accusation, at least, not be levelled at us any longer.'

There was a murmur of amusement across the tiered seats that ringed the chamber of the Amphiophos. Stenwold simply stared, because the stone of those seats was now barely visible. They were all there, so far as he could tell. For the first time since the Vekken siege thirty years before, every single Assembler had answered the call.

He saw plenty of faces he knew, although rather few had any reason to like him. There was such a host of them, four hundred and forty-nine men and women. Of these, more were men than women, and more were his senior than his junior. The entire staff governing the Great College was here, and the prosperous mass of the elected Magnates of the town, the merchants, landowners, factory-owners and the independently wealthy whom the public regarded as the most trustworthy of those who sought office. Thanks to his recent activities, every one of them knew who Stenwold was, and what his grievance. They were not all Beetles, either, for the College staff was varied. There was a scattering of Ant-kinden of differing hues, and amongst them Stenwold caught the eye of Kymon of Kes, the Master of Ceremonies at the Prowess Forum, whom surely he could at least count as an ally. All of the other kinden of the

Lowlands were represented too, even a single Moth named Doctor Nicrephos, who was probably older than Thadspar himself.

But Stenwold's eye was inevitably drawn to a pair present who were not Assemblers at all. One was a Beetle-kinden, but his Collegium-style robes were edged in the Empire's black and gold. The other man was a Wasp-kinden, plain and simple, no doubt a bodyguard or minder.

Thadspar cleared his throat and with a rattling of its mechanism the Assembly's brass automaton ground across the floor towards him, whereupon he plucked two glasses of wine from its tray.

'Master Maker, I don't mind telling you that you have been making altogether a great deal of noise,' the old man said. 'You have been somewhat underhand in procuring this Assembly, and there are those amongst our number who felt that you should indeed be punished rather than rewarded with the, doubtless, great gift of our attention.' He handed a glass to Stenwold. 'However, wiser heads have prevailed, to the extent that we will at least hear the full details of whatever it is that you wish to tell us, before we begin deliberating.'

And the attack on Tark would have nothing to do with this change of heart, of course, Stenwold reflected. He accepted the glass and took Thadspar's place at the podium when it was now offered him.

'The Assembly of Collegium,' Thadspar started, his usual dogmatic lecturing style slowly reasserting itself over his brief humour, 'is known, I hope, for its carefulness in making decisions, by its refusal to be coerced, threatened or tricked into unwise measures. You shall now have your say, Master Maker, and I for one am most interested to hear your words. However, once you have spoken, it is only just that those accused should also speak.' He gestured to the Beetle in Wasp-liveried robes. 'This gentleman, you may recall, is an ambassador from the Wasp Empire who came to our city during the Games. Master Bellowern, I suspect Master Maker's accusations will not be entirely new to you.'

'Some rumours, Master Thadspar, are impossible to avoid, no matter how much one would prefer to,' replied Bellowern, granting a smile for the benefit of the Assembly.

'Master Bellowern will therefore make his defence when you have spoken. You must agree that this is only fair, Master Maker.'

Stenwold nodded tiredly and gazed out across the great mass of faces. Bellowern apart, he knew that there was no great love for him in this audience. He was, in their eyes, merely a troublemaker, and he knew exactly how set in their ways these old men and women could be. Even if he showed them that the Empire was worth making trouble over he would still be little more than an annoyance. And, of course, some of the more venal would have been bribed by the Empire, while others would sympathize with the imperial philosophy of strength and conquest and the Wasps' success in keeping public order. Others still would enjoy lucrative business across the imperial borders with the Consortium, the Empire's merchant cartel. And of course most of them would simply not care.

He gathered his strength together because, of all peoples, his kinden understood how to endure. Physical or mental burdens they could bear, and they had been slaves a thousand years before the revolution had set them free and given them mastery of their own fate. *We are Beetle-kinden, who are tough and hardy, and go anywhere and live amongst all peoples and, wherever we pass, we make and build and better the world.*

If his audience was hostile, greedy and uncaring, then he had his words ready and he would speak his heart and reveal the findings of his twenty years of intelligencing and campaigning. He would give them everything he knew, not twisted as propaganda but honest and true, and he would then hope for their illumination. There seemed precious little to put his faith in amongst those frowning faces, but the *potential* of the Assembly of Collegium was vast.

And so he spoke. He told them everything.

Fourteen

It was a wretched place down by the river that Hofi had chosen to meet at, and Arianna liked it not at all. Swathed in a cloak, her hand beneath it wrapped about her dagger hilt, she was aware that she drew curious looks from those others on the street that evening. It was not simply spies that concerned her, for the thought of robbers and other such lowlifes was much on her mind. Collegium was well policed, but where the river ran, before it met the sea, was a much decayed part of the city. Collegium's goods came in by sea, now, and more by rail, and the warehouses, homes and factories that had been fed by the river trade a generation back had fallen into poverty and disrepair. A quite different neighbourhood had since risen up.

It was a Fly-kinden dive she sought, naturally enough. Arianna looked for the promised name but the legend 'Egel River Rest' appeared nowhere on the peeling facade. Still, she had a good head for directions, so this must be the place.

They were mostly Flies inside, little knots of them playing dice or talking in low voices. They all stopped and stared at her as she came in. She ignored them disdainfully, ducking into the low-ceilinged room and making her stooped way over to an old man who seemed to be the proprietor.

He looked her up and down. 'Reckon I've been told

t'expect you,' he said, tweaking his moustache. 'You'll be wanting the back room. No trouble, mind. That's what I tell them and that's what I tell you.'

She followed the line of his thumb and hunched even lower through a further door. The room beyond was small, but the door on the far side was of a size to let a normal person out in a hurry, or several Fly-kinden at once. Hofi was kneeling on the floor, across from a low table, but Arianna froze when she saw Scadran was there as well.

'Him?' she asked.

Hofi gave her a sly look. 'To tell the truth, he and I weren't so sure about you,' he told her. 'It's an untrustworthy trade and you're not exactly the cleanest of us.'

'Me?'

'Don't play games, Arianna. You're Spider-kinden and treachery's in your bones, useful and double-edged as it is. Scadran and I are mere amateurs by comparison, I'm sure.'

'Hofi, I came here because I thought – and correct me if I'm wrong – that we both struck similar chords at the briefing today. Tell me I'm wrong and I'll go straight back out,' she suggested.

The Fly made a sour smile. 'It is the curse of our profession, isn't it, that we can't quite trust turning our backs on one another. Come in and pull up a floorboard.'

She did so, Scadran watching her without much expression on his heavy face.

'So, we don't trust each other but who else can we turn to?' she remarked. 'And we're not happy, not happy at all.'

'Because the game's changed,' Hofi agreed. 'I suppose we should have seen it coming, but we all of us have been thinking like Lowlanders, when we should have been thinking like Imperial Rekef. Now, are we all speaking the same dialect here?'

Arianna nodded cautiously and Scadran agreed, 'We are.'

'Because it's a very different business, all of a sudden.

I've been here four years, and the pair of you just a couple each. We've been getting into our roles all that time, gathering information to send back. All part of the job. And occasionally some order would come, to find out this or intercept that. We've had our little skirmishes with others, people in our trade but under different flags.'

'Until they stepped it up,' Scadran grumbled. 'Then it became all kinds of work.'

'But all part of the trade, still,' Hofi emphasized. 'Gathering the word, getting the goods, making the odd fellow disappear. And I could still turn a profit shaving a cheek or two, and Arianna went off to her College lessons, and you got to haul crates on the docks. And then Major Thalric' – his voice hushed involuntarily as though the man himself might hear – 'came along, and there was this business with Stenwold Maker. But it was all in a day's work.'

Arianna looked down at the table but nodded, not wanting them to see her discomfort.

'And now we're to help Thalric gut this city like a fish,' Scadran finished. 'Hand it over to the Vekken.'

'Who won't treat it kindly,' Arianna said. 'I think I'm surprised. You've surprised me, both of you.'

'Why?' Hofi raised his eyebrows. 'We're imperial spies now, servants of the Rekef, but for how long? You know that no one who isn't a Wasp has any great prospects in the Rekef ranks. They use people like us because it's necessary, not because they like us. You've seen the way that Thalric looks at us. More, you've seen the way that Graf looks at us, even, who's known me for years. When the Lowlands eventually fall to the armies, what happens to us?' He held up a hand to stop her interrupting. 'You they'll have a use for. With the Lowlands in their grasp it will be the Spiderlands next; heading off south past Everis to the richest lands in the world, or so they say.'

'I will never return to the Spiderlands,' Arianna said flatly. 'I can't.'

'They won't give you a choice,' Hofi said almost cheerfully. 'They won't understand, either, about the Spider Dance, and what happens to those who end up out of step. And Scadran here, what about him?'

'He's part-Wasp, at least,' she said and, before he could correct her, 'And I know that's worse than none at all. Their superiority adulterated. So Scadran's worse than out of a job.'

'Scadran is dead,' Scadran said heavily. 'Scadran knows too much about how the Rekef work. So they'll fix me as soon as the walls come down. Thalric's probably already got orders.'

'And then there's me,' Hofi said. 'It may surprise you to know I was born within the Empire, and my kinden get a decent deal there compared to most. We're good at making ourselves useful. And yet here I am, three years as a citizen of Collegium, and now I've been told to watch the door while the Vekken come holding the knife. Shall I level with the pair of you?' He grimaced at his hands. 'I like this city. I get treated well in this city. I even got to vote for the Assemblers last year, because I'd bought my citizenship. In the Empire I might do better than either of you, but I'd always be considered something less.'

'We can't be claiming that we've come all this way for the Empire and yet not known what it stands for,' Arianna argued.

'Perhaps we never quite did. We've all done well enough from it. And when it was just a matter of protecting imperial interests in the Lowlands, my conscience was clear enough. But now it comes to this . . .'

'I do not want to see this city fall,' Scadran said. 'I have been nowhere else where I have not been treated as an outcast, a half-caste. Here they care less about all that.'

'But you realize what we're saying, both of you,' Arianna told them. 'You're saying we have to . . . deal with Thalric.'

'Kill Thalric,' Hofi corrected. 'Let's not fool ourselves.

We must kill him tomorrow evening, before he leaves for Vek.'

'Graf too,' Scadran said.

Hofi nodded unhappily. 'I've known the man, so I'd – No, you're right. He's a Wasp, and so he gobbles up everything the Empire tells him. We have to kill Graf, too. And the best of Graf's bully-boys are already dead, now. Maker's friends saw to that, so now is our absolute best chance.'

The Assembly had heard Stenwold out. That was the best he could say. Then they had heard Master Bellowern, professional diplomat, spout honey and sugar at them, making them chuckle at his jokes, nod at his sagacity. The Assembly of Collegium, the great hope of the world, had been nothing but fair. It had let both of them speak until their words ran dry.

They were now in closed session, debating what should be done about Stenwold's motion. Also debating what should be done with *him*, if need be. The next he heard of it could be a warrant for his arrest. Still, he would wait for it patiently, sitting here at his table with a bowl of wine untouched before him, his two bodyguards beside him.

'You don't have to stay here,' Stenwold insisted.

'I do. I really do,' Tynisa told him. 'And you know why.'

'I've spoken before the Assembly now.'

'Wasps'll not hesitate to kill you because you're their enemy, Master Maker,' said Balkus, from the other side of Stenwold's parlour. 'Doesn't make any difference where you've been opening your mouth.'

'I shouldn't be like a prisoner in my own home!' Stenwold grumbled. 'Waiting for the Assembly's response is bad enough, but now I'm kept under lock and key, virtually, by my own ward!'

'And what else would you do?' Tynisa asked him. 'Where would you go?'

'I don't know, but I'd like the freedom to do it. Tynisa, I'm not such an old man. I'm capable of looking after myself.'

'Listen to me, Sten.' Tynisa suddenly gripped him by the shoulders. 'Nobody is saying that you can't hold a sword or use it, but nobody lives for ever. I'm worried about Tisamon, right now, and he's as good as they come. But if he dies,' he saw her lips tighten, 'or if I die, or Balkus here, then it will still not matter so much as if you die because, if the Assembly ever does see sense, they will need you.'

'Besides, if they don't,' Balkus added, 'then there could be a squad of their fellows coming after you. You said how they were talking about putting the irons on you.'

Stenwold clenched his fists impotently, and Tynisa slowly released him. 'Is this about . . . her?' she asked gently.

'No,' he said, too quickly, and she gave him a sidelong look before moving away to speak quietly to Balkus.

Thwarted, Stenwold sat and stared at his hands. *These have mended machines*, he thought, *and taken lives*. They were strong hands still, but not young ones. Such a painful admission of something so obvious.

I was young at Myna, that first time. When had the change come? He had retreated to here, to Collegium, to spin his awkward webs of intrigue and to lecture at the College. Then, years on, the call had come for action. He had gone to that chest in which he stored his youth and found that, like some armour long unworn, it had rusted away.

He tried to tell himself that this was not like the grumbling of any other man who finds the prime of his life behind him. *I need my youth and strength now, as never before.* A shame that one could not husband time until one needed it. All his thoughts rang hollow. He was past his best and that was the thorn that would not be plucked from his side. He was no different from any tradesman or scholar who, during a life of indolence, pauses partway up the stairs to think, *This was not so hard, yesterday*.

The aches and the bruises of the last night's action, when he had thrown his baggy body across the warehouse floor to escape Thalric's men, would they not have faded by now, not so long ago? He still hurt and yet they had not actually laid a finger on him.

Not for want of trying! he tried to crow, but he knew it was false bravado. He had simply been staving off the inevitable until Tynisa arrived.

It was all the worse because Tisamon was his age, too, and yet time had done nothing but hone him where Stenwold had rusted. Still, Mantis-kinden lived longer, aged slower and died, almost inevitably, in violence. And besides, was he so sure that Tisamon did not pause on that same stair, once in a while? The other man would never admit it. He would take greater and greater risks to prove himself, until time caught him in the act.

Mantids did live longer, Stenwold reflected. *But I will outlive him, I fear.*

All this inward looking and brooding, it was because of *her*. Tisamon had emphasized the same word to talk of Atryssa, Tynisa's mother, who he thought had betrayed him. Now Stenwold had found a genuine Spider-kinden traitress to apply it to. Like a man who walks blithely from a fight only to find blood on his clothes, he found she had cut him after all.

What an old fool am I.

But she had made him feel young just for a little while, and however false the intention behind it, it had been a great gift to him at the time.

And now Tisamon was going to kill her, as he had every right to do.

★

'You did well there at the warehouse,' Tynisa remarked.

Balkus gave her an odd look. 'I've been in this business since you were a kid, I'd reckon,' he pointed out.

'But I've not known you for long, and I don't know anything about you,' she replied. 'And since Helleron, and that spy, I've been slow to trust people.'

'Fair,' he said. He really was a big man, she realized, almost as tall as Tisamon and much broader across the shoulders, much larger than Ants normally grew.

'So tell me about yourself,' she said.

'Are you doing that Spider-kinden flirting thing?' he asked, apparently seriously.

'No, I am not. I just want to know why I can trust you. Besides, I'm only a halfbreed. Hadn't you heard?'

'I heard you were the Mantis fellow's get, yes, though I don't quite see how that worked out. Besides, Mantids do flirting: this one I knew, when she was looking for a man, she'd kill an enemy of his, just to get his attention. She was mad.' He used the last word as a sign of approbation.

'Well take it from me, I'm not flirting with you,' she said. He was grinning a little and she wondered whether he was actually trying to flirt with her. 'Tell me why you're here, Balkus. I need to know how far I can lean on you.'

'Scuto and me, we go back years.' He smiled suddenly, an oddly innocent expression. 'I took my trade in just about every way a man with a sword and a nailbow could make a living, but it was always good to know that old Scuto was up north with a place to hide out, and some work like as not if times were hard.'

'But you're Sarnesh? That's a long way from home.'

'The further the better,' he said, heartfelt.

'But why did you leave? What did you do?' she pressed.

His smile stayed on, unoffended. 'Just in case I'm a mass-murderer or slept with the Queen's daughter or something, right? The thing is, nobody understands my kinden. You think we're all in and out of each other's minds like everybody's friends every hour of the day. It isn't like that. It's more like you're a kid in a big gang, and if you don't do what they say, then you're no good and they all turn their backs on you. And don't think that they can't put silence into your head as good as putting words.' The smile was fading now. 'Only there are loads of us who just want to do something else, but loyalty is everything, to the city-state. You don't have to *do* anything to get where I'm standing. You just have to *not* do what they say. Once you turn your back on them, you're out, and there's a world of trouble waiting if you ever go back. Even in Sarn, which is better than the rest by a long mile, they don't take kindly to deserters.'

She nodded soberly. 'I see.'

'Oh, and running off with one of their nailbows isn't going to make them any happier,' he added, the smile returning. 'You know what the really mad thing is, though?'

'So tell me.'

'Even when you've escaped, you find you've brought so much of that cursed business with you. You're never free of it. That's why Ant mercenaries are always the best. They're loyal. Nobody ever got double-crossed by an Ant. Or precious few, and not without good reason. So when I got to know Scuto, I got loyal to him. And, now that I'm with your pack, I'm loyal to you. It's just the way we are. So you don't need to worry about trouble from my direction.' He slipped the heavy nailbow off his shoulder and laid it on the table-edge, opening its casing and taking a swab of cloth from a belt-pouch. 'You mind keeping your eyes about you while I clean her?' he asked, and she nodded agreement, thinking about all he had said.

To Arianna they seemed so obviously on edge that she was amazed Thalric did not shoot them all on sight. Her blood and her profession had given her a very good eye to read people and she perceived the taut bonds of conspiracy between herself, Hofi and Scadran as though they were bright ribbons binding them together.

Graf sat at his desk, no doubt dealing with the contracts of the men killed at the warehouse and the few who survived. He looked in an ill temper, barely glancing at them as they filed in. Thalric himself was obviously ready to depart for Vek. He had donned a long coat and there was a pack slung ready on the back of his chair. He did seem to frown a little as the three of them took their places about the room. Hofi moved close to Graf, flicking his wings to perch on the corner of the desk. Arianna herself was leaning by the window, and she knew she was looking casual, nothing in her stance to betray her. Scadran just stood in the middle of the room, and to her he radiated tension.

She supposed they had a lot to be tense about, considering all the changes recently. A lot had happened and a lot had gone wrong. The future held clouds yet to come.

Thalric nodded at them, eventually. He seemed tired, which would work well for them. No doubt he had been busy from the early hours, putting his plans in place.

'I have your final assignments before the Vekken get here,' he told them. 'After that I will try to get word to you, but you'll understand I can't guarantee it. After the siege starts I'll leave it to Graf here, and to your own judgements, how the city's defence can best be sabotaged. A quick victory for Vek will serve us best, although one that kills a great many Vekken troops at the same time would be the perfect result.'

'Excuse me, Major, but what should we do when the walls actually fall?' Hofi asked. 'You won't be able to provide the entire army of Vek with our descriptions.'

His tone was too confrontational, and Arianna guessed he was steeling himself to the task. Thalric's frown returned.

'If you can't extract yourselves from the situation then you're in the wrong trade,' he said shortly. 'If all else fails, defect at the last moment and drop my name to whoever chances to question you. I've not abandoned my people before and I will not do so this time, worry not.'

'What do you have for us, sir?' Arianna asked.

'Well for you, I want you to work your charms on someone in the Collegium militia. One of their senior officers, in fact. They're all old men who like wearing medals and uniforms. Most of them haven't held a sword in ten years. I want information about the military, and you'll be in a position to throw a wrench into their gears when the fighting starts.' He turned from her. 'Hofi, I want you to start spreading rumours amongst your clientele and your peers. Rumours about the military weakness of the city. Rumours that Sarn has become sick of this place. Rumours that Sarn may even be looking to make Collegium merely the junior partner in their alliance. A Sarnesh attack – yes, that might sell well.'

'I see, sir,' Hofi said. 'Lower their morale, you mean. Take away their hope.'

'Indeed. As for you, Scadran, you must look to the port defences. The attack will surely include a naval action, or the Vekken are greater fools than I take them for. Look to see what can be sabotaged at the relevant moment.'

Scadran nodded sullenly.

'Well, I take it we all now understand our tasks, and I wish you good luck with them. Now, I have an appointment with our people in Vek.'

He rose, and just then Hofi slammed his open palm on the desk, their signal.

Arianna had her dagger already clear of its sheath as Hofi drove his own into Lieutenant Graf. The Fly-kinden had been trying to sink the blade over the man's collarbone, but Graf jerked back even as he struck, and Hofi ended up driving it up to the hilt into his shoulder, the Fly's wings powering the blow. Graf roared with pain and reached for his sword.

Scadran was already rushing for Thalric. He had a heavy-bladed sword out, but swung it so wildly that Arianna could not get close to help him. Thalric swayed back, his face set and hard, and as the blade came down again he tried to catch Scadran's wrist. The force of the blow knocked Thalric back into a corner of the room, Scadran's weight and strength pushing him almost to his knees. The big man's off-hand fumbled at Thalric's collar, trying for a hold around his throat.

There was the familiar crackling sound of a Wasp sting from behind her, and Arianna turned to look. Hofi was hanging in the air amidst the glitter of his own wings, and Graf had blown a charred circle into the far wall. Then the Fly slashed savagely with his blade and Graf was reeling back, clutching at his face and screaming. There was blood spitting from between his fingers and Arianna realized that Hofi had gashed the man's one good eye.

She turned back to Thalric. The Wasp was stronger than he looked, every muscle straining to keep Scadran off him, but his halfbreed assailant had the advantage. Thalric's teeth were bared and his eyes bulged, not from Scadran's throttling grip but from his own sheer fury. They swayed back and forth, but with Scadran always forcing him into the wall again at last. Arianna saw her moment. She darted in and rammed her dagger into Thalric's side.

Or that had been the idea. Instead, although the stroke was true, she struck something hard beneath his coat and the blade of her knife snapped at the hilt.

Thalric made a hissing sound that might have been triumph, and kicked Scadran solidly across his bandaged calf. The big man roared in pain, his grip loosening for just a second, and Thalric put a hand under Scadran's chin and unleashed his sting.

Scadran's head simply exploded. There was nothing more to it than that. The body that fell colossally back to the floor was virtually decapitated. Arianna felt her insides lurch in fear and horror but she had her Art-made weapons out now, the narrow claws jutting from her knuckles, and she struck Thalric across the face, gashing his cheek. She had hoped to snap his head round but he took the blow without flinching, and then backhanded her solidly, spinning her to the floor.

He walked past her, and she tried to stand, her head spinning. He had not killed her, which could only mean he wanted to question her or to prolong her death. The Rekef showed no forgiveness for treachery.

She saw Hofi, red with Graf's blood, rise from behind the desk and see Thalric. The Fly-kinden did not hesitate. She had never guessed that the unassuming barber was such a fierce fighter but he hurled himself on Thalric instantly, his wings flinging him across the room. Arianna was on her feet now, swaying, seeing Thalric's sword clear its scabbard and cut across Hofi even as the Fly charged him. The impact spun the blade from Thalric's hand, but trailing crimson as it flew, and Hofi had fallen from the air, striking the ground hard with his hands pressed to the red stain growing over his tunic.

She looked at the sword. It lay beyond Thalric, but a concerted rush might capture it.

Thalric stared down at the writhing Fly for a moment and then raised his arm and finished him with a single sizzling bolt of energy.

Arianna ran. She flung the door open and was out of the room, then out of the building, unarmed and spattered with Scadran's blood.

Thalric sighed heavily. He should have seen this coming, but a lot of things had been demanding his attention recently. He had not thought to look more carefully into the faces of his own people.

That will teach me to trust any inferior race, but in the Rekef Outlander there was frequently little choice. He went to check Graf, in faint hope, but just the sight of the man's butchered body was enough. No help there. Graf had been a good agent, a loyal subject of the Empire. He deserved a better end than this.

Thalric reclaimed his sword, and one hand found the puncture that Arianna had made in the leather of his coat. Beneath it gleamed the links of his copperweave shirt. Though not what it once was, having been pieced back together with steel after Tynisa had sheared it open down the front, it had saved his life again.

Then he stepped out of the room, following Arianna's path, for he had unfinished business.

Fifteen

'Explain to me why these machines are such a threat,' demanded one of the Tarkesh tacticians, sounding irritable. He might even have been the king, for Totho found it difficult to distinguish Tark's ruler, to whom he had been briefly introduced, from the other men on his staff. There were about a dozen of them, men and women, and they all had the same Tarkesh features that made them look like siblings. The king wore no special garments or insignia, just the same plate and chain armour as the others, even here in his war-room, and like them looked as though he was short on sleep. Totho supposed that, mentally, he kept saying, 'I'm the king, I'm the king,' but for outsiders it was impossible to tell.

'It's all to do with flight: Art flight and mechanical flight,' he said, looking from face to face just to be sure. 'I'm afraid I don't fly any more than you, so can I ask my friend here to explain about Art flight?'

One of them nodded, one of the women, and Salma stepped forwards. Totho glanced around to see Parops standing to attention behind them, having persuaded the court to see them at all.

'Your Majesty,' Salma said tactfully, bowing to the correct Ant, 'may I present myself as Prince Minor Salme Dien of the Dragonfly Commonweal, arrived here in common cause with your city-state at the behest of Master Stenwold Maker of the Great College.'

It sounded impressive, but he prompted no awed reaction from the assembled tacticians. Instead they just eyed him suspiciously.

'The Wasps are not strong fliers,' Salma continued. 'With only the wings their Art can summon up, they cannot fly for long distances. They can just about get from their camp across your walls, but they could not simply circle over your city for hours, or even many minutes. Moreover, they could not gain enough height to get out of range of your crossbows without wholly exhausting themselves. You've seen that for yourselves, I'm sure.'

There were nods and a few hard smiles around the war table, and Salma thought, *They actually think they're winning!*

'I'm sure the Wasps have some who are better than that, probably scout squads of their best fliers, but not enough to make a difference. They also have their insect cavalry, and their machines . . . I forget what Totho called them.'

'Heliopters,' Totho supplied. 'The problem is that they don't fly very high either, and they're very exposed to your artillery, because they're big and slow and not as heavily armoured as you might think, because then they couldn't get off the ground at all.'

'We have seen such,' one of the tacticians confirmed.

'But their airships can fly much higher,' Totho explained. 'So high, in fact, that the only thing able to threaten them would be something else capable of flying that high. I don't even know if your orthopters could do it but the Wasps obviously thought they could, which is why they mounted the night attack that saw most of them destroyed. At a great cost to the Wasps themselves, true, but now they can safely attack your city from the air. They can drop explosives on you, or even just rocks or leadshot. They can deploy their soldiers, as well, over any part of the city that they choose. Even though they can't fly up high of their own accord they can glide down without much effort. I am afraid that the Wasps have brought a new kind of war to you.'

Though the tacticians did not exchange glances or confer, Totho sensed the flurry of thoughts passing between them. At last one of them spoke.

'We must destroy them, then, on the ground.'

'That would seem to be your best chance,' Totho agreed.

'An attempt at sallying out with any affordable force would meet with defeat almost immediately,' another tactician warned. 'A sally with sufficient force would merely leave the city wide open, and the potential casualties amongst our troops would be unacceptable.'

'A covert attack would be the only solution,' a third concluded, fixing Totho and Salma with a fierce stare. This, Totho realized, must be the King of Tark.

'We will trust your analysis of the situation,' the man continued. 'You have information and perspective that we lack in this. We distrust new wars, and we see this distrust has brought us to this point. We must mount a swift strike tonight to destroy the airships. Then we must destroy the Wasps in the field before they can construct or import more of them.'

'Your Majesty,' said Salma, 'I would go with your men, if I may?' The tacticians studied him, narrow-eyed, and he shrugged. 'For one, I can fly. I can see better in the darkness than your people. And I am a sworn enemy of the Wasps.'

'We have favourable reports of your fighting in the recent attack.' The King nodded. 'You indeed have talents we lack. Very well. And your comrade?'

'No—' Salma started, but, 'Yes,' said Totho.

Salma goggled at him, wrong-footed for once, and Totho felt obscurely proud of that. 'I may not be the fighter that Salma here is,' he said, 'but I am an artificer of the College, and destroying the airships is an artificer's work.'

'You must stay always with our people,' the King warned him. 'They will know each other's minds, but not yours. You must not stray from them.'

'I will do what is asked of me,' Totho confirmed, and realized Salma was still staring at him, shaking his head slightly. 'I have one other request for Your Majesty, though.'

'What request is this?' The King and his staff were all suspicion again.

'There was a halfbreed scout captured with us, when your soldiers took us in,' Totho explained. 'Her name is Skrill. Please let her out of the city when we start on our sally, so that she can head for Collegium and inform Master Maker what's happening here. He is trying to organize an army against the Wasps, I think, and he may be able to help, so he needs to know exactly what's going on here.'

There was a long silence between the tacticians then, as they passed their narrow thoughts back and forth, trying for a consensus. Eventually, the King nodded slowly.

'It shall be so,' he said.

'Would you mind explaining to me just exactly what you're doing?' Salma demanded, once they were back in their rooms in Parops's slightly skewed tower.

'I don't mind at all,' said Totho. 'If you don't mind answering the same question first.'

'I am going out to fight,' Salma said, 'because I have been trained to fight, and because the Wasps are the enemies of my people, and most of all because I know how to look after myself—'

'That's not it at all,' said Totho. He now felt drained and miserable. The prospect of tonight's activities oppressed him, and he sensed that he had been robbed of choice from the moment he had set foot in Tark. *My last real choice was to leave Che to the Moth.* And what a good choice that had been.

'*What's* not it?' and even to Totho, who had no great ear for such things, Salma sounded evasive.

'You don't care about Tark. No, that's unfair – but you sold yourself long to the Ants. You can fight, but you're no good at destroying airships.'

'The Moths of Tharn can destroy mine-workings. I witnessed that in Helleron.'

'Because they've practised, they've learned particular things by rote. That's not the same,' Totho said. 'But here you are charging out to fight thirty thousand Wasp-kinden, and you don't care about Tark enough to do that. You're looking for her, the dancing girl.'

Salma was quiet for a long time before finally getting his words in order. 'You know, Toth, I really do underestimate you sometimes.'

'All the time,' said the artificer. 'Everyone does. You've not spoken of her, barely mentioned her, since the Ants caught us. I knew, though – I knew you hadn't forgotten. I never saw her but I hope she's worth it.'

'I dream about her,' Salma said, surprising him. 'I can't put her out of my mind. Whenever I'm active, doing something, I'm all right, but then in the pauses she comes back to me. I didn't even know her for long, and yet . . . here I am.' He gave Totho a solemn look. 'I suppose that we're not so very different in that, since you're in love with Che.'

Totho nodded glumly. 'Since almost the moment I met her. Only, Stenwold doesn't much like the idea . . . I even got the courage to ask his blessing, back in Myna, and he didn't say anything much, but his face . . . you could tell. And then that cursed Moth, he just turns up from nowhere as though he's her best friend in the world. And as soon as we got the two of you from the prison he was all over her. You must have seen it.'

'I did,' Salma admitted. 'I had other things on my mind, but I saw it.'

'And she . . . she liked him, I could tell. But it's like Tynisa and the boys from the College. They go to her because she's . . . graceful and . . . elegant . . . and sometimes she leads them on. But I can't believe that *creature* feels anything for Che . . . and I tried to tell her how I felt, but she didn't understand, and it all became . . . I just couldn't stand . . .' He found that he was sniffling now and wiped his eyes and his nose furiously. 'And so I just left, put a note by her pillow and left. I . . . I feel gutted, literally gutted, Salma. Like my insides have been ripped out of me. I'm just hollow. And now all this . . . all the killing, the destruction. You know how I've always wanted to design weapons?'

'I didn't, but go on.'

'I *should* feel that it's wrong – after I've seen what those weapons can do. And yet . . . and yet people would still kill each other with sticks and stones if they didn't have anything else. With their bare hands even. And it would be pointless, so pointless. I . . . I almost think that only the weapons make it all worth anything. At least something is learning from the whole bloody business. The people remain the same, killing and dying and dying and killing, but at least the weapons get better.'

Salma gave him a doubtful look. 'I don't think Che would like to hear that.'

'No, I'm sure she wouldn't.' Totho rubbed at his face, as if trying to erase some unseen stain.

Salma decided to come to the point. 'Listen, Toth, when Skrill makes her move, you should go with her. Get out of here and get back to Stenwold. The Ants have artificers enough. Go back to Stenwold. And to Che, even.'

But Totho was shaking his head. 'You haven't thought it through, Salma. Sorry, but you haven't. What am I supposed to say to her? Yes, I left you on an ill-planned mission that seemed certain to see you dead. Yes, I just ran, at that point, and made sure that my skin stayed whole. That, you see, would look particularly impressive. Che likes you. You and she went through a lot together. When you decided to come here on this fool's mission she was furious, and it was because she was frightened for you. She doesn't like me half as much, I think, nor would she have shed as many tears for me. So if I go back with that story, that I left you to your fate, how could I look her in the face? I know it's not practical, and I'm supposed to be a practical man, but that's how it is.'

'Then don't leave, just stay here. Stay in the city and wait,' Salma said. 'You don't need to go tonight.'

'It makes no difference, because I'd still be in the same position. Anyway I don't think you'll be coming back here afterwards.'

'You can't think I'd just grab Grief and abandon you here.'

'No,' Totho said, 'that isn't what I think at all.'

'Then . . .' Salma thought about it. 'Oh, I see.'

'This is a fool's mission, and these Ants are fools. They didn't understand a word of what you said, or what I said. They have no concept of an enemy that is so much stronger than they are. Their mission tonight will not succeed.'

'I thought in Collegium they didn't believe in destiny.'

'We believe in the odds, Salma,' Totho said, 'and I do not believe that we will win, tonight. I really do not believe that we will survive.' He sounded distant, almost trance-like.

'Well if you believe that,' Salma told him, 'then the question is back on the table. Why are you coming with me? Or is *that* why? Is that it?'

'I do not have that courage, or that cowardice, whatever it is,' Totho said, 'to turn the blade upon myself. But I have . . . nothing left, Salma. I have nothing left. And so I'll let the Wasps do it instead, if it's all right with you. And if I can help you out, or even help the bloody ignorant Tarkesh, then that's good too. But I am turning into something strange that I do not like. And so I think it best that I go with you tonight, and best of all if I do not return.'

Salma had no reply for that, trying to see through the clouds hanging about this man to the student he had once known. Totho had always been gloomy, it was true. He had always been shielding his halfbreed nature against the world – and then there had been his infatuation with Che, which had not helped. Tark had been the forge, though, that had taken the decent ingredients of the man and botched them into something flawed and strangely made.

We can win, tonight, Salma told himself. His own race were slow to admit to the impossible, and the histories of the Commonweal were rife with accounts of one man standing off a hundred, of bridges held by a mere handful, of one assassination bringing down an army or a principality.

We can win, he thought again, trying to convince himself, but in that moment he felt very far from home and the things he knew, surrounded by hard stone and jagged metal, and afraid.

'So how do we get outside the walls without the Wasps spotting us?' Salma asked.

Their leader was Basila, who had interrogated him when he first came to Tark, and then bedded him shortly afterwards. Now she was attired in dark cloth over metal-reinforced leathers, hooded and with a scarf ready to cover her lower face. Both her blade and her exposed skin were blacked.

'Do you think the Wasp-kinden are the only people who have ideas?' she asked contemptuously. 'We are ready for this possibility.'

Salma had accepted an arming jacket from them, and a better-balanced sword, but they had no bows in the whole of the city. For Totho they had found artificers' leathers and another repeating crossbow, not as fine as Scuto's had been, but a serviceable machine nonetheless.

'Follow, and you will see.' Basila led the way, and the two of them fell in with her dozen Ant soldiers all clad as she was. Skrill hopped along at the back, her arm still bound up, looking nervous.

'Listen, Your Highness,' she said. 'I ain't sure about this.'

'Just get to Stenwold,' Totho insisted. 'Tell him what's going on.'

'And what if the Wasps see me?'

'Then run,' Salma said. 'I've seen how you run. You've a turn of speed a horse would envy. Wasps tire fast once in the air, most of them. So run and keep running, and hope.'

'Hope,' she echoed, without much of it in her voice.

They entered one of the city barracks, and almost immediately were heading underground, down into rounded tunnels that the insect colony must have dug under Tarkesh orders.

Nero and Parops had been there to see them off, like a mismatched pair of mourners. Parops had just clasped Salma's hand and wished him luck. There had been little enough hope in his eyes either.

Underground, Salma had no way of keeping track of where they were heading. The Ants seemed to be finding their way simply by touch, for it was so dark that even his keen eyes could make nothing of it. Often they heard the scratchings and skitterings of insects as they scurried out of their way ahead.

'Here,' Basila's voice came to him, and Salma knew they

had stopped when he ran into the back of the man preceding him.

A lantern glowed into life, the dimmest of faint glows. There were two Ant-kinden waiting for them there who had probably even been guiding Basila in with their minds' voices. They carried shovels, and Salma now saw that the tunnel ceiling had a shaft dug into it, with metal bars serving for handholds.

'We have these radiating in every direction from the city,' Basila told him. 'The Wasps have no watch near this one, yet it is close enough to their camp to strike there before we are seen. The Wasps have little light beyond their camp, and we know they do not see well in the dark, no more than we do. These men and I, we have stayed in darkness below the ground since the plan was conceived, making our eyes fitter for this moment.'

One of the Ant engineers was now crawling up the shaft, legs straddling the gap at a painful-looking angle. He began to dig up at the earth above, showering dirt down on them.

'The earth left is shored up, enough to bear the weight of a man,' Basila told them, 'but we will be digging through in minutes. Then we begin.'

She and her team bore their swords, together with little crossbows that were double-strung to give them the power of a normal bow whilst being small enough to shoot one-handed. They had little wheel-locks set above the handle to tension the sprung steel arms.

The Ants waited in silence as the engineer above them dug towards the surface. Totho and Salma exchanged glances, but at this stage neither had anything to say.

Then the lamp was extinguished, and Salma realized the man digging above them must be nearly through. He put a hand to his sword, made sure it was loose enough in its scabbard.

There was a final rattle of earth and the engineer came back down, and went past them with his colleague and, without a word, off into the dark tunnels. Basila was ascending already, hand over hand in a perfect rhythm that all her team picked up, each man climbing with his hands almost under the boots of the man before, and yet not one slip, not one hand trodden on, until they were all above and it was time for Salma and Totho to follow them with far less assurance.

Basila looked between them. 'From now on,' she instructed in a low voice, 'there is no more speaking. I will hear nothing from you, nor you from me. Watch what we do and follow it. No more than that.'

They nodded. Salma drew his sword, painted with weaponblack, and Totho put a magazine into the top of his repeating crossbow. Skrill clasped both of them on the shoulder, a weak gesture intended for what comfort it could give, and then she was off into the night, swathed in her cloak, following the long road to Collegium.

The Wasp camp was lit by picket lamps, a ring of them, twenty yards out from its furthest-flung tent and spaced widely. There were some sentries standing a little in front of them, mere silhouettes to the approaching raiders, and yet others who patrolled along the whole perimeter. Beyond the lamps, after an interval stretch of clear ground, the tents of the camp itself started. Now it was dark there was little activity within.

Grief in Chains is somewhere in one of those tents. Or 'Aagen's Joy', as she had last called herself. Something twisted sourly inside him at that thought.

He saw that several of the Ants had gone, and he moved to ask Basila, but remembered at the last moment that he should not speak.

It was going to be a long night.

There was a sentry out there. Salma wondered at first why they had not attempted to sneak through between the widely spaced guards, but guessed that then the chances of detection would be doubled. The Wasps would know precisely their own perimeter and would leave no gaps.

Another sentry was moving past him now, and Salma watched his progress. The man should probably have been beyond the lights and looking out, but he was walking within them, and so unable to see a thing of the night, but obviously too sullen about his tedious duty to care.

And then he was past, trudging on his way and, even as the patrolling soldier passed the next light, a man rose up out of the night and shot the stationary sentry in the throat. In fact two bolts hit him, the second striking beneath one eye, and he toppled without a word. Quickly a pair of Ants materialized to grab him and then dragged him back to their main group.

Salma heard steps approach behind them, and turned to see a tall Spider-kinden in a short tunic approaching. He looked profoundly unhappy.

'You understand your task?' Basila whispered to him, and the man nodded. Salma realized he must be a slave of Tark. He was taller than most Ants, though, and slave work had broadened his Spider-kinden physique, so when he started to don the dead Wasp's armour Salma understood. A missing sentry would raise questions. Still, as he and the others dashed through the ring of light into the darker shadows of the camp, Salma wondered what they had promised him to make a slave do such a thing. Did they offer him freedom or had he a family under threat? Salma would never know.

The camp was vast, and even at night there were plenty of lone figures moving about it. Many were soldiers, some were slaves of the Wasps or perhaps Auxillians. Basila's little band moved in a series of stops and starts, far more quietly than Salma would have expected. Each tent shadow offered sanctuary, and the dim lights of the sleeping camp were enough for them to find their way. Even Totho seemed to be managing some kind of stealth.

They were making their way gradually around the periphery of the tents, where the least nocturnal activity was. There were lamps glowing through the walls of some of the tents, and low voices talking inside. Salma heard the rattle of dice from one and someone humming an unfamiliar song inside another. These barracks-tents would be carpeted with Wasp soldiers, he guessed. Perhaps others would house the Ant-kinden the Empire had suborned or those giants who last night had carved through Tark's city wall. It would be best, Salma thought, if none of those great creatures were met with tonight.

Miraculously, they had not been spotted. By the ring of lights there were sentries staring outwards, just as their Spider-kinden decoy would now be staring outwards, but the lamps would blind them to what was going on in their own camp.

There was a scuffle ahead but it was over before Salma had a chance to see. A Wasp-kinden had walked within arm's reach of them and paused, casting a bemused glance into the shadows. Basila and another had grabbed him, stopped his mouth and stabbed him into silence. They stowed the body under the eaves of a tent and carried on.

There were lights all over the airfield, so Salma could see the monstrously pale and bloated ghosts that were the airship balloons. They were floating high already, straining at their steel cables, ready to fly at the dawn, no doubt. Totho had tried to explain them to him, how they were not just hot air but some complicated-sounding alchemical air that was better, and which did not need to be hot before it could lift them. Salma had understood none of it.

The Ant-kinden had explosives, he knew. The plan called for them to creep aboard each of the airships and plant them with decreasing fuse lengths, so that they would all explode more or less simultaneously and give the Wasps no warning of their intent. Again, Salma had to take all this on faith as it was beyond his understanding.

They paused again, but this time the shadow they borrowed was cast by one of the heliopters, its squared-off side as high and broad as a poor man's house in Helleron. There was movement and noise from just the other side, the rattle of metal on metal and the occasional curse as some Wasp-kinden artificer worked into the night to get the machine in his charge back into the air. Salma shuffled forwards until he was almost beside Basila, seeing now the broad, well-lit expanse of the field the Wasps had cleared for their flying machines. They had a dozen great lamps to enable the artificers to work, so there were precious few shadows from this point on, just an overlapping plain of harsh artificial light.

The artificers were out in force, and other personnel, too. There were scattered soldiers, men checking the tension of the airship lines, and others counting off stacks of equipment piled beside the aircraft hulls.

Salma realized there were too many people here for the plan to work: they would be spotted the moment they left the heliopter's shadow.

Basila was waiting motionless and he wondered if she was simply hoping for all those people to go away. If that did not happen, as it would not, would they be found here at dawn by the Wasps, still patiently waiting by this downed heliopter?

Totho touched his shoulder and made a motion of counting on his fingers, then a gesture around at their companions.

He tallied heads quickly and sure enough they were a man short.

A moment later something went *Whoomp!* a distance away, but still within the camp, and there was a flash of flame. A second's eerie silence and then the shouting started.

Most of the soldiers took off immediately, running towards the disturbance, and a surprising number of the artificers too, just going to see what the fuss was about.

Basila already had her crossbow in her hand, and Salma actually saw her counting off the seconds: *two . . . three . . . four . . .* and then she was off, running into the light and letting the bolt fly at the nearest man.

Sixteen

And Arianna ran. At first, she ran.

But she knew that running, though it put distance between them, would leave a trail that Thalric could follow. Even at this late hour there were enough people who she jostled, or who stared after her: a young Spider-kinden woman pelting down the street, her pale robes spotted red.

She ducked into a side street, tried to calm herself.

He would be coming for her. She had left him no choice.

She could not believe that Hofi was dead. Scadran she had not known so well, but Hofi . . . She could not say that she had liked him. It was not something that came up, in their business. She had known him for a year, seen him every few days. He was a part of her life and now Thalric had snuffed him out.

She peered back around the corner, seeing only a dozen or so Beetles going about their late errands. Of course Thalric would not be on the street. He would be at roof level, winging his way towards her. She looked up, scanning the sky with wide eyes, but there was nothing.

She had to get indoors. There must be a taverna near here. She moved off, trying to keep to a respectable walk, one hand folded demurely across her breast to cover the worst of the blood. She must have looked like a madwoman, for the locals started when they saw her and quickly got out of her way.

Finally there was a taverna ahead. She could go inside, shield herself from the sky. If they had rooms to hire she could hide out, offering a little extra to keep her secret.

She was almost at the door when she saw him. He was still a hundred yards down the street, but she recognized him instantly. Thalric, in his long coat, with the sword scabbarded beneath it. He began to walk towards her in a patient, purposeful way.

She skittered backwards and took the next side-alley, aware that he was between her and the better parts of town. She was heading into that district where they had ambushed Stenwold, and it had been chosen because the locals cared little about any commotion. Certainly the death of a single Spider girl would excite no curiosity.

She picked up her pace. Glancing behind her she could no longer see him but she had a sense of motion, of being tracked. He was in the air again, she guessed, and could follow her easily, tracing her hurried dashing from street to street as he glided silently over the rooftops.

She stopped under the eaves of a run-down house. Her eyes were good in the dusk, but they seemed to have failed her now. They conspired with her ears and her mind, putting a hundred pursuers on her trail. Certainly she thought she heard the soft blur of wings above, so that he could even be on the very roof of this place, waiting for her next move. And yet surely was that not him, the shadow in the alley across the way? The whole city now seemed to be hunting her.

There was a distinct scrape from up above, and such imaginings fell away. Someone was above her, and who else could it be?

He might not know I'm here. He might not know I'm here. She hugged herself, trying to keep the panic in, but thinking only of Thalric's careful, patient style. He would wait all night.

He might not know I'm here.

But then her nerve snapped and she bolted and, as she broke cover she heard the flash of his energy sting, felt the heat but not the hammering shock of it, as it scorched the muddy flags of the street over to her left. She was running blindly then, and knowing he could fly faster than she could run, but run she did, as fast as she could whip her legs to motion, until she could go no faster. Then she struck against something – something put hard in her path without warning – and she was thrown on the ground. Her head spun from the impact but she forced herself to look up and see.

And she saw his face, and it was the face of Tisamon, cold and utterly without mercy. His claw was over his hand, raised idly to finish her.

Arianna screamed, she could not stop herself, and she covered her eyes.

Tisamon was surprised at himself, because he had wished to see this, the traitress cowering at his feet, utterly defence-less, but now he had it, something drained away inside him.

There had been no fight. He had been expecting a fight.

As that thought came to him he looked up, and Thalric landed not ten yards away, sword drawn, and their eyes met. The shock of recognition was a physical thing, two-edged and cutting. Tisamon remembered the fire and pain, the injury he had still not entirely shaken free of. Thalric, for his part, remembered the wounds he had taken, the wounds he had given, and how Tisamon had simply refused to die.

For a long moment, with Arianna whimpering at the Mantis's feet, they stared at one another. Tisamon's off-hand, as though it had a life of its own, had plucked a dagger from his belt. He had sought them out particularly, those daggers, after the fight at Helleron, and paid a heavy purse for them.

'She is mine,' Tisamon said. 'I claim her.' As he was

speaking a Beetle-kinden pair, a man and a woman, stepped out into the alley, glanced from him to Thalric, and retreated hurriedly back indoors.

Thalric's mind was at war with itself. This was the one confrontation he would normally have baulked at. He had come far too close to dying because of this man, and who knew whether his daughter was lurking nearby? He had a sense, as he was hunting Arianna down, that his were not the only feet on her trail. He had that sense again now, even with Tisamon before him. *Who else is there and where are they?*

He feared. A bitter realization that, but he feared.

Still, he was a soldier of the Empire. He took a step forward and spat a bolt from his palm at the Mantis.

Tisamon hurled himself aside, though the fire scorched his shoulder. But just as Thalric had loosed the bolt the Mantis's hand had flicked forwards and he now saw the Wasp stagger as the dagger struck. A glancing blow, for Thalric had seen the silver flicker coming, but it had been flying straight for his face and, as he dodged, it cut a line across his temple, above his ragged cheek where Arianna had clawed him. He made to launch another bolt, but Tisamon had a second knife in his hand even now, sending the edged darts spinning out one after another, driving Thalric back, back, then up to a rooftop, almost to the limit of his sting's range. Tisamon had a hand full of knives, little hiltless throwing pieces, and there was no way to tell how many he still concealed.

This confrontation could see both of us dead very easily. The thought was in Thalric's mind, but he could see no acknowledgement of it in Tisamon's expression. Thalric was more mobile, the Mantis's eyes better in the darkness.

Stalemate. And Thalric knew that he could not squander his life here, when he was badly needed to further the Rekef plans in Vek. Then let this Mantis see if he could stand against the fall of a whole city.

Thalric's wings blurred into life and he hurled himself into the sky, watching for that next knife at all times until he had put a building between them. Even then he could not have said whether his reason for flight was anything other than a way of disguising his fear.

Arianna felt a brief moment of relief as Thalric departed, but it withered as she looked up into the Mantis's face.

'Please don't kill me,' she begged. Tisamon regarded her impassively. Now the moment was upon him he had expected his earlier passion to be urging him to do it. To his distant surprise it was the other way round. A fickle current of feeling was trying to stay his hand even though his reason insisted he had to kill her.

He dragged her two streets further towards the river, to an empty, litter-strewn square where a body could have lain for a tenday without discovery, casting her down against a windowless wall. He knelt by her, and the flat of his blade was abruptly cold against her neck, a trick he had used often enough to put fear into others, not that this shivering Spider needed it. 'Where are your friends?' he growled at her.

'They . . .' She swallowed, closed her eyes at the feel of the metal moving against her skin. 'They're dead, all of them.'

'You lie.' He twitched, just slightly, but she felt the tiny cut, a bead of blood blooming.

'No, please! Thalric killed them. I'm all that's left.'

He considered this. It should have seemed impossible, but she had been fleeing and Thalric had been chasing her. This was becoming ever more complex.

'Please – please let me talk to Stenwold . . .' she started, and he hauled her up by her collar in sheer rage, slamming her back against the wall. His lethal claw was drawn back, and in that instant all his strength of will went into restraining it.

'Do not even utter his name, traitress,' he hissed. 'You and I, we understand one another. We know the old ways and the old laws, but Stenwold doesn't. He believes in things like conscience and forgiveness, but you and I know better. Some acts of betrayal have prices that *must* be paid.'

He wanted her to scream at him, to fight him. That would have made his decision easy for him, and he liked simplicity. Instead she just hung in his grip, shaking. She was, he decided, a wretched specimen. Atryssa would have held her in contempt.

'Please,' she whispered. 'I need to tell someone . . .' And then her voice dried up, and he saw a reflection move in her eyes, which widened abruptly.

'Watch out!' she yelled, and he whirled around with claw raised high, and when the sword came down he caught it.

It was not Thalric, but a cloaked woman, some complete stranger. She gave him no chance to see more than that, because that sword was coming at him again. Two strong overhead swings, and then a lunge that nearly gutted him as he leapt back and back, turning each blow aside. The sword flashed in her hands, turning through each attack and never still, now gripped two-handed, now passed to her left or right hand, springing at him from all angles.

He had turned a dozen such blows before he gained the initiative, ducking under one swing and lashing at her midriff. She swayed aside, and the tip of his claw scraped against armour, then the pommel of the sword hammered down on him, and he caught it with the palm of his free hand, forced it aside and lashed out at her face with the spines of his arms.

She fell back, not even scratched, allowing him a better look at her. She was some kinden he did not know well but he thought he knew her race, if not her face. The cloak was mostly blown aside, and he could see she was wearing a full suit of armour – but what armour! He had never seen anything like it. Delicate chainmail overlaid with plates of metal that glittered darkly with greens and blues and prismatic metal tones. He nearly lost himself in staring at it, and backed up a dozen steps as she attacked again. Her style was new to him but she was swift even encased in that metal, dancing both with her sword and with him. He met her blade another half-dozen times, taking each blow on his claw or its armoured gauntlet.

The Spider traitress must have run by now, he realized. He would have to hunt her down again. He did not care. This was special.

He turned his next parry into an attack, and he was backing her up once more, his claw tracing lines of swift silver in the air, now sparking off the straight blade of her sword, and sometimes drawing the faintest scratch off that glorious armour when she did not move quite soon enough.

He sought out her face, golden-skinned, composed into perfect concentration, beautiful and fixed as a statue's.

He was under her guard for just a moment, lashing beneath her breastplate. He severed a handful of mail links, cut a tear into the arming jacket underneath. Then she struck him with the guard of her blade, almost catching him with the edge. The blow took him in the shoulder Thalric had already burned and he hissed in pain and fell back. He saw her move after him without a thought.

He found he was grinning, because she was magnificent and he had not fought her like in many years.

Another series of lightning exchanges. Her blade was double-edged and needle-pointed, moving like sunlight and mirrors in her hands, each attack different from the last, without pattern or predictability. He shifted and spun with them, letting his reflexes take him where thinking could not keep up, divorcing his mind from the long-trained motions of his body, letting her advances exhaust themselves till he was driving her back in turn. Three times he struck and failed to penetrate her armour, and once he managed a shallow line of blood across her leg beneath the severed links of the mail.

Her eyes locked his and he knew she would kill him if she could. He would have no choice but to kill her in exchange. It was as it should be and either he would die or he would remember this contest for ever.

Tisamon found he was now breathing heavily, feeling the skin tight across his chest and side, the healing burn where Thalric had caught him at the fight over the *Pride*. His seared shoulder throbbed in agony yet it seemed distant and he could ignore it.

They had reached the endgame. He still had no idea who she was but he would swear now that she was no Wasp agent, for if the Wasps could call on such as this they would rule the world already.

He fell back ten paces, dropped into a new stance, claw held low but angled upwards. She fell into a stance of her own, with that sword gripped double-handed and high, the point aimed downwards. A perfect complement.

He waited for her to come at him.

Whole ages seemed to pass, with the two of them frozen in place, each waiting for the slightest move from the other to set them off. He became aware that the Spider girl had not moved after all, was still cowering back against the wall where he had left her. There was another voyeur, too, a man watching from a doorway. It was all immaterial.

And then she stepped back out of her stance, as though they had simply been playing at a practice bout and she now had other things to do. Tisamon fought the immediate instinct to do the same, holding his pose, but she just stood there now, looking about her, and he could have killed her at his leisure.

She spoke, her face full of confusion. 'Where is this place? This is not Shon Aren.' She saw him there, as though noticing for the first time. The sword in her hand seemed almost forgotten. 'Mantis-kinden? Am I in Y'yen, then? But why?' She approached him, quite without fear or hostile intent, and from the corner of his eye Tisamon saw the man who had watched them darting forwards,

Instantly his claw was in motion, bringing the stranger up short with the edge close to his throat. The strange woman merely watched without alarm or recognition.

A Spider-kinden, Tisamon saw – there had been far too many in his life recently. This specimen was a long-haired man of middle years, his hands empty, teeth bared above the blade that menaced him.

'And who are you?' Tisamon demanded. 'Tell me quickly or I'll have done with you. There are too few answers tonight.'

'Oh, I know of your kind's enmity towards mine,' the man replied, as calmly as he could muster. 'My name is Destrachis and I'm with this lady here, whose name is Felise Mienn.'

'Destrachis!' the woman exclaimed even as he said the name, although not with much love, and with no sign that she saw the claw at his throat. 'What . . . ?'

'We are in Collegium, Felise,' Destrachis explained carefully.

'Yes, you are,' Tisamon confirmed. 'And someone had better explain to me exactly what we were fighting about.'

'You . . .' She seemed to see him again and her eyes narrowed. Instantly his blade was away from Destrachis and he was falling back into his stance again.

'I saw you with him,' she said. 'You must be one of his creatures. Tell me where he has gone.'

'Where *who* has gone?' Tisamon asked her

She spat back, 'Thalric! Thalric the Wasp! Thalric of the Empire. Your master, is he not?'

'He is *not*,' Tisamon said firmly. 'He is my enemy, as he clearly must be yours. You seek his blood?'

She nodded, seeming more lucid now.

'Then if I knew where he was bound I would tell you,' he confirmed. 'And this here is *your* creature, is he?'

She looked at Destrachis coolly, but it was a moment before she responded. 'He . . . I was travelling with this man. He . . . Destrachis brought me here.'

Tisamon began to relax again, until he heard Arianna's voice calling them. All three of them turned to her: a young Spider-kinden girl in a torn and muddied robe.

'You really want to kill Thalric?' she asked hopefully, and Felise nodded in a single sharp movement.

'He will leave Collegium tonight,' Arianna explained. 'He is travelling to Vek.'

The name of that city meant nothing to Felise, it was clear, but Destrachis murmured, 'West of here, along the coast.'

'Then we, too, must go to Vek,' Felise said. 'We must go now. We could catch him on the road.'

'Vek it is,' Destrachis confirmed, somewhat wearily, casting a cautious glance at Tisamon. 'All right if we make our exit? Despite what just happened, we're really not your enemies, honestly.'

'I see that,' Tisamon folded his claw back along the line of his arm.

'I've seen her fighting a few times, now,' Destrachis said, 'and I've never seen anyone walk away from it.'

'It was a pleasure and an honour.' Tisamon stared at Felise thoughtfully. It was as if the woman he had been fighting had been rubbed away, suddenly replaced by this confused foreigner, but to his surprise she turned and gave him a curt bow, bringing her sword, point lowered, up to her breastplate. It was a token of respect he often had used himself in the company of other Weaponsmasters, and he returned it with a slight smile.

Destrachis was already heading away and she followed him with a single backwards glance. Tisamon stared after her, and even as Arianna approached, he waited until the woman Felise was out of sight before he turned his attention to the Spider girl.

'Please let me . . .' She had stopped out of his reach but, having seen him fight now, she knew how fast he could move. 'I really do need to speak to – him. It's about Thalric's plans. Please take me to him . . . in chains if you must.'

He felt the fire of combat drain out of him, leaving him tired and bruised, more thoroughly exhausted than he had felt in a long time. There was no desperate need to kill within him, not now. It had been burned out of him during the fight with Felise Mienn.

'Stenwold himself will decide what to do with you,' he declared, and motioned for her to walk ahead of him.

Seventeen

The Ant-kinden shot all at once, the arms of their cross-bows a vibrating blur with the force of the bolts let loose. Salma saw half a dozen men drop, mostly shot in the head or throat. Even with their targets lit up by the working lamps, it was a fine display of shooting.

Basila and her people were already moving. She took half her force forward with drawn swords, while the others spun the wheels of their crossbows to recock them. Salma had a moment's hesitation before he went with them, catching them up with a flurry of his wings and diving at once into the fray.

Most of the men they fell on were Wasp-kinden artificers, unarmoured save for their working leathers, and some of their slaves. There was no time to distinguish or apply any mercy, though, and Salma knew that the Tarkesh had none to apply. Eight or nine utterly surprised men were caught unawares, cut down where they stood, and then two of the Ants were running on towards the nearest in the line of towering airships.

There was another hollow explosion from within the camp as Basila's tactics of distraction continued. One man, a suicide from the moment he set out, was running through the tents of the Wasps and throwing grenades at random. Salma could only imagine the confusion.

Other Wasp soldiers were coming at them now. Most

came running from the nearest rows of tents, unarmoured, some barely clad, but there were already some in the airships only now making themselves known. A second hail of crossbow bolts raked across the enemy approaching from behind, taking all but two from their feet. Salma turned to deal with those remaining two, who now hesitated, suddenly wrong-footed by their comrades' demise. Giving them no time to react, he stabbed one through the throat and then planted his blade in the other's bare chest. He glanced around for the Ant crossbowmen and saw them advance down the line of airships, loading as they did. Totho was still among them, he was glad to note, busy slotting another magazine into his repeating crossbow.

Basila and her few made quick work of the airship guards. One Ant-kinden was already shinning up the ropes to the first gondola. For a moment Salma wondered why they didn't just cut the cords and let the buoyant machines blow away with the wind, but when he caught Basila up he saw that the lines were twisted steel, three fingers thick and sunk who knew how deep into the ground. Destroying the gondolas themselves was the only option left to them.

An energy bolt crackled past him, signifying that there were more Wasp soldiers on their way. He flung himself into the air, almost by instinct, and met a Wasp coming the other way. Salma grappled with the man as the two of them spun in the air before stabbing the Wasp and letting him drop to the ground.

The Ant crossbowmen were loosing bolts again, but they were being rushed as they did so. Two or three of the Wasps went down, some shots went wild and shields took others. For a moment Salma swung in the air, torn between either helping Basila destroy the airships or aiding Totho. Then he was arrowing down, sword first. Totho had his own blade drawn, crouched low as a Wasp thrust at him with a spear. Salma landed on his feet behind the spearman, thrusting his blade straight into the man's back. He met

Totho's eyes for a moment, and then the halfbreed artificer took up his crossbow again, and immediately Salma sprang into the air.

He had been noted, now, so he twisted and spun to dodge a scatter of sting-shot directed at him, and a couple of crossbow bolts as well. A sweeping glance saw Basila's people moving over to the next airship, and he soared in beside them.

'Faster!' he urged.

'We can't do this faster.' She was climbing a rope even as she said it.

'Can I help?'

'Can you carry me – flying?'

He shook his head. 'The bombs . . . Is it so . . . ?'

'You are not Apt,' she told him, dragging herself over the gondola's side. Two soldiers ran at her immediately, but she had already taken up her crossbow and stopped one with a bolt before he was even halfway towards her. The other's hand spat a dart of gold fire that she sidestepped, and then Salma caught him by one of his armour-straps while Basila ran him through.

She looked across the deck, picking the best spot for the explosive. Salma went to the rail, looking out over it, and his heart sank. There were more soldiers coming, fast. The Wasps had mobilized much more quickly than they should have done. 'I don't think your distraction worked,' he commented.

There was a flight of at least three score enemy heading for the airships. Clearly the Wasps had second-guessed them.

Basila was now kneeling, setting the bomb by clicking at something. A clockwork fuse, Totho had said, but it meant nothing to Salma.

'We don't have much time,' he hissed. She ignored him still, patiently aligning the mechanism.

The first Wasps were at the rail even then. Salma cried

out something wordless and half-ran, half-flew at them, stabbing the leader, driving him to the deck of the gondola. He then slashed up at the next man that he sensed was about to stab him in the back, catching the Wasp across the face. Two more were on him instantly but the sound of fighting behind him heartened him no end. Basila must have finished and they had not caught her unprepared.

They drove him back, and soon two became four, and then he had to take to the air to avoid being surrounded. They followed but he was swifter, skipping past their blades and bolts and leaving a trail of blood whenever he got within sword's reach. He had wheeling glimpses of Basila still fighting on the deck, unable to flee but giving a good account of herself.

The plan had failed. He knew he should now find Totho and try to get both of them out and away from the camp and away from Tark. He knew that he could not abandon Basila, though. With a tight loop in the air he lost the two men still pursuing him, and dashed back for the airship.

Can you carry me? she had asked, but he could not. Not upwards, not even sideways . . .

He screamed as he stooped on them, catching one man in the back hard enough for him lose his grip on the sword. Then he had scattered them, just as Basila finished one more off. With no time for explanations he caught the surprised woman about the waist and ran with her to the rail. He kicked off.

Totho had run out of places to go. As the least bold of the band of saboteurs, so he was nearly the last. Only he and one more Ant remained, and there were now Wasps everywhere.

The Ant loosed his crossbow, bringing down another opponent, but then the enemy were on them again, at sword's length, and Totho stumbled back while the Ant engaged them. Though a skilled swordsman, they mobbed him and, although several of them fell, one of them drove a blade down into his neck, almost to the quillons.

And Totho raised the crossbow his automatic hands had reloaded, and emptied it into them. He saw three men punched back by the power of it as he raked it in an arc across them.

Totho jammed another magazine into the weapon. He was now almost at the camp's edge, and beyond that scattered perimeter of lights lay escape. Surely they could not follow him very far at night. He took another few steps back, raised the crossbow again and pressed the trigger as the closest soldier was almost within arm's reach.

It jammed, and he heard a crack as the shaft of the bolt shattered under the stress. A moment later a Wasp sword was arcing down on him. He held the bow up, cringing, and the enemy blade embedded itself in the weapon, severing the string and sticking itself hopelessly amidst the workings. As Totho let go the snarling Wasp soldier hurled sword and bow away from him. Then he and two of his fellows were wrestling Totho to the ground.

Totho was strong, but so were these professional soldiers of the Empire. One of them struck him in the face hard enough to rattle his teeth. A moment later, groggy, he was being hauled upright to see the gleam of a sword being drawn back to strike.

'Save him!' a voice snapped, and Totho looked blearily into the face of an angry man with a bloodied scalp – an officer who, for all the wrong reasons, had just saved his life.

A moment later a sword pommel connected expertly with the back of his skull, and he remembered nothing more.

It was the kick, more than his wings, that cleared the rail for Salma, and then he was putting all his strength into flight as the burden in his arms dragged him back towards the hungry earth. If she had struggled they would both have been lost, but she clung to him tight and they dropped awkwardly in jolting stages until they found the earth.

'We have to go!' he said, snatching up the first discarded sword he found. When she looked at him all he could see were her eyes, but he thought that she was smiling at him.

'How?' she asked, and then they were both on their feet, fighting back to back. There were a dozen of the enemy trying to get at them in their eagerness to finish it. Salma laid one Wasp's arm open and then cut down one of the stocky slave-kinden who was coming at him with an axe. A Wasp spearman drove the weapon at him, and Salma lunged forwards along the shaft to stab the man in the ribs. When he fell back again, Basila was no longer there.

He felt a single stab of hurt, but he knew that unless he did something quickly he would be just a corpse lying beside hers. His wings exploded from across his shoulders and he launched himself upwards. The enemy were following him and he was growing weary, his Art starting to falter. He landed again and spun round to face them, cutting the first one down even as the man touched ground. They were hanging back now, and he threw himself aside as they began launching their stings, each bolt of golden fire briefly lighting the night.

He turned and ran, looking for Totho but seeing only more of the enemy. He soon found himself deeper amidst the tents, always on the move, running up against little knots of Wasp soldiers and slashing at them frantically, making them scatter.

One pack did not budge, however and he slammed straight into them, losing his second sword. He cracked one in the head with his elbow, rammed his knee into another's stomach. The third man grabbed him, tugging at his arming jacket, but Salma punched him in the face, snapping his head back. Pain burned across his back like the lash of a whip: a sting-blast had scorched him and he reeled, falling to one knee.

He leapt up instantly, wings searching for the sky, but someone grabbed an ankle and dragged him down. Even as he was yanked backwards a bolt of light split the air where he would have been flying. He lashed out blindly with hands and feet but they were all around him now and he met resistance with every blow.

A sword glinted nearby and he grasped the wrist that held it, bringing the swordsman's arm down across his knee with an audible snap. Then the blade was in his own hand. They were furious now, mad for blood, but so was he. He killed the two of them closest to him with brief, brutal moves of the sword.

Another sting-shot flared past him as he ran. He wanted to fly but as soon as he took to the air he would have no cover, and there would be too many shots from all sides to dodge.

Someone grabbed for him and the pair of them tumbled to the ground. Salma was up first, driving his sword down into his opponent then dragging it up in desperate parry as yet another soldier lunged at him. The force of the blow spun him round but, as he staggered back, he managed to get back on his feet. The soldier confronting him paused a moment, sword extended, and then went for him, and for a second they were duelling, just as though they were in the Prowess Forum.

Then another Wasp was close behind and Salma lashed back at him with the sword but only struck the man across the face with the guard. The soldier in front of him took his chance then, and Salma whipped his sword back into line to deflect the blow.

The force of the attack knocked something out of him, the great punching blow to his stomach. Salma gasped, and his world contracted until it contained only himself and the Wasp soldier. No sounds, only dead silence as his sword swept round and lanced the other man through the ribs. His opponent could not parry because his blade was buried deep in Salma's body.

Salma fell forwards into the arms of his adversary, the two of them leaning on each other like drunkards. Then Salma's knees gave way and they toppled sideways together. For a moment their fight was an embrace of brothers.

And darkness rose within Salma, accompanied by a strange cessation of pain.

He was aware again of pain, before he had any idea of where he was. The back of his head was thumping angrily, sending tremors through his skull and into his eyes. Totho shifted awkwardly only to discover that he was lying bound at a strange angle in some peculiar kind of chair.

Growing awareness swiftly furnished his last reliable memory: the night attack. Was it still night? His eyelids told him it was dark, yet he could hear the slightly muffled murmur of a waking world beyond. He was in a Wasp tent.

And tied. He remembered what Che had said, about the torture devices the Wasps had kept in Myna. And that would explain the uncomfortable contours of the chair he was lashed to, its cold metal.

As well as most securely bound, he was stripped to the waist, and when he flexed his body experimentally, he felt the tug and pull of bandages, over rows of surgeon's stitches.

And from somewhere close above him, a female voice stated, 'I think he is awake.'

Totho froze into immobility, but too late. There was no longer anything to be gained from shamming, so very carefully he opened his eyes.

Even the dim light within the tent sent a stab of pain coursing through his brain, but he could just make out a blurred shape looming above him.

Something cold touched his lips, and he twisted his head violently, ringing his skull with agony. The woman's voice said sharply, 'Stop that. It is water only.'

He cautiously turned back to press his mouth against the lip of a cup. The water it contained was so startlingly cold that he felt there must be ice in it. A moment later a damp cloth was put to his forehead.

He forced himself to look properly, to make the vague shapes resolve themselves. The woman who had spoken was young, he saw, and dark-skinned. At first he assumed she was a Beetle, but her face was too flat, her frame too compact. Then he recalled the slave-artificers and recognized her as of the same kinden.

'Where am I?' he finally rasped, and found the ache in his head was joined by another inside his cheek. His mouth tasted rusty with dried blood, so he must have bitten himself in the struggle.

He saw the woman turn and glance at someone behind her, who had not, in all this time, moved or spoken. Merely the thought sent a shiver through him, and then she had stepped aside, and someone else was now standing beside the strange chair. Totho turned his head as far as the pain would allow, and saw a metal-gauntleted hand, exquisitely worked.

The newcomer's voice was quiet and sly, slightly mocking. 'In your position, young man, I would not waste my time with unnecessary questions. What is your name, young one?'

He decided he was not going to answer, and then the gauntlet shifted with a slight scraping of metal and he said quickly, 'Totho. They called me Totho.'

'A Fly-kinden name.' The man sounded amused. 'You must have been brought up in . . . Collegium, I would guess? Well then, my own name is Dariandrephos, but the boorish Wasps call me Drephos. Or "the Colonel-Auxillian", of course.'

'Colonel . . . ?' Totho wrestled with the term.

'In fact I am the only Colonel-Auxillian in the Empire. I know that because they invented the rank solely for my benefit. Perhaps one day they will have to make me General-Auxillian, and then perhaps, what? Emperor-Auxillian. That would be amusing. Where were you trained?'

Totho shut his eyes and said nothing.

'Do you know why you are here – rather than with the other prisoners? Perhaps you do not. We captured three of you, and the other two will be questioned as the Wasps question, as far as their physical capabilities permit. This, as you should have surmised, is not questioning. This is merely a friendly conversation, Totho.'

Still Totho said nothing, and his interrogator clicked his tongue in annoyance. Totho waited for a blow, but instead there was a tugging at his wrists, and then his bonds were loosened. He opened his eyes to see the girl retreating from him again.

'Of course, you require some token of my good will,' said Drephos.

Finally Totho was able to twist around to look at him. He saw none of the man's flesh. The robe and cowl made a tall spectre of him. Only that gauntlet emerged from the folds of black and yellow cloth.

'What is going on?' Totho demanded. 'What do you want from me?'

'You are here because of this.' The gauntlet dipped into Drephos's robe and came out again with a strangely hesitant precision that made Totho wonder whether the hand inside had been injured or burned. On its reappearance it was gripping a small mechanism that he knew only too well.

'And this.' Drephos's other hand, dark-gloved but bare

of metal, appeared briefly to hang a long strip of pocketed leather on the arm of the metal chair. It was Totho's tool-strip, and the device brandished before his face was one of his air batteries, his little pet project he had never been able to finish.

'It is remarkable how much one can learn from the contents of a man's pack,' Drephos continued. 'You have clearly been trained as an artificer, but I could have told that from the calluses of your hands. You were trained in Collegium then? In the Great College?'

Numbly, Totho nodded.

'I would have given a great deal for that privilege.'

'You're an artificer?' Totho seized on that statement. It seemed to offer him some small chance of respite.

Drephos laughed hollowly. 'I am perhaps, though I say it myself, the most skilled artificer you will ever meet. The only reason I qualify that with "perhaps" is your own tute-lage. I am painfully aware that, myself excluded, the Empire is somewhat young in the game of artifice: three generations from barbarism whilst you Lowlanders have a tradition that goes back centuries. Still, one must work with the tools one has.'

'But the Empire must have artificers. Wasp artificers?' Totho said. 'I can't be so special.'

'But you are, because I do not want to rely on Wasp artificers. They are either dull men who have learned their mechanics by rote, or they waste what intellect they have in politics and one-upmanship and care nothing for the sci-ence itself. No, my people, my journeymen, are chosen from other sources. Unless the man be an outcast, I will not have a Wasp in my workshops.'

'You want me to—?'

'I am interested in *you*, Totho. I have never had the honour of a Great College student working for me.'

'I will never work for the Empire!' Totho snapped,

sitting halfway up, then falling back, his head still clamouring.

'I have a case to make.' Drephos sounded amused.

'I know the Empire. I know how they look on other races, even if they aren't halfbreeds!' Totho said through his teeth.

'And what if they are?' There was such dry humour in the man's voice that Totho propped himself up on one elbow to see what was so funny.

Drephos raised his hands, one cased in metal and one without, and slipped his cowl back. The face he revealed was mottled and blotchy with grey, and his eyes had no irises. There were many grades of halfbreed, Totho already knew. A few like Tynisa were just like one parent or the other, and some others managed to combine their heritage into something exotic and attractive. Most were like Totho himself, stamped with an intermingling of bloods that others saw, and then judged them by. Drephos, though, was of those few who seemed actively twisted by their inheritance. His features were lean and ascetic but subtly wrong in their proportions. Even when he smiled the effect was unpleasantly skewed.

'I am aware, young man, that I will win no prizes for my beauty, but believe that I, therefore, judge no man on his face or blood,' he said.

'Drephos,' Totho said softly. 'And that other name, the long one. Moth-kinden names?'

'My mother was left to name me. My father, unknown and unmourned, bestowed on her only so much of his time as it took to rape her. Wasp soldiers are not known for their benevolence towards prisoners or slaves. I suppose few soldiers are.'

'But you said you were an artificer?'

The lopsided smile grew wider than seemed comfortable. 'Remarkable, is it not? And yet something from my father's seed has communicated to me all the workings of the world of metal, for here I am, so much of an artificer that they turn their hierarchy inside out to accommodate me. Without me the walls of Tark would still be whole, utterly unbreached. Yet my mother's people sit in their caves and draw pictures on the wall, and pretend they are still great.'

Totho sank back into the chair. There was a feeling snagged deep inside him, because he was now interested. This maverick artificer, who seemed to have carved out some high station even amidst the Wasp Empire, had caught his imagination.

'Was it your idea,' Drephos asked softly, 'to destroy my airships?'

And *there* was a leading question, and more what Totho had been expecting. It would be better, he thought, to return to familiar ground. 'It was.' He steeled himself.

'Don't be shy of it,' Drephos said. 'It was a well-planned raid. I'd guessed that the Ant-kinden hadn't considered it. I have dealt with them before and there is not a grain of intuition in their entire race. But *you* saw the threat and acted, even as I myself saw our vulnerability. That is why I had two whole wings of soldiers on standby, to rush to the airships the very moment anything disturbed the camp. And just as well I did.'

So that was it: the final nail in the coffin for Totho's desperate plan. He recalled in his mind a brief swirl of images, the fighting, the fury. A sudden lurch took him, and he tried to spring out of the chair. Even before the young woman had moved to restrain him, he was already toppling, the pain in his head making it impossible to stand. Her arms grappled his body, surprisingly strong, hauled him up and sat on him the edge of the chair.

'Prisoners . . .' Totho muttered

'Yes?' Even with his eyes closed he could hear Drephos moving near.

'You said you had taken prisoners. Other prisoners.'

'Two to be precise, although one of them may not recover enough to be questioned.'

'Was there . . . ?' He squinted up at the man. 'Was there a Dragonfly-kinden man? He would have had—'

'I know the Commonwealers, the Dragonflies,' Drephos confirmed. 'After all, the Twelve-Year War was the testing ground for some of my best inventions. I'm sorry, though, but the other prisoners are just Ant-kinden. If there was a Dragonfly last night, he has not been taken alive, nor did any escape, to our knowledge. I am afraid it seems most likely he is amongst the fallen.'

Eighteen

General Maxin took a last moment to understand his reports. They were a secret of his success, these reports. He had very able slaves whose sole task was to compile the wealth of information the Rekef Inlander brought, so he could then look through these few scrolls and read in them all he needed to know. Details could come later. Details he would ask for. For now he had his picture, his mental sketch of who was plotting, who was falling, who was on the rise or on the take.

And his information was not just fodder for the Emperor's ears, either. Maxin had his own schemes. The Rekef was a young organization, created in the very closing years of the first Emperor's reign by the man whose name the spies now bore. The structure and hierarchy had evolved over the next twenty years but at some levels it was still changing. Maxin had his own plans for it.

There were three generals of the Rekef, the idea being that each controlled his own particular section of the Empire, spoke to the others and reported to the Emperor. In practice, of course, those men who were ambitious enough to become generals in the Rekef did not suffer the interference of their peers.

And Maxin himself was winning. That was all he cared about. He was the man who sat amongst the Emperor's advisers. General Brugen was chasing shadows and savages around the East-Empire amidst famine and bureaucracy and the stubbornness of the slave races. General Reiner was wrestling with the Lowlands. For the moment, Maxin was winning and he intended to keep it that way.

Of course there had been setbacks. Brugen was a conscientious man with more small troubles than his staff could conveniently cope with, so Maxin did not fear him. General Reiner was another matter, however. Only recently a man whom Maxin had raised to the governorship of a city, a man well placed for Maxin's plans, had been disposed of by Reiner. The city, its Rekef agents and its considerable wealth, had then been put in the hands of Reiner's shadow, the execrable Colonel Latvoc.

It had been a challenge to Maxin's primacy, of course, but Maxin enjoyed challenges – as long as he won in the end.

He *would* win in the end. He had the Emperor ready to love him like a brother . . . Or perhaps not like a brother. After all, Maxin had overseen the murder of all the Emperor's siblings bar one, and dealt with several other rivals at the same time. Nevertheless he had now presented the Emperor with perhaps the one gift all his Empire could not give him. It would be leverage enough, Maxin decided, to call for a major restructuring in the Rekef, and then Reiner and Brugen would understand, however briefly, that any army could only have *one* general.

He rolled up the scrolls and stowed them in the hidden compartment of his desk, then left to meet the Emperor.

They had moved the slave to a better cell, one with tapestries and carpets, some Grasshopper carvings for ornament, and no natural light. Uctebri had complained at the brightness of the gaslamps, though, and now oil lanterns hung randomly from the ceiling about his chambers, making them look more squalid than ever.

Still, he came to greet them at the first call of his name

and Maxin knew they had been feeding him well enough. This scrawny creature seemed to have a remarkable appetite: it was not clear precisely where so much blood could go.

When the prisoner had presented himself, Alvdan circled him cautiously. Maxin knew the difficulties here were ones of belief. What the wretched old Uctebri had proposed was impossible, quite impossible, as any rational mind well knew. The thing the old Mosquito promised, the golden, impossible dream of sorcerers and ancient kings, belonged in the forgotten folk tales of slaves. When Uctebri spoke of it, though, it was hard not to remember that his very race was supposed to be extinct, to be entirely mythical. While he rasped the words, with his quiet certainty, his strange insistence, it was possible for the rational mind to be tricked into believing, just for a moment, that the quackery was real.

And Maxin now had access to a great deal of information. There was no single stockpile of words in Capitas, no library or archive, but through the channels of the Rekef his hands could reach a long way through the dusty scrolls of all the conquered and subject peoples of the Empire.

The Commonweal conquests had brought a great deal of lore into his possession. Most of it was the simple superstition of savages, but he had become more specific in the questions he was asking. There were a lot of Rekef agents in the conquered Dragonfly principalities who must have wondered just why he was asking them to dig up so much old myth and history.

The Commonwealers were writers whose early histories were given in elaborate, credulous detail. Here he had found signs of the thing the Mosquito had spoken of. Not enough to be certain, but enough to know that there had been something, at some time, that the man's boasts were based on.

'You wish to examine our sister,' Alvdan said.

The hooded head bobbed. 'It is necessary, Your Imperial Majesty.'

'We had understood,' the Emperor said, 'that she was suitable. We believed you had proclaimed her suitable.' He was now suspicious. Maxin liked him to be suspicious. When Emperors were suspicious they came to the Rekef for their suspicions to be eased, and, here in Capitas, Maxin was the Rekef.

'Eminently suitable, Your Imperial Majesty,' the Mosquito said. 'However, there is no room for error. I must begin my calculations. Even now is not too soon, and such things cannot be hurried.'

'This is nonsense,' Alvdan said scornfully. 'We believe none of this. What you claim cannot be done.' He stomped away, but Maxin had heard the doubt in his voice, and he knew the Mosquito had too.

'I am at your disposal,' Uctebri said quietly. 'I am your prisoner, your slave – I shall do as you command. There is none who can offer you this but I. No one else, your great Majesty.'

'Maxin, you cannot really believe this. It goes against all reason,' the Emperor protested, though in his eyes Maxin saw not fear or contempt, but a hunger. *If only it were true*, those eyes said, *what could we do? What could we not do?*

'I have learned that there are things in this world that cannot be dismissed so easily. In your grandfather's father's time, Majesty, our own people had their own strange beliefs. One of which was that we would one day unite and rule the world. Who then would have believed it?'

'But this is different, Maxin.'

'Only in the type of belief it requires, Majesty.'

'So you wish to examine our sister?' Alvdan said, coming back to face the Mosquito. 'And that will discomfort her. It will upset her. *Good*. We are growing to appreciate this plan. But then you say you need more? You do not have here at your disposal all that you need.'

'It is indeed so, great lord. I have not the power, within my own being, for a work so great as this.'

'So your charlatanry needs fuel to make it go, does it?'

'I do not recognize such terms, great one,' Uctebri said, with unctuous humility, 'but I am sure you are correct.'

'Your magic box – that is what you need us to retrieve for you?' the Emperor added derisively. 'If it were so effective, would it be so easy to locate – or even possible to take?'

Uctebri gave a strange whistling sigh and pulled his enveloping hood halfway back to scratch at his head. His red eyes flicked from Alvdan to the general. 'Ruins and ash, Your Imperial Majesty, are all that remains of my people's power, but those who wrought our downfall are now little better. The old days are gone, and shall not come again. Those that were once enthroned on high are cast down, and that which was venerated is spurned in the dust.' His slender fingers intertwined. 'This thing that lords and Skryres and princes would have fought for, when its value was known, is now a curiosity in the hands of the ignorant: ignorant men who profess knowledge, and yet know nothing of what they possess. But it has power yet – power that I can use for your benefit, worshipful Majesty.'

'And if that power is used to our detriment, you know that we shall drain from you each drop of blood that you have fed on, creature,' Alvdan told him. 'Succeed and you shall find yourself most honoured amongst our slaves, but do not dream of betrayal.'

'I am your prisoner . . . your slave,' the Mosquito repeated, 'and you may destroy me with a word, now or later, or when my tasks are done. I am most dependent on your good will, mighty one. When I have proved myself by this great service, you shall think kindly of me, I hope, and know that I can do yet more.'

'Perhaps,' Alvdan said doubtfully. 'I have sent the orders, and they should arrive at the city of Helleron even now. Do you know Helleron? We have no free agents nearer your toy, but Helleron has its store of clever folk who do our bidding. The order has gone out to them. If this Box of the Shadow exists, and is where you say it is, they shall capture it for us.'

They brought the lady Seda in within two bells, as Capitas told time, dragged without warning from her own more sumptuous prison. She tried to fight free when she saw the emaciated, robed figure awaiting her, but the guard forced her in without difficulty, bound her to a chair easily, and now stood behind her, always a shadow in the edge of her vision. The Mosquito-kinden squinted at her, long fingers touching at one another, then parting.

'Light and darkness,' said Uctebri the Sarcad. He moved about the room almost hesitantly. 'That is what life is about: all existence strung between those two poles. Or that is the way that we all used to see it.' Eventually he made his mind up. 'Shutter the lanterns,' he said, and the guard looked at him curiously.

'Sir?' Uctebri was a slave still, with no rank as yet, but he was a man who had spoken to the Emperor and so the guard felt it wise to address him thus.

'I cannot do it,' the Mosquito said irritably. 'Draw the shutters almost all the way. It is too bright in here for what I plan. I trust this will not discomfort you overmuch, Your Highness.'

It was already gloomy in there and, from her vantage point, Seda could see Uctebri as a dark-robed shape that grew less and less distinct as the guard tugged on the cords that controlled the lamps' shutters.

'You needn't call me that,' she remarked drily. 'Nobody else does.'

The last shutter was now drawn nearly closed. She heard the guard carefully finding his way back behind her chair, felt his hand brush her shoulder as he checked her presence.

'And yet I do,' the Mosquito's voice came. When he moved she could just make him out. When he stopped he disappeared in the dark. 'It is the correct form of address for a lady of your rank, I believe?'

She heard a scratching sound from his approximate direction. 'What are you doing, Mosquito-kinden?'

'Drawing. Marking my notes,' emerged his voice. 'Light and darkness, great lady, our whole world is built between them. There are things that can be accomplished in the dark of the moon which are quite impossible at noontime. But it is not the hour that matters, only the light. If I can make it midnight within your mind, then there is nothing I cannot do, but if you have the will to keep the sun burning, then you are quite proof against me. But that art is long lost amongst your people.'

She heard the soft shuffle of his feet, her ears sharpening as she abandoned any reliance on her eyes. When she had come here, she had expected further taunts and jibes from her brother, but he had not been present. Instead there had been this chair, which she recognized from visits elsewhere. They kept chairs like this in prisons, for questioning. There had been none of the other apparatus she associated with the interrogator's art, but she sensed that the Mosquito's desires needed none.

He was very close when he spoke again. 'It escapes the attention of your own kinden – as of other upstart races – that all the great powers of the Days of Lore could see in darkness, to a greater or lesser degree. The Mantids, the Spiders, and of course, best of all, the Moth-kinden and my own people. To know the dark, and not to fear it, was to control the world.'

He was now right at her elbow.

'And then, of course, the great old night ended, and another kind of sun dawned. A revolutionary sun of machines and artifice that burned us all back into our hollows.'

'How bitter you must feel,' she said without sympathy.

'Bitter?' A croaky little laugh. 'My people had already lost our chance for greatness. We were never many, but we had power and a yearning to use it. We had secrets that the Skryres of the Moths have never learned, and some that they might have, but that they deemed us evil, and made war on us to wipe us out, along with everything we knew.'

She gave a little squeak of panic as his pale, cold fingers brushed her cheek, his nails unexpectedly sharp.

'And we are few now, so very few,' he continued. 'And yet they did not completely succeed, for that knowledge is still with us – and your brother is very, very interested in it.'

She had the sense of his eyes fixed on her. They had brought her here unprepared from her chamber, and she wore only a silken gown to keep the night out, and now the night was irresistible. She felt the touch of his fingertips drifting idly down her neck.

'You . . .' From somewhere she marshalled a little courage. 'This is an elaborate scheme of yours, Sarcad, simply to inflict yourself on a woman. Are your own kind so very few, after all?'

His rattling laugh came again. 'Forgive me, Highness. I am an old man, but appetites die slowly in my tribe and you Wasp-kinden are a comely enough people – for an Apt race. You, especially, are a remarkably pleasing specimen of Wasp-kinden womanhood.'

'And this is what it is all about, is it?' She tugged at the straps of the chair, which was a futile enough struggle. 'Or is this just some chance gift to you?'

'Fear not, Your Highness. Your chastity is quite safe from me. The appetites I refer to are not sexual.'

'Blood? Your people really drink the blood of others?'

'As our namesakes do,' he said, 'and I consider myself something of a connoisseur. Royal blood, especially. Although I understand it is in short supply. Your father died not young but not old, yes?'

'That is true.'

'And there was suspicion at that?' He was moving around the back of the chair, she sensed.

'I would not pursue that line of enquiry, Uctebri, lest the guard report your words.'

'Ah yes, the guardsman. Perhaps you could call on him.'

She frowned in the darkness. 'For what purpose?'

'As one ever calls on unknown powers, simply to see if they will come.'

'You have . . . ?'

'He hears nothing, my lady, because I have put a magic on him. He sees nothing, and he hears nothing. Light and darkness, and of these two, darkness has the power. Your brother feared your father was killed. He feared even more being blamed for that death, and therefore no investigation, no suggestion was ever allowed to be raised. Your people's empire is young, its succession untried. Your brother decided that to secure his position he would take drastic measures. He was advised in this by Colonel Maxin – as he then was.'

'Maxin killed my brothers and sisters,' Seda confirmed. There was still no sound from the guard. She knew it was impossible but, in this darkness, with that scratchy voice behind her, she found she could believe Uctebri's claim to magic entirely. 'He only left me alive because, so long as I live, he knows exactly where the threat will come from. If I die, any number of others might rise to be his chief enemy – or all combine against him. My brother feels so secure on his throne that people say he ties himself to it sometimes, lest he slide off in a moment of weakness.'

Uctebri chuckled. 'And your brother has many concubines but, I understand, no children. Not even bastards. Remarkable.'

'He has all of his issue killed at birth,' she said, 'or so I have heard. Bastards have no standing, but even so he will not take the risk of one growing up to be used against him.'

'And no lawful mate. No legitimate issue. A man concerned about his own longevity, should any child grow to manhood. You are his prisoner, but no more than he is his own. Ah, the foolishness of it all.' His voice seemed to be drifting further away. 'Still, you must see why he has, in the end, come to consider my proposal.'

'And what is that?' she asked. 'What is your proposal? You may as well tell me. What am I able to do about it?'

'I have told your brother I can allow him to live far beyond the few years normally allowed to your kinden. Perhaps even for ever? An immortal Emperor of the Wasp-kinden, for ever wise and loved by his subjects. He rather likes the idea, however much he doubts its possibility. He likes it enough to have me try.'

'And should he ever believe he is immortal, I will die that very day,' admitted Seda.

'Ah, alas, your demise would come some moments sooner than his ascension.' He was now speaking right in her ear. 'My people understand blood, for blood is the darkness within our veins. Blood has power. Especially the blood of our kin. Sister and brother, close as close, Your Highness.'

She stiffened as she felt something sharp at her neck, like the razor edge of a tiny blade. She closed her eyes, clenching her fists, and willed it over soon.

There was the slightest arrow of pain, a tiny cut, and then the blade was gone, and for a short while Uctebri remained quiet. Then he said, 'You have quite the sweetest blood I have tasted for some considerable time, great lady.'

'My brother is mad to believe you,' she spat at him. 'You are mad to tempt him with it. After living in fear for eight years I am to be killed on this lunatic's errand?'

'Oh that *is* a shame, Your Highness, that you should believe it impossible.' Uctebri whispered, still at her very shoulder. 'You see, I have my own doubts about your brother's patronage.'

With a start she felt the buckles over her wrists loosen, first one and then the other, and after that he was crouching at her ankles, still speaking. 'I rather suspect that he would be a dangerous man to have around for ever. Or even for much longer. My concern, you see, is for my own kinden and their future, and I cannot say that it would be best served by the Emperor Alvdan. He strikes me as a man neither gracious nor grateful towards those who have helped him ascend to power.'

She was free of the chair now, so at any moment she could leap from it, but she stayed there, transfixed by his words. 'Just what are you saying?'

'Treason,' he explained, and she knew he was standing right before the chair, as if a supplicant. 'Or it would be if I were actually a subject of His Imperial Majesty. You may quibble that I am his prisoner, but ask yourself how long that state of affairs might persist if I did not wish it. No, rather the crown is currently serving me, in requisitioning some piece of desiderata that I have long coveted. What I am proposing is that, whilst I am quite capable of delivering what I promise, the crown of immortality would find a fitter home on another brow than your brother's.'

She did not believe, for a moment, that he could do any such thing. He was a prisoner, and was bargaining for his life with these dreams of longevity. It could even be a trap set by her brother, save that he needed neither excuse nor pretext to have her killed. But possibly, just possibly, it meant that Uctebri the Sarcad represented both an ally and an opportunity.

'I find your words favourable,' she said, and extended her hand into the darkness. When he kissed it, she felt his sharp teeth scratch her skin.

I cannot believe this.

And yet her life had always been bound, not to her own world-view, but that of her brother. If his beliefs led him to the conclusion that she presented a threat, her life would be cut short on the instant. If his beliefs were that she was better off alive, then she would live another day, but only each day at a time. *So why should what I believe matter, in this? When has it ever mattered?*

After Uctebri was done with her she had considered his madness very carefully, while she sat before the glass and repaired her face. This was a whole gaping abyss of madness, like nothing she had ever experienced. Like all the other madness that had so far dominated her wretched life she had to understand it, though. She needed to speak to someone, and that could be no Wasp-kinden. It was not merely a matter of trust, but because her own people could not have advised her, in this. She was beyond all maps.

There was only one name, an old slave of her father's, that she could call upon, so she did so.

He came almost timorously to her room: a lean, grey-skinned man with a long-skulled bald head, his cheeks lined and his head banded with pale, slightly shiny stripes. He always wore such an attitude of melancholy, as though the woes of all the world had come to him. When she was a child he used to make her laugh, when once she had still laughed.

'May I enter, madam?' he asked, his voice quavering. Seda could not suppress a smile at his hesitancy.

'I sent for you, Gjegevey,' she acknowledged, 'so please come in.'

Her prison was a grand one. She had her own chambers decorated with whatever she could get, whatever she could cajole and plead for. There were threadbare tapestries blocking off the blank stone of the walls. She had some plants arranged before the narrow window, in Spider-kinden fashion. Two couches faced one another across a ragged rug of uncertain origin. She had two rooms, this one for receiving guests and, through a doorway guarded only by a hanging cloth, her bedroom. This was the extent of the Empire that Alvdan had left to his sister. His other siblings had fared worse.

The old Woodlouse-kinden stooped to enter her room. He was hunchbacked and inclined forwards, but still he was perilously tall. She knew that his people hailed from the north of the Empire, and that beyond the imperial borders there were said to be whole tribes of them living in giant forests, amongst trees that decayed for ever and yet never fell. She could not imagine there being any other of his kinden than him. How could such stilting awkwardness produce warriors, farmers or anything but vague philosophers?

'You are reckoned a wise man, Gjegevey,' she told him. He waved the compliment off dismissively.

'You are, mmn, kind to say it, madam.'

'You play the doddering old man, Gjegevey, and yet you have been an adviser to emperors since my father's days in power. No slave could survive so, without wisdom.'

He smiled, thin-lipped, never dispelling the eternal sadness that his grey face lent him. 'But there are fools and, mnah, fools, madam.' He pursed his lips appreciatively as she poured him a beaker of wine. 'I know my place, and it is this: that when there is an, mmn, idea in the mind of all my peers, my fellow advisers, that none wish to say, then I speak it. It may then be, mmm, dismantled and matters proceeded with. If I were to ever voice an opinion that none could destroy then no doubt I would be, hrm, killed on the spot. It is a delicate path for a man to walk, but if one's balance is accomplished, then one may tread for many years upon it.'

'Many years,' she agreed, passing him the beaker. He sipped and nodded, and she asked, 'How old are you, old man?'

'I stopped counting at the age of, mnn, one hundred and four, madam.' The wistful smile came back at her wide-eyed expression. 'We are a long-lived people – longer-lived, in any event, than your own. And I am not young, even for my kinden.'

'I want to ask you something. I cannot think of anyone else who might even offer an opinion,' Seda told him, inviting him to sit with a gesture. He perched precariously upon the couch across from her, still sipping at his wine. 'A fair vintage this year,' he murmured, but his eyes were watching her keenly from within their wrinkles.

'On magic, Gjegevey,' she said.

'Mmn . . . Ah.'

'An interesting response. Most would declare, without prompting, that there was no such thing, that it was a non-sense even to raise the matter.'

'Is that what you wish me to say, madam?'

'If I had wished such an opinion,' she said, 'I would not have called you over to speak to me. You are an educated man, and you were educated by your own folk before you ever fell into imperial hands. So tell me about magic.'

'A curious matter, madam,' he said. 'I find myself, mmn, reluctant—'

'Tell me nothing you would not wish repeated. But do not stay from telling me just because such a revelation might not be believed,' she directed. 'Magic, Gjegevey?'

'Ah, well, my own people have uncommon views,' he told her. 'Most uncommon. I will, ahmn, share them with you, but I would not expect you to share them – if you understand – with me.' At her impatient gesture he went on. 'You did not know, I believe, that many of my kinden are Apt. We study, hrm, mechanics and the physical prin-ciples of the world, although in truth we build little, and that must be from wood in the main, metal being hard to come by in our homeland.'

'I did not know that,' she admitted. 'And so, I would guess, that you cannot help me.'

'Ah,' he said, pedantic as a librarian. 'Ah, but yet many of my kinden are *not* Apt and have no gift for machines, and yet follow, hrhm, other paths, the physical principles of the world and so forth and so on, that some might call magic. And so you see, we are in something of a unique position, my kinden. For we are not surging forwards into the, ahm, progress of the world of artifice, nor are we clinging grimly to the darkness of the Days of Lore. We are . . . in balance, I suppose one might say. And these two halves of our culture, they are not two halves at all, for each tries to share its insights with the other, and just occasionally, ahemhem, some gifted man or woman of our kind can understand the both. And so I can confirm to you, within the beliefs and the experiments of my kinden at least, that magic is very real.'

'So why do *we* not believe in it?' she asked. 'If it is so real, prove it to me.' Behind her challenging words, though, excitement was building.

'Ah, but it is an interesting thing, that these things can so seldom be proved. If I were to perform some piece of, hrmf, magic for you, here in this room, you would claim a thousand ways it could have been done. Indeed, those ways might be exceedingly unlikely, but you would cling to them rather than accept the, mmn, the chance that magic, the eternal inexplicable, might be the true agent, and if you were strong enough in yourself, unafraid, unthreatened, here in your own chambers, well perhaps there would be no magic worked at all. It is a subjective force, you see, whereas the physical laws of the artificers are objective. A gear-train will turn without faith, but magic may not. And so, when your people demand, mmn, proof, there is none, but when you have forgotten and dismissed it, then magic creeps back into the gaps where you do not look for it.'

She had a hundred more questions, a thousand, but she bit back on them. It would not do to trust this man too much. 'Tell me, though, Gjegevey,' she said, thinking hard. She must know no more than her brother would expect her to know, but her brother, if Maxin's spies reported this conversation, would expect her to ask about Uctebri. 'Are you aware that, as well as your magic, the Mosquito-kinden are real?'

He regarded her for a second solemnly and raised a hairless brow quizzically. 'The Mosquito-kinden, madam? You must think me very, hmm, credulous.' And yet as he spoke he nodded once, holding her eye.

So, he believes us overheard, though not overseen. 'So some myths are really no more than myths,' she said, feigning disappointment. She had heard that the Spider-kinden had some Art by which they could spin strands of web from their fingers, that they formed these into words and shapes of secret import, while all the time talking about mundane things. She wished she had some similar skill.

'Alas so, madam,' Gjegevey said. 'However, let me alleviate your sorrow at this discovery. Shall I, mmm, show you a little harmless magic?'

Her eyes narrowed. 'You can do this?'

'I would not like to put your hopes too high, and it is some long time since I attempted any such thing. However . . .' He looked down at his hands, grey and long-fingered, and clasped them together, and when he pulled them apart . . . something came with them, something stretching and twisting between his fingers, flashing and flaring with colours.

It is a trick, she thought instantly. *Some chemical or such.* It was pretty enough, for a piece of foolery, and the old man was staring at her so very seriously. She opened her mouth to say something properly polite, and his voice came to her, very clear, without his lips moving or her ears hearing it, the words forming of their own accord in her mind.

The Mosquito your brother keeps, I know of him. Do not trust him. He is very old and wise.

She stared at his face, mouth open. Something lurched inside her. She had the horrible feeling that, in dealing with Uctebri the Sarcad, in coming to an agreement with him, she had stepped slightly out of the world she knew, into a world where things like this could happen.

He is wise, madam, but he is powerful. What he seeks to do is for himself, and not for your brother. Gjegevey's tired old eyes suddenly flashed, throwing briefly into the air the cunning he kept hidden behind them. *And you, Your Highness, may yet find a way to benefit from it. Only do not trust him. Do not trust him unless you have no other choice.*

Nineteen

It was almost true that you could never get a decent spy placed in an Ant city. Ants were fanatically loyal or else they were outcasts with no civic standing. The best any spymaster could do was place a few men in the foreigners' quarter or suborn a few slaves. Even the slaves of the Ants tended to acquire something of their masters' civic pride, though. It seemed incredible to Thalric but, after a generation or so, those born into such captivity seemed to believe that a slave in their city was better than a freeman elsewhere.

He had made good time along the coast to Vek, paying a Collegium sailing master over the odds to catch the wind night and day and thus get him there by the second dawn, so that the rising sun glittered against the great grey sea-wall that sheltered Vek Anchorage as he arrived. He saw the spidery shapes of trebuchets and ballistae positioned upon it, while reports from the delegation had mentioned that there were fire-projectors built into the wall itself.

Behind the sea-wall, his boat was towed the length of the stone-lined canal until it reached the city proper. Docked, and his transport paid for, Thalric made his way through the subdued streets of the foreigners' quarter, following the map he had memorized a tenday earlier. The imperial delegation had made a favourable impression on the Vekken Royal Court, he understood, and a two-storey building had been cleared of a consortium of Beetle importers and assigned for their use. He saw it ahead of him now, the typically spare Ant architecture of flat roof, unadorned walls and small, defensible windows, with a pair of Wasp soldiers standing guard outside. They crossed lances before him, but they could see his race and thus it was just a formality.

'Captain Thalric to see Captain Daklan,' he announced, and they let him through. His name would be familiar, and on being relayed would be translated as *Major* Thalric of the Rekef.

Inside, they had slaves offer him fruit and some brackish local wine. He barely had time to taste either before they came for him.

Captain Daklan of the army, who was also Major Daklan of the Rekef Outlander, was a short, broad-shouldered man a few years Thalric's junior. His dark hair was receding and he had a lined face and a mobile mouth that made him look humorous and easygoing, which was in fact anything but the case. He had entered with two others, a taller Wasp in a uniform tunic who had a writing tablet crooked in his arm, and a strange-looking woman. She must have been close to Thalric's age, and she was a halfbreed, her dark skin swirled in strange patterns of grey and white like water-damaged cloth. The effect was disturbing and intriguing at once.

'Major Thalric,' Daklan said, giving him a cursory salute. 'How is Collegium?'

'Owed a beating,' Thalric said, heartfelt. A slave came in with more wine, some bread and honey, and he topped up his bowl again. 'How do we stand *here*, Major?'

'Well enough. I've heard of some of your own exploits, Thalric,' Daklan said. 'Helleron was a botch, wasn't it?'

Thalric frowned at him, caught with a slice of bread halfway to his mouth. 'Are you authorized to question me about my past operations, Major Daklan?'

Daklan gave him a narrow look. 'Just interested. Word spreads.'

'Then it is your job to stop it doing so, not spread it further,' Thalric said. 'We have enough to concern us here in Vek.' His orders had put him at the head of this operation, but Daklan was obviously an officer who chafed under anyone else's control. Thalric took a chair and sat down, taking his time to finish the bread, smearing it thickly with honey, making Daklan wait. The scribe with the tablet remained impassive but the woman looked very slightly amused at the deliberate delay. Daklan meanwhile shuffled from one foot to the other.

'Major Thalric—'

Thalric, mouth still half-full, held up a hand. 'This honey is very good. Where does it come from?' he asked the halfbreed woman, still chewing.

'Bee-kinden traders bring it from the north, sailing down the coast,' she explained. Her voice was husky for a woman's.

'Naturally,' Thalric acknowledged, wiping his fingers fastidiously. 'Now, Daklan, why not sit down and tell me just who your friends are and exactly how we stand.' At the man's bristling glance he added, 'I'm not your enemy, and if you've heard anything about me it is that my underlings prosper, if they do well by me. I don't care for petty politics within the Empire or within the Rekef. That's why I'm Outlander branch, and I hope you'll be of my mind for as long as you work with me. If you have some prize you hope to see from this operation, then I'll help you towards it if you serve me well. But I have a bad history with uncooperative subordinates.' He smiled, though the thought was painful, 'I'll make that clear to you now.'

Daklan took a moment to think through this, and then sat down, resting an arm on the table. It was not an entirely relaxed position, not for a Wasp whose hands were weapons at need. Thalric decided to overlook it.

'Major Thalric, if we've started badly then I apologize,' Daklan said, not sounding overly contrite. 'This is Lieutenant Haroc, my aide and intelligencer.' Daklan made a vague gesture towards the scribe. 'And this here is our secret weapon. Her name is Lorica.'

Thalric nodded to the halfbreed woman. 'What's your heritage, Lorica?' he asked her.

'My father was a local, sir. My mother was Wasp-kinden. A slave bought from the Spiders, I understand.'

He nodded, digesting this. 'And you can . . . ?' Because there was only one reason that a halfbreed would be here, at this council.

'The Ancestor Art has given me a link to the minds of the Vekken, sir, yes. I can hear them, and speak to them – not that they will acknowledge me.'

'But they are very used to their privacy,' Daklan said. 'And much of what they say is not one to one, but one individual proclaiming to many. And Lorica can hear it, so in negotiations it's of great use to us.'

'I'm sure it is,' Thalric acknowledged. 'So what has been negotiated?'

'The usual preliminaries. A mutual recognition of power. A similarity of aims. They know that we are intent on taking Tark, and they approve. They have had their own designs on Collegium, and we approve. They want Sarn, but they know Sarn and Collegium stand together now, and it irks them.' Daklan smiled. 'May I take it, Major Thalric, that you are here to make the proposal to them?'

'You think they are ready to accept?'

'More than ready. They've not forgotten how Collegium defeated them before.'

'As I understand it,' Thalric noted, 'Collegium simply held them off long enough for Sarnesh forces to reinforce, no?'

He looked to Lorica for a response and she said, 'That is not how they see it, Major. They feel it as a defeat, and keenly so, because Collegium is a place of soft scholars, in their eyes, and they are soldiers.'

'And yet it happened . . .' Thalric frowned, a new thought presenting itself. 'Are we sure that, once this operation commences, these people *will* be able to capture Collegium? It would not serve the Empire if they failed.' He corrected himself. 'It would serve the Empire, by weakening both cities, but it would not serve them as well as breaking Collegium's walls and scattering its people.'

'It is simply a matter of time, Major Thalric, and of preparedness,' Daklan explained. 'The Vekken forces have had a long time to consider that defeat, and learn from it.'

'I suppose even Ants can innovate,' Thalric said, 'given sufficient incentive.'

'You can be sure that they have a plan, sir,' Lorica confirmed. 'Taking Collegium has become their prime civic ambition.' She said it sourly, and he guessed that the civic pride of Vek was something far from her own heart. Halfbreeds were even less welcome amongst Ants than elsewhere.

'Well, then,' Thalric said, 'let us go and make our bid. You can arrange an audience with the Royal Court?'

'Tomorrow evening at the latest,' Daklan confirmed. 'It would not surprise me if they will be marching east in three days' time.'

Oh, it was a difficult enough time to be a Rekef lieutenant. The Fly-kinden te Berro was finding his race's gift for survival becoming strained. Rekef captains tended to have their own followers, their own networks and operations to fall back on. Sergeants and agents were considered just tools, seldom important enough to make the death-lists of those on high. Lieutenants, on the other hand, seemed to have the worst of both worlds.

He had been working in the west-Empire these last few years, even in the borderlands during the preparation for the Lowlands invasion. He had straddled the line, with his diminutive stride, something between Outlander and Inlander. He had hoped to be useful enough to all, and not too vitally useful to any. That line had since become impossible to walk.

All these years he had been General Reiner's man. It had seemed the safest bet. It had got him his lieutenant's bars, some good appointments, neither too dangerous nor too dull. Then things had started going subtly awry. An intelligent man with an inquiring mind, he soon realized that the problem lay within the Rekef itself. The secret service was honing its knives, but its eyes were turned inwards. Two cells of agents that te Berro had worked with had been wiped out by men that should have been their allies. General Reiner was now fighting a war, and that war was not against Lowlanders or Commonwealers but against elements of the Rekef itself.

Then there had been Myna, that gloriously bloody excursion undertaken by Major Thalric, another of Reiner's men. Te Berro's name had been commended in the reports. He had been very proud at the time, but not so long after he had realized that his time was up. The clock of his career in the Rekef had struck, and he was a dead man unless he slid down the pendulum soon and made his goodbyes. He was suddenly a *somebody*, and Reiner's enemies were using his name in pointed ways. He made his researches and his plans, and determined that General Reiner was not in the best position, just now, that there were other men with more promise that a Fly-kinden agent could cling to.

Even before he had been briefing Thalric in the *Cloudfarer*, he had made his contacts, put out tentative feelers. He had got in touch with the agents of General Maxin, Reiner's chief competitor, and offered to defect.

Te Berro was an experienced agent, a useful man, and besides, he had a lot to say about Reiner's people and their operations. He had spent almost a tenday talking to his new friends, until his narrow throat was hoarse with it, and they had written down every word. At the end, knowing that he had nothing left to give, he had cast himself on their mercy.

'Let me serve you,' he had begged Maxin's people. 'Make use of me, for anything.' *But do not cast me away. Do not make of me just one more vanished name from the Rekef books.*

Whether it was this particular mission they had in mind, or whether his breadth of experience recommended him for it, he would never know. A day later they had packed him off to Helleron with his orders, and the implicit understanding that it was his success in this venture that would determine his ultimate longevity.

He had been at pains to show how professional he was. They had told him to recruit agents and he had done so, reviving old contacts with ease to pluck four capable mercenaries from the city's stews and bring them to this private room in a good Fly-kinden taverna. His only problem was in the nature of his instructions and, seeing their hard, professional faces regarding him, he felt that they might tear him apart, or merely laugh at him. They must not laugh, at this. It had been impressed on him that, no matter how bizarre the task seemed, it was in deadly earnest. A great deal hung on his small efforts here.

'These are your orders and I make no apologies for them. They come from the capital itself, from the very palace, so make what you will of them.' Te Berro shrugged, hands spread. 'In Collegium, kept in a certain private collection, there is this item. A box, no more than six inches to a side. Unopenable, or at least you are apparently advised not to open it. A box worked with intricate carvings, vine-patterns and abstract foliage. No better description is provided, but unmistakable, or so they assure me. Given the location and the expertise required this is judged no matter for the regular army. Moreover, by the time you arrive the city may be in some considerable distress, so that your skills may well be tested simply in gaining access. So the Empire calls on you, as freelancers.'

'Mercenaries,' said Gaved. 'Let's wear no flags we're not entitled to.' He was the only Wasp-kinden amongst them and his skill in hunting fugitives had won him an uneasy separation from the Empire, so long as he would always come when they called him. The sting-burn above one eyebrow puckered his expression into a suspicious squint.

'Whatever,' te Berro conceded. 'I have bartered for swift transport to take you to Collegium. The more enterprising gangs of Helleron have realized that the Iron Road is alive and well, so you can be in Collegium in under a tenday.'

'Takes the fun out of the job, but whatever.' The speaker, Kori, had a broad face that held a smile easily. He was Fly-kinden like te Berro, but a barrel-chested, wide-shouldered specimen. He was a treasure-hunter, a raider equally of ruins and of collections such as their current target. Like Gaved and the other two he had a reputation, and no qualms about taking imperial coin.

'Phin?' te Berro asked, and the Moth-kinden woman nodded sullenly. Her name was Eriphinea and she had been part of the Rekef operation in Helleron for some time, an outcast from her own people. What her crime had been she had never disclosed, but she was an assassin by training and more than happy to kill her own kin.

'And you?' te Berro asked of the final hunter. 'It's not quite your line, I realize, but I've read of your skills and achievements. You'd be an asset.'

The man he addressed was Spider-kinden, middle-aged and lean, with a deeply lined face – or that was what te Berro and the others now saw. His eyes narrowed, considering the proposition.

'Master Scylis?' te Berro pressed.

'It sounds diverting,' said Scylis – or Scyla, as she truly was. The name was no more genuine than the face she wore for them, but in dealing with the Empire a masculine visage gave her more of an edge. 'I have some business of my own in that direction, Lieutenant, so while I am there, I may as well help recover your trinket for you.' Scyla appeared elaborately casual but, inside, her mind was working feverishly because the description of the artefact that te Berro had given her rang bells. She now recalled stories and histories she had read decades back when she was still in training: in training as a spy, in training as a face-shifting magician.

Te Berro looked them over. Stocky, blocky Kori in his hardwearing canvas garb, a grappling hook hanging from his belt as the symbol of his trade; Gaved, scarred and lantern-jawed, leanly muscled beneath his long coat; Phin the Moth in her plain robes, grey-skinned and white-eyed, dark hair bound back; and Scylis, an ageless Spider in nondescript traveller's clothes with a rapier at his side.

'For recovery of that box, nine hundred Imperials each, or else the equivalent in Helleron Centrals.' He saw appreciation of that sum register on all their faces save Scylis's. 'I wish you luck,' he concluded. 'If it's worth that much, I suspect you're going to need it.'

'Have you ever seen a sight so splendid?' The speaker was an officer in dark plate-mail, a helmet cupped under her arm, her greying hair stark against skin that gleamed like obsidian. From atop the gatehouse in Vek's wall it was indeed a remarkable sight. Soldiers in perfect order trooped past in their hundreds, shields gleaming on their backs. They marched proudly as if they could march all day, which they could. Some small detachments of cavalry rode up and down this great column on either side, horsemen in light armour who would scout and run messages beyond the reach of the Ants' mind-speech.

Thalric watched critically, his keen eyes seeing strengths, but weaknesses as well. The might of an Ant-kinden army was the steel of its infantry. Taken against their peers they were undoubtedly the best soldiers in the world. That infantry comprised seven out of every ten fighting men of their army, where a Wasp force would have had no more than three of ten as heavy fighters. He watched units of scouts in leather armour pass, and he could guess the use of a scout that could report, silently, as soon as he had spotted his target. He saw also a few squads of Fly-kinden, forty or so men and women in all, but they were the only non-locals in the force.

Now the wall shook slightly as the first of the automotives went through. A few were war-juggernauts, heavily armoured battle machines armed with firethrowers and other anti-infantry weapons, but most were siege automotives for assaulting Collegium's walls. With a harsh metal clattering a pair of orthopters rattled overhead, followed by a handful more. Other than that the air above was clear, and that was what seemed so remarkable. When an imperial army was on the march the sky was alive with men, animals and machines.

Out in the bay the Vekken navy was starting to move as well, the vessels coursing lazily out past the wall. There were big supply barges, iron-plated armourclads packed with soldiers, together with a single metal-hulled flagship twice the length of the others and armed with vast trebuchets. The docks of Collegium were hardly protected by the city's own sea-wall, and so the Vekken hoped for a quick advance by landing their marines on the wharves.

'It's magnificent, Tactician,' Thalric confirmed. Beside him, Daklan nodded appreciatively and added, 'We're looking forward to seeing the army in action.'

The old woman gave them an unfriendly look. 'It has not been decided that you will accompany the army, though Vek thanks you for your assistance and your encouragement.' Her name was Akalia, and she made no secret of the fact that she looked down on Wasps and indeed anyone else not Ant-kinden and native-born to Vek.

'But, Tactician . . .' Daklan said hastily, 'we have our own superiors to satisfy. They will want to know when Collegium has met its deserved fate.'

'Do you doubt us?' Akalia asked. 'Only the armies of Sarn have kept us from crushing that pack of scholars long ago. We have your assurance that your own armies will intervene to ensure Sarn cannot freely aid its allies, so that should be enough for you.'

Daklan exchanged glances with Thalric. A few paces away, Lieutenant Haroc was waiting with his tablet poised to record anything of importance that might be said here. In Thalric's opinion Akalia was right, and there was no need for him to witness firsthand the death of Collegium. Or perhaps it was just that he did not want to see the waste of such a place in the necessary cause of fulfilling the Emperor's ambition. Daklan was keen to be present for the culmination of his work here in Vek, though. He was keen for Thalric to see it too, no doubt as a help towards his own commendation.

'Tactician,' Daklan pressed again, 'imagine yourself in our place. I have no doubt that this mighty force can level the walls of Collegium within days, but if I were to present myself to my superior officers and tell them that I had not seen the fact with my own eyes, they would punish me for failing in my duty, and rightly so.'

Akalia considered this, or rather, Thalric realized, she discussed it with other Ant officers across the city. At last she nodded briefly. 'Very well, your delegation shall accompany us, and it will do your people good to see the Ants of Vek in action.'

Thalric left them then, realizing Daklan would stay to butter up the tactician a little more. It was remarkable how susceptible these people were to the most shallow flattery. He guessed it was because they were used only to absolute sincerity from their own kind. Thalric found himself so easily bored by them, which was an ironic thought. Perhaps he could only feel at ease around those as deceitful as himself.

He came down the stairs within the wall, emerging into its shadow. He was feeling depressed about what must now happen, and he wished that there was some other way, for Collegium was a hard-grown flower that would not flourish again once uprooted. If the Empire could have won its surrender then the world would have been richer.

But he could see how this was needed, for the hotbed of radical ideas in Collegium was just too dangerous to allow to go unchecked.

'Major.' A hoarse whisper. He looked about and saw Lorica lurking against the wall. The halfbreed translator beckoned him over, and he went, cautiously.

'What is it?' he asked her.

'You've a reputation for being good to your subordinates, Major?'

'Only if they do as they're supposed to,' Thalric told her. 'Why? What do you want?'

Lorica smiled. 'I want to give you a warning, Major.'

Thalric felt a familiar feeling rise within him. *What does this remind me of?* His mind returned to Myna, with Rekef orders setting him at the throat of his own people. He felt faintly sick even at the thought. 'Warn me about what?' he asked her.

'Lieutenant Haroc, Major.'

'Haroc? What is there to say about Haroc?'

Almost theatrically, Lorica glanced about her and back up the stairs, making sure they were not observed. 'You should know, sir . . . it means nothing, I'm sure, but you should know: he has been with Major Daklan a very long time, and he's no scribe. His writing is poor, he has others transcribe it instead. He comes from a different branch of the service.'

'What branch is that?' Thalric asked.

'Your guess, Major, but I wouldn't trust him.' She was looking earnestly into his face. 'I'm no fool, Major, and I know that, when the Vekken campaign's done, there'll be no use for me here. Daklan will soon cast me off. He might even throw me to the soldiers here. They'd love to have a halfbreed woman to abuse. You can change that, Major.'

'Yes, I can,' he agreed. He looked at her, trying to see beyond the bloodline. She should not be unattractive, he supposed, but the mixture of her heritage was stamped on every feature, nothing quite as it should be. Still, it did not diminish her usefulness nor, he now supposed, her loyalty.

'I always have uses for good agents, Lorica,' he told her. 'Stay true to me and you'll be rewarded.'

Twenty

Totho was well enough to walk about the next day, but the Wasps kept a close eye on him. He gathered that Drephos was busy with his Colonel-Auxillian duties, whatever they were. The halfbreed artificer seemed to have carved out a strange niche for himself within the imperial army. Totho could see in their faces that the Wasps looked down on him, and yet they deferred to him, and it was not just patronizing. They clearly feared him. Totho did not know yet whether that was fear of the man's own vengeance or what he could call down on them from the higher ranks.

Totho's only real contact had been with Drephos's female assistant. Her name was Kaszaat, and she came from the city of Szar, far to the north, near where the border of the Commonweal had stretched before the Twelve-Year War redrew all the maps in the Empire's favour. She was Bee-kinden, he discovered.

'Are you . . . Drephos's slave?' he asked her, in truth having assumed it.

She gave him a cold look. She was perhaps five years his senior and had not made up her mind about him, whether he was a man or a boy, or to be spoken freely to. 'I am not a slave,' she said sharply. 'I am an artificer.'

'I have not seen many women here . . . I didn't mean . . .'
He had seen precisely two other women and, from the way they had been treated, realized they were being kept as

slaves and for one purpose only. 'Does that mean you're
. . . part of their army?'

'There is no other way,' she confirmed. 'Drephos is
colonel of the Auxillians and I am a sergeant. So I can tell
the common soldiers what to do.'

'Does that work?' he asked, wide-eyed.

She was about to snap at him again, but in the end she
smiled a little, understanding his point. 'Sometimes, but
they do not like it. I am a woman, after all. And inferior of
race they claim. They would have the same problem with
you, for you are mixed-blooded. But you, too, shall have
rank, and so they must obey you, in the last.'

'I . . .' He hung his head. 'I cannot join up with Drephos.
The Wasps are conquerors, tyrants . . . They're evil.'

'No such thing,' she said briskly. 'There is no good, no
evil, only men who do this thing or that thing. And the
Wasps, yes, they do terrible things, things more terrible
than you will have ever witnessed. And they do this because
they can. And yet anyone else who could, they would do
these same things. And so the Wasps are not special, not
evil. They are just the strongest. There will come a day
when it is no longer so, and then terrible things shall be
done back to them, perhaps by those they have conquered.'

'Like your people?' he asked, and her eyes narrowed, all
of a sudden.

'Foolish words!' she told him, but her eyes warned:
dangerous words.

He occupied a sectioned-off area of a tent, with a straw
mattress and a lamp. There were soldiers beyond, always
watching him. Totho might just possibly have crept out,
but then he would be right in the middle of a camp full of
Wasps. If he tried to escape they would kill him.

Salma would have tried, of course, taking to the air
the instant he was outside. He could have seen his way
in the dark and outpaced any Wasp airborne sent after him.
And of course, Salma was dead.

There was a hollow sinking in Totho's chest, each time he remembered that. He had let Salma die. It had been his own idea to come out here, that idea the Ants had so naïvely taken up. It was almost as though he had killed Salma with his own hands.

'I cannot ever join with the Empire,' he replied at last, not emphatically but hopelessly. 'I have lost too much to them.'

Her hand moved so fast he jerked back, expecting to be slapped, but instead she caught his left ear in a pincer grip and dragged his head down to face her. He twisted with pain and surprise, goggling at her foolishly.

'You know nothing,' Kaszaat hissed. 'So your people, who are not even truly your people, may fall to the Wasps. But they are no warriors. Most likely they will surrender, and be spared. My people *fought* the Wasps, year to year, for three years, through all our farms and forts and villages and to the gates of our city of Szar. We are loyal. We would die for our Queen. My father, my mother, uncles, aunts, all gave their lives. Flying into battle. Running into battle. Crossbow, pike and axe. Fight and then fight again. Over and over the Wasps stormed our walls. They must take Szar. It is the gateway to the Commonweal. They did many things. They stood up our fallen on stakes and spears. They poisoned our water. They butchered whole villages to make us surrender. Then they won. Our Queen was stolen away. She is made to be a slave-wife, a concubine to their Emperor. So we became them, and must take their orders and be their soldiers. They rule Szar now, and kill anyone who even speaks against them. They take our men for their armies, and spend our lives like water pissed on dry sand. They cripple us with their taxes. They take everything we have, everything we make or grow. We work in their factories. We make their weapons and armour. We mend their machines. We fight and die for them in places like this

Tark, which we did not even know exists, and so many of us, so many of us shall never see our families and the walls of our beloved city again.' She was staring into his eyes, from just inches away. He looked for tears but saw not one.

'And I work for Drephos, because it is better than not. Because of all the masters in the Empire he is best, because I am an artificer and he treats me as an artificer – not as a woman, not as a slave. So do not tell me how *you* hurt so very badly, and cannot work for the Wasps. Because you know *nothing*, Totho of Collegium. You have no understanding.'

And she released him and spun away, about to leave his little partitioned room then pausing at the door, as if thinking better of it. She did not turn round, though, and he wondered whether she had said more than she meant. He put a hand to his aching ear.

'You're right,' he admitted. 'I suppose I've . . . Well, in Collegium even a halfbreed can train as an artificer. I can't imagine . . . however did Drephos manage it?'

'He once escaped the Empire, he told me once,' she said, turning back to him. 'To where, I do not know, but when he had learned, he came back to them, because . . .'

'Because where else could he truly ply his trade?' Totho realized.

A Fly-kinden messenger put his head about the partition just then, muttering something to Kaszaat.

'He has sent for you,' she told Totho. 'There is something he wishes you to see.'

She followed the Fly outside, and Totho felt he had no option but to follow.

He had clearly lost all track of time, for he had expected early morning and yet it was dusk already, making him wonder how long he had slept, how many hours were missing.

He already felt a traitor to himself and to his friends.

They were treating him here like some honoured guest, instead of Totho the halfbreed. He should have been put in chains, as Che had been.

Or killed, as Salma had been.

The Fly led them to a roughly built gantry that made a tottering tower twenty feet, at least, in height, but close to he saw the joints were solid, the structure thrown up hurriedly but with a kind of stubborn care. He guessed then that it had been Kaszaat's people who had been put to work here. It was not the hands of untrained soldiers that had constructed this.

'Up there.' Pointing, the Fly lifted a little from the ground for emphasis, and craning back Totho could see that there was someone robed and hooded standing at the gantry's narrow apex. Drephos, of course.

Kaszaat had already begun climbing and Totho fell in behind her, letting his Art free to fix his hands as he needed, so that he had no fear of falling. When he was most of the way up there came a flash from far off, but he did not look up or remark on it, concentrating instead on the climb itself until he had reached the top.

There was little room for three of them there and he was uncomfortably aware that he was likely the only one of them who could not fly. Drephos put a steadying hand on him, the metal gauntlet heavy on his shoulder. The other bare hand was already pointing.

'I brought you here to witness some artifice in motion, Totho,' Drephos explained. 'So watch and learn.'

Totho looked up and found the Colonel-Auxillian was pointing towards the city of Tark.

It was now under attack in seemingly the most sedate, detached way possible. High above the city the slow and stately airships swam like ponderous fish. Parts of the city were burning and, as he watched, something blossomed into fiery life above the rooftops, falling like a flaming teardrop until it impacted amongst Tark's streets. He had foreseen this event himself, but never realized how accurate he had been. Like spilling burning oil onto a map, he had said, and here was the map aflame in front of his eyes. Another missile bloomed into vision in the dim air between the zeppelins and the ground, lower this time, and he heard, like the surf of a winter sea, the roar of it striking.

He shivered, clinging there to the gantry-top, because it was a whole new war that was being waged. He felt as though he was watching the years blister and shred, the world reborn in fire into some unimaginable future age. The age of the artificer.

And it was terrible, but it was beautiful. Seeing those drops of flame at such a distance, with no screams, no sight of charred bodies, it was beautiful.

'The airships are a refinement, of course,' Drephos remarked, scholarly. 'The incendiaries are an entirely new plan. I intended to improve on the taking of Maynes, which dragged out over months even after the walls had fallen. Tark will not stand a tenday.'

'Your incendiaries . . .' Totho stammered. 'How . . . ?'

'You tell me, Totho. Let this be a test of your skill. What difficulties do I face?'

'They cannot be accurate from such a height,' Totho almost protested.

'Difficulty the first,' agreed Drephos. 'And a lesser artificer might have persuaded General Alder that accuracy was not necessary.' Another brilliant drop flared and fell. 'And yet it is, and they *are* accurate. So how have I done it, Totho?'

'You could . . . assuming a low wind, such as today . . . you could fix the propellers into the wind, hold the ship as steady as you can . . .' Even as he spoke Totho realized that something in him had responded to the bombing in a way he did not like, something that could consider wholesale destruction as no more than a problem set by a College master.

'Go on,' Drephos murmured and, despite himself, Totho did.

'Then you could attach a telescope – I have seen men use telescopes on the best crossbows, tech-bows and magnetic – to allow them to strike a target at the weapon's utmost range. Something similar . . . with calibrations perhaps, linked to an altimeter?'

'Oh very good.' The metal grasp on Totho's shoulder tightened in an almost paternal squeeze. 'And close enough to how I did it. The calibration required an enormous amount of calculation to get right, what with there being no real opportunity to test it, but my airship captains inform me that they work very well indeed. So, next problem?'

Totho glanced at Kaszaat. She was not looking at Tark, just staring at the rail she held on to. Another flash of fire caught his gaze, and he felt suddenly ill imagining those people he had seen, spoken to, trying to find shelter from such a barrage. The Ants built their houses in stone but still there seemed a great deal on fire down there.

And his traitor mouth continued. 'You would want to control the timing of the missiles' ignition, if you could. A higher ignition would disperse the flame and impact over a greater area; a lower impact would cause more focused damage.' Delivered as though this were some piece of theory for discussion by the class.

'I knew I had read you well. That's excellent thinking, Totho. So solve for me problem the second.'

It isn't as though I'm helping him. He must already have solved it. 'I suppose you could have . . . clockwork fuses or timers?'

'Such as those you were intending to destroy my airships with? And what further problem would you encounter with that?'

Totho still watched, and by some chance three of the airships loosed their charges, that flared into being within seconds of one another before bursting across the city. 'Cost,' he suggested, and Drephos crowed.

'So few artificers even consider it, but we will still have to drop so many incendiaries before Tark is ours. Something cheaper?'

Totho racked his brains, considering all the mechanisms and devices he had learned of. After a moment, Drephos laughed again.

'No matter. You've come far enough to repay my foresight in saving you. You must learn to think simply, where simply will suffice. Tell him then, Kaszaat.'

'Simple cord,' said the Bee-kinden woman. 'Cord of differing lengths—'

'And when it reaches its length, it pulls out a trigger, and ignites the incendiary!' Totho saw clearly, and for a moment was so in love with the elegance of the idea that he did not see a city burning at all, simply a demonstration of artifice and skill. 'That's brilliant—' And he stopped, abruptly shamefaced.

Drephos had not noticed the catch in his voice, but merely watched the airships as they began to make their slow way back to the Wasp camp. 'They will be nearly out of incendiaries now,' the master artificer said. 'And my range-finders do not work well in the dark. I have yet to devise a machine that can see in the dark as well as I can. Do you see my point, though, Totho?'

'Your . . . ?'

'That this is the proper place for you. Here, where the metal meets. You must have guessed the great secret of our artificer's craft, since it comes to all the best minds eventually. *War*, Totho. Think how many inventions and advances come from war. Not just weapons but in all branches of our science. It is war that is the catalyst, that inspires us and whips us on. Artifice feeds off war, Totho. You must see that. And war feeds off artifice, so that each clings to the other, like a great tree growing ever higher and higher. They are the left and right hand of mankind, so as to allow him to climb to the future. War is the future, Totho. War to hone our skills, and our skills to make war.'

'There must be more than that . . .' Totho started. 'At some point war would have to end because the weapons would become . . . so terrible that if anyone used them . . . everyone would die.'

Drephos's laugh came again, no less gaily than before. 'Do you think so? I disagree. There is no weapon so terrible that mankind will not put it to use. On that day that you describe, the end to war would only come after the end of everything else.'

'And that is what you are working towards?' Totho said.

'Look down there, boy!' Drephos's mismatched hands encompassed not only the camp but the fitfully burning city. 'What of that would you save? Take away my machines and they would be at each other's throats with swords and knives instead. Then take away their steel and they would pick up rocks and clubs. There is no saving them: they are merely the fuel for war's engines. Only we, Totho – we are the point, the reason. We, because, alone amongst this destruction, we create, and we create so that they may destroy, so that we may create anew.'

'I cannot join you,' Totho whispered, but something had swelled in his heart, that stopped the words ever being properly heard: something that beat along with Drephos's words, and the pitiless, sterile glory that he spoke of.

'Only think,' Drephos said softly. 'Only think, and watch, and learn. Is it so terrible to be a master of the world – to control, rather than be lost to the current? Come, I will teach you some more that you never learned at the College. I like you, Totho. I see a keen mind, an artificer's mind. That is the most valuable thing in the world, and I would not see it wasted.'

Drephos descended the gantry awkwardly, dark wings

flickering once or twice to keep his balance, and once a hiss of pain as his injured leg locked briefly. Kaszaat had simply floated down on her own, leaving Totho to make the downwards journey rung over rung, wondering if Drephos was humouring him by doing the same, and deciding not.

'The general and his clowns are done for the day,' Drephos observed, making off into the camp with his uneven stride. 'In truth, they are done for the war. All the planning is now here, in my mind. They merely stand slack-jawed and wait for me to hand the city over to them. But I will show you how they play with the toys I have given them. Here!' His gauntleted hand picked out a large tent ahead of them, near the centre of the sprawling camp. The three of them ducked inside, finding the officers' map table and a crudely sketched ground-plan of Tark.

'The battle plan is remarkably simple, as all the best plans are,' Drephos explained to Totho. 'The airships batter a neighbourhood with the incendiaries, and sometimes with targeted explosives if there's a barracks or a similar hard shell to crack. The incendiary material I have devised burns exceptionally hot – enough to fracture stone – but briefly, and so, once an area has been swept clear, the Empire's soldiery can move in without fear of immolation. In this way we secure more and more of the city, a street at a time.'

'But what about the people left behind by the retreat?' Totho asked. 'They cannot be taking everyone with them, surely?'

'You forget the admirable self-possession of the Ant race, Totho. They forget nobody, leave nobody unless they are forced to. Their civilians evict themselves in good military order. And so hundreds, thousands even, will flee their homes, and the remainder of the city becomes more and more crowded. And the results of the next airship bombardment, therefore, become all the more effective.'

Totho stared at the map, seeing red markers for the

latest positions of Ant forces, black and yellow for the heavy hand of the Empire that was creeping in from the sundered wall.

Totho had not slept at all well, yet. The city of Tark had been under the radiant shadow of the airships for four days now. The same savage pattern had been repeated over and over. The Tarkesh formed up against the Wasp advance, the airships drifting in like weather. The Tarkesh then retreated, or they burned. A third of the city was now a blackened ruin, the Wasps' encroachments dark with the ash of their victories.

Totho had not slept well simply because his dreams were troubled with small modifications, innovations and tinkerings, by which this entire process could be made more efficient.

In the day he had a limited run of the camp, because Kaszaat watched over him and there were always guards within shout. He made no attempt to escape, however. He had nowhere to go. *It would be simpler if they killed me*, he thought, but made no attempt to provoke that. Sometimes Drephos would call upon him, and then he would be put to the test, examined on his artifice, or shown again the map table, given some lecture on the order of battle. The very artifice of war, of supply and strategy, in itself held a keen interest for the Colonel-Auxillian.

Drephos rearranged the blocks on the rough sketch of the city, heedless of the damage he was doing to the tactical situation. Everything would have to be moved soon enough to represent the latest advance.

'You see, the Ants don't give ground lightly,' he explained to Totho. 'They fall back and regroup, as good soldiers should, and then they press forward again. And toe-to-toe they're better than the imperial soldiers, make no mistake. That mindlink their Art gives them is a wonderful advantage. Some Wasps have it, true, and the Empire has specialist squads, but not enough to make a difference. Especially as our men at the front are the light airborne, and they can't possibly hold off heavy Ant infantry. So what do we do?'

'I am . . . not a tactician, sir,' said Totho cautiously.

'A good artificer must become one, or at least become familiar with that trade. You must know how your creations are being used, how to best put them to work. Remember, any army officer, given half the chance, will waste any advantage you give him. Kaszaat, explain.'

The Bee-kinden woman glanced at the table, and then looked up at Totho with a bright, challenging look in her eyes. 'When the Ants engage, we target their soldiers directly. In order to use their superior discipline they must stand close, solid formations. Then the airships take them. It is the best time. Our forces are more mobile. Most at least can avoid the fire.'

'Most?' Totho asked weakly.

'What's the matter?' Drephos asked, mocking him. 'I thought these Wasps are your enemies. If their own officers care nothing for their lives, why should we?'

Memories of the bright orange flares, the incendiaries flowering over Tark in all their deadly wonder, lit up Totho's mind, and he shivered.

'Are you going to . . . wipe them all out, destroy Tark?'

Totho had begun to believe it. The fighting had been fierce. The Ants had ambushed the Wasp airborne a dozen times, killing scores of them in each engagement before themselves being wiped out or driven back. The fiery rain over the city continued relentlessly, relieved only by nightfall or when the airships had to return to the gantries for rearming and refuelling.

Though the Ants had tried, they could not adapt to this new warfare. They had been fighting the same set-piece war against their neighbours for centuries. Now the Empire had reinvented the word: 'war' no longer meant what they thought.

'That may be necessary,' Drephos said, evidently none too interested. 'But unless the Tarkesh are very different from the Ants of Maynes, it will not be. You see, they are a pleasingly logical breed, Ant-kinden, and there is an inevitable conclusion bearing down on them: that if they wish to save anything of their people, anything at all, then they must lay down their arms and accept what treatment the Empire gives them. A third of their city is already in ruins, and it will mean years to rebuild what these few days have taken from them. They will realize, eventually, that their destiny as slaves offers them more of a future than their destiny as martyrs. Then they will surrender. Because they are a rational people – an Apt people – they understand the numbers, you see.'

Totho was feeling very cold all over. The logic was icy and unassailable. 'But they are soldiers – every one of them. Surely . . .'

'They are soldiers who cannot fight back. They will eventually realize this. Their civic pride will be heated and cooled, heated and cooled, until it is at last thrust into the waters one time too many, and it breaks. A month to take Maynes?' Drephos clenched his gauntleted hand. 'Now I have given them Tark in a tenday. For that, they will give me whatever they want. Including you.'

'I cannot—'

'You cannot accept it, of course. You would rather be returned to their hands, to be questioned as they call it, or tortured, as I would say. You would rather be a menial slave than an artificer. Morality is not something that has overly plagued me, but I respect it in others. It is your choice, but delay a little before you make it. Once that decision is made you cannot change your mind.'

Twenty-One

There was a rapid hammering on the door of his room and Stenwold pushed himself from his bed and went to answer it. For the first time in a long while he had been doing nothing except stare at the ceiling and brood. No plans, no action or mental juggling of his contacts and agents. He felt depressed, powerless, now that he had finally gone before the Assembly. It was all out of his hands.

He opened the door on Tynisa, who looked agitated. Her sword was already drawn, he saw with a sinking heart.

'What is it?'

'You had better get your gear together,' she told him. 'Arm yourself and go out the back way.'

'Is it the Wasps?'

'No,' she told him. 'Your own people.'

She was off down the stairs, but he bellowed after her, 'What do you mean, my people?' He stomped out, bare-footed, and wearing nothing but a tunic.

'Balkus has just got in,' she told him, halfway down. 'He says there's a squad of Collegium's militia on its way here with one of the Assemblers.'

'Well that's what we're waiting for, isn't it?' Stenwold demanded.

'We want *word* from them, not a whole armed guard. Why would they bring a guard here, if not to arrest you?'

'I won't believe it.'

'Believe it!' she yelled at him. 'You have to leave, now!'

'I won't!' He clenched his fists before him. 'This is my city, and if they will not help me, then there is nothing I can do on my own. I do not value my freedom so very much. Even imprisoned by the Assembly, I may be able to talk them round. I will not leave, Tynisa. But *you* should go – you and Balkus.'

'Not a chance,' she told him. 'Will you at least arm yourself? If things have gone really badly, they may not be coming just to arrest you.'

'I won't believe it,' he said again, but he turned back to his room and took up his baldric, slinging it over his shoulder. The weight of the sword was a comforting burden at his hip.

Balkus and Tynisa were waiting for him below with rapier and nailbow at the ready, as strange a pair of honour guards as he had ever known. He stood between them with hand to sword-hilt and awaited his fate.

Tynisa met them at the door. There were a dozen Collegium guardsmen in chainmail and breastplates, looking uncomfortable and awkward, and in their midst a grey-haired old man in formal robes. After a moment's pause she recognized him as the Speaker for the Assembly, Lineo Thadspar. She supposed this was meant to be an honour, to be personally arrested by the top man.

'What do you want?' she asked him. She had the rapier in her hand but was hidden behind the door. Her tone made the guardsmen tense and she saw a few lay hands on their sword-hilts or mace-hafts.

'Excuse me, what do you want, Master Gownsman Speaker Thadspar?' she corrected, realizing that she had not been helping the situation.

'I had rather hoped to speak with Master Maker, my child,' Thadspar said, seeming utterly unperturbed.

'Then your men can wait in the street, Master Thadspar. I trust that will be agreeable.'

He smiled benignly. 'I can think of no reason why I should need them.' One of his men tugged at his sleeve worriedly but Thadspar waved him away. 'I shall be quite safe. Trust must start somewhere, after all. Now, my child, would you convey me in?'

She stepped back, managing to scabbard her sword without showing the men outside that it had been drawn. Thadspar noticed, though, and raised an eyebrow.

'There have been all manner of affronts done on the streets of Collegium in recent days,' he said mildly. 'Some of which I rather think you were involved in, my dear child. We will have to sort through them at some point. After all, Collegium is a city under the rule of law, yet.'

'Any blood I have shed I can account for,' she told him. 'And don't call me that – I am not your child.'

'I suppose you aren't.' A smile crinkled his face. 'There was some considerable debate, at the time, as to whose child you were. Stenwold was mute on the matter, of course, but as you grew it seemed clear enough to me whose you were. By the time you were twelve years, there were few who recalled Atryssa – but I did, and I knew.'

Caught off-guard, Tynisa paused. 'You knew my mother?'

'I taught her logic and rhetoric for a year. She was an impatient student, a strange trait for a Spider-kinden woman.'

Tynisa would have asked him more, but they had come to the doorway of Stenwold's parlour. Stenwold himself was seated behind the table, waiting with all apparent calm, but Balkus loomed at his shoulder with his nailbow not quite directed at Thadspar.

'Master Maker,' the old man said, and 'Master Thadspar,' Stenwold acknowledged formally, followed by, 'Will you sit?'

Thadspar sat gratefully as Tynisa fetched a jug of wine and a couple of bowls. Balkus was still eyeing the old man suspiciously, as though he might be some kind of assassin in cunning disguise.

Stenwold himself poured the wine. 'I take it you've not come here to discuss next year's curriculum, Master Thadspar.'

Thadspar shook his head. 'You have caused us all a great deal of trouble, Stenwold, and I really rather wish that you had never come back to Collegium to lay this business before us. We will all have a great deal to regret before this is over.'

'So you have come here to do something you regret,' Stenwold suggested. 'And what would that be?'

'You heard Master Bellowern speak, of course,' Thadspar continued.

'Yes, he spoke well.'

'And he reminded us of who we are. He reminded us that Collegium is a centre of thought, of peace, and of law. You would now make us into some desperate mercenary company, springing about the Lowlands in search of a war that is not ours. That was his main point, I think.'

Stenwold nodded, watching him through hooded eyes.

'We have been deliberating ever since, it seems,' the old man said. 'Every member of the Assembly had some contribution to make, and most of it nonsense, of course. Some were for the Wasps, saying that here was a people we could learn from. Some were for you, echoing your assessment of the evils of their Empire. Some others were for you for entirely the wrong reasons, in my view. They were advocating the purity of the Lowlands and the fight against *any* outside influence, malign or beneficial. And some, no doubt, were for the Empire for the wrong reasons as well, because of personal profits to be made, or perhaps even in return for some prior arrangement.'

'Bribes, do you think?'

'I cannot think otherwise. If even a lowly market trader thinks to grease some Assembler's palm to favour his suit, then why not an Empire? That seems to be the way of the world. However, I know a good number of the Assembly who would not take bribes, and I suppose we should hold that up as virtue, in this grimy world.'

'Master Thadspar—'

'Stenwold, I think after your performance today you have earned the right to call me Lineo.'

'Well, then, you came here for a reason, Lineo,' Stenwold said. 'You came here with soldiers, I am told. I am wholly at your disposal.'

Lineo Thadspar sighed. 'So it is come to this at last, has it? Stenwold, you have set in motion a machine that no lever can stop or even slow. More, you have gone about it in an entirely reprehensible manner. You have been agitating amongst the students, you have been brawling in the streets. You have gone out and found an ugly, violent piece of the world, and – hammer and tongs! – you have transplanted it here, where it does not belong.' He grimaced, showing teeth that were white, even and artificial. 'This situation gives me no pleasure, Stenwold, and I regret that I have lived to see it.'

Stenwold nodded, still waiting.

'The Assembly of Collegium concurs with you. It is our duty to resist the Wasp Empire.'

The words, spoken in that tired, dry voice, meant nothing at first. Only as he passed back over them did Stenwold understand what had just been said.

'We have no right to set ourselves up as guardians of the Lowlands,' Thadspar continued, 'but it seems that is what we have become. All through Master Bellowern's speech, his telling us who we were and what we stood for, many of us began to wonder just where he derived his mandate, to limit and define us in such ways. We had slept, I think, for many years, and he was now telling us to turn over and continue slumbering, while meanwhile you were shouting at us to wake up. And in the end, the picture of Collegium that Master Bellowern drew was not entirely to our liking. We have always regarded ourselves as the paragon of the Lowlands, looking down on the Ant-kinden and the others because they lack our moral sensibility. We pride ourselves in how well we treat our poor, our halfbreeds, the disadvantaged of all kinds. And yet we have thereby devised for ourselves a mantle that is heavy with responsibilities. If we truly stand for what we believe is good, the betterment of others, the raising up of the weak and the lowly, then we must take a stand against those with opposing philosophies. In Collegium, we are of a unique calling. There are members from all the Lowlander kinden amongst even our ruling body. Our perspective is broad. We are not the richest of merchants, and yet our inventions keep Helleron's forges busy. We are not great soldiers, and yet we have conquered Sarn with our creed, and won a friend there. We are Collegium, College and Town both, but what are we, if we do not speak out against things we know are wrong?' He shook his head. 'We have therefore informed Master Bellowern that we consider the Empire to have broken the Treaty of Iron by marching on Tark. We were never party to *that* travesty they made the Council of Helleron sign. We have made our stand.'

'But this is marvellous, Lineo,' Stenwold said, but the old man shook his head.

'It is terrible, Stenwold. It means a change that we will never put right. We will look back in future years, if we are so fortunate as to see them, and recognize the moment that you stepped before the Assembly as the beginning of the end of a world, just as the revolution was the end of the reign of the mystics. We have just made history, Stenwold, and I find that I prefer to teach it than to create it.' Thadspar sighed, sipped at the wine that he had not, until that point, touched. 'I should tell you, however, that there are some conditions attached to this.'

'Oh yes?'

'First, as I mentioned to your delightful ward, there has been an embarrassing number of bodies turning up in certain rougher quarters of the city, and I rather think that you yourself may in some way be responsible. If it was you killing Wasp-kinden agents, in self-defence or defence of the city, then all well and good, but our poor guardsmen are going frantic over the matter. I would rather appreciate some clarification in due course.'

'Of course,' Stenwold assured him.

'And second, Stenwold . . . Collegium is going to war. I know that is a very dramatic way of putting it but it is nevertheless true. We are putting ourselves in opposition to the Wasp-kinden and their Empire and, whether it is by words or deeds, that means war. To prosecute this war the Assembly requires a division of labour, and so it has been agreed to appoint certain men and women Masters – War Masters, I suppose, would be the rather unpleasant-sounding term. We have precious few volunteers, and many only willing to put forward the names of others, but, as you have brought this plague down on us, almost everyone is most especially agreed that you should do your fair share. The Assembly wishes to make you a War Master, and if you will not take the post and thus stand by your principles, then I doubt anyone else will.'

'Then I accept, of course,' Stenwold said, 'and I'll do whatever I can. I have some recommendations for others, as well.'

'In good time,' Thadspar said. 'This is quite enough history for one day. My hands are rubbed raw with the making of it.' He drained the bowl, and then poured himself another, looking older now than Stenwold had ever seen him. 'You know,' he said, 'when the Wasp-kinden came to join in the games, I was delighted: a delegation from a savage nation coming to pay its respects. I foresaw Wasp students at the College and Wasp traders in the market. I saw the Lowlands expanded, by a manageable degree, to embrace seven kinden rather than six.' He rubbed at his forehead, stretching the lines furrowed there. 'Why could it not have been as it then appeared, Stenwold? How much easier life would have been.'

Stenwold was about to say something consoling, when they heard the door slam open and both men jumped to their feet, the aged Thadspar just as swift as Stenwold. Into the room came a bundle of visitors, but Tisamon was at their head. He was dragging a girl and Stenwold's heart leapt, to his own great embarrassment, to see it was Arianna. At the rear followed three or four of Thadspar's guardsmen, who had obviously been trying to stop Tisamon barging in, with so little success that he had barely noticed them.

'Tell them!' Tisamon snapped and, whipping out his arm, threw Arianna forwards. He had no doubt intended to cast her at Stenwold's feet, but instead Stenwold found himself stepping forwards to catch her. For a second, the entire room was still, with Arianna trembling against his chest and Thadspar blinking at the Mantis-kinden.

'Master Tisamon of Felyal, if I recall a face,' the old man said. 'Please calm yourselves,' he added, for the benefit of his guards. 'I don't believe anyone is in danger of immediate harm here. Is that the case, Master Tisamon?'

Tisamon nodded shortly. Stenwold glanced from him to Arianna.

'You've come at a good time, Tisamon,' he said. 'The Assembly has agreed to work against the Empire. Collegium is going to war. This is Master Gownsman Thadspar, the Speaker.'

'It's just as well,' Tisamon said darkly. 'Tell them, woman.'

Arianna stood back from Stenwold, not meeting his eyes. 'The Wasps have sent an embassy to Vek,' she said quietly. 'They are encouraging the Vekken to attack Collegium. And it will work, and the Vekken will come.'

Silence fell throughout the room, from the guardsmen hovering in the doorway all the way across to Balkus at the far end of the table.

'Tisamon, is this—?' Stenwold started.

'I found her on the run from her own people,' Tisamon said derisively. 'There's been a falling out, it seems, and right now you're the only thing keeping her from either assassination or execution. So, yes, I think it may well be true. I don't know about Collegium going to war, but for certain the war's coming here.'

To Tisamon it all seemed a colossal waste of time. The War Council of Collegium, it was soon grandly known as, but precious little war seemed to be discussed. There were about forty members of the Assembly present. To the Mantis's amusement they were using a classroom for their meeting, so only one person at a time could take the stand to talk, while the rest sat on the tiered wooden seating and listened like pupils, or more often talked among themselves.

The first matter of business had been whether, after informing the Empire's ambassador that they were now at war, the city should send envoys to the Wasps suing for peace, apparently on behalf of all the Lowlands. Almost half of the men and women there had been for that measure, which had only narrowly been defeated in the vote. They were very fond of such voting in Collegium. The Assemblers themselves were elected by a vote of the city, meaning by anyone of age born there, or who could acquire honorary citizenship. The members of the War Council had similarly been voted for from within the Assembly at large, although it seemed that several people were there, and quite vocal, who had simply been interested enough to come, while others thus voted for were absent.

Stenwold had been hoping for whatever few Ant-kinden belonged to the Assembly to be present now. The duelling master, Kymon of Kes, had made an appearance, as well as a Sarnesh woman. The rest of their race were mostly gone from the city, because Ant-kinden loyalties lay strongest with their own kind. The Tarkesh had gone to help their home city-state, and the Kessen, Kymon excepted, to prepare for when their own time came.

Yet here they were, still choosing roles as though the entire business was some grotesquely disorganized theatrical endeavour. Stenwold himself had become some kind of military commander dealing with the walls. Kymon had been given charge of some of the city's militia. It seemed that anyone who felt himself an expert in war could bag some slice of the city's defences, and any artificer with an invention that could be put to good use was being given whatever was needed to deploy it.

To Tisamon it seemed an utter shambles, but he was only too aware that these were not his people. They had their own way of doing things, and in that way had built Collegium and made it prosper. Until now, at least.

He fidgeted impatiently. Stenwold had wanted him to witness this, and so Tisamon tried to understand what was going on. There seemed to be far too many interminable speeches and not enough actually being decided or done.

Now the talk had finally arrived at what, in his opinion, should have come first.

'We must gather our allies,' Stenwold said firmly, taking his place before the class, 'not only against Vek but against the Empire. Unity or slavery, as I said before. We must impress upon all the Lowlands that their smaller squabbles must be put aside for now, until the greater threat is over.'

'Good luck with that,' someone spoke up, and Stenwold invited the woman to take the podium. She did, looking as though she had not been intending to.

'What I meant is, your pardon, Masters, but we know our neighbours only too well, do we not?' She was some kind of merchant, Tisamon guessed, her bulky frame heavily festooned with jewellery. 'We know them and their prejudices. We of Collegium are broad of mind; can the same be said for many others? The Ants of Kes are no doubt rejoicing to see Tark being invested. The Moth-kinden will not help us because we are Beetles. The Mantids care nothing for anyone save the Spider-kinden, whom they hate. You cannot simply tell these people to stand side by side. It won't work.'

Stenwold took the podium back. 'I thank Madam Waybright for her insight, which has made my point more clearly than I could. The situation of rivalry she describes is the one the Empire is most relying on to win its wars for it. If Vek saw clearly the threat they represented then, as rational human beings, they would not even now be mustering against us.'

There was a rude noise from one of his listeners, and he picked up on it. 'Not *rational*, you say? But they are, Masters. They are strict in their duty and their discipline, as Ant-kinden are, but they are human yet. Had we perhaps made more overtures to them, and not crowed instead about the strength of our walls, then they might not be marching against us now. You see? We are by no means blameless.'

He stared down at his hands, balled them into fists, then looked back up at his audience. 'Let us first speak of those we know will answer our call. No man here can dispute sending messengers to Sarn and Helleron. Helleron especially, for they are closest to the imperial advance.'

There was scattered nodding, and he pressed on.

'I have agents in Sarn already, seeking their help, but they will not know of the threat from Vek, which requires swifter action. Moreover, my agents in Sarn are attempting contact with the Moth-kinden of Dorax, who I know keep a presence in that city. I myself fought alongside the Moths in Helleron, against the Empire's schemes there, and I have some hope that, as they profess wisdom, they will be wise enough to forget, for some short space of time, that they have such grievances against us.'

His audience were less enthusiastic about that but, at the same time, he was asking for no commitment from them, merely unveiling his own existing plans. They could hardly turn down help from outside if it was offered.

'Messengers to Kes, too,' Stenwold continued. 'They have never been our enemies, and they have no love for Vek. More, if they can see past their enmities they will realize that they are the next hurdle the Empire must clear. Their seas will not defend them against a massed aerial assault. A messenger to the island of Kes, surely? What do we stand to lose?'

'The messenger,' someone suggested, but he still had their attention.

'And to the Spiderlands—' he started, but there was a chorus of jeers even at the proposal.

'The Spiderlands are not of the Lowlands, Stenwold,' interrupted another of the College masters, a teacher of rhetoric and political history. 'They will not care and, worse, if we ask for their help they will make us pay for it. If they become involved, they will keep this war going for ever simply for their own amusement. It would suit them well to have us daggers-drawn with our neighbours for generations to come. They would then deal with both sides and only become richer. We cannot invite the Spiderlands to intervene.'

'And besides,' said another, a quiet woman who had surprised everyone by turning up, 'what help could they bring us? Do you think they will field armies for us? They deal in treachery and knives, and we would sully ourselves by inviting that kind of help, even if they could be relied on to turn it solely against the Wasps.'

Stenwold recaptured the podium, hands in the air to

concede the point. 'Very well, no embassy to the Spider-lands.' Then his eyes sought out Tisamon. 'I . . . hesitate to ask this . . . I know the Ants of Sarn have fair relations with their Mantis neighbours, but—'

'But we folk of Felyal are less approachable, is that it?' Tisamon suggested.

There was a murmur of amusement from amongst the War Council. 'Can you deny it?' Stenwold asked.

'Nor would I wish to.' Tisamon strode down the steps until he stood at the front, although he did not seek to take Stenwold's pride of place. 'And, yes, I will be your embassy to my own people, although I can promise nothing. Draw a line from Tark to Collegium, though, and the Felyal lies square in the way. I think my people would be even more unapproachable to the Wasps than to you.'

When the debate was over Tisamon sought out Stenwold again. The Beetle was seated in a spare office of the College, three rooms down from where the War Council had been held, with several pyramids of scrolls stacked ready to hand for the scribes to copy.

'You seem to be keeping them busy,' the Mantis remarked.

Stenwold raised an eyebrow. 'What's on your mind, Tisamon?'

'You should know that I'm taking Tynisa with me.'

'Absolutely out of the question,' Stenwold replied without hesitation.

'She wants to go.'

'That's not the issue.'

'And you cannot stop her.'

'Maybe not,' Stenwold admitted. 'Tisamon, my past record in keeping members of my family from danger is poor, but just think for a moment. I know they are your people, but they will kill her. They will kill her because they'll assume she's Spider-kinden, and if they find out what she *really* is they'll kill her that much quicker. You almost killed her yourself when first you met her.'

'There is a way,' Tisamon said, 'though her stay will not be pleasant, I'm sure. All you say about my people is correct. but they will not kill her out of hand.'

'Tisamon, please—'

'She deserves it, Sten. Her own people, remember. For all they will hate her, and hate me too, no doubt, she deserves to see her father's tribe, if only to reject it.'

Stenwold grimaced. 'I can see this means a lot to you.'

Tisamon smiled bleakly. 'We are not a numerous kinden. If the Wasp army comes to the Felyal, with its machines and its thousands, my people will fight, you may be sure of that. They will kill ten of the enemy for every one of themselves that falls, and yet there will still be more Wasps in the end.'

'You . . . think it will come to that?'

'If the Wasps attack us, it may. I would say they would pay dearly, if only the Empire did not value its own soldiers so cheaply. I can see the Felyal cut and burned, the holds of my people shattered, and for that reason, if no other, I must warn them of their enemy's scale and power. And Tynisa must see them as they are, in case, when this is all over, there is nothing left to see.'

Something in Tisamon's face shocked Stenwold, right then. *Familiarity makes us forget these differences.* Tisamon had been his friend for such a long time that he had become, in Stenwold's mind, almost the tame Mantis, the man half-divorced from his wild people, his ancient, dark heritage. Now, in those angular features, he saw a weight of history that made all Collegium seem like a single turn of the glass, and it was receding, it was fading. It was falling into darkness.

'Yes,' said Stenwold. 'If she will go, I have no right at all to say no. But, Tisamon—'

'Of course,' Tisamon said, a hand on his arm. 'What harm I can prevent, I shall. Whatever harm that is in my power to prevent.'

There was an abrupt rap at the door and Stenwold sighed. 'More war business,' he said heavily. 'You'd better make your preparations.'

Tisamon's hand moved to his friend's shoulder, exerting a brief pressure. 'Be safe, Sten. You've now got what you've been wanting for twenty years. You've got them listening to you, so don't waste your chance.'

Stenwold nodded, opening the door for him, seeing the Beetle woman messenger waiting. He waited until Tisamon had strode out of sight before asking about her business, sure that it was bound to be another burden of the coming conflict.

'Master Maker,' the messenger reported, 'a foreigner, a halfbreed, has come to the city looking for you. She said she has news of Tark.'

'Of Tark?' The wheels were already moving in his mind. 'Her name?'

'Is Skrill, she says, War Master,' the messenger told him, and he felt a shock go through him. The blade that had been held over him, for so long he had almost forgotten it, was suddenly dropping.

'Take me to her,' he ordered. 'Now!'

'And so you left,' Stenwold said heavily, after Skrill had told him her story, with all its wearisome digressions and diversions.

'Weren't my idea. Your man Totho did the plan,' protested the gangly halfbreed sitting across the table from him. She scowled defensively. 'What you think I was gonna do?'

'No, you're right,' Stenwold said. 'It wasn't your fight. You were hired as a scout, not to fight for Tark.'

'Straight up,' Skrill agreed.

'And so . . . ?'

'Once I got far out enough, I stuck around. I thought I'd see the big balloons go on fire like the plan was. Only they never did. Next night I weren't so far off that I couldn't see the city burning.'

'And so they failed,' said Stenwold. He felt physically ill with the strain of it all.

'Looks that way,' Skrill agreed, and then added, 'Sorry,' a little later.

'Hammer and tongs, what have I done?' Stenwold whispered. He heard a sound at the door, the clink of metal, and then Balkus opened it, peering in respectfully.

'Master Maker?' he began.

'A moment,' Stenwold told him, and the big Ant hovered in the doorway as he turned to Skrill again. 'Where are you for now?'

'Well, excuse me, Master Maker, but I hear you got all kind of trouble coming down on you here. I'm for home, which is a wasting long ways from here. This ain't my fight. I'm sorry.'

'I can ask no more of you. I'll see you're paid, and supplied as well.'

She nodded, her narrow face unhappy. 'I liked your boys, Master Maker. Salma especially. He was quite something. I'm sorry it looks like they're gone.'

Stenwold said nothing, and she stood up and slipped out past Balkus.

'Are you . . . all right?' the Ant asked cautiously.

Stenwold shook his head slowly. 'Another two of my own sent to their deaths. Attacking the Wasp camp! What were they thinking?'

'They knew the risks,' Balkus said philosophically. 'I'm sure they knew what they were getting into.'

'But they weren't sent there as soldiers. They were just . . .'

'Spies,' Balkus filled in. 'Better they went as soldiers. That's why I'd never do spy work for Scuto, only strong-arming and the like. Soldiers live rough and die clean, and if they're captured, there's a respect between us men who live with the sword. If they went like soldiers, on the attack, then that's for the best, because spies who get captured don't get any mercy. Everyone hates spies.'

Stenwold shook his head. He wished, fervently wished, that he had a friend left, that he could talk to. Balkus was a loyal man, but blunt and simple of outlook, and Stenwold needed to sit with an old friend, and drink and vent his woes. He had nobody though. Che and Scuto were still north in Sarn. Tisamon, who he could have leant on, was heading east and taking Tynisa with him. He was being left alone here, and the weight of Collegium's woes lay on his shoulders.

'What did you want to tell me?' he asked finally. 'You had a message.'

Balkus nodded. 'Just a little one,' he said with a dour smile. 'They've sighted the Vekken army. Some of your village folk have come in telling of it. Everything's about to spark off around here.'

Greenwise Artector shuffled nervously, finding his lips dry, and aware of a knotting in his stomach. He had come out here in his very finest, his robes embroidered with Spider silk and gold thread, with a jewelled gorget tucked up against his lowest chin. Around him were a dozen others who had done their best to make a good first impression. Some had armour on, either ornately ceremonial or gleamingly functional steel. Many also wore ornamented swords at their belts. They were no soldiers and nobody could mistake them for it. These were the thirteen great Magnates of Helleron who made up its ruling council.

They had chosen for their podium a raised dais in one of the better market places beyond the city proper. It had seen its share of meat, whether the ham of poor actors or the subdued tread of slaves. Now it bore a nobler burden.

Twelve men and one woman, none of them young and none of them slender. The wood had never groaned as much when the slaves were herded across it.

Behind the dais stood their retinues: a segregated rabble of guards and servants. Greenwise glanced back at his own followers, noting in the front rank one in particular.

And they were coming now. A change in the way his fellow magnates stood drew his attention to the front again. Three men approached, a spokesman and two of those common soldiers in their black-and-gold banded armour.

Behind them, off beyond the final tents of the extended city and onto the farmland eastwards, there were rather more than three, of course.

The man flanked by the soldiers was surprisingly young, surely only in his late twenties. Greenwise guessed at first he must be no more than a junior officer or a herald or some such, but there was something in his bearing that gave the lie to that. He had golden-red hair and a bright, open face full of edged smiles. No doubt he was the very darling of the Wasp-kinden womenfolk.

'Are we all assembled?' he enquired, clapping his hands together. Although the city's councillors were raised above him he showed no sign of discomfort. By that demeanour he made it seem that, rather than seeking an audience, he had driven them up there as a wild beast might drive a man up a tree.

Greenwise glanced about him, because there was no spokesman in Helleron's council. All were equal and as such none would trust the role to anyone else. One of his fellows was already stepping forward, though, a corpulent and balding man called Scordrey.

'Young man,' Scordrey said ponderously, 'we are the Magnate Council of the great city of Helleron. Kindly give us the honour of your name and explain the purpose of . . . that presence.' He waved a thick hand in the direction of the army to the east, as though it could all be dismissed so easily.

'My apologies,' said the young man, smiling up at them. 'By the grace of His Imperial Majesty, I am General Malkan of the Imperial Seventh Army, also known as the Winged Furies.' He had an odd way of speaking, self-aware and grinningly apologetic, that Greenwise saw instantly for a device. 'I have come to you with a message and a proposal from my master. A choice, if you will.'

'Now, look here . . . General, is it?' Scordrey started, with the obvious intention of working towards delivering an insult. Greenwise stepped in quickly. 'We are disturbed, General, that you appear to have brought a sizeable force to our gates,' he said. 'You must know that we of Helleron are not drawn into the wars of others.'

General Malkan's smile did not diminish. 'Forgive me, Masters Magnate, but I am unfamiliar with your local customs in that regard. You'll find that we of the Empire tend to carry our own customs with us wherever we go. And, to correct you on one small point, we are not at your gates. You have no gates.'

'Just what do you mean?' Scordrey rumbled.

'Shall I be plain, gentlemen? I am a man of honour and fairness. I pride myself on it. I would not dream of taking advantage of your good natures, just because I have been able to bring twenty-five thousand armed men to within striking distance of your homes without your taking up arms. I will, in the interests of equity, withdraw my men eastwards just as far as they can march before nightfall. Tomorrow, of course, we will return. I trust that will give you sufficient time to prepare yourself for any unpleasantness that might then occur.'

'This is unspeakable!' Scordrey bellowed.

'And yet I have spoken it.' Malkan's smile was now painful to behold.

'Unthinkable!' echoed another of the magnates. 'We have no interest in your wars.'

'We have always traded with your Empire,' added the only female member of the council. She was named Halewright and she had made her fortune in the silk trade. The Spider-kinden always paid better prices to women.

'General!' said Greenwise, loud enough to quiet the rest momentarily. 'You mentioned a choice?'

Malkan gave him a little bow. He was practically dancing with his own cleverness, Greenwise saw sourly. He was a general, he had said. Greenwise did not know whether, in the Empire, that station could be attained by good family alone, or whether Malkan would have genuinely earned that rank in his few years of service. He suspected the latter, unfortunately.

'The Emperor, His Imperial Majesty Alvdan, second of that name, has no wish to force or coerce the great and the good of Helleron,' the general confirmed. 'So he offers you this ultimatum – my error, sirs, this *choice*. When we return tomorrow you shall agree to make Helleron a city of the Empire; you shall make its manufacturing facilities available for the demands of the imperial war effort; you shall place its commercial affairs into the hands of the Consortium of the Honest; you shall submit to imperial governance and an imperial garrison. If all these things are agreed to, without conditions, without the lawyerly quibbles that I am sure you are so fond of, then His Imperial Majesty shall see no reason to disrupt further the everyday business of this admirable city of yours. You magnates yourselves shall form the advisory council to the imperial governor, and you shall be permitted entry into the Consortium of the Honest along with such of your factors as you should wish to so honour. You shall, in short, continue to hold the reins of this city's trade so long as you conform to the requests of the governor and the Emperor.'

The magnates of Helleron stared at him, quite aghast.

Greenwise looked from face to face and saw that no other one of them was going to say it.

'We have heard no choice as yet, General Malkan,' he pointed out.

'Did I forget the other option? What a fool I am,' Malkan said merrily. 'If you wish, of course, you are perfectly entitled to reject these demands and meet us with armed force. I am sure this city can dredge up a fair number of mercenaries and malcontents at short notice. If, however, I am met with a less than friendly reception tomorrow then I have orders to take this city by force. It would make me unhappy if that should come to pass. To assuage my unhappiness I should be forced to ensure that every one of you that I see before me now would be taken and executed in some suitably complex manner. Your families, your business associates, your servants and employees would all then be seized by our slave corps and sent to the most distant corners of the Empire to die in misery and degradation. Before that I would have to see to it that your wives and daughters, even your mothers if still alive, would suffer beneath the bodies of my men, and that your sons were mutilated in the machines of my artificers. I would destroy you so utterly that none would ever dare speak your names. I would remove you from the face of the world, and reshape your city entirely to my wish. Have I made myself clear concerning the precise options you must choose between?'

Greenwise silently watched the three Wasps leave. *Just three*, he thought. There were a dozen men with crossbows in the retinues assembled behind him. They could have stretched General Malkan headlong on the ground and his bodyguards too, but nobody had any illusions about the consequences of that.

He looked around at his own men, who were uncertain and unhappy, and beckoned to a Fly-kinden lad in the fore. Around him the conversation, the inevitable murmur of conversation, had started. He heard one man say, almost apologetically, how he had been trading with the Empire, and they had always settled their accounts admirably.

'A military presence would mean that we would not need to worry about . . .' started Scordrey, and tailed off because they had never had to worry about anything, until General Malkan and his twenty-five thousand.

'The Consortium of the Honest have always seemed sound merchantmen,' said Halewright slowly.

'We would be able to expand our business into eastern markets much more easily,' another added.

Greenwise turned to the Fly-kinden, stooping to speak quietly to him. 'Are you in any doubt,' he said, 'about the response of the Council of Helleron to that general tomorrow?'

The diminutive Fly-kinden always seemed younger than they were, and this one looked barely fourteen, but the world of cynicism in his voice surprised even Greenwise. 'Master Artector, no, sir.'

Greenwise nodded. 'Then you must fly to Collegium, by whatever means you can, and tell the Assembler Stenwold Maker that Helleron has fallen to the Empire, and without a single blow being struck.'

'I am gone, sir.' The Fly-kinden took wing instantly, hovered for a second, and then darted off across the city. Nobody paid him any notice, and there were similar messengers lifting from the ground all around to their masters' orders.

And Greenwise Artector turned his attention back to his peers, and to their slow and patient rationalization of the decision they had already made. The decision he, too, had made, for he was no hero, and he had his own lucrative business to safeguard.

Twenty-Two

Parops's mind, like his city, was on fire. It was a clearing house for a thousand voices: his own calling to his men, keeping them in order; the soldiers with him, relaying their positions from every side; the watchers looking out for the next bomb to fall from the distantly circling airships; the civilians fleeing their homes; the civilians trapped in their homes and who could not escape. Tark was built of stone, but when the bombs exploded overhead they deluged streets in fiery rain that scorched in through shutters and doors, flooded the rooms beyond, and burned and burned. The substance being used was stickier than oil and it clung to walls, to armour and especially to flesh. It did not keep burning for long but even water would not kill it.

Through this constant cacophony the order came to him to fall back immediately. He knew that two score of his soldiers were busy trying to free trapped civilians but he passed the call on, leaden-hearted. Orders were reaching him directly from the Royal Court now, the King's own voice issued them. Even Parops, who thought further and wider than most of his kin, would not dare ignore a royal command.

Fall back to Fourteenth-Twenty-ninth! he instructed his detachment, slinging his shield up on his back. Just then another incendiary charge struck, only two streets away, igniting at barely over roof level, and he felt its impact amongst the men of Officer Juvian, heard the exclamations of fear and horror as it consumed the officer himself and two dozen of his men, scorching the street clean of them. Tears shone bright on Parops's face, but he had his duty. As an Ant-kinden of Tark, he would never shirk it.

His men began falling back in good order. About half of them were regular infantry, properly armed and armoured. The rest were drafted citizens, for every Ant was trained to use a sword from the youngest age. These militia had no shields, but they had no armour to slow them either, and armour proved no protection against this incendiary deluge.

He had lost his tower, almost the first structure to fall. During the evacuation, half of Parops's staff had succumbed to shot or flame, not just soldiers but his messengers, his clerks, his quartermaster. As soon as Parops was clear he had new duties forced on him: to take command of a hastily formed body of men, to oppose the Wasp advance. Yet his progress had been retreat after retreat. He knew that several of the other detachments were advancing slowly and that there must be some grand plan that the Royal Court was working towards, but he himself was not privy to it. He must only hope that it was a good one, so that if he was called upon to give his life for his city, it would not be in vain.

He had always thought himself a bit of a philosopher amongst his people, a man who questioned where others never thought to. Now he discovered that he was, after all, just a soldier. If the orders came to die for Tark, he would do it and gladly. He surprised himself with the thought.

'I've been looking all over for you!'

A blur of motion above, and Parops only just gave the order in time for them to stay their hands before Nero would have been transfixed by a dozen crossbow bolts.

'What are you doing here?' he demanded of the Fly.

The bald man shrugged his shoulders, settling on a

windowsill one floor up. 'Looking for you, you fool! What the blazes are you up to?'

'Obeying orders,' Parops told him shortly. 'You should move back – we're the front line here.'

'Oh, I know that.' Nero wore a padded cuirass, that was an arming jacket meant for a child of twelve, and a short-bow was slung over his shoulder.

'You're no soldier!' Parops insisted. 'You'll get killed if you stay here, probably by us. Go find yourself somewhere safe!'

'You tell me where that might be, and I'll go there,' Nero said.

Parops wanted to argue, but orders came through again at that instant: *Commander Parops. Advance.*

He spared one more upward glance at Nero, then sent this command onwards, watching his men come out from their shelters, from side streets and within buildings. Those armed with shields formed up to the fore, and the rest quickly crowded in behind. Parops took his place, as naturally as any of them. It seemed he had always been trying to find his place in his own city, and it was terrible that only a disaster such as this could show it to him.

But they were now advancing, as ordered, and he knew that the detachments on either side, that were within the reach of his mind, were doing likewise. Ahead he could see a flitting of black and yellow as the Wasps spotted them and began to get into order. They were lightly armoured advance troops, and many were already taking to the air. The first bolts of energy spat towards the front rank of Parops's men, most falling short and fading, and one crackling impotently against a shield.

At a thought relayed from himself the third rank passed their shields up and forward, making a second level of defence against shot from the air. The second rank then levelled crossbows through the gap between the two lines of shields.

Fire at will. Target the airborne, he instructed them, and the crossbows began sounding off with dull clacks. Their range was further than the Wasps' Art-born weapons, and men began to tumble from the sky ahead of them.

'Parops, the airships!' he heard Nero shouting. He had one of his men near the back look up for him, his own range of sky being covered with shields. Two of the lumbering machines were indeed manoeuvring into position above the Ants even as they advanced.

Increase pace. Engage. The Wasps could do one thing or another, he decided. They could drop fire on them or resist their advance on the ground. Anything else and their own men would be forfeited, surely?

The first bomb, plummeting in front of Parops's troop, ignited while still in the air and incinerated two dozen Wasp soldiers. The balance scattered left and right, darting to avoid the spreading flame.

But there was a second airship overhead, and Parops relayed this information to the Court even as his advance continued. The enemy on the ground were falling back, fleeing even, giving up the scorched and blackened streets without a fight.

The next incendiary exploded towards the rear of Parops's formation, amongst those least prepared for it. Ordinary citizens of Tark with swords and crossbows were suddenly ablaze and searing, the hair, skin, clothes of them instantly becoming a torch in human shape – twisting briefly and dying in Parops's mind. His advance continued and in his mind he now heard the yawning silence of a lack of orders. The tacticians of the Royal Court were reeling in shock.

He saw the remainder of Juvian's men under even heavier bombardment, the impact of it cracking their formation, grenades and explosives from on high flinging men – and parts of men – into the air.

He heard the voices of the King's tacticians and for an

awful moment they were talking all together, their orders contradictory: *go forward, go back, spread out, stay tight.* Parops's teeth were grinding helplessly together, his men were looking to him, but he would not relay that babble of panic that was being passed his way.

And then the King's own voice. *Retreat and split up. Retreat!* And he instantly followed the order. His men spread out and began falling back. Wasp soldiers darted in at once, their stings sizzling everywhere, but Parops kept his troops in order, delegating men to turn with crossbows and loose their bolts on the enemy before retiring in good order.

Nothing had been gained. Hundreds had been lost. The battle continued.

The composition of Parops's detachment changed almost hourly. His continuing casualties were balanced by survivors from less resilient squads who came to join him. He picked up a greater number of armed civilians, many now wearing scavenged Ant or even Wasp armour, and even the tail end of a detachment of elites who had been mostly smashed in a fierce day-long engagement in and out of the blackened hulks of houses in the mid-city. They included nailbowmen, men with repeating crossbows, piercers or wasters – and Parops did not know what to do with them.

He had mounted another abortive attack yesterday, only to find the soldiers he was sent to support all dead even as he arrived. Then the airships had loomed and he had ordered a fall-back almost before he heard it directed by the Royal Court. Another street lost. Another battle conceded to the enemy. The numbers of his force might rise and fall, but the ranks of the city's defenders only fell, singly or in their tens and hundreds.

When he allowed himself to think it, Parops had to acknowledge that the situation here was poor, and that he could not see a way out of it. He had to hope that the King and his tacticians had some master plan, something more than a series of futile holding actions.

It was the fifth day, and the surviving population of Tark was packed into the western half of the city, while the Wasps controlled the rest.

Nero was still alive, however. Parops was forever surprised by this, as he had never thought of the man as a fighter. He had turned out to be a true survivor, his Fly-kinden reflexes not one whit dulled by age. Now the ugly little man was again perched on a rooftop, watching the combat that was no longer distant.

The Royal Court itself was under attack, Parops knew that, and his men could not fail to realize it. He wanted to lead them to the Court's aid, but direct orders from the King had countermanded it. As the list of available officers had shortened, so those remaining had become more familiar with their ruler than they would previously ever have imagined. It seemed the ruler of Tark now even knew Parops by name.

I have something I may need of you, the King had told him directly.

'Looks like your man on the right there is losing ground,' Nero called down, though Parops was not sure quite why he bothered. Parops knew exactly the disposition of the officer and his forces, and that Nero was indeed correct.

He sensed another detachment, across the far side of the royal palace, being committed, and saw a change in the movements of the airships as one lazily meandered further in. The outside of the palace was already blackened and burned. The King himself was down below, in the ant tunnels. People had tried the same trick elsewhere in the city, attempting to shelter from the fire, but Wasps had merely approached the tunnel mouths with hand-held firecasters, pouring their searing liquid flame down until everything within, human and insect, was burned or suffocated. Dying in the dark, but not dying alone, because they were dying a death whose agonies were felt by a whole city.

Parops felt his hands begin to shake even at the memory.

They are within the palace. The thought came to him with the voice of one of the King's tacticians, though Parops had the feeling it had not been intended for broadcast. He tensed, getting ready to lead his men forwards. Another firebomb exploded two streets away from the palace walls, no doubt attacking Ant-kinden reinforcements.

Let it be over with, thought Parops, keeping the words to himself. *Let us go in. Let us die. Just let it be over with.* He could not bear to live like this any more.

All officers, report your strengths and position, came the tactician's call.

Here we go, Parops decided, and relayed back that he had eight hundred and sixty-two men under his command, and that he now was at Forty-fifth-Seventh.

And he waited for the call. His tension was clear to his men even if his words had been kept silent from them. They began cocking their crossbows, taking up their shields.

Commander Parops, came the call, and this time it was the King.

Your Majesty, Parops replied, almost breathless with anticipation.

I must issue two commands today that are unthinkable, came the voice of the city's ruler. *I tell you this so that you do not think you have mistaken what you will hear. No monarch of our kind should ever be forced to give such orders.*

Your Majesty? Parops queried uncertainly. *We are all ready to die for you.* With the exception of Nero it was no more than the truth.

I know you are, but I will not have it. Commander Parops,

you are ordered to take those men currently in your command to the west gate, and leave the city by that route. Then break through the Wasp cordon and—

Your Majesty? Parops broke in, agonized. *You cannot mean it.*

These are your orders! snapped the voice in his head. He was seeing shock on the faces of his soldiers now, and realized that the King was making sure that some of them, at least, would hear what they must do. *Break through the cordon. The Wasps are not expecting it. Leave our city. Find somewhere else for yourself and your men. And when the time is right, Parops, whether it be you and your men, or your children or their children, reclaim our city from the invader. That is the task I give to you. That is your order. There is no more than that.*

A great silence had fallen over the city of Tark. It was not any of the normal silences of an Ant city going about its day-to-day business. It was a silence born of loss and shock. In its resounding, thunderous absence one could hear the faint echoes of ten thousand squandered lives.

Half the Royal Court buildings were covered in char, the stone beneath cracked and riven by the sheer heat of the incendiaries. The gates had been staved in during the last reaches of the fighting, splintered by a ram borne by six great Mole Cricket-kinden. The ram-bearers had all died in the attempt, or immediately after it, and their colossal bodies had only just been removed. Not one of their kind was left living in the Wasp army. Every one had given its sad life for the taking of this city.

Before the gates stood two dozen Ant-kinden, still wearing their armour. Their hands and their scabbards were empty. They stood in precise ranks, watching. They were all of the Tarkesh royal staff that remained. It seemed likely that they would be executed, but it was less likely that they cared very much, at this point.

It was Colonel Carvoc who now approached them, with a guard of a hundred light and medium infantry. His face, seeing those defeated men and women, held no sympathy, nor even much triumph. The day did not belong to the Fourth Army, the glorious Barbs. The day belonged to science, and that left a sour taste in the mouth.

He signalled to his men, who remained as wordless as the Ants themselves. One of the light airborne stood forwards and saluted him, carrying a cloth-wrapped lance in his off-hand.

As Carvoc nodded to him the man's wings flared, and he launched into the air, tracing a graceful curve up onto the roof of the Royal Court. There had been no insignia kept there, no emblem or banner to be cast down, so the soldier was forced to hunt across the rooftop, to the gathering silence of the men below, before he found a crack in the stonework that would fit his ambitions. With a decisive gesture he jammed the lance's pointed ferrule in, forcing it down until it was firmly rammed in, lodging deep in the substance of the Tarkesh heart. Then he loosed the cords, and the wind caught the cloth, streaming it out in a billowing gust of black and gold.

The city of Tark had fallen to the Empire after only five days of bombardment.

The Wasps then took control with a firm hand born of long experience. They appointed their deputies amongst the conquered people, giving their orders and leaving the delegation of them to the Ant-kinden mindlink, so that by speaking to a single Ant they could effectively command the whole city. Drephos and General Alder were able to walk through the streets of the conquered city, watching the disarmed inhabitants set to clearing the ruins of their own homes. They worked in silence, and both men felt the shocked quiet that filled the space between their minds: *How could it have come to this?*

'I must confess, I do not trust this silence,' Alder

remarked. He had an honour guard of a dozen sentinels, implacable in their heavy plate armour.

'That is because you do not understand Ant-kinden, General,' Drephos told him.

'And *you* do?'

'I make an effort to know who my machines are to be used against, so that I can better direct that use. They have come to the conclusion for now that to resist the Empire is only to invite greater wrack, so they surrender.'

'They'll rebel in time, then.'

'Every subordinate always does, when given the opportunity,' Drephos said airily, and then qualified it. 'Except for the Bee-kinden. They don't seem to have the knack.'

'And that squad that got away.' Alder shook his head, his plan having not provided for that. Eight hundred men suddenly breaking from the west gate and running his blockade – which, needless to say, had not been expecting any assault and broke almost instantly. He had himself been there to witness the tail end of the fighting and the Ant soldiers making their orderly retreat from their own city, flanked by nailbowmen and heavy crossbows. The pursuing airborne had been cut to pieces, and he had realized that he could not spare more men to go after them just as the Royal Court was being cracked open. So he had reinforced the western perimeter and waited for them to make their vengeful return to attempt to break the siege, but they had not come back. They had simply gone. 'Did they run?' he wondered aloud. 'Did their nerve break, at the end?'

'It was done by design, General. I am sure of that,' Drephos said. 'You've not seen the last of them.'

Alder nodded gloomily. 'Do you believe it about their ruler?' he asked. 'Again, I don't trust it. All these Ants look the same to me.'

'I believe it implicitly, because it is the only way the matter could reasonably be accomplished,' Drephos said.

'While he was King, no matter what order he had just given, his people would still be waiting for his word. They would never lay down their arms. They would always think that some further move could be made in the game.'

'Game?' Alder surveyed the dead Wasp soldiers that were, one by one, being hauled from before the palace gates. 'This is a game for you, is it?'

'For all of us, General, and you can't say you didn't know the stakes. No, the King had to go, and he knew it.'

'So he killed himself, or had his generals kill him,' Alder said tiredly. He had read the report. The first Wasp soldiers had burst into the tunnels beneath the Tarkesh throne room to find their King slain. The tacticians of Tark had been waiting there peaceably, accepting their fate. They had been put to death, of course. There was no sense inviting further trouble by letting them live.

'I've sent a messenger for the Supply corps,' Alder added. 'The administrators, the Auxillian militia, the garrison and the slavers – they'll all be here in a day, perhaps two.'

'And for you the conquest goes on?' Drephos asked him.

'I have orders to move west,' Alder confirmed. 'There are two Fly-kinden communities to take into the Empire but I'm not anticipating a fight there. Then my information is that there is another Ant city-state offshore, and some Mantis savages in the woods that we can root out.'

'I wish you luck with it, General.'

Alder frowned at the halfbreed. 'And where will you be, Colonel-Auxillian, that you're wishing me luck?'

'I have arranged a transfer to the Seventh for myself and my people, General. I have given you the tools to unpick an Ant city, but the Seventh is yet to be thus supplied. They are listed to march on Sarn eventually and, besides, their more immediate destination is of interest to me.'

Alder shrugged, one-shouldered. 'If you have wheedled

such orders, then so be it.' He glowered at the artificer briefly. 'I don't like you, Drephos. You're a worm, and don't think I don't know how much you hate us.'

Within the shadow of his cowl, Drephos smiled thinly. 'But . . . ?'

'But you have accomplished a great deal here,' Alder admitted reluctantly. 'I shall note it in my report.'

'You're too kind,' Drephos said. 'If you do not mind, General, I will return to the camp. I have business to take care of before I bid you a final farewell.'

A few fires were lit, well hidden in hollows to escape unfriendly eyes. They had marched a long way, far enough that they were long out of the reach of the Ant minds left in Tark. Parops and his men had thus no clue as to the fate of their city, but it seemed clear that it would be one of two results: either Tark would bow the knee or it would be overwritten on future maps by some Wasp name, a new town dug out of Tark's ashes.

His men were as dispirited as he had ever seen soldiers be, and he shared their despondency. They were creatures of routine and loyalty, creatures of the city they were born in, conditioned to obedience there, knowing nothing but the will of Tark and its monarch. Now they were alone. Six hundred and seventy-one Tarkesh men and women out in the wilderness, on the road to Merro, with no idea of where they could go or what could be done next.

Between them, they had food for less than a tenday, even if carefully rationed. There were few of them with the ability to live off the land, since it had never been needed, and all of them had left family behind. Parops himself had abandoned his unfaithful mate whom he now missed beyond reason.

There seemed barely any point in continuing, and Parops found the burden of responsibility intolerable. Though ground down with misery, at least his soldiers could look to him for orders. He had never wanted this role. They had made him tower commander simply because he had a good head for logistics and it was considered a position where he could make the least trouble with his unconventional thinking. Now unconventional thoughts were all that could save them, and he could not seem to muster any.

'How are you feeling?' Nero came fluttering down beside him.

Parops gave him a look that was all the answer he needed.

'No sign of any pursuit, anyway,' the Fly said. 'Got other things on their minds, I'll bet. Any thought to what you're going to do next?'

'If I had a free hand,' Parops said flatly, 'I would lead my men back to Tark and attack the Wasp camp.'

'Because that would be suicide,' Nero said.

'Exactly. But my last orders don't allow that, so I have to think of something else.'

'Well I've had a couple of thoughts if you'd like to borrow them,' Nero offered.

'Anything.'

'Get your men to Collegium,' Nero said. 'I've got an influential friend there who's dead set against the Empire. He's on the – what do they call it? The Assembly.'

'Collegium's too far,' Parops countered. 'We cannot travel through most of the Lowlands in the hope that some friend of yours will take in six and a half hundred homeless Ant soldiers. Not to mention that if the Kessen see us tramping down the coast, they'll wipe us out.'

Nero nodded. 'I can see your point there. All right, Parops. I've been a good friend to you – or as good as I could be, yes?'

'For a Fly-kinden, I suppose.'

'High praise there. Right then, I'm going to suggest two courses of action, and you'll not like either of them. All right? One of them is what I'm about to do, and the other one's what you could do. You don't have to, but I'm out of ideas if you don't. First off, I'm going back.'

Parops stared at him. 'You're mad.'

'It's a loyalty thing, Parops. *You* should understand. Not to Tark, I admit: loyalty to my friends. I have always tried to be loyal to my friends. Because I travel a lot and have no certainties, and I never know when I'm going to need a friend, for a bed, for a meal, or to get me out of prison. And Stenwold and me, we go back twenty years.'

'His two agents, or apprentices – the halfbreed and the other one?'

'The Commonwealer, yes. I have to find out what happened to them. Probably they're dead, but I have to know. Because Stenwold would want to know.'

'They'll catch you,' Parops said. 'You'll end up a slave, or dead.'

'They won't catch me,' Nero said, 'because I'm not going skulking in like a thief. I'm just going to walk straight up to them: Nero the famous artist, perhaps you've heard of me? Happened to have a lot of black and yellow paint spare. Maybe you want a portrait. You know the stuff.'

'They will kill you or enslave you,' Parops said firmly.

'You were going to kill me too, at one stage. I'm good at not being killed. I've done it all my life,' Nero said. 'I owe Stenwold, and he would want to know.'

Parops shook his head but found he did not have the strength to argue. 'So what is your suggestion for us? Is it as mad as that one?'

'Madder,' Nero said, giving the first smile anyone there had seen for a long time. In a low voice he explained his plan, and men around them began raising their heads as Parops's mind put out the information.

'We cannot do that. It would be—'

'Suicide?'

'Worse. We'd be slaves. My people would never agree to it,' Parops stated.

'Wouldn't they? There's an Empire coming this way, with armies to spare, and you've got seven-hundred-odd highly trained Ant warriors. So who would turn you away?'

Parops just stared at him.

'Will you at least think about it?' Nero pressed.

There was a moment when Parops did not even see him, when he was concentrating simply on the interchange of ideas flashing between his men, their rapid, silent debate of the concept, of Nero's plan.

'We will attempt it,' said Parops finally. 'What do we have to lose?'

Twenty-Three

He swam in those dark reaches, those vast abyssal reaches that no light had ever touched. No stars there were, and no lamps. There was only the void and the rushing of the wind, or the sucking of the current that sought to draw him downwards.

He had fought free of those depths once already, and now he had no strength for any second struggle. There were monsters in those depths, trawling for ever through the vacant dark with their jaws agape. To fall between the needles of their teeth meant oblivion and surrender.

Not death, because all was death here.

In Collegium it had been the fashion, while he had been resident there, to paint death as a grey-skinned, balding Beetle man in plain robes, perhaps with a doctor's bag but more often an artificer's toolstrip and apron, like the man who came in, at the close of the day, to put out the lamps and still the workings of the machines.

Amongst his own people, death was a swift insect, gleaming black, its wings a blur – too fast to be outrun and too agile to be avoided, the unplumbed void in which he swam was but the depth of a single facet of its darkly jewelled eyes.

Amongst his own people they drew up short poems for a death, and carved its wings into the sides of tombs and cenotaphs, with head down and abdomen tapering towards the sky as it stooped towards its prey. They would paint death's likeness as a shadow in the background, always in the upper right quarter of the scroll, when depicting some hero's or great man's last hours. In plays an actor, clad all in grey, would take the stage bearing a black-lacquered likeness of the insect, which he would make swoop or hover until the time came for it to alight.

He himself could not fly, for his wings would not spark to life. The void hung heavy on him and it clawed at him, howling for him. He swam and struggled and fought, because a second's stillness would see him whisked back to the monsters and the pit. He fought, but knew not why he fought. He had no memories, no thoughts, nothing but this haggard, desperate fight.

And there seemed, for the faintest moment, something hard and distant there in the void, some great presence diminished almost to a star-speck by its separation from him: an insect, but not the death insect. Four glittering wings and eyes that saw everything, all at once: the source of his Art and his tribe; the archetype of his people. He was a spirit lost and that creature was his destination – where he would rejoin the past and be with his ancestors.

And he struck out for it, knowing only that it was right to do so. But it was so far and the void still dragged at him, and that tiny gnat-speck of light was receding and receding.

And then gone.

And with that spark dead, he finally gave up. The fight left him and he swam no more but let the wind catch him and draw him down into darkness.

But there was a light again. Above him there was a light, and it was swelling and growing. A soft light, that was at once pure white and many colours. A light like bright sunlight reflected on a pale wall, and for that reason as he saw it he recalled the sun. He had forgotten that such a thing existed, but now the thought of that once familiar sun surrounded and filled him, and he swam again. He caught the cruel current off-guard and slipped from its grasp. He swam and swam, up towards that lambent ceiling, towards that great spread of light that held back the void.

And he raised his hand to touch it, and his fingers broke the surface.

And he opened his eyes.

For a long time he just stared, trying to make the shapes he saw conform. He was looking upwards and it seemed bright to him but not as bright as it might. The oil lamp in the corner of his vision was burning clearly, not drowned in sunlight. He saw a ceiling, a real ceiling, but it sloped madly away from him.

He wanted to ask what he was doing there, but he could not grasp why he should be anywhere.

Who was he, again? Surely someone had mentioned it.

He reached back, and found his fingers stained with the murk of the void. Was that all? Had he been conceived in that no-place, and vomited forth into this? No, there must be more than that. He felt the weight of the memories penned there inside, and reached for them again.

One by one they fell back into his skull.

He was a child learning his letters, the elderly Grasshopper-kinden woman making their shapes in the earth with her stick, and he copying on his tablet.

He was at the court of the Felipes, competing in foot-races and in the air, learning sword and bow, flirting with the middle daughter of the family. He had gained a reputation already.

News had come of the war. He waited with the two Felipe boys who were his closest companions. The oldest was in his armour. He was going to the front, by choice. None of it seemed real.

The ghost of his father, just the husk of a voice speaking in a darkened room, invisible save for perhaps a wisp of cobwebby substance above the head of the ancient Mantis mystic who was calling the shade forth. It had been so long since he saw the man.

He had been sent to Collegium to study and learn, but he had gone there to escape. The war, the misery, the very thought of that gold and black blot spreading like poison across the map.

The memories began to come more quickly now.

He was duelling with a Spider-kinden girl with fair hair and a sharp tongue, and he beat her because he had been fighting since he was eight, but he knew she was the better—

He was lying awake beside the sleeping daughter of a rich merchant, listening to her father's key turn unexpectedly in the lock—

He was seeing the march of the athletes before the Games with the imperial banner raised high at the rear—

He was watching the great grey bulk of the *Sky Without*, trying to work out why it didn't just fall—

He was leaping from a flying machine to fight the Wasps, and someone nearly putting a crossbow bolt between his shoulder blades by mistake—

He was running through Helleron after a betrayal, trying to keep hold of a Beetle girl with dyed white hair—

Faster and faster the memories came. He was shaking. They poured into him like acid.

More betrayal – he was fighting Wasp soldiers, while her cousin looked on—

He was taken. He was chained—

Her – and she danced for them, for the slaves and the slavers – and they were all free in that moment—

He was breaking free from the cell – the faces of his friends—

His name—

He was Salme Dien, Prince Minor of the Dragonfly Commonweal, but in the Lowlands they called him Salma,

331

because they were all barbarians and could not speak properly.

But the memories were not done with him.

He was coming to Tark with Skrill and Totho, all their names suddenly coming to him at last.

He was making fierce love to Basila in the close and almost windowless room of the tower.

The bloody devastation of the siege, and he was duelling with a Wasp officer while the city burned and the wall fell.

He was attacking the Wasp camp. He was grappling with a Wasp soldier. The blade went into his stomach, all the way up to the hilt.

All the way up to the hilt.

And the pain of it came back to him, and he relived that moment, the searing, burning agony, and the knowledge, the sure *knowledge* that it had killed him. All the way up to the hilt, and the point emerging through his back. His own blade driving into the man, almost as an afterthought because, what did it matter when his world had stopped? The pain of it flooded through him, and he gasped and arched back, and then he really was living it again because the wound across his belly tore open stitch after stitch, and he screamed—

And the void rushed up for him again, the void that had only been waiting in the shadows all this time. The hungry void reached out for him.

Someone plunged their hands into his wound and for a second the pain, which could never get worse, was much, much worse.

And then it was gone. There was something searing and burning through him, but it was distant, like thunder over far hills. And there was light.

He opened his eyes again, but it was still too bright after so long in darkness. He could not look at it.

The same hands were held to his wound, their warmth leaching into him, and he felt – it could be nothing else –

the edges of the wound knit again, the blood cease to spill across his skin, and he felt the ruptured organs find peace and start to heal once more.

It was Ancestor Art, but he had never known anything like it before. He forced his eyes open, forced them to stare into the heart of the sun.

He thought he had gone blind, but it was just the sight of her. She stood over him like stained glass and crystal and glowed with her own pure light, and stared into his face with featureless, unreadable white eyes.

He was weeping, but he did not know it, looking up into the face of the woman who had once been Grief in Chains, and then Aagen's Joy, and so many others in her time.

After they had lain together, they slept awhile. Partway through the night, she had woken and made to go, and Totho had caught her arm and held her there. For a moment he did not speak and she waited patiently, sitting on the edge of the folding bed they had given him in exchange for his straw mattress: the two artificers in darkness, the halfbreed and the Bee.

He had known, when she had come to him, that it was wrong, but she had been so forthright, so open. No wiles, no subtlety, merely an artificer's practical seduction. Kaszaat, in stained coveralls, with smears of oil still on her hands, unbuckling her toolstrip belt in this partitioned space of tent they had given him.

And no woman before had ever offered herself to him. Seeing her there, inexplicably there, he had cursed his memories. He had cursed Cheerwell Maker for running off with Achaeos, and then he reached out for what he could have.

Now, too dark for him to see her deep brown skin, the curves of her body that was lean and compact with the workaday strength of her trade, he asked her, 'Did Drephos make you do this?'

'I am no slave,' she said. 'Drephos does not *make* me.'

'But you are a soldier. You have a rank. He is your . . . superior, or whatever it is you would say.' He did not hold his breath against her answer. He had no illusions.

'He made a suggestion,' she said after a pause, 'but that was not the first time the thought came to me. When one placed above you asks of you something, to go to a man you are interested in already, it is by command? Or it is of free will?' She made to leave again but he held her still.

'Wait,' he said, and then, 'Please.' She settled again, and then he felt her hand brush its way up his arm, trace his shoulder and then rest against his cheek.

He wanted to ask *Why?* but he could not disentangle his motive for the question. Self-pity – or was he seeking a compliment? The latter was another thing his life had been mostly empty of. Totho the halfbreed! Who would have thought it would take capture and imprisonment to bring this fulfilment to him?

He had not realized, until he grappled with her, that he was no longer the awkward, slightly gangling boy he had been at the College. He had not noticed how he had filled out, broad across the shoulders and strong. His Ant blood had made him strong, just as his Beetle-kinden side had allowed him to endure. Kaszaat had seemed small within his arms.

She settled down beside him again and he felt the warmth of her back pressing into his chest and belly. It struck him, and the thought surprised him, that she must feel even more alone than he did. Her city was so far, she had said, and she did not expect she would see it again. She must have been alone now for a long time, with only Wasps and Drephos for company. Perhaps in coming to him she was reaching out for the only contact that might not be a betrayal.

And if Totho accepted Drephos's hand, that proffered gauntlet, would this become a betrayal for her, as if he was no more than a Wasp in truth?

He put an arm about her, his breath catching as it brushed beneath her breasts.

'Once woken, I cannot sleep,' she informed him, although she mumbled it sleepily enough. 'You must talk to me, amuse me.'

So he talked to her. He told her of Collegium, and the Great College. He told her of the workshops there, and the Masters in their white robes. He spoke of the Prowess Forum, and he even spoke of Stenwold Maker, Tynisa and the Mantis Weaponsmaster, Tisamon. Of Cheerwell Maker he spoke not one word.

She left him before dawn, dressing herself in darkness. She explained that she had duties to attend to but he suspected that she did not want their liaison to be common knowledge. She feared the Wasps, more than anything, and she did not want them to think that she was free for the taking.

He dressed himself as the sun rose, in his artificer's leathers, only hesitating as he began to buckle on the toolstrip that Drephos had returned to him. He was no artificer here, not yet. He was a prisoner of the Empire. If he emerged from this tent with his tools ready for use, would that suggest he had committed himself to the betrayal they were urging on him?

For it would be a betrayal of the cruellest kind. They were asking him to design weapons, as had been his dream throughout College. At Collegium his creations would have been graded and discarded. Anything made for the Wasps would be used.

They would be used on his own people.

But they would be *used*.

Something visceral rose up in him, thrilling at the very thought of the work: to undertake the work for the sake of the work, and never ask who it might be for.

When he did emerge there was a messenger waiting. It was strange to see Fly-kinden running errands just as they did back home. Amidst the Wasp army there was a whole cadre of them buzzing backwards and forwards wearing the gold and black of the imperial standard.

'A message for you from the Colonel-Auxillian.' The Fly was very young, perhaps only fifteen or so. 'He'd like to see you in his tent.'

A chill went through Totho as he thought, *Perhaps he will force a choice from me now, and if I refuse, as I must, surely I must, then I will be a prisoner indeed, and they will extract from me everything I know about the Lowlands and Collegium.*

He went nonetheless, because he had no choice and no options.

He found Drephos lying back on the very chair that Totho himself had been secured to, when he first regained consciousness after the raid. It was a complex thing, that chair, and now it moved smoothly, the panels of the back pushing in and out with metal fingers, steam venting from the sides. Drephos had explained earlier how he suffered from particular back pains, so had been forced to devise his own relief. His first love remained the artifice of war but he was not slow in attending to his own comforts.

Kaszaat waited at the rear of the tent but did not meet Totho's gaze.

Drephos opened one eye, and made a signal to the Fly, who darted outside again. The chair made a particularly complex sound and he groaned.

'Bear with me,' he said. 'I am particularly out of sorts this morning.'

The man was not well, and indeed was not entirely whole. He limped when he walked and the arm he kept hidden behind metal must be injured in some way. Totho wondered which of his own inventions had turned on him, or whether this had been the work of his imperial masters.

'You have a visitor,' Drephos announced, although

Totho could barely hear him over the chair and he had to repeat himself.

'A visitor?' Totho looked blank.

Drephos signalled to Kaszaat, who stepped over to the chair and drew the pressure from the boiler, sending steam venting out in hot clouds that forced Totho to stand well back. From that swiftly dispersing mist, Drephos finally emerged, pulling his hood up to shadow his blemished features.

'But look, here he is now.' The master artificer pointed, and Totho followed his finger to see a small figure being hustled in by a pair of Wasp soldiers. It was a Fly-kinden man, bald and lumpy-faced.

'Nero!' Totho exclaimed, noticing the Fly was not bound but neither was he free, for the soldiers were keeping a very close eye on him. He smiled grimly as he saw Totho, but there were mottled bruises across one side of his face and one eye was swollen almost shut.

'Morning to you,' he said. 'And I'm glad to see you. Apparently you may be in a position to vouch for me.'

Drephos interrupted. 'Who *is* this man, Totho?'

'He's a friend,' Totho began, and then realized that this was imprecise. 'He's an old friend of . . . a College Master who was a good friend to me.' Sudden inspiration struck. 'He's an artist, in fact, and I think he's quite well known. We met in Tark,' he added lamely.

'You *think* he's a quite a well-known one?' Drephos sounded amused. 'How well known can he be, if you only think it?'

'I don't know about art,' said Totho stubbornly. 'And I don't know why he's here, either.' He turned to the Fly-kinden. 'Were you captured in the assault?'

'Not exactly.' Nero's wan smile remained. 'I came here to find out what had happened to you, as a matter of fact.'

'Something which the soldiers who captured him did not quite understand,' Drephos explained. 'However, he kept repeating your name and eventually word came through to me.'

'Since when the quality of hospitality around here has definitely improved,' Nero put in, rubbing his wrists for emphasis. 'Well, here's a decent sight. You came through without a scratch, it seems.'

'Without more than a lump,' Totho confirmed. 'But why did you come here? They could easily have killed you.'

Nero shrugged off the risks of it, but the gesture was unconvincing. He had not wanted to come, Totho could sense, yet he had been forced to, and by what other than his own conscience? 'My old friend Sten, you see, we go way back,' he said, sounding almost embarrassed about it. 'We've been through a lot, him and me, what with the College and all.' He glanced at Drephos. 'Stop me if this is getting too sentimental or unmilitary for you.'

'Say all you want, Master Nero. Knowledge is never wasted,' said the Colonel-Auxillian.

'Well then, there was a caper that Stenwold and the others went in for, a long time ago, pretty much the last – the second to last, really – that we did together back then. It's history now, but it involved these fellows.' He jerked a thumb back at the Wasp soldiers nearby. 'And it was too hot for me. I bugged out of there quick enough, told him it wasn't for me. I missed the fun, and then things went sour. Lost one good friend, and another died soon after. And I never forgot how I left them to it, because I didn't like the odds. I know people think my kinden are a spineless bunch, and mostly they're right, but it still didn't sit well. Then, when you and the lad there turned up in Tark, I told myself I'd look after you, keep you on track. And a right job I made of that, too. So here I am still trying to put things right.'

'You didn't have to come,' Totho reproved him. 'I'm . . . holding out fine.' He took a deep breath. 'And Salma is . . . well, he didn't make it.'

Nero looked up at Drephos. 'Shall I say it, or is it going to get me shot?'

'Say all you wish,' Drephos told him. 'I have only refrained from mentioning it because I assumed you would prefer to break the news yourself.'

Nero nodded, his mere expression making it plain he did not trust Drephos one inch.

'The thing is, lad,' he said, 'Salma's still here. He made it, all right – though only just. He's alive and here in the camp.'

Salma was asleep when Totho came to see him. Nero and the others kept their distance, even Drephos, as he went to kneel at his friend's bed.

Only a very slight rise and fall of Salma's chest betrayed the life within him. His once-golden skin was now leaden pale, his cheeks sunken and his lips shrivelled like an old man's. It was hard to see here the laughing, smiling fighter, the nobleman from a far foreign land, who had once brightened the austere halls of the Great College.

'I'm so sorry,' Totho murmured quietly, so as not to wake him. He was acutely aware of all the others nearby, two hundred laid out in this tent alone. All casualties of the war, in one way or another. Most were Wasps, but there were others too: Bee-kinden like Kaszaat, ruddy-skinned Ants, even a couple of Fly messengers who had not flown swiftly enough. Many there, he saw, carried terrible burns caused by the incendiaries, and the Wasp officers' lack of concern for their own men.

Totho returned to Drephos and the others. There was a woman now standing there with them, a severe-looking Wasp-kinden who was scowling at the master artificer.

'Totho,' Drephos said, 'this gentle lady is Norsa, the Eldest of Mercy's Daughters in this camp. Norsa, this young man was a companion of the Commonwealer lying over there.'

Norsa turned a stern eye on Totho, who tried to face up to it. 'He will live,' she said flatly. 'He will recover, now, although at first only *she* kept him with us at all.' She pointed and Totho followed her extended finger to see a robed woman passing along the line of beds, bearing a basin of water. Her eyes were white, and her skin glowed through a rainbow of colours. Totho had never seen her before but, from Salma's words, he knew who this must be.

'So he found her, at last,' he murmured. 'Thank you for aiding him, lady. I realize he is your enemy.'

'I have no enemies,' Norsa replied sharply. 'Mercy's Daughters give aid to whoever they will, however the Empire may take issue with us. Suffice to say that the imperial army knows your friend is here.'

Totho's stomach lurched with the thought and he turned to Drephos. 'Then you must have known!'

Totho caught a sardonic smile from under the hood. 'Norsa here holds me to blame for the injuries done to many of these men. I hear no news from her Daughters, and I heard none from any other quarter. Just be grateful that Master Nero himself thought to look here.'

'But when he recovers,' Totho said, 'they'll . . .'

Drephos finished for him grimly. 'Take him? Question him? Torture him and then enslave or kill him? Yes, they will, for that is their way. A waste of healing, in my opinion.'

'I do not even recognize that sentiment,' Norsa snapped at him, 'although if you were the patient I might make an exception, Colonel-Auxillian.'

Totho glanced from Drephos to Nero, and then back across the room to the unconscious Salma, and realized that some part of his mind had a plan and a decision already prepared for him.

'Colonel Drephos,' he said, although he had found his thought already. 'I need to speak with you. I think you know what about.'

*

Salma drifted in and out of wakefulness. Sometimes he recalled who he was, where he was, and sometimes he did not, perhaps blessedly. He existed in a blurred greyness that was pulled taut between the light of Grief in Chains and the darkness of the void that was still hungry for him.

On one occasion he opened his eyes and found himself looking straight into the face of the man on the next bed. He was a Wasp-kinden with his head bandaged low so as to cover one eye, the wrappings crisp and clean, having just been changed. When he saw Salma looking at him, the other man grinned weakly.

'You,' he said, in a voice just loud enough for Salma to hear, 'are so cursed lucky.'

Salma tried to make a sound, but nothing audible came out. In truth he did not feel so very lucky.

'You should be dead,' the soldier continued, his whispering voice obviously the best he could manage. 'I saw you drop. You were fighting like a maniac but someone got you, and you fell, and that should have been the end of you. I was behind. I saw the point come clean through you, you bastard. She came for you, though, and you were dead, even then, but she came for you as though she knew what had been going on. She ran out and lit the place up and put her hands on you. And you stopped bleeding, right there and then.' He coughed, a wretched, scratchy sound. 'And she's been with you every day, using her Art to keep you alive. I don't know what you mean to her but you're a lucky bastard, so you are.'

Salma tried to speak again, and this time a distant croak emerged, quieter even than the wounded soldier's. 'I came here for her.'

The man's one eye studied him for a minute, before he said, 'Well she's certainly worth that.'

'Salma?'

He had been asleep, or at least drifting somewhere else,

but there was a new voice now, and it carried his name to him.

'Salma, you have to wake up now.'

It was not *her* voice and he did not want to wake up. When he had opened his eyes last, she had been standing there, staring at him. Expression was hard to fathom from those dancing colours, from those eyes, but his heart had leapt painfully just to see her.

He had found her. She had found him. In this mad, war-struck world, they had found each other.

She had sat down at the edge of his bed and, although it was a flimsy folding piece that should have tipped immediately, she barely moved it, making him doubt his senses. He had reached out, though, and she had taken his cold hand in both her warm ones, warm like the sun on a summer's day.

'Why are you here?' she had asked him. 'Why did you come?'

'I couldn't stay away, knowing that you were here,' was his whisper. 'Aagen . . . I spoke to Aagen.'

'Did you—?'

'No. We parted on good terms.' His voice was strengthening, as though healing energies were passing through her hands and into him. Perhaps they were, either by Ancestor Art or by plain magic.

'You should not have come.'

The ghost of his old smile appeared briefly. 'Why?'

'You are hurt. You were already in the hands of death when I found you. All I have done since barely kept you with me.'

'But I am with you.' He was staring at her face. She was beautiful and it was not merely the ordinary human beauty of Tynisa. She was Butterfly-kinden and they were beautiful with the timeless perfection of a sunset or a spring day. He yearned for her even though she was already there right beside him.

She had shaken her head. 'Then I myself have done this to you. I never intended this.'

'No—' But something had come to mind, something the Moth-kinden man had said, or that Che had claimed on his behalf. 'They said . . . did you enchant me? Is this . . . what I feel now, just glamour?'

Her hand had touched his face and he felt a warmth flooding there, and also peace and safety. 'I put a spell on you,' she had confirmed. 'We were penned there as slaves, before the great machines of the Wasps, and I saw your face and knew you were a good man. I needed the help of a good man so I put a spell on you, that still held strong when we were taken by their devices to the city of the slaves. But then you needed help yourself, and I took my spell away. I have no spell on you now.'

Staring at her, he had not known what to think, because his heart still reached for her and he wanted to touch her, to stroke that rainbow skin.

'Then I must love you,' he had said in wonderment, and realized that all this while some part of him had believed Che's claim that it was no more than a spell that made him act this way. Now he discovered it was him, nothing but his own heart.

'Salma! Please wake up!'

He snapped from the reverie – and saw she was not here. Instead there was a man standing by his bed, and it took Salma rather too long to recognize his face.

'Totho . . . ?'

'Yes, Salma, it's me.'

'What . . . what in the world are you wearing?'

Salma registered the tunic Totho now wore, black, and edged with strips of black and gold. It was crossed with two leather belts, one for his tools and the other serving as a baldric for his sword.

'Listen to me, Salma, because we don't have much time,'

said Totho. 'You have to listen and understand what I'm saying. I'm getting you out.'

'Out?'

'Out of here. Because the girl might have saved your life, but you're still not safe. In fact if you stay here you'll certainly die. The Wasps are just waiting until you're well enough to interrogate.' Totho gave a brief bark of laughter in which the strain he was under emerged clear enough. 'What a world! They're waiting for your wound to heal so they can tear you apart. You know how much they hate your kinden. Half of their men here fought in your Twelve-Year War.'

'So be it,' said Salma tiredly.

'No! *Not* so be it! Aren't you listening, Salma? I've bought you out. There's a man, an artificer here, and he wants my service, and he says he can get you out of here.'

'You trust him?'

'Enough for this, at least. You remember Nero? Nero's going with you. He'll look after you until you're strong again.'

'I *can't* leave, Totho.'

Totho glowered at him. 'It's the girl? That dancing girl? Listen, Salma, they are going to *kill* you, as slowly as they can. Would she want that? Because she won't be able to stop them. This nursing order of hers might get to choose whose wounds it heals, but it's got no such say over the fit and well. I've paid the asking price, Salma. I've sold myself just to buy you life.'

'No!' The effort racked Salma with pain, and he knew that everyone down the length of the hospital tent would be staring. 'Totho, no—'

'This way you survive, and live free, and I . . . live too. It's not so bad. I won't be a slave, quite. And who knows what could happen?' *And it's not as if I had much to go back to,* Totho added to himself. *And this way, Che won't detest*

344

*me any more than she already does, because at least I won't
have left you to die, Salma.*

'Totho, you can't do this,' Salma said urgently, feeling
himself worn out just by the effort of this conversation. 'I'm
not worth your doing this—'

'Shut up!' Totho snapped, shocking him into silence.
'Shut up, Salma, because I have already done this. I have
put on their colours and apprenticed myself to these monsters, and I have done it for you, and if you tell me now
that you're not worth it, just *what* have I done all that for?'
His fists were tightly clenched and Salma saw him anew
then: not the shy, awkward youth always tagging along
behind Che, but the man that same youth had forged into.

It came for all of us, Salma thought. *We are all grown now.
Che, when the Wasps enslaved her and put her before their
torture machines. Tynisa when she discovered her birthright.
To me on the point of a sword . . . and to Totho here and now.
We have put childish things behind us, and look at the world
we have grown into.*

There were streaks of moisture on Totho's face but he
was putting on an angry mask to hide the despair.

*I have no right to play the martyr here, nor have I the
strength.*

'I'm sorry, Totho,' he said softly. 'I hope you find that
you have done the right thing.'

Totho had assumed that the Imperial Fourth Army would
be splitting, some to be led west by General Alder and
others staying to secure the half-ruined city of Tark. Garrison duty was beneath the Barbs, though, and a new force
had come tramping out of the desert following its Scorpion
guides. A garrison force, Totho understood, was different
to a field army. It contained more auxillians, for one, usually
around one man in two, and many of the Wasp-kinden
included were veterans who had now earned an easier

assignment than open battle. All this he learned from Kaszaat. The garrison was commanded by a governor who was usually also a colonel in the imperial army. Running a garrison was less prestigious than commanding a field army, but having a whole city at one's disposal, she explained, was an unparalleled opportunity for acquiring both power and wealth. More than one general had willingly taken the demotion.

General Alder was not that kind of soldier, however. He was already busy organizing the Fourth to move westwards. Expecting no answer, Totho had enquired of Drephos, and was surprised when the artificer had told him that the plan was very simple.

'The Fly-kinden settlements of Egel and Merro will be invited to avail themselves of imperial protection. There seems little doubt, given the timorous and pragmatic character of the race, that they will accept. Then the army will proceed on to the island city-state, Kes.'

Totho knew that the garrison force had resupplied the Fourth with more than just rations and ammunition. Two dozen battle helicopters had been assembled on the airfield by the camp, with four hulking carrier helicopters – monstrously clumsy machines that could each hold three hundred men in the open cage of its belly. 'These are just to draw out Kes's airpower,' he guessed.

'Quite,' Drephos confirmed. 'We have a few soldiers who could fly all the way from the mainland, but most of them would tire halfway and drop into the sea. So we will ship them over in droves, to die over Kes and to destroy its flying machines and its riding insects and whatever else shall come against them. Then the airships will drop incendiaries upon the Kessen navy, which I believe is formidable, and drop rockbreaker explosives on its sea-wall and its artillery. After that, the city itself will burn and we will begin landing our forces. I estimate that it will take General Alder three times as long to take Kes as it did to take Tark,

346

partly because the city is naturally more defensible, and partly because I shall not be there with him.'

Totho nodded. That seemed only reasonable.

'We shall shortly be embarking on our own journey, however,' Drephos continued, 'so we shall see none of it. I have faith that General Alder will prove his usual mixture of military efficiency and imaginative bankruptcy.' He went striding with his uneven gait back towards his tent. 'First, though, I have something I would like your opinion on, Totho.'

Totho hurried after him. He was forever surprised to find himself so free just to run around. It seemed the black and yellow that he wore was a shield against persecution, for all that he earned plenty of disparaging looks from the Wasps.

In his tent, Drephos had assembled a little workshop of the most delicate tools Totho had ever seen. There was a grinder for machining metal, a casting ladle and a set of wax moulds, and everything he needed to replace parts and help maintain his devices in the field. Turning, Drephos had something in his hands, long and wrapped in dark cloth, and for once he seemed almost hesitant.

'You are a gifted artificer, Totho,' he said. 'That is, of course, why I plucked you from captivity.'

'At least you hope I am, sir,' Totho said.

'I do not recognize *hope*. Instead I calculate. I gather information,' said Drephos. 'You had on your person certain devices which I guessed were of your own invention, and schematics to incorporate them into a larger plan. A plan that you have never, I would guess, been able to undertake.'

Totho stared at the bundle in his arms and found himself abruptly short of breath. 'Never . . .' he began, then his mouth was sand-dry, all of a sudden. 'What have you done?'

'While you were with your friend, yesterday, and while Kaszaat was making the arrangements for his liberation, I had time to myself, the first spare hour I have had since this siege began. Time weighs heavily on my hands and I hate to be idle, so I took out your plans and did what I could. The results are . . . imperfect. The facilities here are limited. However, I hope it meets with your approval.'

'My . . . ? My approval?' Totho stared into the man's blotched face. 'But, Colonel-Auxillian . . . ?'

'No rank, please, not amongst my cadre at least,' said Drephos. A hard look came into his eyes as they flicked towards the tent-flap. 'Let those outside bandy such words about between themselves. Though we wear their colours we are none of theirs. Indeed, we are greater than them. We are artificers. Call me "Master" if you wish it, as you would your teachers at Collegium, but we are the elite here, and we are above their petty grades and distinctions. And I seek your approval, Totho, because it is your invention – therefore your triumph.'

His bare hand whipped the cloth away, and there lay Totho's long-held dream. It was rough, as Drephos said. His air battery possessed a coarse grip now, and a long tube extended from it. Much of what he had planned was absent, because he had not included it on his drawings, but it was still there in his head, and the prototype could be improved.

'Does it work?' he asked, and Drephos nodded.

'You'll have the chance to test it, of course, and to improve on it. As I said, we have a journey to make. We are going to Helleron, Totho.' He held the device out, and Totho took it, wonderingly.

'Helleron, Master Drephos?'

Drephos was already striding past him. 'Where else should an artificer go when he wishes to work?'

'But Helleron is—'

'Ours, Totho.' Drephos was now outside, and Totho hurried to join him.

'How?'

'General Alder is about to move west along the coast, but I had word yesterday that General Malkan and the Seventh Army were moving on Helleron. They should be there by now. By the time we arrive the city shall fly the imperial flag. Imagine it, Totho! The industrial might of Helleron, all the forges, the foundries, the factories! What could we not do there?' He stopped, abruptly rueful. 'If I were pureblood Wasp-kinden I would have them make me governor. Perhaps I shall anyway. Perhaps Malkan can be prevailed upon. Still, we must do what we can with what we are given.'

And they stepped out again into sight of the airfield and found it had received a visitor, in that short space of time. The most beautiful flying machine Totho had ever seen was roosting in one corner, well away from the gross bulk of the heliopters. An open lattice of light wooden struts, with twin propellers and immaculately folded wings, it was such a work of light and shadow that it seemed hardly there at all, even in broad daylight, He saw Kaszaat inside it already, checking the clockwork engine that crouched aft. She was wearing heavy robes, he saw, despite the warmth of the day.

'We're going to fly to Helleron in that?' he asked Drephos.

'I want to waste as little time travelling as possible. Whatever I have here, I will have sent on. Helleron will have to provide in the meantime, and no doubt it shall do so splendidly.' He reached the flier and ran his metal hand along the imaginary line that would define its flank. 'My beautiful *Cloudfarer*, back at last from running the errands of others. She has been ill-treated, but that shall change, for none can fly her as I can.' He was actually smiling, genuine gladness making his face seem something quite alien. Totho realized that all his other smiles had been just in mockery or pretence.

'We shall be in Helleron in two days, three at the most. Do you believe that?'

'It hardly seems possible, Master Drephos.'

And the smiled broadened, and lost its warmth. 'But we are artificers, Totho. We shall make it possible.'

Twenty-Four

In the chasm of silence throughout the stateroom Sperra clasped her hands together to stop herself fidgeting. They were all looking at her, and most of all the stern-faced woman who was enthroned in their centre, so that Sperra felt very small and frightened.

This was all Scuto's fault and she should never have agreed to it. They had been waiting days now for an audience. Plius the milliner had been doing his best but the Queen and much of her court had left the city of Sarn on the very day that Scuto had met with him. Instead, he had secured a brief interview with some minor official at the Royal Court, and that was when the problem had occurred.

'We've waited long enough,' had been Scuto's position. 'I'll go and see this fellow, whoever he is, and we'll squeeze a better audience out of him and pull ourselves up the chain. By the time the Queen's back, we'll be camping out on her doorstep.'

'Scuto,' Plius had said, 'you might want to rethink yourself.' There had been an odd, slightly amused expression on his face.

'What's wrong with the plan?' Scuto had challenged him.

'The plan, nothing. The planner, on the other hand . . .'

Scuto had folded his hook-studded arms. 'What?'

'Listen to me,' Plius had said. 'I've done my level best to

get you this far, and you are not going to ruin it by going in there and being . . . well how can I put this, Scuto? By being all ugly and spiny.'

'Now, you listen here. I know I ain't any picture, but—'

'Scuto, you've been working where? In the slums of Helleron? And why's that? I know you're a decent grade of artificer,' Plius said. 'So why not get in with the magnates, the propertied classes? No, you're not that kind of fellow, Scuto. And this isn't some Helleron mining baron here, this is the Queen of Sarn. And she won't want to see *you* because, let's face it, no sane person would. And she won't want to see me either, because as an Ant late of Tseni stock I'm barely welcome even in the foreigners' quarter, never mind how things're supposed to have changed round here. So what's your move, Scuto?'

And then he and Scuto had turned and looked at Sperra, but she had refused. She had flat-out refused, protested, complained and objected and, at the end of the day, she had found herself going to meet with a dismissive Ant officer who had sneered down at her because she was a Fly and a foreigner. The next day there had been a better officer who had been sympathetic, but unhelpful, and then there had been a commander who seemed to have something to do with the Royal Court, but very little time. Then there had been a smiling woman, who Sperra had later discovered was a commander involved in counterintelligence, and who had suspected her of being a spy, although spying for whom, Sperra never found out. In any event their conversation had been manipulated so carefully that Sperra realized that she had learned nothing new at all and told everything that she knew, just about.

And then the next day half a dozen soldiers had marched her to the Royal Court, which was where she had been trying to get to all along, but at that moment decided she would rather avoid. She had spent two hours waiting to talk to a serious-faced Ant-kinden who was one of the Queen's tacticians, therefore the highest of the high amongst the city-states. She spoke to him for a full ten minutes, but he seemed not in the least interested in what she had to say. Instead, he quizzed her about the assassination attempt on the Queen.

That was the first she had heard about it, and her surprise must have seemed genuine enough because he did not question her for long. She understood that, whilst the Queen was out hunting with her bodyguards and some of her court, there had been a surprise encounter with a pair of Vekken crossbowmen. The would-be assassins had died resisting capture and understandably everyone was concerned to know what this was all about.

At around that same time the news had come to Sarn that the Vekken were indeed on the march, but that Collegium was their objective. Since then Sarn had been in an uproar, mustering its armies and breaking out its automotives, ready to defend the alliance the city-state had made with its Beetle neighbours.

And the day after, Sperra had been sent for by the Queen. So here she was, a woman of three foot nine inches, in plain and darned clothes, appearing before the Royal Court of Sarn.

Ant-kinden did not need hundreds of spectators to witness their deeds of state. Mind-to-mind, the whole city could be allowed to hear what words were said when it was deemed necessary. There were merely fifteen men and women in that room, gathered around one long table. The height of the table itself demanded that a servant fetch a stool for Sperra to stand on, just so she could be seen.

In the middle of the table's far end sat the Queen herself, and there could be no doubt of her identity. Since their increased dealings with other kinden, the Sarnesh had fully learned the use of symbols and insignia to distinguish themselves. The Queen of Sarn was the one with the crown sitting in the gilded chair, Sperra had divined. Other than that she looked just like any other Ant woman, her unwelcoming features in no way dissimilar from any of her kin. The Sarnesh were a dark-haired, brown-skinned people, but the severe set of their faces was that of Ant-kinden everywhere.

The others around the table were mostly more of the same: tacticians of Sarn, the governing body from among whom, and by whom, the ruling monarch was selected. They were men and women wearing armour, even here, and none of them with a smile to offer her. The grim drabness of this array was broken by a pair of darker Beetle-kinden, both women, whose garments were dreary by Collegium standards but looked positively flamboyant here. They had clearly been around Ant-kinden too long and had borrowed their paucity of expression.

The silence had stretched on for a while now, and Sperra realized that she should probably be saying something. 'Your Majesty,' she began, and her voice was shaking. 'I have come here with a very urgent message from Collegium.'

'We have received messengers from Collegium only yesterday,' noted one of the tacticians. 'We understand that you have been petitioning for this audience for almost a tenday. It seems news has outstripped you.'

'Yes and no, masters,' Sperra said wretchedly. 'I am come from Master Stenwold Maker of the Great College to bring a warning of war.'

'War has come,' a female tactician intervened, almost dismissively. 'We will go to the aid of Collegium and fight the Vekken. You should have no concern over that.'

Sperra coughed, finding her voice dry up. 'There is a greater war than that, ah, Your Majesty and esteemed masters.' She had no idea of the proper address for an entire Royal Court at once, or even whether there was one. 'You must have heard of the Wasp-kinden and their Empire, as they call it.'

That took them a little longer to consider, and Sperra sensed the thoughts flashing between them. At last it was one of the Beetles that spoke up, after a nod of assent from the Queen.

'The city-state of Sarn is not without resources,' she said. 'We have of course had intelligence of these people, and know that they are currently investing Tark, the result of which we await keenly. The extent of their ambitions is unknown but we are considering what threat they may pose to us, should they continue to expand and their ambitions remain unchecked.'

'Then could I say something about what I have seen, and about Master Maker, and Scuto, who's the person that recruited me.' She was aware she was now jumbling it all horribly. 'Only I can tell you what the Wasps want. They're planning to take over all of the Lowlands. They'll do it city by city, you see, and they hope that everyone will just sit back and let them. On account of . . . it's like you said, just then. Tark is under attack and, well, nobody really likes Tark. Anyway. I certainly don't.' She looked from face to face. One of the Beetles nodded, but there was precious little encouragement to be found anywhere else.

'Anyway,' she went on, 'so Tark goes down soon enough, because these Wasps, they've done Ant-kinden cities before. There's a place called Maynes east of Helleron, and they took that years ago, and they're much better at it now. Tark is gone, let's say, and who cares? Only next they head for . . .' She wanted to say Merro, her own home, but that would not have strengthened her case. 'For Kes, say. They get some boats and lay siege to the place. And of course, I suppose you don't get on well with the Kessen either?' She looked at them, and they gave her no response, but this time she waited until a smile twitched the Queen's lips, who said, 'The enmity between the cities of our kinden is well documented, Fly-woman. Make your case.'

'Well it's made, then, Your Majesty,' Sperra said,

'because we're all sitting about glaring at each other, and waving flags every time one of our neighbours gets got, until here they are, at the gates of Sarn, say, and who do we call upon?'

'We are Sarn,' said one of the tacticians shortly. 'Therefore we fight our own wars.'

'But what if they had ten times as many soldiers, and better weapons, and they can fly, and just shoot you down with their bare hands? What then? What if they're too big for any one city to take on? That's what Master Maker keeps saying: there are lots of them, more than any one city could fight.'

A silence. Again she looked from face to face. 'Please, do you not believe me?' she asked.

The Queen shared a moment's glance with some of her advisers. 'Your words are understood, but we have more immediate concerns. You would not wish us, I am sure, to have us rush to the aid of Tark while the Vekken besiege Collegium. We shall remember your words, however. Once our present business with Vek is resolved, then we shall speak further. We see some merit in what you say.'

And that, Sperra realized, was the extent of her royal audience.

'Something's wrong, isn't it?' Che said.

Achaeos sent her a sidelong glance, but then admitted, 'I have not been sleeping well, recently.'

She allowed herself a smile. 'Am I to blame for that?'

'When I do sleep, I have dreams . . . uncertain ones.'

She was about to give a flippant answer but thought better of it. 'I suppose dreams are important to your people.'

'They are, and I think . . . I fear I know where these dreams come from. You remember the Darakyon, and what we both saw there?'

356

'I could never forget.' Although she had tried. It had been after he helped rescue her from the Wasp slave cells in Myna: they had been heading for Helleron and in the way was the knotted little forest of the Darakyon. A Mantis-kinden name, she knew, but no Mantis-kinden lived there now. However, Achaeos had told her that those who had once called the place their home, centuries before, had never left. All nonsense, of course. All superstitious foolishness from a people of hermits and mystics, except that one night he and Tisamon had taken her into that wood and shown her. It had been Achaeos reaching out to her, over the barrier that separated their peoples' worldviews.

And she had *seen*. In glimpses, perhaps, and for that she was thankful, but she had caught sight of what still dwelled between the twisted trunks of the Darakyon, in all its hideous, tortured glory, and her world had cracked, and let in something new.

They were almost at the nameless little gambling den by the river, and there were plenty of shadows that could have hidden anything. She allowed her eyes to pierce through them, calling on her Art, but the shiver did not leave her. 'Are *they* . . . have they come here?' she asked him.

'No. They could not, I think. But these dreams . . . they are calling to me. I do not know why, but I will in time.'

They paused at the door, nerving themselves. The Arcanum, mostly in the person of Gaff, the stocky little man of unknown kinden, had not been forthcoming. They had met with him several times, and sometimes with the Mantis Scelae as well, but received only evasion. Now word had come for them. They had been summoned by the Arcanum. Something had changed.

'Do you think it could be a trap?' she asked, and he nodded glumly. 'But these are *your* people,' she protested.

'The Arcanum are not *my* people,' he said. 'They are the political arm of the Skryres, and they have no one leader

357

but serve many in Dorax and Tharn. Much of the time, it is said, they run the personal errands of their masters, who do not always agree. The Arcanum has turned on its own people before now, so why not against us?'

'What option do we have?' she asked him.

'None – but be ready for trouble.'

They saw Gaff as soon as they entered, in the midst of some game of chance. He noticed them too and made hurried apologies to his fellows, leaving money on the table and hurrying over to them.

'You took your time,' he grumbled. 'Come right with me, sir and lady. There's serious talk to be done.'

He took them into a backroom, heading past the place's owner, and then into a room beyond, that must have been part of the building adjoining. It was dark in there, a single lamp burning on a desk, and it was crowded. When Gaff had taken his place there was quite a gathering of people ranged there facing them. Che felt her hand drift towards her sword-hilt now, though it would now be of no use.

Half a dozen were Mantis-kinden. Scelae was seated on one corner of the desk while the rest stood, lean and hard men and women watching the newcomers suspiciously. One bore a sword-and-circle pin that recalled Tisamon's: a Weaponsmaster, then, who would be more than sufficient on her own to blot them out if she chose. Of the other kinden four were Flies, and three of those were robed and cowled like their masters. One was a Commonwealer Dragonfly. There were only three Moths in all that number. An elderly woman sat on the corner of the desk across from Scelae and a young man stood behind her, in an arming jacket with a bandolier of throwing blades strapped across it. Central behind the desk, though, was the obvious cause of all this assembly. He was thin and balding and, taken alone, his grey, hollow face and white eyes did not suggest any great pre-eminence, but Che could almost feel the crackle of authority surrounding him.

'Master Achaeos of Tharn,' the man said in a precise voice. 'Mistress Cheerwell Maker of Collegium. Your recent careers have been quite remarkable. Do you know what we are?'

Che and Achaeos exchanged glances. 'You represent the Arcanum, Master,' Achaeos said.

'We are the Arcanum, as far as its presence in Sarn now stands,' the balding Moth explained. 'This is all of us.'

The two newcomers exchanged glances, while the assembled agents watched them implacably.

'You have come to us spreading warnings about the Wasp Empire. We are, of course, aware of those savages and we have no wish to involve ourselves in their affairs, either as allies or enemies. Still less do we wish to jump to the call of some Beetle magnate. We have retreated from the ugly and violent world that your kinden have built, and we would prefer that to be the end of it.'

And why get everyone together just to tell us this? Che felt her sword-hand twitch, but fought the instinct down. There was more to be said. There had to be.

'You have no great reputation on Tharn, Achaeos,' the Moth spymaster said, 'and few friends either. Your choice of paramour has seen to that. We have no obligation to you, still less to this woman.'

A missed chance for an insult. Che found that she was holding her breath, and let it out carefully.

'Master, I await your "however",' said Achaeos. 'Or are all of these to be our assassins?'

Scelae smiled at that, and Che saw that she must have been murderess for the Arcanum in her day. The spymaster glanced at her, and then back.

'We had considered it, but we would not have called you to a meeting for the purpose.' The shadow of humour twitched over his face. 'We are not so procedural as that. So here is our "however", Achaeos. Matters have changed. Information has come to us that has forced our hand, however much we resent it. I have spoken, by our traditional ways, to the Skryres of Dorax. They have called me home to take fuller counsel with them. They have said that we must do what can be done, against these Wasp-kinden – for now, until the circumstances change.'

'Thank you!' Che burst out, and he fixed her with a withering stare.

'Do not presume,' he told her, 'that we have any new affection for you or your people. It is the mere chance of our times that we stand together. No more.'

'Chance or fate,' she said, and knew immediately that she had overstepped the mark. For a second there was a tension about Scelae that was likely to become an attack, but the spymaster was not so much angry as shaken.

'Fate,' he echoed. 'Fate's weave has been unclear . . .' His composure seeped back and he shook his head. 'Scelae shall lead the Arcanum here when I am gone, and what can be done shall be done. Tharn has no armies to set against this Empire, but there is little that eyes that know no darkness cannot see. For the moment, while this lasts, those eyes shall be used to see in your cause.'

It was two days before they discovered what had changed the Arcanum's mind. Achaeos and Che came back from an errand in the foreigners' quarter to find a sense of utter despair. Scuto was sitting at the large table in the common room of the taverna they were staying at, with his papers strewn utterly unheeded all about it, and some even on the floor. Beside him was Sperra, looking so ashen that Che thought at first her wounds must have reopened. She was trembling, and if Scuto had been less thorny it seemed she would have been clinging to him. Behind them both, Plius sat like a dead weight in a chair. He had a pipe out and was vainly trying to light it, but his hands shook so much that the little steel lighter kept going out.

'What's happened?' Che asked, and then a terrible

thought struck her. 'Uncle Stenwold! The Vekken? Is he—?'

'No,' Scuto said hoarsely. His eyes were red, she saw, and his hands had clasped each other close enough to pinprick bloodspots with his own spines, the only time she had ever seen him injure himself. 'No fresh news from Collegium.' In truth news from Collegium was coming in all the time. All day great slow-moving rail automotives had been dragging themselves in at the depot with all those residents of Collegium who could not stay to defend their home. Che had expected people from all walks of life, and indeed there were many foreigners, whose lives in the College City had been measured in a few years only, but most of the refugees were children. They arrived with small bags of food, books, a writing kit and spare clothes, and with little notes telling the Sarnesh who they were. The Queen of Sarn was honouring her city's ally in its time of need. With typical efficiency the homeless and the lost, all these displaced children, were found lodgings amongst the Ant families of the city.

But today at the depot had come a messenger from a different direction.

'Sperra, she . . .' Scuto took a deep breath and tried to stop his voice shaking. 'She was at the palace, so she heard it right there, when the Queen did. Helleron has fallen.'

Che gaped at him. 'Helleron fallen?'

'A Wasp army turned up at their doorstep. Not even the ones fighting Tark, but a whole other army. They've put the city under martial law and commandeered the foundries. Helleron is now part of the Empire.'

'Hammer and tongs,' whispered Che. She glanced at Achaeos. His face was closed, expressionless, and she knew he would be thinking of his own mountain city, Helleron's close neighbour.

'They knew,' he said. 'This is the information the Arcanum had received. This is the threat to our people that has made them join us.' He bared his teeth, abruptly feral. 'We warned them that the Wasps would come. An army on the wing, come to Tharn to finish what your people started. The final end of the Days of Lore.'

'That isn't fair,' Che protested.

'Nothing's fair,' he said bitterly.

'But your people, they're magicians. They can see the future. They must have seen some way out of this.'

Achaeos would not meet her eyes. 'You have more faith in them than I do.'

Che embraced him, and he let himself be clasped to her, laid his head on her shoulder. She looked over at Scuto's dull countenance.

'What does it mean?' she asked him. 'What now?'

'It changes everything,' Plius said from behind. He finally had his pipe lit and now did not know what to do with it.

Scuto shook his head. 'I don't know,' he said miserably. 'I don't know what to think. None of you understand. Helleron . . . filthy place. Corrupt, hypocritical. But it was *my city*. I was born in the Empire, you understand, and never stayed two nights in the same place till I was ten. Helleron was the only place that ever took me in. And I had to fight for elbow room even there. I had to break heads and cut throats in my time. But it had a place for me that I could carve out. Founder's Mark, even when the Wasps razed my place and scattered my people, I was always going to go *back*.'

'My home too,' Sperra said quietly. 'More than Merro ever was.'

'It's all falling apart,' Scuto whispered. 'Collegium under siege, Tark falling. Helleron taken. Where next? What happens now? Can we ever pull it back from the edge?'

The question hung in the air. Nobody had any answers.

Twenty-Five

Salma awoke because it was cold, the night cloudless above, and he fought to recall where he was, and then realized that he did not know.

Where is this place? The gloom of the tent of the Mercy's Daughters had become the dark of night, the stars visible above him. He lay on sandy ground with only a thin blanket.

Where is she? Grief in Chains, or Aagen's Joy, or . . . no, it was coming to him.

They had been moving him. Night, again, and it must have been earlier this same night – or last night, was it? But he had been taken from the Daughters' huge tent.

She had been there. He recalled her face, her eyes, radiant. Moth eyes knew no darkness, but hers could stare straight into the sun. She had touched his hand as they took him out. She had said . . . what had she said?

He could not recall it. It was stripped from him along with his health and his strength. The bandages were still tight about his chest, the line of the wound, that she had sealed with her fingers, pulled tautly as he moved, now secured with compresses and surgical silk.

He looked around. There was a scrap of waxing moon up there, enough for his eyes, and there was a fire nearby. They were in a hollow but the warmth was fast leaching out from it, so the cold had sunk into his bones. He made an attempt to crawl closer to the fire, and found he could do that, just. He was capable of it.

He saw Nero, curled up like a child, and indeed looking very like a child bundled in his cloak. A bald child, yes, and to be frank an ugly one, but even his belligerent features attained a kind of innocence in sleep.

Beyond Nero's sleeping form there were two Wasp soldiers in armour. Salma felt his world drop away from him, and he was instinctively groping for a sword that was not there. He sat up, too fast, and hissed in pain, and they looked over at him. One was young, perhaps even younger than he was. The other was greying, forty at least in age, a peer for Stenwold.

'Easy there,' the younger one said. 'How much do you remember?'

'Who are you?' Salma demanded, although he knew he could make no demands that he could enforce.

'My name is Adran,' said the younger of the soldiers. 'This is Kalder.'

'Lieutenant Kalder,' the older man rumbled in a particularly deep voice. 'We're still in the army, boy.'

'You're Salma, right?' Adran nodded absently. 'So what do you remember?'

Salma acknowledged the point. 'Assume I remember nothing.'

'Then you're out,' Adran told him. 'They got you out.'

'They?'

'The halfbreed artificer did it,' said Lieutenant Kalder. 'Arranged for it, anyway. He's got some pull, that one, for all that he's just a piebald bastard.'

'Halfbreed?' *Totho?* And it came back to him then, what Totho had done for him, the price that had been paid for Salma's life and liberty. So the artificer Kalder meant was the other one, the man who had wanted to keep Totho as his slave.

'So why are you . . . ? What are you going to do with us?'

'You don't need to worry,' Adran said, but Salma shook his head.

'What is going on? I see Wasp soldiers before me. Look at me, I'm in no position to cause you any trouble, so at least tell me the truth.'

Adran and Kalder exchanged looks.

'You probably think we're all monsters in the Empire,' said the younger man.

Thinking of Aagen, Salma said, 'Not necessarily, but until proved otherwise.'

'Right.' Adran poked at the fire. 'Have you heard of the Broken Sword?' Kalder started to speak, but Adran continued, 'He might have done, if he was in the Twelve-Year War.'

'He's too young for that,' Kalder objected.

'I've never heard of any Broken Sword,' Salma told them.

'It's . . . We're a group within the Empire, who don't altogether agree with what it's doing. Don't get me wrong. I'm proud to be Wasp-kinden. But things are changing, and never for the better. We've always fought. We're a martial people, just like the Ant-kinden or the Soldier Beetles of Myna. Back before the unification and the Empire, though . . . we might have lived in hill-forts and stolen each other's daughters and cattle, but it was different then. It was . . . natural, almost.' His halting way of exploring what he was trying to say reminded Salma unbearably of Totho.

'The Empire, though, it's wrong. The way it works now, the way it has to keep expanding, further and further, just to stop everything collapsing. You might not realize it, but every Wasp-kinden freeman past thirteen is in the army, and has a rank, and can be sent hundreds of miles away from home because the Emperor wants to bring some foreign city under his control. Nobody gets to choose otherwise. And then there are all the Auxillians, who have it even worse.'

'The people you go and fight don't exactly have a good time of it either,' Salma said weakly.

'No, they don't,' agreed Adran. He had a tremendous sincerity about him, and that in turn reminded Salma of Che, when she was on some moral mission or other. What Adran was saying really *mattered* to him.

'The Empire imposes its will on dozens of other kinden, and it destroys them by making them behave like us. And that's wrong. It's evil, in fact, and by making us do its work, it makes all of us evil.' He glanced at Kalder. 'Or that's what I think, anyway.'

The expression on the older man's face said so clearly, *These young soldiers today* that Salma had to smile. 'As for me,' Kalder took over, 'I just got sick of it. I fought your lot, right? And before that it was putting down insurrections amongst the Hornet tribes. And before that I was a sergeant fighting the Bees at Szar. And I did garrison duty at Jerez even before that. I had a family, once, but I haven't seen them more than six months in twenty years. And now we've just taken Tark, and no sooner have the fires burned out than they're marching us out again, the bastards, for some other forsaken place. It never ends. They just grind you down and abandon you when you drop. So what the Broken Sword is really about – rather than what it means to idealists like young Adran here – is men like me, soldiers who just want the fighting to stop. We want to go home to our wives, our farms. But even if we could, some of us, we wouldn't, now, because by staying put we get to help others who think the same way, help them to get out and away. And it's not just Wasp-kinden. Soldiers are soldiers, whether they're imperial, Auxillian, or whichever poor bastards we might be fighting.'

'But what if they find out?'

'Then they take us apart an inch of skin at a time,' Kalder said. 'Because the Empire, the Rekef especially, hates none more than quitters like us.'

'But we're safe,' Adran broke in. 'We're scouting, you see. Or that's what they think. Drephos the artificer, he arranged for people to be looking the other way, but it was the Daughters' Eldest, Norsa, who knew who we were and called us. The Daughters and the Broken Sword see eye to eye, and Norsa's a favourite of the general.'

'We can take you another day out from here,' Kalder added. 'After that you and your Fly friend are on your own. You'll be far enough from the army to be as safe as anyone can be, but I don't know where you can go next.'

'If we were closer to home then we'd have safe-houses, Wayhouses and the like,' Adran said. 'We're at the edge of the Empire, though. Just don't head south and don't head east.'

'Or north,' Kalder said slowly, 'from what I hear. So I suppose you don't have many options.'

The scout touched down virtually on the bonnet of the transport automotive, startling the driver, who cursed him. The scout made no reply but caught his balance quickly and saluted General Alder.

'Report on the soldiers ahead, sir.'

Alder rose from a cramped conference he had been having with Major Grigan of the engineers and Colonel Carvoc, in the narrow space right behind the driver and ahead of the freight.

'Tell me,' he demanded. He had been informed earlier that an advance scout had spotted a force about two hundred strong encamped right in the path of the Fourth Army, and maybe it was about time someone told him what they intended. 'It's the Tarkesh fugitives, yes?'

'No, sir. I've made contact with them, sir,' the scout reported.

Alder's one hand grasped a strut to keep him standing as the automotive lurched over some difficult ground. All around him, before and behind, the mighty strength of the Imperial Fourth Army was on the move. There were automotives and pack animals, horses, giant beetles and even desert scorpions, all moving in great columns that probably still stretched most of the way back to Tark. The infantry marched in shifting blocks, while the officers and artificers rode. Sometimes heliopters thundered overhead, sweeping the terrain to watch for ambushes, and a multitude of the light airborne performed the same function, squads of them jumping forwards half a mile and then waiting for the army to catch up.

'Tell me what's going on, soldier,' Alder demanded. The scout saluted him again.

'It's an embassy, sir.'

'You spoke with them?'

'They hailed me as I passed over, sir, so it seemed reasonable.'

The man had a sergeant's tabs on his shoulders, and presumably had been picked out from the crowd for some quality or other. Alder now hoped it was his sound judgement.

'Imperial intelligence says the Kessen won't meet us in the field,' Alder said. 'So what's going on?'

'It isn't the Kessen, sir. There are Ant-kinden amongst them, but they're mercenaries. It's the Spider-kinden, sir. Or at least, some Spider-kinden and their retinue.'

Alder's expression did not change but inside he felt uneasy. The Empire's stretching borderlands had only touched near the Spiderlands in the last year, and had no established relations. The Scorpion-kinden of the Dryclaw normally acted as go-betweens in any trade the Consortium conducted with the wealth of the Spiders. It was fabled, that wealth, though probably entirely fabulous. Certainly it was unsubstantiated at least. In fact, as he considered it,

Alder realized that he knew almost nothing for certain about the Spider-kinden holdings situated south of the Lowlands. They were rich. They were clever. Their lands extended on beyond imperial maps. That was the imperial reservoir of knowledge on the subject.

'This could get ugly,' he murmured.

'They want to speak with you, sir,' the scout reported.

'No doubt. You are dismissed, soldier.' As the scout's wings ignited into life and he kicked off from the automotive, Alder was already gesturing to a Fly-kinden messenger.

'Get me Major Maan,' he instructed, because he urgently needed to know imperial policy regarding the Spiders, and it was an ill-kept secret that Maan was Rekef Inlander. 'And get me any Scorpion-kinden we've still got with us. I want to talk to them.'

After two hours in further conference he felt no wiser. Major Maan had simply emphasized that all travellers' reports confirmed that the Spiderlands were very extensive, that they were varied in geography and peoples, and that the chief interest of their rulers seemed to be in conspiring against one another. The Lowlands had never presented a threat to the Spiders, as the Lowlanders were also notably self-involved and divided. There was a brisk trade along the Seldis road to Tark, Merro and Helleron, but beyond that it was remarkable how little reliable information could be found.

'They're subtle, sir,' Maan had warned, as if that explained everything.

And so here he was now, General Alder of the Barbs, with his own retinue of two hundred Wasp soldiers and, nearby, another five hundred of the light airborne ready to move in on his signal if things got as ugly as he feared. He had Maan with him, for all the good it would do, while behind him the main army was setting up temporary camp under Carvoc's command.

And ahead were the Spiders. The ground here was hilly, and patchily wooded, and the Spider commander or lord or whatever he might call himself had chosen a little dell to pitch his tent in. It was barely a tent, by Alder's standards, just a peaked roof of silk held up on poles, tugged lightly in the wind. A small knot of people were gathered beneath its shade, and the rest of the retinue were at military attention, waiting for him in immaculate parade-ground fashion. It was, he admitted, a clever piece of theatre.

At least half of them were bronze-skinned Kessen Ants in gleaming chainmail and helms of like colour. Their shields bore a device of abstract flourishes that Maan loudly informed him was the crest of Seldis.

Some of the others were Flies, and most of those seemed to be nobles or wealthy citizens, as richly clad in felt and silks as many a magnate of the Consortium of the Honest. Others there were Beetle-kinden soldiers with heavy cross-bows. An honour guard of a dozen hulking Scorpions, stripped to the waist, leant on swords almost as high as they were. Then there were the Spiders themselves.

There were almost a score of them, and they seemed all elegance and poise, each one regarding the approaching Wasps with a slight and individual smile. If the Flies had been dressed well, these were magnificent, and yet they trod a thin line between the ornate and the excessive. They were, Alder had to admit, the very soul of taste, wearing their fine silks and gold, their embroidered brocades and their jewels, as though the garments were simply casually thrown on for no special occasion. Himself an old soldier who had never cared for gaud and glitter, Alder found himself moment-arily dowdy, travel-stained and awkward, but he thrust the thought away angrily.

It was clear to see who the leader was, and to Alder's surprise it was a male: a further victory for Major Maan's intelligence because Alder had been assured that they were always led by their womenfolk. This particular Spider-kinden lord reclined languidly in a solid-looking gilt chair, high-backed and fantastically carved. A couple of young women of his own race sat at his feet, and the others stood around him, not as a formal court, but in little groups and cliques. They were all beautiful, men and women alike. Even the oldest amongst them possessed an austere handsomeness, while the youngest glowed with the fruits of youth. Some were pale, others tanned, and their hair was fair or red or dark, more varied than most other kinden ever were, but all with the same ineffably delicate sophistication about them.

The soldiers arrayed behind the Spiders tensed slightly, waiting to see if the armed men coming towards them meant mischief. Alder turned to his troops and signalled for them to take their ease.

'Major,' he said. Maan glanced from one Spider-kinden to the next, swallowing awkwardly.

'Remarkable, General. One does hear—'

'Just listen, Major. Only speak when I consult you.' Alder went forward, with Maan dogging his heels, followed by two sentinels for bodyguards and a scribe to make records.

The Spider leader stood up as they approached. He looked younger than thirty years, and he wore a crimson shirt with ballooning sleeves beneath a green jerkin filigreed in gold thread, and loose-fitting dark breeches above knee-high boots that sported silver spurs. He made a flourishing gesture of welcome that was part wave and part bow, rings glittering on his fingers. His neat, dark beard made his smile flash all the more.

'Do I have the honour of conversing with a general of the Wasps?' he asked. 'That is the title, is it not?'

'General Alder of the Imperial Fourth Army, known as the Barbs,' Alder replied, restraining an urge to salute.

'The Barbs? Charming. I am the Lord-Martial Teornis of the Aldanrael and I am delighted to make your acquaintance, General Alder.'

The second name meant, Alder recalled from his briefing, that this man was of the Aristoi – from one of their ever-feuding noble families. The name itself meant nothing to him though, and he had no clue as to how the Aldanrael might rank in the grander scheme of things.

A couple of the well-dressed Flies came forward at this point, and Alder turned to them to greet them formally, before seeing that they were bearing a flask of wine and a large platter of honeyed meat, shredded and laid out like unreadable script.

Servants? he wondered, noting their finery, and then, *slaves?* Major Maan had stressed how the Spiders had a thriving slave trade, but these little attendants were more richly dressed than most Wasps of good family at the imperial court.

He allowed a goblet to be pressed into his hand, with that, his thumb feeling idly at the small gems that encircled its stem.

'You are here as an embassy from the Spiderlands?' Alder enquired, determined to regain the initiative.

'From Everis, Siennis and Seldis, certainly,' Teornis said, 'but it would be somewhat presumptuous of me to speak for the Spiderlands entire. Yes, General. We have been watching your Empire with some approbation recently. Our agents have reported on your conquest of Tark, and it seems you have done the impossible with embarrassing ease.'

Alder allowed himself to nod. 'The Emperor commands and the Empire obeys, Lord . . . Martial,' he said, stumbling a little over the unfamiliar title.

Teornis permitted himself a wry smile. 'You are a military man, General. A direct man.'

'I try to be. So I will ask again, what is the purpose of your embassy?'

'We are concerned, General.' Teornis signalled for a

chair to be brought forwards for Alder and, with that politeness accomplished, slouched back into his own. Alder decided that standing would give him the advantage, but then changed his mind when he saw how Teornis took his ease, and found to his embarrassment that it was inexplicably too late to sit. He felt surrounded by an invisible net of unfamiliar manners.

'We have no quarrel with your Empire,' Teornis went on, regardless. 'We wish you well, in fact, should you decide to sack any other Ant-kinden cities. We are certain, from our intelligence gathered, that you will make us better trading partners than the Tarkesh ever did. I only wish to make sure you understand our position.'

Alder nodded. Matters were falling at last into a recognizable pattern. 'You want to be sure we're not coming for you and yours.'

'Precisely, General.'

'Well then that's simple,' Alder said, now anxious to conclude the interview as quickly as possible. 'The Empire wishes the Spiderlands nothing but peace. Our business is with the Lowlands only.'

'Splendid.' Teornis smiled dazzlingly. 'I thought as much, but our women back home insisted I put together this expedition and talk to you about it directly.'

Alder allowed himself the smallest answering smile. 'I had expected to be dealing with a female of your kind, Lord-Martial.'

'They have better things to do,' said Teornis, 'than play soldier.' It was only later, much later, that Alder recognized this as an insult. At the time Teornis's tone and expression suggested only one man joking with another. Then the Spider continued, 'So I anticipate Kes will be your next conquest.' Alder glanced at the Ant soldiers behind him, but Teornis waved his concerns away. 'Mercenaries, General, worry not. I am afraid we are a terrible influence on the young men and women of Kes. They see, you understand, that even a servant of ours lives better than a lord of theirs.'

It was hard to deny. 'Then Kes it is,' Alder admitted. 'After we have secured Egel and Merro of course. There will be no forays further southwards, never fear.'

But Teornis's smile had evaporated and a whole sea-change had blown across the entire Spider embassy, as though sudden winter had rushed in off the coast. 'Pardon my impudence, General,' Teornis said, 'but you contradict yourself.'

Alder resisted the urge to check that his men were still close behind. 'How so?' he asked.

'Egel and Merro are not part of the Lowlands. They are ours.'

Alder stared at him. 'Not on my maps,' he said.

'Your maps aside, General, both Egel and Merro have been holdings of the Spiderlands almost since they were settled. Our own histories are very clear on that point.'

Alder risked a glance at Major Maan, who interpreted that as a chance to speak. 'I am afraid,' he said firmly, 'that you are quite mistaken. Our agents have been informed by the very occupants of those towns that they are Lowlanders.'

And Teornis laughed at him, not scornfully but so politely as to cut to the bone. 'I am afraid that your agents have fallen victim to one of the local Fly-kinden pastimes, which is to playfully misdirect strange travellers. Let us hope that they did not also purchase any priceless gems or talented slaves at bargain prices. I am afraid that the Fly-kinden of these two towns, if indeed they are not simply one town with two names, find it convenient to claim themselves as either Lowlanders or subjects of my own people, depending on the asker. They are a duplicitous and untrustworthy people, and no doubt we would best be rid of them, but nonetheless they are our subjects. Any attempt to impose your Empire's rule over them would amount to a declaration of war. I am no great strategist, but such a development would I think weaken your Empire's position.'

'War, is it?' Alder growled.

'I hope it need not come to that. Perhaps you would provide us with your maps and we can then correct them,' suggested Teornis innocently.

'You have a mere two hundred men here, Lord-Martial. What do you think would happen if I decided I should send a definite message back to your people?'

Teornis shrugged, slinging a leg up over the arm of his chair. 'Oh, you'd send them my head in a box, no doubt, which is another reason I'm doing this thankless job and not, say, my sister or my mother. And we would then have to muster our armies, which is a tiresome enough proposal to make me glad that I would be dead by that point. And then we would fight, I suppose.'

Alder narrowed his eyes. 'Perhaps you should be more concerned, Lord-Martial. I have automotives here, flying machines, artillery. Your people are Inapt. Will you bring bows and arrows against us?'

Teornis's smile broadened. 'It's true,' he replied, 'I wouldn't know what to do with a crossbow, if someone should thrust such a distasteful object into my hands. We do not trouble ourselves with all that greasy machine-fondling that some kinden seem to find so irresistible. No, we have – how shall I put it? – people to do that for us. We have plenty of Ant-kinden and Beetle-kinden hired with us, and many more within our satrapies further south. The Empire is not the only one to have subject peoples. Do not think, General, that we cannot field all that clanking metal palaver if we need to.'

'So your position is clear,' Alder said grimly.

'It is, and it is one of the open hand of friendship – or, as you are Wasps, the closed hand, I believe, is more appropriate. We wish nothing but peace and trade with your mighty and admirable Empire.' Teornis sprang from his chair effortlessly to look Alder in the eye. 'But if your hand comes against Egel or Merro or any of our holdings, then you and I, General, shall be at war, and nobody shall profit from that in any way.'

Back in his camp, Alder called his officers together and gave them the situation.

'I think they're bluffing,' he explained, but he saw from their faces he had few takers.

'A war on two fronts would be disastrous, sir,' Carvoc said. 'To take Kes we will need to concentrate all our efforts.'

'Even if we bypass the Fly townships,' one of his field majors remarked, 'they could attack anyway, cut our supply lines.'

'And we just do not know what they can field,' Major Maan added. Teornis' people seemed to have particularly impressed him. 'The Spiderlands are, we know, very large, and they could bring in troops by sea—'

'Yes, Major,' Alder interrupted heavily. Just this morning his world had been so simple. Now his conversation with Teornis had struck it a severe blow and crazed it with far too many complications. He was a soldier, not a diplomat, and he did not want to be the man to go to war with an unmeasured enemy nation.

'Send the fastest messenger we have back to Asta,' he said. 'I need to know imperial policy on this.'

And in the meantime the Fourth Army would sit idle.

The *Cloudfarer* had reached Helleron through clement weather, but it was not the same city that Totho remembered. Not that he remembered it fondly, but the city that came to his mind instead was Myna, with Wasp soldiers and Auxillians everywhere on the streets, and a hunted look in the eyes of the locals.

General Malkan had come to meet them at the airfield in person, clasping Drephos's gauntleted hand. Filled with enthusiasm, he seemed barely older than Totho himself.

'Colonel Drephos, a pleasure,' he said. 'Since I heard you were expected here I have had clerks taking stock of every foundry and factory in the city.'

'Most kind, General,' Drephos said. 'Have my people arrived yet?'

'And your machinery. They all came in with the garrison force.'

'Excellent.' Drephos turned to Totho. 'You have had a chance to consider the plans?'

'I have, sir.' In the freezing air that the *Cloudfarer* flew in, he had been hunched close by the windbreak of the clockwork engine, scribbling his alterations and additions. *All for Salma* he had reflected. *I made this bargain, and now I must keep it.* But beyond those sentiments his busy mind had been concerned only with the calculations, the mechanical principles.

'Then let us unleash them on Helleron,' Drephos said eagerly. 'It's not often I have a whole city to work for me. General Malkan, pray show me what you have for us.'

How long I have wished to see the factories of Helleron, was the ironic thought as Totho entered one. *I had not thought it would be like this.* He meant as an invader, an imperial artificer, but he also meant as a master rather than a menial. As he and Drephos, and Drephos's ragbag of other picked artificers, came in, the factory work had been totally stilled. A great crowd of workers were gathered there, the staff of three factories waiting to receive their new orders. Malkan had been quick in providing Drephos with whatever he should need and Totho knew that the general was one of a new breed of Wasp officers. Malkan was not just a slave to maps and charts and the slow movements of troop formations. He actually liked artificers and the way they could

377

win wars more efficiently, more quickly, than ever before. Drephos was the Empire's most gifted artificer on the western front, and Malkan was keen to see that he was kept happy.

'My name is Colonel-Auxillian Dariandrephos,' the half-breed announced, his voice ringing from the gantry he stood on across the echoing factory floor. 'You will refer to me as Master, or Sir. Most importantly, you will do what you are instructed without needless question, without debate, without retort. I want you to have no illusions about your situation here.' He cast his narrow gaze over them, the working men and women of Helleron. He had his cowl thrown back leaving them no doubts about what he was.

'These men and women with me,' Drephos told the workers, 'are my elite staff. You will address them as 'sir' and do exactly what they instruct you. In my absence, they are my voice.'

Totho could feel the resentment boiling up from these hard-working men and women whose lives had come under new management. It was not that this was a new factory owner telling them what to do, nor even that he was a foreigner. What rankled with them was that Drephos was a halfbreed and, worst of all, a Moth halfbreed, born partly from that superstitious, primitive tribe that raided their mine-workings north of the city. Here he was, claiming to be an artificer, and appalling chance had placed him as their superior.

'I myself will have no illusions here. You hate and resent me,' Drephos continued. 'I, on the other hand, have no feelings whatsoever concerning you, collectively or individually. I wish you to think about precisely what that means. It means that if any one of you comes to my notice in a way that displeases me, or any of my people here, then that man or woman shall become my object lesson. Work hard and well and you shall escape my notice, which shall be best for all concerned.'

They still stirred rebelliously, and so he smiled at them lopsidedly. 'You may have heard from your leaders that some amicable arrangement has been reached between your people and the Wasps of the Empire. It is not so. We own you. You work at our command. I invite any of you here to dispute it.'

He signalled, and a dozen Wasp soldiers came to attention. 'Now get these people back to their work,' he said. 'Bring all the foremen up here, though. I have one final thing to say to them.' He turned to Totho and the others, seeming very pleased with himself.

'Your comments?'

'They will not serve you willingly,' Kaszaat said. 'Not at first. Surly and angry, they are.'

'It's only natural,' Drephos said, not a bit daunted. 'They are a skilled workforce, though, and only in Helleron is such skill so taken for granted. Nowhere else could you lay hands on so many trained people. We must therefore ensure that their talents are put entirely at our disposal.' He turned again as two men and one woman were brought up to the gantry. 'Well now,' he addressed them. 'You are my foremen, are you?'

Two of them merely nodded but one of them was quicker on the uptake and said, 'Yes, Master.'

'Master,' Drephos echoed. 'Such a versatile word, is it not?' They looked at him blankly, and he elaborated. 'Amongst your kinden, of course, it is a great term of respect. Your College scholars, your magnates, the great among you, are called 'Masters'. Among the Wasp-kinden it is any man who owns a slave, and therefore has rights of life or death over that slave.' His smile was thin and hard-edged. 'So it will now be the choice of you and your workers just what interpretation we shall apply to that word. Do I make myself understood?'

He had, and they nodded unhappily, and murmured the title for him.

'I am anticipating troublemakers,' he told them. 'The lazy, the impertinent, the disobedient, the talentless.'

'Oh no, Master,' said the woman amongst them. 'We'll be sure of that. No slackers in our houses. No backtalk either.'

'You misunderstand me,' said Drephos. 'I am *anticipating* them. There are such in any body of workers, perhaps a dozen in every factory.'

The foremen were exchanging glances, approaching the point of denying it and then drawing back.

'I am *anticipating*,' Drephos explained happily, 'that they will be singled out by you there, and reported to my soldiers. I am anticipating that my guards will have some three dozen such malcontents brought to me within the *first five days* of work here. Choose those who contribute least, or stir up trouble, or whom you personally dislike, whatever you will, but I will be very unhappy if my anticipations are not borne out.'

The two men nodded slowly now, looking as miserable as Totho had seen anyone in a long time, but the woman said, 'Excuse me, Master, but . . . what shall be done with them, once your guardsmen have them?'

'They will be allowed to participate in other parts of the creative process,' Drephos told her. She paled a little at that, and then the soldiers began ushering all three away.

'Some promise there, I think,' Drephos mused, glancing back at his cadre of artificers. Besides Kaszaat and Totho there were two Beetle-kinden that must surely be twin brother and sister, a halfbreed that looked to mingle Wasp and Beetle blood, and a hulking nine-foot Mole Cricket whose weight made the whole gantry creak.

'Master Drephos . . .' Totho started, feeling deeply uneasy about it all.

'Ah, Totho,' Drephos said. He was clearly in a fine mood today. 'You have seen the prototype?'

'I have, Master Drephos, but . . .'

'What do you think?' Drephos began descending the stairs to the factory floor where the workers were being given their new machining projects, designs and specifications for unfamiliar parts and pieces.

'The new loading mechanism seems to work very smoothly,' Totho said, drawn from his original intent by the need to discuss the finer aspects of the technical work. 'It will need to be machined very exactly on the finished version, though. There will be little room for error, to avoid jamming.'

'That would be a problem anywhere else,' Drephos agreed, 'but here in Helleron the skills and the equipment have come together in glad harmony. In the Empire we would have had to compromise, but the Emperor's generals have made their plans as if they had my very wishes in mind, because Helleron is ours, and here we are.'

'Aside from that, I think we may have to redesign the grooving within the barrel, or at least test variations of spacing and angle.'

'Granted,' Drephos said. 'Test it then. Conclusions in two days. By then we should be ready for the spiralling lathe work on the first batch.'

'First *batch*, Master?' Totho enquired.

'You weren't thinking of making just *one* of them, surely?' Drephos grinned at him, teeth flashing in his motley-coloured face. 'Like a showpiece? A museum curiosity? What do you think these factories are for, Totho?'

'All for . . . you can't mean it, surely?' Totho felt weak, stumbling on the stairs so that Kaszaat had to reach out and grab his arm to steady him.

'Explain to Master Totho how we do things,' Drephos flung the words over his shoulder.

Kaszaat was grinning, and most of the others smiled at least a little, their newest colleague still learning how things were done.

'One project at a time is the rule,' Kaszaat explained.

'When we really get to work, when the war effort calls, all resources are devoted to one project. This time you're the lucky one. It's *your* project. Three factories, hundreds of workers, all of us, all concentrated on your devices.'

The thought made his head swim. It was all happening far too fast for him.

'I had better start my testing,' he said. The other artificers were already fanning out across the factory, each heading to his or her own task. Kaszaat was about to go as well, when Totho caught her arm.

'Tonight I . . . Could I talk . . . come to talk to you, tonight? I need . . . I just need . . .'

'You just need someone,' her smile was ambiguous, 'and I can be that someone. Perhaps I need a someone also, sometimes.'

Twenty-Six

'The gates are sealed,' said Lineo Thadspar. He looked older than ever.

'Did the last train get away?' Stenwold asked him.

'No, they were too long in loading it.' The Speaker of the Assembly sat down at a War Council that was greatly different in constitution to the first one. As the Vekken army had neared there had been many who had decided that war was, after all, not for them, and others had surfaced in whom an undreamt-of martial fervour had been kindled. The stone seats were lined with College Masters, artificers and city magnates who had found in themselves the means to greet the hour. And that hour had now come.

'They were still leaving by the western gate until an hour gone, but the Vekken are just outside artillery range of the walls on all sides now, and anyone leaving would fall straight into their hands,' reported Waybright, one of the survivors of the original council. 'They have not totally encircled us, but they have set up regularly spaced camps.'

'They'll want you to try to attack them at the gaps, to see them as divided,' Balkus said seriously. Nobody had exactly invited him here, but he went where Stenwold went, and unlike most there he had experience of Ant war firsthand. 'But we – the Ant-kinden – we're never divided. You should remember that.'

'We're in no position to attack them, in any event,' Lineo Thadspar said.

'Precisely how strong are these gates?' Kymon asked. He had a rough map of the city before him and he traced its boundaries with a stylus. 'This is a weak city against force of arms. The walls are pierced all over. You have a river, the rail line, the harbour. The gates themselves, how strong are they?'

'We learned a few tricks after our last clash with the Vekken,' Thadspar said.

'Likewise the Vekken,' Stenwold cautioned.

'That's true, but I hope we've learned faster than they. It is, after all, what we are supposed to be good at, here at the College.' Thadspar leant over Kymon's map. 'Our gates have secondary shutters that slide down from within the wall. My own father's design, as it happens. They are of dense wood plated with bronze, and they should withstand a hefty strike from any ram or engine you care to name. There is a grille that has been lowered where the river meets the city and, while they may eventually break through it, they will at least not surprise us by assaulting that way. We have gates across the rail arch, too, and I have engineers buttressing them even now. The harbour . . . has certain defences. What is their naval strength, anyone?'

'Nine armourclads, plus one really big one,' someone reported from the back. 'And two dozen wooden-hulled warships. Plus four dozen small vessels and half a dozen very large barges that they're holding back. Supply ships, I suppose.'

'They will attack the harbour soon,' Kymon cautioned. 'I myself have been given the west wall to command. Who has the south?'

'I do,' Stenwold confirmed. He could feel the tension in the room slowly screwing tight, the image in everyone's heads of Ant-kinden in perfect step making their encampments around their city of scholars. 'I'm open to any suggestions.'

'What about the supply situation on our side?' Waybright asked. 'We've had people leaving in droves these last few days, and yet there have never been so many within our walls. All the satellite villages west of here have emptied, some of the people have come here with nothing but the clothes on their backs.'

'We have always husbanded our harvests well,' Thadspar said. 'We will ration what we have, and we need hold only until the Sarnesh arrive to relieve us.'

'Masters,' Stenwold said, 'I will now say something we have all thought, to ourselves. The Vekken were defeated last time because the Sarnesh relieved us, although we held them for tendays before that happened. The Vekken know this. Even they are not so blinded by pride and greed that they will have forgotten.' He looked around at them, face by face, and so few of them would meet his gaze.

Kymon did. 'You're saying that the Vekken believe Sarn will not aid us. Or that even Sarn's aid cannot tip the balance.'

'A secret weapon?' someone suggested.

'All speculation,' Thadspar insisted. 'Why should Sarn not aid us?'

'We have no idea of the situation,' Stenwold insisted. 'It is simply this. The Vekken are here. They do not relish defeat, and so they must believe they can win.'

'Perhaps they seek to capture the walls before Sarn can even get its army here,' Waybright said. 'If they already had the city, Sarn might turn back.'

'All I am saying is that we cannot fight this war on the assumption that the Sarnesh will rescue us sooner or later,' Stenwold said. 'If we fight, we must fight to drive them away with whatever strength we have ourselves.'

They did not like that. He could see that none of them wanted to accept it. A holding action, they thought, just until . . . Kymon met his eyes and nodded.

A messenger burst in, a young Beetle girl quite out of breath. 'Their artillery is shooting at us!' she said. 'What do we do now?'

Kymon stood. 'All officers to your posts!' he snapped. 'Stenwold?'

'Here.'

'If the harbour falls, the city falls, and they'll attack it, tomorrow or the next day at the latest. Everybody listen: if you have someone coming to you with means to defend the harbour, send them to Stenwold. Everything will count.'

The Vekken were very efficient in their mustering. When Thalric and Daklan had put the Empire's invitation to them an army had been raised in mere days. The Vekken, like all Ants, were soldier-born. The soundless call had gone out into the city, and without a spoken word it had been answered by the thousands of the war host of Vek. There had then been the matter of material, machines, supplies. It was a matter long settled, though, for Vek had been looking for this war for decades, awaiting the moment when Sarn's protective hand was lifted from the reviled city of scholars. The supplies were already laid in, the machines in readiness, the crossbow bolts and engine ammunition neatly stockpiled. Each year the tacticians of Vek had convened and added what further elements they could to the plan, while their artificers continued their patient progress.

So, when they had arrived and surrounded the city, it had been a wonder of discipline. There was not a man but who knew to the inch where his place was. The engineers had begun instantly bringing forward their machines: lead-shotters, catapults and scorpions, trebuchets and ballistae, a great host of destruction of every kind that the artificers of Vek could conceive of. The smaller machines were unloaded from carts, or had progressed under their own mechanical power. The larger were constructed on the spot even as the artificers made their calculations, their crews untiring and careful to a fault. To the watchers on the walls of Collegium it seemed that the Vekken battle plan unfolded as smoothly as a parchment, spreading out and around their beloved city.

Akalia did not watch her men prepare. She had no need. They were already in her head, each section and squad informing her of its readiness. They gave her a perfect map of the field in her mind's eye, the composite of all that each soldier saw. Sitting in her tent she was also everywhere her forces were.

There is no time like now, she instructed her people, and called for her tacticians. They responded almost as one, alert for the order. At the same time her engineers were tensioning and charging their siege weapons, all of them, all at once.

Test your ranges, she told them mentally, and one from each battery loosed, sending rocks or shot spinning high towards the pale walls of Collegium. *Attend me*, she told her officers, and stepped out into the afternoon light to see the first plumes of stone dust that her ranging shots had raised from the walls, or the dust from the earth where they had fallen short.

Correct your ranges, she instructed, feeling the artificers all around making their measurements, their practical mathematics of elevation and angle.

Loose one round, she decided and, even as she sent the order out she felt the ground quiver beneath her feet as all her engines rocked back simultaneously with the force of their discharge. A fair proportion of the machines still lacked the range, but this time more missiles found the walls than failed. The city of Collegium was briefly swathed in puffs of stone dust, as though it were letting off fireworks.

What damage? she asked. Forward of their artillery positions were officers equipped with telescopes, raking the walls for any weaknesses, and their reports were rapidly passed back: *None, sir. No damage sighted, sir. Some slight scarring, sir.*

She had expected nothing less, because Beetles, for all their inferior characteristics, knew how to lay stone on stone. The tacticians of Vek had counted on that when they designed this expedition. They were still assembling much of the artillery: great trebuchets, leadshotters and rock-throwers to attack the walls; grapeshot ballistae to rake the battlements clean of soldiers at closer range; engine-powered rams and lifting towers for the troops to take the walls. There were even experimental grenade-throwers, delicate, spindly things designed to throw small, volatile missiles deep into the city beyond.

The fleet had blockaded the rivermouth and was now waiting for her signal to make its assault, but the walls would come first. She was a traditional soldier, and she preferred traditional methods to the unknown concerns of a sea landing.

Let it all come down, she sent out the order. *Pound the walls until sunset. Let the dawn tell us the result.*

'Soldiers off the walls!' Kymon bellowed, though he was ignoring his own advice by striding along the east wall as the missiles came in. Many landed short, throwing up plumes of earth from the fields or impacting amongst the straggle of buildings out there: Wayhouses, storehouses, farmers' huts, all abandoned now. Some struck the wall itself, and he felt the impact shudder through his sandals. A few even flew over to smash stonework in the city below.

He stopped and backed up a few steps, waiting, and a lead ball clipped the very battlements ten feet ahead. He had found a disaffected Kessen youth amongst the volunteers and put him to good use. Now Kymon could walk blithely amongst his troops and inspire them with his disregard for the enemy, whilst all the time the boy was watching the incoming assault and giving him warning.

The walls of Collegium had their own artillery, but the Vekken army had brought up a whole host of it, more than even he had thought they possessed. The defenders' engines were outnumbered four to one along the west wall, where the brunt of the attack was concentrated. Soon, he well knew, the barrage would begin to creep towards the wall-mounted weapons so as to clear the way for the Vekken infantry.

But where Vek had strength, Collegium had intelligence. Here before him was a team of artificers working at one such weapon. As he watched the great catapult began to revolve, descending foot by foot into the stonework of its tower with a groaning of gears and a hiss of steam. Further along the wall they were winching great iron shields into position about a repeating ballista.

Kymon dropped to one knee and peered over the city side of the wall. There was a detachment of some three hundred city militia below and he shouted at them, 'Clear the way!' He gestured furiously. 'Left and right from me! Clear the way!'

Most of them got the idea and just ran for it, dodging to either side. A moment later a great rock whistled over Kymon's head to spin past them and smash into the wall of the building beyond, pelting them all with a shrapnel of fist-sized stones. He saw a few fall to it, but most were clear. It was far more frustrating than he had thought, to command soldiers he could not commune with mind to mind.

And they were such a rabble too. They brought determination and enthusiasm, but little discipline. Some were the city militia, decently enough armoured but more used to quelling taverna brawls and catching thieves than to fighting wars. The bulk of Collegium's armed force was simply those citizens bold enough to put themselves forward for it. Some brought their own weapons, others had been armed from the College stores. Anyone with any training as an artificer had been given something from the workshops: repeaters, piercers, nailbows and wasters, or whatever 'prentice pieces were lying around. Some attempt had been made to sort them into squads similarly armed, but the mess of men and women beneath Kymon bristled with a ragged assortment of spears, swords, crossbows, clubs and agricultural implements.

He stood again, waiting for despair to wash over him, but instead found a strange kind of pride. If these defenders had been Ant-kinden of his own city it would have been shameful, but they were not. They were Beetles, mostly, but there were others, too: Flies, rogue Ants, Spiders, halfbreeds, even some Mantids and Moths. They were truly the host of Collegium, the city which had opened its gates to the world.

He came to the catapult emplacement to find the weapon more than half hidden now, steadily grinding itself down below the level of the wall. There was a man, a College artificer, crouching by the battlements with a telescope and some kind of sextant, making quick calculations.

'Is this going to work?' Kymon had forgotten the man's name, but when the goggled face turned up to him he recalled him as Master Graden, who taught applied fluid mechanics.

'I am assured it will. Not my department, obviously, but the mathematics are simple enough,' Graden explained. 'Incidentally, Master Kymon, my invention – have you had a chance to consider it? The sand is to hand, and my apprentices have it ready to place on the walls.'

It seemed that almost every artificer in Collegium believed that they had an invention that could help the war effort. Kymon was no artificer, but the mention of sand jogged his memory further.

'Have it ready,' he said, more as a sop to the man's pride than anything. 'Every little thing may help.'

He passed on towards the next emplacement. Behind him another lead shot struck the wall, making it shiver beneath his feet like a living thing.

'It doesn't look like they're coming,' one of his soldiers said to him. Stenwold shook his head.

'They're coming, but not just yet. I need the chain ready in time. It must be our first line of defence.'

'But the mechanism hasn't been used in—' The soldier waved a hand vaguely. 'I don't know if it's ever been used, Master Stenwold.'

'Oil it, fix it – replace the cursed thing if you have to. Don't be the man whose failures make the city fall.'

It was unfair, but the man fell back, face twisting in shame, and ran off to do his job. Stenwold turned briefly to the men who had answered his call, but his attention was drawn back to the sea. This had been the harbourmaster's office, and the view from it would have been beautiful if not marred by the ugly blots of the Vekken fleet. The armourclads, iron-plated or iron-hulled ships with mon-strously powerful engines, formed the vanguard, waiting out in anchored formation with smoke idling from their funnels.

'How are we going to stop them?' Stenwold asked, for Collegium had no navy. The few ships in harbour were only those which had not seized the chance to flee before the harbour was blockaded, and they were definitely not fighting ships.

'The harbour has its artillery defences, as well as the chain, Master,' reminded Cabre, a Fly who was an artificer from the College. 'They were designed with wooden ships in mind, though, and they've not been updated in thirty years. You know how it is. When Vek came last it was overland, and nobody thought . . .'

'And we'll now pay for that lack of imagination,' Stenwold grumbled.

'We don't know if they could even dent the armourclads out there,' Cabre admitted, scratching the back of her head.

'What else have we got?' Stenwold asked.

'Master Maker?' It was a Beetle-kinden man who must be at least ten years Stenwold's junior. For a Beetle he looked lean and combative.

'Yes, Master . . . ?'

'Greatly, Master Maker. Joyless Greatly. I have a cadre of men, Master Maker. Some twenty in all. I have recently been working on an invention for the Sarnesh, but I cannot think that they would object to our using it in our own defence.'

And he does not add, 'until they get here', Stenwold noted. Joyless seemed to him a name of ill omen. It tended to denote children named by their fathers after their mothers had not survived the infant's birth. 'Go on, Master Greatly.'

Joyless Greatly stared challengingly about the room, at a dozen or so artificers who had been sent to Stenwold's care. 'I have developed a one-man orthopter, Master Maker. I have one score and ten of these ready to fly, though only my twenty men are trained to fly them.'

It seemed impossible. 'Thirty orthopters? But where . . . ?' Stenwold asked him.

'They are not what you think, Master Maker. These are worn on the back, as you will see. When the fleet approaches, or when the army comes to our walls, I will take my men out. We will drop grenades and incendiaries on them. Their ships may be hulled with iron, but they will not have armoured decks. We can drop explosives into their funnels, or on their weapons.'

'They will shoot you down,' Cabre warned him, but there was a fire in Greatly's expression, of either patriotism or madness.

'Let them try, for I will outrace their bolts and quarrels.

Master Maker, we may be your second line of defence, but we *shall* attack.'

'There are other flying machines as well,' ventured an elderly Beetle woman Stenwold could not recall, save that she had something to do with the airfield. 'Some two dozen of various designs that have been brought within the city. With the assistance of Master Greatly's force we might at least harry them during their advance.'

'And meanwhile I can train new pilots for the other machines,' added Joyless Greatly.

'Do so,' Stenwold agreed. 'More, please. Anyone?'

'Excuse me, Master Maker.' The speaker was an Ant-kinden with bluish skin, and Stenwold had no idea even where he came from, never mind who he was. He was no warrior, though, despite his race. Inactivity had left him thin from the chest up and broad below.

'Yes, Master . . . ?'

'Tseitus, Master Maker.' The Ant's gaunt face smiled. 'I have an aquatic automotive which, Master Maker, I have been working on for many years.'

'One boat, Master Tseitus—'

'Not a boat, Master Maker.' Tseitus glanced around suspiciously at the others as though they would, at this late juncture, seek to steal his idea. 'It goes *beneath* the waters.'

Stenwold stared at him. 'A submersible automotive?'

'She is beautiful, Master Maker.' Tseitus's eyes gleamed. 'I have taken her into Lake Sideriti. You would not believe what wonders there are beneath the waters there—'

'But for now you'll put her into the city's service?'

'This city is my life, Master Maker. And if there might be any funding, in the future, for my project—?'

'Yes, yes,' Stenwold said hurriedly. 'Let us just save the city first, and then I cannot imagine that the Assembly will not reward its saviours. Your submersible boat, what can it do?'

'Go beneath the waters,' repeated Tseitus, and then after

a brief, awkward pause, 'Drill into the hulls of their ships. Attach devices that others here may devise. Is there some explosive that may work underwater?'

'I haven't—' Stenwold started but, as though summoned magically by the concept, one of the other artificers was already raising a hand.

At dusk, Akalia called for the Vekken artillery to be stilled. There was no sense wasting their ammunition in speculative and inaccurate night-time shooting. By the last light, her spotters had confirmed some light damage to the west wall where she had been heaping most of her missiles: some ragged holes punched in the crenellations, and a few patches that might repay a barrage over the next few days and even open up the whole wall. And once the wall was down in even one place her real assault could begin.

There had not been a single answering shot. It had been somewhat vexing the way most of the artillery positions atop the wall had been protected from her own, but it made little enough difference if they were content to hide behind their walls until she battered them down.

There would be casualties to the Collegium artillery when the assault went in, but no war was without casualties and her men understood that.

They cannot have the range to match us, one of her commanders had suggested. She could only shrug at him. For whatever reason, though, the Collegium artillery had remained silent.

Her commanders had secured the camps, in the highly unlikely event that the Beetle-kinden were planning some kind of night raid, and so finally she retired to her tent. The Wasp-kinden Daklan wished to speak with her, she knew. She had considered letting the foreigner stew but decided that, as matters were progressing so well, it would do her good to remind him of the superiority of those he was allying his Empire to.

'Commander Daklan,' she addressed him, and then looked to the other man. 'And it is Commander Thalric, is it not?'

'It is, Tactician,' Thalric said. It pleased Akalia that he did not try to deny the Ant rank. In her mind she was doing him more honour than he deserved.

'And you are pleased with what you have seen, so far?' she asked the two Wasps. 'Your vengeance against Collegium will soon be accomplished, will it not?'

'Indeed, Tactician,' said the other one, Daklan.

'One might wonder what the foolish Beetles have done, to inflame such a far-off enemy,' she said, her eyes narrowing.

'You know the Beetle-kinden, how they can never leave well enough alone,' Daklan said quickly. 'The Empire has its actions focused east of here, as you know, and it seemed likely to us that Collegium would interfere in some way.'

'They are a pack of meddling old men,' Akalia agreed derisively. 'Look at what they have done to Sarn, and in so short a time. They've gelded an entire city with their absurd ideas!'

'True, and well put,' Daklan concurred. She sneered at his ingratiating manner, but it was fitting, she supposed. It was certain that they feared her and wished her to think well of them.

'Tell me, Tactician,' said the other one, Thalric. 'How do you consider that first bombardment? It seemed to be a little . . . unorthodox to me.' Daklan glanced at him sharply, perhaps because this was something they had agreed to leave unsaid, but Akalia shrugged. 'You are imprecise with your words, Commander Thalric. With us Ant-kinden you must say what you mean. What do you mean?'

Thalric was ignoring Daklan's frown. 'Their wall artillery, Tactician.'

'That was curious,' she agreed. 'I have asked my artificers for possible causes. It may be that they have let their artillery become useless with age, although that seems unlikely even for Collegium. However, they are not a valorous race. Perhaps their engineers did not dare take to the walls to man them under our shot.'

'Perhaps that is it,' Thalric said, but she could see a look on his face that she did not like.

'You are here only on sufferance,' she reminded them. 'I shall have no impertinence from you foreigners.'

'Of course not,' Daklan said quickly. 'We are merely . . . unused to such a great display of artillery. Our wars work in different ways.' She saw Thalric's face twitch at that sentiment, but she could not read his reaction.

'You are dismissed,' she told them suddenly. It was late, anyway, and she would need a rested night, to command on the morrow. She must consider what to do with these Wasp-kinden, too. Perhaps it might be best if they became casualties of war. She watched them walk away, a tension between them, men who would be arguing as soon as they were out of her sight. Another divided and chaotic kinden, then. When the time came they would be no match for the perfect order of Vek.

Akalia went straight to her tent and had a slave unbuckle her armour. Then she fell asleep in anticipation of the morning's work.

She was awakened instantly by the first crash and sat bolt-upright, feeling the ground shake beneath her. Her entire camp was awake, but for a terrifying moment nobody knew what was going on.

Sentries report! Her mind snapped out, but there was no answer amongst the babble of replies. Her sentries knew of no attack, and yet the camps were under attack. Men were dying, snuffed out instantly, but very few of them. Instead she was hearing a waxing tide of alarm from her engineers, from her artificers.

What is going on? she demanded of them, sensing them rush about in the darkness, that clouded, moonless pitch-darkness. Fires were being lit, men were rushing into formations with still no idea of what was going on. One unit of a hundred men was abruptly half its number down, a great rock having found them in the night, crushing the heart from their battle order.

Report! she demanded once more. *I will have executions for this. It is intolerable.*

Then the word came rushing through the army like wildfire. Their artillery was being destroyed.

How? she demanded. *How are they attacking us?* It must be men, some stealthy team sent out, but even as she thought that, the ground shook once again.

And the impossible answer came back, *They are shooting from the walls.*

For a moment she could not think. She had no answers, and none of her officers had any answers, and so the entire army was paralysed by indecision. The ground shook again, and once more, and the artificers' minds passed on to her the sound of smashed wood and crushed metal.

At last the only remaining course came to her. *Move the artillery back. Disassemble it if it cannot be moved!*

On the walls of Collegium the artillery had either been winched back up or uncovered, and now the artificers of the most learned city in the Lowlands practised their art. All day they had taken their measurements and worked out their angles. Men used to the classroom and the lectern had crouched behind battlements and scribbled their calculations. Some of them had died, crushed by shot, raked by stone splinters. Now the fruits of those labours were borne on the air by the engines of Collegium. The night was almost moonless, and small specks of fire were all that was revealed to them of the Vekken encampment, but the engineers and artificers of Collegium held lamps by their sheets of calculations and adjusted their angle and elevation by minute degrees.

And the catapults and ballistae, leadshotters and trebuchets of the Collegium walls spoke together, flinging hundredweights of stone and metal at the invaders.

Some of them missed, of course, either by chance or bad calculation, but all around the city the Vekken army was awoken by the sound of its own siege emplacements being destroyed: trebuchets splintering under blindly targeted rocks, and leadshotters ripped apart by explosive-headed ballista bolts. The thinking men and mathematicians of Collegium, carefully and without passion, set about undoing any gains that the Vekken army had made during the previous day.

When dawn came, it was clear that more than three-quarters of the artillery the Vekken had so carefully placed the previous day had been smashed beyond hope of repair, and although the invading army had more to bring forward, it seemed any chance of simply knocking down Collegium's walls had been dealt a fatal blow.

Twenty-Seven

In his dream Achaeos was deep within the Darakyon: not on the outskirts, where he had taken Che to show her the darkness of the old world, but in the heart of it, where he had been just that once before. He was there, in the crawling, twisted heart of the shadow-forest, whose inhabitants he had impudently demanded aid from – whose inhabitants had arisen to his call, but not at his command. The cold of their touch as they had then rifled through his mind was still burned on his memory like a brand. And in return for showing him the way to where Cheerwell was imprisoned, they had exacted a price.

He *owed* them, and such debts were always honoured, and seldom repaid happily.

In his dream, Achaeos stood surrounded by the knotted and gnarled trunks of the Darakyon's tortured trees, and he had seen, with the night-piercing eyes of his kinden, the things that dwelt under their shadow. Never had he more wanted to experience the blindness, the darkness, that other kinden complained of. These denizens had been Mantis-kinden once, he knew. Something of that remained, but it was overwritten in a heavy hand by crawling thorns, by pieces of darkly gleaming carapace, by the spines of killing arms, by rough bark and tangling vines and glittering compound eyes.

They were legion, the things of the Darakyon, and they

stared at him mutely. Their whisper-voice – pieced together from all the cold, dry sounds of the forest – was silent. There was a message, though, in their wordless scrutiny of him. He sensed reproach. He had disappointed them.

In his dream he cried out to them, demanding to know what it was he had done, or had not done, and still they stared, and their meaning decayed from mere dissatisfaction to despair. No words yet, but he heard them clearly still, from the very way they stood: *Why have you forsaken us? Why have you failed us?*

'What must I do?' he demanded of them. 'Tell me what has gone wrong.'

Overhead, in the gaps between the twining branches, the sky flashed with lightning, back and forth: the night riven over and over with golden fire, yet never a rumble of thunder to be heard.

They pointed, each and every one of them, fingers and claws and crooked twigs dragging his attention towards one tree, that seemed the same as all the rest, and he strained his eyes to see their meaning.

Something bloomed on the shrivelled bark of that trunk, and at first he thought it was a flower, a dark flower that shone wetly as the lightning danced. Then it quivered and ran, thick and flowing, down the tree's length, and he saw that it was blood. Of all the horrors of the Darakyon he recalled, this was new – this was unique to his dreaming.

Achaeos opened his mouth to question, but he saw now that *all* the trees, every tree in the forest's dark heart, and then all the trees beyond, were bleeding, the stuff welling up from invisible wounds and coating the trunks, pooling and oozing on the forest floor. Overhead the bright lightning lashed back and forth, gold on black, gold on black.

He stepped back as that encroaching red tide reached him, but it was rolling forth on all sides, and the things of the Darakyon were melting into it, still regarding him with an air of betrayal.

'What?' he called out to them, and it seemed that his Art-made wings opened without him willing them, so that he was lifted high into the stormy sky, seeing the Lowlands spread beneath him: the Lowlands and then the Empire and the Commonweal and beyond. The stain spread out from the Darakyon, the tide of blood heedless of boundaries and city walls: Helleron and Tharn were gone, Asta and Myna. Now, across the map that was so impossibly presented to him, fresh wounds appeared in the face of the world – Capitas, Collegium, Shon Fhor, Seldis – cities drowned in blood that arose in fountainheads from the depths of the earth, and in those wounds there were crawling things like maggots, long twining many-legged things that should never have been allowed back into the light.

The next morning Achaeos looked more pale and drawn than Che had ever seen him.

'Still not sleeping?' she asked.

He shook his head. 'Sleeping, but dreaming.' He sat down heavily beside her. 'The Darakyon. Something troubles it. It . . . wants something of me, but I cannot make it out. The voices are confused.'

Che regarded him, worried. 'And if you could, would you do so?'

He stared dully about the taverna's common room, which was now mostly empty. 'I must, for I owe a debt – and the things of the Darakyon are creditors I cannot ignore. But I cannot hear them clearly, and so I cannot act.'

Scuto and Sperra were already breakfasting. Neither of them looked much better than Achaeos did. *I should feel as bad*, Che knew. It had not sunk in, though, what might be happening to her own home. She wondered if the Vekken had reached the walls. That seemed very likely.

Be safe, Uncle Sten, she willed silently, for he would

always forget that he was no soldier. She had visions of him striding along the walls of Collegium and waving a defiant blade at the Ant horde.

There had been Sarnesh soldiers assembling for two days now, forming up their expedition, their automotives, their artillery and supply train. They would go by rail about half of the way, but closer to the siege the Vekken were likely to have undermined the tracks, and the army would proceed on foot. Nobody could march like the Ant-kinden, though. They were tireless on campaign and they would send the Vekken back home stinging.

An officer came into the taverna that very moment and marched over to them, his chainmail clinking. He looked about the table and said, 'Which one of you is named Sperra?' An unnecessary question, because it was a Fly-kinden name, and she was the only Fly there.

She raised her hand timidly, and the Ant looked at the rest of them. 'You must come with me. Your associates also. If any of these here claim not to be your associates, then they will be taken into custody pending investigation.'

'Now wait a minute,' Scuto started, rising.

'We are all her associates,' Che said. 'What is going on, officer?'

The Ant had been staring at Scuto, more in horrified curiosity than anything else. 'You are summoned to the Royal Court immediately. You must come with me.'

'Why?' Scuto demanded.

'You do not question the commands of the Queen,' the Ant snapped. 'I don't know what kinden you are, creature, but I will have your spikes filed blunt if you speak out of turn again.'

Scuto bared his snaggled yellow teeth at him, but said nothing. The officer stepped back, and one by one they filed past him. There was a squad of a dozen soldiers waiting just outside to escort them.

'What on earth is going on?' Che demanded in a hoarse whisper.

'Nothing good,' Achaeos said, before the officer again shouted for silence.

The Queen herself met them without any of her tacticians or staff. The belligerent officer had virtually pushed Scuto and the rest into her presence: just a single Ant-kinden woman standing at the end of a long table. Until Sperra whispered it, they took her for just another Ant in armour.

There was only one other there, a Fly-kinden man of middle years, wearing on his arm the badge of his guild, a figure-of-eight endlessly looping within a circle, which signified: *Anywhere within the world.*

The Queen of Sarn regarded them coolly, her gaze dwelling long enough on Scuto that he began to shuffle

Eventually he spoke up: 'Listen, Your Highness—'

'Your Majesty,' Sperra hissed.

'Your Majesty,' he corrected himself. 'What it is, I'm a Thorn Bug. No, you don't normally get my kinden around these parts. Yes, there are others. No, it doesn't hurt. Is that about it, Your Majesty, with all respect?'

The others held their breaths, but what would have seen Scuto dead by now if spoken to a Spider lady or Wasp officer passed without reproach here, for the Ant-kinden knew little of standing on ceremony.

'Save the matter of how you fell in with a Beetle named Stenwold Maker,' she said.

Scuto shrugged. 'He got me set up in Helleron when there was no one else to turn to. He picked me out as being good for something, Your Majesty, and since then we've done a lot for each other. Is there news of him, if I might ask?'

'Some of the last reports to come in from Collegium give his name as one of their . . .' there followed a pause, in which some unseen aide was obviously briefing her, '. . . War Masters, we believe the term is.'

'Do you know if the fighting has started yet, Your Majesty?' Che burst out.

'It seems certain. You four are his agents, then, in my city. You are the delegation sent to win us over to join your fight against the Wasps?'

'We are, Your Majesty,' Che confirmed.

'Then consider us won, but in no way that you will appreciate,' the Queen declared with heavy irony. 'You have heard that the Empire is already in possession of Helleron. We believe they are coming here next.'

'Here, Your Majesty?' Scuto goggled. 'To Sarn?'

'At the moment,' she said, 'there is a running conflict between my artificers and those of the Empire. Mine are destroying the tracks of the Iron Road while theirs are replacing them. There will inevitably be a battle. Our agents inform us the Empire's armies are mustering for a march on my city even now.'

They stared at her. The whole room seemed unutterably still.

'You must understand what this means,' she continued.

But they did not. They could not understand. Too much was happening too fast.

'I cannot therefore send my soldiers to Collegium,' she said, almost gently. 'I must defend my own city, my own people.'

Che gasped. 'But – Collegium cannot stand against the Vekken. Our citizens aren't proper warriors. Your Majesty, please—'

'It pains me to make this decision,' the Queen interrupted, in a voice that brooked no argument. 'Collegium has been our ally, and it is an alliance we have profited by. If I could be sure that I could hold the Wasps with half my soldiers, I would send the other half to your city without delay. I would maintain that my forces are the best equipped and best trained in all the Lowlands, but now the Lowlands have changed. It is not just that Vek is at the gates of Collegium, or that Helleron is in the hands of the Empire. News comes from Tark, at last, and all word states that the city has fallen. An Ant-kinden city. A city-state like mine. I cannot afford to wait for the Empire to come right up to my walls, lest my city suffer the same fate as Tark. My soldiers are trained for open battle, battle on the field. We shall meet them in the open, and then see if we are still the soldiers to put the world in awe.'

'But what about Collegium?' Che cried. 'What about Stenwold?'

'Do you know what a Lorn detachment is?' the Queen asked them. Surprisingly, it was Sperra who had the answer.

'It's a suicide detail, Your Majesty.'

The Queen's lips twitched. 'That is not exactly how my people would describe it – but a desperate assignment, certainly. I will send a Lorn detachment to Collegium. Solidarity should demand more, but no more can I afford to give. Three battle automotives with crew, though I can ill spare them.' She turned to the Fly messenger. 'Master Frezzo?'

He stood forward. 'Your Majesty?' He looked pale, and when he risked a glance at Che she saw her own distress mirrored in his face.

'It was you brought me the news of the Vekken army from Collegium,' the Queen told him. 'Now you must take this reply back, though one that I am loath to make. The Vekken will almost certainly be at the walls by the time you arrive.'

'It will present no difficulty, Your Majesty,' Frezzo said firmly. Che knew that he had the honour of his guild to uphold.

'Then go,' the Queen ordered him, and he saluted her and ran from the room. The ruler of Sarn turned back to

Che and her companions. 'You may stay here or you may leave,' she told them. 'Save that there is no safe passage guaranteed to Collegium any more.'

'Someone should go with the Lorn automotives,' Scuto said.

'It is your choice.'

'Then it should be me,' Che decided. 'Stenwold is my uncle.'

'You and Achaeos need to continue your work here,' Scuto advised her. 'It's looking more important all the time. Stenwold's going to need *me*, though. A War Master indeed? You know how he is, always forgetting himself and playing soldier.'

'Scuto, no—' started Sperra.

'Yes,' he said. 'Your Majesty, I'll go. I'm an artificer and I never knew an automotive that couldn't use another decent pair of hands.'

'Scuto!' Che reached for his arm but stopped just short of the spines.

'Che, listen to me,' Scuto insisted. 'Stenwold is going to need to know what's going on here, and I don't just mean what that messenger can tell him. What's going on with your work – stuff I wouldn't trust to paper. I'm our best bet. I'll be a good hand on the automotives, and I'm tough as a bastard. Remember the *Pride*, when it went up? Think you'd be standing here if my hide weren't between you and that mess? And yet here I am, healthy as anything.'

'You had better bloody be right about that,' Sperra hissed. 'Nobody as ugly as you was meant to be a hero.'

Salma opened his eyes to sunlight, and for a brief moment he thought it was *her*.

Then he recalled. The Broken Sword. Himself being smuggled out of the Wasp camp. He was about to sit up hurriedly, but remembered his wounds and eased himself up with care. The injuries tugged less than before, and he felt stronger. Looking around he saw Nero sitting close.

The Fly nodded to him. 'You're looking better than you have for a while.'

'Where are we now?' Propping himself up with one arm was about all he could manage, however improved he might look. Salma looked around, seeing a scrubby hollow and a dozen or so other people. There were a few feeble fires going, and an earth mound that smelled like bread, and that he realized must therefore be a scratch-built oven. 'What's going on, Nero? Who are these people?'

'They're on the run, like us,' Nero said. He pointed out a mismatched trio in Ant-style tunics: a Spider, a Fly and a Kessen Ant. 'They're slaves who got out from the city before it surrendered—'

'Tark surrendered?'

Nero grimaced. 'I suppose you never heard. You never saw, either. The Wasps . . . they just took the city apart from the air, like your friend said they would do, until the Ants knew there was nothing for it but to give up, or to see Tark rubbed from the map. That's how they deal with Ant-kinden, apparently. Anyway, those three were lucky enough to make a run for it, and now they've got nothing – just like the rest of us. As for them—' He indicated the woman tending the oven, who had three small children holding close to her skirt. 'They used to farm at a waterhole on the Dryclaw edge. Now Tark's gone, though, the Scorpions are raiding unchecked, and there are dozens of little farmsteads, and whole villages, that are getting attacked and left burnt out. She thinks her husband might be alive, but he's a slave of the Scorpions if he is, and being dead might be better.'

There were half a dozen young Fly-kinden sitting close together at the lip of the hollow, staring suspiciously at all the others. 'They were slaves of the Wasps,' Scuto identified them. 'I get the impression they were a gang of some kind, probably from Seldis. They sell off their criminals down Seldis way. Anyway, they're completely lost. They know the Wasps are going to take Merro and Egel, and they don't want to go back to the Spiderlands in a hurry, and so they're pretending they're not part of our troupe here, but they're sticking around all the same. And the gentleman and ladies behind you . . .'

Salma made the laborious effort of turning himself over to look. There was a covered cart there, he now saw, and a bearded man seated on the footboard was carving something in wood. A girl of around twelve was stretched out across the back of their draft-animal, which was a big, low-bodied beetle with fierce-looking jaws. Another girl of nearly Salma's age was nearby, picking over the half-hearted bushes for berries. They were all white-haired and tan-skinned, and they wore loose clothes of earth-tones and greens. The older girl sensed Salma's attention and glanced his way. She had a heart-shaped face and bright eyes, and she smiled timidly at him.

'Roach-kinden,' Salma identified them. 'I didn't think you had them in the Lowlands, but they roam all over the Commonweal.'

'And the Empire too, although the Wasps really hate them,' Nero agreed. 'Oh they're not seen much, but I hear they come south past Dorax from the Commonweal into Etheryon, and even down the Helleron–Tark road and west towards Felyal. The Mantis-kinden seem to tolerate them, or so I understand. These poor fools were found by the Wasp army as they were travelling, and a pack of scouts decided to do a little free-range looting. They don't know what happened to the rest of their family.'

'Refugees,' Salma whispered, and he remembered how it had been during the Twelve-Year War. As the Wasps advanced they had displaced hundreds, even thousands, onto the roads of the Commonweal, to be preyed on by bandits or descend to thievery to feed themselves. The

Commonweal's rulers had done their best but there had been the war to fight as well, and the scale of the exodus had been unthinkable.

And now it seemed certain that it would happen here as well.

'What can we do for them?' he asked, and Nero laughed harshly.

'Do? You can't even stand, boy. What do you expect to do?'

Salma stared at him, and then slowly forced himself up to his knees. His head swam briefly, but he pressed his hands flat on the earth for balance. Whilst Nero looked on uncertainly, he rose slowly, first one foot beneath him, then the next, and then, forcing his legs to obey him, he raised himself upright. Pain shot through him from his wound, but he clenched his teeth and ignored it.

Now he was standing. Nero had stood up, too, hands ludicrously spread to catch a man twice his size.

'I . . . can . . . stand,' Salma got out, though he had to fight to keep his vision in focus. He knew that he might topple any minute, and placed a hand on Nero's shoulder to steady himself. 'Tomorrow, or the next day, I will walk,' he said. 'And then I shall be ready to act.'

A man called Cosgren joined the refugees a day or so later. He was a Beetle-kinden, but huge – the largest Salma had ever seen, and monstrously broad across the chest and shoulders. For the first day he was with them he was quiet enough, watching his travelling companions carefully and even fetching wood for a fire. The next day he waited until they were all awake and then addressed them: 'Right, look at you. You don't know the first thing about where you're going, do you? So it's going to be like this. I'm in charge. And because I'm in charge, I'll get us to somewhere, but you all better do what I say, and that means I get what I want.'

The Fly-kinden youths huddled closer and looked at him rebelliously. They all had their hair cropped short to their skulls in androgynous fashion, and they carried weapons of a sort, if only sticks and stones. Cosgren must have weighed more than all of them put together, though, and eventually they let their gazes drop sullenly.

Cosgren's rule lasted almost peaceably for that same day. He took what food they had, with the pretence that he would distribute it, but everyone knew, and nobody said, that his own capacious belly would be filled first.

And then, at dusk, he wandered over to the wagon and the three Roach-kinden.

'Old man,' he began. The father of the two girls eyed him cautiously. He was not so very old, not really, but his white hair and beard made him look it.

'You hear me?' Cosgren demanded. 'Then say so.'

'I hear you,' said the Roach. His voice was surprisingly soft.

'I'm going to make your life easier, old man. I'm going to take your daughter off your hands.'

'My life's easy enough, and I thank you for your kind offer,' the Roach said.

Cosgren smiled, and a moment later he had knocked the man down with a simple motion, almost thoughtless.

'I'll give her more than you can,' Cosgren said, grinning down at him. 'You, girl, come here – unless you want your old dad to get hurt some more.'

He was, Salma realized, speaking to the younger of the two girls, not that it would have mattered either way.

Salma was on his feet, without quite realizing how he had got there, and Nero hurried over to him, telling him to be careful.

'You're in no state,' the Fly said. 'Just wait a moment . . . there are ways . . .'

'I know.' Salma approached Cosgren's lumped back with

410

dragging steps. 'You there!' he called, and the big man swung on him.

'You get back in line, boy. Don't want those wounds opened up again, do you?'

'No,' Salma said. He felt the line of his life stretched taut here, a moment of dread and then peace. In this wasteland between wars, in this meaningless brawl, and why not? Why not indeed? He had been given his moment, reunited with Grief in Chains, and then it had passed him by, and here he was. 'I'm going to stop you,' he told Cosgren, conversationally.

For a second the big Beetle did not quite know what to make of it, this drawn-looking invalid threatening him with . . . what? With nothing. Then he grinned.

'A lesson for boys that won't do what they're told,' he said, and he picked Salma up effortlessly, huge hands agony about his ribs, and Salma poked him in the face.

The world was briefly a very painful and noisy place, and then dark, blessedly dark and quiet.

He came to with the sense that little time had passed. There was an awful lot of noise nearby, but the pain in his chest and abdomen was too much for him to focus on it. Nero was kneeling beside him, asking over and over if he was all right.

There should have been another blow coming from Cosgren, but there was nothing. Perhaps the beating had finished, in which case he had got away lightly, but Cosgren would still be free to pursue his tyranny unchecked.

The sounds were screaming, he realized, and a man's, not the child's.

'What's going on, Nero?'

Nero grimaced. 'You . . . kind of cut him, Salma. Don't look so confused. That's what you meant, right?'

'Cut him? What . . . ?'

Nero took one of Salma's hands and brought it before his face. The first thing he saw was that it was covered in blood. Then he saw the claw, a sickle-shaped thing that curved from his thumb. Even as he watched it retracted back until there was barely a sign of it. Curiously, he flexed it back and forth, and felt its companion on his other hand do the same.

'I never had these before. When . . . ?'

'I noticed them on you back in the tent of the Daughters,' Nero told him. 'I couldn't remember then whether you'd had them before.'

There was a sudden shifting around them, of people coming together. Salma turned over and forced himself to sit up. Cosgren was standing, one hand clapped to a face slick and red. His eye, his one remaining eye, was staring madly.

'You little bastard.' The voice was choked with pain.

Salma saw a movement beside him, a glimmer of metal. The Roach man had drawn a thin-bladed knife, hiltless but sharp. They had all gathered around him, even the Fly gangsters. When Cosgren took a step forward, a flung stone bounced off his shoulder.

Half weeping with the pain he stared at them: the Fly gang, the Beetle mother, the ex-slaves and the Roach family. By that time, Nero had his own long knife out, and was holding it casually by the tip, ready to throw.

Cosgren snarled something – something about their not wanting his leadership, then let them starve – and he stumbled out away from them, off into the barren terrain.

Tension began to leach out of the refugees. The Roach man knelt by Salma, offering him some water that he took gratefully. Behind their father, his two daughters stood, staring curiously.

Salma glanced around at the others. The Flies had gone back into their exclusive huddle as though nothing had happened. The three slaves had drifted away as well, and he saw that they had found their own new hierarchy, with the Spider as their spokesman, as though they were still compelled to live within rules of obedience.

He should feel weak after his exertions, he knew, but he felt stronger than he had in days.

The next day there were bandits. A dozen rode in, half of them mounted two to a horse. Their leader, though it was little satisfaction to see, was wearing Cosgren's leather coat.

He was a Beetle himself, or nearly. His skin was a blue-black that Salma recognized from his recent travels. The refugees had been travelling at the wagon's steady pace, most walking but Salma lying in the bed of dry grass it carried, staring up at skies that promised unwelcome rain before nightfall. Then the thunder of hoofs had come to them, and they had stopped dead, and most of them had looked to Salma.

Am I riding here on the wagon because I am weak, or because I have become their leader now? They needed no leader – except perhaps in moments such as this. Salma got down, pleased to find his legs holding him without a tremor, and watched as the intruders' eight horses made a very crude semicircle before the wagon. The draft-beetle hissed at them, swaying its jaws from side to side, but the bandit leader ignored it, looking over the ranks of the refugees.

'Let's keep it simple,' he said. 'These are troubled times, nobody's where they wanted to be, everyone's a victim, so on, so forth.' He spoke with the accent Salma recalled, and refined enough that he seemed testament to his own words, a man not originally cut from this kind of crude cloth. 'So let's see what you've got. Let us just take our pick and then you can go on your way.'

Salma looked over the bandit's men. They were a motley band, but not as raggedly dressed as might be expected. These were not just desperate scavengers driven to robbery. Most had some kind of armour: leather jerkins and caps, padded arming jackets, even one hauberk of Ant-made chain. There were axes and swords amongst them, and a halfbreed at the back, who looked to have Mantis blood, had a bow ready-strung with an arrow nocked. Salma's own army had some knives, some clubs, and the staff that Sfayot the Roach had cut for him.

He leant on it now, grateful that it would disguise how weak he really was. 'So what do you imagine we have?' he asked. 'Perhaps you think that we all had time to pack, before we were driven out, before we escaped.' Salma planted his staff in the ground, firmly enough. 'If you're slavers then we will fight you, and you can sell our corpses for whatever they'll bring you. But if it's goods you want, we have none. Less than none. Come down here and see for yourself.'

'We're not slavers,' the bandit leader replied. 'Too many of us have been on the wrong end of that market to risk trying to sell there.' He smiled, teeth flashing in his dark face. 'Commonwealer, aren't you? I've known enough of your kind in my time.' He swung off his horse, and Salma heard the clatter of a scale-mail cuirass beneath Cosgren's coat. Without needing orders, two of his fellows got down off the horse they shared, and the three of them walked past Salma to peer into the wagon.

'You're slaves yourselves?' Salma asked. As his fellows prodded through the grass in the bed of the wagon, the leader turned back to say, 'Some of us.'

Salma had spotted the colours of that scale-mail, then, and the design of the sword the man bore. 'You're an Auxillian,' he said.

For a long moment the bandit leader regarded him fixedly, until at last he said, 'So?'

'There are no friends to the Empire here,' Salma explained. 'I was a prisoner in Myna myself, once.'

'There's nothing but the wagon,' one of the bandits said. 'And even that's nothing you could borrow money on.'

'Excuse me, sir,' said the Roach Sfayot. 'But we have nothing, no goods. No food, even, until we stop for the evening and forage.'

'You have women,' the bandit leader noted. 'Roach-kinden, isn't it?'

Sfayot regarded him narrowly, waiting.

'You sing, dance? Anything? Only I remember your lot as being musical.'

Sfayot nodded slowly.

'Well then we'll deal,' the bandit leader decided. 'We have a commodity for trade: safe passage on this road. In return, you'll trade us some entertainment. And we'll break our bread together, or whatever you can find. And then we'll decide what we're going to do with you.'

Twenty-Eight

The morning began bright and cloudless, and Stenwold had the dubious pleasure of being able to see it. Balkus had kicked at his door an hour before dawn, and then carried on kicking until Stenwold had arisen.

Now he was in his temporary base in the harbourmaster's office, the harbourmaster himself having taken ship at the first word of the Vekken advance. Around him were his artificers, his messengers, and a fair quantity of others whose purpose and disposition he had no ideas about. Balkus stood at his shoulder like some personification of war, his nailbow in plain view, and Stenwold tried to imagine what would happen when the naval attack actually took place.

The harbour at Collegium had been designed to be defended. There was a stubby sea-wall sheltering it, and the two towers flanking the harbour entrance held some serviceable artillery, if not particularly up to date. There was a chain slung between these towers, currently hanging well below any ship's draft, that would serve when raised to prevent a vessel crossing that gateway, or that was the theory. Defence had been a priority in the minds of the architects, certainly, but they had lived two centuries ago, and had never heard of armourclads, or even of ships that moved by the power of engines rather than under sail or with banks of oars. Since then, defence had been a long way from anyone's mind right up until the Vekken had turned up with a fleet.

Out-thought by Ant-kinden, he cursed to himself, trying to find some gem of an idea that might save the day. If the Vekken could land their troops, those superbly efficient paragons of Ant-kinden training, then the docks would be lost in half an hour, and the city in just a day.

'They're moving!'

The shout roused Stenwold from his ruminations. He rushed over to the expansive window of the harbour-master's office and saw that the funnels of the armourclads had now started to fume in earnest. Four smaller vessels were beginning to make headway towards the harbour, whilst the huge flagship had begun to come around with ponderous but irresistible motion. The small ships of the fleet began to tack around it, some by engine power and a few by sail.

'Is the artillery ready?' Stenwold demanded. 'Where's Cabre?'

'Gone to get the artillery ready,' said one of the soldiers with him. 'It's in hand, Master Maker. All you need to do is sit here and watch.'

'No,' muttered Stenwold, because he had to *do* something, and yet what was there to do? 'Master Greatly, is he . . . ?'

'He said that he was ready, although I don't believe a word of it,' said one of his artificers, the man with the underwater explosives. 'He did say you could go and watch the launch if you wanted.'

'Yes, I do want,' Stenwold decided. He looked around for Balkus. 'Where's . . . ?'

There was a dull thump from quite close by, and he felt the floorboards shudder. For a mad second he was two decades younger and in the city of Myna, with the Wasps' ramming engine at the gates.

'What was that?' he demanded, but nobody knew, so he

rushed to the window and saw three buildings away a warehouse burning merrily, its front staved in.

'Sabotage!' someone shouted and, even in the moment that Stenwold was wondering coolly who would sabotage a warehouse, a second missile was lobbed from the great Vekken flagship. It flew in a shallow, burning arc, and it seemed impossible that it would not just drop into the water, but their range was accurate, and in the next moment another of the dockside buildings had exploded.

Most of the Collegium dockside was wood, Stenwold realized dully, and then, *They must be sighting for our artillery*. There was only a brief stretch of sea-wall at Collegium, but the two stubby towers that projected were already launching flaming ballista bolts and catapult stones towards the approaching armourclads, sizing up the distance. The siege engines on the Vekken flagship must be enormous, though, the entire vessel a floating siege platform. Collegium's harbour defences could not hope to match the range.

Something flashed overhead, and Stenwold saw a heliopter cornering madly through the smoke. It was a civilian machine, some merchant's prized cargo carrier, but its pilot was putting it through manoeuvres its designer had never anticipated. Behind it barrelled a sleek fixed-wing flier, propellers buzzing, and then a heavy Helleron-made orthopter painted clumsily with a golden scarab device. The airfield had begun to launch its defences. He should go and see how Master Greatly was doing.

And someone called, 'Look out!'

He turned, idiotically, towards the window, just in time to see the whole wall in front of him explode. The incendiary blast hurled him away in a raking of splinters, knocking everyone else off their feet. He hit his own map-table, smashed it with his weight, and a wall of heat passed over him. He could hear himself shouting out some order, but he had no idea what.

Then he was being helped to his feet, and for a moment

he could not see, and his face and shoulder were one mass of pain.

'What's . . . ? Who's . . . ?'

'Steady there.' The voice was Balkus's but there was a lot of other noise, too – the crackling of flames, the cries of the wounded. He let Balkus guide him blindly away and prop him against a wall.

'Now hold still,' the Ant said. People kept running past, jostling him, and he felt stabs of pain as Balkus plucked the worst of the splinters from him. He wiped his face, feeling blood slick on his hand. The injured were still being hauled from the harbourmaster's office, even as the room burned.

'Is everyone . . . ?' he started, and then realized: 'The fleet! Is the chain up?'

'No idea,' Balkus said, and Stenwold staggered away, thumping down the stairs with blood seeping into his eyes again, and Balkus trying to keep up. From somewhere there was another explosion, another flaming missile from the Vekken flagship.

He staggered out into the clearer air, that was nevertheless blotched and stinking with smoke, onto the flat open quayside. Ahead of him was the calm stretch of the harbour, and the two stubby walls with their artillery towers, with the great open space of water between them.

Only it was open no longer, for the first ships of the Vekken navy were fast crowding into it. Three of the armourclads were powering forwards, and he could hear above all of it the thump of their heavy engines. To either side of them, wooden craft knifed through the water, coursing ahead of the cumbersome metal-hulled vessels, their catapults and ballistae launching up at the harbour towers.

The towers were loosing back, however and Stenwold saw one skiff swamped by a direct hit from a leadshotter, its wooden hull simply folding in the middle, the mast toppling sideways. The men that fell from its sides were armoured Vekken soldiers, as were most of the crews of the approaching navy, and Stenwold thought they must be mad to dare a sea assault.

And yet here they came, and the chain was still nowhere to be seen.

'Raise it!' he shouted, with no hope of being heard across that expanse of water, amongst such commotion. 'The chain! Raise the chain!'

Beside him Balkus was slotting a magazine into his nailbow, which at this distance was as futile as Stenwold's own shouting. By the time the weapon would mean anything, it would be too late.

And then Stenwold saw a gleam in the water as something was cranked up from the seabed: the great spiked chain that closed off the harbour mouth. There were engines three storeys high in the paired towers to drag the great weight of metal through the water, but they were engines fifty years old. Here it came, though, and Stenwold ground his teeth in agony as it seemed that the powering armourclads would be past it before it was up in place. They were bigger ships than he had thought, though, and further away, but the fleetest of the wooden vessels now surged forwards, trying to cross the barrier before it was finally raised.

The chain caught the ship before a quarter of its length had passed, and it abruptly began rising with it in a splintering of wood. The spikes on the chain were busy rotating, each set in opposition to the next one, chewing and biting into the vessel's hull even as its bows were lifted entirely out of the water. Then the craft began to tip, spilling men out, even as its engine mindlessly pushed it further over the chain. A moment later it slid back, entirely heeling onto its side, to lie awash in the water directly in the path of the armourclads.

'Nice work!' Balkus exclaimed. Stenwold shook his head. 'They didn't even have armourclads when that chain was made. There's no telling whether it will stop them.'

Out there, the cargo heliopter he had seen earlier was veering over the armourclads, and he saw it rock under the impact of artillery fire, half falling from the sky and then clawing its way back up. The Helleron orthopter was turning on its wingtip, and a man at its hatch was simply tipping a crateful of grenades out to scatter over ships and sea alike, exploding in bright flashes wherever they struck wood or metal. A moment later one of the flier's flapping wings was on fire, the orthopter's turn pitching into a dive. Stenwold looked away.

'Master Maker!' Stenwold turned at his name to see Joyless Greatly and a group of other Beetle-kinden lumbering towards him. They lumbered because they were wearing some sort of ugly-looking armour, great bronze blocks bolted to their chests, and man-length shields on their backs.

'Ready for action, Master Maker.' Greatly was grinning madly.

'You said you had orthopters!' Stenwold shouted at him. 'Where are they?'

'We're wearing them, Master Maker.' Joyless Greatly turned briefly, and Stenwold saw now that his back resembled a beetle's, with curved and rigid wingcases, elytra that almost brushed the stone of the quay.

The block weighting his chest was an engine, Stenwold realized, and it must have been a real triumph of artifice to make it that small. There were explosives hanging from it, too, on quick-release catches. The expression on Greatly's face was quite insane.

'Good luck,' Stenwold wished him – these being insane times.

Greatly gripped a ring on his engine and yanked at it, twice and then three times, and suddenly it shouted into life. Stenwold fell back as the wingcases on his back opened up, revealing translucent wings beneath, and then both wings and cases were powering up, first slowly but gradually threshing themselves into a blur.

And Joyless Greatly was airborne, his feet leaving the quay and, beyond him, the score of his cadre were up as well.

Beetles flew like stones, so the saying went, but Greatly had overcome both nature and Art. His wings sang through the air and sent him hurtling out across the water, utterly fearless and weaving for height, until he became just a dangling dot heading towards the oncoming bulks of the armourclads, which had reached the chain.

The sky above them was busy now, as the airfield sent out its fliers one after another to attack the encroaching fleet. Airships wobbled slowly overhead and dropped explosives and grenades or simply stones and crates, while orthopters swooped with ponderous dignity. There were fixed-wings making their rapid passes over the oblivious ships and loosing their ballistae, or with their pilots simply leaning out with crossbows. Stenwold felt his stomach lurch at the thought, but there were men and women out there, Fly-kinden mostly, but a Moth here, a Mantis there, even a clumsy Beetle-kinden, all darting with Art-given wings, shooting at the Ant sailors and soldiers and being shot at in turn. The air that Joyless Greatly and his men were entering was a frenzy of crossbow bolts and artillery, of sudden fiery explosions and scattershot.

The lead armourclad now struck the capsized wooden ship and crushed it against the chain, forcing it half-over and then shearing through the planks until it itself met the grinding teeth of the chain. They scraped and screamed as they hit the metal, scratching at it but unable to bite. For a second Stenwold thought the ship would be lifted up by it, but its draft was too deep, and its engines kept urging it forwards. Explosive bolts from the tower artillery burst about its hull in brief flares, and then one of the towers was enveloped in a firestorm as the flagship found its range. The tower was still shooting, even though some of its slit windows leaked flame.

And the armourclad strained, and for a second its stern was coming around as the chain stretched taut, but then a link parted somewhere and the chain flew apart in a shrapnel of broken metal and the armourclad's bow leapt forwards, making the entire ship shudder.

There was now nothing between it and the harbour. Stenwold knew he should move, but he could not. He just stared at the black metal ship as its unstoppable engines thrust it forwards. The repeating ballista mounted at its bows was swivelling to launch blazing bolts at the buildings nearest. Meanwhile another missile struck the east tower and caved a section of it in.

Impossibly small over its mighty decks, the miniature orthopters of Joyless Greatly swung hither and thither like a cloud of gnats. They had the swift power of a flying machine but the nimble size of a flying man, and Stenwold saw them dart and spin about the deck of the armourclad with their artificial wings blurring, releasing explosives one by one from their engine harnesses.

The cargo heliopter shuddered past, trailing smoke now, a trail of incendiaries falling behind it that were mostly swallowed by the sea. Stenwold longed for the telescope he had at Myna, but he had not even thought to bring one. He strained his eyes to see one of Greatly's men dodge and tilt over the armourclad's deck, leaving a trail of fire behind him.

'Will you look at that!' shouted Balkus, pointing. Stenwold followed the direction of his finger to see something glint beneath the surface of the harbour.

'Tseitus's submersible ship!' he exclaimed. He had expected something like a fish, but jetting out from beneath the quay came a silvery, flattened oval as long as three men laid end to end, with six great powering paddles that forced it through the water in uneven jerks. It was fast, though, for with half a dozen of those laborious strokes it was most of the way to the armourclads. He lost sight of the submersible as it passed beneath the lead ship.

'Everything we have,' he heard himself say. 'It must surely be enough.'

There was a spectacular explosion of fire and stone, and the east tower simply flew apart, some strike of the flagship having found its ammunition store. The flying debris battered the nearest armourclad, rolling it violently so that its starboard rail was almost under water. With a dozen great dents in its side, it began to drift towards the shattered tower, its engine still running but its rudder ruined.

Cabre had been in that tower, Stenwold recalled. He suddenly felt ill.

The lead armourclad was still forging forwards but it was on fire in a dozen places from Greatly's ministrations. Even as he watched, Stenwold saw one of the diminutive fliers hover neatly by its main funnel. It was too far to see the descent of the bombs, but a moment later there was a cavernous bang from within the vessel, and the funnel's smoke doubled, and redoubled. The flier was already skimming away, and the others were leaving too, making all ways from the stricken ship. Stenwold saw at least one of them falter and fall to the Vekken crossbowmen, spiralling over and over, out of control, until the water received him.

Balkus grabbed Stenwold and threw him to the quayside, more roughly than necessary, and then the stones beneath him jumped hard enough to throw him upwards an inch and smack the breath from him when he came down.

A single piece of jagged metal was thrown far enough to clatter onto the docks, but the centre of the lead armourclad had exploded into a twisted sculpture of ruined metal and burning wood that clogged the mouth of the harbour. Beyond it, through a curtain of smoke, Stenwold could dimly see other ships of the fleet making ponderous turns, still under attack from the air. One of them was listing already, its wooden hull holed beneath the waterline in what must have been Tseitus's blow for Collegium.

The fliers began to return home, and there seemed so very few.

The powerfully-built Fly-kinden stepped from the dockside house, watching the ships retreat, his vantage a slice of sea and sky viewed down a narrow back alley. 'I want my money back,' said the treasure-hunter Kori to the women behind him.

'Go to the wastes!' the Madam spat at him. 'You filthy little monster!'

He leered at her, lounging in the doorway, oblivious to the smoke on the air. 'Come, now, the world's about to end isn't it?' he demanded. 'The city's about to fall. Your ladies should be giving it out free, just for the joy of their profession. I'd thought I'd find some proper dedication to your trade here, in this city of learning.'

The old Beetle woman regarded him venomously but said nothing. Kori laughed at her. 'Instead, what is there? The moment a little disturbance happens, and four streets away mind, all your girls lose their nerve and start crying and whimpering and begging for their lives. I mean, it's not that I don't enjoy that sort of thing but, still, if they won't *perform*, what is there? The trade's fallen into a sad state. It's no wonder they call this a house of ill repute.'

'You brute!' the old woman said. 'This is our home, our city! We can't all just fly away through the air when the walls come down.'

'Well, exactly,' the Fly agreed. 'But will you make the best of it? No, you will not. You could have had a few coins from me, woman, and they might have stood you in good stead. I'm sure there's a Vekken Ant with a venal soul somewhere out there. My ardour has cooled though, so my purse remains shut. I leave you only with my own disappointment.'

He walked away from them, whistling jauntily against the misery of the city around him. He felt it incumbent upon him to at least keep his own spirits up. So Collegium was on the rocks these days. That was no business of his. Let the Ants and the Beetles sort their own lives out, so long as he got what he came for.

The other hunters were still outside the city, waiting for his return and report. He had decided that he was the most experienced man amongst them, and therefore that he should be their leader. So far, at least, they had followed his suggestions. He knew a few of them by reputation, had met with Gaved the Wasp once before in a bitter dispute over an escaped slave. There were no hard feelings, though. They were both professionals.

He holed up in a taverna until dusk, enjoying being the only unconcerned man in a panicking city. The prices were cheap but the service was poor, because the innkeeper's son and daughter had both run off to join the army. That thought made Kori smile at the foolishness of the world. It was not that he feared risk, since risk was his business, but he always made sure that he was suitably reimbursed for any risks he took, and made sure he could always fly away if things got messy. In a world turned so badly on its head, there was no better life than that of a mercenary agent.

As dusk fell he made his silent exit, flying fast and high above the Vekken encampment, beyond any Ant-kinden's view or crossbow's reach, out into the hills beyond until he had tracked down his fellows' camp.

'You're late,' Scylis informed him, when he landed.

'I set the clock, so I'm never late,' Kori said. 'I've been biding my time, is all.'

'Well?' asked Gaved.

'Well I visited Collegium once before,' Kori said, 'but I don't recall it as being quite so crawling with Ants.'

The four hunters looked over the camps of dark tents that had spread like a stain around the city. From their hilltop retreat they had heard the loudest sounds of conflict, the roars of the leadshotters and other firepowder weaponry.

Gaved had spent the day spying out the walls with his telescope. 'Well, they warned us to expect trouble.'

'This is more than just trouble,' the Fly considered. 'This complicates things. We should be asking for more money.'

'That's your answer to everything, isn't it, Kori?' observed Phin the Moth, looking amused.

'Never found a problem it couldn't solve yet,' he agreed. 'You reckon this is the Empire, then?'

'Vekkens,' Phin corrected him.

'Yeah, but that maggot patron of ours in Helleron knew there'd be trouble. So I reckon the Empire's been stirring, eh?'

'Of course it's the Empire,' Scylis, Scyla, told them. Her companions talked too much, and she was fed up with all of them. She always worked best alone. Phin and Gaved had even slept with each other a couple of times, which she viewed as unprofessional. There was no real affection there, she knew, just physical need, but it still irked her. Perhaps it was the price of her wearing a man's face most of the time.

'I reckon the Empire wants all of this,' Gaved said distantly. 'They're starting fires like this all over, so they can just come over and stamp them out. Going to be a bleak enough place when the black-and-gold gets here.'

'You? What will you have to worry about?' Scyla asked him. 'They're *your* cursed people.'

That made him frown at her, and sharply too. 'If you had any idea how hard I've fought to be free of their bloody ranks and rules, you wouldn't say that.'

'Still living off their table scraps, though, just like the rest of us,' she jibed.

'Yes I am. So what's the plan?'

'Plan hasn't changed,' Kori explained. 'Go in, get it, get out – just the usual. A little war won't stop us.'

'And if there's anyone here who can't get himself in past the Vekken then he shouldn't be doing this job,' Scyla added.

'Well, Master Spider, and when did you grow *your* wings?' Phin asked acidly.

'Don't you worry about me,' Scyla told her. 'I'll be through the Ant camp and up the wall, and they'll never even know it.'

'Best if we all make our own way, then,' Kori said. 'You need to find the main marketplace of the middle city. That's about three streets south of the white College walls,' he added, because none of the others had been there before. 'There's a taverna called the Fortune and Sky, a merchant's dive, so we'll meet out back of that. For now, let's all pick our points of departure, as close to the action as you like.'

Gaved looked at Phin and Scyla, seeing them nod in response. 'Agreed then,' he said. 'Luck to all, and no stopping for stragglers.'

Kori's Art-conjured wings flared from his shoulders even as he spoke, lifting the stocky Fly-kinden into the air. Phin's wings, when they followed suit, were darkly gleaming, almost invisible.

The warden obviously recognized him, a balding, portly man doing his best to stand to attention, as another balding, portly man came to call. Stenwold waved him down.

'No formality, please. I have just escaped from a meeting.'

Memory of that meeting would stay with him for a long time, because the War Council had degenerated into a room full of people who had lost their grip on how the world worked. There was no continuity between them. Stenwold had seen the dull, aghast faces of men and women present who had fought on the wall when the Ants made

428

their first sortie. There had been artificers manning the artillery, who had first experienced war when dozens of Ant-kinden died beneath the scatter-shot of their weapons. Then there had been those, in these sharp-edged times, who had found a new purpose: men whose inventions were finally being put to work, men who had always dreamed of taking up a sword, and now found that the reality was better. Stenwold would always remember Joyless Greatly, even when every other memory had gone. The Beetle aviator's dark skin had been soot-blackened, and his calf was bandaged where a crossbow bolt had punched through it, but his eyes shone wildly, and he grinned and laughed too easily. He was *living*, Stenwold realized. He was consuming every moment. Flames that burned so brightly never burned for long, but Joyless Greatly, artificer and aviator, was burning so fiercely that it seemed he would not outlast even a tenday.

Kymon had been there, the lean old Ant-kinden become a soldier again after years in an academic's robe, and Stenwold even found Cabre in the crowd, bandaged and burned but alive. When her tower had fallen she had escaped through a window so small that only a Fly-kinden could have managed it. Others had not been so lucky.

And Stenwold had made his excuses as soon as he could but found he had nowhere to go. Not his own house, certainly. They would find him there, and bother him with papers and charts when he really had nothing further to contribute. He needed a break. Most of all, he needed someone to talk to.

'Has anyone been to see her?' he asked the warden.

'No one except the staff,' the man said. 'I go in and talk to her a little, sometimes.'

'Good,' said Stenwold. 'What about charges?'

'None,' the warden said. 'She's your collar, War Master. They're leaving her to you.'

'Don't call me that, please.'

The warden looked surprised, himself obviously a man who would love such a grand title. He shrugged and unlocked the door of the cell.

She was being well enough looked after, he saw. Save for the bolted shutters on the window the room beyond the locked door hardly seemed a prison at all. There was a rug on the floor, a proper bed, even a desk provided with paper and ink. *For confessions, perhaps? Last testimonies and defiant speeches?* This was certainly not the room of a common felon. Stenwold had made no particular arrangements, but he wondered whether his recent rise through the city's hierarchy had effected this good treatment.

'Hello Stenwold,' said Arianna. She was sitting on the bed, dressed in her old student's robes, her arms wrapped about herself. 'I wondered when you would . . .' She stopped herself. 'I suppose I wondered *if*, really.'

Stenwold crossed slowly and turned the desk chair to face her, lowering himself wearily into it. 'Things have been difficult,' he said.

'I've heard.'

'But you can't imagine,' he said. 'Just two days now and – the College halls have become infirmaries, and every student who ever studied medicine is there, doing what little can be done. And there are artificers that have fought all day who will now be working all night, on the artillery, on the walls. There were girls of fifteen and men of fifty who were out on the walls today and many, enough, who never came back to their mothers or their husbands or wives. And the Ants keep coming, over and over, as if they don't care how many of them it takes. And they'll get over our walls if they have to make a mound of their own dead to do it. Have you heard that?'

Numbly she shook her head.

'And I . . . I'm here because – who else can I tell? I've sent them all away, my friends, and I keep asking myself whether it was to help, or just because I wanted to try and keep them safe. Because I have a record, there. I have a real history of sending people off to keep them safe. I even seem to have thought that two of them might be safe at Tark.'

For a long time he sat in silence, grasping for more words and finding none, until she said, 'Stenwold – what's going to happen to me? You can tell me that, can't you?' She bit at her lip. 'I keep expecting your Mantis friend to turn up as my executioner.'

'Or your Wasp friends to pull you out,' he said bitterly. 'No, that's right, you told Tisamon you were fighting amongst yourselves, you . . . imperial agents.'

'Rekef,' she said. 'Say it. I was a Rekef agent, Stenwold. Not a proper one. Not with a rank, or anything. But I was working for them. And, yes, we fought. We tried to kill a man called Major Thalric.' She watched his reaction carefully. 'You remember him?'

'We've met,' Stenwold allowed. 'I wish . . . I wish it was so simple that I could just . . .'

'*Believe* me? But of course, I'm a Spider and I'm a traitor. Twice a traitor therefore. I'm sorry, Stenwold, really I am. I . . . seem to have done a very good job of cutting myself off, here.'

He looked at her, at the misery in her eyes, the hunched shoulders, and knew that he would never be able to discern what was truth and what was feigning. By race and profession she was doubly his better at that game.

'There were three of us in the plot,' she said slowly. 'If it helps explain. It happened when Thalric told us the Vekkens were getting involved.'

He shook his head. 'I don't understand. You were working against us. You sold us out to the Empire. I don't understand why the change of heart.'

'Because the Empire is different,' she told him flatly. 'We were expecting an imperial army to take Collegium. Not this year, probably not even next, but eventually. And

431

the Empire *conquers*, and if you conquer, then you make sure that you leave the place standing so you have people left to push around. They would probably even have let the College go on, so long as they got to control what was being taught. And Collegium would still be Collegium, only with a Wasp governor and Wasp taxes, and Wasp soldiers in the streets. That's what we thought. But the Vekken hate this place. It's a reminder of a defeat, so they'll not leave a stone standing given the chance. And that made us think and realize just what the stakes were. And we broke away, Hofi, Scadran and I. We tried to kill Thalric when he came to brief us. We killed his second, but the man himself was too good for us. He got the other two, and I'd have been next if your Mantis hadn't found me. Lucky for me, wasn't it? A quick and private death swapped for a public execution. Or perhaps just death at the hands of the Vekken when they burn this place around me.' She stood up suddenly, and he knew she was going to ask for his help, to demand it, to impose on him in the name of the lies she had once shared with him. But the words dried in her throat and she just made a single sound, a wretched sound.

'I cannot vouch for the Vekken, or the Empire,' he said. 'There will be no execution here. Even in these exceptional times, the Assembly won't break a habit of ten years just for you. The irony is that you'd probably be exiled, eventually, but that currently presents us with technical difficulties.'

Her fists were clenched, and he saw the small claws there slide in and out of her knuckles. There was more in her eyes than mere pleading, and he felt her Art stir there, the force of it touch his mind, trying to turn him, to make him like her and pity her. That Art was weak, though, sapped by her own despair, and he shrugged it off almost effortlessly.

'You know . . . I could have easily killed you,' she got out.

'I'd guessed it. You cannot spin that into an obligation.'

'No.'

'Do you regret not doing it?'

She stared at him. She was obviously at the very end of her leash, stripped of her strategies and schemes, more and more transparent in her desperation. 'No,' she said, and he wished that he could believe her.

He felt a sickening lurch inside him at the thought of what he was going to do, all the perils and unspeakable foolishness of it. Tisamon, for one, would never speak to him again.

'You're being held here to my order, and therefore I'm going to set you free,' he said, speaking fast so that he could get the words out before he changed his mind.

She was silence itself, awaiting his next words.

'What more do you want me to say?' he asked her. 'You're going free. No conditions. You've already been questioned, and I have no more questions for you. I'm not even going to ask you to go back to the Rekef and work against them on my behalf, even if you could. I cannot know the truth of it now; I would not know the truth of it then. I . . . just . . . You can walk out of here as soon as I tell the warden, and I'll tell him as soon as I leave.' He got to his feet, feeling ill and sad. 'Which is now.'

'Wait,' she said. There were tears in her eyes and he wondered dully if they were genuine.

'I'm waiting.'

He could feel her Art touching him again, feeling at the edges of his mind and trying to find a way in. It must have been just instinct for her, her last defence, still trying to sway him because she did not really believe what he said. She thought this was a trap. Her lips moved but she said nothing.

'No words,' he said tiredly. 'No thanks, even. I'm sorry but I don't even know if I could believe that.'

He turned and walked out, and then told the warden

that she could go. As he reached the door he looked back and saw her emerging cautiously from the cell, testing the first steps of her freedom.

He left then, set off for his house at last. He had probably made a mistake, and he hoped he would be the only one to suffer for it. It had been lies and pretence, and he had been a fool, as he still was, but for the few days that she had been with him she had made him feel young, and made him happy.

Nothing he had done in the defence of his city had sat well with him, the horrors of the naval assault recurring over and over, but he found that, when he remembered that he had freed her, the pawn of his enemies, he slept easily.

The next day the Vekken came against the wall in force. During the night they had brought up their remaining artillery, and the dawn saw great blocks of their infantry assembled behind their siege engines. There were massive armoured ramming engines aimed, three each, at the north and west gates, and both those walls already had a full dozen automotive towers ready to bring the Ant soldiers to the very brink of the walls.

The harbour mouth was still blocked by the pair of ruined armourclads, and the buildings nearest the wharves had been abandoned after the incendiary shelling from the Vekken flagship. Stenwold had Fly messengers on the lookout who would fetch him if the ships started moving again, but he could not meanwhile just sit idle. Against Balkus's protests he made his way over to Kymon on the west wall.

There had been some fighting here the previous day. The Ants had made assaults at the gate, and one of the siege towers stood at half-extension, a burned-out shell only ten yards from the wall itself. The wall artillery had obviously been busy, and would be still busier today.

Stenwold made his hurried way along the line of the

defenders. Most of them now had shields, he saw, which he knew was a reaction to the crossbow casualties of the previous day. The Ants had advanced far enough on one earlier assault that some of those shields were the rectangular Vekken type the attackers used.

'War Master,' some of them acknowledged him, to his discomfort. Others saluted, the fist-to-chest greeting of the city militia. They all seemed to know him.

Out beyond the wall, without any signal that could be perceived, every Ant-kinden soldier suddenly started to march. The engines of the rams and towers growled across towards the defenders through the still air.

'They're coming in faster this time,' Kymon said, striding up to him, and it did seem to Stenwold that the engines were making an almost risky pace of it, bouncing over the uneven ground. Close behind them the Ant soldiers were jogging solidly in their blocks.

'Ready artillery!' Kymon called, and the same call was taken up along the wall. 'They're going to rush us!'

'Master Maker!' someone was calling in a thin voice, and Stenwold turned to see a man he vaguely recognized from the College mechanics department.

'Master Graden,' he now recalled.

'Master Maker, I must be allowed to mount my invention on the walls!'

'This isn't my area, Master Graden.' But curiosity pressed him to add, 'What invention?'

'I call it my sand-bow,' said Graden proudly. 'It was made to clear debris from excavations, but I have redesigned it as a siege weapon.'

'I'm not an artificer. Do you know what he's talking about?' Kymon growled.

'Not so much,' Stenwold admitted.

Then the Ant artillery started shooting, and abruptly there were rocks and lead shot and ballista bolts falling towards the wall, and especially towards Collegium's own emplacements. Stenwold, Kymon and Graden crouched under the battlements, feeling more than hearing as their wall engines returned the favour. Stenwold risked a look at the advancing forces and saw, almost in awe, that Kymon had been right. Behind the speeding engines, the Ant soldiers were no longer in solid blocks that would make such tempting targets for the artillery. Instead they were a vast mob, a loose-knit mob thousands strong, surging forwards behind their great machines.

And they would be able to form up on command, he knew, each mind instantly finding its place amongst the others.

'Can it hurt? His device?' he shouted at Kymon over the noise.

Kymon gave an angry shrug and then ran off down the line of his men, bellowing for them to stand ready, to raise their shields.

'Get the cursed thing up here!' Stenwold ordered Graden, and the artificer started gesturing down to where his apprentices were still waiting with his invention. It looked like nothing so much as a great snaking tube thrust through some kind of pumping engine.

'What will it do?' Stenwold asked. Another glance over the wall saw the Ants' tower engines ratcheting up, unfolding and unfolding again in measured stages, with Ant soldiers thronging their platforms and more climbing after them. Crossbow quarrels started to rake the wall, springing back from shields and stone, or punching men and women from their feet and over the edge, down onto the roofs of the town.

'It will blow sand in their faces!' Graden said enthusiastically. 'They won't be able to see what they're doing!'

True enough, Stenwold saw that one end of the tube had a vast pile of sand by it. The other was being hauled onto the wall, with the great engine, the fan he supposed, hoisted precariously onto the walkway.

The nearest tower was almost at the level of the wall-top as Graden's apprentices wrestled the sandbow into place, and then the artificer called out for it to start. All around them the defenders of Collegium, militia, tradesmen, students and scholars, braced themselves for the coming assault.

Twenty-Nine

Parosyal had white beaches, a sand that gleamed as brightly in the sun as the sun itself. Nothing on the mainland could match it, nor any other isle along the coast. A hundred Beetle scholars had written theories to explain it.

There was only one safe harbour at Parosyal, Tisamon had explained, and she had understood that by 'safe' he was not referring to anchorage or the elements.

Parosyal was a mystery, and one that history had ignored: the sacred isle of the Mantis-kinden. The slow march of years had seen Collegium scholars baffled by it, Kessen fleets avoid it, and opportunistic smugglers or relic-hunters disappear there, never to be seen again.

'Every one of my kinden seeks to come here, once at least in a lifetime,' Tisamon explained, and she knew he was confirming that she, too, was his kinden. 'They come from Felyal, from Etheryon and Nethyon. From across the sea, even. From the Commonweal.'

'That's a long haul,' she said.

He nodded. 'This is our heart.'

'But why?' she asked. 'Surely not . . . gods?' She knew that, long ago, some ancient peoples had tried to make sense of the world by giving faces to the lightning and the sea. Perhaps some savages still did, in lands beyond known maps, but in these days nobody halfway civilized held that they were subject to the will of squabbling and fickle divinities. Achaeos had told her that the Moth-kinden believed in spirits, but ones that could be commanded, not ones that must be obeyed. And then of course there were the avatars of the kinden, the philosophical concepts that were the source of the Ancestor Art, but they were just *ideas*, aids to concentration. Nobody thought that they actually *existed* somewhere.

'An ancient and inviolate communion,' whispered Tisamon, and a shiver went through her. It was not the words themselves, but because she heard quite clearly some other voice saying that exact phrase to him, when he was younger even than she, and as some previous boat was approaching this same harbour.

She felt sand scrape at the boat's shallow draft. The vessel's master, an old Beetle-kinden, called for any to disembark that were intending to.

She took up her single canvas bag, slung her swordbelt over her shoulder, and splashed down into thigh-deep water.

The bay of Parosyal held a single fishing village that was huddled between the water and the treeline, facing south across the endless roll of the ocean as though it had turned its back on the Lowlands and the march of history. The houses were constructed of wood and reeds, and built on stilts to clear the high tides. The villagers were a strange mixture that Tynisa had not been expecting.

There were only half a dozen Mantids there, and they seemed mostly old, their hair silvered, and with lines on their faces. The other villagers comprised a whole gamut of the Lowlands population: quite a few Beetles, including one in the robes of a College scholar, some Fly-kinden, a few Kessen Ants. There were a surprising number of Moths passing back and forth between the huts and the boats, or conferring in small groups.

No Spider-kinden, though, she had expected that.

She set foot now on the sand of the beach, shaking a

little water from her bare feet, and she was aware that many of them were staring at her. Staring at her, especially, in company with Tisamon. Her blood was mixed, but her face was her mother's. In fathering her, Tisamon had dealt his own race the worst blow, having committed the ultimate sin against their age-old grievances.

But she had expected worse than she received. Looks, yes, and a few glares even, but nothing more. Tisamon was standing in the centre of the little village now, watching a pair of young Moths put a small dinghy out onto the water. He was waiting for something, she could see.

Where is it all? she asked herself, because surely this collection of hovels could not be *it*. This was not what all the fuss was about. And then she looked past the huts towards the wall of green that was the forest that covered most of Parosyal and she knew *that* was it.

Tisamon's stance changed, just slightly, alerting her to the approach of an ageless, white-eyed Moth-kinden man. His blank gaze flicked to Tynisa, but her appearance drew no change of expression to his face.

'Your approach is known,' he said softly to Tisamon. 'Your purpose also.' He looked to her again. 'It is not for me to judge, but . . .'

'The Isle will judge,' Tisamon said firmly, but his glance at his daughter was suddenly undermined by uncertainty.

'Indeed it will,' said the Moth. 'It always does. The Isle has never seen one such as her. We can none of us know what may be born, or what may die . . . even if she has made the proper preparations.'

Tisamon's look was to the dark between the trees. 'It must be tonight. We have no time.'

'Are you sure she is ready? She is very young.'

'I was her age, when I came here to be judged.'

The Moth shrugged. 'The Isle will judge,' he echoed, and then, 'Tonight, as you wish.'

*

She had expected some grand ceremony: drums and torches and invocations. They had meanwhile taken up residence in one of the shacks, many of which seemed to be empty. Tisamon had set to sharpening his claw, over and over, and she knew it was because he was merely keeping his mind off what would happen.

He could not tell her, she knew, for it was forbidden. Mantis-kinden seemed to live their lives in cages of air, held back at every turn by their own traditions. Tisamon had broken free from that cage once, but he would bend no more bars of it now, not here.

He was worried about her, she realized. He had tested her as fiercely as he could, killed her a hundred times in practice duel, measured her skill and her will to fight against his own. He believed in her, but she was his daughter and he worried. She, in her turn, could not ask him for reassurance, could not even speak to him lest he hear her voice shake. That was pride, she realized, a refusal to bend to the common demands of being human. It was *Mantis* pride.

Out there, in the village's centre, they were brewing something in a small iron pot hung over a beach fire. The Moth that Tisamon had spoken to and an older Moth woman were talking to one another in soft voices. *Are they casting spells? Is this magic?* But Tynisa did not believe in magic, for all that it seemed to turn the wheels of Tisamon's life. Che, poor credulous Che, believed in more magic than Tynisa could ever allow into her world.

Tisamon looked up. The sky above the island had now graded into dusk, into darkness. Tynisa had barely noticed.

'It is time,' the Mantis said. He looked her over, noting her rapier, her dagger, her arming jacket. He had told her to be ready for war.

When the time came to drink, she baulked at first. Whatever they had boiled up over the beach fire was thick and rotten-smelling. They waited patiently. They would not force her. If she did not drink, she would fall at the first challenge.

She took the warm clay cup from them, suppressing a revulsion that seemed more than rational, some deep abhorrence that she could not account for or place.

As quick as she could, she drank it. The liquid was shockingly sweet, both cloying and choking, and she fought herself to swallow by sheer willpower. The reaction in her gut doubled her over and she reached for Tisamon for his support, but he was out of arm's length already. *You are on your own from here.*

Tynisa regained her balance, wiped her mouth. Her stomach twisted sourly, and the two Moth-kinden seemed to shift and blur in her vision.

'What . . . ?' she began to ask, but they were already heading for the forest, so she stumbled after them, the ground suddenly unpredictable. Tisamon was still near, but too far to take strength from him. He did not even look at her.

The forest verge loomed dark. The Moths had vanished, either into it or just away. She glanced once more at Tisamon, but he would give her no clues. When she stepped forward she felt the shadows as a physical barrier that she had to put her shoulder to and force aside.

He was with her when she stepped between the trees. He was with her but, as she forged her way through the trees, he fell away and fell away, until she could not find him anywhere near her. There was motion, though, all around. In the darkness that her eyes could half-pierce, that motion showed her path to her. The rushing of others on either side kept her straight. She caught glimpses. They were Mantis-kinden, keeping pace with her, guiding her. They ran through the trees easily while she struggled to keep up. They were always overtaking her, passing on into the heart of the wood, whilst more were always rushing up from behind. She saw them in her mind: young, old, men, women, familiarly or strangely dressed, or naked and clad only in the shadows of the trees.

Real? Or has their drug done this to me? She had no way of differentiating, for everything she saw *looked* real to her. Her normal judgement had been stripped from her.

They were herding her. She ran and ran, deeper and deeper, and knowing herself led like a beast, or hunted like one. She could not be sure.

And at last she was afraid.

It had taken its time, that fear, stalked her all the way into the denseness of this forest, for which there had to be some other word. *Jungle* was that word, Tynisa realized, for this piece of another place and time that was hidden away on the island of Parosyal.

It was dark now, and so dark between the trees, beneath the knotted and tangled canopy, that even her eyes could not penetrate it. She felt her way by touch as much as sight, and still went on, knowing only that she was being led.

She had lost sight of the ones leading her, or they had gone ahead or gone out of her mind. She was alone, and yet she could sense they were still there. She was totally at their mercy, lost in this torturous place.

When had the night grown so dark? She wondered if there was ever day in here. She had to force her way through the trees at times, through gaps a Fly would fight to negotiate, and at others there was a great cathedral of space about her, a cavern of twisted boughs and green air.

This was no natural place, and surely no place for her. She knew now that this had been a dreadful mistake. On whose part? On Tisamon's, for certain, and he had gone. She had lost sight of him.

Because she was on her own now. He had told her as much. This she must do *alone*. He could not be there to hold her hand.

Father!

443

But what a man to have as a father – cold as ice, distant, bloody-handed. No, Stenwold was her father, in all but the blood. Stenwold the civilized, city-dwelling, scholar and philosopher. Stenwold the kind, the understanding. She had been raised in Collegium, studied in the white halls of the College itself. What madness had brought her here, into this maze of green and black?

She stumbled down a dip, splashed through a stream, took a second to look about her, but it was still no use. She had the sense of things moving, urging her on, but nothing came clearly to her eyes.

If she stopped now, she would be lost for ever. They would never find her bones.

The madness that brought her here was one she carried with her. It was the madness that took her when she drew a blade in anger. A cold madness like her father's. Because she loved it: not killing for its own sake but killing to prove her skill. Killing to prove her victory. Blood? She was steeped in it.

With that same thought came the faintest glimpse of one of her escorts, a brief shadow between the trees, and she knew it was not human at all.

She rushed forwards to keep pace, struggling up the steep bank that the stream had cut, hauling herself up by the hanging roots it had exposed.

And she was there – and she saw the idol.

An idol? There was no other word for it. A worm-eaten thing of wood, taller than she was by at least two feet, with two bent arms outstretched from it, a great cruciform monument so worn by time that no detail of it could be made out clearly. Even the trees had been cleared from around it, or perhaps they had never taken root there.

This was it. She was at the heart of the Mantis dream, the centre of the island, the centre of the forest, of the kinden's heartwood.

She approached the looming thing slowly, stepping over

the lumped ridges of roots, feeling movement in the trees all around. They were watching her, and waiting. What was she to do? What was she to make of this . . . thing?

Close now, almost within arm's reach. She had never believed in magic but something coursed from this crude and decaying image, some distant thunder beyond hearing, a tide that washed over her, lifting her and dragging at her.

She put out a hand to it. Would it be sacrilege or reverence, to touch this thing? What light the revenant moon could give her was shy of it, but her eyes hoarded the pale radiance against the darkness and she drew her hand back sharply. The idol was crawling with decay and rot. Worms and centipedes coursed through its crumbling wooden flesh. Beetles swarmed at its base, and their fat white grubs, finger-long, put their heads into the night air and wove about, idiot-blind. It was festering with voracious life, perishing even as she watched it. She saw then where new wood had been added as the thing fell apart, making good and making good but never replacing the dark and rotten heart of the effigy, so that whatever was jointed in was simply further prey for the rot, over and over, decade after decade.

And she saw that was the point, that the thing before her, a dead image, was also a living thing, a festering, fecund thing, life consuming death and death consuming life.

She took her knife from her belt. She had seen gouges where the thing's breast would be, if the angled spars that jutted from it were arms. This was the test, was it? She raised the blade.

She felt the power, that invisible tide, as it rose to a peak about her. Above her thunder rumbled in a clear sky.

And she stabbed down.

She did not believe in magic, but lightning seared across the stars in the moment that her knife bit into the worm-eaten wood – and she saw the second idol, the glare of the lighting burned it on her eyes: the tall, thin upright, the two hooked arms.

The flash had blinded her, but she sensed it move ever so slightly, swaying side to side, and she froze.

Not an image, but the original. Even without sight, she saw it in her mind. That triangular head eight feet from the ground, vast eyes and razoring mandibles, and the arms, those spined and grasping arms. An insect larger than a horse, easily capable of snatching her in its forelimbs and crushing her dead, scissoring into her with its jaws. They killed humans, in the remote places where they still lived. They killed even people who came hunting them with bows and spears. Everyone knew this.

Was she supposed to kill it now? She blinked furiously, seeing only shapes, blurs, and she felt it move again, swaying slightly, fixing her with its vast, all-seeing eyes.

And she stood still and waited, the knife useless in her hand.

It was close. She could see the shifting motion as its arms flexed on either side of her. She was almost within its embrace.

Sister.

The voice came like a stab of pain in her skull.

Sister.

She could see enough now, the towering, swaying mantis before her. The voice seared through her, but she knew it was some latent Art awakening, just for this moment. The Speech – she had heard of this: Art little seen these days, but to command the creatures of one's kinden was known. To hear their simple animal voices and to order them . . . but not this—

Sister, you have come far.

They were not human words. Some other intelligence was prying into her skull, forcing itself upon her, and her poor mind was forming the words as best it could.

You have come to prove yourself.

Had she? She had forgotten why she had come.

Turn, sister, the voice speared into her mind, and she turned and saw him there.

He was just a moving shape in the darkness, leading with the tip of a blade splashed pale silver by the moon. Her rapier had cleared its scabbard even as she saw him, and she felt the shock of contact, real as real, heard the scrape and clatter as the metal met.

He drove her before him, lancing and slashing in dazzling, half-seen patterns, a shadow-shape that she could not pin down. Her body knew the dance, though, or at least her sword did. Even as she felt the rapier vibrate with her parries, it was as though she was feeling its history, all the swift patterns it had ever moved through, as though the fight she was engaged in was running along grooves worn deep by centuries of use.

And she stared at the face of her opponent, which shifted and blurred before her, and tried to read it, but it changed and changed again. Now she was fighting Tisamon, his blade the darting metal claw, and murder on his face as he tried to blot out the unforgivable crime of having sired her. Now it was Bolwyn, whose shifting visage masked the faceless magician who had betrayed them in Helleron. He was Piraeus, seething with hate for her, treacherous and mercenary but poised and skilled despite it. The blade cut close to her face, and then she felt it pluck at her arming jacket, not deep enough to draw blood, but close enough.

Always the figure was a fraction faster than her attacks, displaying Tisamon's cold rage, or the face of Thalric with the fires of the *Pride* reflecting in his eyes. Her adversary was every man she had ever fought, every man she had loved or hated, one at once and all together, a shifting chimaera of faces and styles and blades. He was the half-breed gang-leader Sinon Halfways with his marble skin, and Captain Halrad who had tried to own her; beautiful Salma who she had yearned for and yet who had never given himself to her; Stenwold, who had hidden her past from her; Tisamon, always Tisamon.

And then, there was an instant in which the face was a woman's, and she could not have said if it was her own, or that of her mother, and she lunged with a wild cry and felt the rapier's keen-edged blade lance through living flesh.

She was lying on her side before the idol, and the world seemed to be fading in and out around her so that she could almost see through the trees. There was a whispering chorus in her mind, but no words, just a susurrus of constant, muddled thoughts. She was exhausted: every muscle burned and twitched with it. The rapier's hilt was still tight in her hand, and she felt it almost as the clasp of a lover.

Her head swam, but she seemed to understand things she had not comprehended before, though she knew this knowledge would leave her when she regained her full wits. In that drifting but infinitely lucid state she saw how Tisamon must be able to call his blade to him, and how Achaeos had known where Che and Salma were being taken, and many other things.

And there was a figure kneeling by her now, a Mantis woman with silver hair, proffering an ornate bronze bowl gone green in places over the years. She took it without hesitation, sitting up to drink, and she knew it was rich mead mixed with the blood of whoever or whatever she had slain before the idol, and the ichor, freely given, of the great mantis.

And it was bitter and sharp, and it burned her, but she forced it down, because it was strength, and skill and victory.

And when she awoke again, as dawn crept between the trees, there was something sharp cutting into her closed left hand. A brooch of a sword and a circle: the token of the order of Weaponsmasters.

*

Tisamon was waiting for her on the beach, and when she saw his face she realized that he had not been certain, despite all his promises to Stenwold, whether he ever would see her again.

She now wore the badge of his order on her arming jacket, and when the thought occurred, *Did I really fight . . .* she had only to touch the rents that the unknown blade had cut there, almost through to the skin. She was left only with the question, *What was it that I fought? What blood did I drink?*

The thought had come to her of those shadow-creatures in the Darakyon forest that she had seen that once when Tisamon led her through its margins. They had known his badge and his office, and stayed their hands for him.

There was a darkness at the heart of Parosyal, she understood, and it was best not to ask questions.

Tisamon's eyes flicked from the brooch to her face, and he smiled just a little. She knew he would never ask, just as she could not ask him about his own experience all those years ago.

'There is a boat that will take us over to Felyal before noon,' he told her.

'What do you hope to accomplish there?' she asked him.

He shrugged. 'Perhaps nothing, but I will see what can be done. It will not be easy for you.'

'This will help?' She touched the brooch lightly.

'It will keep them from killing you out of hand,' he told her, 'but you may still have to prove yourself to my people – as may I. With last night behind you, I have no doubt that you can.'

Thirty

'You don't strike me quite as bandits,' said Salma. 'Or perhaps you've not been in the trade long.'

The brigand leader shrugged. 'There are two or three that have.' He had given his name as Phalmes, and the total of his band was fifteen men and one Ant-kinden woman. They had a fire lit in a farmhouse that had been torched at least a tenday before, and the band of refugees was huddled close together in their midst, watching them suspiciously. Sfayot played pipe, though, keeping time on a drum with his foot, and his daughters danced. It entertained the bandits, but Salma found it lifeless compared to other dances he had seen.

'Most of us are getting out from under the Empire,' Phalmes said. 'Deserters like me and some slaves. Others are rustics running away from home, or who've been burned out. The Empire's on the march and that pushes a tide of flotsam ahead of it. We've got to live, and banditry's as good a living as any.'

'I've seen bandits,' Salma observed. 'It's a wretched life.'

'I imagine you have, being from where you're from,' Phalmes agreed. 'And I'd ask just what a Commonwealer like you is doing so far from home. Not great travellers normally, your people.'

'It's a long story.'

'It's going to be a long night.'

'Tell me a short one first,' Salma said. 'How do you come to know the Commonweal?'

Phalmes just smiled sourly, and Salma immediately understood. 'You fought there?'

'Five years of the Twelve-Year War,' the bandit agreed. 'After they drafted me for their Auxillians. I was apprenticed for a mason, before that. So much for the futures we think we'll have. So tell me, Commonwealer, tell me your long story.'

And Salma told him, the bones of it anyway. He could not place any real trust in this man, he knew, and so he held off the names and the details, but he told Phalmes about the College and about his being recruited by a Beetle spymaster. He recounted his journey on the *Sky Without* and their escape, and their foundering in Helleron. He told of the betrayal and their capture by the Wasps.

Phalmes had listened without interruption, but it was when the tale reached Myna that he held a hand up. 'How long ago?' he asked hoarsely. 'When was this?'

Salma counted back. 'A couple of months at most, since I was held there. Then my friends got me out – and the governor was killed, I heard.'

'The Bloat?' Phalmes said. 'They killed him?'

'Yes. And I met the woman who is running the resistance there. She was freed at the same time I was.'

'She? What's her name?'

'Kymene. Do you know her?'

Phalmes shook his head. 'Heard of her, though. So *your* lot let her out. Well, now, that's bought you safe passage and a half, more than any song and dance.'

The elder of Sfayot's girls came, then, and sat down next to Phalmes, who regarded her without expression.

'Your father sent you here to me?'

She nodded, watching him.

'There's a man with a realistic view of the world,' said

Phalmes tiredly. 'Your friend here has just bargained your freedom, girl.'

She shrugged. 'We knew he would.'

'And why's that?' Phalmes asked her, like a man humouring a child.

'Because he is such a man,' she said. 'My father has keen sight.'

Salma shifted uncomfortably. 'It was nothing but chance.'

She shook her head stubbornly, and then turned her attention to Phalmes. 'What will you do?' she asked him. 'Your men are unhappy. They fear the Wasps.'

'Do they, now?'

'They should,' she told him. 'My father has seen it. They are just north of here. The great city of the chimneys has fallen to them already.'

'Does she mean Helleron?' Phalmes demanded.

'It's the first I've heard of it,' Salma said, and then reconsidered. 'Or no, I'd heard that northwards wouldn't be a good destination. I hadn't thought . . . Things are moving fast, then?'

Phalmes nodded gloomily. 'It's looking as though this country won't be good even for bandits any more. There's plenty of my lads here who need to keep themselves well out of the Empire's hands, and I put myself squarely in that number.'

The girl leant into him unexpectedly, almost pushing him against Salma. 'You're not a bad man,' she said. 'My father sees many things.'

Salma's eyes sought out Sfayot near the fire, and found the white-haired man looking at him with an unnervingly clear stare.

'I'm as bad as I need to be,' Phalmes told her. He seemed about to push her away, but then decided against it. Salma could see that he was already worrying about what to do with his followers next, because where could he lead them now?

'You should come with us,' the Roach girl told him.

Phalmes stared at her levelly. 'Should I? And where are you all going that is such a wonderful destination?'

'I don't know,' she said, and then looked over at Salma. 'Where are we going?'

'I'm not leading us anywhere,' Salma said, but realized, even as he said it, that this was not quite true. They had been looking to him since he had driven Cosgren away, because Cosgren had made himself leader, and then Salma had displaced him. That was the way things worked.

And if he was leading them. he should know where they were going, and why.

'What else has your father seen?' he asked. Phalmes gave an amused snort, because magic was just a word to him, but Salma had seen magic in his time and he believed in that moment that Sfayot could indeed be a seer.

'That you will find something,' the girl said. 'You will find what you seek, perhaps.'

'Does he know you're telling me all this?'

'He wanted me to,' she said. She was close to his own age, thin and pale, with her white hair cut short and ragged. She was pretty, though, and she looked at Phalmes with a smile that he did not know what to do with. In that moment of awkwardness, Salma saw him as though he had known the man all his life. A solid working man, ripped from his trade, his family, his life, only to be driven further and further as he fled the rolling borders of the Empire, and yet here he was, still trying.

'They made you an officer in the Auxillians,' he guessed.

'So you're a magician as well now, are you?' Phalmes demanded. 'I was Sergeant-Auxillian, if you must know.'

'And you're still trying to look after your men.'

'Just like you are,' Phalmes confirmed, 'but what of it? A man's got to have some purpose in his life.'

'Yes, he does,' Salma agreed.

'Why not come with us?' the Roach girl asked Phalmes again.

He merely shook his head tiredly.

But the next morning, as the refugees set off westwards, Phalmes and his bandits were riding uncertainly alongside them. They were far enough apart to maintain their sovereignty, but they rode a parallel path, and took care not to get ahead.

Something was happening, Salma was aware, though he was not sure just what. In the meantime, as he waited for it to happen, his little band of fugitives lived day-to-day and relied on one another. When they were hungry, the land or the leavings of others sustained them. When they were weary they stopped and scavenged wood for a fire.

Then, one afternoon when they were in sore need of food and shelter, one of Phalmes's scouts reported back that there was a small village ahead. They had been following the Sarn–Helleron railroad, and it was some little hamlet built around a rail siding. Passenger trains had stopped here, so there would be inns, farmland, an engineer's workshop with a single enterprising artificer. But there had been little traffic of late, and most of the opportunists had headed away, looking for fatter pastures, leaving only a skeleton of a place, inhabited by those that could not or would not leave.

Phalmes gave a signal and the bandits began to ready their weapons.

'What are you doing?' Salma asked him.

'We need food,' Phalmes said. 'What's more, there are roofs out there that we can make use of.'

'There will be no pillaging here,' Salma told him. 'There's no need for that.'

454

'You're right, so long as the locals there are sensible.' The Mynan gave him a hard smile. 'So long as they understand that we have the power to take, all we need to do is ask.'

'Let me at least talk to them first,' Salma insisted.

'Whatever you want,' said Phalmes with a shrug. 'But those around you now are *your* people. They're looking to you to provide, like my men look to me. They're short of everything and hungry each evening. What are you going to do about that?'

Salma looked out at the village and thought, *Was it Cosgren that brought me to this?* It had to be something more, but he could not put his finger on the moment when he had shouldered this responsibility. It was now on his shoulders, nonetheless.

It did not turn out as Salma had planned, none of it.

They had gone to the village, all of his ragged band: the farmwife and her child, the Fly gangsters and the escaped slaves, Sfayot and his daughters and – like a dark and brooding tail – Phalmes's deserters and brigands. The village would have no wish to play host to such a pack of vagabonds, and yet the numbers Salma led in were great enough that they could hardly resist.

Taking Phalmes and Nero along with him, Salma had met with the village headman and bartered for food. Some of his barter had been in coin, some in promised labour, or services. He was aware that he had desperately little to offer and that, even with Nero's practised haggling, they should have been turned away immediately. Instead, the headman made an offer that was generous by any means, and Salma understood then how he was participating in banditry. Banditry of a civilized sort, but Phalmes's men were all well armed, and this village was small.

They would camp within the village boundaries, Salma explained. They would chop the promised wood, draw the promised water, all the other meaningless tokens of their agreement. The headman tried to wave it away, but Salma had insisted.

He had not intended to become a brigand, but it seemed that it was easier than he had guessed to slip into that trade.

He had not intended to defend the village, either, but nevertheless it had happened. He had less control over his fate than he had ever imagined.

The real brigands had come thundering down on the settlement at night, with swords and burning brands. There were a score and a half of them and they were not here to make deals, or even to threaten or intimidate. They came for quick loot, a handful of whatever they could grab.

Instead they found Salma and his followers. Even while the villagers were putting their children out of the way, reaching for their staves and spears, Salma was rousing his band, sending them out with blades and sticks and bows. He went out himself, too, seeing by the slice of moon far better than the attackers, making savage work with the staff that Sfayot had made for him, and then ultimately just with the claws of his thumbs.

He discovered he was strong enough to fly again, using his wings to leap into his enemies, kicking and raking, and then jump back before they realized what was happening.

These were the sort of mixed ruffians he remembered from Helleron: Beetles and rogue Ants and halfbreeds, driven but disorganized. The fighting was fierce.

When they were finally chased away, at least half their number struck down, Salma walked amongst his own people to assess the damage. Two of Phalmes's men were dead, and one of the Fly-kinden youths. Others were wounded, and Sfayot and his daughters did what they could with charms and herbs and bandages made from torn and boiled cloth.

Then Salma went to face the headman.

'We did not bring them down on you,' he said because,

all through the fight, that had been his thought, of what the villagers must surely believe.

'I did not believe you had,' said the headman, a Beetle-kinden, like most of the villagers. There was a cut across his balding scalp that one of his own people had bandaged. 'Why did you come here?'

Salma shrugged. He was feeling haggard and worn down and his wound ached. 'We saw your houses and we were hungry.'

'Take the food,' the headman said. 'I have some money, too. We have done well here until the troubles.'

Salma wanted to refuse, but he thought of Phalmes and knew that he had at least that much responsibility – even to bandits and deserters.

The dawn brought a sight that made him shiver. Without ever discussing it, his followers had taken the arms and armour of the slain bandits. The Fly-kinden had swords and daggers now, and the Beetle-kinden farmwife had a crossbow. The three slaves had covered their tunics with studded leather hauberks. Sfayot's eldest daughter had a short-hafted axe thrust through her belt. She had accounted for herself well with slung stones, the previous night.

Phalmes approached Salma and held a shortsword out to him, hilt first.

'I saved this one,' he said. 'I know a bit about swords and here's a good one. Helleron-made, and they know their business there.'

Salma accepted it gratefully. The balance was good, better than the Wasp-kinden weapon he had carried for so long. It felt good to have a proper sword in his hand again.

Two nights after the village he dreamt of home: riding out of the elegant palace of Suon Ren in the Principality of Roh, and seeing the landscape spread out before him in gentle tiers that centuries of careful cultivation had made into a picture of perfect beauty: the green and gold of the

457

fields under the blue of the sky. It was autumn, near harvest, and the cold breeze that was blowing promised an early end to those warm days. The northern landscape revealed more snow on the mountaintops than a tenday ago. The Lowlanders knew nothing like this in their dry land of bronze and dun and yellow.

He had ridden out and through the fields, and through the small villages built of golden wood that stood safe within sight of the castle. On the horizon was the shadow of the Gis'yaon Hold where he had guested twice with the Mantis-kinden, renewing the bonds of fealty and solidarity between them and the Principality of Roh – and through Roh to the Monarchy itself.

As he passed through these villages, the people bowed to him in honour and respect, and his horse tossed her head in reply.

Last winter the predators had come down from the hills, and Salma had ridden out with Felipe Shah to deal with them. The body of the Commonweal was groaning with parasites, and those parasites were brigands. In its thousand-year history there had been times of strength and times of recession, but never such a difficult time as this. The Monarch's realm was patchworked with rot like a blighted leaf. Some roads were so preyed upon that even the Crown's own messengers could not pass safely. There were loyal principalities cut off from the court by lawless lands. Some castles were the home only of robber barons who played at the prince but were nothing more than bandits grown fat unopposed.

Where now is that golden sound our strings once gave unto the dawn? had sung the old minstrel at Felipe's court.

Where now is the ancient blade for many years so boldly drawn?

The mist of autumn leaves its tears,
The weeping of the ending year,

Of maidens for their husbands lost, of children into darkness born.

And Felipe and Salma and their men had gone to fight, from horseback, from the air, with spear and punch-sword and bow, because the principality was like a garden, and a gardener had a duty to ensure the health of his charges.

Duty and responsibility, of course. A duty to protect those in the principality who could not protect themselves, because Salma was a Prince Minor of the Commonweal.

The next day, Phalmes rode along next to Sfayot's cart and spoke to Salma, although it was at Sfayot's eldest daughter that he looked most. Nero sat up beside Sfayot himself, in between his occasional flights about the surrounding countryside.

'Did you ever hear about the Mercers?' Salma asked.

'How could I not?' Phalmes said. 'While fighting in the Commonweal, you got to hear a lot about the cursed Mercers.'

'And?'

'And what? I could never work them out. Your people, your peasantry, seemed to worship everything they did, but the pissing *Mercers* weren't averse to cutting throats when it came to it. Nobody wanted to fight them. At least there weren't so many of them.'

'Thousands, really, but you would have seen few enough' Salma said. 'They do more than fight invaders, though. In fact that's barely what they do at all. They protect the Commonweal, and that means mostly from its own worst impulses. They go wherever brigands have made the roads unsafe, where princes are cruellest to their subjects, or have rejected the wisdom of the Monarch. And they work against invaders, and their agents, but they defend the Commonweal first and foremost. They are heroes.'

459

Phalmes shrugged. 'Well, you asked me what I knew about them. So what of it?'

Salma smiled slightly. 'Where will you be in five years, Phalmes?'

'In an unmarked grave, probably,' replied the ex-bandit. 'Possibly the same in just five days. It's an uncertain time. I'd prefer to go . . .'

'Home?'

'Myna, yes. But I can't see that happening.' A shadow crossed his face, and Sfayot's eldest inched forward to look at him more closely. 'Ever,' he added. 'Even if Kymene starts a revolution, the Wasps will only put it down within a month, or even a year, and what difference would that make? And then everything will just be worse. So, if I do live out five years? Who knows? I don't feel that I myself have much of a choice in the matter.'

'And if I gave you a choice?' Salma said.

Phalmes frowned at him. 'Meaning what?'

'I'm a prince,' Salma reminded him.

'Good for you, Your Worship. So what?'

'In the Lowlands they don't understand it. In the Empire too I'd guess. I'd almost forgotten it myself, but I am a prince and that still means something, wherever I am.'

The messenger brought Totho to a long practice hall attached to one of Drephos' newly commandeered factories. There were targets of wood fixed to the far wall down a long arcade, scuffed and scratched and painted with range-markers.

The master artificer was there already, along with his entire cadre of followers and a few Wasp soldiers as well. Totho found himself the last to arrive. There was no resentment, though, only a barely concealed excitement about them. Totho sought out Kaszaat but her expression conveyed a warning.

Drephos was smiling, as lopsided as ever. He had his hood fully back, with no cares about his malign features amongst his own people. In his hands was the snapbow.

Totho had originally called it an airlock bow in his designs but, after the sound that it made, the term snapbow had stuck, from the artificer's old habit of calling any kind of ranged weapon a 'bow' of some sort, despite the lack of arms or string. This was the tweaked and adjusted article, perhaps destined to undergo another iteration, perhaps to be presented as finished. Each of Drephos's artificers had been given a chance to make further changes and test them. The last day or so had already seen a dozen separate prototypes tried and forgotten.

Now Drephos proffered the weapon and he took it, feeling how light it was, a sleek and deadly-feeling creation, like a predatory animal that found its prey by sight from on high. The curved butt fitted to his shoulder and armpit to steady it, and he was able to look down the slender length of the barrel, using a groove in the folded crank of the air battery itself to correct his aim.

'Any complaints, Totho?' Drephos asked him.

'It's beautiful, Master,' Totho said, wonderingly.

'You have the best of them, as is only fitting,' Drephos said. At his gesture the big Mole Cricket-kinden began handing out the others, until all the artificers had a newly finished snapbow in their hands.

'We are almost at the end of our stretch of road with this device,' Drephos told them all. 'Next will be the training sergeants. General Malkan is preparing to march, but he is leaving me two thousand men here and every factory in Helleron if I need it. When we walk out from here, if we are satisfied, this entire city will be devoted to your invention. It's a rare privilege.'

'I understand, Master.' There was something he was missing, he knew, some underlying tension he could not account for. He glanced at Kaszaat and saw that she alone of them was not smiling. 'We're here for the final tests?' he asked.

'We are,' Drephos said, and signalled to the soldiers. One of them went to the far end of the range and pulled a door open.

There were two dozen people behind the door, and they were pushed out onto the range quite quickly by Wasp soldiers, who closed the doors and stood nearby, hands open and ready. Totho frowned. Afterwards it would appal him that it took him so long to work out what was going on.

They were Beetle-kinden, mostly, with a few halfbreeds or Flies, and they looked as though they were going to a costume party all dressed like warriors. Some wore leather cuirasses or long coats, others had banded mail, or breast-plates, or chain hauberks in the Ant style. There was even Spider-made silk armour and a suit of full sentinel plate that the wearer could hardly move in. None of them was armed.

'What . . . what's going on?' Totho asked.

'We are going to test your invention,' Drephos explained, 'and you should have the honour of going first.'

He knew even then, but he said, 'I don't understand.'

'You have made a machine for killing people, Totho,' Drephos said gently. 'How else can it be tested?'

It was a long time with him staring at those confused men and women before he said, 'But I can't just . . . shoot at them. They're . . .'

'Troublemakers,' Drephos said crisply. 'The lazy, the malcontents, the unskilled, the grumblers – all those picked for me by my foremen, though fewer than I had hoped. Still, it will have to be a sufficient sample for this test, because we have little time.'

'But they're *people!*' Totho said.

'Are they any more people than the soldiers your weapons

will be used against? Did you think you could bring such a weapon into the world and keep your hands clean?' Drephos asked him. 'I hate hypocrisy, Totho, and I will not tolerate it. Too many of our trade are ashamed of what they do, and try to distance themselves. You must be proud of what you are. War and death are the gearwheels of artifice, remember? This is meat, useless and replaceable meat, no more.' His gauntleted hand fell on Totho's shoulder paternally. 'You have made this beautiful device. You must be the first to give it purpose. Now load it.'

His hands trembling, Totho thumbed back the slot at the breech of the weapon and slipped a finger-length bolt into place, the missile's presence closing the slot automatically. He remembered a sleepless night designing that very mechanism, with Kaszaat breathing gently beside him. He was thinking, *I will not do it. I will not do it*, but his fingers completed the now-familiar task with a minimum of fuss.

'Charge it,' Drephos said quietly. Totho's hand was already on the crank, and five quick ratchets of it pressurized the air in the battery.

'Ready your bow,' Drephos said, and slowly he raised the snapbow, feeling its snug and comfortable fit against his shoulder. *I will not do it*, his mind sang again.

'Shoot,' Drephos said, and Totho was frozen, his fingers on the release lever. 'Shoot!' the master artificer said again, but he could not. He was shaking, his aim veering. The range of targets at the far end of the hall had not yet realized what was going on.

'This is a test, Totho, a test to see whether what I purchased was worth the price. Remember our bargain. Your friend is alive and free, and in return you are *mine*.' And on that word his metal hand clenched on Totho's shoulder like tongs, and Totho pressed the trigger.

The explosive snap of the release of air echoed down the length of the hall. He had been aiming, perhaps unconsciously, at the most heavily armoured target, the man (or was it a woman?) in the heavy sentinel plate. Now he saw the clumsy figure fall backwards. He could hope that just the impact against the metal might have knocked it over, but there was no movement, and he thought he saw a clean hole had been thrust through the steel.

'Loose at will,' Drephos decided, quite satisfied, and all around them the artificers loaded and shouldered their weapons.

Totho lay sleepless in the dark and he shook. His mind's eye was glutted with the work of those few seconds, the ears still ringing with the discrete 'snap-snap-snap' as his inventions – the work of his own mind and hands – had gone about their purpose.

Drephos had been ecstatic, declaring the test a complete success. Even at the range they were firing, the bolts had not scrupled to pierce plate armour or punch through rings of chainmail. Only the Spider-kinden silk armour had at all slowed them down, the fine cloth twisting about the spinning missiles and preventing them penetrating. They spun, of course, because of the spiral grooving Totho had instituted on the inside of the snapbow barrels, giving the weapons greater range and accuracy. It had been an innovation that Scuto had made to Balkus's nailbow, he recalled.

A skilled archer, Drephos estimated, could make five or even six accurate shots within a minute, a novice perhaps two or three. Their use was easy to learn, and in Helleron they were even easy to make. There were factories working day and night now to produce the quantity Drephos wanted. As soon as they were manufactured and tested they were handed to the waiting soldiers that Malkan had detailed to Drephos' project. It took barely a day of constant practice for them to be smoothly loading and shooting as though they were born to it. The snapbow was a weapon for the common man, just as the crossbow had been, which had thrown off the shackles of old mystery centuries before.

But all Totho could think about now was that armoured figure falling, some innocent Beetle man or woman who had caught the foreman's ire. And then they had all been dropping, and the spears of the soldiers had stopped them fleeing, and in the end the last few had tried to rush towards the waiting line of artificers, giving Drephos his chance to see the damage of a point-blank shot.

I did this. He, Totho, had brought this thing into the world. *I have found my place here now. I have earned it.*

He clutched at his head. He felt as though that part of him he had always thought of as himself was dropping further and further away, slipping down some well or shaft, never to be seen again.

He must flee. He must escape from Helleron.

And do what? His own mocking voice in his head. *And go where?*

I will find Che.

Who is in the arms of her savage lover even now, and does not think of you.

I don't care. I love her.

Fine way to show it, joining her enemies and sleeping with a Bee girl.

His fingers knotted in his hair, unable to blot the thoughts out. *I love Che! I always have!*

You cast-off. You sorry failure. All your life you have been nothing, despised and ignored. Now you have been offered something real: a place, a reason to live. Drephos understands you.

He cannot. He doesn't even know what love is.

Of course he does. He loves with a passion you have never known. He loves his work. He loves progress. All the things you once professed.

I am not like him.

You are his heir in all things.

He threshed on his bed, kicking at the blanket. The voice in his head was like a person there in the same room, calmly

465

and patiently dismantling everything he had ever thought. It was all the worse because the thoughts came from nowhere save within him. This cold world that had opened up to him in Tark, when he had seen what war and artifice could really do, had become the world he must live in.

I cannot go on, he insisted. *The guilt will destroy me.*

Guilt? hissed the voice in his head. *Do you not realize that you can let go of guilt now, and shame, and love? You have been clawing at them all this while, when there was a chance you would return to what you were, but you have taken the final step now. You can never be the man you used to be. Your hands have become true artificer's hands, to build or destroy without conscience or remorse. You can let go of guilt, now, and relax. You are across the barrier of mere humanity and over the other side. It's all meat now, expendable and replaceable meat.*

And Totho writhed and twisted, but had no answer to that.

Thirty-One

Master Graden had taken his own life.

Stenwold sat in the War Council's chamber with his head cradled in his hands and thought about that.

They had put the sandbow, Graden's much vaunted invention, up on the wall. The enemy crossbows had raked the battlements even then, and shafts had stuck into shields and sprung from stone, or punched screaming men and women off the edge of the wall. Kymon had been shouting for them to ready themselves for the strike. The tower engine had almost reached the height of the walls, with sixty Ant-kinden warriors waiting on its platform and more ascending from below. Another two towers were close by, the Ants hoping to swamp and then hold this section of the wall. Ant artillery was pounding at the wall emplacements which were returning shot, or scattering loads of scrap and broken stone into the Ant soldiers below.

Graden had been so enthusiastic, running his apprentices ragged to get the sandbow into position, the great tube and its fan engine. Then he had told them to turn it on.

The great engine had started, and the mountain of sand below the wall had begun to disappear. Once he had seen it work, Kymon had been shouting for those below to fetch more sand. Sand, grit, stones, anything.

On the north wall the fighting had been fiercest, and the defenders had died in their droves to prevent the Ants keeping a foothold on the walls. It was guessed, because there were men in Collegium who were ready to count anything, that two of the city's impromptu militia had died for every Ant casualty, quite the opposite of the normal balance of a siege.

On the west wall, where Kymon commanded, the numbers had favoured the city much more. Master Graden had saved the lives of hundreds of his fellows. Those Ants that had gained the walls were shaken by what they had seen, and their legendary discipline bent and broke before the defenders. Stenwold himself had sent one man hurtling over the edge.

In the retreat, when the Ants conceded the day, the sandbow had been destroyed by artillery fire before it could be brought down from the walls, its casing smashed by lead shot, and two of Graden's apprentices had been killed.

And, a day later, Graden had quietly mixed a solution of vitriolic aquilate and drunk the lot, and died quickly if not painlessly. It was not the deaths of his apprentices, however, that had driven him to it, but the sight of what he himself had wrought with his artificer's mind and his own two hands.

It was an image that would stay with Stenwold until his last days, as with so much he had seen lately. Nobody on the west wall would ever forget those Ant soldiers with the flesh pared from their bones, faces blasted into skulls in the instant that the sandbow loosed, or the armour and weapons ground into unbearable shiny perfection, the mechanisms of the siege tower whittled to uselessness, the entire host of organic and inorganic detritus that was all that was left after the arc of the sandbow passed across them.

Graden had been shouting at them to turn it off, even as Ant crossbow bolts rattled on the stones near him, but Kymon had taken charge of it, and had it aimed at the next-nearest tower, and thus saved the wall.

It was two days later: two days of desperate fighting on

the wall-tops. The shutters over the gates were bent, holding, but never to open properly again. Artillery had cracked the north and west walls but they still stood. The Vekken flagship had almost razed the docklands, burning the wharves and the piers, the warehouses and the merchants' offices. Collegium would never be the same again.

Today they had come by air. Vekken orthopters flapping thunderously over the walls as their artillery started launching once again, dropping explosives on the men on the wall, masking the oncoming rush of the infantry. The aerial battle had been as bloody as any other. Stenwold had stood impotently and watched as the Ant fliers had duelled laboriously with Collegium's own, that were more numerous and more varied. The Ant machines had flame-throwers and repeating ballistae, and of course they never lost track of their comrades in the confusion of the skies. The defenders had been joined by a swarm of aid from the city: Fly-kinden saboteurs, Joyless Greatly's cadre of one-man orthopters, clumsy Beetle-kinden in leaden flight, Mantis warriors attacking the armoured machines with bows and spears. Because he was War Master now, Stenwold had forced himself to watch, and he had no excuse to turn his head when Fly-kinden men and women were turned into blazing torches by the Ant weapons, or when flying machines spiralled from the sky to explode in the streets of his city.

It had made him ill. He had barely eaten these last days. He felt that he had brought this down on them, for all he knew that it would have happened anyway, whether Wasps or Vekken.

Joyless Greatly was dead. He had died in the fighting that day, unseen and uncounted until a reckoning could be made later, just one more mote falling from the sky. He had been a genius artificer and a pilot without equal, and the thought that he had died as he would have wished was no counterbalance to the loss that Collegium had suffered in his death. Joyless Greatly was dead, and Graden had killed himself, and Cabre the Fly artificer had died defending the last remaining harbour tower, even after she had so narrowly escaped from the other. Hundreds on hundreds of other people of Collegium had fallen in the air and on the walls or out over the sea.

And now Stenwold sat with his head in his hands after the War Council had adjourned, and there was a long-faced Beetle youth waiting to see him.

'What is it?' he demanded at last, because this young man was another of the lives in his hands and he had no right to ignore him.

'Master Maker – excuse me, War Master, you should see this. In fact, you have to.'

Stenwold stood up, seeing that the youth was torn between emotions, unable to know what to think next. Stenwold had seen him before, but could not place him.

'Take me, then,' he said, and the young man darted off.

'It's Master Tseitus, War Master,' the youth explained, and Stenwold placed him then: an apprentice of the Ant-kinden artificer.

'What does he want?' Stenwold asked.

'He has . . . he . . . I'm sorry, Master Maker—'

Stenwold stopped him. 'Just tell me. It has been a long day. I have no time.'

'He made me promise to say nothing, Master Maker,' the youth blurted. 'But now he's gone and—'

'Gone?' Stenwold demanded. 'Gone where?'

'You have to come and see!' And they were off again, and the youth was definitely heading for the blasted wastes of the docks.

'He was desperate to do something,' the youth explained. 'The bombardment was all around here. So he took her out.'

'Her? What? You mean the submersible?'

'An hour ago, Master, only we didn't know if there was

enough air . . . enough range . . . We never had a chance to properly test her.'

What he had to show Stenwold was an empty pool with access to the harbour. A lack of submersible.

'What has he done?' Stenwold asked, and the apprentice spread his hands miserably.

It became apparent the next morning, when Stenwold was dragged from his bed by an excited messenger who pulled him all the way back to the charred docks.

The Vekken flagship was sinking. It was sinking slowly, but by the dawn a full half of it was below the waves, despite all the pumps the Ants could lay on it. Supply ships and tugs were taking on men and material as fast as they could, but the vast vessel itself was foundering, slipping beneath the waves, heeling over well to one side so that the water was grasping at the closest of its great catapults that had wreaked so much damage across the harbourside of Collegium.

Of Tseitus and his submersible there was no sign. Whether he simply had not had the stocks of air, or had been destroyed by the Ants, or whether he had become locked to the metal hull of his victim and gone with it to the bottom, it was impossible to say.

Doctor Nicrephos was an old man, and very badly in fear for his life. He had listened for days now to the stories from the wall, about the patience and gradual Ant advance, the implacable faces of the Vekken, the diminishing resources of the city. He had lived in Collegium for twenty-five years. He knew no other home. For twenty of those years he had been the College's least regarded master, clutching to the very periphery of academia, teaching the philosophy and theory of the Days of Lore to a handful of uninterested and uncomprehending students each year. Magic, in other words: something in which Collegium, as a whole, did not believe. There had always been calls to remove his class from the curriculum. It was an embarrassment, they said. There were always those Beetle scholars who believed that the past should stay buried, and that it was an insult to the intelligence of their people that a shabby old fraud like Doctor Nicrephos should be given his tiny room and his pittance stipend.

And yet it had never happened. There was too much inertia in the College, and he still had a few friends who would speak up for him. He had clung on, year in, year out, in this nest he had made for himself, and expected to die in office and then never be replaced. For a man who did not love the company of his own kinden, that would have been enough. His business was the past. He had no care for posterity.

And now it was all falling down. He would suffer the same fate as all the others if the Vekken breached the wall, either put to the sword or sold into slavery, and who would buy such a threadbare thing as he?

But he could not take up arms and walk the wall. He was barely strong enough to fly and his eyes were weak save when the room was darkest. There was something he could do, however, or there might be something: to gather his pitiful philosophy with both hands and make a weapon of it, and brace himself for the inevitable disappointment. He had been a seer of Dorax once, but throughout his years of teaching it had been a rare thing to even attempt to pluck at the world's weave. He feared that, after so long, true magic was beyond him.

'Close the curtains,' he said, and one of his students did so, drawing the patched blinds to cover the falling sun. He had four in his class now: one other Moth who had likewise found his home society unbearable, a cynical but gifted Spider girl, a dysfunctional Beetle youth who could never sit still, and a Fly who came every tenday but never seemed to learn anything. He would need them all now, for whatever faint help they could give.

'We are going to embark on a ritual,' he told them, when they were all seated on the floor of his room. Between the walls and his desk there was so little room that their knees were all touching in their circle. 'This ritual is to attack the Vekken army in ways that the material and mundane defences of this city are incapable of. Precisely what effect we can manifest I am unsure but, as I have taught you, the power of magic stems from darkness, fear, uncertainty, ill luck. All those gaps between the lighted parts of the world.'

'All things that can't be tested,' said the fidgeting Beetle youth. 'That can't be proved.'

'That is so,' Doctor Nicrephos agreed, 'and very close to the heart of the mystery.'

'Doctor, is this going to work? I mean, really?' asked the Spider girl. She cared, he knew, more for her politics and her rumours than for her studies.

'Yes, Doctor, because I was thinking about finding myself a sword and going onto the wall,' the Fly added. 'I don't see we can do any good here.'

'But that is the very attitude you must banish, if we *are* to do good,' Nicrephos insisted. 'Belief is what you require. If you go into this without belief then, yes, we will fail. You must open your minds to the possibility, allow room for that uncertainty.'

That they looked doubtful was an understatement. With no other option, though, he pressed on. 'Listen to me, close your eyes, all of you.'

With poor grace, they did so.

'I require your help, your thoughts, your strength in this. It is a great magic that I intend, that I could not manage on my own. I want you to bend your thoughts on the Vekken camps. Many of you must have seen them from the walls, or from the air. Think of all the Vekken soldiers, hundreds and hundreds of them, with their tents all in lines so very exact, and inside those tents their palettes laid out just so. Imagine them going to sleep there at night, all at the same time, like some great machine. But they are not machines. They are men and women as we are. They have minds, although those minds bleed into one another. I want you to imagine that mind as though you could see it, the mind of all the Ant-kinden there, like a great fog hanging about their camp.'

He could see it himself, in his mind's eye, a great shining jelly-like creature that squatted in and about all those orderly tents, the minds of all the Ant-kinden, touching and connecting.

'We are going to insert something in that mind,' he went on, after he had given them a good long chance to picture it. 'We are going to put something dark in it. There are always areas of the mind that are ready to accept darkness. These Ants love certainty and order, and so they must fear doubt and chaos. You must think of all the doubt and chaos that you can, imagine taking it from your own minds and placing it within that great lattice-mind of the Vekken. All your fears, all your worries, all your pains and guilt, you must dredge these up for me and project them into the mind of the Ants.'

He stopped talking, feeling the pull of concentration build up between them. He was straining now, his heart knocking in his chest. It was so very long since he had done anything like this, and it was like trying to gather a great thing and push it up a steep slope. His students were little help, doubtful, embarrassed, reluctant to look at the darkness within themselves, and more than that, there was the great and overarching ceiling that was Collegium, city of progress and science, of merchants and scholars and artificers, and a hundred thousand people who did not believe.

It was no good, he realized. He had not the strength to force his own will out of the city, let alone onto the Ants. He was too old and had been too long amongst these people.

Now his one chance to aid in the defence of his home

was faltering. His students were beginning to shuffle as the silence dragged.

He called out, in his mind, *If there is some power that hears me, please help me, for I have not the strength! I will promise what you ask, but help me, please!*

He heard one of them, the Spider girl, draw her breath in hurriedly, and then there was a sudden pain in his skull that made him arch his back and choke. It was cold, pure cold, reaching along his spine and prying its way into his eyes. He felt tears start and freeze on his cheeks. Something had grasped him with thorned hands that thrust into his mind.

And, despite all this pain he heard the words in his mind, a monstrous, mournful chorus that said: *What is this that calls? What is this that begs of us?*

I am Doctor Nicrephos of Collegium, he said desperately, because the pain and the pressure combined were on the point of stopping his heart. *If you have strength then lend it to me, for my city is under threat and I would send my thoughts onto our enemy. Please, if you know any pity, lend me your strength!*

How bold you are, the voices said. *Old man, you have not so many breaths yet to draw. Why seek to save that which will so soon outlive you? We have no pity but we do have strength. What claim have you on us?*

Ask what you will, Doctor Nicrephos promised. *Please aid me, and I shall do as you ask.*

He felt his request hang in the balance. He knew his students had all felt this change too, that the room was cold enough for frost to form on the curtains, and that their breaths were pluming visibly in the dim air.

We shall aid you, but you shall perform a task for us – and it may mean your death that much sooner.

He would have agreed, he was sure, but they were not seeking his agreement. *The compact is made,* the dirge of the voices continued, and he felt the cold, that had already tested the limits of his tolerance, double and redouble, flood into the room, through his students, and then out, across the city and the walls, to poison the minds of the Ants. It fought its way clear of the great mass of disbelief that cloaked Collegium, and set about the work he had planned for it, and he knew that the Ants would not sleep easily tonight, nor for many nights to come, because the nightmares that his new ally could bring forth were worse by far than the feeble horrors that he and his students could dream up.

Home at last. Stenwold made himself a cup of hot herb tea, hearing Balkus stomp into the spare room and collapse on his bedroll, probably still wearing his armour. He should have been bodyguarding all day, but Stenwold had told him to fight up on the wall, and Balkus – Sarnesh Ant-kinden at heart – had been only too happy to empty his nailbow at the Vekken. More than that, of course, as there had been savage close-quarters fighting there and Balkus had been in the thick of it, holding the line on the north wall. A head taller than almost all the other fighters, with a shortsword in one hand and a captured Vekken shield in the other, the man had provided a tower of strength for the defenders.

Stenwold sipped his tea, found it bitter, and poured more than a capful of almond spirits into it. He needed to sleep tonight, because tomorrow would be no more forgiving to his nerves. Perhaps Balkus would die, or Kymon. Perhaps he, Stenwold, would.

Tired as he was, he toyed with the idea of it actually being a relief. With Graden's suicide, though, he could not fool himself that way.

He drained the cup. He knew he should be hungry, but he was too tired for it, too numbed by exhaustion.

I am not cut from this military cloth. The sight of the dead sickened him, whether their own or the enemy's. Brave men and women all, doing what they were instructed was right, and Stenwold, of all people, knew how history wrote over such victims, and the truth of whether they had been right or wrong got washed away in the tide of years.

I hope Tisamon is doing better than I am. He felt the absence of the Mantis-kinden keenly. Yes, the man was intolerant, difficult and primitive in his simplistic concepts of the world, but he was loyal, and could be a good listener, and Stenwold had known him a long time.

He levered himself up and trudged his way up the stairs, kicking his ash-blackened boots off halfway, knowing that he would trip over them in the morning but too depressed to care. He left his leather coat hanging over the banister. His helm remained downstairs on the kitchen table.

He slogged on into the darkness of his room, unbuckling his belt, and stopped.

He was not alone.

In the darkness, with even the moon tightly shuttered out, he felt fear. A Vekken assassin? A Wasp assassin? Thalric, perhaps? He had been given no time, these past days, to brood on such danger. What better opportunity than this to do away with him? Stenwold reached for his sword and recalled that it was still with his coat, ten yards and as good as a thousand miles away.

And then another part of his mind whispered something. Was it a familiar sound, or a scent, that informed it?

'Arianna?' he said hoarsely. When there was no reply he fumbled for a lantern and lit it with three strokes of his steel lighter, his hands trembling.

She was sitting at the end of his bed, a young and slender Spider girl with ginger hair cut short, gazing at him with wretched indecision.

'Did . . . they send you to . . . ?' he got out.

'No,' she whispered. 'Stenwold, I . . . didn't have any-where else to go.'

Ludicrously, he felt his unbelted breeches slipping, and

tugged them up hurriedly. 'But . . . you could have escaped?'

'The Vekken would have killed me if they caught me – all the more so because Thalric is with them now. And . . . I have nowhere to go, Stenwold. I am outcast from my homeland and a traitor to the Rekef. And to you, also. I have *nobody* left to turn to.'

'Except me?'

She looked up at him. He momentarily thought that she might try to flirt with him, or speak of the connection they supposedly had shared, but there was now nothing but mute pleading in her eyes.

'Arianna, I—'

'You can't trust me, I know. I could be an assassin. I could still be spying for the Rekef. Stenwold, I am at the end of everything now, and I have no more. Because I tried, in my stupid, small way, to save Collegium – and I got it wrong, just like everything else.'

He put the lantern on his reading table, words failing him. There was too much, far too much, going on within him. He no longer felt tired, but more wide awake than he had been in days. He was trying now to navigate through a maze of pity, caution and a lecherous recollection of their time together that shocked him with its potency. He had thought himself past such yearnings, and yet seeing her here, against all odds and beyond any common sense, was an aphrodisiac, a tonic to an aging man.

If she is my enemy, I cannot give in to these feelings. And if she was truly as desperate as she claimed, how wrong would it be to take advantage of that? Of Arianna the student of the College.

But, also Arianna of the Rekef, the imperial spy gone off the rails. Impossibly, the thought of the risk she could present only seemed to spur some part of him on.

She stood up abruptly. 'I'm sorry,' she said. 'I – I thought . . . I have no right . . .'

Without warning she was trying to dart past him, but he caught her by the shoulders and held her there, practically in the doorway. 'Wait . . .' he began.

The lanternlight brought out the glint of tears in her eyes, and he knew that she could feign it all, being what she was, but his heart almost broke with the strain of it.

She stared up at him, the small breasts beneath her tunic rising and falling. 'Stenwold . . .'

I am carving my own coffin. Perhaps it was the fatigue of these last days, or the need to find some spark of life in such dark times, but he had now lost the reins that could hold his desires in check. He bent down almost fearfully, as though she were venomous, but he still kissed her, and she thrust her lips up towards him.

When he awoke the next morning and he turned over to find her there, warm and soft and alive, sharing his bed, it all flooded back in on him, the pleasure he had taken, for which a price was surely yet to be paid. Yet this morning, with the Vekken army already assembling for its next assault, he felt more rested, more vital, than he had in so very long.

Then there was someone rapping on his front door downstairs, and he foresaw the chain of circumstance exactly: Balkus answering the door and lumbering upstairs to deliver some message, then not comprehending why his employer was sleeping with an enemy agent. He pushed himself out of bed and slung a robe on.

He hurried downstairs in time to intercept Balkus, recognizing the thin, bent figure that had come to see him this morning.

'Doctor Nicrephos?' Stenwold asked blankly. Could matters be so desperate that they were drafting such an ancient Moth as this to be a messenger? 'Is it the wall? What news?'

'Master Maker . . . Stenwold,' Doctor Nicrephos hovered awkwardly on the threshold. 'We have known each other for . . .'

'We've done business for years,' Stenwold agreed. 'But why . . . ?'

'I need your help,' the old Moth said, 'and I know no one else who might even listen. Tell me, what do you know of the Darakyon?'

The Vekken woke like clockwork. Thalric had witnessed it each morning of the siege. Each morning, at precisely an hour before dawn, every single soldier in their army arose and drew on his armour, buckled on his sword. No words, no sound but the clink of mail. Walking down their lines of tents, Thalric felt a shiver at the sheer brutality of their discipline, that strode roughshod over everything in its path.

Except perhaps this siege was starting to tell on them, he reflected. This morning they seemed a touch off-kilter, their timing fouled by something. A few of them were even running late, hurrying with their buckles, no doubt under the withering scorn of their peers.

For some reason the Ant-kinden had passed a troubled night, he decided, and that was curious. Still, the siege had been now many days in the making. The casualties amongst the Vekken had been, in Akalia's words, 'acceptable', though, to Thalric's eyes, seeming far too high if these Ants were as good as they were supposed to be. Even Ant-kinden would get their edges blunted eventually, under such punishing treatment. Still, it seemed strange that, on this morning, a malaise should be so marked amongst them.

Ant-kinden, he thought, mockingly. *They even go off the rails in unison.*

He saw Lorica threading her way through the Vekken towards him, unconsciously falling in with their mechanical rhythm, getting in no one's way and finding her path without having to seek it. She too looked out of sorts, though, and was frowning.

'Something wrong?' he asked her.

'Possibly.' She rubbed the back of her neck, her eyes still heavy with lost sleep. 'You should know, Major. There's been a visitor to the camp.'

'Speak.'

'A Fly-kinden messenger came in, for Major Daklan's ears only.'

Thalric let his breath out in a long sigh. 'That could mean many things.'

'He was from the Empire, I'm sure of it,' Lorica told him. 'Imperial Fly-kinden have a kind of a look, and they hold themselves a different way. They know they're onto a good thing.'

Thalric nodded. Outside his tent he could now hear the louder pieces of Vekken artillery launching at the walls of Collegium. The actual fighting was just a distant murmur beyond.

'You've cast your lot,' he told the halfbreed. 'I don't know if you'll regret it, but I hope not.'

'I respect you, Major Thalric,' she said candidly. 'And I hope you value me, since Major Daklan certainly doesn't. Do you know what's going on, sir?'

'For certain? No.'

'But you suspect.'

'I have seen this before, and too many times,' said Thalric, wearily thinking, *And most of the time I have been on the other side of it.* Secret messages from the Empire, and for Daklan's ears only. 'Perhaps it's nothing significant.'

'You don't believe that, sir.'

'No, I don't, but that doesn't mean it isn't true.' He stood, shaking his head. 'How do you think the siege is going, Lorica?'

She had stood watching with him, now she frowned. 'I'm no strategist.'

'If you'd asked me yesterday I would have said well. Now something's changed, and this message doesn't make me any happier. I'm going to talk to Daklan.'

'Is that wise, Major?'

He managed a smile. 'Lorica, I am a simple man. Nobody ever believes me when I say that, but it's true. I like my life simple. I am for the Empire, and I should therefore stand shoulder to shoulder with everyone else who is, and face with a drawn sword all those who are not. That is simple. you see, but someone is trying to complicate my life. I'm going to talk to Daklan, to discover precisely what he's not telling me.'

He found Major Daklan out by the artillery positions, with Lieutenant Haroc nearby as his constant shadow.

'Major, how goes the war?'

Daklan's face was so devoid of guile that it was evidence of guilt in itself. 'Well enough, Major Thalric.'

'The Vekken seemed slow off the mark this morning, I thought,' Thalric said. Daklan gave a glance over at Haroc and then nodded.

'I cannot explain it. I heard some talk of disturbed sleep, no more.'

'You don't think they're losing their stomach for the campaign?'

'Not at all.' Daklan shook his head. 'Tactician Akalia seems satisfied with their progress. Every day they are closer to breaking the wall, or taking it by storm.'

'She's a cold woman,' Thalric observed. 'I've heard some of the casualty figures.'

'That's Ants for you,' said Daklan dismissively. 'The ships, the artillery, the men – she's only looking for the victory. Whatever has unsettled her men clearly hasn't reached her yet. Perhaps the Collegiates have developed some kind of mind-affecting gas that has drifted over here. Ant-kinden are strong of body, but they lack our strength of will. They would be more easily swayed than we.'

Thalric nodded carefully, and then said, as offhandedly as he could make it, 'I hear there was a messenger from command.'

Perhaps there was a moment's flicker in Daklan's eyes. 'Nothing to worry youself with, Major. Helleron has fallen to our troops, or rather, has capitulated. The Winged Furies now threaten Sarn and so the siege here will not be relieved.'

'Good,' Thalric decided. 'Then all we have to do is wait.' He turned and walked back towards the camp, knowing coldly that Daklan had been lying, and that his days of cherished simplicity were gone.

They had been shadowing the Vekken army since it first came in sight, and had been given an unexpectedly good view of the first day's festivities. All that time, he had kept his head low, which was a skill he had acquired over many years of doubtful company, while Felise Mienn had gone about her business as freely as she pleased.

Living off the land, Destrachis considered, was a game for fools and peasants. And, inexplicably, for Dragonfly nobles.

He had watched her. With the cloak blunting the sound and shine of her armour she could freeze to near-invisibility while standing amongst trees or crouched against the scrub. She moved as though she was part of the landscape, and she would always come back with food. He himself was, he suspected, eating better than he had in the fiefs of Helleron.

When she came back this time he had to put the question to her. For all that questioning Felise was a dangerous game, it was time to air some facts

'You were a Mercer, were you not?'

She looked at him as though she didn't know who he was, which was always a possibility.

'What do you know of the Mercers, Spider?'

He smiled. She scared him badly a lot of the time, but he knew he must never show it. 'I have done my stint in the Commonweal. That was what attracted me to your cause in the first place. I therefore know the skills a Mercer needs in going about her business. There's a lot of open country in the Commonweal: woods and farmland and marshland and hill country. Lots of villages but lots of space between them, and the roads not so good, and half the Wayhouses lie empty and rotted. Keeping the peace, tracking bandits, carrying the Monarch's word: it means spending a lot of time in the wild, doesn't it?'

'It does that,' she agreed, then she sat and dumped a bagful of roots beside the fire, together with some grain biscuits she must have taken from a farmhouse. He took out his smallest knife and began to peel, aware that she was looking at him with more curiosity than usual.

'Destrachis,' she said at last, and he allowed himself to relax, because when she could actually remember his name she was least likely to threaten him. 'What was a Spider-kinden doing in the Commonweal?'

'My question first,' he pressed, carefully not looking at her.

'Yes, I was a Mercer, when I was very young. I wanted to . . . but it changed when . . .'

He sensed a shift in her and said hurriedly. 'I drifted north of Helleron years ago. Ended up in Myal Ren and then travelled a little, plying my trade, stitching and quack-salving.'

'I saw him today again,' she said, without warning.

His knife stopped for a second and then went on. Looking down onto the Vekken encampment, he had caught a glimpse of a couple of men in black and yellow armour, but her eyes were better than his and she now swore she had seen Thalric.

Her patience impressed and appalled him. She had been stalking this entire army for almost a tenday now.

'So when are you going to make your move? Are you going in there after him?'

He had missed the change, but she had snatched her sword out. 'So many questions,' she said. 'Why? What are you hiding, Spider? Who are you working for?'

'You,' he said, still peeling although his hands shook slightly. 'Or, if you won't have me, for myself. I'm not your enemy, Felise.'

'No . . . you're not.' The sword was hovering just in the edge of his vision. 'But I do not know what you are . . .'

Why did I ever agree to this? But he was here now and there was no getting away from it. He would rather cut his own thumbs off than risk becoming a target for Felise Mienn.

'I will have my moment soon,' she said. 'Thalric cannot hide amongst the Ants for ever. Or perhaps *I* will go in and get him. We shall see.'

Thirty-Two

There was one matter only before the imperial advisers today. The tangled news of the Spiderland intervention in the progress of the Fourth Army had been flown to Capitas as fast as a chain of messengers and fixed-wing flying machines could fetch it. It had thrown them all but, while most were still reeling, General Maxin had been able to find his moment. After all, there were few setbacks for the Empire that he could not turn into his personal opportunities. Life was a ladder, and if he clung on when everyone fell back a rung, then he was inevitably closer to the top.

Of course, he must be seen to be deeply concerned. He had even brought an expert to speak before the council, which meant a double victory for him. Not only was he himself shown to be so committed to the Empire's progress, but his witness was formerly in General Reiner's camp, until she had seen the way the wind was blowing and come over to Maxin's side.

She was a Spider-kinden named Odyssa, a Lieutenant-Auxillian in the Rekef, and she had been telling the advisers and the Emperor what she knew about the Spider military potential. The summary was that it varied.

'The Spider ladies and lords prefer to hire or levy their armed help when needed. There are personal retinues but no real standing army,' Odyssa explained. 'The various cities of the Spiderlands all have provincial forces that can be called on and, as there is always plenty of work for mercenaries and fighting men in the Spiderlands, there is always a sizeable pool to draw on.'

'Perhaps we should simply avoid these Fly-kinden places,' one of the Wasp advisers said. 'What glory or profit can there be in vanquishing Fly-kinden?'

'Merro is a keystone in the Lowlands trade routes,' one of the Consortium factors intoned drily. 'Also a large proportion of black-market and underworld trade passes through the hands of the Fly-kinden. There is a great market at Merro in which, it is said, anything can be purchased for a price.'

'Moreover,' put in old Colonel Thanred, 'we have no guarantee that the Spiders will not simply disrupt our supply lines and attack our rear, with or without the cooperation of these Ant islanders.' Thanred was the nominal governor of Capitas, a ceremonial position accorded to a war hero, and his sole advisory role seemed to be to deride other people's ideas.

'Is that likely?' an adviser asked, and Odyssa then explained to them about Spider politics, or at least so far as they could be made comprehensible to outsiders.

'The Spiderlands,' she said, 'are like the Empire in that they have a fair number of subject peoples within them, although those territories, I would think, are more than twice the size of the current imperial holdings. Unlike the Empire there is no central rulership. Individual cities have families that vie for control, and so do whole regions, and then groups of regions and so on. And all these families are constantly working against each other, playing one another off, changing alliances or enmities. Spider-kinden, when engaged in politics, cannot be second-guessed. Therefore they may decide that General Alder's army represents a threat, and thus attack, or instead they may not. You can only be certain that you will have no clue of what they will do before it happens.'

487

'A load of good that information is,' the Consortium factor grumbled.

'What about that city beyond the Dryclaw, what is it called? Our recent find?' someone asked.

'Solarno,' Maxin completed for them: a city that Wasp exploratory expeditions had contacted only months before, that seemed to represent the north-east corner of the Spiderlands. 'It may repay long-term investment,' he suggested. 'Unfortunately it seems to have seceded unilaterally from the Spiderlands, with no attempt to recapture it. More politics, I suppose.'

'Long-term investment?' Thanred jeered. 'We have an entire army sitting at the mercy of these backstabbers.'

The Consortium factor bristled. 'And what if they *do* attack? We need Merro. It's a prize second only to Helleron. So let's fight the Spiders. What could they muster, realistically?'

'If I could, mnn, speak,' said the old Woodlouse Gjegevey. Maxin turned a narrow gaze on him, because he had not entered the debate until now.

'I have not travelled in the Spiderlands, but have read, nonetheless, of their, mmn, kinden. There is record of a Spider lordling who mustered an army with the, ahm, intention of conquering at least part of the Lowlands – Tark and Kes and the Fly warrens at least. It came to, mnm, well, he was defeated by the machinations of his political rivals amongst his own kinden, but the, mmn, reports regarding the force he raised placed its size at over one hundred thousand soldiers.'

There was a thoughtful pause amongst the other advisers.

'I cannot vouch for the quality of their troops, but you will understand that this was a single lord. If our precipitate, mnn, action should prompt a unification amongst such families, well . . .'

It was help from an unexpected direction, but Maxin

would take it. He turned to the centrepoint of the advisers' crescent of chairs and asked, 'Your Imperial Majesty, what would you have us do?'

Alvdan started from his reverie. He had taken no part in the discussions, and Maxin knew just what it was that so consumed him. What the Mosquito was offering him, impossible as it sounded, far outweighed these mundane debates. 'What would *you* advise, General?' the Emperor responded eventually.

'Perhaps an official embassy should be sent to these Spider-kinden. No doubt they want something from us, some recognition or tithe. We can buy them now and take back our gold at our leisure. We have done it before.'

There were no strong objections, and the Emperor put his seal on the plan. The Fourth Army would stay put, and General Alder would fret, but Alder was Reiner's man, Maxin knew. The glory of the Lowlands would go to General Malkan when he took first Sarn and then Collegium. But Malkan had always been one of Maxin's retinue, and he was the youngest and keenest general the Empire possessed.

Maxin was careful not to leave in Odyssa's company, for that would have raised too many questions. He met her eyes, though, and nodded to show that he approved of her performance. He gave a nod to old Gjegevey too, before he left.

As for Gjegevey, he made a great show of being slow to rise and the last to leave, and when he left, Odyssa was waiting for him.

'I thought it must be you,' she murmured softly. 'My message was that the Lord-Martial had a man amongst the imperial advisers.'

'As you yourself said,' Gjegevey murmured, 'any man who plays politics with the, hmm, Spider-kinden, is liable to find himself caught in webs.' He smiled. 'What a pair of, mmn, traitors we are.'

'To who?' she asked. 'Do you honestly think, O scholar, that you know where my loyalties lie?'

Even speaking to her I feel myself ensnared, Gjegevey thought.

Felyal had an uncertain relationship with the sea, and held no firm borders. The wall of greenery their boat coasted past was inundated now, the brackish waters reaching far inland with the high tide. When the waters receded, the trees would be left suspended on their spidery roots amongst a mudscape of burrows and discarded shells.

Outsiders used the name and made no distinction, but Tynisa learned that 'Felyal' was the Mantis Hold, and that 'the Felyal' was the wood itself, just as that other place far north-east of here was *the* Darakyon. There had been a Mantis hold there as well, once.

Their boat tacked closer and then further away, the Moth-kinden fisherman shading his eyes and watching the water carefully. At last he found a channel running into the wood, and guided the boat twenty yards along it before throwing a line out to loop over a branch.

'This is as far as I can take her,' he explained. Tisamon paid him a handful of coins, and then stepped out onto one of the arching roots, holding an arm back for Tynisa to clutch at.

It was an awkward journey until they passed the high-tide mark, stepping half in muddy water and half on the projections of the trees, seeing the swirl of creatures moving in the murk, and slapping at mosquitoes that hung in the air as big as hands. They clambered and scrambled inland with best speed, walking from root to root, jumping channels that were thick with mud and motion. The air glittered with life. Dragonflies skimmed the waters for fish drawn in by the tide, and butterflies like ragged brown cloaks hunted through the canopy for the open blooms of flowers.

They reached land, at last, and if it was not dry it was at

least solid, past the furthest intrusions of the sea. The trees progressed from the stilted marsh-dwellers to broader and more familiar breeds. There was a weight to them, an ancient crookedness, that returned errant thoughts of the Darakyon to Tynisa, and she shook them off uncomfortably.

'What lives here, besides your people?' she asked.

'Our namesakes,' Tisamon said briefly. 'Beyond those two, there is nothing to worry you.'

'No ghosts?' she asked. 'Spirits?'

Tisamon turned back to her. 'The mystics teach us that there are ghosts and spirits everywhere,' he said. 'But no, this is not like *that* place.'

She would have asked more, but then the Mantis-kinden found them. She only knew about it when Tisamon moved, the metal claw abruptly in place and at the ready. She had the sense of sudden flight, the sound of metal on metal.

Everything stopped. She could see nothing, though her sword had leapt to her hand. Claw cocked back, Tisamon was standing before her, tense as a taut wire.

There, by his feet, was a broken arrow. It had been meant for her.

'Where is your honour?' Tisamon shouted out, genuinely angry. 'Come forth that I may see what my kinden have become!'

There were five of them, three women and two men, all of them within a few years of her own age. They had bows, strings drawn back to the ear, and not the little bows of Fly- or Moth-kinden, but bows as tall as they were, and they were all of them tall. They were fair too, as Tisamon was, and as she was also. Her features were Spider-kinden, though, while theirs were composed of the same angles as his: sharp-chinned, sharp-eared, narrow-eyed. A kind of austere grace, like a statue's, was theirs, but without the warmth to make them seem human. They wore greens and greys, and one had a cuirass of black-enamelled metal scales.

Their leader stared at Tisamon with eyes narrowed. 'What filth is this? What do you want here?' she asked, regarding Tisamon without any love. Then her gaze passed to Tynisa and she spat at her feet. 'No Spiders in the Felyal,' she said. 'We had thought that decree would not be forgotten.' The other four arrowheads were directed unwavering at Tynisa's head, waiting only for the nod.

'Look again at her,' Tisamon urged quietly. The Mantis woman shot him a hostile glance, but her eyes twitched over Tynisa, and came to rest on the brooch.

'What is this?' she demanded.

'We must speak to the elders of Felyal,' Tisamon said calmly.

'And if they will not speak to you?' The woman's comrades were slowly lowering their bows, relaxing the strain on their strings. They could see, from that one badge, that this situation was more than they themselves could decide on. There was a wildness to their eyes, though. That the mark of a Weaponsmaster could be borne by a Spider was hateful to them, Tynisa understood. She saw also that they did not even consider that she might have acquired it by forgery or theft, that badge. That she sported it meant that she had earned it, and she wondered just what might happen to any unwise thief who tried to claim such a symbol undeservedly.

'If they will not see us, then that shall be what they choose,' Tisamon said. 'I myself know the way, but if you wish to escort us, so be it.'

'You, perhaps, but *she* may not come. She may live this time, but send her back to the sea,' the woman snarled.

Tisamon shook his head. 'You cannot deny that symbol, and don't make either of us prove it to you.'

The Mantis woman looked rebellious for a further moment, her jaw stuck out aggressively. Then she signalled, and one of her band ran off into the trees.

'We are watching you,' she hissed at Tynisa. 'If you try to run, we shall kill you.'

'Why would I need to run?' asked Tynisa, trying to muster icy disdain and meanwhile hoping her nerves did not show. She had always known this, how Mantis-kinden hated the Spiders. Everyone knew it and nobody knew why, but the grievance went back deep into the Days of Lore, the enmity's roots impossible to tug out and examine.

And now she was here and amongst them, and they hated her. She could feel all four of them hating her, just patiently waiting for the word. The brooch she wore seemed a feeble object to hold up as a shield.

She hoped Tisamon knew what he was doing and, glancing at him, saw that he was by no means as certain as she had previously thought. His anxiety was now as much for his own sake as for hers. She was the abomination that he had produced, and thus they were guilty side by side.

He strode ahead, though, forcing the other Mantids to keep up with his pace. He was coming home, but it had been twenty years, and how much did he really know about the current regime? Or perhaps nothing ever changed here, in this deep pocket of the past.

And she realized that they were already within the Mantis community, the Hold, and she had not noticed. All around them lay a village, but the Mantids had not cleared any ground to accommodate it. Instead their houses were scattered around and between the trees, light structures of wood that barely touched the ground, with rounded walls and sloping roofs that funnelled upwards into openings that were both chimneys and doors. She could not count them, half-hidden in and out of the trees, but it seemed everywhere she looked there was another, situated further out between the distant trunks and branches, until she wondered whether the entire wood was riddled with them. So this was the Mantis-kinden, their idea of a town.

But of course, they could not live one on top of another. Basic lessons of economics were coming back to her from the College. Where were the farms? Where was the cleared land? Of course there was none, for Mantis-kinden were not farmers. They must hunt and gather their way through the Felyal. They could never form great compact towns or cities, and how many of them could even this wide-stretching forest feed? And how scattered they must remain, just to support themselves.

It only struck her then that this was something from another time, another world. Here was where the claws of the past had dug in and held tight. The revolution had never happened here, where the Days of Lore still dragged their timeless way along.

And here were the Mantis-kinden themselves. The advance messenger had drawn a fair crowd of them, perhaps a hundred or more. There were suspiciously staring children, holding wooden stick-swords that were not toys but practice blades, and there were some silver-haired old men and women, and there was a host in between, for the Mantids lived long and aged late. They surprised her, and mostly because of the amount of metal they displayed. Many of them had donned armour, either the leaf-shaped scales or curving, fluted breastplates and helms: the much-coveted carapace style that no other kinden had been able to duplicate. Black and brown and green and gold, and old, the armour and the weapons were the work of generations, handed down and handed down, and always keeping the past alive. She almost felt the ancient blade at her own side shift in sympathy.

One of the older women was stepping forwards. She walked as though she were young, with the same grace as all of them, and she had a beautifully sleek rapier hanging from a cord loop at her belt.

'What do you want here?' she asked. 'Why have you come?'

'My name is Tisamon, Loquae, and I have come home.'

Tynisa glanced at him and realized with a shock that she had never thought him afraid before, but he seemed so now. Moreover, he was revelling in it, feeding off it. It stretched his mouth into a taut grin as tension twanged through his entire body. He was as alive and alert as he had ever been, and unmistakably thrilling with it.

'There *was* a man called Tisamon once,' said the Loquae, for Tynisa knew this word was a title, not a name. 'He left many years ago, hearing the call of the world. Perhaps he *might* have sought to rejoin his people.' Her eyes were slits as she stared at Tynisa. 'But he would never have brought a Spider here with him. By what right does she bear that badge?'

'By the only right that anyone can,' Tisamon said, his voice all calm, his stance all readiness. 'And she is not a Spider. She is my daughter.'

The words speared through them like steel, like a wind lashing at trees and bending them backwards. There were blades in hand instantly, rapiers and long knives, and claw-gauntlets being buckled on. Even the children hissed their disapproval at him, and the Loquae wailed, 'What have you done? You have made an abomination! What have you become?'

Tisamon watched her, grinning still with pain and tension.

'You cannot be one of us,' the Loquae spat at him. 'You are not one of us!'

'Then I must be an intruder.' He brought his hand up, and his gauntlet was on it now, though it had been bare a moment before, with the blade unfurling. 'And you will have to kill me.'

Even as he said the words, three of the Mantis-kinden sprang forth to challenge him, and Tynisa assumed they would all set about him at once. By some signal or concord she did not catch, two of them stopped short and one just kept moving, her own clawed gauntlet slashing out at Tisamon's face. He had no moment of confusion, for he was part of their world and had known instantly who his real opponent was. He was a step back before she had even completed her move, her blade passing uselessly between them.

There was no moment of breath, he was attacking instantly, and Tynisa saw what few outsiders had ever witnessed, the vicious, graceful dance of the mantis claws. Tisamon and his opponent shifted like dappled sunlight, moved like dancers, like insects skittering over the surface of a lake. Their claws were cocked back behind them, and then lashing forth in complex patterns, dancing and spinning, using every joint all the way to the fingers to make them pirouette and wait and stoop as though they were living things in their own right, like silver dragonflies hovering and darting, and their bearers nothing but an abstraction.

Tynisa kept her hand clutched tightly about the hilt of her rapier, and never realized that she did so. She had seen Tisamon fight so many times before, but until now she realized she had never seen him fight anyone so *good*. The Mantis woman moved with him and Tynisa could not tell who led and who followed. They fought as though they had rehearsed it, blades cutting air, striking against one another high and low, and their off-hands flashing too, the spines raised on their forearms, raking and cutting. They were far too close, not the distance of a rapier duel but almost chest to chest most of the time, constantly in one another's shadow, and never touching, ducking and spinning past one another, and even when turned away each knew the other's precise stance and position.

Then it was over. Tynisa blinked. She had barely seen it, had to review the last few moves in her mind to see that, yes, the reason that the woman's arming jacket was now flooding with red across her stomach was precisely *that* move of Tisamon's, not his last move, but one three moves before, and nobody, not even his opponent, had realized.

His victim made a shocked sound, and doubled over, striking the ground heavily, but Tisamon paid no heed to her because the second challenger was upon him. This was a man a little over Tynisa's age, driving for Tisamon with a short-hafted spear. Tisamon was already moving, even before the luckless woman struck the earth, lashing out with his claw, trying to close.

This fight was different again, a fight of space and distance, with the spearman trying always to keep Tisamon at the end of his reach, and Tisamon forever closing, forced to be the aggressor, sweeping the spearhead out of the way time and time again in his effort to step in, so that the whole contest seemed to happen backwards as the spearman retreated, step-perfect and never looking behind him, to keep away from the flashing edge of Tisamon's claw. He never blocked, either, and Tisamon was the same. The two weapons seemed to exist in different worlds, meeting only when Tisamon struck at the spear itself. Always it was drawn back, the claw springing away from the head and not splitting the shaft.

Tynisa risked a glance at the other Mantids, and saw no hatred there. They did not cheer the fighters on, or wager, or discuss. Their entire attention was fixed on the battle, with nothing short of reverence.

And Tisamon caught the spear with his off-hand, just behind the head. The spearman had the chance for a moment's surprise, started to drop the weapon and fall back, but Tisamon's sweep cut the haft in two, and then he lunged forwards and the point of his claw caught the man outside the collarbone, driving deep into his shoulder so that the younger man's already pale face went white with the pain and he fell back into the crowd.

Tisamon was already turning, claw crooked back again, as the third challenger came for him. She was armed with a rapier, and Tynisa saw that it was a match in style for the weapon she herself bore, down to the leaden-coloured, slightly shortened blade. Tisamon rose to meet her with an expression that was madness and ecstasy combined, a bloodlust and a joy in the fight that chilled Tynisa and called to her equally.

They were faster now, twice the speed of the first duel, as Tisamon changed pace to keep up with the flickering of the rapier's narrow blade. The woman across from him was older than the previous two, but a good ten years his junior nonetheless, and she did not fence as Tynisa had learned, with careful feet and a rapid hand. Instead she flew, figuratively and literally. She made her sword into a lattice of steel about her, using the edge more than the point, letting its momentum lead her body where it would, and then the wings would explode from her back and carry her over Tisamon's head, landing and thrusting or cutting even as he turned, and they were moving faster and faster, until Tynisa could not breathe.

She never realized that her own face had slipped into the same almost religious expression worn by all of the others, or that she had released her rapier hilt to clasp her hands over the brooch of sword and circle.

Tisamon ducked and drove in, trying to step inside the reach of his adversary's blade, and she would not let him, and yet when he walked into the razoring steel of her guard, he stepped through it unscathed and she fell back as the spearman had, before driving him away again. Her eyes were almost closed. The patter of steel on steel was a constant staccato that had almost become music.

She took flight again, and this time Tisamon leapt with her, lashing out with his full reach, and they came down together, frozen in a single slice of time.

His claw was over her back, folded so that the point touched near her spine, but held just short, cutting her cuirass but not her skin. The spines of his right arm had drawn blood where her shoulder met her neck.

Her blade was along the line of his throat, his head tilted back so that the flat was against his cheek, the point running through his hair. Her off-hand and his were locked together, spines meshed with spines, between their bodies. Only then did Tynisa notice that the woman wore the same badge that Tisamon did – that she herself did.

The Mantis woman's wings flickered and died, and they stood very still, both looking past her at the Loquae.

An almost crippling sense of vertigo hit Tynisa, because she recognized that look, recognized the moment. It took her back to the Prowess Forum, duelling some other student with wooden swords, and at the end of the pass they would look over at Kymon to see how they had done, to read his reaction.

Just a game, she thought, but the woman he had fought first was dead, and the man badly injured, and now there was a razor edge to Tisamon's throat, and yet he was looking calmly at the old woman to see how he had done.

The Loquae closed her eyes for a moment. She was clearly not happy, but something had been resolved. 'You are one of us,' she said at last. 'What you have done is a heinous thing, but there is no denying that you still have a place here. What would you ask of us, Tisamon of Felyal?'

'That you give my daughter the same chance to prove herself,' Tisamon said simply, as the blade of the rapier was withdrawn and he stepped away from his opponent.

'You should not have come back,' the Loquae reproached him. They were in her home, a hut cut into two rooms by a wall pierced by a common firepit. 'Whatever you have proved, to us, to yourself, today, it would have been better if you had never returned.'

Tisamon listened to the clatter and scrape of sword on

sword, keeping a watchful eye through the doorway. 'If it had just been myself, Loquae, you would not have seen me again. But I have a responsibility to her. She is mine.'

The Loquae made a scornful noise. 'None of her looks.'

'Watch her,' Tisamon urged: Tynisa was fighting, rapier to rapier, against a Mantis youth of her own age. It was her third bout: the other two had ended with blood, almost to the death. She had taken two shallow cuts, to her shoulder, to her side. She had not deigned to acknowledge them.

'The Spider-kinden woman that broke you must have been remarkable,' the Loquae said drily.

'She was not like others of her kind.'

'You mean she was able to fool you,' the Loquae said. 'Be careful not to presume too much on our acceptance, Tisamon. You were given a fair and balanced chance to prove yourself. If I had decided to draw my own blade against you, matters would have been different.'

Tisamon nodded, conceding that point. For a moment the two of them watched Tynisa catching her opponent's blade in hers and twisting it from his hand. The Mantis-kinden watching her wore expressions of loathing, but still they watched.

'She can never be one of us. She can never be more than abomination,' the Loquae reiterated. 'Still, you have given her our skill, and she cannot be denied the badge.' She sighed. 'So, Tisamon, what do you want? I know you have not come here solely to flaunt your halfbreed daughter.'

'I wish to speak to the elders,' Tisamon said. 'All of them. It is possible they will never hear a more important word spoken.'

They gathered in the hall that was the only building there built even partly from stone aside from the smithy. Stones that had been laid in the Age of Lore centuries before rose to four feet, and wood often replaced made a broad and sloping roof from there on up, so that, to be upright, all but the smallest had to stand along the central line. The Mantis-kinden spent much of their lives outdoors, beneath the trees, and they were not builders.

Nine of the Felyal elders had gathered there that night, seven women and two men. This was not all of them, but all of those who could be reached in such short time. Several of them wore the badge of the Weaponsmasters. Tynisa was kept outside, hunched by the door to hear, but barred from the council itself. She had not been perfunctorily slain, and she understood that she had reached the limit of Mantis acceptance thereby.

'I am come to speak with you of the Wasp Empire,' Tisamon began. 'You have heard of them, surely, these Wasp-kinden from the east?'

'We have,' said one of the elders, the youngest of the women there, though still a dozen years Tisamon's senior.

'You may also have heard then that they have attacked the Ant city of Tark,' Tisamon said.

'Tark is fallen, this we have heard too,' said one of the men. 'Those fleeing its destruction have passed our Hold. We have not heard more yet of Merro or Egel but it is possible that these too have fallen.'

This news shook Tisamon. 'Then matters are worse than I had feared. They will come here.'

'They have already come here,' said the Loquae, who was an elder in her own right. 'They have sent men to speak with us and make their peace.'

'You must not believe them,' Tisamon told them. 'They will tell you that they only wish harm to others, perhaps even to our enemies, to the Spiderlands even, but they lie. They wish to conquer all of the Lowlands. They do not recognize allies or peers, only enemies and slaves.'

'You have a good grasp of their talk,' said the Loquae.

'At least the talk of their second emissary. The first was slain on entering the Felyal, by one of our huntsmen who had no time for diplomacy.'

There was the slightest murmur of amusement at this. It was a Mantis joke, Tynisa realized, for what it was worth.

'And the second?' Tisamon asked.

'He spoke the same words you just put into his mouth. He told us we were warriors and so were his people. He offered us respect, admired our blades. All the while, our seers were looking into his thoughts. He was thinking, "*Savages, living in trees and hunting wild beasts. Savages, and ripe for conquest.*" When he was here his eyes could never be still for trying to guess our numbers and our strength.'

'You slew him,' Tisamon said.

'We let him return to his people. He could not tell our strength and what report he might give of it would merely weaken their understanding of us,' said one of the other elders.

Tisamon took a deep breath, feeling in this strained diplomacy that he understood Stenwold a little. 'You must not fall into the same error that he did,' he told the elders. 'The Wasps are rash and foolish, and they understand little, but they are strong, and there are more of them than anyone here can know. I have been into their Empire. I have seen how they storm cities. They have armies comprising more soldiers than there are women, men and children in all of Felyal. If they come here with swords and their Art-fire, then we will slay hundreds of them, and tens of hundreds, but they will still send more. They will burn the forest and bring close their engines of war, their flying machines, their artificer's weapons. Do you understand what I mean?'

'We understand, Tisamon,' said the Loquae. 'You tell us nothing we have not thought for ourselves.'

'And they *will* come here,' Tisamon went on, yet the emotional response he had been expecting was not evident.

'They can tolerate no land that has not felt the stamp of their heel. We hate the Spider-kinden for many ancient reasons, but amongst those causes we hate them because they seek to control, and because they live off the sweat of their slaves. The Wasps have a lust to conquer and rule that the Lowlands have never confronted before, and they hold more slaves, and more wretched ones, than any Spider Aristoi. And when they come here, despite all our skill and speed, they will sweep Felyal away as if it had never been. You must understand how we cannot ignore them. We must act.'

'Must we so?' said the oldest of the elders, a woman whose silver hair fell past her waist, and whose face was lined deeply as the very old of other kinden were, and not simply become taut and gaunt as most Mantis became with the years. 'We know all of this already, Tisamon, and yet we ask ourselves *if* we should resist. For what would be the good? We cannot hold back time any longer. It has been five hundred years since the Days of Lore and the greatness of our race. We have dwindled and withered since, and become a pale ghost of the warriors we once were. Look at us now with unclouded eyes, and you will see a dying people.' She paused and eyed him before continuing.

'Where once we were sovereign and unchallenged, now we become adulterated with every generation. Our young men set sail not for sacred Parosyal but for the harbours of Kes to sell themselves as mercenaries. They turn their backs on their homes for the touted wonders of Collegium, the grimy wealth of Helleron. The Beetles cut wood at the edge of our forests and poison us with their gold, which buys those parts of us we cannot sell. Their peddlers visit our Holds and bewitch our young with their toys and their gauds, and they take their gold back from us again, without ever returning to us what we sold. We are become their shadows, become the savages that they take us for. Each generation is less than the last, until soon we shall be nothing but beggars sitting before their tables, bartering thousand-year skills for what crumbs they deign to give us. Faced with that, Tisamon, can you not see that a good clean death at the hands of *warriors* might be preferable. Let the Wasp-kinden destroy us, and finish the work that all the years have been doing. At least we can then die as the brave die.'

Tisamon knelt before them with head bowed, and Tynisa, craning her head around the doorpost, thought he was defeated. She felt the weight of their words herself, and she did not even belong to these people. Tisamon had one shot left, though.

'I shall take a boat east along the coast,' he announced.

'For what purpose?' asked the Loquae.

'To see their army, and discover whether it is at Merro or Egel, or elsewhere,' he said. 'To see, that is all.'

'And what then?'

'Then I shall return,' he said. 'I will have a plan, by then, a proposal. Will you hear it?'

'We can do no less,' she said, 'though we shall likely do no more. I imagine you will do what you think is right.' Her eyes narrowed at the thought of where Tisamon's judgement had led him in the past.

Thirty-Three

They made camp that evening in a half-burned Wayhouse, which seemed to Salma like a physical mirror to his own thoughts of late. There were a dozen charred corpses within that they hauled out and burned properly outside. It seemed likely that the destruction was Wasp work, for the Way Brothers kept rest-houses all over the Lowlands, and they turned nobody away and maintained only peace within their walls. Many a bandit had used them as a place of refuge, so they were seldom robbed or attacked by thieves either. The Wasps obviously had no such traditions, and Salma found it easy to imagine a scouting or foraging party descending on the place, killing, looting and then setting a half-hearted fire as they left. There was a Wasp army on the long road to Sarn, north of them, and Wasp soldiers were neither the most disciplined nor the most restrained.

It had pushed him to a decision, and before dusk he had lit some torches, and then stood on Sfayot's wagon to address his followers.

They had gained well over four dozen since the defence of the village, so that Salma now had to pause before matching a name to a face for many of them. There were villagers that had actually followed after them, stout young men and women looking for something more than subsistence farming. Then there was the Fly-kinden engineer, and her whole extended family, who had fled Helleron before the Wasps seized it; the five Sarnesh crossbowmen who must have been deserters from some mercenary company; a lean old Spider-kinden archer and hunter who went on ahead each morning to stalk game; a Moth woman with a haunted face who had not given her name or said a single word to anyone since joining them.

He glanced at Nero, who nodded encouragingly, though the Fly did not know what he was going to say.

Salma was not entirely sure of that himself. What scared him was that they were now all listening, waiting for it. He looked from face to face: at the Fly gangers still clustered together, the escaped slaves, the bandits, their leader Phalmes with his arm about Sfayot's eldest. The pair had slept together the night after the defence of the village, but Sfayot himself had not seemed to mind. 'He's strong that one, in lots of ways,' the Roach-kinden had said of Phalmes. 'She could do worse for a while.'

'You've followed me this far,' Salma began to address them. 'I didn't ask you to. I didn't ask to be your guide or your leader, but here we are, all of us, and it seems to me we cannot go on like this. We cannot just drift aimlessly and finally end up beached somewhere not of our choosing. We need direction. Thus far you have looked to me for that. So from now, if you will let me, I will accept the mantle you have offered. I will offer you leadership, purpose and direction. Let me tell you what direction I would be taking you, though. Then you may not wish to continue with me, but we will see.'

He left a pause there. *How did this come about?* He had no answer but, as he said, here they all were.

'Sfayot,' Salma indicated, and the Roach-kinden man nodded. 'If we came across more of your family, you would want to help them wouldn't you?'

'Of course,' the Roach said. 'No question.'

'Of course,' Salma echoed, 'because they're your family. We all understand that. So tell me . . .' He looked over at the Fly youths and singled one out. 'Chefre, if we ran into more of your gang, you'd want to look after them, surely?'

She nodded cautiously, saying nothing. They were close-mouthed, that lot.

'You would,' Salma confirmed, 'because there are ties and obligations. That is what makes us who we are. And Phalmes, I have spoken to you. I feel I know you. You cannot escape who you are or where you come from. If we met a Mynan on the road, a man of your city, you would aid him. You would have done so even before you fell in with us. Can you deny it?'

'I cannot, nor would I,' Phalmes said clearly, though wondering where this was going.

'Family,' Salma stressed for them. 'Family is family, whether it's blood, or brotherhood, or citizenship, or even kinden. And we look after our family, and they look after us. I used to think that family was a Commonweal thing, and that only my kinden really understood it. But that was just because I did not understand what held the Lowlands together. *Family.*'

He paused, bracing himself for the mental leap he would have to make.

'We are all part of the largest family in the Lowlands, and it is a family that grows larger every day. It was never small, but it has never been as large as it is now. That family is the dispossessed, the victims, the cast aside, the ill-used. Look at us all, from different lands and different cities, different trades and races, and yet we are all family, and there are thousands of brothers and sisters, uncles, aunts, children who are our family, and who now need our help. Our help against the men who would do this to them.' His sweeping gesture took in the burned Wayhouse, the cremation pyre. 'They are our enemies. Let us become theirs.'

'Just what are you talking about?' Phalmes demanded. 'We can't exactly take on a Wasp army!'

507

'Can't we?' Salma said, and the certainty in his voice shook them. 'We can attack their scouts, take their supplies, aid their victims. We can strip the land so they go hungry. We can nip at them and draw a tiny bead of blood, a hundred ways. We can force them to change their plans, because of us: divide their forces, hesitate, falter. Or that is what we shall do if you follow me. We can take the war to them, without ever meeting them on the battlefield.'

Some of them were aghast at the idea, some were keen, most were simply bewildered. 'I shall give you tonight to consider all I've said,' he told them. 'Anyone who wishes to find their own path is free to do so. Those who are still with me in the morning will have cast their lots in with me. In the Commonweal there are men called Mercers who ride the roads and keep them safe. Those who stay with me shall become my new Mercers.'

And he turned from them and headed for the Wayhouse. The others had made their camp in and around the broken building, and those that wished to go could do so without feeling that he was watching them.

Salma slept easily that night. He had met the burden of his responsibility, and his conscience was clear.

When he awoke it seemed very quiet beyond the drape. He knew what that must mean. He rose and dressed slowly, then took up his staff. Finally, he pushed the drape aside with the point of the staff and went out into the stark dawn light.

They were all there. Not one of them had gone. More, they had been joined by someone new.

She was there, radiant with her own light even in the sunlight, glowing with rainbows, and gazing only at him. Grief in Chains and Aagen's Joy – and who knew what other names she had gone by – had come for him.

He could only imagine how it had seemed to Phalmes and the others, this vision striding in with the first rays of dawn – a sorceress, a mirage, and here for Salma only. It must have seemed like a sign for them, the final augur in his favour.

As she approached him now, he felt blinded by her beauty. Her lightest touch on his arm thrilled him. 'I've found you at last,' she said.

'How?' he asked.

'You came so far for me,' she whispered. 'How could I do any less for the one I love?'

Food was arriving, in cartloads, in baskets, in handfuls. Men and women who had tilled their own land, or the land of those that had owned them, were heading out now daily to reap vacant fields. Children swarmed through abandoned orchards like locusts. Farmhouses were raided with the thoroughness of the truly hungry. When they found the hastily abandoned country seats of the rich in their isolated estates, they climbed the walls and broke down the gates, coming back with armfuls of expensive delicacies or coal for the fires. Traders and peddlers threshed and ground, while artisans built the clay ovens to make bread. Hunters came back dragging their kills or driving errant livestock.

Nobody was eating well but nobody was starving, and Salma could have asked for no more.

'So what's your next move, lad?' Nero asked him.

'Our next move is to move, then to keep moving,' Salma said. 'Otherwise we'll exhaust what's around us. We're still just scavenging, though on a greater scale. The bulk of these non-combatants need to find sanctuary, and Sarn or Collegium remain our best chances.' He watched the woman Grief in Chains as she moved through the people. She spoke to few of them, barely even acknowledged them, but her shining presence changed them as she passed. Just looking at her brought a smile to Salma's lips, and he knew it would remain the same however dark the times became.

She called herself 'Prized of Dragons' now.

'News has been short from westwards,' Nero reminded

him. 'And that army north of us can only be heading for Sarn.'

Salma nodded. 'And yet what option do we have?' He looked at his hands. It was something Stenwold did, when he had difficult decisions to make. 'Sfayot! Phalmes! I need to speak to you!' he called out.

The Roach and the Mynan came over, and it was clear that both of them had been expecting something from him for a while.

'We're moving, tomorrow,' Salma informed them. 'Sfayot, you must take the needy onwards, at your own pace, gathering and foraging as you go.'

'Of course,' the Roach agreed.

'If scouts from the Empire spot you, they'll see no more than refugees on the move.'

'And we can defend ourselves, if we have to,' Sfayot added. 'And I take it you two will be campaigning, yes?'

'It's about time we drew our swords,' Phalmes agreed. 'Where are we bound?'

'I want to see what's happening north of us. We'll probe the Wasp army, see what we can learn, and what good we can do,' Salma explained. 'But information first, action later.'

Phalmes nodded, his expression suggesting that he had no doubt about the latter. 'And your girl?'

Salma faltered for a moment. 'I had thought she would stay with Sfayot.'

'She can close wounds with her bare hands,' Phalmes pointed out. 'We've all seen it, and Butterfly-kinden Art is like nothing else. Besides, after all the ground she's covered, do you think she'll agree to stay behind?'

'True,' Salma realized, knowing that he had no right to hide her away while he put himself in danger.

'As for you,' Salma turned to Nero, 'I have a special task.'

'I'm one of your soldiers now, am I?' the Fly asked.

'As good as, yes,' said Salma. 'But I want you to go to Collegium.'

Nero nodded slowly. 'It's been a while, but I can still find my way there.'

'Find Stenwold, or at least get word to him. Let him know what I'm doing.' After a moment he added, 'And tell him about Totho, too. He'll want to know.'

They entered his tent carefully and, from his hidden vantage point, Thalric saw the brief glint of steel as they pushed aside the flap.

There was a moment's pause and then he stepped up behind them, startling the two soldiers Daklan and Haroc had brought with them. 'Were you looking for me?' Thalric asked.

Daklan and Haroc came back out of his tent quickly. They had come quietly and without armour to catch him asleep. He thought it possible they might regret that.

'Ah, Major Thalric,' Daklan began.

'You had a message for me, at this hour?' Thalric prompted.

'Of sorts. I have received orders from Capitas, Major, which concern you.'

Thalric nodded. It was no more than he had anticipated. 'Perhaps you want to reveal them, Major Daklan?'

Daklan glanced at the Vekken tents all around them. 'I think we may have some grounds for argument shortly, Major, and I would hate for our allies to see officers of the Empire in disagreement. Perhaps we should step off beyond the sentries.'

'Into the dark, you mean?' Thalric clarified.

'There's a moon. Or are you frightened of the dark, Major Thalric?'

He smiled at that, watching the two soldiers stand uncertainly to one side, and Haroc and Daklan step apart a little, anticipating his move.

But of course they were right. A brawl between Wasp officers would damage the Empire's reputation with the Vekken, and Collegium had not fallen yet.

He felt suddenly very cold, as though his life was already bleeding away.

'My loyalty is always to the Empire,' he said softly. 'If the Empire truly requires this, then who am I to put my own interests before those of my Emperor?'

'Very patriotic,' said Daklan, who did not believe him, but without another word Thalric turned and headed towards the outer edge of the Vekken camp, leaving them to follow.

He stopped only when they were barely still in sight of the camp lanterns. There was enough moon to see the shapes of Daklan and Haroc, who held a sword in his hand now instead of a scroll. The two soldiers trailed behind, obviously trying not to hear anything that might prove bad for them.

'I admire your resolution, Thalric,' Daklan said, tensely, expecting a trick. Thalric saw clearly that, had his name been on the death-list, Daklan would not go so quietly.

'I have served the Empire all my life,' Thalric said. 'In its service I have done deeds that, if I had done them in my own name, would have driven me mad. Only by knowing they were for the greater good could I drive myself to accomplish them.' He fixed Daklan with a stare that made the man shift uncomfortably. 'I have burned books and executed friends, tortured women and killed children, all in the Empire's name. What would I be if, when my own life came before that same judge, I was to reject the Empire's will and obey it no longer?'

Daklan shifted uncomfortably. 'This isn't personal, Major. I won't pretend that I'm fond of you, but orders are orders.'

'Of course they are.'

'You are to leave the service of the Rekef, and as suddenly as possible – their exact wording. You know what that means,' Daklan said. Thalric saw his teeth white in the moonlight as he grinned.

'Can I ask why?' Thalric said. 'If you know.'

'I know well enough. The orders are from General Maxin. That's a name you must recognize.'

'He's your patron?'

'I plan to do well by him,' Daklan confirmed. 'There are changes happening in the Rekef, changes at the top, but the ripples come down to lowly soldiers like us. It's known that you're General Reiner's man.'

'I am the Emperor's man.'

'The Emperor doesn't give a curse, Thalric. You're Reiner's man, and Maxin is having a little cull of Reiner's people just now. You're a major, so you're important enough to get noticed, in all the wrong ways.'

'I don't think General Reiner has any love for me,' stated Thalric sadly.

'Obviously not, or he'd have protected you,' Daklan agreed. 'You're big enough to make the list, but small enough to be sacrificed. Bad luck, Major Thalric. Now, I've got sleep to catch up on, so let's put you out of your misery.'

Daklan was tense again, expecting an explosion of anger or desperation, but Thalric carefully lowered himself to his knees.

I have always served the Empire, so let this be my last service. And yet even as he thought this, even as Haroc stepped over with hand raised, something began turning deep inside him. *This was the will of the Empire? Simply because some distant general was grabbing for power? Because the Rekef was tearing at itself? The Emperor would never condone this if he knew.*

He heard the crunch of Haroc's sandals on the ground right behind him.

How does this serve the Empire? But, above and beyond this plaintive call, he heard a voice he had almost forgotten cry out *How does this serve* me?

Cut off, run out, left hanging, abandoned to the butchers – and something stirred within him that had been fettered for decades.

I want to live.

He twisted, so that Haroc's sting scorched the side of his face rather than caving in the back of his head. Almost distantly, he felt his own hand flare with fiery energy, and saw one of the soldiers immediately arch backwards. Daklan was running forward with drawn blade, furious at being fooled. Thalric staggered upright, smashing Haroc across the face with his elbow. The man moved with the blow, though, and then his sword lashed across Thalric's side, grating against the copperweave mail beneath his tunic that once again saved his life.

Thalric let his wings flare open, lifting him up, intending only to get away from here. Haroc was on him, grappling with him in the air, and a moment later the two of them crashed to earth with Haroc on top.

'Kill him!' Daklan was shouting now, heedless of the Ants within earshot. 'Kill the bastard!'

Thalric struck Haroc still harder across the side of the head, but the lean man ignored it, slamming his own fist into the seared skin of Thalric's face, and then getting a hand on his throat, the other hand raised with palm open.

'Goodbye, Major,' he grunted – and then Daklan screamed in pain and Haroc's head whipped round.

Thalric was bringing his own hand up already, while Haroc's palm was now pointing back the way they came. Energy spat from it and Thalric heard a woman cry out.

He loosed his own sting, and Haroc was already twisting to avoid it, but the blast caught him across the shoulder and chest, throwing him off Thalric, who now staggered to his feet.

The last soldier was running for him, casting a bolt of energy that sizzled over his head. With sick regret Thalric shot him directly in the chest, then watched him pitch over, roll once and lie still.

Daklan was down, trying to prop himself up with one hand, the other one reaching round for the knife buried in his back. Beside him, Lorica the halfbreed lay curled up into a ball, after Haroc had blasted her in the stomach.

Thalric was about to turn back to finish Haroc, but Daklan was suddenly on his feet, making a jagged, staggering run with sword extended. Thalric swayed to one side, reaching for the sword and letting Daklan's momentum spin him round. Then he saw Haroc standing, hand extended, and Thalric let go of Daklan to launch a desperate shot at him. Haroc loosed his sting at the same time.

Haroc's head snapped back, his face a blasted ruin. His own bolt passed between Daklan and Thalric, burning them both, and then Daklan's sword pierced the copper-weave and sliced into Thalric's side.

He gasped in agony and dropped to his knees. This was bad. He had suffered enough wounds to know this was a bad one. If Daklan had drawn the sword from his flesh then there would be more blood than he could have stanched, but Daklan was now stumbling away, loose-handed, then falling. Thalric saw a shudder overtake him before Lorica's knife-blow finally did its work.

Beyond Daklan, he could hear Lorica's quiet whimpering.

He himself was hurt, hurt enough to die, without some help soon.

But of course, there would be no help, because the Empire had put him on a death-list. He certainly could not seek refuge with the Vekken for, to his pain-racked mind, they were the Empire near enough.

He began to crawl towards Lorica. Haroc's shot had been a solid one and Thalric guessed she must be on the very brink of death herself. His hand touched her ankle, then worked its way up until he could grasp her hand.

She could not speak, and he himself had nothing to say, but despite his own suffering he clung to her until her sobbing stopped and she relaxed into the calmness of death, because Thalric had always looked after his subordinates whenever he could.

When she was silent, the whole world was silent. The sleeping Ant camp made not a sound. Thalric released Lorica's cooling hand. He was breathing in fractional stages, each one a burning ruin.

Dying, thought Thalric, and then the fierce thought, *No!* He would not surrender to this. He would fight. He would fight. He would . . .

He levered himself to his elbows, rolled onto his good side, and then he gave a short, retching cry as he got to his knees. The world loomed dark for a moment, but he clung to consciousness. If he lost it now, it would be for ever.

Have to fight!

He crawled over to Daklan, leant on the knife-hilt to drive it another inch further into the man, hissing with spite. *Now comes the hard part.*

He took the hilt of the sword still lodged in him and closed his eyes. It took him three long breaths to begin.

It should be done slowly, he knew. With a strangled gasp he dragged the blade from his own side, feeling the motion far too deep. The darkness clawed for him again as he clasped one hand to his blood-slick flesh. He leant heavily on Daklan's corpse once again, fighting for every moment.

From the uneven tear in the other man's tunic he began to rip cloth in long, ragged strips. The idea of pulling a binding tight made him sick with weakness. Instead he awkwardly stuffed cloth in the jagged torn gash in his mail, feeling the fabric grow instantly warm and sopping with blood. Thalric just kept tearing and stuffing until the oozing blood had begun to cake and set, making the whole side of his body a grimy clotting mask. Then he sat back and waited for his shaking to stop.

Have to fight. He was Thalric the spymaster. He had plans to make. He was never without a scheme. He needed to find somewhere to hide. *Somewhere to die?*

Lurching drunkenly to his feet he instantly doubled over about the wound, then began stumbling away, no clear direction or destination, just away into the night.

Thalric's mind faded in and out, so that the night became a series of brief moments of lucidity amidst constant descents into chaos. Every so often, like now, he had to stop to remember simple things like his name, or what he was doing, or why his side was running with blood.

He could not tell how far he had gone, but he did not dare look back in case he saw the bodies of Lorica and the others still clearly in sight.

The night was turning grey to the east, now. *My last day, do you think?* He had been making a shambling progress on knees and one hand, hunched over the other hand pressed to his side, just managing a crippled-insect pace across the dusty terrain.

Betrayed. He had known it would happen eventually, because he lived in a world of betrayal. He had been ready to kill his mentor, poor Ulther, after all, and lied to himself that it was for the Empire's good. *Am I any better than Daklan, for all my protestations?* Worse, perhaps. At least Daklan had accepted the true darkness of what he did, while Thalric had blithely convinced himself that he was still a loyal servant of the Empire, and not just the tool of some faction.

He stumbled, and the wound flared in his side, and for a moment he could not breathe. Inside him, something howled for his lost Empire, like a child ripped from its parents. *Where did I go wrong? What can I do to make them take me back?*

But it was too late for that. There was only one thing the Empire wanted from him, and he would oblige it shortly and settle his account. All he had accomplished through his conscientious loyalty was to make himself expendable, and ultimately be expended.

He did not feel he had the motivation to get up again. He had always been a tough and leathery creature, and he would spend a long time over dying. He felt he deserved it.

But there were footsteps approaching, cautiously. No doubt the Vekken had tracked him. They might put him out of his misery, or take him back and try to save him. He wanted neither option.

Thalric lifted his head to see who was coming. He saw booted feet, shimmering blue-green greaves and the hem of a cloak.

With a great groan he fell onto his back, staring upwards, his gaze following the armoured lines until he came to her face. The sight of it stripped raw something in his mind, something branded into his memory, never to be forgotten. He heard a wordless, ragged cry, and knew the voice was his own.

Fate, he realized, had truly found a fitting end for him.

'I've found you at last,' said Felise Mienn. That was the last thing Thalric heard for some time.

A pain in his hands woke him, shooting cramps that let Thalric know his clenched fists were bound shut so that he could not use his sting.

Everything seemed unexpectedly, appallingly bright. He had been trying to find somewhere to hide. Now there was sun so dazzling he could hardly open his eyes. Though his hands were bound, his arms were free, but he could barely lift them. He tried to sit up,

The stitches now inserted in his side pulled alarmingly, and he remembered.

Ah yes, Daklan. Daklan and his far-distant general, and the Empire.

He could barely even remember the name of the general who had ordered his death. It hardly mattered, what with so many generals and so many agendas.

Forcing his eyes open, he saw that he was not alone. He lay in a room that had been recently looted. The shutters were torn from the windows, a chest at the foot of his bed had been smashed open, and the wooden panelling had even been ripped off one wall. The design was Beetle-kinden, and he guessed that it was some farmhouse within sight of Collegium that Vekken soldiers had gone over whilst encircling that city. The man sitting beside the bed was no Beetle but a Spider-kinden with long greying hair, wearing a Beetle robe that was smeared with blood.

'Who?' His voice was a dismal croak. 'Who are you?'

The Spider smiled, his features lined with a weary humour. 'You have a remarkable constitution, Master Thalric. I don't think many people in your position would even be breathing, let alone talking.'

'You . . . know my name, but who are you?'

'My principal knows your name, and she's been most anxious to meet you. However, she wanted me to get you in a state where you would be fit to meet her.'

'Curse you!' With a supreme effort, Thalric forced himself into a sitting position. He saw a flicker of surprise in the man's face. 'Tell me who you are!'

'My name is Destrachis, Master Thalric, but does it mean anything? No? Are you happier now? Or let me elaborate: I am a traveller, something of an opportunist, a scholar, and a doctor of medicine, which is why you are even in a position to ask these questions.' Destrachis stood. 'You'll be leaving soon, when you're strong enough to walk. A day or two, who knows? You are remarkably resilient, and I see from the patchwork you've made of your skin that this is hardly the first time you've been wounded, although perhaps the worst.'

Thalric hissed in rage. 'Tell me,' he demanded, 'what is going on.'

Destrachis, pausing at the door, smiled back at him. 'She wants you to run, Master Thalric. She wants to feel her victory over you. She wants you dead, but she wants you to appreciate just why – and by whose agency – your death will occur. I can't claim to understand it myself, but she wants satisfaction, and skewering a sick man while he's dying on the ground is not apparently very satisfying. So, after chasing you all the way across the Lowlands, she ordered me to make you well enough to run again. Perhaps that makes some sense to an imperial mind?'

'The Empire and I have parted company,' Thalric muttered. 'But she . . . ?'

'Her name is Felise Mienn,' the Spider informed him. 'A Dragonfly-kinden noblewoman. I have no idea why she hates you quite this much.'

Thalric slumped back heavily in the bed, feeling his strength drain away all at once at the very sound of that name. She had been hunting him. All this time, she had been hunting him, and he had never been aware.

The Commonweal during the Twelve-Year War . . . when the Rekef Outlander agents such as himself were moving ahead of the army, disrupting any resistance the Dragonfly-kinden could mount: raids, sabotage, rumours.

And assassination – dark deeds that he had performed gladly, knowing that the impenetrable shield of the imperial will kept him safe from guilt or blame.

'I killed her children,' he recalled hoarsely. 'And I made her watch.'

'Yes, that would do it,' Destrachis said, quite unmoved by the thought, and left him there to reflect.

Thirty-Four

'We've been seen,' Tynisa said. The black shape in the sky had wheeled back past them and was now darting off.

'Some time ago,' Tisamon confirmed. 'Fly-kinden, which tells us little because even the Empire uses them as scouts sometimes.'

They took refuge in a hollow that was carpeted with shoulder-high thorny bushes. Out here in the hill country east of Merro there was little enough cover.

'Just a local, do you think?'

'Any local would be keeping his head down, with an army on their doorstep,' Tisamon remarked. Except, of course, that it wasn't. By all reason and logic, the Wasp army that had sacked Tark should already have been all over Egel and Merro, and probably at the gates of Kes by now, but aside from those possible scouts, there was no sign of it.

Felyal had provided a boat, a little one-handed skiff that Tisamon had handled ably enough, with the air of a man for whom old skills came back easily. Mantis-kinden made swift boats, this one with such a broad sail and so little hull that Tynisa was constantly clutching at its mast for fear of the water. They had kept close to the coast, running easterly in good time, creeping past the lights of Kes one dark night and then beaching in a secluded bay, all the while looking for signs of the imperial advance.

From then on they had just been watching and waiting, but it was almost as if the Wasps had simply decided to head back north after taking Tark.

'We couldn't be *behind* their lines, could we?' Tynisa asked.

'If so, we'd know it. Wasp-owned land has a feel to it. And they'd be all over here, taking stock, taking slaves. No, they're still ahead, and I can't understand it.'

They rose from the hollow and soon put another two hills behind them. Lying flat on the crest of the second hill, Tisamon squinted into the distance.

'Is . . . that looks like a camp. A big one.'

Tynisa joined him, spotting a dark blot on the horizon. The land was more wooded around here, patches of cypress and wild olives and locust trees that sketchily followed the lines of streams, with cicadas half the size of a man screaming like torn metal at irregular intervals. It seemed to Tynisa that the darkness Tisamon was pointing to could just be more of the same green, but he seemed convinced that it was an army.

'And camped there, in broad daylight,' he said. 'And it's just a field camp, a temporary pitch-up. No fortifications, nothing. The army's just sitting there eating up its rations. So what is going on?'

'The scout's back,' Tynisa noticed.

Tisamon risked a look upwards. They were both wearing green and earth tones, camouflaged against the dusty ground. So had he detected them again? Yes. The scout circled a moment and then seemed to be coming down.

Instantly, Tisamon's claw was in his hand, but Tynisa murmured, 'Wait.'

The Fly landed twenty yards away, glancing about cautiously. He was dressed outrageously, they saw, and certainly no imperial soldier.

'Is that what they're wearing in Merro these days?' Tisamon wondered. The little man was approaching them nonchalantly, pretending that he was just meandering and had not seen them. As he passed by he let a paper drop from the hands clasped behind his back. He was actually whistling tunelessly as he stared out with apparent satisfaction across the hillside. Then he took a deep breath, exhaled it, and was in the air again, darting off eastwards.

'What in blazes was that all about?' Tisamon demanded, but Tynisa had plucked up the discarded message and was reading it curiously. It was elegantly written in a florid script, and seemed so familiar from her College days that she wanted to laugh.

'It's an invitation,' she said. 'Someone wants to speak with us. It says to come down to the big grove.' She pointed. 'They must mean that one way down there.'

Tisamon did not seem amused. 'It's a trap,' he decided.

'A long way to go for a trap.'

He shrugged. 'Some people think like that.' His eyes narrowed. 'This is Spider-kinden work – the clothes, the details, I know it.'

'I suppose we are a bit close to the border up here,' Tynisa allowed. 'Are we going to go down?'

'We are – but with weapons drawn,' he decided. 'I don't trust any of this.'

Approaching the grove they saw there was a sizeable body of people within it, and making no attempt to hide themselves. There was enough armour visible for them to see that none of it was in the Empire's black and gold. They paused at the very edge of the trees, uncertain whether their stealthy approach had been observed or not.

'Head west as fast as you can if this goes badly,' Tisamon decided. 'If it goes really badly, get yourself to Merro and send a messenger to Stenwold.'

'Assuming Stenwold is in any position to receive one,' Tynisa said, remembering the Vekken army.

Tisamon shrugged. 'We must make that assumption.'

Then he stood up and walked forward openly, his claw folded along his arm. Rapier held loosely in her hand, Tynisa followed.

There was an instant stir amongst the guards on the perimeter, but they obviously knew to expect visitors. The Ant-kinden there drew a little closer at the sight of Tisamon, and the Spiders lounging beneath the sideless tent smirked a little, and murmured barbed comments to one another. But when Tisamon stood proudly before them, looking down his nose at them all, not one was willing to challenge him.

'I believe someone wanted our company.' Tisamon pitched his voice so as to carry to all of them. Tynisa looked about them, reading their stances, their faces. They were not expecting a fight, she noted. Not an ambush, then, or not immediately. She turned to see a richly dressed Spider-kinden stand up from amongst his fellows. He was a strikingly handsome man, neatly bearded and with a very white smile. Something about him sent a shiver through her, though, not one of attraction but of warning. If it was her Mantis blood that governed her battle instincts, now her Spider blood took over. This was a man to be reckoned with, she knew. He was Aristoi, therefore political through and through.

When he smiled at her, though, she liked him despite herself.

'Won't you come a little closer?' he offered. 'It would be crass of me to conduct my business at the top of my voice, but I'm loath to scald myself beneath this wretched sun.'

'I do not fear you,' Tisamon informed him, and stepped on until he was just outside the little pavilion. He left enough room around him for fighting unhampered, Tynisa noticed. The legendary Mantis dislike of the other man's entire race was rigidly evident in every line of his body.

'My scouts shall be disciplined,' the Spider said. 'They told me two Mantids, but I see only one, albeit as much a

Mantis as one might wish to encounter, and one remarkable woman. Pray allow me, sweet lady, to have the honour of naming myself.'

He was expecting a response, but she did not know what to offer, and so she shrugged. He took that as satisfactory, and made a remarkably fluid and elegant bow while never quite taking his eyes off her. 'I present myself as the Lord-Martial Teornis of the Aldanrael, and I offer you the solemn bond of my hospitality.' He saw the twitch in Tisamon's face and his smile turned rueful. 'Ah well, I admit that in certain circles the Aristoi's iron word bears a trace of rust, but you would accept wine, surely, if I offered it? And some refreshment. If you will not trust my open intent, you may rely on my love of indulging my own luxuries.'

Tynisa smiled at him despite herself. 'I am Tynisa, and this is Tisamon of Felyal. I will drink and eat with you, Master Spider, on the condition that you do not ask my companion to.'

'A lady of compromise,' Teornis observed. 'Delightful.' With a gesture he caused a cloth to be laid out on the ground, with silk cushions strewn around, and a low table bearing an assortment of dishes, most of them not immediately familiar. The other Spider-kinden had moved back a little to make space, and were now sitting or lying, watching the two newcomers slyly.

Tynisa knelt at the table, knowing that Tisamon would stand there like a hostile statue until this ritual was done, or until something went wrong. She decided it would be best if she herself spoke for them.

'This seems an unusual place, and time, for an Aristos of the Spider-kinden to ride out merely for pleasure,' she remarked. A Fly servant put a goblet in her hand and she sipped, finding wine as rich and potent as any she had ever tasted.

Teornis settled down facing her across the table. His

gaze on her was still admiring, though just as certainly she knew that it had been donned with as much care as his shirt or his boots. 'Pleasure, my lady Tynisa? Why this is a military outing. Surely you won't deny we make a fearsome spectacle?'

'Military? To what end? Have the Spiderlands been invaded as well?'

'Because my curiosity is raging, first please tell me how a Spider-kinden lady comes to be travelling with one of those who have, all unjustly, declared themselves our mortal enemies?'

Best not to put any further weapon in his hand. 'We are simply old friends, Tisamon and I.'

'You are rich in your choice of friends, obviously,' Teornis remarked. His fingers hovered over the spread of food, and he plucked at a mound of candied somethings. 'Tisamon of Felyal, you say. Is it Felyal you have now come from? I have an ulterior motive in asking, as you see. I seek someone to carry word for me. I fear Felyal would be of little use, since none there would credit a word I have to say.'

'Surely you have followers enough to bear a message, Lord-Martial?'

At the sound of his title, no expression crossed his face, no pride at her using it. 'Alas, I am caught in my own nets. These are wicked times, and when word comes from the Spiderlands, who will accept it at face value? Hence I hoped to convince you of my pure heart and true motives, and send you back to your home or your employer with my news, and hopefully your own words to plead my suit for me.'

'Well then,' she said. 'I am come here from Collegium, my home.'

He raised an eyebrow. 'Far abroad indeed, and shame on me, I should have marked the accent. I now see how you must have overcome the age-old hatred of my kin to allow this man into your confidence. Collegium? My lady Tynisa, perhaps you may be of use to me, if you would?'

He is very carefully stopping himself from calling Tisamon my servant or slave, or my possession in any way. It had been a long time since she had sat and sparred like this, weighing every word spoken, but the skills came back to her, as much part of her as the lunge of a sword.

While she considered, Tisamon interrupted shortly, 'What do you want of us?' His tone made it painfully clear that his trust was far from won.

'I cannot believe that you're travelling in these parts and have not heard of the Wasp Empire's recent actions,' Teornis explained. Noting their reactions he nodded. 'More than merely heard, I see. Well then, if you were, in a moment of childish enthusiasm, to climb to the top of the tallest tree in this grove, you would see from there some thirty thousand Wasp-kinden soldiers and their followers, who have been camped for some time, and whose destination is Merro and Egel first, Kes second, and one imagines the world, from then on, in any order they please.'

'What keeps them there?' Tisamon growled.

'You are a Mantis, and therefore a fighting man,' Teornis observed. 'Yet I claim a glorious piece of military history for my own kinden, since I have stood their thirty thousand off in open country with just two hundred men – and I still do.'

That breached Tisamon's reserve, and for a moment he forgot that he was talking to an enemy, a hated deceiver. 'It can't be done.'

'All the same, I have done it. If my kind were remotely impressed by such entertainments I would be taught in the academies. My problem now is simply that I cannot go on doing it for ever. They are currently waiting, I am informed, for word from their leaders. My people are meanwhile doing their best to make sure that word is slow in coming, but come it will, and then they will move.'

'And you and yours will be swept away like chaff,' Tisamon finished, sounding unnecessarily satisfied at the prospect.

'All things are possible,' Teornis allowed. 'Have you means of returning to Collegium, my lady Tynisa? Because if you would sail today and inform them of the events transpiring here, I would count myself in your debt.'

'You're serious, aren't you?' Tynisa could not have said just what had convinced her, and this could be another elaborate charade, but something had struck true. 'You're sitting here feasting on candied nuts and pickled scorpions, even though one day soon they'll come over that hill. And you need help.'

'The mysterious Spiderlands, the subtle Spiders,' he said. 'Not so mysterious nor subtle that when a vast army of mechanically inclined savages pitches up almost at our borders we do not sweat a little. There is a sizeable force gathering even now at Seldis, soldiers and sailors both. If the Wasps head west, though, I cannot say that they will do anything but still gather there. But if you were to get word to Collegium . . .'

'You are apparently short on news, Lord-Martial,' Tynisa interrupted. 'By now Collegium is certainly under siege.'

She had him. For the slightest moment his mask dropped and he looked genuinely and utterly surprised. 'The Wasps?'

'The Vekken, but the Wasps have put them up to it. Collegium is therefore in no position to answer your call, Lord-Martial.'

'Ah well.' His composure was intact again. 'I will have to think of something else, that's all. Life is a bouquet of surprises.'

'I have thought of something,' Tynisa said. The idea had unfurled full-grown in her mind without her ever guessing that it was cocooned there. 'But I must consult with Tisamon first. Then I may just have a thought for you to mull over, Lord-Martial.'

The field lying east of Sarn was a mass of well-ordered soldiers and machines, as the might of the Ant-kinden prepared for battle. Walking out through the gates, with Achaeos and Sperra close behind, the sight stopped Che in her tracks. She had never seen such a vast assembly of fighting men and women, and every one of them preparing calmly, no orders, no confusion. They queued for their rations and to have their blades sharpened. They handed quivers full of crossbow bolts down the line, and assembled themselves into square formations of hundreds of soldiers apiece. These were soldiers with dark helms and chainmail hauberks and long rectangular shields, with short stabbing swords and light crossbows. Amongst these greater blocks moved smaller squads of specialists: nailbowmen, heavily armoured sentinels, fast-moving scouts with big sniping crossbows, grenadiers and artificers with powder-charged piercer and waster bows. Spanning all ages from sixteen to fifty, both men and women, in the clear morning light they all looked alike, all of them ready to march without question against an enemy they had never seen.

Like fortified towns in this carpet of soldiers were the automotives. The Sarnesh battle-automotives were huge slab-sided things, frames of iron and heavy wood riveted over with armour plates and with only the bare minimum of windows for the crew to see from. The poor view mattered little because the soldiers outside would be able to mentally give them a picture of the battlefield. Even now artificers were crawling over them, making last-minute repairs and adjustments, tightening the clawed belts of their tracks, directing swaying crane rigs in order to lower parts into place. Each automotive had a swivelling tower positioned on its back, though these were currently being swapped with others fresh from the Sarnesh workshops.

Che went over to the nearest machine, even as the new tower found its resting place. 'What are you doing?' she asked.

The artificer supervising did not look back at her. 'Your Wasps – they fly, we understand,' he said, watching carefully as his apprentices bolted the new tower into place. 'Well we have a surprise for them. All our automotives have been fitted with forward repeaters, and the new towers house twin nailbows in place of the ballista. They'll soon learn they can't just steal the skies from us when we begin to rake them with these.'

'That's . . . good thinking,' said Che, a little numbly. The newly fitted tower turned first one way and then the other at the cranking of the men within, its nailbows gleaming with oil.

'Look.' Achaeos was pointing to another unit of soldiers marching past. Che couldn't see what he meant until he added, 'The two ranks.' The Ant infantry had been formed of alternating ranks: shieldmen and crossbowmen. There would be a lot of eyes on the sky when the battle came, and what one Ant saw, they all saw.

There were other automotives approaching now, huge many-legged vehicles with open backs that soldiers were already climbing up into. Che understood that between these transporters and the train carriages, the entire army would be able to travel to the point where the rail line had been broken, and there they would wait for the Wasps to arrive.

'Orthopters,' Sperra said, and Che saw flat, wheeled carriages being pushed out down the rail line, with the flying machines lashed down to them, their wings detached and laid alongside them. They were decked out with nailbows fixed above and below them and to both sides.

So much technology, she thought, and it gave her some small pride to know that it was Sarn's alliance with Collegium that had made it the best-equipped Ant city-state in the Lowlands.

'Cheerwell Maker!' she heard a voice. She expected this to be Plius, perhaps, but instead it was an anonymous Sarnesh Ant officer, waving her over. He looked agitated and, even as she saw it she realized that the demeanour of everyone around her had changed, all the surrounding Ants pausing for a fraction in what they were doing.

And many of them now seemed to be looking at her.

What has happened? 'I'm here! What's the matter?'

'The Queen needs you urgently!' the officer called out to her. 'And your Moth consort too.'

Che gaped a little at this choice of phrase. Achaeos, beside her, merely looked perturbed. Surrounded by thousands of Ants, though, there was precious little they could do if things went wrong.

With Sperra tagging anxiously along behind, the pair of them were led through the impeccably disciplined chaos of an army pulling itself together, and then towards another of the armoured automotives. There were no markings to indicate it as anything special but, when its side hatch was pushed open, Che saw the Queen standing within dressed in full plate armour.

'What is the meaning of this?' the woman demanded shortly, not from Che but from Achaeos himself.

'I do not understand, Your Majesty,' Achaeos said, genuinely puzzled, and two soldiers grabbed and manhandled him around the bulk of the automotive so that he could look towards the land rising north of the city.

There hundreds of soldiers could be seen, approaching the Sarnesh force in a straggling mob. Achaeos strained his eyes, but the sunlight was very bright and his kind preferred darkness. He did, however, see that the first rank of Ant soldiers nearest the advance had already locked shields, while those in the second rank had their crossbows levelled.

'I don't understand,' he repeated, and then Che cried out, 'Mantis-kinden!'

'Not just Mantids.' The Queen was stepping down from

the automotive. 'My scouts say there are Moths there as well. What do they intend? Is this your doing?'

Achaeos opened his mouth to deny this, but Che cried out, 'Yes!'

They all turned to her, astonished, Achaeos and Sperra included.

'Your Majesty, when we first came to your city it was with two purposes. Whilst Scuto and Sperra were to seek out audience with yourself, Achaeos and I were to contact . . . those allied to the Moths of Dorax. When last we met them they had heard of the fall of Helleron, at which they were much concerned. They were going to speak with their masters and I think . . .' The feeling of hope swelling within her made it hard to breathe. 'I think they may be friends.'

The newcomers could now clearly be seen as Mantis-kinden. Compared with the rigidly organized Ant army they seemed a ragged host, and far fewer in number. Che studied them individually, though, and saw them differently: lean, hard men and women with spears, bows, swords and claws just like Tisamon's. No two were alike in their weapons, nor in their armour: she saw leather coats, cuirasses, crested helms, breastplates, scale-mail, even a few suits of fluted plate that looked as if made for another era entirely. They all had about them the same air, though. These were warriors, and they were ready for war.

One of them stepped forward, approaching the rigid Ant line without fear. At some unheard signal from the Queen, it parted to let the envoy through. Che's heart leapt when she recognized Scelae. The slender Mantis-woman wore a long coat of scales, backed with felt to silence the clink of metal, a tall unstrung bow was slung across her back and she walked confidently through the staring Ants and made a respectful bow to their Queen.

'Your Majesty,' she said. 'I bring you greetings from the Ancient League.'

'And what might this League be, that you speak of?'

asked the Queen, still not entirely trusting this new force. 'I have never heard of it.'

Scelae smiled slightly. 'The name has an irony to it, as the League has existed just these last five days. The traditions it pledges to are ancient, though, for in the face of our changing world we have renewed some old ties. Just as your city is now ranged with the Beetles of Collegium, so the holds of Etheryon and Nethyon have come again to seek the wisdom and guidance of Dorax and the Moth-kinden.'

'A new power on my doorstep,' observed the Queen. 'Should I rejoice in this?'

'I am no seer and I cannot tell the future,' Scelae said, 'save in one thing: this force you see was gathered in one day, made up of all those ready to hear our call. We march with you now against the Empire.'

'How many?' the Queen asked and, before Scelae could answer, some word came to her from scouts who had been counting all this while. 'Eight hundred. Eight hundred Mantids – and perhaps a hundred Moths as well. And you will fight alongside us?'

'We will fight,' Scelae assured her. 'There is nothing in the world you may be more sure of.'

Thirty-Five

That day, Stenwold had cause to remember how he had told Doctor Nicrephos that it could wait until evening because of the urgent duties he had to fulfil.

He remembered particularly in the first few hours after dawn, when the remaining Vekken armourclads made another pass at the harbour, grinding their engines to breaking point to try and nose their own half-sunk siblings out of the way, whilst simultaneously their artillery lashed the harbourfront again and again. As Stenwold's role was to defend the harbour, he had waited there with a few hundred soldiers, crouching behind every piece of cover that was available and watching while the great ships shoved repeatedly, and the sound of their engines groaned across the water.

Over sixty of his men had been killed during the bombardment because, at that range, if he had pulled them far back enough to be out of the way, the Ants would have been able to establish a presence on the waterfront itself before he could have formed up enough men to stop them.

And then, mid-morning, the armourclads had given up and reversed their engines, pulling back into open water. To Stenwold, however, it did not seem like a victory.

He had thought about going to Doctor Nicrephos at that point. The old man had been very agitated, talking about some artefact that must be given over to his own protection.

He knew it was somewhere in the city, and he believed he could even divine its location. He had obviously been very serious, but to Stenwold it had made very little sense.

But then a messenger had come for him from the north wall, saying that he was needed there urgently. There was never any time.

His journey across the city had been nightmarish. Over the last day the Vekken had begun using special trebuchets, far out of range of any armaments on the Collegium walls. They were incredibly spindly contraptions, his telescope had told him, and they flung handfuls of grenades arcing from their slings. These exploded over the city, showering it with fire and shrapnel, or else burst in flames on the roofs of buildings. It was a random barrage, doing little damage, but it meant that nobody in the city was ever entirely safe. Those few who braved the streets had to keep one eye on the sky, and Stenwold, passing through the streets of his home city, felt the doom of the place keenly, like a cloud hovering above him.

'I'm starting to wonder about how this is going to go,' he had told Balkus, and the big Ant only nodded.

In the hour before dawn a messenger had got through to the city. His name was Frezzo and he had been expected days before, but an Ant crossbowman had shot him down, and he had been resting within sight of the city walls, building up the strength to fly again. However he had insisted, with the honour of his guild at stake, on giving his news before they treated his wound. The news itself was just one more burden for the defenders. It appeared Sarn was not coming to their aid. They all knew that Helleron had gone to the Wasps, but not even Kymon had made the logical step that a westward-moving imperial army would occupy Sarn's attention and thus prevent any chance of rescue from the north.

Kymon and his soldiers were down off the west wall today, but only because there was no immediate assault.

Instead, what artillery the Ants had left was pelting the wall mercilessly with rock and lead shot. The artillery on the tower emplacements was returning the favour in daylight now, and most of it was second- or third-generation, as more and more engines were smashed by increasingly accurate incoming missiles. Stenwold had seen some machines being fixed in, during the pre-dawn, that were just the previous engines reassembled with desperate haste, and therefore sure to fly apart after a few shots.

The north wall was bearing the brunt of it today, with tower engines and rams and legions of Vekken infantry. Stenwold came at a run, expecting disaster, but then he found himself cornered by an enraged academic.

'Master Maker! Or I suppose I have to call you War Master now.'

'Call me what you want, Master . . . ?'

The Beetle-kinden was squat and balding and enraged. 'I am Master Hornwhill, and I demand that you discipline these military fellows! It's an outrage!'

'What's an outrage?' Stenwold asked, trying for calm. Hornwhill was so incensed by whatever had outraged him that it took Balkus looming menacingly at his shoulder to calm him down.

'Master Maker, my discipline is in the mercantile area. I design barrels, and they are not meant for military use!' the man protested. Stenwold goggled at him.

'What are you talking about?'

'This!' Hornwhill stomped over towards a row of catapults that the north wall commander had set up, and which even now were launching their shot in a high arc, right over the wall and onto the men and machines arrayed on the far side. Hornwhill grabbed one of the missiles from the engineers and brandished it fiercely. 'This is my double-hulled safe-passage barrel intended for breakable goods!' the excited artificer exclaimed. 'Five hundred of them have been seized from my warehouse and I demand restitution.'

'Who's in charge here?' Stenwold called out, and a dirty-faced engineer popped his head up above the winding winch of a catapult.

'Here, War Master!'

How is it that everyone knows me? 'Why are you throwing barrels at them?' Stenwold asked him.

'Got precious little else to throw,' the engineer said cheerily. 'Besides, these beauties are just what we need. They crack open when they hit, but they don't damage their cargoes, just release them all cosy like. They're lovely.'

'Cargoes? What cargoes?' Stenwold said, trying to block out Hornwhill's jabbering complaints.

The engineer grinned at him, still winding back the catapult. 'Well, I figure we might as well use every dirty trick in the book, War Master. Last night me and my lad raided every menagerie, animal workshop and alchemist's store in the city. I got the lot in these barrels. I got scorpions, poisonous spiders, stinging flies, glasses of acid, explosive reagents. I got the Vekken doing a real guessing game with what's going to land on 'em next.'

'Balkus,' Stenwold said.

'Here.'

'If Master Hornwhill doesn't shut up and go home, throw him in the river.'

Nothing was going quite as it should. Akalia was becoming increasingly aware that, in the estimates of the Royal Court of Vek, Collegium should have fallen by now.

It seemed impossible that a city-state of tinkerers and philosophers could hold off the elite of Vek, the most disciplined soldiers in the world. Still the walls stood, though, the defenders rushing to throw back every incursion. The Beetle-kinden and their slaves seemed indefatigable, never-ceasing. Every time it seemed the walls would be taken, the Beetles dragged out some new scheme, and thus held her off for yet another day.

She shook her head. It had been a run of disturbed nights for her, and for her men as well. Her ill dreams had communicated themselves to her army, or else she had been infected with theirs. She *feared*. In waking moments she would not even have acknowledged it, but she feared. She feared the derision of her peers, that no Ant-kinden could escape. She did not fear that Collegium would never fall, but she feared that she would not take it fast enough, that, had the King chosen differently, a more skilled tactician would be within the walls by now.

And those Wasps had run mad and killed one another. It should be expected from a weaker race, but still it shook her. She could see no logic to it, no sense at all. Without warning they had left the camp and butchered each other to the last man. The report of her sentries had been easily brushed off at first, but the event had returned to prey on her mind. *Was this some ploy, some new weapon, some contagious insanity? Will it happen to us?* Her artificers had assured her that it was impossible, but she found herself losing faith in them. *Clearly the Collegium scholars know things that we do not.* In her mind, in the hearts of all Apt people, there was a tiny worm so deeply buried that it would never normally see the light. It was a worm born many centuries before, in the Days of Lore before the revolution – those days when her kind and the Beetles had both been slaves. It was fear of the unknown, of the old mysteries. In now facing the scholars of Collegium, Akalia was rediscovering her fear of the unknown.

Tactician, word arrived from her engineers.

Report, demanded Akalia. In her mind's eye she saw the west wall of Collegium as her scouts could now see it through their glasses. The patient voice of one of her artificers guided her through the stress fractures, cracks and damage that her engines had done to it over the last few days.

The wall is holding out better than we had anticipated, the artificer explained. *The Beetle-kinden mortar remains semi-solid indefinitely, and so there is a great deal of flexibility in the wall. However, damage to the stones themselves is now quite widespread. There is considerable cracking and, even with the artillery left to us, we have been able to accurately expand the stress areas that you see here.*

Just tell me when, Akalia snapped at him.

There was a moment's pause in which the artificer conferred with his colleagues.

We think today – late today or early tomorrow. We were considering holding until tomorrow in any event, to give us more time for the assault, and—

No! she ordered. *Today! If we can possibly be within Collegium's walls today, then we must make all efforts. The artificers of Vek have so far proved themselves inferior to these Beetle peasants on every level. You know what you must do to change that.*

The artificer capitulated hurriedly. She had the sense of him hurrying off to order an increased barrage from the siege engines.

This had gone on too long already. The greater Wasp city-state must have already done its job, because her scouts would have spotted Sarn's approach by now, but she still felt that the scholars and merchants of Collegium were laughing at her behind their walls.

Not for long, though. The King of Vek had given her free rein on how to punish the resistance of the city, after she had taken it, and that thought was her only consolation as she waited for the walls to fall.

'Master Kymon!' the man was shouting. 'They're coming!'

He panted to a halt and Kymon just had to stare at him and wait for his wind to return. If this had been an Ant-kinden defence he would know already what it was the man had seen, not only in words but by the very image. His halfbreed Kessen watcher was dead, though, and he had to rely on word of mouth. This was unbearably frustrating.

At last he snapped, 'What did you see? Troops? Engines?' Above them the Ant artillery was still pelting away at the wall. Each shot made the stones shift and shudder so that Kymon had pulled his cowering soldiers back from them in case they suddenly fell, even though Collegium's architects had assured him that they were far from cracking.

'Engines, Master Kymon, with soldiers behind. Ramming engines, I think.'

Under cover of the bombardment, Kymon knew. The Vekken had already tried rams against all the gates on and off, and the metal-sheathed shutters had dented but never given in. They would be disappointed again.

He was suspicious, though, for even the Vekken had some sense of strategy. 'What about towers?' he demanded.

'Back with the men,' his lookout reported. 'The rams are in front.'

'And these rams? Like the ones we've seen before?'

'I'm not an artificer, but—'

'Just tell me!' Kymon barked. He would never have had to shout at Ant-kinden either, but sometimes, with these slow city people, it seemed the only way.

'Not quite, Master Kymon. Bigger, with a different end to it.'

Kymon cursed the man silently for not being able to just *show* him. Even so, his military instincts were telling him bad things.

'Pull back from the wall!' he shouted.

'We're already—'

'Further, you cretins! Or I will personally flog every last one of you!'

His men began to shamble away, talking amongst themselves and lagging. Kymon bared his teeth and fought down his temper.

'What's going on?'

He rounded on the speaker and almost shouted down his throat before he saw it was Stenwold.

'The Vekken are trying something new,' he explained shortly. 'How long before they reach the wall, boy?'

The lookout spread his hands helplessly.

'Well, how fast were they moving?' Kymon asked him, thinking that—

He picked himself off the hard flags of the street, head ringing, and saw all around him that his men, even Stenwold, were strewn about, similarly jolted off their feet.

'Get up!' he bellowed at them, hearing his own voice as strangely distant. They looked dazed, stunned. Stenwold's eyes were wide.

'They sent a petard against the wall!' Kymon informed him, knowing that he was speaking too loud. Even as he said it, another explosion rocked them from a hundred yards south, and a third followed on its heels. The Vekken were using engine-mounted explosives driven directly into the stones so as to crack the city open. He turned fearfully, looking for the wall.

The Beetles of Collegium had done well, for it still stood, but it was obvious that it would not stand for very much longer. He watched how the latest explosion rippled the stones like canvas in a breeze.

The Vekken artillery kept on launching, and he saw great chunks of stones still bound with mortar falling out to crash onto the streets right in front of his men.

'On your feet, all of you!' he screamed at them, and there was something in his voice at last that reached them. They were clustered together too close, they were shaken, terrified, even. As more stones fell from the wall he strode out before them, shield on one arm, drawn sword in his right hand.

'Listen to me!' he shouted at them. 'The wall will fall

and it was always going to. You, boy!' He pointed at the ashen lookout. 'Go to the other walls, get men with the right materials to repair a breach. Go now!' As the lad ran off Kymon glared at the rest of them. 'You, though, you're staying here with me, and those Vekken bastards are going to be inside *your* city in minutes, you understand? They're going to punch a breach in that wall with their engines and then come flooding through, soldiers in better armour than yours, with better training than yours, and you know what you're going to do? You're going to hold them at the wall. You're bloody well going to stop them getting into *your* city. You understand me? Not *my* city. I'm a Kessen and I wouldn't have a city like this to defend for all the wasting world, but *your* city, and the only people in this whole city who can keep it *yours* are *you*! You men and women standing before me now!' He was conscious of a greater shattering behind him which was echoed in the stir of the soldiers before him – and that Stenwold Maker now had a repeating crossbow in his hands and had cranked back the string.

'When they come through,' he bellowed at them, 'they will loose their crossbows first, to try and clear the way. I want shieldmen at the front, everyone with a decent-sized shield. Behind them, crossbowmen, Master Maker here will take his shot when he sees the best time, and you all shoot when you see him do it. There will be a lot of rubble. They will have to move forward over it. You will just have to stand still, so make that count for you.'

He stared at them, seeing city militia, artisans, shop-keepers, factors and merchants, dockworkers, porters, immigrant labourers, street-brawlers, black-marketeers and a handful of professional mercenaries.

You'll just have to do, he thought, and then, *If I had a command of Kessen marines we'd sort these bastards out.*

And he turned, and the wall came down.

It was so close on evening, the sky darkening almost

visibly. The Vekken had left it to the last minute, but their artillery had finally done its job. The widescale weakening created by the petard engines and the incessant pounding of the trebuchets and leadshotters had first knocked holes in the wall and now it was tumbling, great clots and sheets of stone peeling away until the wall before and to the left of him was dissolving into an utter chaos of tumbling masonry.

'Go!' he shouted at his men and, when they did not move, he went himself,. trusting to their shame to carry them with him.

The rubble had barely finished shifting when he began to climb it, and for a terrible second he thought he was the only one there. Then there were shields to the left and the right of him, a motley collection of a dozen different styles, and now he was at the top of the breach, seeing Vekken soldiers hauling themselves up towards him.

'Brace!' he shouted, and ducked behind his own shield. Most of the men around him did the same, but there were always a few who were slow or who thought they knew better, and this time it proved fatal. Crossbow bolts slammed into his shield, three or four actually punching their square-sectioned heads through to gleam like diamonds in the backing.

Then Stenwold was at his shoulder, raising his crossbow so that it almost rested on Kymon's shield and then pressing the trigger, and a score of crossbows fired with him, and two score more a heartbeat afterwards. The Vekken were climbing the rubble with their shields held high, but a dozen fell anyway, the close-ranged bolts sticking in their armour, and more fell amongst their crossbowmen following immediately behind.

Then the Vekken were making a final push up the shifting stones, and Kymon braced himself again, feeling his heart hammering out to him its message that he was too old for a battlefield by ten years at least.

He rammed his shield forwards into the first man that came his way, impacting so hard on the man's own that the Vekken was sent tumbling back down. Another man took his place, though, one of a stream of Vekken soldiers that was pushing forwards up into the breach, and the serious business of killing at the blade's point then began.

The harsh hammering of a nailbow sounded nearby as Stenwold's bodyguard elbowed his way into the second rank and began to shoot the enemy indiscriminately in the face. Kymon was absorbed in his own trade, though. He was a trainer of men, a College Master, but most of all he was a swordsman. These Ants coming against him were soldiers, but he had always been something more than that, and he showed them. He taught them a dozen fatal lessons of the shortsword, his blade striking like a scorpion's sting, forward, left and right, so that the soldiers advancing near him began to pay him more heed than his fellows, thus becoming easier prey for the men either side of him.

All down the line, though, the battle was shifting. The defenders of Collegium were laying down their lives. They were selling them dearly, giving no ground, and making the Vekken pay for each inch they climbed, but the Ants fought as an impeccable unit, while the defenders fought like a ragged line of individuals. Kymon could feel the tide turning, no matter how many he killed or how skilled his blade.

'Hold!' he bellowed. 'Hold for Collegium!' He was aware, when he could pause to think, that the defenders were still faring far better than they should, and that the Vekken were not fighting with that sharp edge that Ant-kinden usually possessed. There was something in their faces, something haggard and bruised, that was blunting them.

For a second the line swayed forwards again, whether from his words of encouragement or from the defenders' own desperation. Ant soldiers went backwards, lost their footing, and it seemed that the advance might be halted, but then they gathered themselves, as Ants always did, and surged back up.

'Hold!' Kymon shouted once again and, miraculously, something went out of the Vekken advance. Abruptly the men attacking the breach were no longer backed by hundreds of others. The Ant attention had been somehow split.

He felt something strike him in the chest, clipping the rim of his shield. At the base of his vision he could see the quilled end of a crossbow bolt that had driven through his mail. It seemed to hurt far less than it should.

His line was failing, even though all the Ants beyond the foot of this hill of rubble were turning north, trying to move out of the way but constricted by their neighbours, their minds all obviously sharing the same focus.

Something struck him in the head, ringing from his helm, and he found himself falling back . . . no, Stenwold had him. Stenwold and his Sarnesh bodyguard, carrying him back.

'The line . . .' he managed to gasp.

'Hold still,' Stenwold told him. There was more said but, although the Beetle's lips moved, Kymon could hear none of it.

He drew his breath to demand that Stenwold speak up, but there was no breath to draw, and he understood that the bolt had pierced his mail, had pierced his lungs, perhaps. The sky above them was growing dark far faster than the oncoming night alone could have managed.

He sent his mind out, futilely, for some last contact with his own kind, but he was the last man of Kes remaining within the walls of Collegium, and when he died, even clasped in Stenwold's arms, he died alone.

Stenwold looked to the line, then, but incredibly it still held, and the Ants seemed to be trying to retreat, and there was a great cheer that Sarn had come, Sarn had come at last.

Stenwold rushed forwards, and in his mind's eye there

was a vast host of Sarnesh soldiers crowding the horizon, but instead he saw merely the shapes of Sarnesh automotives powering towards the breach in the wall. There were two still moving, and the caved-in wreck of a third some distance back, where the Vekken artillery had found it. The remaining two were driving in at top speed, though, their clawed tracks chewing up the dusty, bloody earth, and he saw the Vekken soldiers at the fore linking shields, bracing themselves ridiculously against the charge.

Artillery began bursting around them, and Stenwold saw one of the machines take a terrific blow that stove in one side and yet did not stop it moving. The machines were loosing their own weapons now, repeating ballista bolts smashing the Ant shield-wall full of holes. The Vekken had a siege tower out there, half-extended, and the undamaged automotive struck it a terrible blow that dented the whole front of the machine, but smashed the tower's lifting gear totally, spilling men and broken machinery in its wake.

Stenwold wanted to close his eyes as they struck, but he could not – he could only stare. The Vekken artillery was smashing into its own infantry in its haste to destroy the automotives, and then the unstoppable momentum of the machines had taken them right into the main block of soldiers, and hundreds of the Vekken shieldmen were simply crushed beneath them.

The damaged machine was meanwhile slewing away from the city, one of its tracks jammed, and a moment later Stenwold saw fire break out around it, the fuel tanks for its engine catching light. The Vekken were fleeing from it, and it exploded, scything through them with jagged metal. The final machine was still driving for the breach, scattering the Vekken in its wake. A leadshotter struck it a glancing blow, spinning it round so that it was facing away from the city, and Stenwold saw Vekken Ants climbing onto it, swarming over it like their very namesakes, and prying hatches open.

With a final effort, the last of the Sarnesh Lorn detachment threw its tracks into reverse and began to climb the rubble backwards. The Vekken had clawed their way on board before it was halfway up, and Balkus grabbed Stenwold's arm and pulled him back, fearful for his safety.

Doctor Nicrephos was waiting for them, the frail old Moth looking impossibly out of place so close to the front line. 'It is time!' he was shouting. 'We must go!'

'Anywhere but here,' Balkus agreed.

Stenwold looked back to see the last automotive slew backwards into the breach, using its armoured length to bridge the gap in the wall. There was a thump and flare from inside that must be a grenade going off, and then the mauled machine fell still.

Beyond the wall the Vekken began to retreat to their camp for the night, but they would be back again in the morning, perhaps for the last time.

The Fly-kinden, Kori, ducked in and closed the door solidly behind him. In the moment it was open they could all hear the distant sound of exploding grenades.

'Well this is lovely!' he exclaimed. 'I do hope the Empire sends us someplace nice like this again!' He hooked his cloak off and cast it into the corner of the taproom. They had the taverna to themselves after the owner had gone off to fight.

'You've taken your time,' Gaved snapped. 'We'd about given up on you.'

'Big city, Wasp-boy, so even a man as talented as me takes time to get around it. And this whole Ant invasion gets in the way sometimes.' Kori stretched. 'Someone get me something to drink. I feel a need to toast the Emperor.'

'Over a fire, no doubt,' muttered Eriphinea the Moth. She slung him a wineskin, which he caught on the wing while hopping up onto a table.

'Have you located it?' Scyla demanded of him. The other two were also on their feet now, waiting for his report.

'Relax, I've found the building,' the Fly assured them. 'Private collection? Barred and bolted, more like. No simple job to get in. Briskall, the old hoarder, he's obviously gone to ground with all his treasures. Won't come out until the siege is over, or the Vekken come to break down his doors.'

'Can *we* break through his doors?' Eriphinea asked doubtfully. 'These Beetles and their locks . . .'

'I'm the knees with locks,' Kori told her. 'I'm the utter knees. I'm more worried about finding our trinket once we get in there.'

'Don't forget,' Scyla said disdainfully, 'we can't miss it. That's an imperial guarantee.'

'Oh sure, sure.'

'We'll have no difficulties locating it,' the Moth insisted flatly. That silenced them, and they stared at her. Her blank eyes gave them nothing back.

'Would you care to qualify that, Phin?' Gaved asked her.

'Not in any way that you could comprehend,' she said, not harshly but as a simple statement of fact. 'He knows.' She pointed at Scyla. The Spider, finding their attention on her, scowled.

'She's right,' Scyla said shortly. 'We'll know it. Her and me.'

'Well whatever,' said Kori. 'You sniff it out, and I'll get us in, and the Wasp here can watch the door. We have the place and the means.'

'Let's go, then,' Gaved said.

'Let's wait till dusk, shall we, so people don't see us housebreaking,' Kori suggested.

'There's a war on! Who's going to care?' the Wasp demanded.

'Night-time is always better,' Scyla said. 'In war they kill looters out of hand, in my experience, which is just what we'd look like.'

'Darkness is always best,' Eriphinea confirmed.

The Wasp threw up his hands. 'Nightfall it is,' he said. 'Always assuming we can even get the thing out of the city.'

'Neither Ants nor Beetles fly, so they seldom watch for fliers,' Scyla reminded them. 'We got in. We can get out.'

'Unless what they say about Ant women is true,' Kori said.

'And what is that?' Phin asked him archly.

'That they can fly non-stop for a whole night the first time you knock them up.' The Fly grinned lewdly.

'And you believe that?'

'No, but I could have a lot of fun putting it to the test.' He rubbed his hands. 'And we've got a few pleasant hours to wait, assuming the Vekken don't kill us. Anything to eat around here?'

'Are you sure this is the place?' Stenwold asked.

'Yes, yes,' Doctor Nicrephos insisted. 'You cannot understand, but I am driven – drawn – and I know not by what, but this is definitely the place.'

'Keep calm, Doctor,' Stenwold advised him, but Nicrephos was obviously anything but calm. Something had a hold of the old man, something that was now shaking him to his very bones.

There were four of them there loitering outside in the street and looking suspicious. Stenwold had brought Balkus, of course, and because he had gone home first to wash, because he could not bear the thought of Kymon's blood on him, Arianna had joined them and was here too. He was not sure whether she entirely understood what was going on here but, when Stenwold had left for this errand, she had been tagging along behind him.

He spared her a fond smile, and resisted the urge to reach for her hand. 'This is Master Briskall's place,' he said, belated recollection coming to him. 'I knew I recognized it.

He used to be an archivist at the College, but there were questions as to where some of the exhibits were disappearing to . . .'

'We have to go in,' Nicrephos insisted. '*Please*, Master Maker.'

'Are we expecting trouble here?' Balkus hefted the nailbow. 'Want me to send Master Briskall a warning shot?'

'No!' Stenwold snapped. He did not understand why this whole venture felt like something criminal, but maybe Doctor Nicrephos's furtive manner was beginning to infect all of them. 'I am a Master of Collegium, therefore we'll knock.' He turned to say more to the Moth, but the grey-skinned old scholar was wringing his hands and silently baring his yellowed teeth.

'Well if you want to do things the hard way,' Balkus muttered, 'I'll get them out of bed.'

The big Ant went up to the reinforced door and his fist descended, a single booming thud that had the door already swinging open on its hinges. The others crowded forwards instinctively.

'Oh—' the big man said, and then swept back one arm, knocking all three of them, even Stenwold, off his feet. A second later there was a flash, and Balkus staggered back, tripped on Stenwold and sprawled out in the street.

'That was a Wasp sting!' Arianna cried out. Nicrephos was desperately trying to get up.

'Balkus?' Stenwold called in dismay.

The Ant sat up, a patch of his chainmail now fused together over his chest. 'Bastard!' he shouted, and unslung his nailbow.

'They are trying to steal it!' Nicrephos shouted in alarm. 'We must stop them! Please, Stenwold!'

'All right!' Stenwold drew his sword, took a second to steel himself, and then flung himself in. The expected bolt sizzled past him and he hit the floor awkwardly, trying to roll away. A moment later the very floor seemed to shake as Balkus discharged his nailbow three times through the doorway, and then moved in to take cover behind a side-table whose exquisite vase he had just shattered. They were in an entrance hall with a door at the far end, and another in each of the long side walls. Stenwold saw movement ahead as the unknown Wasp drew back, and he took advantage of this. All of a sudden he was no longer tired, no longer the War Master, but just Stenwold Maker and free to make his own mistakes, with his own life as the only stake.

The Wasp, out of uniform in a long coat, reappeared with his hand spread, but Stenwold was already far too close and moving too fast for that to work. He had knocked the arm up before the man loosed his sting, and cannoned into him with enough force to send them both sprawling. Stenwold had the better of the collision and already had his sword stabbing down at his opponent. The Wasp twisted agilely out from under him so that the point of the descending blade chipped the floor tiles, but Stenwold managed a quick reverse and caught the man under the chin with his pommel as he tried to rise, sending the Wasp reeling backwards.

'Beware!' he heard Nicrephos croak. 'Someone here has power!'

Stenwold smacked the Wasp across the back of the head with his sword-hilt, sending him back to the ground, and then something snaked past him and caught about his throat. Its claw hooked sharply into his armpit, dragging him off balance.

A grapple! he realized, before seeing a stocky Fly-kinden across the room holding the other end of the rope he was just about to pull. Trying to brace himself, Stenwold got one hand on the rope about his neck, so that he was only pulled off his feet and not strangled with it. Then Balkus burst in with the others right behind him.

The rope tightened, the barbed tines digging into him,

and then the Fly had a shortsword drawn and was flying straight towards him, even as Stenwold choked and tried desperately to dislodge the hook. Balkus was . . .

Balkus was staring strangely, his nailbow hanging loose in his hands. Stenwold shouted at him for help, but his face had gone slack, utterly devoid of expression.

The Fly was abruptly crouching on top of him, his sword clutched in both hands like an outsized dagger. Stenwold groped for him, seeing only a careful concentration on the man's flat face. With one hand still on the entangling hook, Stenwold got his other hand on one of the Fly's wrists. For a moment the man was pushing down against him, the tip of the sword descending until it touched Stenwold's chest.

There was a woman pointing at Balkus, a Moth woman. She was approaching him with a dagger in one hand, but her other was directed at him, so that the power of her Art held him immobile as she approached. She was speaking words that Stenwold could not hear and the big Ant just stared back at her with a glazed expression. In the Moth woman's hand the dagger's glistening blade was smeared with something black. She was smiling all the while.

With a supreme effort Stenwold halted the sword's further descent, locking his own arm and pushing up against the smaller man's wrist whilst still hauling at the hook with his free hand. The Fly-kinden's teeth were bared in a snarl and he was remarkably strong for one of his small kind. Suddenly he grinned and simply took up the sword one-handed, leaving Stenwold clutching the useless wrist of an empty hand. Stenwold yanked at it furiously, putting the man off his stroke so that the sword just clipped his ear, but then the Fly's wings flashed out to steady him, and he drew the blade back for one final strike.

Arianna's knife flashed, and the Fly-kinden arched backwards, the weapon spinning from his hands. She struck again and again in fierce desperation as he screamed and bucked, knocking himself off Stenwold's chest. For a moment he was scrabbling about on the floor to retrieve his dropped sword, his back now a welter of red, and then finally she drove her blade into his side up to the hilt with a cry of revulsion.

Stenwold was aware of Doctor Nicrephos shouting something, and he felt a wave of cold surge through him that had every hair on his body standing on end. The Moth woman cursed in frustration, and lunged her dagger forwards just as Balkus snapped out of his trance. It was a hasty blow she delivered that skittered harmlessly from his mail, and in automatic response the nailbow boomed, sending her flying backwards with a bloody hole punched all the way through her.

'Stenwold!' the old Moth cried. 'Help me!'

Stenwold staggered to his feet, looking around for the old man. For a brief moment he saw Doctor Nicrephos wrestling with a shadowy figure, and then a blade flashed and the Moth was reeling back, his robe bloodied. Stenwold had a brief glimpse of a Spider-kinden man – no, a Spider-kinden woman? It was impossible in that moment to tell. He roared out a challenge, and Balkus shot another bolt at the same time, but the Spider dodged nimbly, running for the open door with something under his – or her – arm. As Stenwold charged, she – it was definitely a she – turned and flung something at him that struck him in the chest and instantly he was falling, tangled and stuck in strands of fine, sticky silk. A moment later, the Wasp-kinden man was running after the Spider, slipping through the door just before Balkus' nailbow destroyed the door-frame in three separate places.

Arianna crouched by him, her eyes wide.

'Who was that?' she gasped. 'What is going on?'

Only Doctor Nicrephos knew that, Stenwold thought painfully, for he could still see the old man from where he lay, and there was no doubt that the Moth was dead. *As for who that was, though . . . surely it can't be . . .* It could *not* be, he decided. It must be some other of the same order, for Achaeos had sworn that he had killed the face-shifting spy who had plagued them in Helleron.

A spy in Helleron. A spy in Myna. Now a spy in Collegium. The coincidence was there already, so how much further for it to have all been the work of one man – or one woman? And how difficult was it for a master of disguise to play dead?

Arianna was patiently disentangling him from the Art-made web, and after a moment Balkus joined them, slotting a fresh magazine into his nailbow.

'Any idea what they got away with?' he asked.

'None,' said Stenwold helplessly. 'And no understanding of this at all.' He took a good long time to recover his breath, leaning back against a wall of Briskall's entrance hall, staring mournfully at the body of Doctor Nicrephos, whose last desperate request had cost the old man his life – and achieved nothing. Arianna crouched beside him protectively, her head on his shoulder. She had saved his life, he realized. He had hardly noted it in all the confusion, but the Fly-kinden would have had him if she had not stabbed the man first. Spiders played deep games, but he allowed himself to hope that this was it, this was all, and at last the womanly concern she presented to him was the Arianna that really was.

He was unspeakably grateful for her company at that bleak moment.

There was the dead Moth woman to consider, as well. This mixed bag of raiders had all the hallmarks of a mercenary team. The presence of a Wasp did not guarantee they were imperial, nor did it seem likely they were Vekken.

It was all rather more than he could disentangle.

He heard Balkus's clumping tread, and then the big Ant was back with yet another body slung over his shoulder. As he lowered it to the floor Stenwold saw an elderly Beetle-kinden who had been killed by a single knife-blow to the back of the neck.

'Master Briskall *was* at home then,' Stenwold said weakly. 'What else did you see through there?'

Balkus shrugged. 'Bit of a mystery, Master Maker. There's a nice big lock on this door, and all manner of stuff behind it that any thief would go out of his mind to steal. Some of it's in locked cages or behind glass, but there's plenty there just for the grabbing, only they didn't.'

'We interrupted them?' Stenwold suggested.

'That Spider had something with her when she ran off,' Balkus pointed out, and he had obviously made his mind up about the sex of the escapee. 'There's one thing gone, something square and about so big.' His hands made a shape no more than six inches to each side. 'It was just out on a stand, though – nothing this old boy wanted locked away.'

'Just an opportunistic grab, maybe,' Stenwold suggested, but an odd thought came to him: *Or something Master Briskall did not know the value of.*

The three of them then carried the bodies of Briskall and Doctor Nicrephos to the nearest infirmary, although they were both beyond all healing. Stenwold told a reliable-looking soldier about the other bodies, and advised that Briskall's house should be secured against thieves. Then the three of them returned to Stenwold's home, to find a messenger waiting on his doorstep with even worse news.

Scyla realized, as she left, that her only regret was that Gaved had escaped. She worked alone for preference, so she had taken no joy in the company the Empire had forced on her.

And she had no intention of sharing a reward with anyone. If this box was so important, then the Wasps would just have to pay the full amount to her alone.

Within a street she had taken on the guise of a portly

Beetle woman, easy enough to do under cover of darkness, and was heading towards the nearest city wall. Getting through the Vekken lines would be harder, but she was adept at her craft.

Though heavily carved, the box was otherwise as unassuming as she had been told, but she had been given no time yet to make a detailed examination. If she could find out what was so special about it, then maybe she could raise the asking price. The Empire had a lot of money to throw around, and with a thousand faces at her disposal she had no worries about making enemies. Perhaps she should even impersonate Gaved? Now that would be amusing.

She guessed that Gaved would now be circling the streets looking for her, but between her disguise and his pitiful Wasp eyes, he had no chance at all. He would give up in the end and get himself out of the city before dawn, heading back to the imperial masters he constantly disavowed but would never quite escape.

Some part of the back of her mind was aware that those who had originally taught her would despair at her behaviour. Theirs was a noble and ancient calling of spies, and now she was a mere profiteer prostituting the gifts they had awakened in her just for spite and for gold. She had long ago lost sight of any higher goals she might have had, any lasting achievement she could make. Now it was just the getting and the gaining and, most especially, the joy of outwitting – making bigger fools of all the fools out there, who looked no further than another's face.

She reached the city wall and stood close to it, seeing no one around, no airborne shape hovering above. Calling on her Art she swiftly scaled the stonework, hands and booted feet clinging easily to its smooth stone. Flat against it, near the top, she waited as a sentry passed by, with eyes only for the Vekken camp beyond. She crawled onto the walkway and the battlements and, like a shadow, face downwards, to the earth below.

Now came the real challenge. She could have crept from darkness to darkness, and thus avoided the Vekken lanterns, but she wanted to complete her victory. She wanted to fool a whole army.

She focused her concentration and changed her face and form, taking on the obsidian hue of a Vekken Ant, even down to the dark chainmail and helm. Ants could not be fooled by mere appearances amongst their own kind, though, and she stretched her powers and gifts, feeling tensions and strains within her mind as she worked with it, reaching out towards something that was a distant and foreign concept, an ideal, a mere idea, but something that was the fount of Ant-kinden Art.

And the night was full of voices. She heard the rapidly passed reports of sentries, the chatter of artificers working on the artillery, questions from officers, and the complaints of a few who simply could not get to sleep, and she walked into it and, when she was seen, she simply greeted them, mind to mind, as any Ant would. If they had asked her questions it might have been difficult, in an army where any stranger could be identified so quickly, but it never even occurred to them to be suspicious, for she was doing the impossible, counterfeiting them so well that they could not conceive that she was not one of them.

Blithely and openly, she walked straight through the Vekken camp and out into the night.

By dawn she was far from the Vekken camp, back to the easy guise of a Spider-kinden man of younger years. When she had first called up this face he could have been her twin. Now he was a decade younger than she was.

The local people around here, solid farmers all, had heard about the siege of Collegium but had no idea what to do about it. They were simply awaiting the outcome, and if that meant Vekken soldiers coming down the road then they would take it as it came. Even the Vekken needed farmers to till the land, and Scyla suspected life as Vekken slaves would not change their rural ways so very much.

She found a barn where two placid draft-beetles were stabled, and climbed up to the hayloft. It was time to examine her prize.

Nothing but a box carved in wood – that was her first impression. The carvings were strange, though. They drew the eye in a way that seemed to ignore the angles and corners of the thing, as though whatever they truly encompassed had no real edges at all, and they led on and led on, and as she turned the thing over in her hands she could see no end or beginning to them, coiling and twining traceries of thorny vines and ragged-edged leaves that overlapped and overlapped and only emphasized the depths of the spaces in between them, depths that seemed, by some trick of light and shadow, to fall into recesses far further than the small box itself could readily accommodate.

In her intense concentration she did not notice the light wane within the stable, or hear the increasingly uncomfortable shuffling of the big insects below.

But how remarkable, she thought, that those lines split apart again and again, and yet whatever path she followed only turned and twisted, while all the others flourished with leaves, and carved insects, beetles and grubs and woodlice and other things that dwelled within rotten wood. Over and over she turned it, trying to unravel the essential mystery. A box it was, and light enough that it must be hollow, and yet there was no lid, no catch, no way of working her way into it, save to follow, follow, follow the carved patterns laid over and under one another, round and round the seemingly endless sides of the box.

There was a flickering within her mind, like shadows when the candle flame is blown, a flickering and a dancing, and at last she looked up, and saw shadows moving of their own accord across the walls of the barn, shadows that her eyes picked out of the darkness. Warrior shadows, with spined arms and stalking gait, the shadows of great clawed insects, forelimbs clasped in solemn prayer, robed men raising daggers to a shadow moon, and ever the interlacing, clutching branches of the encroaching trees. Shadows overlapping with yet more shadows, so that whatever was being enacted around her and within her mind was lost, save for the emotions that flooded and coursed through her, beyond her beck and call, as wild and furious as a storm tide: rage, betrayal, loss, a seething sense of bottomless hatred.

She was aware that she was holding her breath, and that seemed only wise because these shadows – or some at least – were Mantis-kinden who had no love for her kind, and she felt that she had no disguise sufficient to cloud their eyes to what she really was.

But too little, too late, for one such shadow had turned to her, if shadows could turn. There were no eyes, but as it gazed on her she was aware of a shadow thing part woman, part insect, part twining plant, but also the very shape that hate might take if some alchemist could distil it and then make it flesh.

She had a sense that this unfolding of power – this long-denied awakening that she had provoked – was not going unheard, and just as the things from the box stretched their serrated limbs, so distant minds that had been searching for this moment were sparked into wakefulness. *The imperial contract*, she thought, and in her mind was the instant image of a pale, emaciated man with bulbous red eyes, the skin above his forehead shifting with blood. One long-nailed hand was reaching for her, his face cast into a covetous scowl . . .

And she gasped in shock, and it was gone, they were all gone, and the sun was shining back through the hayloft hatch, and the beetles below were straining at their tethers, clawing at the walls, with oily foam welling between their mandibles, causing enough ruckus to bring the farmer. She ducked out of the hatch and climbed down the outside wall.

She was no true magician, no seer, but her people had their women and men of magic, just as the Moths did, and she had learnt a lot from them back when she was young and willing enough to subjugate herself to others. She had no idea what this box truly was, but she realized that it was *powerful*. The magic trapped within it, from the Days of Lore for sure, was of an order she had never encountered before. She had no idea what the pragmatic Wasp Empire could want with it, but one thing was clear: she was being offered only a pitiful fraction of the true value of the thing. More, the Empire, ignorant as it was, would never come forward with a fitting price.

She knew places she could take it where a proper buyer might be found. Once word was out, then there was still gold enough within Moth haunts, still collectors of the arcane, rogue Skryres, Spider manipuli, all willing to bid for what she possessed. To the wastes with the Wasps. She would go find her own buyers and name her own price.

She did not stop to ask herself where this thought of betrayal, so natural to her, had first sparked, and whether the idea was really hers at all.

Thirty-Six

They were three days out of Sarn, moving at the speed of the slowest automotive. The Queen was unwilling to let the Wasps bring the place of battle any closer than their current camp, and Che read from this that the Queen wanted the battlefield to stay as far away from her city as she could get it. She supposed that this was to protect the farmland and villages on which Sarn relied, but another thought suggested that Sarn's ruler was already planning where to make her next stand, if her army lost the contest here.

Che and Sperra had been packed in with the rest of the non-combatants. This was Sarn's trade-off for doing things Collegium's way. In exchange for the mechanization and the superior weaponry, they had inherited a baggage train of foreign artificers and support staff doing jobs that would normally have been done by Ant-kinden soldiers.

She had seen little of Achaeos since the journey began. He was liaising between the various Mantis and Moth leaders of the newly formed and fragile Ancient League. Che understood that the League itself was still settling, and that neither of the kinden concerned came easily to placing their sovereignty under the leadership of others, even others of their own kind. Achaeos was worried about the battle, she knew, and whether things might go badly wrong even without the Wasps' intervention.

And then the train itself was abruptly slowing, with an unmistakable forward-lurching as the brakes were applied.

'Perhaps it's a broken line,' Sperra suggested, but there were Ants in the carriage with them that had stood up instantly and, as soon as the train was at rest, were flinging the doors open and ordering everyone to get out as quickly as possible. That was when Che realized that they had sighted the enemy.

It was really tremendously civilized, she supposed. The Wasps had arrived by train too, as though this were merely some polite meeting of diplomats. The Queen of Sarn had sent a big block of crossbowmen and nailbowmen out to screen the army from airborne attack, but the rest of her men were pitching tents methodically, checking the engines of the automotives or fitting the wings on the fliers.

'What about the Wasps?' Che wondered.

'Too late in the day for a battle,' an Ant told her. 'If they come for us, we'll be able to form up in time, but there's no sense in just waiting.'

Of course they would be able to simply stop what they were doing, all at once, and begin to fight, for a single order could mobilize the entire Ant army. Che realized this was a luxury the Wasps did not have, so their soldiers must be currently preparing for a possible attack, and would have to stand ready at least until nightfall. Their tents were already pitched, though. Moth scouts reported that they had arrived at this point – where the rails gave out – some days ago, and had been steadily reinforcing their numbers ever since. She tried to get a better view of them, but they remained just a black stain on the horizon, further down the gleaming and interrupted metal line.

Achaeos suddenly dropped out of the sky beside her, making Che jump.

'You should witness this,' he told her. 'The Queen and Scelae are having their first command conference. I think we should be there, too, in case they have a falling out.'

The three of them rushed through the Ant camp towards the Queen's tent. The guards barred them momentarily, but then the word obviously came to let them pass. They did not even need to demand admittance before they were being ushered inside.

Within the barely furnished tent was a single table, with one map pinned upon it. Behind stood a handful of tacticians gathered up about their Queen, a clutch of sibling-similar Ant-kinden wearing partial plate-mail but with no other sign of rank or precedence. On the near side of the table were Scelae in her scaled armour, and a single grey-robed Moth-kinden. The way they looked at the Sarnesh was more adversarial than allied.

The Queen acknowledged their arrival with a brief nod. 'It is as though you are truly part of my army,' she said drily. 'I only have to think of sending for you, and at once you are summoned.'

'We have a certain responsibility for this meeting,' Che said boldly. It was what Stenwold would have said, were he himself here.

The Queen nodded. 'Cheerwell Maker,' she said. 'Sperra the Fly-kinden. You shall be our translators, should we need them. I do not know, as yet, whether this Ancient League shall speak a language Sarn understands.'

She looked to Scelae, who shifted stance slightly, ready for a confrontation.

'Speak, O Queen,' the Moth said, quietly, 'now that you have called us to you.'

Che sensed hostility radiating from the tacticians, at a possible lack of respect, and only the Queen herself seemed wholly calm. *This alliance is so brittle, still, and they have marched side by side for only days*. She could sense relations between their different cultures straining and stretching.

'So tell me,' the Queen of Sarn invited. 'What will our battle order be on the morrow?' She met Scelae's sharp Mantis glance without hesitation.

The other woman shrugged. 'We will fight the Wasps alongside you. We know how to fight.'

There was no sound or expression from the tacticians, but Che felt their disapproval deepen until the tent almost reeked of it. The Queen shook her head. 'We are grateful for your assistance and your support, but we cannot dispose of this matter so casually. Tomorrow shall stand or fall on precise details such as this. The strength of Sarn is in its order, its discipline, each man and woman knowing exactly where they are supposed to be, what they are doing, and what the rest of the army is doing all around them. Your people are known as great duellists, archers, killers. I do not dispute it. They are indeed warriors, but they are not soldiers. In that field, my own kinden have no rivals. Not the Wasps, not the Mantis. Do you deny it?'

Scelae's expression, her brief glance towards the open flap of the tent, indicated the great numbers of the Ants all around, and the few followers she herself had brought. That was the only superiority she would recognize, but she said nothing. The Queen smiled thinly.

'Your people will fight their own battle tomorrow, each one of them alone,' she said, softly but firmly. 'My people will fight *my* battle all together, united, for that is our strength. So, tell me, how shall we use you?' As the Moth opened his mouth to speak she raised her hand in a gesture of such simple authority that she silenced him. 'I do not cast your alliance back in your faces. I value, more than I have words to say, that your people have come to honour us in this way. I ask the question for no other reason than that I need to know the answer. You cannot move with us. You cannot hear my orders in your minds, even if you were disposed to follow them. Tell me how I may make use of you. Show me, that I can make my people understand.'

After that speech there was a space of silence. Scelae and the moth exchanged glances, and Che found herself thinking, *So it is not just the old races that can practise subtlety.*

The Mantis woman cleared her throat. 'I have lived in Sarn for many years,' Scelae began, 'and I have some idea of how your kinden think. You are right, of course. In the heat of battle, your orders may not seem right to us, so I cannot guarantee that my people will follow them, even if we could hear them. Tell us then how are you intending to progress the battle tomorrow?'

'Aggressively, we have decided,' the Queen said, after a brief silent word amongst her surrounding advisers.

Scelae nodded. 'Then let's be plain with it. Any fancy planning and contingencies we come up with now won't survive a meeting with the Wasp battle line. We cannot hope to react to your sleights and changes and tactics. You, however, can react to ours.'

'Explain,' said the Queen.

Scelae leant over the map, but it was obvious that she could make little sense of it. 'I will split my force and place one half on each of your flanks. We will screen your advance with our bows, and our wings. We will prevent their flying soldiers from wrapping your lines. I have many skilled archers amongst my people. Then, when we're close to the enemy, we will attack, draw them out, break their lines. Wasp discipline does not match your own. They can be provoked, dispersed. With your mind-speech, you will be able to take advantage of what we can give you. Let us be the spearhead, then. Give your orders based on how we strike. That way you can make best use of us.'

The Queen considered this, still surrounded by the silent counsel of her tacticians. She nodded slowly, a deliberate affectation simply for the benefit of the other kinden there. 'The idea has merit, although you take a great deal of risk on your people. If you yourselves break rank, to charge or pursue, we may not be able to save you.'

Scelae tilted her head on one side. 'We are warriors. We fight. We understand all that means.'

The Queen looked down at the map-tables, then up at Cheerwell, the shock of eye contact startling in its intensity. *And how many others now look at me out of her eyes.* 'Your comments?'

Che opened her mouth, trying to think, but Sperra said, 'Messengers, surely.'

'Little one?'

'Messengers. If it goes wrong you can send someone out to the League soldiers,' the Fly-kinden said. 'You can call them back, put them elsewhere.' She spread her small hands. 'Not that I know the first thing about war, anyway, but that's what I'd do.'

'You wouldn't need actual messengers—' Che broke in suddenly.

The Queen found a smile for her. 'Yes, we have the same thought. I shall place a few of my fleetest soldiers with each half of your warriors,' she told Scelae. 'They at least will be able to hear me, and they can tell you what I . . . suggest that your forces do. Many things can happen in a battle, and we can never predict them all. I may have need of your warriors in ways we cannot yet consider.'

Scelae glanced at the Moth-kinden, who nodded.

'Agreed,' she said, and moved to go, preparing to explain to her people a plan that all the Ants already understood.

Che coughed pointedly. 'I have . . . something to say, I think. Something that my uncle himself would say, if he were here.'

The Mantis stopped, looking back at her.

'Speak,' the Queen directed.

'This is something that stretches beyond the battlefield of tomorrow,' Che said, sounding to her own ears unbearably awkward and pompous. 'We're writing history, right now, here in this tent. The three cities of the Ancient League, and Sarn, and Collegium, are all standing together and of one mind. We must remember our common cause. We must. If we turn the Wasps back, then it would be all too easy just to go back to trying to ignore each other, to forget how we have stood here, all together, for one purpose. We should remember that, for as long as we can.'

Scelae, who had so long been a spy in the Queen's city, smiled bleakly. 'I am not sure even the threat of the Wasps can bring us to that degree of unity. Let us defeat them first, and see what remains.'

Che slept that night in Achaeos's arms, clutching at him for security, while Sperra lay as a curled and lonely shape at the other end of the tent. The morning woke Che not with dawn light but with his absence.

'Achaeos?' she called softly. There was a noise from outside, not loud, but a constant and steady sound of the Ants getting ready to fight: preparing armour and weapons, the engines of the automotives, the propellers of the fixed-wing fliers, and not a single human voice to be heard.

'Out here,' he said finally. Sperra was slowly uncurling as Che put her boots on. Stepping outside made her head swim because of the sheer quantity of movement all around. The entire Ant force was afoot, forming into its traditional tight units of shield and crossbow. There were several thousand infantry in her view alone, and every single one of them knew where he or she should be.

Sperra ducked out after her just as the engines of the flying machines began to settle into a low grumble beyond the tents and the machines themselves to slowly crawl across the ground.

'Apparently the Wasps tried to attack at dawn,' Achaeos explained, his voice sounding oddly empty. 'A strike force of fifty or so intended to destroy the fliers. The Queen had put the Mantis-kinden on guard, though. They can see well in the dark, and their bows can shoot further than any Wasp sting.'

'Are you all right?' Che asked him. He sounded shaken and numb.

'Our scouts came back,' he said. 'The Empire outnumbers us by about three to two, but the Ants don't seem to think it makes much difference. It's tactics and discipline, not numbers, apparently.' There was a ragged edge to his words, emerging as though he had not the least interest in the conflict that was about to unfold.

'Achaeos, what's wrong? Tell me!'

'I have dreams, Che,' he told her. 'Terrible dreams. The Darakyon is hounding me but I cannot understand it. It is going mad, it seems, over something new that it cannot get through to me. Something terrible is going to happen, Che.'

'Here? In the battle?'

'Something dire enough to make this battle look like children brawling,' he said.

The engines of the automotives roared suddenly, and the entire Ant army set forth together, every single man and woman of the infantry marching precisely in step. Sperra poked her head further out of the tent and swore in a small, lost voice, as thousands of men and women all around them were suddenly on the move and falling into place. It felt as though the whole world was leaving them behind.

Technically, all three of them had been seconded to join the field surgeons, as they each had some experience of medicine in various forms. There would be a blessed pause before any casualties came back, though, and Che wanted to see for herself exactly what was going on. She looked around for a vantage point and picked one of the transport automotives, empty of everything except rations now. With a clumsy flick of her wings she cast herself up at the overreaching cage of struts that defined its cargo area, clung tight and hauled herself up until she could stand on them, looking out over the battlefield. She was just in time for the first of the orthopters to drone overhead, just taking off but still going fast enough for the downbeat of their wings to buffet her. She sat down hurriedly just as Achaeos and Sperra joined her on her perch.

Plated with shields, the units of Ants were themselves like great crawling insects. The centre of the Sarnesh battle array was made up of them, square after square plodding forward with a single will. Interrupting these black metal lines, armoured automotives drove forward at walking pace, their brand-new nailbows glinting proudly in the sun.

On either side, the soldiers of the Ancient League were a diffuse cloud, now getting a little ahead of the line, now being reined in again. Che pictured all those Mantis-kinden, all running as individuals, some with arrows to bowstrings, others brandishing swords, claws or lances. She saw in her mind's eye the tight clusters of Moth-kinden with short-bows and knives and blank white eyes.

Ahead of the Sarnesh advance, the Wasp army moved like a living thing. Behind their soldiers, blocky flying machines began to lurch into the air.

'The scouts said they had "armoured heloropters" or some such,' Achaeos reported.

'Armoured heliopters,' Che corrected. 'A stupid idea, really.'

'Why?' Achaeos asked. 'Not that I don't think the same about all these machines.'

'We were all worried that the Ants wouldn't think like fliers, but it seems the Wasps have been guilty of the same thing. You can armour a heliopter all you like, but you can't armour the rotors, and that's what keep the machines in the air. The Sarnesh fixed-wings will be able to shoot them down and—'

Her words failed in her throat, because the Wasp army had just exploded. Its entire front ranks were now in the air, a great buzzing cloud that was sweeping forward on to the patiently advancing Ant line, filling the whole sky.

*

Sperra had a telescope but did not care to use it, handing it mutely to Che instead. Putting her eye to it, Che saw a slice of the world wheel crazily, tilted and blurry. Then she had the battlefront focused, a wall of flying Wasps surging forward like a breaking wave to smash against the front lines of the Sarnesh.

One instant it seemed that no force on earth could withstand that great rushing charge, a thousand men of the light airborne, hands extended to sting, wings sweeping them down the valley of the rail line. Then her point of view was filled with lancing rain, but rain lashing *upwards* in near-solid sheets, and she heard Sperra gasp and Achaeos curse. Only then did she realize that it was the crossbow quarrels from the leading Ant-kinden, sleeting upwards at a range that the Wasps' Art weapons could not match. She wished, then, that she had seen it all, as the other two had, that sudden black flash of bolts, shooting in absolute unison, from the forward Ant formations.

And the Wasp charge was now in chaos. It was nothing she could follow with the glass and so she took it from her eye, trying to make sense of the mad buzzing clots of men that the charge had been broken up into. From her vantage point she could see the carpet of dead which that first round of quarrels had produced, still some distance ahead of the inexorable Ant advance, but the remainder of the Wasps were heading in all directions. Some were turning and fleeing back to their own lines, others over on the flanks were still attacking, trying to take the Ants in the side. But as they swung around they met the long arrows of the Mantis-kinden, and the Mantids themselves, wings flashing to life as they drove upwards with blades flashing into the suddenly scattering Wasps. Many of the Wasps just tried to push on through, streaking over the Ant formations with their stings flashing down as points of golden light, mostly to crackle uselessly over raised and overlapping shields. They were being slaughtered even as they flew, for the formations behind the leading edge of the advance had their crossbows too and even at this range Che could hear the bang-bang-bang of nailbows from infantry and from the automotives.

The Wasp heliopters were looming large, now, lumbering through the air to get above the Ant-kinden and bombard their tight formations, but the Ant fixed-wings flashed past them, nailbows blazing. One of the cumbersome machines was clipped from the sky almost instantly, tumbling forwards with enough time for half a revolution before its armoured lines split asunder against the ground. With shaking telescope Che saw the sparks of nailbow bolts striking against the armoured hulls of the others, while the heliopters' ballista and leadshotter fire kept trying to pin down the swifter Sarnesh fliers.

The Ant advance had not slowed, even now that the lead heliopters had begun to drop explosives on them. Flame and shrapnel flowed in broken chains across the Ant soldiers. The formations quickly broke up as the heliopter was directly over them, and then massed back together once it had passed, but there were undoubtedly gaps being blasted into their lines. There were too many soldiers in too close a space to avoid it all. Che saw one of the heliopters falter in the air suddenly, struck by nailbow shot from the automotives, and then plummet down amongst the Ant soldiers without warning, smashing an entire unit apart with the impact.

Beyond it, a fixed-wing exploded in mid-air, showering burning metal. The Wasps had pivot-mounted leadshotters behind their lines and were starting to lob missiles at the flying machines, and also in long curving arcs over the heads of their own men and into the Sarnesh advance.

And yet the Ants did not falter, not even for a moment. Their formations flowed like water, breaking under attack, reforming a moment later. They were still moving at the steady, patient pace that they had started with, despite the casualties that were starting to mount.

The Wasps had drawn up a battle-line now, with five score of armoured sentinels in the centre, and shield-bearing infantry with spears on either side. More of the light airborne were flocking over to the flanks, and Che saw them swing wide of the Ant advance, coming to attack the rear. On one side the Mantis warriors were holding back deliberately, sending out their arrows but keeping their places. On the other the Ant liaisons had been killed, and about half of the Mantids suddenly dashed out – on the ground or in the air – and attacked the Wasp airborne as they passed over, making an entirely separate swirling battle that quickly fled away from the main one.

The opposing lines were closing, the telescope told her. She felt Sperra and Achaeos take wing to drop down from the automotive, and realized that the first casualties were being carried in, but she could not stop watching. There was crossbow- and sting-shot being exchanged all the way down the line, with the Wasps taking the worst of it. Their shields were smaller, and they lacked the Ants' great advantage that every man was looking out for all the others as the enemy shot came in.

The Ants at the rear of the advance suddenly reversed face, raising their shields against incoming airborne that had swung round behind them, and the crossbow quarrels started sleeting up again. Then the Mantis-kinden who had been holding back were suddenly there, dashing across the ground more swiftly than Che could believe, or leaping into the air with a flare of wings, and the Wasp light airborne broke as the Mantids tore through it, and individual Wasps were darting away, trying to get back to their own side.

She dragged her attention to the lines, and caught them just as they clashed, the Sarnesh suddenly upping their pace to a thundering run, hundreds of armoured men throwing their weight behind their shields and crashing into the Wasp line. Some fell to the Wasps' levelled spears but their shields managed to turn most of the spearheads or even shattered the shafts, and then they were smashing into the Wasp line, swords stabbing frenziedly, and to either side the second-rank formations were deploying, turning the line of the Ant army into a pincering curve.

Another heliopter – and she thought it might be the last – trailed fire over the Ant ranks, and the Wasps were fighting furiously, their line buckling slowly but hundreds of their soldiers coursing back and forth over the heads of the enemy, lancing down with their stings at any visible weak point. The telescope was revealing too much to her now, all the bloody work that war was, dripping red swords and faces twisted in pain. More and more Wasps were rushing into the fray to shore their line up, until their full numbers had been committed and they could stop the Ants from encircling them. The warriors of the Ancient League were scattering all over the field in knots of ten or twenty, launching sudden attacks against the Wasp flanks and then falling back, or sending arrows high to kill unsuspecting soldiers in the centre of the Wasp lines. Che sensed that all that had gone before was but prologue to this moment, the soldiers of both sides now dying in their hundreds. In the air were the remaining flying machines, surrounded by the Wasp light airborne that latched onto them and cut at their cables and controls, and also by giant insects – the Wasps' own namesakes – that were urged on by unarmoured riders brandishing lances and crossbows.

She heard the roaring of the automotives even over all the clamour of battle, and then the Ant lines were splitting, as if by some pre-planned clockwork mechanism. A lead-shot strike caved in the front of one vehicle, which began to gout smoke. Another shot punched into the packed Ant lines, smashing through the centre of one formation, and then raking the side of the one immediately behind, leaving three dozen dead at a stroke. The Wasps surged forwards at some points, held back at others, and the automotives drove on like hammers, nailbows shooting until they jammed, and the Wasp line was broken like porcelain, all its unity lost.

In the centre the remaining sentinels had formed a fighting square and were contesting to the last with pike and shield, seeming nigh-invulnerable in their all-encasing armour, but there were Wasps fleeing backwards all along the line, getting in each other's way, even fighting with one another, and the Ant advance continued as steadily as before.

Thirty-Seven

The city was running short of places to house the wounded, let alone the dead. Where the messenger took Stenwold was one of the College's workshops where apprentice artificers had toiled and studied in happier times. Into a small room beyond a long hall that was almost carpeted with the ice-packed dead they had brought the body, and laid it on an artificer's work table. This unknowingly appropriate gesture affected Stenwold more deeply than anything else.

They had not been able to get Scuto's body to lie flat, of course, what with the hunchback and the man's other deformities, and so it was resting on its side, looking as awkward in death as life, propped up on its own projections that had scratched long lines into the wood as they had worked him off the stretcher. Amidst all those spines and thorns and burned, blistered skin, they had not cared to remove the three quills of crossbow bolts that were sunk deep into Scuto's flesh. Stenwold was sure that they had been the final death of him, and not the grenade that had scorched across his nut-brown skin and smashed one of his hands. Scuto had always been a tough one.

His mockery of a face, that had resembled nothing more than a grotesque puppet carved idly from wood, was locked in a grimace that showed all his hooked teeth. Stenwold put a hand out to close his friend's eyes, but managed only to spike himself on one of the Thorn Bug's points.

Scuto had been pulled from the Sarnesh automotive that had blocked the breach, and Stenwold realized that if he had stayed a moment longer he would have witnessed it himself. Scuto had been dead before they had ever drawn him out, though. There would have been no last words, no farewells. Stenwold understood that only one of the Sarnesh Lorn detachment had survived, and she was not expected to live long despite all the doctors were doing for her.

'Why?' Stenwold asked. 'Why did he come?' He looked up at Balkus, and saw the man's normally solid features twisted in grief. Balkus, he recalled, had known Scuto a long time, at least as long as Stenwold himself.

'He always looked after his people,' the Ant said. 'He must have heard about the siege here. We were his people, Stenwold – you and me. Waste and blast the bloody man. Did he think I couldn't take care of myself?' Balkus's fist slammed down on the table. 'You stupid, stupid bastard! What did you think you were doing?' There were no tears on the big man's face, but his voice, the utter loss in his voice, more than made up for it. Ants grieved privately and mind to mind, Stenwold knew, but Balkus had been away from his own kind for many years, had forgotten the touch of their company, and his pain came out in words just like any other kinden's.

Stenwold tried to picture those last terrible moments in the automotive, the desperate fighting hand to hand, the grenade's explosion, the driver trying to keep control of the racing vehicle, trying to get it within the walls of Collegium, past the Vekken soldiers and their crossbows.

It came to him that for once he had done the right thing in sending all the others off: Che and Achaeos, Tisamon and Tynisa. For once, at least, where Stenwold now was had become the place *not* to be.

I am running out of friends. Scuto was the oldest and the closest of the dead, but he had Kymon on his conscience too, and poor Doctor Nicrephos, and so many of the faces that he had been introduced to so recently, only to have them snuffed out in the fighting – people like Joyless Greatly, like Cabre who had manned the harbour defences, or Tseitus in his submersible.

'What time is it?' he called out. 'Anyone know?'

'I think I heard the third clock not long ago,' Arianna said. She had been keeping prudently out of the way, by the door.

'Until dawn, then?'

'Two hours and half an hour more, Stenwold. No more.'

'We should try for at least some sleep,' he said tiredly. 'The Vekken will be back with the dawn, and they have made a breach now. I do not know how we can keep them out of it.'

'I'm not going to sleep, not tonight,' Balkus said flatly. 'I'm going to go to that breach, and when they come I'm going to kill every bloody Vekken I see. And when I run out of ammunition I'll use my sword, and when that breaks I'll use my fists.' He was a stranger then, broad-shouldered and threatening, an Ant setting about doing what Ants were best at, which was killing their own kind.

Stenwold had thought that the Vekken would have to come over the crashed automotive to take control of the breach, and he had his soldiers lined up with crossbows ready to shoot them as they crested the top, but his lookout had just called from the broken wall and told him that they were bringing up a ram. A ramming engine, if they could coax it up the mound of debris, would punch the automotive aside in just a few blows, leaving the breach wide open for the Vekken infantry to rush in. Taking over Kymon's command, Stenwold had gathered every man and woman who could hold the line and placed them here, but the Vekken soldiers were better at close work by far. This would be the last stand, he knew, the last moment before the Vekken surged into the city and overran it.

The Great College, he thought, *the Assembly, the Sarnesh alliance.* All the centuries of innovation, philosophy, art and diplomacy that had been hatched within these walls, and now the ignorant hands of the Vekken would carry it away and dismantle it.

'Artillery's ready, War Master,' one of his artificers reported. The wall had been judged too unsteady to mount more engines on it, but they had found from somewhere a pair of ballistae, and he had them flanking his forces on either side now. One was a light repeater, the other a massive and ancient Ant-made piece they must have dredged from a museum. It would probably do no more than loose a single bolt.

'Angle so that you can hit the ram, when it starts to push the automotive out of the way,' he told them, knowing that by then it would already be too late, that the breach would be well opened.

On the walls, in place of the artillery, he had posted everyone else: old men and women, the injured, the young and a plethora of Fly-kinden who would only get trampled underfoot in a ground-level melee, all up there with whatever they could get their hands on. Some had crossbows, but others had hunting bows, stonebows, even slings and rocks for throwing. Some industrious citizens had even carried a few dozen of the fallen stones from the wall up to its top, to pitch over onto the Vekken.

Even as he looked up at them the shooting started, men and women of Collegium putting their heads over the battlements to let slip a bolt or arrow or stone and then ducking down fast. The clatter of answering quarrels came fast after, and Stenwold saw several, the slow or the unlucky, hurled back from the wall within the first few seconds.

'Stand ready!' he called to his forces. He wanted to deliver an encouraging speech, such as the one Kymon had given, but he, whose life had been measured in words often enough, found himself without them.

He had already found a greying militia officer to be his second in the all too likely event that something happened to him. Third in command was Balkus because, if it came to that, they would need the man's fighting spirit more than any gifts of leadership.

'Heads up,' the Ant muttered to him, and he scanned the wall, looking for some new threat. Balkus was glancing backwards, though, and he turned to see Arianna running to join him.

'No!' he shouted at her. 'Wait for me back at the house, please!'

'What kind of fool do you think I am?' she asked him. She had found a leather cuirass from somewhere, and there was a strung shortbow over her shoulder. 'If you fail here, do you think they won't kill me anyway?'

'But . . . I want . . .' *I want you to be safe.* He stared at her helplessly, and with pointed determination she took her bow and nocked an arrow to it.

'Let her fight,' Balkus said. 'We need her. You've seen all who's left here. We need everyone.'

'The ram's coming in!' the lookout shouted. A glance at the archers on the walls showed that they were shooting almost straight down now, and that others were heaving great stones up to the lip of the battlements.

'Artillery ready!' Stenwold shouted, and drew his sword. Between the Vekken and Arianna, he did not see the strength his followers derived from that simple, calm motion.

There was a hollow boom, and the automotive jumped a foot forwards, and then slid another foot down the loose stones, and Stenwold could hear the ram's engines straining, imagined its toothed wheels clawing for traction.

'And loose!' shouted the artillerist artificer, and the repeating crossbow began its work, sending bolt after bolt, as fast as Stenwold's heart was beating, into the gap the ram had created between the automotive and the wall. The big old ballista had misfired, and six men were frantically rewinding it, cranking the string back while the bolt was replaced.

'Shields ready!' Stenwold called out, and his rabble of citizens and militia formed up into a mockery of a military formation. Every single man or woman with any kind of shield stood in the front rank, some with no more than a few nailed-together planks on a leather strap as a handle. At each end stood the archers, crossbows levelled shakily, or arrows ready at the string. Arianna had run to join them. The look of desperate bravery on her face made his heart ache, and all the more so because it was mirrored on every face around her.

With a tremendous crack the ancient ballista hurled its eight-foot bolt forwards, the wooden arms shattering into pieces with the force, but the missile drove straight through the ram's hull, and Stenwold saw a sudden venting of smoke and heard the engine squeal in protest and then die.

There was a great cheer from the defenders, for the ram had gained a gap of no more than four feet either side of the automotive for the Vekken to press through, but then the Vekken were coming regardless, surging through the gaps in tight order with their shields raised. The repeating ballista slammed its bolts into them, knocking them back two or three at a time, and stones were pushed off the battlements above to crash down into the packed intruders, battering their shields aside. Arianna and the other archers needed no further orders now. They were shooting into the Vekken as they came, arrows and bolts and slingstones bouncing from shields or whipping past them. For a moment, one mad moment, it seemed that the Vekken did not have the force to seize the gaps, that they would be driven back so that the defenders could retake those narrow breaks and hold them against all comers.

They were Ant-kinden, though, and in the simple business they were engaged in there were no finer soldiers anywhere, and once that moment of hope had gone, they pushed through, despite the bolts and the stones, and over the heaped bodies of their kin, and onto Collegium ground.

As soon as he saw that the archers could not hold them, Stenwold drew a great breath and cried out, 'Forwards!' and, because there was no time to wait, he was first in, trusting to them to follow where he took them.

He met the Ants with their shield-line, and without expectations, but he was an old fighter. No Ant soldier, but he had held a blade for longer than these Vekken men and women had been alive. In those first seconds he surprised himself by killing two of the enemy, lunging past their shields as they skidded on the last loose stones. On either side the mismatched shields of Collegium pressed, and there was still a fair barrage falling on the enemy from above.

And there was no more to think about, no regrets, no worries, just the savage, simple business of putting his blade into as many Vekken as he could reach. It was turned by shields, turned by armour or by other blades, but he did not let up, stabbing and cutting with a fury, because this was *his* city and these were *his* people and if Collegium fell, then the whole world fell with it into a dark age that would make the Age of Lore seem like enlightenment.

He was dimly aware that Balkus was now beside him, the only other man in the front rank without a shield. Balkus, with a shortsword in each hand, battering down Vekken shields with brute force, always keeping an eye out for Stenwold, as if some mindlink had joined them in their extremity, so that he could anticipate each blow even as Stenwold registered it, putting a sword in the way to deflect it.

They were losing ground, but not as swiftly as they should. The sheer savagery of the Collegiate charge had shaken the attackers, put them back on the shifting stones. Ant faces were impassive at best, but Stenwold thought he could see something like bafflement within their eyes. They were soldiers, superior in every way to this mixed-race rabble that confronted them, so how could they be held up for even a single minute? They locked shields and pressed, but they were confronted with men and women who were totally cornered now, nothing to lose and nowhere to go. They died, of course, those defenders of Collegium. Tradesmen were run through, merchants wearing ill-fitting armour were hacked down, labourers and militamen fell with crossbow bolts buried deep. There was not one of them who went easily, though, and even as they fell they dragged at their enemies, pulled their swords down, hooked shields with their fingers. A thousand acts of final bravery and defiance, shaking the Vekken advance, if only for a moment.

And seeing this hesitation, Stenwold's heart soared with pride in his city, and a lunging Ant laid his arm open and he fell back, sword falling from his grasp. Balkus killed the man who had wounded him that same instant, and already a shield was raised to take his place, but Stenwold was reeling, being passed back through the crowd until he was standing clear, with Arianna descending on him and swiftly tearing a strip off her robe to bandage him.

'I can fight!' he insisted, but she dug her fingers into the wound until he stood still enough for her to finish. 'I can fight!' he said again, looking round for a sword.

'War Master!' someone was shouting and, feeling dizzy, he turned to look. A man he felt he should recognize was running towards him, waving his arms. 'War Master!'

'I'm here! What news?' He could barely hear himself over the fighting behind him.

He knew this man – one of his own soldiers from the harbour guard—

His heart sank and he could have virtually mouthed the words along with the man: 'War Master! The harbour! They're coming in at the harbour!'

Stenwold turned, torn by doubt, seeing the line surge back and forward, the final throes of Collegium's defence. He was responsible for the harbour, though, and there were people needed there.

He hoped that Balkus would be enough for them. The big Ant was still standing, splashed with blood, working himself into a frenzy.

'Take me there!' he commanded, and the harbour man ran off, leaving him to lurch in his wake, with Arianna holding his good arm to help him along.

The sight that met him at the harbour was worse than he had feared, though, and worse than he had dreamed possible. There were already two tugs dragging the drowned armourclad out of the way, and beyond it the sea was full of ships, painted across with dozens of sails.

Thirty-Eight

The bulk of the Wasps could retreat far faster than the Ants could follow, and they took flight down the rail track towards their camp, their rail automotives and their massed artillery. The sentinels and many of the armoured shield-men, however, could not simply fly away. Faced with no choice, and with a fierce desperation that left a lasting impression on their enemies, they stood their ground, holding up the Ant advance still further so that their comrades could escape. In a tight square of armoured men, surrounded on all sides by the implacable Sarnesh soldiers, they fought on with bitter determination until every last man of them was dead.

The Ants re-formed their lines, their shield-lined formations, with some of them that had sustained heavy casualties breaking up to form new groups. Others near the back began to move the wounded out. Two automotives had been smashed before the leadshotters had been silenced, and a third had ground to a halt with artificers hurriedly prying armour off to get at its engine. The Sarnesh went about reassembling their battle order with the minimum of fuss, with calm deliberation. The Wasps were allowed to fall back, to exhaust themselves in the panic of flight. The Ants would follow at their own inexorable pace.

The warriors of the Ancient League were another matter. They had not stopped when the Sarnesh had redrawn their lines. They harried the Wasp-kinden mercilessly, chasing them in the air, raking them with arrow-shot. It seemed at first that they might continue their hunt all the way to Helleron. Che, trying to focus her telescope on the nimble figures in green and grey, abruptly overshot them. There was nothing but black and gold now in her field of view. She took the glass away, trying to see what was going on.

The Mantids and their allies were now falling back, surging to meet up with the plodding Sarnesh lines. Beyond them the Wasps were making a new stand, rallying into another wall of shields and ready airborne. Behind them . . .

She felt just then that things had started to tip, although she could not have said why. She was no tactician, but something spoke inside her.

A rail automotive had pulled in to the broken end of the rails in a great plume of steam. More Wasp soldiers were rushing out of it, hurrying forwards to join the battle. Reinforcements from Helleron, she saw, but something new had communicated itself to her. She could not be sure what.

There were Ants all around. One word to them would be a word to the whole army. She had no words, though. She had nothing she could warn them of.

Still. 'You should take care,' she said to the nearest Ant surgeon, 'your people at the front.'

He was washing blood from his hands and he stared at her as if she were mad. Out on the field, transport automotives were removing the bulk of the wounded. The worst would be treated here, the rest removed to Sarn. The surgeons were hard pressed to keep the pace.

'The Queen is consulting with her tacticians,' the surgeon said suddenly, and Che realized that she had been heard after all. The man's eyes unfocused for a moment, and then he said. 'We will press ahead. We must destroy them, drive them until they can fly no more, and then wipe them out. We must break their siege engines in order to protect our walls.' He nodded. 'It will be a long, hard fight.' She realized the last words were his, and the rest had been the Queen's.

During the first clash of the battle the Wasps had been able to bring forward more of their siege train, another batch of leadshotters and a few of the smaller catapults that could be wheeled out intact rather than needing assembly on the spot. The Sarnesh automotives would have a harder time of it from now on. Even as Che watched, the first artillery engines began to discharge, their shot mostly flying wide or short, and the Sarnesh advance continued with the same patient progress, the wide sweeping wings of scattered Mantids and Moths surging a little ahead of it.

The next batch of the wounded had now arrived, and she gave up her watching, went to do what good she could with bandages and needle. It unnerved her, tending these wounded Ants. They did not curse or scream, because each was taking strength from all the others, from their suffusing solidarity. Somehow a show of pain would have been more reassuring to her. All around her the Ant surgeons worked in skilled communion, linked with each other and with their patients. It made Che feel clumsy and awkward. They even gave her the least of the wounded to tend.

There was a moment – she remembered it well later – when all the soldiers around them stopped, just for half a second, all at once, and she knew that out on the battlefield something new had happened. She tied off the wrapping on the man she had been working with, and took up her glass again.

The Ant advance had stopped as they tried to work out what had happened. The fresh Wasp troops from the rail automotive had formed a double line ahead of them, but at a range that a heavy crossbow would find stretching. They had loosed some manner of weapon, though. The rattle of missiles had struck all the way along the Ant line, short darts like nailbow bolts that had bounced from shields or got stuck in armour, although a few unlucky soldiers had been injured in the face. Beside them, a few of the lightly-armoured Mantids had fallen.

The Sarnesh started their march again, the automotives grinding solidly along beside them. Wasp artillery-shot was falling sporadically about them, and another of the armoured vehicles was brought to a halt when a stone shattered its left track. The advance was undaunted, though between the officers at the leading edge of the Sarnesh army a quick analysis was taking place of what new weapons the Wasps possessed and how they might work.

The twin archer lines of the Wasps suddenly sprang forward in a flurry of wings, covering ten yards in a great flying leap. It was a chaotic display, obviously unpractised. For a moment they were everywhere, in utter confusion, and then they were struggling to get themselves in place as the other troops, who had so recently fled, moved forwards again to back them up.

As one the Ant soldiers picked up their pace. The leading officers could see more of the weapons now, and they seemed to be firepowder bows of some sort, like nailbows, but there had been no smoke and no sound other than a distant crackle when they had loosed.

Drephos had driven him hard in order to be here now. It was only because the foundries of Helleron were so well supplied, so easily turned to any mechanical endeavour, that it had worked at all. Totho had been working day and night, and forcing his workforce through the same punishing schedule. Towards the end he had allowed them three or four hours of sleep at most. How they had hated him, the halfbreed that fate had set over them, and now Drephos's right-hand man.

The factories were still working now, of course, but Totho had left them to the care of other hands. Drephos had come to him one day, after his life had become just a murderous round of unceasing manufacture, and told him, 'It's time.'

'Time for what?' Totho had asked dully.

'Time for the real test, Totho.' The master artificer had earlier been radiant with enthusiasm, eagerly rubbing his disparate hands together. 'The soldiers have practised. They are passable, and the efficiency of your invention easily makes up for the deficiency in their training. We are ready to take your gifts to General Malkan.'

'You want me to go with you?'

'Are you going to tell me you don't deserve it?' Drephos had asked him. 'Totho, I am very proud of you. I made absolutely the right decision when I took you in. The least I can do is let you witness your creations in action.'

Which means the warfront. Totho had opened his mouth, and a host of words had thronged there, as he stood looking into Drephos's expectant face. *I don't want to go to war. I don't want to see my work killing other people.* But he had remembered Drephos's words about hypocrisy. *I am a weaponsmith. I owe it to my victims to be there. As a personal service.*

'I'll go pack, Master,' he had said, and Drephos's answering smile had actually cheered him.

The rail journey would have been intolerable had he not been so tired. They had crammed every soldier they could into the pirated carriages, their kit, their supplies and disassembled war engines, spare parts for fliers. It had been a mobile war waiting ready to be deployed. Drephos and Totho had been given no more space than the soldiers, huddling shoulder to shoulder with bad-tempered Wasp artificers and officers. It would have been intolerable if Totho had not slept through almost all the journey, awaking with an artificer's senses only when the automotive began to slow.

There had been a great deal of babble at that point and when Totho had asked what was going on, a gesture from

Drephos had silenced him. The master artificer was already on his feet, armoured hand clutching a leather strap to steady himself and listening hard.

'The battle's just begun,' he had announced. 'We cut matters a little fine.' Pitching his voice higher to carry across the crowded carriage he had called out, 'Now, listen, I have orders! I want a messenger to bring General Malkan to me instantly. I want all the snapbowmen ready to engage immediately. I want them drawn up in ranks beside the rails, loaded weapons to hand. Pass the word back!'

Although the entire journey had been a protracted grumble about Drephos and his presumption, when he did give an order the officers moved briskly. The automotive ground to a screeching halt and began spilling Wasp-kinden from every door, doing their best to find their places. Totho could see the bulk of Malkan's army trying to re-form, evidently severely bloodied by the Sarnesh troops. *It's exactly like the stories*, he thought, *arriving just in the nick of time to save the day.*

The snapbowmen that were Drephos's new experiment made their ragged ranks, but he drove them forwards, forwards until they had passed the fleeing host of the first engagement, until Totho, running with them, could see the dark line of the Sarnesh advance, the great wall of shields.

One of them loosed, perhaps just a fumble of the trigger, and abruptly they were all shooting, together and individually, and Drephos was shouting at them. The master artificer had his breastplate on over his robes, but he still looked nothing like a soldier or an imperial officer. He cursed the soldiers with utter fury, though, threatening them with impalement on the crossed spears unless they reloaded and stood ready.

When he turned back to Totho, though, he was calm personified. 'Well out of effective range here,' he said, 'but did you see?'

'See, Master?'

'Our bolts reached the Ant lines,' Drephos confirmed, and he was smiling as though he had just been given a present. 'Within range, from here. The Sarnesh even stopped for them. Your remarkable invention, Totho!'

Abruptly he was all business again, looking around at his soldiers. 'On my order, I want a ten-yard jump forwards to put us properly in range. Ready yourselves!' His eyes narrowed. 'Now!'

Totho had to run, to catch up with the line again, but Drephos flew. He flew badly, very awkwardly, like a wounded man, but he put himself through it nonetheless to stay alongside his secret weapon. *Totho*'s secret weapon. By the time they arrived, the Wasps were just about in order, forming their two lines, one kneeling and one standing. It was a familiar formation that crossbow units all over the Lowlands used.

'Stand ready!' Drephos called. He had officers for this task, of course, but they stood there dumb whilst he made his own voice hoarse. He was quivering with excitement, uneven features stretched in a mad grin. 'Charge your bows!'

In ragged unison the Wasp snapbowmen cranked back, pressurizing the air in the weapons' batteries. Totho could see in his head just how they worked, the designs he had made when he was still an apprentice at Collegium.

'The rest is trimming,' Drephos had explained to him, after the first test. 'Your battery is the revolution! We could put a firepowder primer there instead of your device, and use the long tooled barrel, but firepowder is clumsy. The discharge rocks the weapon, and so you have no accuracy at any range, and it's dangerous and expensive to boot. Your discharge of air barely makes the weapon shudder as it vents, and it is both safe and free. A revolution, Totho! War marches on another step!'

There was something obscene about Drephos's expression now. The excitement that shook the man was almost sexual.

'Loose!' he yelled.

The leading edge of the Ant advance simply disintegrated, men and women collapsing backwards with nothing but surprise and pain. There were round holes punched in shields, split rings in chainmail, and soldiers all the way along the line were abruptly dead without warning, even as the snap-snap-snap of the bows sounded all around Totho.

In a split second, the Ant tacticians must have made their decision, for the Ant lines were abruptly charging forwards with all speed despite the distance, going from a steady plod to an outright run without warning and without confusion. They outstripped their Mantis allies for a moment, and they avoided their own fallen without fail, not even slowing. For any other army, moving in full armour over such a distance, it would have been madness, but they were the strongest soldiers in the world, wearing mail for years until it became a second skin. It could be done, and they did it.

On the flanks the Mantids decided they were not to be outdone, and soon made up the distance, dashing along in their light armour, their leather and their scale, rending the air with their war-cries over the utter silence of the Ants.

They had taken the new weapons as crossbows, imagining the Wasps desperately reloading, winding them back, while seeing the approaching Ants closer and closer. One more round of bolts at close range and then the charging Sarnesh would break them.

The next salvo of snapbow bolts ripped through them, catching men in the second, the third and fourth ranks. Sarnesh soldiers at a full run were brought to an instant halt as their fellows ran into them, too close in their tight formations to stop or turn. On the flanks there were Mantis soldiers spinning and falling, jerked suddenly back by the power of the bolts. The Ant advance stumbled, faltered, and then surged on into the next lash of the snapbows.

Totho's stomach lurched, and he felt his hands clenching uselessly. He wanted, he wanted so very badly, to look away, but he fixed his eyes upon what was unfolding throughout the Sarnesh lines. *I have a responsibility to my victims.*

'The tests already told us, of course,' Drephos breathed, even as his soldiers reloaded. '*This* is the true experiment, though. All those Ants in their metal armour, and when our bolts strike metal, they flatten or even bend, and yet they *still keep going.* They spin, even. A man without armour might have it lance straight through him and leave no more than a hole, if it missed his bones, but any armoured man whose armour fails is a dead man there and then.'

Totho stared. He felt nothing except cold, as if someone had stabbed him somewhere vital, and he was simply waiting to die. He felt nothing, and he realized that meant not even guilt or remorse.

At the Great College they had told him that he would never amount to anything.

'Loose!' the master artificer called once again.

At close range, the twin ranks of the snapbowmen stopped the advance in its tracks. So many men and women fell in that one instant that those behind were caught, trapped now with a tangle of dead comrades before them who a moment ago had all been living and breathing, had been kindred minds within theirs.

'Down bows and back!' Drephos told his protégés. 'General Malkan's move, I think.'

'Why stop now?' Totho asked hopelessly.

Drephos smiled at him. 'Ammunition, Totho. Have you any idea how many bolts we've loosed in the last few seconds? Let Malkan spend his men instead, since they are more easily replaced.'

Already the Wasp soldiers of Malkan's army were rushing

past on either side of the firing line, both on the ground and in the air, descending on the battered Ant-kinden with sword and sting.

Before setting out, General Malkan had left Drephos two thousand soldiers in Helleron, but in the end the foundries, though working day and night, had produced only twelve hundred snapbows, and so Drephos had done the best he could with what he had.

Back among the surgeons, Che was tying another bandage when the invisible wave of news washed over them. In an instant all the Ants were up, and beginning to move the wounded onto the transport automotives. They worked as carefully as they could, but there was an edge of haste to them that she had never seen in Ants before.

'What is it?' she asked them. 'What's happening?' but they had no answers, just grimly took up each wounded soldier who still had a chance of survival and stretchered him or her away.

Sperra took her telescope back from Che and leapt into the air, putting it to her eye and holding place with her wings.

'They're retreating!' she called, her voice shaken. 'The Sarnesh are falling back!'

'What?' Che asked. It made no sense. They had been advancing steadily. 'What's going on? Tell us, Sperra.' Beside her, Achaeos patiently strung his bow.

'The men at the front are standing their ground, but the Wasps are all over them, and the rest are ... they're running. They're actually *running*. They're keeping their shields over their heads, but they're coming back fast.'

All the remaining automotives were pulling up, and there were men throwing open the doors of the train. Che stared at it all in disbelief. 'This can't be happening!'

'The Mantis-kinden on the right edge are still fighting,' Sperra was saying, her voice sounding less and less steady.

'They're fighting like madmen, I've never seen the like, never – but they're all fighting alone. They're killing them, killing the Wasps, but there are so many coming at them now – they're falling! All of them, they're falling!'

'What about the left flank?' Achaeos called up to her.

'They've drawn back with the Ants. The Sarnesh who stayed to hold the line, they . . . they're being overrun! What can they do? They can't get all the way back here before the Wasps catch them!'

The last Ant adjutant assigned to the Mantis left-side company saluted Scelae. He was shaking slightly, but nothing else in pose or voice told anything more of the horror that was in his mind.

'They suggest you pull back,' he told her. 'Two companies are going to stand here and hold them off, to allow our people to reach the automotives and the rail line.'

'Will that be enough?' Scelae asked.

'They say it will have to be. We must fall back towards the city.'

Scelae cast around. She had lost no more than a quarter of her force because, spread out as they had been, the new Wasp weapon had whipped mostly into empty air around them. 'You!' she called, pointing to one of her Moth-kinden, a girl and one of their youngest. Scelae had no time to assess her fitness for the task, time only to give the order.

'Get on to that moving rail-machine,' she said. 'Then fly on to Dorax when it stops. Fly, and keep flying until you're there. They must know of this. Go now.'

With a look that was close to tears, the Moth darted off.

'I need help,' Scelae said to the other Moths, a mere dozen gathered close to her. 'I need what help you can give me. I know I cannot command it, but you see what must be done here.'

'We see what a Mantis must do here,' said their eldest,

an old man of more than sixty years. 'We shall give you what we can.'

'What can we do?' one of the others demanded. 'The sun is out! What can we achieve, in broad daylight?'

'You forget yourself,' said the eldest. 'Magic is fear, uncertainty, doubt. Where better to find these things than on a battlefield? Now join with me.'

Scelae turned from them, trusting them to do what they could. To the expectant Ant adjutant she said, 'When your companies make their stand we shall stand with them. Tell your masters that.'

'That is *now*,' the Ant said, and indeed the Wasps were approaching, on the ground and in the air, a wave of the Wasp soldiers who so recently had been fleeing, but were now howling for revenge.

The nearest Ant companies had formed a long shieldwall two men deep, with crossbows levelled at the rear. The soldiers braced for the impact of the Wasps, knowing that in their sacrifice, their inevitable deaths, they would buy their kin time to run for home.

When that was all they had to give, they gave it gladly.

'Ready!' Scelae called. Already there were Wasp airborne streaking overhead, diving on the running troops, their stings crackling, or racing onwards towards the auto-motives.

She had lived a long enough life, she decided. Spying for the Arcanum in Sarn, she had not thought to be given this honour at last: to die as a Mantis ought.

'Hunt out your deaths!' she cried out to her warriors, and they raised their weapons and rushed forwards.

'I cannot see—' Sperra gasped. 'No! I see some soldiers staying behind to hold them back. The Mantis ... The Mantis-kinden are fighting on the left. They have charged the Wasps—' She choked on the words for it had been like watching sand disappear before a wave. They were in there, though, spinning and slashing, inside the Wasp formation, cutting and killing, and dying. 'They are holding them!' she cried out. 'I think . . . I think some of the Wasps are fighting with each other! They are falling on each other, butchering each other in mid-air.'

The first of the running soldiers were past them now, heading for the train. The wounded were still only half loaded on board.

'I think—' Sperra continued, telescope still to her eye, and just then the first of the Wasp airborne struck her, sending her tumbling from the sky. He had been lunging blade-first, but in his haste only his shoulder had struck; he swung round for another pass and an arrow sprouted beneath his armpit, and he spiralled away with a yell.

Achaeos nocked another to his bow. The Ants doubled their pace with the wounded soldiers, knowing that some would die from the exertion, but more would if they did not.

'Ach!' Sperra was now holding her ribs, cursing but desperately trying to find her telescope. Che lifted her bodily onto the nearest automotive, despite her protests.

'Go!' the Beetle told her, and then the machine *was* moving, grinding off, as soldiers flooded along beside it, filling the train neatly from the front carriages back, orderly even in defeat.

Achaeos loosed his second arrow, and then a brief moment of desolation and despair swept over him. Out on the field, the madly fighting ball of Wasps had swept over the little group of Moth-kinden, silencing what magic they had raised against the minds of their enemies.

He put a third arrow to the string and drew it back, but the fire of a sting-blast washed past him, struck him to the ground. He heard Che scream but it was distant, very distant, because his pain was so large and so immediate.

It hurt so much more when they lifted him bodily onto

the automotive's flatbed amongst the wounded he himself had been tending. 'Che!' he cried out, and he had a vague glimpse of her face even as the vehicle began to move, but his out-thrust arm was clutching at nothing. He was leaving her behind. The train was moving now as well, and there was only one automotive left, and it seemed full to him. 'Che!' he yelled again, through the searing pain. She was shouting something back at him, but he could not hear it.

Che looked round, and saw that she had left it very nearly too late to do the sensible thing. She ran for the last big transporter, clutching at the rungs and slats. It had already started to move, and she felt her grip slipping. She called out, but the driver was only listening for the voices in his head. She stumbled helplessly—

One of the Sarnesh inside leant over, caught her by her belt and lifted her in effortlessly. There were Wasps passing over them now, but most were starting to turn back, not wanting to get too far from the main body of their army. The vehicle's driver flung the machine forwards over the uneven ground, aiming for the line of the rails, and Che heard a kind of whistling noise that she barely had time to register.

Something caught her a massive blow across the head, the slats of the automotive's side slamming into her as the ball of metal from the leadshotter ripped through the back of the automotive in a maelstrom of jagged shards. The automotive was suddenly veering around. All around her the Sarnesh were leaping out even before the vehicle had come to a halt. Che was too stunned to follow, lying in the automotive's belly with her head spinning. A moment later there was a muffled crack from the engine and the machine was enveloped in smoke.

Choking, gasping, Che drew her sword, half jumping and half falling from the back of the vehicle as it ground to a stop. Everywhere she looked, there were Wasps. Behind her the train and the automotives were retreating towards

Sarn, and she had the single candle-flame of comfort that at least Achaeos was on one of them. The others who had been unlucky enough to be on the last automotive out were fighting already, falling to the swords and stings of the Wasps. She felt herself begin to tremble, her sword shake in her hand.

So ended what would become known as the Battle of the Rails.

Thirty-Nine

In the last few days Stenwold had become an old hand at estimating the numbers of soldiers. Now he looked at the citizens of Collegium who had joined him at the wharf front and knew he had less than one hundred and twenty.

The armourclad had been hauled around now in the harbour, and a great, wide-beamed ship was coasting through the gap, with grey sails piled far higher than the ruins of the harbour towers. Its bow was square and there were men there manhandling a folding bridge, and beyond them the rails were lined with armoured forms.

'We have no chance here!' Stenwold told his tiny force. 'The Vekken are breaking in at the west wall even as we speak, and we cannot hold them here. Go back to your families. Go back to your wives and husbands and children. There is no sense in your staying here.'

'What will you do, War Master?' one of them asked him.

'I will remain,' Stenwold said heavily. 'When they dock I will see if the word of one Master of Collegium can yet carry weight, but you must go, all of you.'

He heard some take him up on his offer, but when he looked round he still had more than a hundred remaining.

The great ship was coming in, coasting with a terrible grace. The sails were being furled and there were two anchor-chains in the water to slow her as she approached the charred wood of the wharves.

'Stenwold,' Arianna said in awe. 'That isn't a Vekken ship.'

He looked from her to the approaching vessel, and back again. 'How do you know?'

'Because that's a Spiderlands ship out of Seldis, and I ought to know my own people's work.'

Stenwold gaped at her and then at the ship. The bridge was coming down now that the ship was yards from its berth. 'Hold your shot!' he told his men.

A Spiderlands ship. He saw her sleek lines, the pattern of waves and arabesques that decorated her rails – but those rails were lined with Ant shields.

The bridge struck the wharves, and his men began backing up nervously, fingering their crossbows and swords. *If it is the Vekken, then a surrender offered here, without a shot loosed, may buy these men their lives.* 'Hold still!' Stenwold told them.

And the Ant-kinden coursed out onto the Collegium docks, forming up even as they did so into a fighting square. They were not the glossy onyx of Vek, though, their skins were pallid, pale as fishbellies.

Tarkesh Ants. What is going on? Stenwold moved forward, more to keep a distance between these newcomers and his own ragged followers. His people were nervous, and seeing these new Ants assemble, moving from shipboard to land in impeccable order, was not helping them.

'Identify yourselves. You are on the soil of Collegium!' he shouted. He had the feeling of every set of too-similar eyes on him, all those swords and crossbows, directed straight at him.

One man broke from their ranks, slinging his shield. He regarded Stenwold without expression, unknowable conversations passing through his mind. 'You speak for Collegium?' he asked.

'I am Master Maker of the Great College. What is your business here? We are not at our best to receive visitors,'

Stenwold said, thinking, *If this goes badly, then I take the brunt. At least Arianna has a chance to get clear of it.*

The Tarkesh officer smiled grimly. 'I am Mercenary-Commander Parops, formerly of Tark. I hear you have a little Vekken infestation.'

One of Stenwold's men exclaimed and pointed, and then they were all rushing to the broken edge of the wharves to stare out to sea. The Ants shifted, but only to give them a clearer view. Something was burning out on the water, sheets of flame shooting forty feet in the air, and Stenwold saw that it was one of the Vekken supply barges. There were little copper-hulled ships out there, darting through the waters with steaming funnels, gallantly doing battle with the remaining Vekken armourclads and blazing away with flame cannon at the other barges, which were already starting to smoke. Stenwold saw one of the little ships blown apart as a leadshot from an armourclad struck its steam engine, but the others were nipping nimbly through the hail of shot and loosing their own weapons.

Larger, flat-hulled boats were meanwhile driving through the waves to make a landing west of the city, packed with soldiers, and beyond them all another half-dozen of the elegant Spiderlands galleons were tacking wide of the fighting, whilst smaller sailing ships with high forecastles made passes against the armourclads, showering the Vekken sailors with arrows. It was only for a moment that Stenwold watched that slow melee, the sails of the Spiderlands frigates a nimble elegance against the lumbering ironclads. He saw one of the Vekken ships listing, Spider-kinden marines fighting on its decks with grim desperation. The wooden ships were fleet, but when the Vekken caught them they were matchwood in short order. Still, the sea was full of sails. It was an entire fleet that the Spiderlands had sent them. The Vekken navy, already diminished by its assaults on the harbour, was falling to their numbers and to their grace.

'Stenwold,' Arianna hissed to him. 'The wall!'

'Commander,' Stenwold said, bringing his mind back to his responsibilities. 'The Vekken are in at the west wall.'

'Take us there,' Parops instructed him. 'And we shall turn them out again.'

The Vekken rushed into the city, desperate to flood their soldiers past the breach, to set foot at last on the conquered enemy ground. When they were past the wall there was a moment of confusion. Akalia's plan had gone so far and no further. The wall was down, the city was therefore taken.

But the people of Collegium did not see it that way. There was no surrender. Even as the Vekken formed up in the wall's curving shadow, the arrows and the sling stones fell on them, rattling from their shields, bouncing from their mail. There were men, women and children at the windows of every house, throwing rocks, loosing cross-bows. Impromptu lines of citizens formed before the orderly Vekken advance, armed with clubs, with spears. Every house became an archer's platform, every street a choke-point. The Vekken advance was never halted, but it was slow, so slow. Two streets from the wall and a house they were passing suddenly erupted in fire and stone, razored shards scything through the tight-packed Vekken ranks, killing scores of them. As the invaders recoiled and recovered, the people of Collegium were in the next houses, shooting down at them. Girls of twelve, old women of seventy, Fly-kinden publicans and fat Beetle shopkeepers, grocers and clerks and cooks swarmed from doorways and alleyways, holding their knives and chair-legs, their scavenged waster bows and stolen Vekken shields. In the fore, always in the fore, was a giant Sarnesh Ant-kinden with a nailbow and paired shortswords. He became the man the Vekken hated most, the man they needed to kill. A cross-bow bolt found his shoulder. A sword-stroke had riven the armour over his hip. He refused to fall. To the Vekken it seemed that he even refused to bleed.

Another house detonated to the Vekken rear, and every building of Collegium had become their enemy. The call was going out for artificers, but the streets were so full of Vekken soldiers, their advance backing up all the way to the wall, that no engineers could have got through.

A grey-haired Fly-kinden woman almost fell on Stenwold and his new allies in her eagerness to intercept him. With commendable precision she got out her report on what the people of Collegium were sacrificing for their city. The persistence of his own people astonished Stenwold, and even more so because by now there was no command, nothing from the Assembly that could order the defence. The street-by-street stalling, the sabotage of their own homes, this all represented the men and women of Collegium taking their fate into their own hands.

Parops digested the situation quickly. 'Have people lead my men to each major thoroughfare before their advance,' he said. 'People who can explain that we're on your side. We will hold the Vekken as long as we need, and holding them is all that needs doing.'

Stenwold recalled the landing craft he had seen. 'There are a great deal of Vekken out there, Commander,' he warned.

Parops's face lacked something human in it. 'That's my employers' problem, Master Maker, but they have brought a great many troops.'

'But *why?*' Stenwold demanded.

'Does it matter? Now let us do our work,' Parops cut him off.

Arianna clung to Stenwold's good arm, practically dancing with glee, watching the Tarkesh rush into their time-honoured calling of killing the Ants of other cities.

★

Tactician Akalia stared at the flames of her barges and could not understand what was happening to her war. An open call had gone out to every man and woman of her officers to explain it to her, and not one had the answer. A mass of ships had crept up on them at night from who-knew-where, and was going about the savage business of finishing her entire fleet. There were little sparks in her head that were the masters of her vessels, and they were flickering out, one by one, each giving his life and his ship for the greater glory of Vek, and leaving nothing but ripples in his wake.

Tactician! We must withdraw troops from the siege!

No! We are inside the wall, she threw back.

But, Tactician, they are coming for us! And she saw through the eyes of the officer the approaching ships already close to beaching on the shore. The soldiers left in the camp were already rushing to intercept them, but the vast majority of the Vekken force was up about the walls of Collegium.

Bring the force back from the north wall, she decided. *Our men here will hold the enemy until then.*

Even as she thought it, her men at the beach were dying. For a panicked moment nobody realized why, but then she saw that there were repeating ballistae mounted on the front corners of the flat-bottomed craft, and as the Vekken soldiers came to repel the beachhead they were being systematically shot down. Some managed a ragged shield-wall, and began to return shot with crossbows, but then the first of the craft had ground on the sand of the beach.

Men with skins like burnished copper were leaping out. They wore long hauberks of the same colour, mail with rings of incredible fineness, and long oval shields with a distinctive notch cut into them. Many of them were fitting repeating crossbows to those notches even now, advancing on the diminishing Vekken while they began to loose. Others were lifting the ballistae from the bows of their boats and running forward with them to where artificers were setting up three-legged mounts for them.

She instructed the men coming back from the north wall to pick up their pace.

Tactician, we are encountering heavy resistance within the city!

No excuses! she snapped. There could *be* no excuses, now, for failing to capture Collegium: not these newcomers of unknown kinden, not the new ships, not any device of the Beetle academics.

But, Tactician, we are facing soldiers from Tark, several hundred at least.

The situation began to slip from her fingers. Tarkesh, in Collegium? Even as she considered it, the last of her men at the beach died. Too few to mount a proper defence, they had been outflanked and shot down. Now the enemy was rushing up the beach, and two hundred yards inland lay the Vekken camp, all but undefended.

Withdraw all from the camp and join the northern force, she decided. *Then we shall sweep them back into the sea.*

Tactician! The eastern force is under attack!

From who? she demanded, stalking out of her tent with her greatsword balanced on her shoulder.

A mixed force, Tactician: Flies, Scorpions, Spider-kinden, others I do not know—

And the speaker was gone in a brief impression of shock and pain. There were others there clamouring for her attention, but she blocked them out. With the remainder of her staff she headed north, and it took all her control not to run.

Joined by the forces reclaimed from Collegium's north wall, she tried to make a decision, but she craved only an outcome that would enable her to sack Collegium, and that goal was fast receding. Her eastern force was pinned against the very wall they should have been taking, under attack from the defenders above and from the inexplicable new forces that had come in off the sea. Her western force was held in the city by the Tarkesh, and under attack from the rear by the copper-armoured strangers. She had but a third of her army left to her name.

We will attack. If she returned to Vek with this disgrace, then she would never have the respect of her kind again. She began marching her forces back towards the city walls. The breach was still there, so she would force her way into the city and then proceed to hold it against the newcomers.

Ahead, a force had gathered to oppose her. There were Tarkesh there, and the copper men, and many, many diverse men and women of Collegium, Beetles and all other kinden. They outnumbered her surviving force by more than three to one.

They were not Ant-kinden in the main, though, so they could not stand together and fight together as Ant-kinden could. What were such odds, therefore, compared to the iron discipline of Vek?

Shields to the fore and stand fast, she ordered, for the enemy were charging now, coming for her people at a run, hoping to break them. Obedient to her will, her soldiers closed ranks, crouched behind their shields, and waited to weather the assault. *Crossbows. Volley fire.*

She saw the first sheet of crossbow bolts strike them, saw some parts of the attacking force crumble back, others press on. The Tarkesh held, and so did the copper men, while the exhausted locals were knocked back, thrown into confusion. Many of them had not even possessed shields.

Hold firm. Throw them back.

She sensed the realization go through the enemy Ant-kinden that their assault had failed before contact was made. Almost immediately they were making their withdrawal, the enemy force falling back piecemeal to its starting point and leaving its dead behind. She herself had suffered barely a dozen casualties.

Artillery! came the warning in her mind. The repeating

ballistae had now been brought up from the beach, and the copper-skinned artificers were setting them up with grim efficiency. The Vekken force was well within their range.

Shields, she ordered. *Advance. Drive them into the sea.*

The mass of Vekken infantry, her prize soldiers, the finest in the world, locked shield to shield, before them and overhead, and marched forward in double time towards the enemy line. *Let them use their ballistae when it has become sword against sword*, she thought.

The artillery was now launching, the bolts peppering her lines, punching through shields, knocking holes in her formation that were quickly filled. There was still confusion as her enemies tried to arrange their line. She saw, to her surprise, that they were going to charge again, to try to halt her by the sheer force of their momentum, to wrap around and take her force in the flanks.

An Ant-kinden army has no flanks. The men at the sides would simply turn to face their aggressors like pieces in the machine. Collegium could still be hers.

They were in crossbow range now, both sides loosing a torrent of bolts to thud into shield or stab into armoured flesh. Then she saw her enemies gather what courage they had left and charge her.

Hold, she instructed, and then, *Cut them to pieces—*

Something loomed just then over the enemy force, something dark in the great span of sea and sky behind them. It was rushing towards her army, coursing with and around and between her enemies: a great barbed shadow cast by nothing at all, but thorned and spined and shifting like the shadows between great trees, and Akalia screamed, in her mind and out loud, as it descended upon them.

It was a trick of the light, or a moment's hallucination, but every man and woman of her army saw it just as she did, and they shifted and started, and their shields slipped, and then the enemy struck them.

*

It was a long time ago. It seemed a hundred years ago. It seemed like yesterday.

They were already rebuilding, Stenwold knew with satisfaction. They were planning the regeneration of Collegium, from the wounds it had inflicted on itself, and the wounds the Vekken had dealt it.

And I would rather be out there with them, but that was not true. *I would rather be at home.* He did not want to be here in the Amphiophos in his formal robes.

'Master Maker, can I introduce the Lord-Martial Teornis of the Aldanrael?' asked Lineo Thadspar, stepping into his view.

Stenwold managed a weary bow to the immaculate Spiderkinden Aristos. This was the one who had commanded the fleet, he realized: the man who had saved Collegium.

The Amphiophos was full of new faces today, but most keenly he felt the lack of so many of the old ones. The Assembly, like the city it governed, was peppered with holes. Where now was Waybright, who had fallen to a crossbow bolt on the east wall? Where was Doctor Nicrephos, and where was the stern old visage of Kymon of Kes?

'Lord-Martial, I have no words to thank you,' he said, all too truthfully. 'I had not thought the Spiderlands would be such a supporter of our city.'

'The Spiderlands holds no single opinion as one entity, nor takes any single action, War Master,' replied Teornis drily. 'However, I myself see sufficient advantage in trade and political futures to go so far on behalf of your city. You must thank another, though, for the invitation.'

Stenwold could see, from Thadspar's face, that this was something new, and he made a politely enquiring sound.

'You are acquainted with a most enchanting member of my kind named Tynisa, are you not?'

'You've seen Tynisa?' gasped Stenwold. 'Where?' The world was making no sense to him now. *Is it because I am so tired, or it is really all nonsense?*

'The full story I shall tell you when we can find more leisure,' Teornis promised. 'It is unfinished as yet, for she and her companion had some small matters to attend to before their own return, or else I would have offered them space on my flagship.'

Stenwold nodded, mind still reeling, and thanked him again before looking for a place to sit down. It was five days since the Vekken army had been defeated and Collegium saved, but people still moved about their city as though there was a war going on. There were a great many foreigners here, and the locals regarded them nervously. If Teornis had wanted Collegium for himself he could have made a serious attempt on her, Stenwold knew, and in their negotiations the day after the battle the Spider had pointedly not quite said as much. Stenwold knew a little of the trade concessions that the Aldanrael family would reap from this, the loans and the technology and the student places at the College, even two Master's seats that were also seats on the Assembly.

'Commander Parops,' Thadspar said, drifting past. The Tarkesh officer was still in his armour, and he shook Stenwold's hand heartily. 'You're Stenwold Maker!' he said.

'I am indeed,' Stenwold admitted. He still felt that he should sit down, but just now he was supposed to be a diplomat. It was a wrenching change from being a soldier, and after an hour of this he was not sure which he preferred.

'You know a Fly-kinden, name of Nero,' Parops informed him.

It was obviously a day for name-dropping. 'Yes, I do,' Stenwold said, 'although it has been a long time since I've seen him.'

'Then I have a lot I can tell you,' said Parops. Then, seeing Thadspar anxious to introduce him to others, he grimaced and added, 'Later, though.'

I can see I'll not have many evenings free for a while.

Stenwold allowed himself to lean back against a convenient wall, before he saw another Assembler approaching him, leading a copper-hued man of rangy build.

'This is Artificer-Commander . . .' the Assembler started, and the name had obviously evaded him.

'Dariaxes,' said the copper-coloured, copper-clad man whose eyes were a startling red.

'Commander Dariaxes is Fire Ant-kinden from Porphyris,' the Assembler announced excitedly. 'This is the first-ever formal contact between our cities. Isn't that remarkable, Master Maker?'

Stenwold tiredly conceded that it was. 'I am only pleased our first meeting is under such amicable terms, Commander,' he said. 'Your men are . . . mercenaries for the Spiders?'

'My city is a satrapy of the Spiderlands,' Dariaxes corrected. It was a word Stenwold was only vaguely familiar with but the context told him more than he was happy with. How different was a satrapy from a city the Wasps had conquered? He supposed that the chief difference would be that the Spider-kinden, who could convince anyone of anything, had probably persuaded the Fire Ants that they were perfectly content with their servitude. They were not the only ones, though, that was clear. The Spiderlands were vast – unmapped as far as any reliable atlas of Collegium went – and the Fire Ants had not come alone. Stenwold had already been introduced to a Dragonfly soldier whose ancestors in the Days of Lore had fled so far from the Commonweal that the Spiders had taken them in.

Sour thoughts were easy to hold, with the scars of the war still so fresh. Dariaxes's men had died outside the walls to make his city safe, and there had been Spider-kinden amongst the dead too, along with Scorpion mercenaries and a dozen other races.

'Collegium thanks you,' he told Dariaxes, whose smile

told him he had guessed at some of the thoughts in Stenwold's mind.

Stenwold glanced around the room, seeking escape, and he picked Balkus out of the crowd – a full head over anyone except the Scorpion captain. The big Ant was, at least, enjoying himself. He had a bandage on his face, still, where a Vekken sword had cut open his cheek, but he was still managing to form a smile around it, and there was a young Beetle-kinden woman, an artificer of the College, hanging adoringly on his arm. Stenwold could not begrudge him that.

There was a touch at his elbow, and he turned to see Arianna, with one hand resting on the sling that marked his own war-wound.

'Ah,' he said, with false jollity, 'you're here to tell me there's something urgent I need to attend to.'

'Yes, I am,' she said, with such intensity that his stomach lurched.

'Something's happened?' he said, instantly worried. 'What?'

There was such a serious look on her face that it could be nothing good. 'You had better come with me,' she said. 'Some of the guardsmen outside have picked up someone who came asking for you. You need to see this.'

She led him outside, while he was still trying to figure out who it could be. True, everyone seemed to have learned his name during the war, but he had hoped to return to obscurity as soon as it was over.

'In here,' Arianna guided him, tense as a taut wire, her hand seeking her knife-hilt. Stenwold's mind was full of wild speculation as he looked inside, but none wild enough to prepare him for what he saw.

Sitting at a table, between two men of the city militia, was none other than Major Thalric of the Rekef.

★

Beyond the wide tiered steps of the Amphiophos, where the Assembly of Collegium met, there was a broad plaza where ancient statute forbade any market trader to set up stall. In former times the people of the city had gathered there to hear proclamations from their most respected leaders, but more recently it had been a good vantage point from which to protest, wave banners, shout obscenities and throw things at the Assemblers as they hurried inside.

Now it had been returned to its original purpose. The people of Collegium packed it, wall to wall, shoulder to shoulder, with their children held up high to see too, and Fly-kinden thronging every window-ledge, and the roof-gardens packed with even more, since residents were allowing complete strangers up through their houses to enable them to witness this gem of history being cut and mounted.

Stenwold, one of that gem's key facets, had a hard time bringing his thoughts to the moment. When Thalric had told him that the Wasp major had fled from his own people, Stenwold had not believed him at first, despite the deep wound in his erstwhile enemy's side that some Inapt healer had neatly dressed. Then Stenwold had recognized the livid mark across the man's face as the result of burning from a Wasp sting, and had begun to think. Arianna had urged him not to believe anything the man said, for Thalric was subtle as a Spider, she said, and Stenwold had no doubt that was true.

But even Spiders, it was said, got caught in their own traps, every so often.

Lineo Thadspar led them out onto the steps, and the roar of approval seemed to shake the very marble beneath them, making Stenwold stagger a little until Balkus caught his good arm to steady him. There were no words in that roar, but the unadulterated joy of a people freed from terror. Ever since the previous Vekken attack had retreated from the city before the arrival of a Sarnesh relief force, in the days when these grown men of Collegium were but boys, there had been the knowledge that the Vekken would try again. Now the Vekken army had been smashed so decisively it would take that city a decade to regain its strength.

Thadspar had been intending to speak but the crowd just would not be silent, continuing to thunder its approval for the saviours of the city. A junior artificer had hurried forward and passed Thadspar a speaking horn, but there was not a device invented that would have made his voice clear over that joyous throng, and so he waited. Stenwold, who had always taken the old man for a shrewd politician, saw tears in his eyes.

Back in a guest suite, and under heavy guard, was Thalric – Major Thalric of the Rekef – who had limped into the city with Stenwold's name on his lips. Major Thalric, who had nowhere else to go, by his own story, and so had finally come here.

'What would I do with you?' Stenwold had asked him sharply. 'We are enemies, you and I.' He could not rid himself of what this man had been ready to do to his niece Che, when she had been in his clutches.

'I have only enemies left in the world,' Thalric had admitted. He was a man fighting to control his circumstances, not drowning but not swimming either. The next adverse wave could swallow him. 'The fact that I am sitting here talking to you shows that you are less my enemy than those I once called friends. As for what I can do for you, I know something about what the Empire may do next. I know a great deal more than you about how the Empire does things.'

'And how can I trust you?'

'You'll never know if you can,' the Wasp had said, 'and I'm sure that little traitress on your arm will urge you to put me to death but, really, will you ever have a better chance?'

Stenwold frowned, now, in retrospect. He did not want this, to be here at the focus of all this cheer and attention.

Instead he needed to deal with Thalric and make his decision. He hated unfinished business.

Still, if he put those nagging thoughts aside, just for a moment, there was some strange satisfaction in finding himself here in a jubilant scene that would surely be recorded in history books to come. The saviours of Collegium, the defiers of Vek. Thadspar stood with the other surviving members of the War Council, fewer than might have been expected, and a handful of other citizens who had led the defence: militia officers, stalwart merchants and artisans, and College artificers, even Master Hornwhill, who had been so very reluctant for his inventions to be used at all. Balkus stood shoulder to shoulder with the Tarkesh commander, Parops, and beside them was the slighter, rangier form of Dariaxes, with his constant copper smile. Then there was Teornis of the Aldanrael, dressed as soldier-gone-fop in a gold breastplate, jewelled gorget and a helmet adorned with glittering wings. His expression was one of modest contentment, which drew attention to him far more than waving and grinning ever could. There were others, too, of his own company: Scorpion, Fly, Dragonfly, Spider. The steps before the Amphiophos were crowded today.

At last the crowd had quieted enough for Thadspar to be heard, and he left it another beat before he spoke.

'Citizens of Collegium, this day shall be recounted to our children so that it never be forgotten,' he said, his voice booming metallically from the horn. 'To teach them, we must learn many lessons ourselves. We might learn from this that we are strong in ourselves, for it is true. Most important, we may learn that we are strong in our friends – you see those around me, do you not? There is not one man or woman standing before you who has not earned their place on these steps but, in truth, if all who had earned such a place were given it, then we would need steps that spanned our whole city! I see those before me who have shed blood for their city. I see the peaceable citizens who took up the sword and the crossbow without fear or complaint. This victory belongs to every one of us.

'But look again at these who stand beside me, familiar faces and strangers both. Our true celebration must not be for the destruction of the Vekken who, but for their misguided envy, should not even have been our enemies. Instead, it should be for this alliance, this company you see before you. When else, in all the years this city has stood, known as Collegium of the Beetles or even as Pathis of the Moths so long before, has such a band of allies been ranged together? You see here Ants from the city-states of Sarn and Tark who have fought side by side for Collegium. You see lords of the Spiderlands, and the allies they have brought with them whose faces have never been seen in our community before.

'And more than this, I look into your faces, and I see Fly-kinden, Mantis, even Moth. And more, I see in my mind all the faces of those who cannot be with us, who have been cut down in this war, and they were many, and of all kinden, and this day is also theirs. We must never forget all those who gave everything for us. Where you stand now there shall be a memorial carved, and I wish every one of you to bring us the names of those you knew who fell, and each one shall have its place. The gate of the west wall, whose shutters, I am informed, can never rise again, shall never be reopened, and a new gate will be built where the Vekken made their breach. In this way, by including it into the very structure of our city, we shall never forget our friends, or our victory.'

Thadspar accepted a bowl of wine from a servant, drained it, and handed it back, pausing a moment before continuing.

'Many of you will have heard that in the east a new power is brewing,' he told the crowd. 'They are Wasp-kinden, and they call themselves an Empire. You may even have heard that they have taken the city of Tark for their personal possession, and we know this is true. Their forces even now threaten Sarn.

'We have never seen their like before. Some of you may know that War Master Stenwold Maker has been warning of their power for many years, and I say now, as Speaker for the Assembly, that it is to our shame that we did not heed him sooner. The Wasps wish to see us destroyed, and why? Why us? Look upon these men and women ranged beside me, and that is your answer. All of us, standing here, we are the Lowlands entire, and to conquer the Lowlands, their Empire must first conquer us!

'We have won a battle,' Thadspar told them finally. 'We still must fight a war.'

Stenwold thought that he should feel triumphant, that his warnings had finally been heeded, that Collegium was at last committed openly to opposing the Empire. Instead he just felt tired, heading back with Balkus and Arianna to speak once again to Thalric – to interpret the foreign script of his prisoner's face and try to master its grammar.

'Good speech,' Balkus rumbled beside him. 'Of course, I'm not really Sarnesh any more. I did wonder why they wanted me up there.'

Stenwold was about to reply when he saw a young Beetle waiting to see him as he approached Thalric's suite.

'Master Maker!' he got out. 'There's someone to see you. Says it's urgent!'

Then a Fly-kinden had bolted past him, virtually bouncing off from Stenwold before she had come to a halt.

'What's—' Stenwold started, but Balkus got out, 'Sperra!'

Stenwold stared at her, seeing a thin and grubby Fly woman who looked as though she had neither eaten nor slept for days.

'But you were in Sarn . . .' he said stupidly.

Balkus knelt quickly towards her, and Sperra leant against him gratefully. She looked half-dead with exhaustion.

'The Sarnesh have fought the Wasps . . . field battle,' she got out. 'They lost, pulled out . . . when the train got us back to Sarn we had news from here that the Vekken had been turned. I got on a train to get here right away – didn't stop for anything. I brought the Moth-boy. He got himself hurt. They put him in a Wayhouse hospice nearby.'

Something in her manner, in the words left unsaid, had crept up on Stenwold, and now he said softly, 'Slow down now. What about Cheerwell?'

'Master Maker, I'm sorry,' she said. 'Che was supposed to be in the last automotive off the field, only . . . it never made it back to the city. I'm so sorry.'

Forty

It was the greatest magic, from the very ebbing shores of the Days of Lore.

Here, within these close-knit tree trunks, treading ancient paths through the forest, they came on a moonless night. Tramping lines of grey-robed figures made their unfaltering way through the pitch-dark with their heads bowed. There was a sense of desperation about them, of tattered pride held up like a standard. How much had already been lost, to have brought them to this state?

Watch closely, little acolyte.

There were lamps ahead, though dim: wicker baskets crowded with fireflies lending an underwater radiance to the tree boles, and not even touching the shadows between them. Figures waited there, tall and stark. There was black metal there, scale armour, spearheads. This grove was sacred, and the idol to their Art that they kept here was a mere stump, the relic of a thousand years of rot and busy agents of decay. Around it the Mantis-kinden stood, like statues themselves, and with some were the great hunched forms of their insect siblings, their killing arms folded as if in silent contemplation.

Watch closely, little neophyte.

In solemn procession the robed men and women wound their way between the trunks to them. Night was all around them, yet a dawn had come to the world that no shadows could resist. This was the end of the Days of Lore, and across the Lowlands their dominion was shrinking by the day. Their ancient cities were overthrown: Pathis, Tir Amec, Shalarna and Amirra had fallen as the slaves rebelled, and not all their craft, not all the killing steel of their Mantis soldiers, could stem that tide. The slaves, the dull-witted and the ugly, the graceless and the leaden, had cast them off. They had made themselves armour and terrifying new weapons, and they had declared themselves free.

Pathis, Tir Amec, Shalarna, Amirra.

And Achaeos's mind called up the counterparts: Collegium, Tark, Sarn and Myna. And how many more had been the haunts of his own Moth people, that none now even remembered?

And when unity was most needed there had been schism. Centuries of strife had held the Moth-kinden together. They had raised armies against the Centipede-kinden who had erupted from the earth. They had staved off or defeated the machinations of all the other sorcerous powers: Spiders and Mosquitoes, the sly Assassin Bugs and the ancient buried kingdoms of the Slugs. The revolt of the slaves had struck at their very being, and they had flown to pieces. Some counselled peace, some retreat and isolation. Factions and parties grew, and when blades were raised they fell brother on brother, and all the while the inexorable tide of history was sweeping them aside, leaving little sign that they had ever existed.

You have seen some of our stones in Collegium that still stand, and the sewers at Myna that the Mole Crickets built for us. What else remains?

And so this. At last, this. This last attempt to summon the guttering forces of the old magic that the Moths had once lived and breathed – this most ambitious of all rituals. They were renegades, of course. Even those in Tharn or Dorax who advocated war and bloody retribution would have nothing to do with this. These outcasts had vowed to risk anything, to use up all the credit their kinden had amassed. They had come to the Mantis-kinden with stories of revenge, and the warrior-race had listened to them. Thus they had come here.

To Darakyon.

To *the* Darakyon, Achaeos thought. The Darakyon is a forest. 'Darakyon' alone would be a Mantis hold, and there is no such hold there.

But there was.

Here was the hold of Darakyon, seen in brief glimpses in the darkness between the trees, and here was its heart, its idol, once as sacred as that of Parosyal, a place of pilgrimage, of reverence.

They were gathered about it now, those robed shadows, and the Mantis-kinden stood proud and strong, their beast-allies beside them, and waited for the might of the Days of Lore to smite the unbelievers, to fragment their minds and terrorize them.

It was the darkest and the greatest magic ever plotted, to put a shadow on the Lowlands that would last a hundred years, to shatter the spirits of the people of the daylight and drag them down into slavery. A spell to taint the whole world

620

and wash away the revolution, even down to the ideas that had fermented it. A spell that would sicken the world to their children's children's children, or for ever.

It was the greatest magic, the darkest magic, and it went so terribly wrong.

I do not want to see this, Achaeos pressed, but the whispering chorus of voices was unmoved.

You could not understand, little seerling, so we must show you.

And he watched, without a head to turn aside, without eyes to close, as the ritual reached its bloody peak and the magic began to tear apart. He saw the deed that wiped the hold of Darakyon from all maps and made the forest of that name into the place of dread that even the lumberjacks of Helleron or the Empire would not approach, and he screamed, but chill hands held him and forced him to see it all, every moment of its demise.

And he saw what was done to the men and women of Darakyon, and how they were made to linger beyond time in that place, forever hating, forever vengeful and in pain.

But most of all he saw what they made of the rotten idol, and all the unfathomable power and evil that their ritual released. He saw it, small and deeply carved and potent beyond the dreams of Skryres, and knew that it was abroad in the world again, a tool for whatever evil hand should find it.

In the form of the Shadow Box. The soul of the Darakyon.

'So tell me,' Stenwold said, 'why I should take the appalling risk of keeping you close, or even keeping you alive.'

Thalric smiled, reclining easily behind the table as though he were back in his own study. 'You should start thinking like a man of your profession, Master Maker, and not just a Lowlander. I was a spymaster once. We both know the value of an enemy agent turned.'

'I couldn't trust you.'

'You have the craft to weigh what I tell you. I can be of more value to you than ever your Spider girl turncoat is.'

'No, you cannot,' Stenwold said flatly.

Thalric raised an eyebrow. 'Is it like that, then? Well then, do you want me to tell you about her? The truth? You must be still wondering whether the subtle Spider has spun a straight line?'

'Thalric,' Stenwold said warningly, and found his hand at his sword-hilt, and the Wasp's gaze followed it.

'I did not take you for a killer of unarmed prisoners.'

'You're Wasp-kinden,' Stenwold pointed out. 'Therefore you're never unarmed. What do you *want*, Thalric?'

Thalric stood up from the table, a little of his casual ease sloughing off him. 'I have been alone before, and hunted, but never so much of both at once. There was always the Empire. Now I find that the Empire I knew is a hollow egg. The insides are rotting with factions and I, who have disdained them, have become a casualty of politics. You believe, Stenwold, in something beyond yourself?'

'I believe that it is the duty of the strong to help the weak, and of men and women to live in peace and to build together,' the Beetle said, without even thinking. That was the doctrine so much of Collegiate thought was based on.

'I believe in the Empire, but it did not bear the weight of my belief,' Thalric said.

'So you're more imperial than the Empire now, is that it?' Stenwold shook his head. 'I can't see you as such a thorough turncoat.'

'I had my chance to die for my beliefs, Master Maker,' Thalric said with surprising emotion, 'but when they came for me, at the last, I fought them. I made my decision then. I can no longer claim now to be a loyal son of the Empire, having failed to follow its last command. I have to *live*, Maker, and you know as well as I the fate that awaits an agent cut loose by either side. He falls, Maker. He falls and is gone. So employ me, make use of me, while you still have me.'

'Sit down again,' Stenwold said, and then, 'Let's talk.'

Thalric returned to the table, glancing up at Arianna's hostile gaze. 'She would still see me dead, I observe.'

'Perhaps she has more sense than I do,' Stenwold said. 'What do you know of the forces currently marching on Sarn?'

Thalric raised his eyebrows. 'From what I recall, the Seventh had the honour set aside for it – General Malkan's Winged Furies. Malkan is the Empire's youngest general, and very ambitious.'

'What is the Empire's attitude to taking prisoners after a field battle, Thalric?'

The question was obviously not one the Wasp had expected. 'It depends on the battle. A battle against Ants would see few prisoners taken. If the fighting was bitter then the soldiers may leave none alive to be taken, whether they have surrendered or not.'

Stenwold found himself gripping the table, imagining Che surrendering with hands out in supplication, yet the swords still coming down.

'So the Sarnesh have lost a battle,' Thalric mused. 'Who did you have with them, Master Maker?' When Stenwold did not reply, he said, 'Not your niece?'

There was no mockery in his tone, so Stenwold nodded.

'I am sorry,' said Thalric, and when the Beetle glared at him he continued, 'She impressed me as a woman of intelligence and resource.' He seemed to brace himself before adding, 'Do you want me to go and find her for you?'

'You?' Stenwold demanded, puzzled.

'With appropriate help,' Thalric said, and it was clear that he was wrestling the idea into shape even as he spoke. 'I might be able to achieve it, for I am at least of the right kinden, and among the thousands in Malkan's army, I could appear just one more foot soldier, one more of the light airborne.'

'I must think,' Stenwold said, standing.

'At least consider the offer.'

'I must think,' the Beetle repeated, and left the room. Arianna sent Thalric a last poisonous glance before she followed.

No more bad news, please. No more messengers. Stenwold was still haunted by the stricken look on Sperra's face, when he had told her of Scuto's death. *Home, now.* No more war business. No more shaking hands. Home, was the plan. No more of the heavy marble halls of the Amphiophos. Home and try to find a path to save Che. *Any path that does not involve me placing trust in Thalric.* It might be that there was no such alternative. *And how to keep him mine, once he is loose? If the Empire would accept him back then he would betray me without a thought.*

He stomped wearily down the steps of the Amphiophos, hearing a ragged cheer as some late celebrants recognized him.

'This won't go away, will it?' he said gloomily.

'My kinden scheme all their lives for such recognition,' Arianna said.

His sharp glance left her instantly contrite. 'I'm sorry, I know that's not what you want to hear.'

'It's what I am, though, isn't it,' said Stenwold. 'I'm as much of a web-spinner as Teornis. The difference is that the people who get caught in my webs are my own. My own friends, my kin.'

The frightened expression appearing on her face had his

hand to his sword instantly, turning and drawing. He froze, then, hearing two or three people cry out in shock at the bared steel.

'So they're still calling you War Master,' said that oh-so-familiar voice, that twenty-years-familiar voice, and Stenwold sheathed his sword numbly, noting that neither father nor daughter had so much as flinched at the threat of it.

He put out his hand, noticing it tremble slightly, and clasped arm to arm with Tisamon, feeling the man's spines flex. 'You've no idea how good it is to see you,' he said. *I've missed having a mad killer by my side.* The thought made him laugh out loud, and he went to embrace Tynisa like a true father. But she took a step back, and then he noticed the sword and circle brooch she bore – saw in her haggard features the cost of that honour.

'Tynisa . . .'

'I live,' she told him flatly.

'The Mantis-kinden?'

'I live,' she said again.

Stenwold felt Arianna flinch at the thought. *A nation of Tisamons, how could that ever work?*

'And Collegium is still standing,' Tisamon observed. 'You Beetles will always surprise me.'

'I am told,' Stenwold said, 'that you are not entirely free of guilt in that.'

That dragged a smile from Tynisa. 'We didn't know if Teornis would get here. We didn't know if he would even try.'

'I am surprised,' Tisamon admitted. 'And at what cost is the city saved?'

Stenwold nodded. 'At least we are here to pay it. The Spider Aristos has saved Collegium, as much as anyone has, and we cannot deny him that.'

'The world,' Tisamon declared, 'has turned upside down.' His gaze sought out Arianna, recognizing her for the first time beyond the College student's robe. The claw was on his arm, as simple as that.

Stenwold put a hand on his shoulder as though he had not seen it, facing the man's hostility head-on. 'She has stood by me,' he said. 'She has saved my life and fought for my city, and she could have betrayed or killed me at any time. She is' – *Mine, she is mine* – 'loyal,' he finished, at last. 'And she did warn us of the Vekken, and we put that time to good use.'

'Trust comes slowly,' Tisamon agreed as Arianna regarded him cautiously.

'I see you didn't trust them enough to sail here with them,' Stenwold observed.

'As to that . . .' Tisamon looked sidelong at Tynisa, 'we had other engagements.'

'A little job to do,' Tynisa confirmed. 'We'll know, soon enough, if it has worked.'

Haldred was a Wasp of good family, a captain in the imperial army and a man whose preferred career path would have placed him securely in the imperial city of Capitas all his life. For a rising star in General Maxin's retinue, however, there came some tasks that could not be avoided. A great deal hung on this, he had been told, and success in achieving it would be remembered. His name would be commented on to the Emperor himself.

He had passed the camp of the Fourth Army with a brief word to General Alder, and now he was flying with his escort of soldiers over the scrubby terrain, looking for the camp of the Spider-kinden. He had a mouth full of fine words for them, and a pouch full of documents for alliance and mutual benefit. The Empire and the Spiderlands were two giants only just met, and still testing each other's strengths. This was one of only two places where they could now see directly eye to eye. Given a choice, Haldred would have preferred the city of Solarno, with all the decadence of the Spiderlands ranged beside a vast and beautiful lake stretching beyond the horizon, but instead he had been sent out here into the wilderness, and he had to make do with what orders came his way.

Dusk was closing on him, though, and he had yet to find the Spiders. It seemed impossible, in this barren country, for two hundred men to hide so effectively, but he had been searching for some time without success.

One of his men suddenly called out something, pointing, and Haldred saw what could be a group of men sheltering within a copse of trees. This must be them, he decided, and began to descend.

He and his men landed before the trees, and approached it cautiously. There was no fire alight, no obvious splendour of tents. He stepped within the shadow of the branches, still seeing nobody and nothing there.

'I speak for the Wasp Empire,' he called out. 'I have an embassy to the Spiderlands.'

'Do you indeed?' said a voice softly, almost in his ear. He jumped back – looking up into a pale, fierce face.

They were not Spider-kinden, after all. He was in a different net altogether.

In his tent, General Alder looked over the most recent numbers reported from his quartermasters by lanternlight. The supply situation was growing desperate. The Scorpion-kinden were slow in bringing supplies across the desert, and those caravans the Wasp-kinden themselves sent out were plagued by bandits, who were most likely the selfsame Scorpions. *Wretched barbarians*, Alder sneered inwardly. *Give me the order and I'd have the lot of them in shackles*. That order would not come in his lifetime, though, because the Dryclaw desert offered nothing the Empire wanted save a right of way, and even that meant just a quicker step than skirting it.

This interminable waiting was death to a fighting man:

each long day not knowing whether the next day would see them finally march. His men had made their temporary night camp when the cursed Spiders had first been sighted. They had been here ever since, sending back to Tark for supplies over and over again. The soldiers were restive, fighting amongst themselves, grown complacent. It was very bad for discipline, but Alder was an army man to the core and he needed his precise orders.

Now at last the imperial emissary had arrived, that preening little puppet Haldred, and surely tomorrow they would take the Merro road. His men meanwhile were out of all order, growing fat and idle.

Major Maan had stepped into the tent, saluting. 'You sent for me, sir?'

'Any sign of that diplomat, Major?'

'He must be staying with the Spiders, sir,' Maan reported, in a tone of voice that suggested envy. The splendour of Teornis's tent and servants, the womenfolk especially, had impressed him.

The Spider had moved around a lot, like any travelling noble, pitching his tent on hilltops and in hollows, now within sight of the sea, now virtually overlooking the Wasp camp. Alder did not trust him for a moment. 'Where is he camped tonight, Major? What have your scouts reported?'

'I've had no word, sir.'

Alder had sighed. 'Well find me word, Major.'

Rather than ceding him the privacy of his own tent, Maan simply sent a soldier off for a lieutenant of the watch, and then sat down obtrusively while they waited. When the lieutenant arrived it was a blessed relief.

'Your scouts, Lieutenant, have they reported on the Spider lord's current dwelling?' Maan asked him.

'They've not returned yet, sir.'

Alder narrowed his eyes. 'What, none of them?'

'My squad has not returned, sir,' the lieutenant repeated implacably.

'It's no great matter, Major, but when I ask a question I'd like an answer.'

Maan saluted and left the tent, with the lieutenant in tow. A short while later he was back.

'General, none of the scouts has returned.'

Alder stood slowly. 'What do you mean?'

'No scouts have returned, General,' Maan said, tongue licking his lips nervously. 'I'll let you know—'

'But it's dusk already,' Alder remarked. He put his head out of his tent and then corrected himself. 'It's dark. You're telling me that *none* of our scouts is in?'

Maan gaped at him. 'I . . . I have spoken to at least half of the watch lieutenants . . .'

Alder just stared at him and then went back inside his tent.

His swordbelt was hanging to one side and he went over to it and drew the blade.

At the periphery of the Wasp encampment, sentries patrolled outside a regular ring of lit torches, stopping to exchange a brief word whenever they met. They relied on the fires behind them for their night-vision, because Wasp-kinden were day creatures.

The first arrow came out of the night without warning, silent on chitin-shard fletchings, burying itself in a soldier's neck above the line of his armour. He gaped at it, spear falling from his hand, and fell, and the two sentries nearest to him just stared.

The sound of three hundred shafts splitting the dark air was just a whisper, just a whisper, until they struck.

General Alder heard the first screams as he emerged from his tent. 'What—?' he started, and stopped, the words drying on his lips. He could see, through the line of tents, the torches of the west perimeter and they were winking out, and there was now a wave of darkness surging into his camp. A wave of dark bodies that could see clearly by the waning of the moon and held blackened steel in their hands.

He heard officers try to sound the alarm, to call them to the defence, but he heard none of them even finish the sentence. Arrows were slicing down around him, punching randomly through the sides of tents, or picking off men as they struggled, half-armoured or even unarmed, into the open.

'To me!' Alder shouted. 'Form on me!'

'Form on the General!' Maan added his voice. 'All troops form up and—' Then he was down, clutching at an arrow that had gone so far through him it had pinned him to the ground.

There were soldiers enough, though, some in armour and some near-naked, and he saw the flashes of stings crackling into the tide of the attackers, and caught split-second revelations across their line. They were spread out, no disciplined block of troops, and he was aware of Wasps trying to form a line ahead of him, to defend him. It would not be enough, surely, though he still had no idea who was attacking his camp. *The Spider-kinden, it must be.*

He noticed the Ant-kinden of Captain Anadus formed up with more discipline, but they now were making a slow retreat, shields locked and manoeuvring between the tents, losing men to arrows even as they did so. If there had been more of them left from the siege of Tark then perhaps they could have made a difference, but now all that Anadus was trying to do was leave.

The invaders struck the Wasps' half-formed line and Alder's soldiers began to go down. He raised his blade and lunged forwards, parrying a rapier as it snaked towards him and, with a skill that belied his years, binding under the enemy thrust to drive the blade into his opponent. There was a further volley of flashes as several of his men fired their stings at once, and looking down he saw the face of a Mantis-kinden man ashen in death.

Mantids? he thought, utterly bewildered. *From the woods beyond Merro? What have we done to provoke them?* All around his camp was falling. The Mantids were in amongst the packed artillery now, firing whatever they could with oil spilled from the Wasps' own smashed lanterns. Major Grigan and his artificers were being hacked down even as they ran to douse the flames.

'Form up on me!' Alder shouted again, feeling his voice hoarse with the smoke that was heavy on the air. He saw another group of men trying to join up with his own, with Colonel Carvoc at their head, but they were getting whittled away like wood. They were still ten yards away when Carvoc himself reeled back with an arrow through him, and his squad immediately disintegrated.

Alder's sword came up swiftly, catching the curved blade of a claw as it sliced down on him, but then a spear drove into his side, shattering ribs and embedding itself deep into his body. He cried out and tried, with his last strength, to kill the man – no, the woman – before him, but the spear-wielder pinned him to the ground, stamping on his chest to free the spear-point and, as she passed over him with barely a pause, the Mantis woman stabbed again, this time through his throat.

'We asked them how many warriors Felyal could muster, all told,' Tynisa explained to Stenwold, 'and they thought about a thousand or fifteen hundred, meaning everyone except the children, really. And they agreed that even a thousand warriors could not hold off the army of Wasps that was out there, if it attacked, since it was an army of about twenty, thirty times that number.

'And then we asked them how many Wasps they could kill if *they* themselves attacked. Attacked without warning, at night, after a long wait had left the enemy distracted, bored . . .'

'And they thought about thirty each,' Tisamon finished, and he was smiling now, a particularly Mantis smile.

★

And across the field of the Wasp encampment the warriors of Felyal raged, and where they found Wasps or their allies they killed, never slowing or stopping or giving their foe any time to realize that the force that attacked them was barely an army at all. A mere warband a fraction of their size, but that ravaged through their tents with a ferocity born of long years of smouldering grudges against the Apt masters of the sunlit world.

They left nothing untouched. They were Mantis, so they took no prisoners, they kept no slaves. They expected no mercy and they gave none. When they came to the tent of Mercy's Daughters, Norsa faced them in its doorway, unarmed, and for a moment it seemed that she would turn them aside, but they were mad for blood, and not known for leniency, and neither healers nor wounded escaped their blades.

Those soldiers who escaped, for the Mantids were not equal to their boast in the end, would make conflicting and broken reports to their interrogators, and none would forget that night. Even those that questioned them would thereafter sleep uneasily, their imaginations fired by the dreams of blood and shadows, as though the night itself had teeth and they had fallen into its jaws.

Of the soldiers of the Fourth Army, the Barbs as they had been known, scarcely one in four survived.

Stenwold shook his head at this news. The Wasp army that had been ready to rampage up the coast was gone. Teornis had already told the story of how it had been held back, first by the Lord-Martial himself, and then by a close cousin of his whose face would pass, when suitably made-up, for Teornis's own, with a mere two hundred men. He had only hinted at other plans for the Fourth Army, because he did not wish to boast about matters still in the brewing.

Stenwold found that he was grinning at Tisamon. 'You chose a good time to show Tynisa her heritage.'

Tisamon did not smile in return. 'They will not fight for Collegium, Sten – but they will fight. The south coast road has gatekeepers, and the Wasps will come again.' The thought of that future was grim in Tisamon's eyes, and Stenwold was about to find some reassuring words to offer when Arianna plucked at his robe.

'Stenwold!'

She was staring back up the steps leading towards the Amphiophos entrance, which still saw a fair traffic even at this hour.

'What is it?' *Assassins,* he thought instantly. *Who has she recognized?*

'Stenwold, you want Thalric, don't you?'

'Yes, why?'

'Get soldiers, as many as you can,' she hissed. 'If you want him, you'll have to fight for him. Now, or it will be too late!'

Soldiers? When I have Tisamon. 'With me,' he growled, rushing back up the steps, and Tisamon was instantly in step with him, claw hinging out. He heard Tynisa and Arianna behind, knew that his ward would have her rapier clear. He felt much safer with these escorts than with a score of Parops's Ant-kinden.

'What is it? Tell me?' he demanded, as they clattered through the corridors of the Amphiophos.

'I saw her!' Arianna was saying. 'She's here for him!'

'Who?' Stenwold demanded, out of breath already.

'The Dragonfly! Tisamon knows!'

And she was suddenly ahead of them, standing before the guards of Thalric's suite, a Dragonfly woman, her cloak thrown back to reveal scintillating armour. The Beetle-kinden guards clearly did not know what to make of her, seeing her possibly as one of Teornis's foreign troops.

They had their shields half-up, frowning, and abruptly there was a long, straight sword in the woman's hands. The curtain to Thalric's chamber was drawn half-back, as though Felise had first tried to simply walk between them.

'Let me pass,' she demanded, in the tone of a final warning.

Stenwold shouted, 'Stop!' skidding to a halt beyond reach, or so he hoped, of that oddly-styled blade. Instantly she had shifted stance, the arc of her sword now covering the guards and Stenwold both, and for a second there was silence as the tension in the woman coiled up to a crisis.

'Lady Felise.' Tisamon had come to Stenwold's shoulder, claw at the ready, but there was a strange expression on his face.

The Dragonfly stared at him, something changing behind her features.

'Lady Felise,' Tisamon said slowly, 'we have met. Do you remember?'

'Did we fight?' she asked, almost in the voice of a child.

'You gave me that honour,' said the Mantis, giving the words special meaning only for him and for her.

Something shifted behind her face again, something trying to be heard, but then again it was that perfect mask, beautiful and terrible all at once, and the guards clutched at their maces and raised their shields. 'I have found my prize,' she said coldly. 'He is within this room. I will not let anything keep me from him. Not even you, Mantis.'

Tisamon's voice was a whisper. 'What . . . what's in the room, Sten?'

'Tisamon, please—'

'Because I *know* who she's hunting, Sten.'

There are better and easier ways to break this news to Tisamon, Stenwold reflected. The dreadful tension of the Dragonfly woman was like a shrill sound at the very edge of his hearing. Bloodshed was imminent.

'He's here,' he confirmed. 'Thalric is here. He gave himself up. He claims the Empire has cast him out and tried to kill him.'

'Does he indeed?' said Tisamon, without sympathy. 'This woman wants Thalric dead, Sten. She wants to cut his throat and probably dance in his ashes. I have no issue with that, myself.'

'We . . . need him,' Stenwold whispered. He could see the Dragonfly, Felise, standing perfectly still, focusing inwards and inwards. *I have seen that look before, in Tisamon.* There was another there as well, hanging back further down the hall, a long-haired Spider with a wry smile. Stenwold could see how they had gained access: the two of them, travelling together on this day, would seem like just more of the rescuers from across the seas.

'What is this?' Felise demanded, taking a better grip on her blade. 'Fight me or stand away from me. I will have his blood. I will have the blood of any that stand in my way.'

It was a gesture that always seemed a good idea at the time but never quite worked out so. Stenwold stepped forward and walked towards her. Past the two guards he caught a glimpse of Thalric inside his room. Something had gone out of the man, some hope of a last chance.

'Stenwold,' the Wasp said, half warning, half imploring, 'remember Cheerwell—'

Without warning the woman's sword was at Stenwold's neck. He looked into Felise's eyes and saw madness gathering there like stormclouds.

This was not a good idea. 'I am Master Stenwold Maker of Collegium. This man' – his nerve almost failed – 'is in my care. Why do you wish to kill him?'

The blade jumped, the edge cutting an inch of shallow blood. 'Ask him,' she hissed. 'Master Stenwold Maker of Collegium. If it is not enough that his people have raped my homeland and slain my people in their thousands, ask him what it is that he has done against me.'

Remember Che, the thought came. Thalric might be his only chance of seeing the girl again. 'Thalric?' he asked faintly.

'Stenwold, you need me.'

'Only if I can trust you for the truth,' Stenwold said flatly, and he saw something pass across Thalric's face. Here was a man in a trap of his own making. The Wasp knew what would now happen even before he spoke, and in that fatal moment Stenwold finally recognized some virtue there, beyond all the principles the Empire had built in him, because despite what would follow he said, 'I killed her children, Master Maker. The Empire wanted a certain noble Commonweal bloodline extinguished, and so I went into her castle and killed all her children. She had no sword then, when we surprised her. She was taken for a slave. I suppose she escaped.' Thalric's voice sounded flat, sick.

Stenwold pictured Che, either dead now or incarcerated in a Wasp cell, or at the mercies of their artificers, and he looked into Felise's face and reassessed her. This was the face, he decided, of a mother who had loved her children and who now wanted solely to avenge them.

I have no right, he knew, and he gestured to the guards, who stepped back in evident relief. Felise spared him one more brief glance before passing through the doorway.

Forty-One

Her captors had found a little cluster of farm buildings nearby, stone-built and solid, with a big storage cellar that they had cleared out, throwing away everything not immediately edible or useful. Che hoped that the farming family who had once lived here had been given the chance to flee before the black and gold storm.

In the cellar their artificers had been busy even before the battle, and wooden beams from a dismantled house had been used as bars to mark out a pen that would hold a dozen prisoners at most. A few dried stains of reddish-brown suggested she was not the first.

She was the only one now, though – the only prisoner they had taken out of those that had failed and fallen in the Battle of the Rails.

When she had tumbled from the stalled automotive, she had her blade ready in her hand, certain that death was moments away. She had imagined herself then as a Tisamon or a Salma, ready to die striking a blow and enjoy a soldier's honourable end.

But all around her the Wasps were swarming along the rails, blackening the sky above. These men, who had been fleeing so recently, were back, with a vengeance that could be sated only with blood. Everywhere, Wasp soldiers were stooping on the survivors to slaughter them. They hacked down the Sarnesh field surgeons whether or not they lifted blades against them. They killed the wounded, swiftly and brutally, just as their comrades were doing over all the battlefield.

She had felt the sword slip from her fingers, her mind filled with the horror of it, and she realized, then, that she had been lying to herself for a long time. This was the real face of war, and she could never be a true soldier.

Che had stood there motionless, unnoticed and unthreatened, with the Wasps massing back and forth all about her. It had been that total stillness that saved her, though her head had spun. The stillness, and her empty hands, until at last a Wasp had dropped before her, seeing a wide-eyed, unarmed Beetle girl, assuming her a slave, perhaps. He had called two of his comrades to wrestle her away, and she had not resisted them. A moment before, she had wanted to die as brave warriors died, but when she saw what that looked like, repeated over and over all around, she very much wanted to live.

She had not necessarily accomplished that, either. She had been confined in here more than a day, now, and they had given her water but no food. She could hear, from sounds above, that the Wasps were resetting their camp, and seemed in no hurry to chase the Sarnesh back to their city walls, but nobody had come to question her, or rescue her, or even to look at her.

Slavery, she told herself. Would it really be so bad? Perhaps some kind master would buy her. After all, she had a Collegium education. Perhaps she could teach Wasp children.

She knew that a life of slavery could be bad, and she knew equally that there were worse fates by far.

There was a rattle at the hatch above, chilling her heart, because her water bowl was still half-full.

There had been pitch-darkness in the cellar before, which would have been a terror to her if her Art had not penetrated it and allowed her to see. The sheet of sunlight that now splashed down the stone steps was a harsh glare at first, and she shaded her eyes. She heard sandalled feet descending and forced herself to look.

A Wasp soldier was peering doubtfully at her, by the bluish light of a mineral-fuel lantern.

'This is her,' he said, to someone standing above him, and then came all the way down to the cellar floor to make room.

The man following took the stairs awkwardly, limping and holding to the wall. He wore no Wasp uniform, being swathed instead in a hooded robe, and he seemed to need no lantern when he peered at her.

'Just one prisoner,' he said tiredly. 'Well the intelligencers will suffer more than I. And she will be theirs, I suspect, unless I press my claim on Malkan. You say she had some tools on her?'

'Only a few, sir,' the soldier below him said, 'not a full artificer's set, but she is a Beetle, sir. They're reckoned good with machines.'

'Not without proper tools, they're not,' grumbled the hooded man. 'She's probably a worthless slave or something. Or did I hear that the Sarnesh keep no slaves?' He glanced up at a third man who was standing higher on the steps, and obviously saw him shake his head. To Che this last imperial was just a slouching silhouette.

'You don't want her, then?' the soldier pressed, and Che felt her throat go dry. She had little idea of what they were talking about, but she feared what any Wasp intelligencer might do with her.

'Excuse me, sir,' she got out. 'I am a scholar of the College. I know history, politics, economics—'

'Are you an artificer?' asked the robed man sharply, as though speaking to an idiot child.

'I have studied mechanics a little . . .' She was crippled with honesty even at this moment.

For a moment he studied her. 'No. Let them rack her

for answers. I won't deprive General Malkan of her.' With halting steps he turned round and made his way back up towards the sunlight.

It was only when they had gone, and taken most of her hope with them, that she realized that they had not all been strangers.

Why here? It seemed impossible. The sight of her echoed in his mind. Che, down below behind the timber bars.

Oh, Totho could string a sequence of events together, surely. The horror of speculation was wondering what he did not know. Whose bodies now lay amongst the Sarnesh dead on the battlefield? Stenwold perhaps? Tynisa?

Perhaps the Moth Achaeos had perished too.

That thought sent an ugly little thrill through him. If Achaeos was dead . . .

But Che would be dead all too soon, once they had finished cutting and twisting her flesh. General Malkan's interrogators would undoubtedly want to know everything she could tell them about Sarn, in preparation for his next campaign.

Totho stood and watched Drephos in conversation with one of Malkan's officers. The general himself was conducting any communications through intermediaries at the moment. That was, Totho had realized eventually, because he was embarrassed. Anyone with eyes could see that Drephos had turned the battle for him, turned the iron tide at the point when Malkan's men were at their weakest. Drephos had broken the Ant advance and given the Wasps new heart.

Or rather, Totho thought wryly, *I did, and nobody knows.*

How happy he was for that, and it was not that Drephos had snatched the praise from him, but Totho had hidden away from it, for he had witnessed as closely as he cared the monstrous effects that his inventions had on meat and metal.

Amongst primitive peoples, like the Mantis-kinden, contracts and agreements were sealed with a drop of blood. Well, his contract with Drephos and the Empire was well and truly sealed. He was wading in it, up to his waist already, and with further still to go. And here was Che, suddenly come like his conscience to remind him of all that he had betrayed.

It would serve her right. He hardened his heart. She had never taken the time to think about what she was getting into. Or perhaps it would be a form of justice on Stenwold for sending his own niece into the tempest. Or on the wretched Moth for luring her from safety into this dangerous place. Justice for someone, surely. And that would make some sense of it all.

'Totho?'

He looked up sharply, seeing Kaszaat walking towards him with concern in her eyes.

'You're brooding more than usual. What's wrong?'

Now here was a woman worth his attention, he told himself. Not too proud to lie with a halfbreed. And she obviously cared about him.

Because Drephos told her to.

'Totho, what's wrong?'

She reached out, and he flinched away without thinking.

The look of hurt on her face could have been genuine, and he realized how much he had been poisoned by Drephos, by the Empire, so that he would never be able to be sure with her – or with anyone else – what was real and what was feigned. He had been adopted into a world where everything was weighed in objective scales, valued coldly and then put to work. His credit here was his artificer's skill and, though he had valued that more than anything, he found it was short measure for his whole life. He was now merely a pair of hands to make, a mind to create: not Totho of Collegium but some working annexe to Drephos's ambition.

And is that so bad? Because he had lived his entire life, surely, on similar terms. He had worked with the debased currency that his mixed blood could buy him. He had worked twice as hard as his peers, getting half as far. Men with less talent at their graduation than he had possessed from the start had walked straight from the College into prestigious positions of wealth and respect, whereas he, with only real skill to his name, had been accorded nothing. Even amongst Che and Stenwold and the rest he had been the fifth wheel that nobody really needed.

Well, at least here he *was* needed, and if he was to be valued merely as a commodity, at least Drephos had placed that value high enough to spare Salma's life in exchange.

But that deal was done, and he had nothing left to barter for Che. *I cannot save her.*

A simple thing to say, and surprisingly easy.

I cannot just let her die, without a word.

And there was the barb that now caught him. Must he plunge a blade into his own guts by revealing to her what he had become? Or instead live with that emptiness inside him, that lack of a final meeting with her before the end? *Or do I merely want her to see that at last I've made something of my life?*

He clenched his fists, and his mind conjured up the last throes of the doomed Sarnesh charge, bright blood springing from sheared metal as the bolts drove home.

I am become the destroyer. What can I not do? What limits me now?

Che heard the hatch move, but no sun flooded in. Clearly night had come and she had not realized.

One man only, this time, with a covered lantern giving out a fickle light, but her eyes saw him well enough.

She could not be sure of his identity until he had stopped. It was a young man, broad-shouldered and sturdy-framed and marked by mixed blood, and she did not quite know him. She saw the trappings: a toolbelt such as he had always wanted and could never afford, black and gold clothes, a sword and a rank badge. She recognized none of that. It was only when he stood in the cellar, on the other side of the bars, that she was sure.

'Totho . . . ?' Her voice emerged in a quaver, not quite believing what she saw. 'Is it you? It can't be you.'

He stared at her, and his features were harder than she remembered. Still, there had been harsh times for both of them since they last parted.

'Totho, don't just stand there. You have to let me out. You must know what they'll do to me.'

His face tightened further. 'I don't have the keys,' he muttered, and continued to stare.

'Totho . . . what are you doing here?' she asked. 'You went off to Tark . . . why are you wearing that . . . uniform?'

'Because it is mine,' he stated, and she began to feel her brief surge of hope draining away.

'You mean . . . how long?'

He realized that she was seeing their history together unravel backwards, trying to recast him as a spy during all that time, because poor Che didn't realize that people changed.

'Since Tark,' he said. He found it mattered to him that she knew she had already cast him off before he had found his new calling.

'But why?' she said, still trying to whisper but her indignation getting the better of her. 'They're the enemy, Totho! They're monsters!'

He felt his anger grow in him. 'I did it to save Salma,' he snapped, 'because otherwise they would have killed him. Or don't you think that was worth it? Perhaps I should have just died alongside him.'

'But that's . . .' She gaped at him. 'But you're free,' she said, still determinedly marching up the wrong street. 'You could run, surely, run to Collegium and tell them what happened here.'

'You have absolutely no idea what happened here.' He felt she was trivializing the sacrifice he had made, and suddenly he was on fire with it. He had never impressed her as a companion, as a warrior, most certainly not as a prospective lover, for all that she had once been life and breath to him. 'Do you want to know,' he asked her, voice shaking slightly, 'what *happened* here?'

'I don't understand, Totho.'

'*I* happened here, Che. That's the simplest thing. Those dead Ants out there – I killed them. When the city of Sarn falls it is I who will break it. When this army or another like it is at the gates of Collegium, it will be *me*, do you understand? When the Lowlands becomes just the western wing of the Empire, then by rights my name should be on the maps.'

She was backing away from the wooden bars. 'Totho?'

'All my doing, Che.' As she retreated so he had moved up to the bars himself, gripping them as though he were the prisoner here. 'What your uncle dismissed as a toy back in Collegium, they have made into a weapon here. You remember how I always wanted to make weapons? Well now it's happened, and my weapons win wars.'

Backing against the far wall of her cell, she stared and saw him at last, as not friend, nor lover, but enemy.

'You?'

'All me.' Now he had her attention, his lust for recognition was leaching out of him, leaving only a hollow bitterness. 'So I can't just walk away from this, Che. I have *become* this. I have paid in blood, and none of it my own.'

'Oh, Totho . . .'

He waited for her condemnation that he surely deserved, the last gasp of her defiance before the interrogators pried it out of her.

'I'm sorry,' she said. 'I'm so sorry.' And the expression

on her face told him, beyond any shadow or suspicion, that her concern was purely for him, for her lost friend.

Something was building in him, that hurt worse than burning, but he clamped down on it. He was Drephos's apprentice. There was no emotion he could not master. 'Stop saying that.' He heard his voice shake. 'I've found my place now. There's nothing to be sorry for. Feel sorry for yourself. You know what they'll do to you.' In his mind arose the words, from the depths of his own soul. *What they will do to her is nothing, compared to what they have done to me.*

She was moving back to the bars now, and one hand slightly extended, as if to touch his own. He suddenly felt that, if he was to feel her skin on his, he might die. He stumbled backwards, until he felt the incline of the steps behind him.

'It's over,' he said. 'Everything's over.' He tried to suppress the next words, but they forced themselves out anyway. 'I'm sorry, Che. I'm sorry it turned out like this.'

She was standing at the bars when he left her, and the lantern's last shine glinted on the tracks down her face, and he thought they would be the only tears ever shed for him.

And where is the damned box? was the thought of Uctebri the Sarcad, stalking the bounds of his comfortable cell. It had gone wrong. Not irretrievably wrong, but wrong nonetheless.

He had been at pains to keep his antennae out, groping around for the Shadow Box's location. It had mouldered in Collegium for a long time, but the Darakyon itself was becoming restive. It had sensed his interest and there was always the chance that it would find some champion for its cause. *Reaching so far into the Lowlands is dangerous,* his own people would have told him, had he cared to consult them. *The Moth-kinden have not forgotten us.*

No, that was true. In some decaying archive of Tharn or

Dorax would be found the name of the Mosquito-kinden, and the time when the Moths broke them, hunted them down, and tried their best to wipe his entire kinden from history. These days the Moths had other matters on their minds, though, so a clever old man might stretch his arm as far as Collegium and cause no alarm, sound no warnings, especially if that old man was working through an Empire blinded to the magical world by its own Aptitude.

But the Empire itself was being coy. They had not sent some squad of soldiers or Rekef men to retrieve the box. The political situation, the distances, had all militated against that strategy. Instead they had hired hunters.

And one of those hunters knows too much. Uctebri had felt the touch of her mind, just briefly. Someone with training, with a gift for sly magic, was now in possession of his prize. In that brief contact of minds the acrid taste of betrayal was in his mouth. *She will not bring it to me. She recognizes its value.*

But she could not hide it, not a thing of that power, now that it had been awakened. He could sense her moving about, with that appallingly powerful treasure in her hands. Her deceits would hide her exact whereabouts, but he could have drawn a circle on a map and known for sure that she was within it.

He heard movement outside, knew before the man even entered that it was the Emperor. The ruler of the Wasps was in an ugly mood.

'Your Imperial Majesty, you honour me with your presence.' Uctebri the Sarcad bowed sinuously as the Emperor marched into his new suite of rooms.

'We demand to know what progress you have made,' snarled Alvdan the Second. General Maxin had come in behind him, but stood at the door as though he was no more than a guard. Alvdan had found himself relying more and more on that man recently, what with troubles in the Lowlands and similar. He reserved his own main attention for this, though: the Mosquito's ritual that would elevate him beyond the misery of his father and his grandfather, and remove from him the one blight that had constantly mocked his reign and stolen his joy.

The matter of his succession: which potential traitor, from a nest of venomous things, should he take to his bosom, or even breed himself? His successor, the heir that would stand like an executioner beside his throne as soon as the child was born or the decision made. But if Uctebri's ritual should achieve its impossible end, he need never worry about his successor again, because he would need none. He would live for ever.

He was impatient to start.

'Your Imperial Majesty, it wants but the time, the most auspicious date.' The Mosquito glanced between the Emperor and General Maxin. 'And the box, of course. We must have the box. Gifts such as you seek must be had only with the correct materials.'

'It is coming,' the Emperor said. 'Our agents carry it to us even now.'

'I hesitate to correct His Majesty in his proclamation,' said Uctebri, turning to the nearest wall to make another few chalk scratches.

'You are not to use your sarcasm on us, creature,' Alvdan snapped. 'Explain yourself.'

'I am naturally concerned at the progress of this most puissant gem, Great Majesty, but my arts have told me that all is not well. Your agents have miscarried, have been suborned or have turned traitor, for the box is no longer being fetched here.'

'General?' Alvdan demanded, suddenly unsure. This news was as impossible as the mooted ritual, but he had already accepted *that* as possible, and so how could he feel sure that this creature could not know?

'In truth, Your Imperial Majesty,' Maxin said slowly, 'I had expected before now to hear from my agents.'

'But this is not good enough,' Alvdan reproached him angrily. 'If we must possess this thing then we will have it. Uctebri, where is it now? Your arts have surely furnished you with that knowledge?' He tried to make his tone mocking, but his uncertainty sounded through it.

'It has gone into the lawless lands around Lake Limnia, where the Skater-kinden live and where many things are lost and found – or change hands. My arts, alas, can be no more exact.'

'You have heard,' Alvdan turned to General Maxin. 'Send your hunters there. Stop at nothing. Obliterate every cursed Skater if you have to.'

'As you wish, Your Majesty,' replied Maxin.

'And, Worshipful Majesty, if I might ask . . .' Uctebri began softly.

'What is it? Speak.'

'I require the opportunity to further examine your sister in closer detail.'

Alvdan smiled. 'Oh, as close as you wish, monster. Of all the things I have to give you, she is least precious by far. I give her to you for whatever you need.'

The Mosquito's answering smile contained a hard edge that promised those words would not be forgotten.

Forty-Two

Thalric loosed his sting at her even as she came into the room, and Stenwold assumed it was over then, an absurd anticlimax. The impact rocked her back, but the crackling energy just scattered from her glittering armour, leaving black marks like soot. Then she was on him.

He had the table between them and Stenwold saw him try to get up quickly, and tumble backwards over the chair, face suddenly twisting in agony as his unhealed wound racked him with pain. With a single downward swing Felise cut the table in two, shearing the wood across the grain in a way Stenwold would not have thought possible.

Thalric had lurched to his feet, and his hands spat fire again, but she turned, shielding her face with her pauldron and, although she had to brace herself against it, again the crackling blast just danced off her mail.

If Thalric had been whole and well, he might have stood a chance. He was a resourceful man, but his wounds hobbled him. Even this much exertion had a fresh spot of blood leaking through his tunic. When he raised his arm again the strange sword nearly took the hand from his wrist, instead laying open the skin along the back of it. Thalric hissed, and went for her, and in a moment of cool decision she reversed the sword and smashed him across the face with the pommel.

He fell back against the wall and slid to the floor, dazed,

and she thrust the sword into one tilted half of the table, as sickle-claws folded out from her thumbs.

He had his uninjured hand extended at her defensively, but she lanced it through the palm with a lightning jab of one claw and he gasped in pain and withdrew it. For a second she regarded her talons, one bloody and one clean.

She placed them, very gently, so that they pricked him in the hollows beneath his jaw, and began to force him upright. For a moment he seemed about to resist, but then, as they drew blood, he was struggling to his feet, digging at the wall with his elbows for purchase until at last he was standing, face to face with her at last, and so close they might be lovers.

She showed no expression.

Stenwold stood at the doorway with Tisamon watching over his shoulder, but now someone was pushing in on the other side of him. It was Felise's Spider-kinden companion.

'Who are you, anyway?' the Beetle asked him, as Felise held Thalric by the points of her thumbs, staring into his face.

'Destrachis, doctor.' The Spider was watching the woman intently, waiting for something.

Thalric studied the face of his antagonist, pushing his thoughts through the pain in his side, the pain of his hands. 'Before you kill me,' he said, and even that drew some fresh blood as his throat worked against her talons, 'tell me one thing.'

Her face neither denied nor permitted his request.

'What will you do next?' His last gambit, his last chance, and once the words were out he closed his eyes and waited.

Destrachis leaned forward, but Felise made no move. There was no sign that she had even heard the words.

'What is going on here?' Stenwold demanded in a hoarse whisper.

'This man Thalric has a good mind,' Destrachis said. 'He has got to the heart of it.'

'Next?' came the voice of Felise, uttering the word as though it was wholly unfamiliar to her.

'We took him outside your city, you see,' Destrachis went on. 'But he was near-dead, and so instead of killing him she had me patch him up and send him on ahead. Because revenge on a dying man was not what she was looking for.'

'This is hardly better,' Tisamon observed from behind.

'He fought back this time.' Destrachis shrugged. 'Now we must see if she can bring it to a close.'

'Spider, I should have slain you before,' said Felise, still holding Thalric up on his toes, holding her perfect pose without the slightest tremor. 'What is this Wasp to you?'

'Nothing,' Destrachis said. 'I have never been the Empire's.'

'But you are not mine either,' she said. 'Who is it that pays you, Spider?'

Destrachis pursed his lips. 'Must there be someone?'

'You are no gangster from Helleron, and it was no mere chance that we met. Do not take me for a fool.'

'Or I will be "next"?' Destrachis wondered aloud. His voice was casual, but Stenwold could see how tight his face had become with controlling his expression. 'But you're right, of course. I spun my way into the fiefdoms of Helleron. I engineered it so that I would travel with you.'

Stenwold could see Thalric watching with the utter concentration of a man whose life is being extended by every word spoken.

'Mantis warrior,' Felise said. 'If I asked you to slay that Spider there, would you do it?'

'Without hesitation,' Tisamon said, and Destrachis went pale all of a sudden, feeling a subtle change of stance in the man beside him. The claw was abruptly raised to hover over Stenwold's back, the point pricking the nape of the Spider's neck. Stenwold himself had gone very still. He had been about to protest, to remind them that they were in

Collegium, in the very Amphiophos – but they were not. At least Felise and Tisamon and Destrachis were not. The place they shared was infinitely older, where such things as this were done.

'If he gives me no answer, you may slay him,' Felise decided. She was still staring into Thalric's face, had not once taken her eyes off him. 'Who has hired you to plague me, Destrachis?'

'Arante Destraii, your aunt,' Destrachis said, still holding tenuously on to calm. 'Ask me no more questions, Felise.'

'I do not believe that,' she said. 'Shall I tell the Mantis to kill you? Tell me the truth. Tell it all.'

'Please, Felise, you do not—'

Thalric hissed in pain as her claws dug into him a little, and Felise got out, 'Mantis—'

'Wait!' Destrachis got out. 'You will kill me if I tell you, and have me killed if I do not. Is that justice?'

'Why is it that only the unjust cry for justice?' Tisamon said. His claw twitched, drawing a spot of blood.

Stenwold felt himself trapped in a world he suddenly did not understand. 'What is going on?' he asked.

'Precisely, Beetle-kinden. Explain all, Destrachis.'

'I am hired by your family,' he said quickly, 'and that is no more than the truth. Not your husband's noble line, for the Wasps made sure no drop of his bloodline remained. Your own family was not great enough to be extinguished, so you were taken alive. Do you remember being a prisoner of the Empire, Felise?'

'I was never a prisoner.'

'Of course you were, and you were to be a slave, but the Arantes rescued you and . . .' He stuttered to silence.

'Speak!' she commanded.

'You were . . . broken.' He waited to see if the words would kill him. 'You were not well, in your mind. So your own family took you into their house and hired doctors to make you well, but we . . . they could not. They tried so many ways, until eventually one used an ancient craft to bring your mind back to the place where it had snapped, and stitch that broken end onto the present day – or thus I can best describe it. Shall I go on?'

She remained silent, but Tisamon shifted behind him, and so Destrachis continued. 'It did not go well. It was not well done . . . better not to have meddled, would be my opinion now. But you remembered, at least, the name and face of the man who had done those atrocities to you, and you determined you would have your revenge, whatever the cost. Your family were concerned. They . . .' And he stopped again, and Stenwold was surprised to see the Spider's eyes glitter with tears. 'Felise . . .'

'I remember,' she said slowly. Thalric saw something surface then in her eyes, and she looked at him anew. 'I remember you now. You are the man who slew my children.'

He could not nod, would not speak, but something in his face confirmed it.

'I remember,' she said again. 'What have I done?' She took her hands away abruptly, looking back at the bisected table, at the upright sword, as though they were quite strange to her.

Thalric, shifted, sagging an inch, and faster than Stenwold could follow she whirled back to him, thumb jabbing at his face. It raked a line of blood down his cheek, but that was all.

'Why can I not kill you?' she screamed at him. Her clawed hands hovered right before his face, twitching and shaking, but still she could not strike. In the echo of that cry her onlookers were silent. Stenwold saw, in sidelong glances, the same stricken expression appear on the faces of both Tisamon and Destrachis.

Thalric let out a long, slow breath. 'Because I'm all you've got,' he replied between gritted teeth. 'I wondered that, when you had me before. How many chances do you need? I'm right here now, so why not just do it? If you want me, what better chance can you possibly look for?'

In a voice almost lost, in the utter silence that followed, she whispered, 'Help me.'

Destrachis moved forwards solicitously, but it was Tisamon who pushed past to clasp her by the shoulders. Her claws twitched at him but never reached him, although he made no move to stop her.

'Come,' he said. 'I shall find you some food and drink, then a bed.' He looked back at Thalric. 'This man shall die at your command, I swear it.'

He led her from the room, pausing only to look Destrachis straight in the face. The Mantis made no threats, though, and after a moment looked away.

They did not come for Che the day after that, either, and she was even provided with a scant meal of soup and broken biscuit. The Wasp army camp become slowly a more permanent affair. She heard the sounds of rough carpentry overhead and guessed that the farmhouse was being extended and fortified. She kept her ears open because, if she could somehow later speak to her friends, she wanted to have something to report to them.

General Malkan, she overheard from the guards, was not moving the army onwards. Though hot-blooded, he was no fool. The casualties the Seventh had sustained meant that they would stand little enough chance before the walls of Sarn, even if Sarn stood alone. What she learned hardly raised the spirits, but it did give some small sliver of satisfaction.

And Sarn was unlikely to be standing alone. Malkan and his officers must be concerned enough about that for the news to filter down to the lowest and the most luckless in their army and, through their bitter gossip, to Che.

Collegium was free of the Vekken, she also learned, and could therefore lend aid to Sarn if needed. Moreover there were fearful whispers of the Ant-kinden's newest allies. Word was out about the Ancient League and the soldiers were rife with rumours of some age-old secret society binding all the Inapt of the west together, which the Empire's presence had now brought into the light. Like all Apt races the Wasps had their dark past, when the old kinden had terrorized them with wizardry and nightmares, and some vestige of that remained even now. There was a current of fear running through the Seventh at the thought of having to confront such a thing as the Ancient League.

The more level-headed, however, put the problem as Malkan would see it: if, even with an army at full strength, he pitched against the walls of Sarn, the warriors of Etheryon and Nethyon could simply swarm down from the north, catching him in a pincer movement. If he attacked them first, the Sarnesh would sally forth from their city. It was not the individual elements, but their combination, that concerned him.

I did this, Che thought to herself. Though she would meet her fate soon enough at the hands of the Empire's minions, she would at least have the satisfaction of knowing that she had accomplished so much. Faced with the resistance she had helped to build, the Seventh was now going nowhere, merely waiting for another army to be freed to aid it and the Fourth in the conquest of the Lowlands.

Yet she had heard more recently that some problem had arisen with the Fourth and that messengers were not arriving as expected.

In lieu of better information or opportunity, the Wasps were knuckling down and waiting, and their energies were now invested in making their camp defensible. For this entire day they had therefore not been able to spare an artificer interrogator to rack poor Cheerwell, or perhaps they were waiting for the right torture machinery to be sent down the rail from Helleron.

On one occasion a short, dark woman of a kinden Che

did not recognize came down and stared at her with hostile eyes for some time, before returning up to the sunlight without uttering a word.

Then the bustle of the camp quieted at last and the conversation she could make out from above was that of sentries only, so she knew it must be night again – and she had survived another day.

I will resist. I will fight. I will fly. But she knew she would do none of these things. She had not that kind of strength.

I wish I could have seen Salma once more. Last time she had been behind bars, he had been there with her, providing her with a source of resilience to draw on, and she was not enough on her own, she realized.

There was a rough sound as the hatch opened, but for a long while nobody entered. Then she caught the faintest gleam of a shuttered lantern and Totho, still in Wasp uniform, came stomping down the steps. As before, he simply stopped and stared at her.

'I'm still here,' she said unnecessarily.

'Do you want to talk?' he asked. A sharp reply came to her tongue, but she realized that, yes, she did. Another human voice, in whatever circumstances.

'Please,' she said.

'We've . . . grown up, at last, don't you think?' He seated himself on the lowest step, right across the room from her, but the stone walls carried his voice perfectly.

'Is that what this is?' They had hatched out of the College, with its protective walls, and into a harsher world than they had dreamed of. 'I'm not fond of it.'

'It's about making choices,' he said. 'Or . . . that's how I see it.'

'You've made your choice, clearly' she said, too quickly, and instantly regretted it. She saw a shadow pass across his face, and for a moment he seemed about to rise and go, but in the end it all washed past him, just as with the Totho she knew of old.

'Do you know where the others are now?' he asked.

'Is this some kind of interrogation?'

His lip curled. 'Do you think the Empire gives a bent cog where a few graduates of the College are?'

'They were all still in Collegium, when I left: I mean Stenwold and Tynisa, and Tisamon. Scuto must be back there by now, though he came to Sarn with us at first.' She was about to name Achaeos too, but decided better of it.

'I'd give a lot to be back there, with none of this having happened.' He frowned. 'But on the other hand . . .'

'What, Totho?' she demanded. 'What do you have here, amongst these monsters?'

'A purpose,' he said, and after a pause, 'Che, back then . . . did you ever . . . could you have, if I had been . . . bolder . . . could you have loved me, ever?'

'I always loved you,' she said simply. 'But not as you mean, not as you wanted. I'm sorry, Totho. I wish I could say something else. I wish I could lie to you about that, but . . . I owe you the truth. You were always my friend, and maybe I took you for granted, but . . . not that.'

He sat for a long time as the minutes of the night passed them by, his hands clasped together, without any expression she could interpret, until at last, without a word, he turned and went back up.

She sagged away from the bars, wondering if a lie, even a forced and obvious one, might have bought her something more.

Then he was back, with something slung over his shoulder. He dumped it – a sack, she now saw – on the cellar floor, and went over to the bars. He looked only at the lock. The Wasps had made a hurried job of these cells, and the door was a section of heavy lattice that could be lifted out, secured by bars merely padlocked into place, nothing too complicated.

He opened the shutters on his lantern and took some rods from his toolstrip, crouching down by the first lock. It had been a matter of constant dismay to the College masters how many of their students learned to pick locks, until no Master's office, private chamber or strongbox was safe from the pranks of their young scholars. Totho had never been the prankish kind, but he made up for that with his understanding.

'The problem is, Master Drephos looks at people and sees meat,' he said, as if to himself. 'Something to test machines on. Life has no value for him, and I could come to appreciate that. See the world like that, and you don't get hurt all the time. I hurt all the time, you see, because I haven't let go. Let go of you.'

The first lock sprang open, and he stood to attend to the second.

'You see,' he went on, 'it doesn't matter what you feel about me. Because I can't seem to shake myself free of you. I don't think any Spider temptress, any cursed charlatan-magician or Butterfly dancer could have her hooks in as deep as yours are in me. Because I still love you, despite everything, and you came just at the right time to destroy my life one last time.'

And the second lock came free, and he lifted out the lattice with a grunt of effort. Not knowing what to say, she slipped out of her cage.

'Can you get yourself out of the camp?' he asked. 'I can't help you there but in the sack I've put food and water, and a uniform, too. Mostly they'll just see another Auxillian, but you'll have to creep past the sentries, and if they catch you . . . well.'

'I won't reveal who freed me,' she said hurriedly.

'You will once they ask hard enough.' His face was bleak.

'Are they watching the skies?'

'No, not so much. They're expecting Sarnesh heading down the rail line, if anything.'

'Then I'll fly out,' she said, and saw his surprise. 'But you . . . you can get past them, can't you?'

'No.'

'Totho, you have to come with me.'

'No,' he said. There was no give in him. 'Once you are gone, I have no further ties. I will die, if they find me out, or I will live on here as Drephos's apprentice, devising newer and better ways of turning men into meat.'

'Totho, you're mad! You have to come with me back to Collegium!'

'Collegium has nothing to interest me any more. Not unless I come to it with an army,' he told her.

She felt her blood turn to ice, looking into that so-familiar face and seeing only a stranger.

'But because I do seem to be a traitor by nature, I have still one betrayal left to make. Or perhaps you will see it as one last act of loyalty – to you and Stenwold.'

'Totho—'

'Listen.' He reached into his tunic and produced a scroll, rolled up and then pressed flat. 'If you do manage to escape, you must take this to Stenwold. Or maybe to Sarn.'

'What is it?'

'The design for my snapbow,' he said. 'The weapon that broke the Sarnesh.'

She took it hesitantly, as though it might burn her. 'You realize what you're doing,' she said softly. 'You know what this means.'

'It means I am giving the Lowlands a chance,' he said. 'A small chance and no more. You'd better change clothes, Che. You don't have as much time as you think.'

He watched her as she changed, and she wondered if he was considering some other future in which she donned this uniform for real, and stayed with him just as she had pleaded for him to go with her.

Forty-Three

She stood at the east end of Collegium docks, charred wood crunching beneath her feet, knowing there was all too little time to do what she must.

Down the line of the wharves they were already cutting out the worst of the damage, replacing it with good treated wood, sinking new piles for piers with machines she had never seen before and could not comprehend. These folk were nothing if not industrious, and there was building work like this going on all over the city, not just replacement but improvement.

Felise Mienn stared down into the water. Collegium was a deep-water port and it was black down there, a vertical drop providing enough draft for the bulkiest freighter. What secrets must be buried there, in the silt deep below: what forgotten bones and treasures?

Destrachis would be looking for her, she was aware, but perhaps he would not think of looking here until it was too late. She wished she had not made him speak up.

Thalric had been right when he asked her what came next. Her future, as she had been able to imagine it, ended with his death, so what could she do after that? Once he was dead nothing would have changed, the dead would not be revived, and she would have to turn away from a blank and pointless future to confront the past.

The past was a gnawing horror to her, and just as she

had chased Thalric all across the Lowlands, so it had been chasing her.

What had been left unsaid? Destrachis could have spoken more – she could feel the shape of it, though her mind denied her the details. What else was left to know?

Far better not to know. If she stepped off here, the water would embrace her like a lover and draw her down. Her armour would fill with it and, even if her volatile mind changed yet again, there would be nothing she could do to resist. She would finally have taken her fate in her own hands. Let Thalric live, because he would not be able to hurt her any further.

Her reflection was faint in the water rippling below. She could see the outline of her shoulders, her draped cloak. Her face, though, was just a dark oval.

She stepped forwards to let her momentum topple her towards the sea.

Someone caught her cloak by its trailing edge and hauled her back. For a moment she was suspended ludicrously, at some bizarre angle, and then she felt rage at him, the wretched doctor her family had set on her, and her wings exploded from her back and she turned and stooped on him with claws bared.

She had lashed out at him three times before she realized this was not Destrachis. Instead it was the Mantis Tisamon who was dodging backwards, although a shallow line across his forehead bore witness to her first strike.

She froze instantly, and Tisamon fell back into a defensive stance, waiting for her. On the periphery of their attention, a dozen dockworkers were staring at them, unsure whether this was a fight to the death or just some kind of theatre.

'Why?' she demanded, as though he had done something terrible to her.

'Because you are worth more than this,' he replied.

'You do not know that.'

'I know. I have spoken with the Spider doctor and he has told me many things.' The knowledge Tisamon had been given sat heavily on him, for the story Felise had choked out of Destrachis was but one half of it.

Her golden skin had turned pale now. 'No, you cannot . . .'

'You understand what that means,' he insisted, and though he had never stinted at cruelty before, he winced now. 'You cannot wash it away with your own death. Nor can you blot out the knowledge by killing that Spider creature. You cannot even achieve it by killing Thalric – though that would be a service to everyone. *I* now know, and I would rather I did not, but I *do* know. To take that knowledge from the world you must kill me, before you cast your own life away.' Destrachis's conclusion of the tale was raw in Tisamon's memory: how Felise, having awakened with the thought of Thalric's death obsessive in her mind, had found herself barred up, with her room in her family's house made into an asylum to protect her from herself.

And she had killed them, all the other doctors and, more than that, she had with her own hands made herself the last of her line. Her aunt, her cousins, all left dead at her hands, as she strode through her own house in blind fury wielding her husband's sword.

He was poised to act, knowing his clawed gauntlet was his to call on the moment she drew blade.

Instead, she said, 'I don't wish to kill you. I don't understand you. What is it you feel?'

Her face was all confusion, and that touched him. 'I had a love, Felise Mienn, as you have had, and just as yours was taken, the Wasps took mine from me. We are alike, then, and so I think I understand you, perhaps even better than your Spider does. If you seek a purpose, then the Empire still stands and we must fight it. I would be honoured to fight beside you.'

Her stance softened noticeably, and at last he allowed himself to relax.

It was good to find a time and place when messengers were not currently seeking him out, or at least if they were they were not finding him. Now it was just Stenwold and Arianna dodging the public acclaim that so many other Assemblers were soaking up whether they had earned it or not.

But Stenwold was not a politician by choice. He was a soldier, an agent, a spymaster, all in one, and he played his own games that had never needed any public approval.

The game was at a halt, for now, the pieces patiently waiting. The Wasp army had not assaulted Sarn, or not according to the last messenger's report. The Fourth was in no position to assault anything, so Merro and Egel were spared Wasp occupation. Teornis had sent messengers back to his family and its allies, urging them to strengthen the border, and with word of the Collegium concessions too, just to sweeten the pot. He was a likeable man, professionally so, though Stenwold was not sure whether to like him or not.

Achaeos had awakened at last, though still very weak. He had been frantic about something, not Che's fate but something else, something he would not quite explain to Stenwold. He had begun asking for Tisamon, instead, but the Mantis was off somewhere on his own inscrutable errands. Stenwold had his own plans for Tisamon. The Mantis and his daughter would go with Thalric, to see if they could track down Che. Stenwold had no genuine trust in Thalric of the Rekef, but Tisamon and Tynisa would keep him in check if anyone could.

For now there was a pause, a heartfelt pause, in all that business, and he had brought Arianna to one of the best-kept secrets of the Amphiophos. Behind the domed building itself there was a garden, walled so high that it was always in the shade, and yet the artificer's art, with glass and lenses, had funnelled the sun there, so that plants from all across the Lowlands thrived in a wild tangle that the gardeners daily needed to cut back. Here little pumps made water run as though a natural stream passed through, and there were statues that had been old when the Moths fled the city, and stone seats and, by tradition, nobody raised their voices or quarrelled here.

The rain was spotting down through the broad gaps between the glass but there was shelter enough amid the trees, and Stenwold took Arianna to a lichen-dusted seat, where she looked about her in astonishment.

'I'd never even heard of this place,' she said.

'The Assembly prefer not to talk about it overmuch. A little selfishness, I think, that can at least be understood. I always thought this was the only worthwhile reward of belonging to their ranks, though I never had the time to appreciate it. And I won't have any time again, I'm sure. Tomorrow the war begins anew for me.'

'For me as well then,' she said.

'I wouldn't ask it of you.'

'And you wouldn't have to. I'll fight your war, Sten, even if all that means is being there for you when you need me.'

He looked at her and, out of habit, thought, *But can I trust you?* He realized though, that he did trust her, and the final piece of that had fallen into place not when she saved his life at the Briskall place, but when Balkus had accepted her. He decided that Balkus, that big, solid and unimaginative man, could see more clearly than Stenwold himself on this subject.

'Stenwold,' Arianna said, and when he turned to look at her, her eyes held a warning in them. 'We're being watched. I'm sure of it.'

He stood swiftly. 'Some other Assembler, no doubt.' But he did not believe that.

Then a voice came from amid the tangled undergrowth. 'I could have put an arrow in your head, old man. Not that there's much chance you'd notice.'

Stenwold reached for his sword and discovered that, yes, he still wore it at his waist, so familiar now that he donned it automatically. It slid easily from its scabbard. 'How did you get in here?'

The sword was not all that was familiar. He knew the voice too, when it replied, 'I got in here because I'm a Fly and your clumsy pack of kinden don't even understand what 'fly' means.'

The speaker emerged: a bald-headed little man with his ugly face and knowing smile, and Stenwold said, 'Nero?' in tones of sheer disbelief.

'It's been a while, Sten. Who's the lady?'

'This is Arianna,' and the awkward pause as he thought of how to introduce her obviously told Nero all he needed to know, for the mocking smile was even broader now. 'And this is, Nero, the artist,' Stenwold explained to her awkwardly.

Nero grinned at Stenwold. 'You get bigger and fatter every time I see you.'

'And you're still ugly.' Stenwold's retort came without hesitation from twenty years away. 'You've no idea how good it is to see you. Why are you here? Are you staying long?'

'Just a messenger boy, me,' Nero explained. 'With a message from a friend of yours, though, and there's a whole cartload of news, so you and your lady better sit back down and listen.'

In the darkness that she could now dismiss with a thought it had been remarkably easy to break away from the Wasp camp. With Totho watching, she had simply tiptoed past the occasional Wasp sentry, invisible in her uniform to men who saw Auxillians merely as slaves – ubiquitous and acceptable. When she had got in sight of the camp's perimeter she had waited carefully until nobody was looking her way, then simply taken off, let her wings lift her high, over the ring of torches and sentries and out into the night.

Totho watched her leave and was torn, when she flew, between relief and guilt. His night's work was not done, though. He turned and went back to the farmhouse, opened up the hatch and returned to the cellar with his shuttered lantern. He would replace the bars, close the tumblers of the locks. *Give them something to wonder about.*

He was just getting down to the task when a voice intervened: 'Well now, what have we here?'

He turned, flicking the lantern shutters wider, but he already knew who he would see: the emotionless face of Colonel-Auxillian Dariandrephos, flashing pale and mottled from within the confines of his cowl.

'A good artificer makes his plans carefully in advance,' Drephos reproached him. 'He does not need to come back and finish up, Totho.'

'How . . . ?'

'I watched. Perhaps you forget that for me it is never dark. I watched and saw quite clearly. You came out with the girl, you let her loose. I watched because I thought it likely you might do so. Kaszaat warned me that you were acting strangely, and she was right. And so I came to see what else you might have been up to down here.' He raised an enquiring eyebrow and moved closer. 'So, what else have you done?'

'Nothing,' Totho stammered. Drephos was still advancing on him, but he knew he himself was the stronger, and the master artificer was not even armed.

'She . . . she was my past, and I found I could not cut it loose so easily.'

Drephos laid his gauntleted hand on Totho's shoulder. 'And what else have you done? How else have you betrayed me?' His voice was very soft, not angry, not even sad.

'I swear—'

Drephos gripped him by the shoulder and Totho cried out in pain as the narrow fingers dug like pincers into his flesh. His entire arm was instantly locked, so he grasped Drephos's wrist with his other hand and tried to pry it free. To his horror there was no movement at all, only an inexorable tightening of Drephos's grasp.

'What else, Totho?' Drephos asked, as he still struggled and tugged. 'Is there an explosive, perhaps? An incendiary planted? Or were you to kill me? Kill the general? Tell me, Totho. I won't be angry, I promise.'

Totho was now whimpering, feeling the bones of his shoulder grind. Unable to shift those imprisoning fingers he slammed his hand up against Drephos's elbow as hard as he could.

He struck metal, as hard and solid as any armour. With ragged breath he dragged at the sleeve of the man's robe, until the shoulder seam gave way and he bared Drephos's entire arm.

It was metal, all of it, not just armoured but an arm entirely of metal, and he could only guess at the delicacy of the mechanisms within that gave it life. Even in the extremity of his pain, something stirred in him at the sight, the artificer's instinct in him that could never quite be denied.

'It was a savage accident,' Drephos explained conversationally. 'And worse was having to devise this replacement one-handed. But I see you like it. I'm glad.'

He pushed, and Totho, all strength gone from him, fell back against the wooden bars. 'Tell me what you have done,' Drephos said. 'I am a Moth, at least partly, and I can read it from your face. What is it you have done?'

'I gave her the plans,' Totho gasped, all resistance ebbing out of him. 'The plans for the snapbow.'

667

Drephos stared at him for a second. And he laughed. Laughed and laughed and let go his grip so that Totho slid down the bars to the floor. And still Drephos laughed and laughed as his apprentice looked up at him, bewildered.

'Oh that's good!' Drephos got out. 'That's very good. And I suppose you thought it was young love that made you do it, or nostalgia, or any of those other things that we'll soon breed out of you! My dear boy, you gave her the plans, did you? Why that's excellent!'

'What do you mean?' Totho demanded. His shoulder was still agony, but at least he could move the arm. Nothing was broken.

'Don't you understand?' Drephos crouched before him. 'What will they do with the plans? Why, they'll build snapbows of their own. Can you imagine the look on Malkan's face when he finds out they have his new secret weapon?'

'This is just to spite the generals?' Totho asked, baffled.

'But what will the generals do, Totho, when that comes to pass? Who will they come to, and what will they ask?'

'They'll come to you,' said Totho slowly, 'and they'll ask you to . . .'

'Build them something even better!' Drephos crowed. 'And the science advances one more step. Oh, you may have thought you had all kinds of airy motives, Totho, but in your heart you're an artificer. You're a man of progress just like I am. How hard would it have been for me, myself, to get that weapon into the hands of the enemy? Just think how much time you've saved me. The war goes on, Totho, back and forth, year to year, and how much better for us two that it does. If the Empire ever wins outright then will it continue to let us use its foundries and its workshops? Will it lend us further resources for our work?' He then took Totho by the unhurt shoulder and hauled him to his feet. 'Do you bind yourself to me, boy, truly? Once before I thought I'd read truth in your face, but I can be deceived.'

One last chance, Totho realized, for him to stand against the bloody flood, to reject the metal and choose the meat – to do something Che would be proud of.

'I am yours,' he said soberly. 'I bind myself to you.'

Che had set off walking away from the camp and not stopped until dawn began to colour the eastern sky. She discovered she had been heading a little east of south. It occurred to her that she had no idea where she was, and that the food and water Totho had scavenged for her would not last for very long. The one building she came across was a barren shack that was possibly once some rich man's hunting lodge, but it had been picked bare already.

She now had a problem, and realized that she should have fled the camp westwards along the rail line, which would have led her infallibly to the gates of Sarn and to safety. Instead, she would have to work her way northwards as best she could, and hope to encounter the rails again. Northwards and westwards, then, so that she did not simply walk straight back into the Wasp camp. And, even so, they would have scouts out, so she would camp out during the height of the day, and then walk all night, trusting to her Art to keep her eyes sharp.

For now, she simply trudged on until the sun became too hot, and then she rested, and in the evening she trudged on again, looking always for a sign of the rails ahead of her, like the cut or rise of the railside bankings. But the rugged, scrubby terrain went on endlessly, punctuated only by knots of trees wherever water had gathered beneath the earth, or the ravaged plots of ploughed farmland when the ground became fertile enough. She found no buildings that had not been systematically sacked and burned, which told her she was still too near to the Wasp camp, wherever it was, for comfort.

Towards dusk, she found a stream that had cut a channel through the land, capable of hiding her from enemy eyes. It was cooler, too, and edged with green that was a welcome change from the drylands that extended between Helleron and the woods of Etheryon. Its course ran too straight to be natural, and the land either side was flat and had obviously once known the plough, but she could not tell how long ago, or whose hands had refashioned the soil here.

She was still heading along the channel when she heard something buzz overhead like a very fast-moving insect. There had been a knife amongst Totho's gifts and she seized it in her hand, trying to crouch into some kind of martial position, but she could see no one, certainly nobody in black and gold armour.

She was just thinking that perhaps it was an insect after all, when something struck the side of her head in a blaze of pain and she dropped face-first into the stream.

When Che recovered, she found her wrists and ankles bound with strips of cloth torn from her own clothing – not the uniform tunic she still wore, but her real clothes that had been in the sack, and were now spread out with the rest of its contents around an almost smokeless fire. A low, wide tent had been pitched beside a pool that the stream flowed into, and then out of, on its artificial course.

Some bandit or wanderer, she guessed. *I can promise a reward. I can probably make them be reasonable.*

And then she heard a footstep and turned, and almost cried out in dismay, for he was a Wasp – not in uniform, but a Wasp with a scarred face, in a long leather coat, coming with a string of fish in one hand and eyeing her speculatively.

It had been something as commonplace as a slingshot that had brought her down, a stone aimed at her from the undergrowth.

His name was Gaved and he was obviously no ordinary Wasp as Che was used to them. No uniform and no rank, and he had all the marks of a loner about him. When she eventually questioned him about what he did, he told her he hunted men and women for a living.

'And now I've caught you,' he said, 'a nice, plump deserter. Well, it's about time my luck changed. I was robbed by a bastard Spider-kinden and I'm still on his trail, but I reckon I can now make some pocket money by returning you to your masters.'

'If it's money you want, if you get me to Collegium . . .'

'Girl, I've just come from Collegium. I'm not even sure it's still standing by now.'

'It is, the . . .'

'And *anyway*,' he said, speaking over her, 'I've got no wish to retrace my steps, not with my Spider friend still out there hoping to claim my share of the loot. So, if it's all right with you I'll just hand you in and go about my business.'

'They'll kill me.'

'They'll whip you, certainly,' he said unsympathetically. 'Maybe they'll kill you too, if they want to make an example, but probably you'll just get a whipping, an Auxillian abandoning her post. Why not tell them you got lost?'

'I'm not a deserter,' she protested. 'I'm not an Auxillian.' She fell silent, knowing that whatever she said could only make her position worse. The same understanding was in his eyes, too.

'I'm sorry,' he said, with a shrug. 'A man's got to make a living, and it's not easy sometimes.'

He had taken her into his tent, come nightfall, with the fire left to burn itself out by the opening, and she had assumed he would take advantage of her. Instead he just made sure she was tied too tight to escape, and then lay down at whatever distance from her the tent would allow. She realized that in some perverse feeling of concern he had brought her inside to keep her warm.

'Please,' she addressed his back. 'I promise you more

money than the Wasps will pay. Just take me to Sarn. Sarn can't be too far out of your way.'

'Don't make me gag you,' was his only reply.

Gaved woke with the dawn, as he always did. It was good to be travelling alone and in the wilds. It had been fun going along with Phin for a time, but in the end other people tended to crowd him.

And yet here I am, so self-sufficient I'm doing the Empire's work still. The cursed Spider, Scylis, had seen right through his vaunted independence, and he could do without some mercenary telling him things he already knew.

He remembered his last sight of Phin, sprawled dead with a nailbow shot straight through her. She had deserved better than that, but then so did most people who died.

The girl was awake and staring at him and obviously about to start pleading for her life again. That would only depress him. 'I'm going out to water the place,' he told her, 'but I'll be watching, and if you make a move it won't be a stone this time, but a sting, you understand?'

She nodded, and he went outside into the growing sunlight, smiling to greet it, as he always did. Then the smile slipped and he growled, 'Who in the wastes are all of you?'

Che watched the Wasp re-enter, with an odd expression on his face. He had a small knife in one hand, and she opened her mouth to scream, but he said, just above a whisper, 'Now I'm going to cut you free. No sudden moves, all right?'

The knife sawed through the bonds at her ankles, and then at her wrists, and a moment later he backed out of the tent again, and she saw a flash of reflected sunlight as he ~st the knife point-first into the ground.

~he crawled cautiously out after him and saw that they ~ot alone, that there were at least a dozen other people crouching or standing around the tent. They had swords and bows and crossbows, and they came from all kinden, and they distinctly had the look of the bandit about them.

'Well,' Gaved said. 'I suppose she's yours now.'

'Don't move, Wasp. We've not done with you,' said one of the bandits – and a moment later Che was running forward, throwing herself into his arms with a cry of joy, because under the grime and the tarnished cuirass and the rough clothing was none other than Prince Salme Dien, who she thought she would never see again.

'Salma! How can you be here? How can it be you?'

'I had some help in finding you,' he replied, embracing her gently, and glanced back towards one of his own people who was muffled in a cloak. Then the hood was pushed back to reveal that the face beneath was bright and rainbow-hued.

'You found her?'

'And then she found me,' Salma confirmed. He looked at Gaved the Wasp. 'Did this man hurt you?'

Gaved visibly tensed, knowing that her answer would seal his fate.

'No,' she said. 'Nothing like that at all.'

'Then pack up your tent, Master Wasp. You're coming with us.' He turned again to his followers. 'Phalmes?'

A tough-looking Mynan stepped forwards. 'Yes, chief?'

'We're heading back for camp, and then I want a messenger sent to Collegium.'

Che then thought about the plans that Totho had given her, the plans still concealed inside her tunic.

The war was far from over.

Visit **www.panmacmillan.com** to read more about all our books and to buy them. You will also find features, author interviews and news of any author events, and you can sign up for e-newsletters so that you're always first to hear about our new releases.